THE WINE
OF
SAN LORENZO

BOOKS BY HERBERT GORMAN

THE FOOL OF LOVE

THE BARCAROLE OF JAMES SMITH

THE PROCESSION OF MASKS

THE PETERBOROUGH ANTHOLOGY
(*With Jean Wright*)

JAMES JOYCE: HIS FIRST FORTY YEARS

GOLD BY GOLD

THE TWO VIRGINITIES

A VICTORIAN AMERICAN:
HENRY WADSWORTH LONGFELLOW

NOTATIONS FOR A CHIMÆRA

HAWTHORNE: A STUDY IN SOLITUDE

THE PLACE CALLED DAGON

THE INCREDIBLE MARQUIS: ALEXANDRE DUMAS, *père*

THE SCOTTISH QUEEN

JONATHAN BISHOP

SUZY

THE MOUNTAIN AND THE PLAIN

JAMES JOYCE

BRAVE GENERAL

THE WINE OF SAN LORENZO

Introductions to

THE CABALA *by* THORNTON WILDER
(*Modern Library, Inc.*)

THE MARBLE FAUN *by* NATHANIEL HAWTHORNE
(*Limited Editions Club*)

A PORTRAIT OF THE ARTIST AS A YOUNG MAN
by JAMES JOYCE
(*Modern Library, Inc.*)

THE SON OF THE THREE MUSKETEERS *by* CAMI
(*Farrar & Rinehart, Inc.*)

The Wine of San Lorenzo

By Herbert Gorman

FARRAR & RINEHART, INC.

New York   Toronto

This book has been manufactured in accordance with paper conservation orders of the War Production Board

"Manifest Destiny"

"Why, were other reasons wanting, in favor of now elevating this question of the reception of Texas into the Union, out of the lower region of our past party dissensions, up to its proper level of a high and broad nationality, it surely is to be found, found abundantly, in the manner in which other nations have undertaken to intrude themselves into it, between us and the proper parties to the case, in a spirit of hostile interference against us, for the avowed object of thwarting our policy and hampering our power, limiting our greatness and checking the fulfillment of our manifest destiny to overspread the continent allotted by Providence for the free development of our yearly multiplying millions."

From an article on the Texas question in the July-August issue of the Democratic Review of 1845. Internal evidence would seem to indicate that this article, in which the historic phrase "manifest destiny" appears for the first time, was written by John L. O'Sullivan, the editor of the Review.

Contents

Prelude

ALAMO

Alamo

THE thudding cannonade stopped abruptly about ten o'clock and the unexpected silence that followed was like a suspended menace. There are moments when Time appears to grow rigid and then stretch back on its black haunches for a fatal lunge and this sudden cessation of sound was like that. The threat poised, frozen in air, and the visible world, a world of ragged cottonwoods, gray mesquite, mud-colored streams and deserted houses, crouched motionless beneath it. One was hurled incontinently from a familiar frightening noisy chaos into a clammy void where the very nothingness became an unbearable threat. A pall of acrid smoke, sulphurous and stinking, hung low in the night air between the blunt-cornered oblong of the Alamo and the March clouds that obscured the moon. At the slanting southeast corner that stretched from the old mission church to the solid south wall where the big gate was reinforced by tipped logs, a sort of picket line of crisscrossed sapling lengths, a primitive chevaux-de-frise, thrust ax-sharpened points toward the dry ditch and behind it Crockett and his buckskin-coated dozen lounged, red-eyed, half-asleep, half-awake, their hands close to their old Kentucky rifles. There was a hint of rain in the air that was like a cold kiss.

In the chilled airless sickroom, which was in the south end of the long stone barracks and close to the gunpowder storehouse built against the mission church, the ailing and wounded murmured querulously and swore fervently as Dr. Pollard moved the heavy tallow candles from blanket to blanket. These men were frightened. They were intensely aware of the sudden silence and it disturbed them more than the buffalo bellow of the big guns that had been firing for more than a week. That discordant eruption had been something they could understand. They could recognize their own guns, a score or less of various calibers, including one bull-mouthed eighteen-pounder, that thrust their gray-black snouts at irregular intervals across the four sides of the heavy walls, for these spitting monsters spoke with an awful immediacy that shook the shattered windows and crashed against their weakened eardrums until they thought they would go mad. But they didn't. One never goes mad from what one understands. Santa Anna's guns were farther away, firing up from the abandoned stone and adobe town of Bexar, from the ruined millsite to the northwest of the Alamo, from the west and from the east, and their explosions did not strike the aching heads with such deafening impact; but the grinding clash of the cannon balls on the hard-baked walls and against the stone barracks was like the crunching teeth of some terrible giant.

And now there was silence. It was not right that there should be such silence and the sick men experienced a sort of dull confused scared anger at it. God damn it to hell! Let there be the customary noise; they could understand that; but this unreasonable stillness . . . Something inexplicable had occurred and their helpless startled irritation before the mystery aggravated their usual restlessness. It made their wounds ache more violently than ever. They complained, turned, rustled the straw beneath them, shivered in the cold night air and cursed with a congenital colored fluency that brought the ghost of a smile to the exhausted doctor's tight lips. The boy from Nacogdoches opened his eyes very wide and endeavored to make out the design on the discolored ceiling. His thin features were so sprinkled with brown freckles that one might imagine a huge peppermill had been ground above his face.

"Doctor," he said in a high-pitched voice, "you're not goin' to fool with my foot, are you?"

Pollard glanced down at the shapeless bundle of rags. It was as large as a big cabbage.

"No," he replied shortly. "Not tonight."

He was chewing an unlighted cheroot that stuck like a rat's tail out of his mouth. He was impatient. It angered him to think that the boy was here at all.

"The toes are all squashed together," said the boy.

The doctor shrugged his shoulders and moved on.

"Doctor," said the boy again, half-afraid to speak and yet more afraid of the silence. "What's happened? Why ain't they firin' no more? Has Santy Anny pulled out? Did Houston git here? Where is he?"

The doctor, experiencing a bitter helplessness, rubbed his unshaven chin and spat his cheroot to the floor.

"How in hell do I know where Sam Houston is?" he snapped. "Maybe he's at Refugio. Maybe he's at San Felipe. Maybe he's on the Brazos. I can tell you where he isn't, though. He isn't here. Now shut up and try to get some sleep."

But the boy had to talk. By saying words, any words at all, he kept the silence away from the place where he lay. He said:

"I saw Sam Houston at Nacogdoches. I saw him twice. Jesus, but he's a big man. 'Bout eight feet high, I should guess. First time he was with Missus Sterne. She's the alcalde's wife. Real pretty, too. Second time he was walking down the street to Brown's Tavern with a Creek Injun. He wore moccasins and he was awful drunk. He fell plumb into the hitchin' rail and yelled, 'Git out of my way, you God-damned, pigeon-toed, ring-tailed, cockeyed, web-fingered son of a—' "

"Oh, shut up!" begged the doctor wearily. For two clakos he'd chop off the young cock's foot. In spite of the cold damp air he was perspiring. Don Samuel, indeed.

The boy was silent for a moment, meditatively moving his jaw as though he was chewing something, an undigested sentence perhaps, and then he turned on his side with some difficulty. He had to do it without moving his foot for every time he did that the pains shot up his calf from his ankle until he thought he would scream. Everything was busted down there, all right. The man next to him was voiding into a battered spittoon. The receptacle sloshed as he slapped it down on the hard earthen floor. He was a big man with a gray-stubbled face, a veinous nose and very sharp blue eyes set in the midst of numberless tiny wrinkles and creases. A bandage completely covering the top of his head concealed what hair he might have had. Sinking back with a grunt upon his blanket he observed the boy from Nacogdoches for a brief interval in puzzled silence.

"You come in with the men from Gonzales?" he asked abruptly in a thick slurred voice.

"Yes," replied the boy eagerly. "Five days ago I come in. We rode in 'bout two-three in the mornin'. Thirty-three of us. 'Bout eight hours ahead of Mister Bonham. We could hear the guns on the Cibolo. They didn't want me to come along, leastways Ensign Kimble didn't, but I came anyway. Say, it's funny the firin's stopped, ain't it?"

The blue-eyed man ignored the question. He fumbled in the straw beneath his blanket, extracted a chocolate-colored quid of tobacco as big as a plum and popped it into his mouth.

"Wear your didies when you come in?" he inquired, and then, without waiting for an answer, shot another question at the boy.

"Hurt your foot, sonny?" he asked.

"Yesterday," the boy explained. "Yesterday afternoon. I was standin' near the west wall in front of the well when one of Santy Anny's cannon shots landed plumb in a pyramid of our balls. They flew all over the place and one bounced on my foot. All my toes are squashed together. I'll prob'ly lose my foot."

He said it with some pride.

"Lucky you didn't lose your head," remarked the older man with elaborate gravity. "I seen a Texian's head shot right off once. He just stood there without no head at all, his own mother wouldn't've recognized him, and then he took a step and fell down."

The boy nodded.

"I know," he admitted. "I seen chickens run around after their heads was chopped off. Where'd you see that happen?"

The man squinted upward as though the picture he sought might be etched on the murky ceiling. Then, turning his head, he spewed forth a long stream of dark-brown tobacco juice. It flew in a graceful arc and landed directly in the center of the spittoon. The boy gazed admiringly at this feat. The man shook his bandaged head and said: " 'Tis funny there's no firin'."

Then as though to fight back the troublesome silence he began to talk in a dogged insistent voice, hardly glancing at his youthful auditor.

"I'm O'Hare," he announced. "Dennis O'Hare. Ever heard of the O'Hares? I come from the Redlands. We're all born with full sets of teeth up there. I was with old Ben Milam here in Bexar in December. We took the town in five days, bejasus, but old Ben was killed on the third day. Shot in the guts, he was. 'Who'll go into Bexar with old Ben Milam?' he asked and three hundred of us went in with him. We fought right through the streets and across the plaza. We came hell-bent through the Mexican gunfire. Cos surrendered fourteen hundred men to us, bejasus."

"I heard about it," interjected the boy.

"Yes, by God," went on O'Hare without pausing. "Three hundred of us took fourteen hundred greasers and sent 'em back across the Rio Grande with their tails between their legs. Ever hear about old Ben Milam? Ever hear about Francis Johnson? We was out there five days, five days by the river, and Burleson said Bexar couldn't be taken without artillery. But we took it, didn't we? We took it with our rifles and our knives. We fought like Comanches."

"I heard about it," repeated the boy.

Of course, he had. It was the news of that fight that had started everything and sent him off on the wild-goose chase now ended in the sickroom of the Alamo. Lying on his side and vaguely aware of the strong sour ammoniac smell of the man beside him his little knowledge, a disturbing irritant of hearsay, observation, conjecture and blind intuition, seemed to rush simultaneously into his consciousness. It was all there at once. The recollection of the excitement when the dusty messengers galloped into Nacogdoches was an agitated reality in his restless mind. He had been carrying a newly slaughtered suckling pig to Colonel Henry Raguet's imposing house on that December day when the hard-riding Texians had reined in their foam-flecked horses before the Cantina del Monte. Miguel Cortenoz, coffee-hued, pockmarked and bowlegged, had run out to question them. The noisy crowd gathered,

Americans, Mexicans, Spaniards and Frenchmen from Louisiana, boisterous Irishmen, fat Germans, Negro servants, even a few itinerant Indians in dirty blankets, all the queer human debris that populated the mud and adobe hovels of La Villa de Nuestra Señora del Pilar de Nacogdoches. The boy saw the black-bearded old rascal answering to the name of Monsieur Gervais who swore he had shipped with Jean Lafitte in the Gulf. He saw, too, the Ring-tailed Panther, an ex-Missourian who frightened little boys by telling them how he ate the raw hearts of Indians. Don Francisco Garrero, the barrister, was there as well, standing on the pointed toes of his boots and staring with dark intensity over the bobbing heads. The jabber of voices was terrific, like a swarm of excited birds over a cornfield.

Then the crowd swirled on down to Brown's Tavern overlooking the plaza, decimated, of course, by deserters who preferred to stamp into Señor Cortenoz's dance hall and gambling saloon and ignite their tortured interiors with fiery liquids. From there the mob proceeded to the alcalde's house. The alcalde, not a jailer but the director of the civic affairs of the heterogeneous community, a mayor, if you will, was Don Radford Berry, successor to Don Adolfo Sterne, the plump squat little Rhineland Jew whose wife had been observed so often in the company of Don Samuel Houston. He came to his door and listened. The boy, hanging on the outskirts of the crowd and still clutching the slippery cadaver of the suckling pig, heard fragments of the report. Yes, sir, a great action. In five days Bexar had capitulated and now there was not a Mexican trooper of Santa Anna's command north of the Rio Grande. Texas independence was a reality. Don Radford Berry nodded his head while a perplexed and dubious expression crept across his usually stolid face.

Nacogdoches was a queer place. The boy knew this but he could not explain it. It was really two communities in one, two civilizations overlapping, existing side by side and yet mutually suspicious and, at heart, antagonistic. On the one side was the English-speaking group, about five-sixths, now, of the rapidly growing town's population, powerful, planning, inexorably linked to General Jackson's United States; on the other side was the Spanish-speaking group, small but shrilly articulate and morally sustained by the undeniable legality of its position, pro-Mexican, almost to a man, and resolute to adhere to the ancient ties of its mother country whose center of authority was in the Palacio Nacional in Mexico City. It was Roman Catholic, Spanish and Indian in culture and psychology and helplessly indignant at the aggressiveness of the tough gringos who were pouring in from the States. The predominant English-speaking group (and big conniving Don Samuel Houston testified to this) was twenty to one in favor of the separation of Texas from Mexico. The boy had vague ideas about this angry division in his own town but from the age of ten (and he was now sixteen) he had heard constant argument and observed violent fist and knife fights in the dusty streets, behind the taverns and in the cantinas of the Mexican quarter. That was sufficient to convince him that the problem was like a red-hot coal. Tossed back and forth it burned everybody's hands.

The boy was bewildered but earnest. He was a Texian (so all about him pronounced the proud word) although long ago his widowed father had made the long trek from a mysterious place called Agawam, Massachusetts. This father, long-lipped, religious and dryly repellent, labored for some years in Nacogdoches as a harness manufacturer and then a convenient fever swept his soul, presumably, to heaven and his body, certainly, to the graveyard on the edge of the town. The boy, then about eleven, became the charge of one Eustaquio Archuleyte, a butcher. Eustaquio's place of business, near the old Mission Nuestra Señora de Guadalupe, was a small corral guarded by a shapeless log office and there he slaughtered chickens, turkeys, pigs and skinny steers. The boy delivered the carcasses and joints to the taverns and the big houses and in those places he listened to more than one angry disputation concerning the state of the world in general and the future of Nacogdoches in particular.

There appeared to be several aspects to the separatist feeling. Colonel Henry Raguet, for instance (whose charming daughter, Miss Anna, played the French harp), preached the gradual independence of Texas from Mexico. He was a Pennsylvanian of Swiss descent and naturally suspicious of drastic gestures. "Move slowly and by legal steps," was his advice. But those swashbuckling brothers, William and John Wharton, who came often to Nacogdoches to consult with Don Samuel Houston, were emphatic in their declarations that Texas must eventually become an integral part of the United States. "The sooner the better," they announced to all who would listen and they did not conceal their willingness for violent action. Don Adolfo Sterne, however, outlined the vision of a self-sufficient Texan Republic that belonged neither to Mexico nor to the States and that would eventually stretch from the Gulf to the Pacific Ocean. It appeared to the boy that the larger portion of separatist feeling favored this solution. But then, he didn't know. There were undercurrents he could sense but could not fathom.

Passion mounted and Nacogdoches assumed the aspect of an insurgent community. How it was in the rest of Texas the boy did not know for he could neither read nor write and the few broadsides and ancient newspapers (including Colonel Raguet's New Orleans *Bee*) were complete mysteries. He could listen, though, and he suspected from what he heard that all Texas was seething. It was. The

lid blew off the bubbling pot when General Santa Anna, president
of the Republic of Mexico, fully revealed himself as a determined
dictator obsessed with destroying the Federal Constitution of 1824
and establishing a centralized government throughout all of his country, including Texas. His ruthless campaign through rebellious Zacatecas was a portent. The Texians felt the hot wind roaring up from
the south and acted accordingly. There were hurried meetings, secret
conferences, loud speeches and violent pamphlets. The Wharton brothers, Don Samuel Houston, Henry Smith of Brazoria, James Robinson
of Nacogdoches, Dr. Archer, a dozen others, pounded the primitive
roads on tough little horses.

At San Felipe a protest meeting was held and the chairman, R.
M. Williamson, electrified his angry audience when he declared, "General Santa Anna, instead of being your president, has been invested
by the General Congress with the absolute powers of the dictator.
Elected president by the Republican party, he no sooner took his seat
than he threw off the veil of disguise, and to the amazement and consternation of the Republican party he exhibited himself the friend and
supporter of the aristocrats and defender of the clergy." Williamson
pointed out that Santa Anna's brother-in-law, General Martin P.
Cos, was advancing toward the Rio Grande with thousands of armed
men. He cried, "For what, fellow citizens, are they coming; in the
name of God, say not speculation. They are coming to compel you
into obedience to the new form of government; to compel you to give
up your arms; to compel you to have your country garrisoned; to
compel you to liberate your slaves; to compel you to swear to support
and sustain the government of the dictator; to compel you to submit
to the imperial rule of the aristocracy, to pay tithes and adoration
to the clergy." It was these words and many more like them, mouthed
in taverns and on street corners, that blew like kindling sparks through
the muddy lanes of Nacogdoches during the autumn of 1835. The
boy's mind took fire from them.

Early in November, while Cos was closing in around Bexar, a
consultation met in San Felipe and declared the provisional independence of Texas under the Constitution of 1824. "Whereas, General
Antonio López de Santa Anna and other military chieftains have by
force of arms overthrown the federal constitution . . ." Nacogdoches
was transformed with patriotic fervor and the pro-Mexican element
walked very softly along the back alleys. The lines were clearly drawn
now and big Don Samuel Houston, elected commander in chief of
the practically nonexistent Armies of Texas, set about recruiting his
undisciplined forces. The boy promptly volunteered to Mr. Thomas
J. Rusk, who was raising the Nacogdoches Company, and Mr. Thomas
J. Rusk promptly refused his services. The future senator explained

that there was no room for suckling pigs among his tusked boars. Rumors came riding in on the backs of the tough little horses. Stephen Austin's forces were said to be camped five or six miles from Bexar. Sandy-haired Jim Bowie, leading ninety hard-riding, hard-drinking Texians, smashed four hundred Mexicans at Mission Concepción. Jim Fannin was commissioned inspector general of the new army. The general was sitting on his tail in San Felipe and endeavoring to organize a durable military establishment. Or he was squatting at a council fire with The Bowl, war lord of the Texas Cherokees. He was advising caution, pleading for planned organization, drill, equipment, preparation and a concerted scheme of campaign. He had not forgotten the lessons learned in the regular army of the United States. It was during this high pitch of excitement that the messengers had galloped into Nacogdoches with news of the storming and capture of Bexar. So, to the devil, then, with all caution. The hotheads had been vindicated.

It was while he was listening to the messengers outside Don Radford Berry's house that the boy decided to go to Gonzales. He would be close to the heart of things there and by the heart of things he meant Bexar. He could worm himself into the army there. At Gonzales or Bexar the officers would not be stiff sticks like Mr. Thomas J. Rusk. All he needed was a horse and a gun and a poncho. The horse he could wheedle from the one-eyed foreman of Colonel Henry Raguet's big corral with the payment of his life's savings of eight American silver dollars and a promise of future payments; the gun he could obtain by the simple expedient of stealing Eustaquio Archuleyte's long rifle from its place above the door in the log office; and the poncho he could get by exchanging the suckling pig he carried for an old garment in the Mexican quarter. His mind made up he pushed his way through the gesticulating crowd. Don Radford Berry, still perplexed and dubious in expression, had gone into his house with three of the messengers, leaving one outside to hold the bridles of the exhausted mounts. He was a tall thin man in dark-blue trousers, bright yellow shirt and decorated Mexican boots. His long straight black hair hinted at a certain degree of Indian blood.

"Hello, sonny," he said. "Huggin' your baby?"

The boy glanced down at the carcass of the suckling pig and grinned.

"It's for Colonel Raguet," he said, knowing that Colonel Raguet would never see it. "Are you ridin' towards Gonzales?"

"No," replied the messenger disgustedly. "We'll be crossin' the Sabine into Louisiana by mornin'. We been to Gonzales. Cut up from there to the old San Antonio Road. Look here, sonny, we could use that pig o' yourn."

The boy backed away in polite haste.

Early next morning he started out for Gonzales, riding the twenty-two-year-old jaco the one-eyed foreman had reluctantly stolen for him. Eustaquio Archuleyte's long rifle was attached, muzzle down, to the wooden saddle that was his seat and over his thin back was flung an ancient tattered poncho that smelt of urine and chicken droppings. His progress was uneventful as he pushed across river after river, the Angelina, the Neches, the Trinity, the Navasota, the Brazos, the Colorado, passing through vast deserted stretches, stopping at small settlements and isolated holdings, working a day here and sleeping a night there and imbibing an awe-struck realization of the vastness and diversity of Texas. At Gonzales, which he reached in February, 1836, they didn't want him in the army, either. The recruiting officer looked down at the thin figure and small pointed freckled face and burst out laughing. "Might be I could get ye a job as ramrod in some cuss's musket," he said as he walked away. The boy was still in Gonzales on the twenty-fourth, loitering in the plaza, when J. W. Smith and John Sutherland rode in with the frightful news, already suspected, that the Alamo was under siege and that Travis wanted men and wanted them in a hell of a hurry. It was a new chance. Like a leech the boy attached himself to the small group that rode out on the twenty-seventh to reinforce the young redheaded lawyer who commanded at Bexar.

It was the sum of all this, an incoherent mass of partially apprehended facts, tall tales, and spontaneous gestures revolving in his mind like a ball of hair in a cat's stomach, that was circumscribed in the reiteration of "I heard about it."

What he was hearing loudest of all, however, was the silence that had settled over the Alamo and the dogged insistent speech of Dennis O'Hare from the Redlands, paradoxically enough, seemed to make it more manifest. The accustomed background had been snatched away and the futile nakedness of human voices was pitiful in its stark loneliness. Presently O'Hare stopped describing Ben Milam's death, and, placing both hands to his bandaged head, began to swear in a low monotonous voice. A man, lying farther away, yelped abruptly as Dr. Pollard fumbled with his crushed arm and the sound was like the unexpected explosion of a firecracker. A low grumbling chorus surged through the sickroom. The boy felt the pains increasing in his calf and resistless tears rushed into his eyes. He flung his arm across his face but the damp smell of his shirt was no comfort. It was terribly hard to be a man when one's foot was smashed and the audible world had been suddenly snatched away. Tomorrow there would be weak sunlight, the color of pale butter, in the plaza at Nacogdoches and Miss Anna Raguet would bend her head toward her French harp. The boy lay quiescent, his skinny hairless arm in the damp shirt sleeve concealing his weakness while a swift sour nausea mounted from his stomach. When he began to vomit over the side of his blanket nobody seemed to notice.

In the mission church, beside the hastily reared wooden scaffolding from whose top a precariously wedged gun poked its round snout out of a small second-story window, Mrs. Dickinson stood quietly alert and appeared to be listening to the silence. It was dark and drafty in the hollow belly of the old edifice, once the temple of worship of the mission padres of San Antonio de Valero, and the few small shaded lights glowed dully against the enormous gloom. The baby, Angelina, named, of course, for the river, slept as soundly in a coil of weathered hemp rope as though she were cradled in one of the fine new cribs that were manufactured in Philadelphia and brought overland in the big creaking wagons. At eighteen months life has few problems. In a far corner, quite invisible, little Charley Livingston and the "touched" Indian, Juan Diego, conversed in low tones, or, rather, the man conversed and the boy listened. Mrs. Dickinson could hear the faint murmur of Spanish syllables and she knew that the Indian was repeating again the strange story that he was the reincarnation of that peon who had talked with the Virgin Mary upon the hill at Guadalupe. Juan Diego was loco, "loco rematado," averred the priest who had fled from Bexar. He was a small wizened Indian, perhaps forty, perhaps sixty years old, one could not tell, and nobody paid any heed to him except little Charley, and, perhaps, Joe, Colonel Travis's Negro boy.

The woman shivered, and not from chill alone, as she leaned against the scaffolding, listened to the silence and wondered what was happening around Jim Bowie's sickbed in the corner room of the west wall where her husband, the captain, had gone in response to a hurried call for a consultation from Colonel Travis. She was not frightened but she was fatalistic. That strange wave of *what is to be must be* that had swept through the Alamo during the past week had engulfed her as it had men like Travis, Crockett, Bonham and her own husband. Perhaps some of the nameless fighters were frightened. She did not know. But if they were they concealed it beneath a surprising display of sang-froid. One thing she did know and that was that there would be no surrender. A contemptuous cannon shot had answered that insolent demand days ago. By a lucky accident the black iron ball had embedded itself in the wall of the Múzquiz house in Bexar where Santa Anna had established his headquarters. How the Texians roared with delight at that lucky hit!

Mrs. Dickinson was petite, dark-haired and pretty. She was young too. But as she leaned against the scaffolding a curious agelessness permeated her small features and at the same time she appeared to be both eighteen and eighty years old. A little more than a week of suspense and horror had done that to her. To disentangle the days of that short period was an impossibility for they all flowed into one maelstrom of incessant agitation. Since the morning that Santa Anna's vanguard had entered the deserted plaza of Bexar with bands playing and standards flying the only peace for the less than two hundred Texians who had fortified themselves within the Alamo had been the fitful and uncertain hours of exhausted sleep. Through the windows of the mission church Mrs. Dickinson had observed the continual arrival of enemy troops, the slow investment as the besiegers deliberately spread their lines about the fortress, the digging of trenches and the placing of howitzers, the bridging of the turbulent San Antonio River with planks torn from the wooden houses of Bexar, the grumbling and constant bombardment, the raising of the blood-red flag upon the stone-built church in the town (*that* meant that the warfare was against rebels), the cutting off of the water supply, the unsuccessful sally of the Texians for fuel wood, the miraculous arrival of the thirty-three men from Gonzales, the blazing campfires at evening with small black shadows (almost within pistol shot) passing back and forth, and the cold stars and threatening clouds gazing down at it all. These things ran together in her mind like a spumy cascade and it was difficult to separate one from the rest. She felt as though she were on an island lost in the midst of a rising storm and now that there was an evil lull she forced herself to endure it without even a ghost of hope. She did not even think of Fannin or Houston any more. She knew that they would not arrive in time. What she *was* listening for, she could not say. Perhaps eternity.

In their dark corner Juan Diego, the Indian who was loco, told his story for the twentieth time to little Charley Livingston.

"Tú eres buen muchacho," he declared with the familiarity of an elder to a child. "Thou art a good boy. Therefore, I will tell thee again of the coming of Our Lady to me on the hill of Tepeyac by Guadalupe in the days when Zumarraga was archbishop of Mexico. This happened in a faraway time before thou wert born. It was in this way. My father lay upon his mat for many days and would not move. His flesh fell away from him until the bones of his body stood forth like the ribs upon the steers in the corral behind the barracks. So I said, My father, this is an evil thing and it comes from thy neighbor, the pateta, who desires thy cornfield.' My father closed his left eye and I knew that he would not have it so. So I said, 'My father, I will go to the medicine man who lives in Tlaltelolco on the other side of the hill and ask him to raise thee from this mat.' My father closed his right eye and I knew that he would have it so, Pues y qué? I went up the hill of Tepeyac early in the morning . . ."

The slow light footsteps of Mrs. Dickinson sounded near and Juan Diego paused for a moment and squinted into the murkiness. Little Charley Livingston sat with his back to the cold stone wall, his eyes gravely fixed on the shadowy face of the Indian.

"He aquí!" exclaimed the storyteller. "A marvelous thing happened. A cloud came down from the high air and from it stepped Our Lady in a garment of blue terciopelo with stars of bright gold all over it. The light of her face was such that I could not look upon it and I lay down on the tawny rock and covered my eyes with my hands. Our Lady spoke many words to me. She told me that she was to be the patron saint of the Mexican Indians and that she would take them under her loving protection. She would watch over their huts and their corn and their beans and their hunting and the sicknesses of the old men and the childbearing of the women. Then she told me that I should go to Mexico City and tell the archbishop that he must raise a church at the foot of the hill and dedicate it to her. I could not speak for my tongue grew large in my mouth. He! Like a bubble exploding she vanished into the morning air and there was left an odor like gardenias and I rose to my feet and ran without stopping for my lungs were filled with the divine breath of the Mother of God. Art thou listening, little one? I ran all the way to Mexico City. I ran to the great casa of the archbishop of Mexico. I ran through the gate and the padres in their big black hats could not stop me. I ran into the comedor which was all white and gold and there at a great table sat the archbishop of Mexico with the leg of a fine turkey in his hand and an embroidered napkin under his chin. I fell upon my knees and told the archbishop of Mexico what I had seen and heard. I laughed and cried at the same time. The archbishop of Mexico put down the turkey leg and nodded to the padres who had followed me from the gate. 'This man is enloquecido,' he said. 'He does not have a good smell.' So they threw me into the street and hurt my knee. I did not run when I returned to my father."

Mrs. Dickinson paused by the sitting figures and listened without interest. She had heard it all before. But the monotonous sound of Juan Diego's voice was less than the inaudible summons of eternity and that made it more endurable. It was familiar and she could support herself by it much as a seaman might support himself by a thin rope stretched across a reeling deck. To hold tight to it was to preserve one's footing. It did not occur to her that Juan Diego was an unreality. It was said that he had been the mozo of the provincial of the Brethren of the Profesa, one of the best-loved orders of monks in Mexico, and had even been taught to read and write. Mrs. Dickinson was not certain of this for the Indian had never given evidence of any such talents. The one thing she did know was that Juan Diego was

loco and, being a good Presbyterian, she suspected that his derange-
ment could be traced back to a religious exaltation that had snapped
his simple mind. One cannot beat the holy drum too hard.

"My father lay upon his mat and would not speak," continued the
Indian, his little black snake eyes dimly shining in the hollowed
wrinkled pouches of his lids. "So I told him my story and fell down
beside him and covered my face with my hands. During the night
my father coughed twice. I took this as a sign and in the morning ran
to the hill of Tepeyac again and knelt on the red rock and prayed to
Our Lady. Mirad. There was a sweet wind and a tinkling sound and
she stood before me and her garment was of blue terciopelo with
bright stars of gold all over it. With my hands before my eyes I told
my story. I wept. Then she spoke to me. 'Climb the porphyry rock
beyond you,' she said, 'and fill thy tilma with the roses thou shalt find
there and take them to the archbishop of Mexico and tell him that this
is a sign from Me.' Válgame Dios! little one! Hast thou ever heard
of roses growing out of the smooth porphyry? So I climbed the rock
and all about me were great red flowers with many petals and I picked
them and filled my tilma with them and ran toward Mexico City."

By leaning forward and peering through the gloom Mrs. Dickinson could see the intent face of little Charley Livingston. It was a
small face and it seemed even smaller because of the mop of brown-
black hair untidily parted in the center that sat like an old-fashioned
cap on the boy's head. Charley had wide hazel eyes and a little out-
thrusting chin. Mrs. Dickinson, who was particularly familiar with his
immediate past, thought that he, too, had been caught up in that web
of fatality that had become a sort of negative support to the men in
the Alamo. With his father dead and his brother lost to him, his
present a series of removals from temporary home to temporary home,
he yet maintained a gravity that was little less than mature. Nothing
surprised him. No one had ever seen him weep and no one had ever
seen him frightened. He moved quietly with a detached air about the
beleaguered mission-fortress and when he paused to converse it was
generally with one of the few Mexicans who had crowded into the
fort. Perhaps that was because his Spanish was so much better than
his halting English. Perhaps again, he liked the Mexicans best. She
did not know. She did know, though, that she had promised to find
a home for him . . . and now . . .

"Once again I passed the gate of the great casa of the Archbishop
of Mexico," went on Juan Diego. "And as before the Holy Father sat
at his table but this time he held no turkey leg in his hand. He was
eating a fine fish flavored with hazelnuts. 'What!' he cried. 'That bobo
again. Where is my stick of lime-wood?' I threw my tilma open and
the roses poured like a red river across the carpet. In a rapid voice

I spoke while the padres, who had pursued me, pushed me toward the door. I told everything. I told it three times. The archbishop of Mexico sat as still as though an Otomí sorcerer had turned him into stone with his feathered wand. He stared at my open tilma which lay spread on the carpet with all the roses about it and his eyes seemed to pop out of his head like the eyes of an escarabajo. I was hurled into the stone corridor before his mouth opened and the words flew out of it. 'Bring that Indian back,' he said and his voice shook like the cloth awnings over the market in the wind. So the padres, one of whom had kicked me in the belly where it is not good to be kicked, pushed me back into the comedor and there I saw it, too. I saw it with these eyes that now see you in this darkness."

Juan Diego touched his eyelids and then closed his lips tightly.

"What was it, taita?" asked Charley Livingston in a clear voice. He was following a customary formula.

Juan Diego opened and shut his mouth three times (which everybody knew was for the Father, the Son and the Holy Ghost) and placed a bony tobacco-colored hand on the boy's knee.

"It was Our Lady," he said solemnly. "The image of Our Lady gazed out of my old tilma at me. She was as I had seen her on the hill of Tepeyac in a garment of blue terciopelo with bright stars of gold all over it. Framed in roses and smiling she looked out upon me and I fell to my knees and wept. I peered through my fingers—so—and she was still there. All in bright colors. Ah, hijito, this was a marvelous thing."

It did not seem incongruous to Mrs. Dickinson that these two should be sitting on cold stone in the shadows and talking about miracles while a besieging army crouched beyond the walls on all sides. Nothing seemed incongruous any more. If the sun had suddenly started to shine by night she would not have been surprised. Or if Don Samuel Houston himself, in Cherokee coat and buckskin vest and high-heeled boots with three-inch spur rowels patterned from daisies, had ridden through Santa Anna's crowded camp and followed by a thousand shouting Kentuckians it would not have drawn an exclamation of high relief from her. This was the land, high and low and broad and slit by rivers and streaked with mesquite and chaparral, where what happened happened without reason and one accepted it as shriveled Juan Diego accepted Our Lady of Guadalupe. Or as she accepted the fact that this was the end of the world. All the same, even with the world ending, children must sleep. She stretched her hand toward the small boy.

"And then what happened, taita?" asked little Charley Livingston. The Indian shook his head in a gesture of perplexity.

"The clouds float across me," he said. "There is much smoke in my eyes. I cannot see clearly. But the Archbishop of Mexico raised a great church before the hill of Tepeyac and in it they hung my tilma in a frame of pure gold and around this another frame that weighed one thousand kilos. And out of the two frames Our Lady of Guadalupe watches the Indians as they come and go. And where she stood and spoke to me a spring of healing waters gushed from the rock and over that they raised a Capilla del Pocito with three domes of blue and white Puebla tiles."

Suddenly he turned his head and stared at Mrs. Dickinson.

"It is very still here," he said. "I do not like this stillness."

"Taita . . ." began little Charley Livingston.

There was a rapt earnest look in his hazel eyes.

"No, no," interposed Mrs. Dickinson. "That is enough. You must sleep, Charley. You must go back to the barracks and sleep. Juan Diego will go with you. Juan?"

The Indian rose obediently and helped the boy to his feet.

"Keep close to the wall," said Mrs. Dickinson.

She walked back slowly to the scaffolding after they had left and resumed her attitude of listening to the silence.

In the northwest corner of the enclosure two small stone and mud buildings stood side by side close to the outer wall. The one nearer the mission church was the habitation and headquarters of William Barret Travis, the redheaded, explosive-tempered, twenty-seven-year-old lieutenant colonel who commanded the meager forces in the Alamo. The other was a chamber of discontent and the smell of death for in it lay Jim Bowie, helpless, emaciated, his great strength shorn away. It was here that the little group of officers was meeting, not so much to devise plans (for there was nothing that could be devised) but rather to emphasize their oneness at this somber moment and to present a unified front to the ominous silence. This silence, which had clapped down on the besieged garrison like a heavy iron lid, did something to the voices of the men. It instigated them to speak louder and more distinctly and then made them acutely conscious of the lonely stridence of their words. Travis noticed this as he stood beside Bowie's pallet bed and shifted his gaze from face to face. The glances he encountered were grave and stubborn. If only God or Fate or Destiny, whatever It was, would give them a little time . . .

Bowie reached a long arm under his bed and pulled forth an empty whisky bottle.

"God damn it!" he said vehemently and flung the bottle against the stone wall. It crashed and split into fragments.

"That made a little noise," said the sick man.

The others shifted their booted feet and Travis glanced down pityingly at the yellow-haired giant from Georgia. Bowie, Travis knew, had ceased to be a responsible man. He was suffering from three maladies and any one of them was sufficient to destroy him. They were grief, alcoholism and a pair of rotting lungs. During the last week he had lost strength and weight at a terrifying rate and now as he lay there in the sickly yellow glow of the tallow candles he looked like a collapsed scaffolding. Not so many months before he had been a pillar of strength, a man to lead hardy enterprises and scare the wits out of disaffected Indians and troublesome Mexicans. That was before his wife's death. Bowie, the swashbuckler, the duelist, the Indian fighter, the slave smuggler, the land speculator, had ridden high, wide and handsome until he met and succumbed to the charms of Ursula Veramendi, daughter of one of the vice-governors of Texas. After their marriage he had become a changed man, joining the Church and settling in a big house in Saltillo. His old companions saw him no more. He became a father. The wild days were slowly forgotten. Then Fate, almost a native of Texas, stepped in. A plague swept Saltillo and carried off with it Ursula Veramendi Bowie and her two small children. The home with all its present and potential joys and transquillities exploded like a bubble. Almost crazed with grief and an ineradicable bitterness Bowie plunged into the maelstrom of the Texas struggle and an unceasing series of bouts of heavy drinking that aggravated his diseased lungs. He was trying to kill himself, unconsciously perhaps, and he was succeeding. The gray augury of death was in his face at this moment.

Travis shifted his eyes from Bowie and studied the expressions of concern on the features of Crockett, Bonham, Dickinson, Patton and Kimble, his little staff of officers. The concern was all for the sick man and not for themselves. He knew that. He cleared his throat. Without anything to say he had to say something.

"I am certain they will attack before dawn," he declared, running his hand through his uncut red hair.

It was a remark he had made on each of the three preceding nights and it was a way of saying what he thought a good general would do. Indeed, there was no one in the room who could explain Santa Anna's delay.

"They've been building ladders all day," remarked Dickinson. "I could see them from the church window. Just out of pistol shot. I could hear the hammers."

"If we can hold out another twenty-four hours," said Bonham, "perhaps Smith . . ."

Bowie laughed discordantly. The sound was ugly.

"You'll never see Smith again," he announced savagely. "Smith's gone back into the world and he'll stay there."

He was sick enough to want to hurt anybody.

"Fannin may come up," argued Bonham reasonably.

Bowie continued to laugh. The ugliness was touched with hysteria.

Travis glanced sharply at him.

"That's enough, Jim," he snapped. "Here we are and here we'll stay even if all Mexico rides over us. Christ! There is only one thing we can do and that is to fight like the devil and hope that Houston or Fannin or somebody will arrive in time with reinforcements. We've got to do it. There isn't a man among us who isn't a match for a dozen Mexicans. You know that. We've proved it again and again. Why, Jim, at Mission La Purísima Concepción you routed half a thousand of them with ninety men. They ran like sheep before you. They can't stand up to cannon. We've got guns and we've got ammunition and—"

"But nó food," broke in young Trimble.

"We've got corn bread and red beans left," insisted Travis. "We can hold on—"

"We don't need food," Crockett interrupted. "Leastways, not much. I've traveled ten days on a pouch of dried corn no bigger than my fist. If we kill enough of them we won't be hungry. It's right exhilaratin'. Every time I see one of them go down I feel as though I'd taken a bite out of a big steak. Just pull your belt tighter, Trimble."

"I wasn't complaining," replied the young officer from Gonzales with some indignation.

"Nobody's complaining," said Travis shortly.

He glanced at Crockett and there was a faint amusement in his eyes. The colonel had arrived in Bexar a week or so before with a dozen men from Tennessee. With a characteristic gesture he had adopted Texas and its cause. Travis recalled how the famous fighter in buckskin had mounted a goods-box in the Civil Plaza and harangued the cheering populace, declaring that not long since he had been a candidate for Congress in his native state and that during the canvass he had told his constituents that "if they did not elect him, they might all go to hell and he would go to Texas." "And, fellow citizens," he had shouted to the men of Bexar, "I am among you. I have come up to your country, though not, I hope, through any selfish motive whatever. I have come to aid you all that I can in your noble cause. I shall identify myself with your interests, and all the honor that I desire is that of defending as a high private, in common with my fellow citizens, the liberties of our common country." One became a Texan as easily as this. The will was all.

"Any special orders?" asked Patton, breaking the short pause that followed Travis's remark.

Travis shook his head.

"We all know what to do," he replied briskly. "You all have your posts and you all know your men. If they assault hold your fire until you can see them clearly. Perhaps you'd better tilt your cannon a bit. We don't want to fire over their heads. And watch for those ladders. If there's a breach send for Patton and his twenty-five men. He'll be by the well acting as a reserve. If they get over the walls in great force run for the barracks. Every corridor and room is barricaded and you can pile them up there. Fight from room to room. Don't let a single man fire at random. Whenever possible pick off the officers. When . . . Well, that's all, now. We'd better disperse. I'm going to make a round."

He clamped his jaws together and turned toward the door. He had to get out into the night air. There was a sickliness in this close chamber that he did not like, a smell that reminded him of coagulating blood. The others, relieved to have their minds limited to the imminence of positive and practical action, crowded after him. It was the Now of it that mattered solely and not the Tomorrow of it. They were almost cheerful as they filed into the courtyard. Even young Trimble was laughing at some grumbling comment from Colonel Crockett. Bowie alone, unable to move, remained in the domain from whence they fled—that terrain of shadows haunted by the phantoms of the mind, fears, despairs, premonitions and regrets. He watched the men passing out one by one, Crockett bowing his tall figure to pass under the low portal, and his large helpless hands, hands that had once thrown a knife farther and harder than any Comanche or Kiowa, grasped at the sides of the cot. He could see something that they could not see but he would not put in into words. Let them find it out for themselves. All he could do was rail and curse and swear to himself that he would not die of sickness in a bed. God would not permit that. With a convulsive effort he struggled to rear himself upright and the exertion plunged him into an agonizing fit of coughing. He spat the blood and phlegm from his mouth and it spattered his bare chest. With a long wheezing sigh he sank back on the damp blanket. It was no use. Let them go, then. Let them go without him. They were living, for they could move; he was lifeless, for he was bound to a space no larger than a grave. He gazed after them with hunger and loathing and love and was quite unconscious of the tears that flowed down the streaked furrows of his face.

The boy from Nacogdoches lay back and wiped his sour mouth weakly with the back of his hand.

Dennis O'Hare, who had stopped swearing to himself, observed him through small noncommittal eyes.

"I never got took that way," he said after a moment. "Leastways not since I was a tadpole. Back in Ireland, it was, when I was seven years old. I tried to drink a jug of my da's poteen an' I puked for three days."

"I shoulda thought it would have killed you," murmured the boy miserably.

"We got strong stummicks in Ireland," replied Dennis O'Hare. "Strong ones in the Redlands, too."

Dr. Pollard's slow steps, the steps of a tired man, approached across the sickroom and the boy shut his eyes tightly and pretended to sleep. He was still afraid that the doctor would fool with his foot, unwrap the bundle of bandage, perhaps, and let the crushed toes drop out, or cut them away, or something like that. He didn't trust doctors. They said they wouldn't do something and then they went and did it. Pollard paused by the boy for a moment and then passed on to the next recumbent form. He was whistling softly to himself, a listless sort of whistle that sounded as though it was coming out of his pursed lips without conscious volition. What a damn curious thing to do in this silence, thought the boy. It was like tempting fate. But perhaps the doctor was whistling to make certain that there was such a thing as sound. It wasn't sound that came from sick folk. At least, not exactly. It was just noise. Sound came from strong people, from well people, from people who . . .

"Know that tune?" inquired O'Hare's rough voice. "Alligator horses, eh?"

The boy from Nacogdoches continued to pretend that he was asleep. He was afraid the doctor might come back. Doctors had a way of popping out at one from behind beds and concealed doors. They popped out with steel knives and iron probes in their hands and sometimes they had pincers and saws. His stomach was feeling funny again. Like a pan brimful. If he moved ever so little it would spill.

"That's an old one, bejasus," went on O'Hare. "Heard it before ever I came this way."

He began to sing in a growling flat voice that sounded like a file cutting a chain:

> Ye gentlemen and ladies fair,
>   Who grace this famous city,
> Just listen if you've time to spare,
>   While I rehearse a ditty;
> And for the opportunity
>   Conceive yourselves quite lucky,
> For 'tis not often that you see
>   A hunter from Kentucky.
> O Kentucky, the hunters of Kentucky!
> O Kentucky, the hunters of Kentucky!

He interrupted himself long enough to announce, "My uncle Mike, the one they shot down Washita way for stealin' horses, used to sing that one," and then went on murdering the song. The boy from Nacogdoches kept his eyes shut although the squeezed lids began to hurt. He could not hear the doctor but there was a possibility that he might be lurking and watching. Ready to jump for him as soon as he opened his eyes. Dennis O'Hare grated:

> We are a hardy, free-born race,
>   Each man to fear a stranger;
> Whate'er the game we join in chase,
>   Despising time and danger;
> And if a daring foe annoys,
>   Whate'er his strength and forces,
> We'll show him that Kentucky boys
>   Are alligator horses.
> O Ken—

Suddenly he stopped.
"Younker," he called in a low urgent voice.
The boy from Nacogdoches did not reply.
"Ah, the hell with it!" exclaimed Dennis O'Hare.

When Travis stepped out of Jim Bowie's chamber the onrush of chill night air blew the fetid smell of the sickroom out of his nostrils and his mind. It was too late to be sorry for anyone or anything. Fate, or destiny, or the stubborn will of man, or whatever one chose to call it, had directed a course and it must be followed to the end. So much was sure in a world of constant uncertainties. He stood for an instant buttoning the neck of his jacket and adjusting his heavy belt from which swung one of the knives named after Bowie while he stared across the dim expanse of courtyard where the well loomed like a crouching Indian in a blanket. He was a stern-faced little man with a straight back and combative shoulders. Hope was dead and yet something hard as agate and unequivocally convinced within his soul would not let him yield. In the first place, he regarded his stand to the end as a warranty of the liberation of Texas from the despotism of Santa Anna and his Centralists. It was possible to win a cause by losing a battle. As Thermopylae spoke for Greece, so would the Alamo speak for Texas. What his inward dream might be was indefinite in his mind but he could feel its presence as sharp as a wound and as sweet as the spring winds in the high valleys. *I shall never surrender or retreat.* Such faiblesse was not in the dream. He had written those words to *the People of Texas & all Americans in the world.* Yes,

Americans . . . ! *I am determined to sustain myself as long as possible . . . Victory or death!* One wrote like this in the passionate fever of the instant. But one did not say such words to a hundred and eighty grim unshaven men. There was no need of it.

Beside the inevitable purpose that could not be denied there were lesser factors to be considered as well. It was still possible (though not probable) that Sam Houston or Fannin was marching to his relief and if he held out for a few days (a week, perhaps) they might arrive in time. His reason doubted it but his heart desired it. It was something to clutch at though not to lean on and in this great sprawling country the impossible had been known to happen more than once. Then, too, he doubted the mercy of Santa Anna. Even if he surrendered (which was unthinkable) it would not guarantee the safety of his garrison. There was the plundering and murders that followed the Zacatecas campaign last year to give an idea of the merciless side of Santa Anna. No, he was caught. Time had picked him as a symbol.

He moved slowly along the north wall observing the mounds of earth that had been raised to support the five guns and the tired men who were dozing beside them. A few were finishing a late ration of corn and beef and Travis automatically reflected that the supplies were almost exhausted. It was lucky they had found the supply of corn in the Mexican jacales before they tore them down for firewood. At the barracks, which came flush to the north wall, he turned and walked southward before the east front. Each doorway was barricaded by piles of sandbags. Men were sleeping there, too, and there were men on watch as well. He could hear faint movements, the thud of a rifle butt dropped to the cold floor, a cough (so many had contracted colds), even a low sibilance of voices in the darkness. And midway in his southward journey he paused at the sound of a plucked guitar and a low voice singing. He recognized the air. It was "The Yankee Girls," an old song that dated back almost to the War of 1812 and his lips mutely shaped the words.

> Not England's daughters rosy-cheeked,
>   Nor Scotia's lassies fair,
> Nor Erin's blooming maidens can
>   With Yankee girls compare.
> Though what they tell us of their charms
>   All very true may be,
> They'll not compare with Yankee girls;
>   The Yankee girls for me.

Well, they were all done with girls. Behind the barracks, to the east, were the cattle and horse pens, now pitifully denuded of livestock, and he knew that cannon were set along the farther wall there, as well, and that watchers were straining their eyes to catch any Mexican movement in the mesquite and chaparral country beyond.

He passed the sickroom without glancing at it and turning the corner to the east came to the gunpowder room. Two silent men resting upon their rifles stood by the closed door. Without moving, like frozen caryatids, they watched him pass and he was about to turn back and speak to them, though of what he had no idea, when two small forms indistinct in the heavy shadows of the buildings slipped by and vanished around the corner. They were evidently bound for the barracks. The moment before they disappeared Travis recognized them. The crazy Indian, Juan Diego, and little Charley Livingston. His lips tightened as he thought of the ten-year-old boy for he was well-acquainted with Charley Livingston's story. As he moved slowly toward the door of the mission church, from which the couple must have come, that story fleetingly absorbed his mind and momentarily freed him from the incubus of his responsibility.

He had known the boy's father. David Livingston had come to Texas from Massachusetts about 1827 or 1828 with a rather faded and discontented wife and two small lads. He was the only son of a New England merchant, a dealer in fabrics and furniture, and a Frenchwoman of gentle birth who had fled from her native country during or shortly after the great Revolution. It was this mixed blood, possibly, New England and French, that was responsible for the restless and somewhat incoherent attitude of David Livingston toward life. Anyway, after his father and mother had both perished in a fire that swept away their Cambridge home and the family business had crashed like an empty walnut shell underfoot the son had packed his few valuables and set forth with his wife and children for the Southwest. He landed in San Felipe and there he established himself as a dealer in general merchandise. He was not a good businessman and he did not prosper. Perhaps the restlessness of his nature came between him and the steady routine that was necessary for the success of his affairs. Perhaps, too, a particular affection for strong liquors had something to do with it. In 1829 his wife, who had grown steadily more discontented and morose as time crept on and brought her none of those luxuries that she remembered from Massachusetts, died and he was left with the two small boys, David, Jr., aged seven, and Charles, aged three. He did not trouble his head much about them. Instead, he turned them over to a Mexican housekeeper of ample figure and easy morals while he passed most of the time that he did not reluctantly devote to his business in his favorite taverns.

When Travis first met Livingston in San Felipe in 1832, about the time of the Bradburn troubles, he found him to be a somewhat seedy individual with an intelligent mind but lacking in all ambition to better himself. Unlike the majority of settlers who were pouring into Texas regardless of the regulations and loud in their declarations of what they would accomplish, David Livingston confined himself to securing the most comfortable chair in the tavern and remaining there until he had to go home to bed. The Mexican housekeeper and her daughter attended to the general merchandise. Also, Travis found, to his intense disapproval, that the Livingston boys, now aged ten and six, spoke Spanish much better than they did English. When he protested about this to Livingston and heatedly declared that the children were being denationalized the father merely wagged his finger and said, "My boys are not Americans. They are Texians. And Spanish is the official language of Texas." Yet Travis liked Livingston. He was like something fine that had been flawed by circumstance.

He liked him even better in the spring of 1835 when revolt swept over Texas and men seized their rifles to defend a newly declared independence. David Livingston, rising for once with alacrity from the tavern chair, was among the first. It was almost as though he had found a way out. He brought his two boys to Gonzales, entrusted them to a Tennessean friend who was in the land business, Alphonsus Ewing, swallowed his last drink and rode away with Jim Bowie's men. At the Mission La Purísima Concepción on October twenty-eighth Bowie attacked and defeated a body, some four hundred strong, of Cos's troopers. The Mexicans lost their cannon and fifty killed. Bowie lost one man out of his ninety-two. That was David Livingston.

When Travis heard of it he thought that it was a fitting end for a lost man. At least, Livingston had died for something and that was better than collapsing on the splintered floor of some third-rate tavern. It was always good to die for *something*. So many men who had labored assiduously all their lives expired for nothing. He wondered vaguely about the two boys and it was not long before he heard. David, now fourteen, had been taken to Tennessee by Alphonsus Ewing, who preferred to return to his native state and enter politics there rather than stay in Texas and live through a civil war. Charley, ten years old, was brought to Bexar by Captain and Mrs. Dickinson. It was their intention, they said, to find a home in Texas for the quiet undemonstrative child. "If I did not have all I can handle with this baby of mine," Mrs. Dickinson explained, indicating her infant Angelina, "I would keep the boy myself." To find the boy a home, then.

As Travis paused for a moment before the door of the mission church he thought, perhaps you *have* found a home for him, Mrs. Dickinson. Then he put little Charley Livingston out of mind. He decided not to enter the church and directed his steps toward the ditch that guarded the southeast corner of the Alamo. A score of men rested beside their rifles. Farther on, by the log picket barricade that ran southwestward into the south wall he came upon Crockett who had just rejoined his dozen Tennessee boys. They were conversing in low voices but stopped when they saw the young redheaded lieutenant colonel emerge from the shadows.

"No sound at all?" Travis inquired absently.

He knew very well that there had been no sound from the Mexican lines.

"No, Colonel Travis," replied Crockett in his drawling voice. "But you can be certain for sure that the black devils are up to something. When a Mexicanner is quiet look out for him."

"D'ye think Smith got through?" asked one of the Tennesseans without any particular interest.

John W. Smith had been sent out on March third to seek for aid.

"Why . . ." began Travis.

"We can always hope," broke in Crockett testily. "You ain't a mite low in your britches, are ye, Tyler Jasset?"

Unconsciously they subdued their voices to the silence. It was like talking in church or in the president's antechamber.

"What does it matter?" went on Crockett angrily. "We'll fight anyway, won't we?"

He ran his hand lovingly along the barrel of his Kentucky rifle.

There didn't seem to be anything left to say. Travis teetered on his boot heels for a moment. One could not be heroic with these men for they saw as easily through histrionics as they did through flattery. They had accepted their responsibility and that put a natural end to talking about it.

"You'd better post two men and try to get a little sleep," said Travis as he turned away.

Crockett growled something inaudible in reply.

Travis passed along the south wall, noting that the large gate had been bulwarked strongly with earth and tilted logs. He came to the west wall. This presented a broad front the full length of the enclosure. To Travis it seemed to be the obvious spot for an onslaught by Santa Anna's hordes. Heavily packed mounds of earth supported six guns and on the roofs of the small buildings reared at unequal intervals against the wall men sat staring out into the darkness. Others slept close to the guns. These heavy weapons, one an eighteen-pounder, had been captured from Cos after his surrender the previous December. Travis walked slowly, observing the cannon and the piles of ammunition below them. He saw that the covers of the powder kegs had been loosened, that squat filled bags lay beside them and that the barrel mops and rammers rested against the wall. There was a discordant sound of snoring punctuated occasionally by the scrape of a boot or a sharp cough. Everything appeared to be in such order as was possible under the most hopeless conditions. Whatever happens, thought Travis, the Mexicans will know they have been in a fight.

Moving along deliberately, his boots hardly sounding at all, he reached the door from which he had emerged so short a time before. He paused with his hand resting against the weather-worn wood and glanced up into the night. He could not see the heavens. The moon, that had shone weakly earlier, had disappeared and a pall of mingled smoke and mist had settled over and around the Alamo. Travis had the sensation that he was standing in a black iron dome, one of those arching covers, perhaps, that are placed over joints of meat to keep them warm. He was as trapped from the sky as he was from the great rolling leagues of unbesieged Texas. But, instead of frightening him, this enclosed feeling aroused no more than a brief flicker of urgency in his resolute mind. We must take it as it comes, he thought. What is Santa Anna doing at this moment? I would give a barrel of Pennsylvania whisky, if I had it, to find out.

General Antonio López de Santa Anna was sitting in the large ground-floor living room of the Múzquiz house in Bexar surrounded by his generals and listening to the reports of runners from the various detachments he had spread about the Alamo in a rough circle. A dozen candles illuminated the sparsely furnished room and lighted the swarthy faces of the officers. Santa Anna, just past his forty-second birthday, was drinking cup after cup of black coffee which was being served him by an attentive Negro servant. Juan Almonte, his favorite aide and reported to be a bastard son of the priest Morelos who had fought with Hidalgo for the independence of Mexico, stood at his shoulder. At this time the general was an impressive-looking man. Not tall, of middle stature, say, and sturdily built, he appeared to great advantage in uniform. His sallow face, animated by large dark expressive eyes, was almost distinguished and if it had not been for his thick Negroid lips and black bushy oiled pompadour he might have been considered handsome. When in repose an expression of melancholy aloofness softened his features and it was for this that he was sometimes called the toro triste, the sad bull.

At the moment he was not sad at all. He was anxious and he was fighting against sleep but he was already savoring in optimistic advance the triumph which he was convinced was almost in his grasp. His brother-in-law, Martin Perfecto Cos, who had been ingloriously defeated more than once by the Texians, and General Castrillón had urged him to wait until the seventh of the month, just another day, when two twelve-pounders were expected, before he attempted a frontal attack in force with escalading ladders on the Alamo but he had obstinately refused. He would launch the assault at four o'clock on the morning of March sixth and that was less than four hours away. It was for this reason that he had silenced his guns. In the darkness and as silently as possible his men were taking their final positions. The defenders of the Alamo were inextricably trapped and nothing remained but to rush in for the kill. Some four thousand men were waiting for the signal, the degüello, that wild trill on the bugle that was the "fire and death call," the "throatcutting," the summons that meant "no quarter," nothing less than complete extermination.

Santa Anna pushed his cup toward the Negro servant, wiped his lips with a napkin and surveyed the faces of his officers as he listened without comment to the report of the latest runner. His tactical plan was simple. He had divided his forces into four columns. The first, commanded by Cos, consisted of the Permanent Battalion of Aldama (except the company of Grenadiers) and the three right-center companies of the Active Battalion of San Luis; the second, commanded by Colonel Don Francisco Duque, included the Active Battalion of Toluca (except the company of Grenadiers) and the three remaining center companies of the Active Battalion of San Luis; the third, commanded by Colonel José María Romero, was composed of the Permanent Battalions of Matamoros and Jiménez; and the fourth, commanded by Colonel Morales, was made up of the light companies of the Battalions of Matamoros and Jiménez and the remainder of the Active Battalion of San Luis. These four columns were to converge on the Alamo from different points at the sound of the bugle. In reserve, under the personal command of Santa Anna, were the Battalion of Engineers, the five companies of Grenadiers of the Permanent Battalions of Matamoros, Jiménez and Aldama and the Active Battalions of Toluca and San Luis. The cavalry, under Colonel Joaquín Ramírez y Sesma, was stationed at the Alameda of the Alamo with orders to scout the country when the attack began and to make certain that no Texan escaped. Not one of the generals, not Santa Anna, or Castrillón, or Cos, or Amador, regarded it as excessive that such planning and such quantities of troops were employed against a hundred and eighty-odd men cornered in an old mission fortress. They knew their Texians.

When the runner ceased reporting (he had brought the news that Ramírez y Sesma proposed to saddle up at three o'clock) Santa Anna nodded and turned to his brother-in-law.

"The ladders were all distributed?" he demanded.

Cos nodded.

"Yes, general," he replied. "The first column is carrying ten ladders, two crowbars and two axes; the second, ten ladders; the third, six ladders; and the fourth, two ladders."

"The fourth should have had six ladders," said Santa Anna. "They must escalade the north wall. Well, well, it does not matter. Enough will get over. Y bien. Here is a general order. The men will wear neither overcoats nor blankets or anything that may impede the rapidity of their motion. The commanding officers will see that the men have the chin straps of their caps down, and that they wear either shoes or sandals. Por Dios! I am tired of bare feet."

He drained the fresh cup of steaming coffee that had been set before him.

"That is all," he announced. "You may return to your posts now. Tell your men that the honor of the nation is involved in this engagement against the bold and lawless foreigners who are opposing us. I expect that every man will do his duty, and exert himself to give a day of glory to the country, and of gratification to the supreme government, who will know how to reward the distinguished deeds of the brave soldiers of the Army of Operations."

The officers saluted and passed out of the living room into the night with a great crunching of boots and rattling of sabers. Santa Anna was left alone with young Almonte and the Negro servant. The general studied the empty coffee cup for a long minute. There was a half-puzzled, half-satisfied expression in his eyes like that in the eyes of a child who has received an unexpected gift and does not quite know what to do with it.

"Well," he said in a brisk tone as he recovered himself and glanced up at his aide, "so much is so much. Perhaps we had better go out and walk for a while. It will keep us awake."

"This direct attack will be costly, general," remarked Almonte with the familiarity of a favorite as he picked up his cloak and flung it about his shoulders.

Santa Anna rose abruptly.

"It is of no importance what the cost may be," he declared. "It must be done."

He started toward the door and then paused and turned.

"Just a moment, Juan," he exclaimed. "Just a moment."

He crossed the living room and pulled open the door to an inner chamber and passed in. Before the door closed again behind him Almonte heard a surprised exclamation in a young feminine voice. He scowled at the blank portal. His devotion to the general was genuine but this was one side of his nature (and a big side, too) that he did not approve. Love was all very well; the troops never marched without their soldaderas, their campwomen, who added a florid and extravagant aspect to their bivouacs; but this particular affair of the general smelled to heaven. The girl in the inner chamber, Beatriz, was the daughter of a middle-aged widow of Bexar. Castrillón had happened upon her a few days before when he was directing the dismantling of several houses to bridge the San Antonio River, then in a turbulent flow, and he had brought back to the general an enraptured description of her beauty. Santa Anna's amorousness, always oozing through the surface when attractive women were around, was aroused and he desired Castrillón to bring the girl to him. Castrillón explained with studied politeness that procuring did not come under military orders and the general, after he had seen the girl himself and found her to be surprisingly pretty, turned to Colonel José Miñón, one of his most sycophantic officers and a sly rascal as well. Miñón undertook the mission. With a cavalryman's bluntness he put the proposition to the girl's mother, who flew into a rage, threatened to faint, declared that she was respectable, swore that her deceased husband had been an honorable officer in the Mexican army and announced in a voice surcharged with emotion that Santa Anna's only way of getting Beatriz was through a marriage ceremony. As the general had been married for twelve years to Doña Inés García, this appeared to be a positive checkmate to his amorous propensity. However, Miñón, anxious to please, had a solution. In one of his companies, he explained to Santa Anna, was a smart and well-educated scalawag who was remarkably skilled in impersonations. Why not make a priest out of him? "When he apes the archbishop of Mexico," declared Miñón, "you laugh until the tears roll out of your eyes." The general ran his tongue over his thick upperlip, chuckled, sent a squad to the church in Bexar to seize the vestments and missal and announced the date of the bogus marriage. It had taken place in his headquarters two days earlier and perhaps that was one reason why Santa Anna was so sleepy. It was a bad, bad business and Almonte did not like to think of it.

He waited, frowning, and presently Santa Anna came out of the inner chamber and carefully closed the door behind him.

He was smiling.

"She is exquisite," he said, rolling his eyes at Almonte. "I shall send her to San Luis Potosí and keep her for my old age."

Juan Almonte threw open the outer door.

"Shall we go, general?" he asked briefly.

Santa Anna stepped into the darkness and glanced upward.

"Caramba!" he exclaimed. "The stars are not watching tonight. But it is just as well. Where the devil are the horses? Give me your arm, Almonte."

In a small corner storeroom on the second floor of the barracks Charley Livingston lay on a pile of dried cornhusks and dreamed that he was running across a plain of red porphyry. His brother David was running after him. As David was four years older he ran faster and the distance between the two steadily diminished. Charley's lips were dry, his heart beat like a drum and his small legs moved up and down in an incessant pattern that was maddening. He did not know why he was running or where he was running but the imperative need for escape from something or someone charged his body like the steam in a railroad engine. It was not particularly from David that he was running for David had always been kind to him and made him a bow and some arrows and taught him to shoot the old musket with the split butt and often brought him quantities of nuts. It was toward something or someone, then, that he was running. He could hear a mingled roaring in his ears and presently he observed that it was not the wind or the speed of his flight but a number of people who were either urging him on or shouting at him to stop. As he raced along their faces floated about him and he recognized some of them. There was his father opening and shutting a wide mouth in a very red face and calling to him to go on, to go faster. There was fat Belita and her daughter, Enriqueta, and they, too, were cheering his speed. The thin discontented face from whose lipless mouth came a constant "Stop now! Stop now!" must be his mother. He did not remember her very well. And there was Mr. Alphonsus Ewing, long-lipped, ox-eyed, with flowing curls, who boomed, "That's enough, lad. Come back now. Come back to Tennessee." There were others, as well, Captain and Mrs. Dickinson, Juan Diego, Joe who was Colonel Travis's boy, men and women of San Felipe and Bexar, all of them crying "Faster! Faster!" or "Stop! Stop!" David was gaining on him. David could almost reach out and grasp him by the collar of his jacket. He sucked his breath in painfully and urged his legs to greater speed. Quite suddenly he tripped and fell forward into complete darkness. He fell for a long time and his stomach seemed to rise up into his throat. And then he landed softly upon what he knew was a great bed of roses. He knew that they were roses although he could not see them. They rustled beneath him.

For a long time he lay without moving, his face buried in cool petals, and inhaled the ineffable odor of the flowers. Then he raised himself on his hands as though he had been summoned, although he had heard no voice. Staring before him he saw a little light, a little light in the distance no larger than the eye of an ox. As it approached it grew in circumference until it was a wide circle. There was a shape in the circle and it turned its head and looked steadfastly at him. The scent of the roses was mingled with the scent of gardenias. It was a woman and her garment was of blue terciopelo with bright stars of gold all over it. Her lips moved and though no sound issued from them he could hear what she was saying. "I am thy Mother. Thou art my Son. I will watch over thy hut and thy corn and thy beans and thy hunting and the sickness of thine old men and the childbearing of thy women. Go then, my Son, to the bishop . . ." He began to crawl forward and as he crawled forward the words died into a thin music that died into a soft sighing like the morning wind in the poplar trees. "Mother!"he cried, rising to his knees and stretching out his hands. But her smile became fixed and timidly reaching he touched the hem of her blue robe with his finger and knew that it was hardened clay. At that moment she began slowly to tip forward and unafraid he gazed upward and watched her topple down upon him. She crashed all about him and through him although he felt nothing and the loud sound of her crashing caused him to start upright on the bed of dried cornhusks in the small corner storeroom. As he rose to his feet there was another crash from the courtyard. Wide-awake he ran toward the door.

Where there had been silence there was terrifying sound. In the sickroom the boy from Nacogdoches started upright as though an iron spring in his back had been suddenly released. He had not been sleeping. He had heard Dennis O'Hare sing interminably and then snore interminably and sometimes he had heard a groan from the darkness or the slow steps of Dr. Pollard who seemed never to sleep at all. He had been waiting, not knowing for what he had waited, and with the first crash he was absolutely sure that this was it, that this was exactly what he had attended. He forgot all about his smashed foot. He turned to the man beside him.

"Mister O'Hare," he called in a high voice. "Mister O'Hare."

There were two violent crashes in rapid succession and dislodged plaster from the ceiling fell in a shower on the floor.

Dennis O'Hare had swung his legs sideways and kicked over the battered spittoon. A stream of urine ran along the hard earth. The man from the Redlands was getting up. In the dim light from the candles the boy from Nacogdoches could see O'Hare's gray-stubbled face and his sharp blue eyes almost popping out of their sockets. He stood for a moment swaying as though dizzy with his head thrust forward and the loosened bandage sliding down on his forehead. A clamor of cries, oaths, exclamations and movement swirled in the fetid chamber.

"I can't git up, Mister O'Hare!" cried the boy despairingly.

Without turning his head the Irishman reached down a muscular hand and yanked the youth upright, where he stood like a stork on one leg.

"'Tis an assault, bejasus!" O'Hare said hoarsely. "The bastards are on the walls. Where's my gun?"

He lumbered away leaving the boy from Nacogdoches teetering on one foot. And now the boy could hear the rapid cracking of musket and rifle fire and a tumult of shouts from the courtyard beyond the closed door. Barely conscious of what he was doing he began to hop along the earthen floor and once when he lost his balance and had to put his bandaged foot down he screamed with the awful pain. It was as though a thousand red-hot nails had been driven into him. No one seemed to notice him. At the door a half dozen men, including O'Hare, were struggling to get through and their combined pressure finally shot them out into the night like a cork from a champagne bottle. The boy from Nacogdoches went with them. Protecting the door was a triangle of sandbags waist high and behind it three or four men were firing wildly at the dark rim of the west wall. O'Hare, as though by tacit consent, immediately took charge.

"Watch out for our own men, you cursed fools!" he exclaimed.

"They got ladders," declared a voice in the darkness. "I can see the poles. We're shootin' between the poles."

The boy from Nacogdoches collapsed against the cold adobe wall and tried to adjust his eyes to the murky confusion before him. Men seemed to be running in every direction. The cannon on the walls bellowed at intervals. The rattle of musketry sounded like good-sized stones hurled against a barn door. It was difficult to see in the darkness but by straining his eyes and with the aid of the flashes from the cannon the boy could finally make out a jagged line of shifting heads and arms and clubbing muskets and slender poles that shot up beyond the wall and then suddenly disappeared. For some mysterious reason the shouting did not seem to come from this fringe of action but from above it and around it. It was loud enough, though, this outcry that seemed to be both a protest to heaven and a defiance to all malevolent powers. It rose into the starless immensity of the night like a cry that would go on forever.

The boy from Nacogdoches edged along the cold wall of the sickroom toward the sandbags that protected the door on the side toward the barracks. He could think little better than he could see or make sense of the sound he heard but he did reason that if he reached the barracks he could get a rifle, maybe, and shoot a few Mexicans. That was it. In spite of his foot he would have to shoot a few Mexicans, four or five, at least, for that was the reason that he was here. He slipped between the sandbags and the wall and hopped north toward the nearest barrack door. There were heavy boots rushing by him but he was too intent on his objective to notice who were in them. It was only a short distance. There was no feeling in his bandaged foot but all the same he did not dare to put it down again. He balanced by resting one hand against the rough wall. This would be the barracks wall. The door was quite near. He could see the shape of the sandbags there in the glow of light that poured from the interior. Perhaps he could get inside and fire from a window and then after it was all over he would go home and be a hero. Like some of the men he had seen in Gonzales. He would walk up and down the streets of Nacogdoches and perhaps Colonel Henry Raguet's daughter would smile at him as she passed in her carriage. His hand just touched the sandbag barricade to the nearest barrack door when a boy's small form shot over it and knocked him flat on his face.

"God damn ye!" shouted the boy from Nacogdoches as tears of anguish spurted out of his eyes. "You've fair kilt me!"

He rolled over and tried to wrap his arms around the shapeless bundle that was his foot.

Charley Livingston knew that he had knocked somebody over but he did not stop to see who it was. He had one objective and that was the old mission church where he was sure that he would find Mrs. Dickinson and maybe Juan Diego. The Indian always returned to the church after he conducted the little boy to the barracks door. Somewhere in the darkness there he had his lair where he slept and dreamt of Our Lady of Guadalupe. And Mrs. Dickinson slept in the tiny room where the padres had once kept their vestments in ironbound leather chests. She slept there while the captain sat up on the scaffolding by the gun and looked out of the window into the darkness beyond the walls. Charley ran through the din of voices and exploding weapons without looking to left or right. He did not see the fringe of figures on the wall or the men retreating to the sandbags by the building's doors. He did not even know that the infrequent sharp buzzes above his head were bullets that smacked into the hard adobe. All he sensed was a dark chaos in which moving shapes were illuminated by bright flashes.

As he ran past the sickroom door someone shouted to him but he did not stop. In a second he was around the corner and tearing by the powder room where several men were rolling out small barrels and boxes and a moment later he was dashing under the heavy front and into the mission church. It was dark in there but the gun on the scaffolding was firing and its thudding reverberations echoed through the hollow edifice. There was a sickening stench of gunpowder in the air. Captain Dickinson and his men were up there, then. They were shooting through the window. That was why the scaffolding creaked and groaned so. But Mrs. Dickinson . . . He ran across the stone floor to the little room and called her name. There was no answer. He saw a solitary candle burning on the little table, a disarrayed pallet and the box in which Angelina slept at night. That was all. Mrs. Dickinson and the baby had vanished.

Charley stood in the middle of the room breathing heavily. His small fists were clenched. He had awakened from a dream into a nightmare and for the first time in his short life he was terribly frightened.

It was not the firing; he had heard that before and while it had startled him it had not aroused any real fear; but this was different. After the unexpected silence it came like a long-expected threat. It was something behind the firing that frightened him, something he could feel without touching and see without eyes and know without thinking, something evil that swelled in the darkness and was all shapes and no shape and all sound and no sound and all silence and no silence. It was just . . . something. His slight body started to shake as he turned and stepped softly back into the murky vastness of the old building. He wanted to find Mrs. Dickinson but he did not know where to look for her. He wanted to find Juan Diego, too, but he did not dare to explore the shadowy recesses of the mission church. Reluctantly, trembling violently, he crept toward the outer door. Behind him the gun on the scaffolding banged away at regular intervals.

It occurred to him that in his flight from the barracks he had seen nothing, nothing, at least, but shapeless running forms and sudden flashes. He had just fled blindly and instinctively from being alone with the fixed purpose of finding the comforting nearness of Mrs. Dickinson. He liked her because she let him alone and did not talk to him or try to caress him as some of the Mexican women did and he liked Angelina because she smelt of milk and sometimes of vomit. He did not like to be touched or kissed but now he felt that it would be good to slip his hand into Mrs. Dickinson's and perhaps even be kissed by her. That terrible something . . . It was so near . . . Peering out the door he could see the crazy design of the picket line of saplings a short distance to the front and right and the constant flashes from rifles. That would be where Colonel Crockett and his men were. Even as he looked, his eardrums spinning from the uproar, a veil seemed to be clawed away by an invisible hand and human figures shaped themselves clearly against the crisscrossed logs. It was getting lighter. Dawn was coming, then. He could see the backs of the buckskin-jacketed Tennesseans as they fired and reloaded and fired again. They worked automatically like beavers. There was Colonel Crockett himself, the big man who was firing as regularly as any of the others. He turned his head and his wide mouth was opening and shutting. He was singing, that's what he was doing. And though Charley could not hear a sound from that mouth he knew what Crockett was singing, his favorite song, the air he trolled as he walked about the courtyard in the evening.

> Will you come to the bow'r I have shaded for you?
> Your bed shall be of roses, bespangled with dew.
> Will you, will you, will you . . .

The boy crouched against the outer door while a whirlwind of explosions and shouts beat about his head. He was still trembling violently but not because of the noise. It was the lack of someone and the fear of something that he could not comprehend. This was not the first time he had heard firing or seen men fall but it was altogether different. It was as though the iron dome of the starless sky was closing down upon him and taking his breath away and stirring erratic reflexes in his skinny body. For instance, his knee kept jumping and would not stop. His hands shook and there was a sensation of tiny cold feet crawling along the back of his neck. He wondered fleetingly whether or not he could move and if he did move if his knees would bear him up. He made the attempt and staggered like an old man with palsy toward the barricade of sandbags that half enclosed the entrance to the mission church. Just as he reached them and spread his arms along their cold hard surface the inconceivable occurred.

Simultaneously with a loud explosion a portion of the picket line of saplings split into fragments and an instant later a stream of agile figures darted through the breach. Others came pouring over the criss-crossed logs, dropping like apples from a heavily fruited tree in a gale and the space before the boy's distended eyes, a space of gray light and fire-shot darkness, merged into a mass of struggling bodies. Swords clashed, rifles exploded, weapons were swung like clubs and screaming men fell constantly to the earth. This mass of desperately engaged humanity sagged slowly backward toward the mission church and constantly enlarged as the invaders sped through the broken logs or dropped from the picket line. There was no end to them and the boy had the feeling that all the world was pouring into the Alamo, a dark vicious world of dark men in bright uniforms who surged onward and drove the little group of Crockett's Tennesseans back by sheer bulk of numbers. It was like a burst dike. It was like a whirling mass of inconceivable matter that was only human when it broke into recognizable elements. One of these elements separated from the monstrous body and dashed straight toward the mission church door. It was a man in a red mask. He was screaming like a hurt horse. He ran blindly into the pile of sandbags, caromed off them and continued to run obliquely across the grand plaza toward the west wall. As he passed Charley saw that the man was not wearing a red mask. He simply had no face at all. A powerful impulse jerked the boy from his semiparalyzed state and he turned and raced back into the church.

Near the northwest corner of the wall not far from the chamber where Jim Bowie lay helpless Travis stood beside a disabled cannon, his drawn sword in one hand and a rifle in the other, and waited for the inevitable. He had expected it from the beginning. Behind him the Negro boy Joe, his black face now as gray as the reluctant dawn, crouched on the ground to make himself as small as possible. At this moment Travis understood everything. He was aware that all was lost and all was won. He knew that it was not the army that survived that always gained the battle. A mysterious light from a source outside himself illuminated all that had brought him to the place where he was and much more that he had not understood before. In no sense of the word introspective or prophetic he now found himself lifted to a plane above the struggle from whose vantage point he could gaze both backward and forward into time. He saw himself at last as the dogged physical expression of an urge, a necessity, a destiny that was greater than he and that gloriously vindicated the arbitrary sacrifice of himself and the hundred and eighty souls who had stayed here because he had stayed here. He had nothing to reproach himself with. It did not matter that neither Houston nor Fannin had come up. That was not in the scheme of things. It would have been a setback. If they had relieved him there could have been no sacrifice and if there was no sacrifice there would be no victory. It was very clear to him and it made him gravely lighthearted.

It was with great calm, then, that he watched the north wall and the fringe of tired men with hot guns and a few ball cartridges apiece who stood on the earthen mounds and waited for the third onslaught of Santa Anna's men. Since four o'clock when the degüello had blown in the darkness there had been two attacks. During these he had been everywhere, running from the picket line at the south to the west wall, then to the north wall and through the barracks and across the cattle and horse pens to the east wall, firing a rifle here and directing a cannon there, encouraging his men at the guns as they loaded grapeshot and scrap iron and blasted it into the ranks of the advancing Mexicans. It had been pitch-black, then. No light but the flashes of the guns. The first attack had faltered at the north wall and then to the west, east and south and the Mexicans had fallen back in confusion, leaving the countryside dotted with prostrate forms. The Texans had roared their exultation at that but Travis had experienced neither exhilaration nor optimism. He knew. The light that had fallen across his mind had made everything clear. Within half an hour the Mexicans had advanced again on all sides in battalion order, trumpets blowing and drums beating, their scaling ladders slanting forward and the artillery behind them hammering the stone buildings and the grand plaza of the Alamo. This time the defense had been more difficult. The besiegers reached the terrain so close to the thick walls that the clumsily placed cannon could not rake them and discharged their grape and scrap iron over their heads. At the south and north walls ladders were actually placed and men started to climb but those above, fighting with clubbed muskets, swords and bowie knives, cut them down as rapidly as they appeared over the parapets. Finally the Mexicans had broken again

and fled incontinently to the farther ground beyond rifle range. For the
second time the Texans had cheered loudly and again Travis, his face
grave and composed from the satisfaction of his revelation, had neither
smiled nor cursed. Knowing perhaps less than he it was better for
them to go down cheering.

And now it was time for the third assault.

It came even as Travis stood beside the disabled gun and watched
the north wall. It started like the roaring of surf or a wild wind in tall
pine trees, a growing bellow rising to an hysterical screaming and
punctuated by the thud of cannon and the staccato reports of muskets
and rifles. Travis dropped his sword and half-crouched as he swung
his rifle up. He could tell by the sound that Santa Anna had massed
the bulk of his forces before the north wall and was flinging them forward with a new ferocity. The vanguard was already in the deep
shadow of the wall and Travis knew that the cannon could no longer
be trained upon it. He knew, too, that the Texans could not use their
rifles and muskets with accuracy for the wall had no inner banquette.
In order to fire they had to stand on the top, presenting themselves as
living targets to be mowed down by a score of Mexican bullets at once.
Travis watched them drop like hit ducks. His eyes were steady and his
face composed as he saw the slaughter. He was no longer William
Barret Travis of Georgia but a symbol of the Texas that was to be.
*I shall never surrender or retreat. "Thou therefore endure hardness,
as a good soldier of Jesus Christ."* But there was no hardness. There
was only the splendid fact. The crouching Negro boy jabbered with
fright but Travis poised on light feet with lifted rifle and did not turn
his head.

He was not surprised when the Mexican troopers came tumbling
over the wall like sheep. They were driven as they were driving, pushed
on by the masses behind them and for every one that landed upright in
the plaza five sprawled dead. The early dawn caught the red flashes of
swords, bayonets and bowie knives and the bright brass glitter on the
accouterments of the coffee-colored invaders. The high roaring was
like a tornado that snapped tree trunks and hurled great boulders down
rocky ledges. Travis raised his rifle to aim it. The Texans were breaking now, those that were still alive, leaping from the wall and the gun-
mounds and running for the long barracks where the sandbags barred
the doors. Behind him he could hear running feet, too, a merging of
all the living in the stone heart of the old fortress. But not for him.
He watched for a target, the butt of his rifle resting gently against
his shoulder and his eye alert along the dark barrel. He wanted an
officer. A high-ranking officer. Oh, God, give him a high-ranking
officer. Santa Anna himself. And then he saw his man standing on the
wall, silhouetted against the gray morning, a captain, maybe, or a

colonel in a gold-frogged white tunic and a red-plumed hat. With a sword in his hand. He would do. Travis took careful aim overanxious for fear of missing but instead of firing he dropped the rifle with a clatter and pitched forward upon his face. A chance bullet had struck him squarely between the eyes. The Negro boy, Joe, bent almost double, ran like a rabbit toward the barracks.

On the north wall Colonel Miñón shouted for his men to bring up howitzers.

The candles, mere stumps of yellow tallow, had long flickered out in the little chamber where Jim Bowie lay in the stagnant darkness staring at the closed door and listening to the end of the world. With the repercussion of the first shots he had striven desperately to rise but there had been no response in his flaccid body. Even the slight strength that had enabled him to fling an empty whisky bottle against the stone wall a few hours before had departed. His body was dead. Nothing remained but that mysterious something which watched and listened and feebly reasoned and was dumbly aware, a slight thread attached to his moribund flesh and inexorably weakening while the tumult mounted in the courtyard. As the sound swelled the thread thinned and soon it would snap. That was good for it was already past the perfect time. It was not right to outlive the body even by a second for every instant of such existence was an aeon of horror in itself. He tried to moisten his lips with his dry tongue but he could not do it. He exerted his will to make an audible sound but nothing came forth except the faint wheezing of his lungs and they functioned laboriously and apart from his will like an alien machine that someone had placed in his breast. He had nothing to do with it and that was fortunate for if he had he would have stopped it. He endeavored to think but even that was impossible. The pictures spun crazily and merged into one another, a yellow road becoming a cobbled street and faces, Travis, Houston, Ursula, joining like the smoke of campfires into one face that hung furtively over him and then became the darkness. It was there and it was not there.

But he could hear.

He could hear the cannon fire and the whacking sound of rifles and muskets and the shouting and the running feet. The noise drew near and departed and then drew near again as though it was lowered and lifted and lowered by some gigantic hand. Sometimes the sounds were separate and sometimes they were all a part of one sound. They were outside the door and then they were inside the door. They came through his ears and they issued from his lungs. For an instant he would be caged by them and a second later they would be caged by him. Now he was flowing along with them as though he was being carried on the frantic current of a river full of rapids. The speed was terrific. He was rushing through a tunnel and there must be an end to it for there was a pale early-morning glow at the end of it. All the faces and places rushed along with him but it was that glow, metal-hued like a knife blade, that must be his terminus and his liberation. He was approaching it. He was dashing upon it. Then the last fragment of his reason, upblazing like the last effort of a guttering candle, recognized it as the open door to his chamber and all the faces that had become one face became many faces again. They were dark and angry faces that seemed to rush in on the wings of a strong wind, a froth of tobacco-colored bubbles on a spate of sound and fury. It struck him on the head and the thin thread snapped.

The Mexican trooper, a yellow-brown burly Indian from as far south as Chiapas who had burst Bowie's skull with the heavy butt of his flintlock musket, wiped the dark wood on his stained trousers and grunted.

"*Jesucristo!*" cried the man behind him. "You have spattered his brains all over the wall!"

"His skull was as thin as an eggshell," said the Indian. "Drag him out. He has the nose of a jefe. The general will want to see him."

The boy from Nacogdoches whimpered like a frightened puppy as he crawled along the ground close to the barracks wall. He had not been able to stand up since the flying body of the boy had knocked him flat on his face and now he was scared for fear he would never be able to stand up again. At least, it felt like that. Every time he tried to straighten his leg the pains ran up from his foot and felt as though some animal with steel teeth was biting into it. It was terrible. He had passed the first barracks door unconsciously for the anguish had blinded him but now, by raising his head sideways, he could see the sandbags ahead that were his goal. He could see the flashes of fire from them and by turning his head sideways the other way he could see the Mexicans tumbling over the west wall and forming a dense mass that was advancing slowly to great yelling. It was plenty light now to see all that. The Mexican officers were screaming and beating their men forward with the flat sides of their swords and the men refused to move fast. That was because the Texians were firing from behind the sandbags that ringed the door and from all the windows of the barracks. They were firing from the church and the sickroom and the powder room and the roofs. They were firing from everywhere and for every shot a Mexican fell on his face or his back. But the bulk kept advancing. There weren't enough bullets in all Texas to stop that. There were still some of the defenders running toward the sandbags but most of the space between the barracks and the mass of invaders was clear except for the men lying on the ground. He would have to move faster if he was to reach the barricade before the narrowing space was blotted out. When he reached the door maybe they'd give him a gun or else he'd crawl through the barracks corridor and come out on the other side where the back sheds and cattle pen were. If there was any fighting there he could not hear it. The din was too infernal. He tried to move faster but it was hard. His foot bumped on the ground and the pains ran up his leg and plunged into his crotch. There was no control there. He began to urinate and a wet streak smeared the earth beneath him. There was something whining and panting beside him and it took him a minute to realize that it was himself. Jesus, but they were coming fast now! He wouldn't look at them. He wouldn't look ahead either because he didn't want to see how far away he was from the sandbags. They must be right ahead although he couldn't hear any firing from them now. Perhaps the Texians had retreated into the barracks. Whimpering, gasping, urinating, he crawled onward like a monstrous lizard and suddenly he was in a flickering chaos of stamping feet. They rose and fell all around him. The noise was unbelievable. It was like a burst dam. He ceased to crawl and buried his face in the cold ground, tasting the flinty flavor of crushed rock. Maybe they would think he was dead. Maybe they would just rush over him. A sharp boot heel crunched his outspread fingers and he screamed high and shrill like a hurt horse. He thought he heard a woman screaming, too. "No! No! No!" It was like a woman's hysterical voice. He rolled sideways regardless of his foot and his dilated eyes caught the flash of something blue like a woman's skirt. Then it was gone. A second later he felt the bayonet plunge into his kidney and with the last reaction of self-preservation he flung his arm out in a gesture of defense. The smashed fingers were outspread like a red starfish.

The remnant had been forced back into the barracks and here Dennis O'Hare found himself fighting furiously the resistless wave of Mexicans that flowed through the door and windows. Beside him a score of powder-blackened, blood-besmeared comrades whirled their muskets like Indian clubs and brought them down with hollow thwacks on the heads of the invaders. There was a sound like bursting melons. O'Hare, his bandage fallen about his neck and the reopened wounds on his head spurting gore, had secured a sword and slashed with it viciously at the dark faces that crowded toward him. They were innumerable, these faces, and as fast as one dipped and fell three or four others took its place. They sprouted in the gloom of the corridor like evil mushrooms, seeming to split, form in wholes and split again like a demon growth that increased faster than it could be destroyed. He had seen fires in the Redlands like this, a fringe of destruction creeping and rushing and spreading and mocking with its hot breath the puny efforts of men to control it. And the smoke-dense air of the corridor increased the likeness. The Mexicans still had plenty of powder and ball and they fired constantly into the retreating melting clot of Texans. O'Hare, pushed back with the rest, passed door after door where his own men were waiting with knives, bayonets and swords behind the heaped bodies of their dead. He could hear the deafening reverberations of the muskets and see those valiant few cut down as they held the doorways for a moment and then were crushed beneath the sheer weight of numbers. The acrid atmosphere was heavy with the smell of new blood.

Presently they would reach the farther wall, the last room beyond which there was no retreat. There would be nothing to do then but to face as they faced now and fight until their arms could no longer swing and thrust and the bullets of the Mexicans had mown them all down. One last pile for the liberation of Texas. A sacrifice to the god of the future. O'Hare did not word it so to himself as his hairy arm darted forward and the sword ripped into the throat of an advancing trooper but he had the exalted feeling that the last room would be something that Time would remember as long as men fought for a fairer world. He had been with old Ben Milam down there at Bexar and now he was with Travis at the Alamo. The Keltic gods would not forget that. The blood streamed down into his eyes but he was too busy to wipe it away. The man beside him fell against him but he merely stepped away and let him fall like a sack of corn to the floor. A bullet ripped along his shoulder but he hardly felt it. The gray stubble on his brick-red face was wet and his sharp blue eyes were half-blinded by a viscous substance but he continued to lunge and parry, to retreat step by step, to bawl orders that no one heard and to bellow for the sheer sake of bellowing. He had never felt better in his life. A queer gorgeous joy possessed him and in it he felt invulnerable to wounds and ricocheting musket balls. He could go on fighting like this until Fannin or Houston reached Bexar, until all the Mexicans in Mexico were slaughtered, until . . . Simultaneously he was struck in the sword hand and the left knee and he slumped downward into a sitting position. There was a bewildered glad expression on his spattered face as he heard the men behind him. They were scrambling into the last room and hauling some old lumber forward to make a barricade. That was it. Hold them there, Texans. Hold them. He lifted his bloody hand and tried to wipe his eyes and then through a crimson mist he blinked and peered along the corridor and was surprised to see that he was not engulfed by Mexicans. For an instant he thought they had retreated and was about to raise his hoarse voice in a bellow of triumph when he saw the squat monster leveled directly at him. By

God, they had hauled in a howitzer and were going to fire it down the corridor. They were stuffing its upturned maw now and he saw the flash of the lighted match. He wanted to laugh. Bejasus, they had to bring up a howitzer to kill him. They couldn't do it with muskets and swords and knives and pistols. They had to bring up a howitzer. He sat there with his mouth wide open laughing uproariously when the thundering crash came and he was enringed with a bright flashing circle of crimson and gold.

In the northeast corner of the mission church where a portion of the roof had been destroyed by round shot and fire some time before lay a huge haphazard pile of stones and collapsed wall and it was in the midst of this debris that Charley Livingston crouched and watched the dawn spread across the sky colored like a fish's belly and continually suffused with a lemon-hued light. When he had run back into the building from the barricade of sandbags he had instinctively sought this heap of damp masonry and popped into it like a rabbit into a hole. Now he squatted in a miniature fortress all his own and watched the sky and listened to the noise. He couldn't forget the man without a face. It was all red like meat and with a black hole in it. The man couldn't see. That was why he ran into the sandbags and bounced off like a ball thrown against a wall. Probably, he was bouncing all around the plaza by this time, hitting buildings, walls, people, anything at all, and never knowing what he hit because he didn't have any eyes. There was a bird that had got caught in one of the barracks rooms that acted like that. But the bird had eyes. It could see but it didn't seem to try to see. It was too scared. Sometimes people couldn't see when they were too scared. But it was different with the man who had bounced off the sandbags. Charley knew that he could see if he stood up and peered over the wreckage but he didn't feel like standing up. He just wanted to sit or crouch where he was until Mrs. Dickinson or Juan Diego came and found him. They would come sometime because they always did.

His feet beneath his small bottom began to go to sleep and so he twisted about and sat down with his back against a large rough piece of cornice. He didn't tremble any more but he was still frightened. The noise had been like a great giant rushing around and slamming doors and butting into walls and knocking things over. It was blind, too. Sometimes it came very close to him and then it went away again. It was all one sound but it was made up of different noises. It was made up of musket shots and cannon explosions and pieces of wall falling and men yelling. He could recognize Captain Dickinson's gun on the scaffolding for when that went off it shook the inside of the church and bits of stone fell about him. After a while he didn't hear it any more. But he heard the men who ran into the church and fired their

muskets and shouted and then ran out again. When that happened he
had crouched as low to the ground as he could and the trembling in his
limbs had started again. Then there wasn't any noise in the church at
all and as the minutes crawled along he had stopped trembling and
even been tempted to peep over the big oblong stones. But he hadn't.
He was afraid that he would see something he did not want to see. The
noise was all outside now, bumping against the walls and pouring into
the unroofed portion of the church. It was day up there, a lemon-
colored day that brightened all the time and flowed in a slanting shaft
into the somber interior of the building. He could see thousands of
particles of dust dancing in that impalpable shaft. He could smell the
smoke that impregnated the day. It was like burning hair or charred
leather. Quite suddenly he realized that it was cold and with the realization his teeth began to chatter. He crossed his arms and shut his eyes
as he leaned his head against the rough cornice. He would have to wait.
That was all there was to it. He would have to wait until Mrs. Dickinson or Juan Diego found him. The minutes passed and the noise
lessened. Presently he heard heavy footsteps and a murmur of voices
and his eyes opened quickly. He stared at the broken masonry before
him and listened. The footsteps continued, a lot of them, and they
spread about the church, scraping, thumping, echoing, approaching.
The voices were speaking in Spanish. One of them exclaimed,
"Cabrón!" and another angrily retorted, "Más que babieca!" They
were very close now and abruptly a silence fell and there were no footsteps at all. For a moment Charley continued to stare fixedly at the
stone before him and then some inexplicable power forced his eyes
upward and he looked directly into the black eyes and brown face of a
Mexican sargento.

The sargento reached over and plucked Charley up like a puppy
and set him down beside him. A half dozen sullen-looking soldiers, one
of them with a still-bleeding cut across his cheek, gathered around and
inspected the boy with some interest.

"What are you doing here, muchacho?" asked the sargento.

"Maybe he is the comandante's son," said one of the soldiers.

"Be quiet, majadero," ordered the sargento. "The comandante had
no son."

He squatted down until his face was level with Charley's eyes.

"What is your name?" he asked. "Can you speak Spanish?"

The boy's voice wouldn't come. He stared into the copper-colored
heavy face and nodded.

"Shall we slice him up?" suggested the soldier with the bleeding
face. "We have orders . . ."

"I give orders," declared the sargento, straightening up. "We will take him to the general. The general will want to see him. Come on, now. Vámonos."

He grasped Charley firmly by the arm and steered him across the empty shell of the church. The boy could see that there were a lot of Mexican soldiers in the church now. They were poking about in the shadowy corners and exploring the little side chambers. Except for an occasional sporadic shot from outside there was no noise, nothing but the clacking of the soldiers' feet and the swift sibilance of their spoken words. Near the scaffolding that supported the gun there was a small group and as the boy was thrust past it he saw that it was looking down at several bodies. He looked, too. Captain Dickinson lay on his back with his mouth open and his head so far back that his chin thrust up like a male duck's tail when it drinks. The front of his belly was all covered with blood. He lay with his leg crumpled under him as though he had fallen from the scaffolding. Something, perhaps the fear that was already convulsing Charley's small body, froze and from the instant he saw the dead face of Captain Dickinson there was no longer any animate emotion,. fear or horror or disgust, in the boy's mind. He had seen death before but never in this way. The hushed decency was gone and in its place was the unsuspected ugliness and meanness of a slaughtered jack rabbit on a butcher's block. From the instant that Charley saw the distorted body of Captain Dickinson he ceased to function as a normal boy who can be frightened or horrified. Instead, he became a vacant eye, a stunned observer, a moving automaton without impulse or emotion.

"Vámonos," repeated the sargento, pulling the boy along roughly.

They passed over the broken stone slabs of the church pavement into the daylight. A weak morning sun, obscured by lifting clouds of gray-brown smoke, shone down on the courtyard. There were bodies before the sandbags, bodies by the smashed picket wall, bodies spotted over the earth around the well, and through these prostrate figures moved Mexican soldiers in bright uniforms, their bayonet-tipped muskets poking and thrusting at the clots of disordered and blood-stained garments. Near the entrance to the powder room stood a group of officers and it was toward them that the sargento thrust Charley. The sargento wanted to attract the attention of one of the officers, the one who was leaning over and examining a naked cadaver terribly slashed with bayonet wounds, but he was afraid to attempt it. He kept pulling Charley hither and thither in the hope that they would be observed by the officer. The officer straightened.

"Bowie was much too brave a man to be treated like a dog," he said crisply, averting his eyes from the cadaver.

Then he shrugged his shoulders.

"Pues no vale la pena!" he declared. "Well, it is of little consequence."

The sargento pushed Charley a little nearer.

"Almonte!" called the officer. "See that this body is put with the rest. Are they bringing up the wood?"

"Yes, general," answered a young man in a blue and red uniform. "The cavalry is cutting timber and in Bexar . . ."

"Good," said the officer. "We shall have such a fire that all Texas will feel the heat of its flames. What is it, Martin?"

A stout man in uniform, who had come up hurriedly, began to speak in an urgent indistinguishable voice, spreading his hands pleadingly as the words poured out.

"No, no, no!" broke in the officer savagely. "My order was to kill every man in the Alamo. Seę to it, then, General Cos."

He swung on his boot heel and Charley saw his dark bloodshot eyes.

"What's this?" demanded the officer. "What have you there, Juan Becerra?"

"Excelencia, it is a boy," explained the sargento in a frightened voice. "It is a gringo boy. I found him in the church. Would you like to look at him, Excelencia? Shall I . . ."

Two scattered gunshots echoed from the barracks.

"Dale!" exploded the officer. "There are some rats left over there, then? Clean them out, Castrillón. Every one of them. What's that, Juan Becerra? A boy? Well, take him down to headquarters. Take him to the Múzquiz house. Perhaps I will have time to look at him there. Almonte! Where the devil are you, Almonte?"

Charley observed the flushed and bloodshot-eyed officer without interest. He was a colored picture like all the rest and the boy saw him merely because he came before his eyes.

"Move, now!" ordered the sargento, tightening his grip on Charley's arm. "Do you hear what su Excelencia says? We will go into Bexar."

Su Excelencia was still shouting orders as they moved toward the broken gate.

There were seven in the group of captives who stumbled along the rough ground, leaving behind them the breached Alamo and moving downward toward the fringe of houses on the riverbank that was Bexar. A dozen mounted cavalrymen surrounded them and urged them forward. They traveled slowly, constantly stepping aside for the soldiers bearing logs, branches and house plankings who passed in the opposite direction. A heavy dust, curiously oillike in odor and agitated by the hoofs of the horses, rose to the waists of the adults and made them seem in the dull morning light like floating upright torsos on a sullen sea. Three of the seven had children, Mrs. Dickinson carrying Angelina, the Mexican wife of Dr. Alsbury clutching tightly to the hand of her son whose head bobbed along on the dust waves like a jettisoned melon and Señora Eufemia Marmolejo, the other Mexican, who carried her eight-year-old daughter with some difficulty. The seventh captive was Joe, the Negro boy.

Mrs. Dickinson, hatless and with disarranged hair, moved with her head bowed and eyes half-closed. She had the feeling that she was reaching the end of one nightmare and approaching the beginning of another. Since the sudden gunfire at four o'clock had roused her from slumber and she had snatched up Angelina and fled to the barracks in search of Charley Livingston she had been aware only of action and the arrival of an attended moment. The end of the world. That was the attended moment. She had known it at midnight when she stood beside the scaffolding and listened to the silence and dimly heard the touched Indian, Juan Diego, tell his strange story to the small boy. And now' it was the end of the world'. Time was falling in fragments all about her as she trudged along in the dust and was supremely indifferent to her destination. It was time to die, then, for it was both stupid and cruel to outlive one's world. She was sorry that she had not found Charley. He had not been in the barracks and she had not seen him behind any of the sandbag barricades. Perhaps he had fled to the horse pen or the farther cattle pen. She had not dared to look far.

Everything had happened suddenly like a great explosion. The night had burst into a great flower of flame and smoke through which she heard the cannon and rifle fire and the terrible shouting of men. Enlarged figures had rushed by her and she had stumbled over prostrate bundles that had yielded to her foot and had been men. She had smelt blood and urine and gunpowder. The echoes had pursued her along the corridor of the barracks and back again into the courtyard where the early dawn was tumbling over the walls with the Mexican soldiers. There was the boy with the great blood-drenched bundle of rags on his foot who lay with his face pressed to the earth while the invaders swung their bayonets at him. An instinct had flung her forward to his rescue but brown angry hands had thrust her away. What had happened after that? A blind man had knocked her down as he caromed along the sandbags. Joe's black face touched to clay gray had bobbed out of the smoke. Travis was dead. Crockett was dead. Bowie was dead. Patton was dead. Pollard was dead. Bonham was dead. Dickinson . . . Ah, yes. She had known that from the beginning. She had known it even before the cannon in the church ceased firing. It was there that her mind stopped. There was no path to travel beyond that point. And no reason to travel, either. Thinking and not thinking she stumbled along in the dust, clutching Angelina tightly to her breast and only vaguely aware of the soldiers bearing bundles of wood, logs, branches and planks, who streamed past her on all sides.

It was only after a long time that she became dimly conscious of a figure padding softly beside her and sometimes pressing gently against her arm. With the reluctance of the stunned she forced herself to glance sideways and down and saw the incredibly ancient wrinkled face and black glittering pouched eyes of Juan Diego, the Indian who was loco. "Loco rematado," the priest had said. The priest had not been loco. He had run away. The sight of this dark face with the map of eternity engraved upon it recalled something to Mrs. Dickinson and after a moment it became plain.

"The boy?" she asked with fear in her voice. "Where is little Charley, Juan Diego? Where is the boy?"

The Indian's twisted mouth, like a knife slit in weathered leather, moved soundlessly as though he was chewing his answer.

"With Our Lady," he said finally. "They are all with Our Lady." He waved his hand backward at the Alamo.

"Oh, no!" Mrs. Dickinson exclaimed. "They wouldn't do that. See. There are three children here."

Juan Diego put his thumb and forefinger together and placed them against his lips. Then he blew sharply through them and opened his hand.

"With Our Lady," he repeated.

After that he would not speak again. He seemed not to hear as he padded along softly beside her and sometimes pressed gently against her arm. The sickly sweet smell of his aged unwashed body rose to her nostrils and it appeared to her that here was the smell of death, too. Presently a cavalryman urged his horse closer and lashed at the Indian with the side of his saber.

"Ah bribón!" he shouted. "Fuera! Clear out or I'll chop your ears off!"

Juan Diego disappeared into the dust.

"He daid," chattered Joe, who was just behind Mrs. Dickinson. "Oh, yas, missis. He daid long time. He sho daid now."

Dumbly she accepted the fact. She accepted the fact that everybody who was not walking with her was dead. That was what the end of the world meant.

They were nearing Bexar now and she could see the muddy glister of the river not so far ahead. Suddenly the brassy notes of a regimental band crashed into the smoky air and it was to triumphal music that she turned in obedience to the mounted cavalrymen and directed her steps to the makeshift bridge that Santa Anna's engineers had flung hastily across the San Antonio.

In the back chamber of the Múzquiz house Charley Livingston stood against the wall and silently watched the young woman in the white lace dress puffed out with many petticoats eat bananas. First she pulled the skins off and threw them on the table and then she put the end of banana into her mouth and kept pushing until it was all gone. After that she licked her fingers. The solemn observation of the boy made her laugh and when she laughed he could see the pink end of her tongue dancing in her mouth.

"Eh, hijito," she said, "come over here and sit on my knee and I will give you a banana."

He shook his head.

"Are you afraid of me?" she asked. "Do not be afraid of me. I am Señora Beatriz Sosa de Santa Anna. I am the wife of the general. I am very fond of little boys. How old are you?"

Charley compressed his lips tightly and continued to stare at her.

"I don't think you have any tongue," she said, laughing. "Stick it out and let me see. No? What a stubborn child you are. I think you must be a Yanqui. Are you a Yanqui? Perhaps you cannot speak Spanish. Can you speak Spanish? What? Well, you are a bad child. You are not a chiquito. You are a chiquitico. No, you are a chiquirritico."

She reminded him of a young parakeet except that she was prettier. Her teeth were small and white and her nose had a little hook in it. He decided that she could not be much more than half a dozen years older than himself. She would be sick if she continued eating bananas.

"I was frightened at all the noise," she said. "Were you frightened when the guns went off? I wanted to crawl under the bed. But after a while they stopped and now it is all over. The general is going to make a great fire and burn up all those bad men and then he is going to drive all the gringos out of Texas. I wanted to go with him because I am the wife of the general. But he thought the journey would be too hard for me. He is going to send me to San Luis Potosí in a beautiful coach and I am to live in a great house there that is full of servants and jewels and flowers and . . . oh . . . everything. Would you like to come with me and be my little boy? If you do you will have to promise to talk to me. What is your name? How old are you?"

Charley maintained his silence. He had not heard such a flow of words since he had blundered into Belita's room and found her standing in the wooden tub taking her monthly bath. That was a long time ago. Belita had clapped the washcloth into her crotch and screamed such a frantic stream of expostulations that his father, who was sleeping by the stove in the kitchen, had waked up and fallen off the chair in a fit of laughter. It was funny that he should think of that now. It was such a long time ago. Papa and David and Belita and Enriqueta. He could see them clearer than the people he had been living with only the day before. They lived beyond the stunned space in his mind like bright figures in a colored picture-book but yesterday's and today's people were in the stunned space. For the moment he could neither see nor feel them.

"Oh, what a wretched child you are!" cried the girl. "You are like a stick of wood. You should be thrown into the fire under the oven. How would you like that? You must not forget that I am the wife of the general and that when I bid you speak you must answer. I shall have many servants in San Luis Potosí and I shall direct all of them to beat you if you are not a good boy."

Good boy. Tú eres buen muchacho. Who . . . ?

"Do you see this bracelet?" asked the girl, extending her thin arm. "Do you see all the stones in it? They are emeralds. The Mexicans call them quetzalitzli. The general, my husband, gave me this bracelet. It is very beautiful. He will give me many others like it. If you are a good boy I will let you hold it in your hand. Come now. Tell me your name?"

Of course. He remembered. They were sitting in the church . . .

"Juan Diego," he said aloud, nodding his head.

The girl burst into laughter. She was funny. She laughed all the time like a hungry parakeet.

"That is not your name," she insisted. "How can your name be Juan Diego?"

His observation of her became puzzled. He had not said that his name was Juan Diego. How could it be? His name was Charley Livingston. He had merely remembered who had called him a good boy.

"Juan Diego," cried the girl, clapping her hands together. "Juan Diego."

Well . . . if she desired it that way. He let his eyes shift from her to the closed door behind which he could hear raised masculine voices. There was a regimental band playing out in the plaza and its music was strident and gay. He could hear it above the girl's chatter and the grumble of the men's conversation. It would be near noon now. He was tired and hungry and a little dizzy. Under him he could feel his legs weakening and it required an effort to keep from slipping down into a sitting posture. There was no reason not to sit down but he did not want to. There was no reason not to accept a banana, either, except that he had never eaten one and was afraid of them. But he didn't want to. However, he couldn't resist looking at the girl again as she peeled another and put it to her mouth. The banana was firm and creamy white and her mouth around it was red and moist. It slid slowly up and disappeared. There was something rather sickening about the process but the girl seemed to like it. She opened her eyes very wide and showed her little white teeth when she laughed. She was laughing now

"Juan Diego," she said. "Juan Diego."

Why not? The repetition of the name brought the gnarled little figure of the Indian back into Charley's mind and he saw him clearly sitting on the cold stones of the church with his back to the thick wall. There was much smoke in his eyes, he said. "And out of the two frames Our Lady of Guadalupe watches the Indians as they come and go." He could remember that, too. If he thought hard he would remember more. But not while the girl was laughing and she was laughing all the time. Like a parakeet. She looked at him and laughed and thrust her tongue out and laughed again. And now she was reaching for another banana. She would surely be sick. It was not good to eat too many bananas. Perhaps, though, the general had brought her these bananas all the way from Mexico City for a marriage gift. In that case . . . He continued to stare at her gravely while she laughed and made faces at him.

Bexar was crowded with Mexican troops and in the Civil Plaza a regimental band was brassily playing gay airs. A stand of colors ruffled in the breeze before the church. Mrs. Dickinson, hurried along with her fellow captives by the armed guards and entering the town for the first time since that frantic twenty-third of February when Travis had removed the garrison and its women to the Alamo, saw a community that had boldly shifted from a sullen acquiescence to an undisguised elation. As she passed up the main thoroughfare to the Múzquiz house she was not surprised to note the triumph on the scores of brown faces that lined the way and laughed as the humiliated gringos stumbled by. She was not surprised and she was not humiliated. She was not even astonished that her numbed faculties accepted all this horror as something that had been expected and would have to be endured. A portion of her mind seemed dead or in a mortal trance but the lesser part of it could observe in a detached and casual fashion. She could see the faces and the flags and hear the cries and the music but she could not think about her predicament or her future or what all this meant to her life. Those emotions appeared to lie beneath a hard shell of ice and she was convinced that when the ice broke, as it would have to break, she would die. Through the splintered ice would rise the corpses, swollen from immersion, of everything that had made life worth living and she would die. Everything except Angelina. She, at least, was lying warm against her frozen heart, a small living impulse in a world of death and through that impulse she, the mother, could live and breathe for a little while. Until the ice broke. Until the pallid corpses pulled her down into the freezing depths.

Now they were at the Múzquiz house and halted in the crude sunlight while a crowd of officers with jingling spurs, heavy sabers and plumed hats passed in and out of the guarded door. Some distance away a boisterous gesticulating mass of Mexican civilians observed the little group of captives and called to them in jeering tones. Some of the faces seemed familiar. And Mrs. Dickinson automatically recalled the last day she had passed in this town. The twenty-third of February. Neither hot nor cold. It had begun to a sudden excitement, a flurry of movement, inhabitants of every class hurrying to and fro in the streets, houses being emptied and their contents piled into carts that rumbled off into the countryside, barefooted laborers shouldering their effects and slipping out of the buzzing hive. Colonel Travis had issued an order forbidding any departures from Bexar and backed it up by a series of arrests of fleeing residents. It had not stopped the exodus. By ten o'clock fully two-thirds of the population had decamped. It was not until eleven o'clock that a friendly Mexican had informed the commandant that Santa Anna's cavalry was at León only eight miles away and that messages had been sent to the native population warning them to evacuate the town as it would be attacked the next day. Travis had acted quickly after receiving this information. He had sent John Sutherland out to scout and Sutherland had returned in a half hour with the disturbing news that a body of some fifteen hundred mounted men wearing polished breastplates and carrying lances were little more than a mile and a half from Bexar. The alarm bell of the old church was rung and it was then that the garrison had retired behind the thick walls of the Alamo, taking with it only what it could carry in its hands.

It had been a day of fear and flight and now these men who had fled not to the Alamo but into the countryside to secret caches with their furniture and goods were back again to fawn before the peg-legged conqueror and gloat over the few remaining victims. They were waiting for the wine and the dances. There were scores of them, big-shouldered and capable, who might have handled a gun on the besieged walls but that was not in their ignorant scheme of things. They had always been disaffected to the liberation of Texas and suspicious of settlers from the States. "Let us alone," they seemed to say. "Let us suffer persecution if we choose. Let us speak our own language and live our own lives and worship our own God." Mrs. Dickinson saw their brown stubborn faces and dark eyes and glittering teeth and vaguely acknowledged them to be a distant and alien race. There was something wrong somewhere. There was nothing that could be done now. There was nothing that could be done tomorrow. There was nothing that could be done until the bitter smell of blood was washed clean from this land.

A hairy sargento tugged roughly at her arm and she turned, holding Angelina tight against her breast. Mrs. Alsbury and the other Mexican woman had gone with their children. Only Joe stood disconsolately by the door, his black face still tinged with the gray of fright. Shaking her arm free from the sargento's grasp she mounted the steps and passed into the large living room of the Múzquiz house. A dozen officers were clustered about a table but at her entrance they spread apart and she found herself facing a seated officer who lifted his head from a paper and fastened two large melancholy eyes upon her face. She stared dumbly at him.

"Come closer," ordered Santa Anna in a low voice.

She advanced until her skirt touched the table at which he was seated.

"You are the Dickinson woman," he said. "And this is the baby. What is her name? Angelina? You see, I am well-informed."

He leaned forward and thrust a blunt finger at the child. Mrs. Dickinson instinctively started to shrink back and then she arrested the movement. What did it matter? She watched the muscular hand with its two rings from which winked large stones fall softly upon Angelina's tiny wrist.

"It is a beautiful baby," said Santa Anna.

She could tell from the sound of his voice that he meant it.

"Mrs. Dickinson," he went on in the same low easy tone, "I beg you to have no fear. You are quite safe. The ends of justice have been accomplished here and treason has been punished. But I do not war against women."

He paused and waited for a reply but she said nothing.

"Do you hear me?" he asked pleasantly. "You are not deaf, are you?"

She ran her tongue across her dry lips.

"No," she replied, "I am not deaf, General Santa Anna."

"Good," he said, smiling. "Then we can converse."

He seemed incapable of taking his eyes from the baby's sleepy face.

"I commiserate with you upon the unfortunate death of your husband," he declared. "I understand that he fought valiantly to the end and I am always prepared to acknowledge the bravery of an antagonist. I am also merciful where mercy is justified. If this had been war I would have treated your men as honorable soldiers and prisoners of war. Unhappily it was not war. This was a treasonable rebellion of criminally-minded subjects of the Republic of Mexico and certain American outlaws who plotted against the safety and integrity of my country. I had no other course. The law was clear. If I had dealt with this shameful rebellion in any other way I would have been a traitor myself to Mexico. Do you understand?"

Mrs. Dickinson said nothing.

Santa Anna cleared his throat and caressed Angelina's chin with his brown finger.

"Was she frightened?" he asked in a sympathetic voice.

"No," replied Mrs. Dickinson.

"Did she sleep through it all?" he persisted.

"No," answered the mother. "No, she did not sleep through it all."

Her reply was punctuated by several triumphant shots from the street.

Santa Anna expelled a deep sigh.

"She is a beautiful baby," he repeated. "How small her hands are."

Mrs. Dickinson closed her eyes.

"What do you plan to do, señora?" demanded Santa Anna softly.

"I have not thought so far," she replied in a thin tight voice.

Suddenly she was terribly frightened. Vague memories of stories of captured American women crawled like cold little snakes into her mind and for an instant she thought she would lose consciousness. But perhaps they had not been true. There had been so much lying that it was impossible to separate the true from the false. And Santa Anna was not an Indian. She placed her hand on the table to steady herself and the weight of the child was heavy on her breast.

"You are a widow now and life will be difficult for you," said Santa Anna gravely. "Perhaps you have no money. Or few friends. You must not be afraid of me, Señora Dickinson. I am very soft-hearted where women and children are concerned. Let me make you an offer. Your little child needs a protector. Permit me to place her in my own family and educate her. It would please me very much. I will provide well for her future and if you like you may come with her."

For an instant Mrs. Dickinson was speechless at the effrontery of the offer and then she thought that it must be some trick. She stared accusingly into the eyes of Santa Anna. There was a softness and earnestness there that were unmistakable. This man meant what he was saying and the realization of it aroused a revulsion in her that caused her to turn her head away. She could not look at him.

"No," she said in a barely perceptible voice.

Santa Anna sighed for the second time.

"As you will," he replied.

There was an instant's silence and then the general turned his head decisively.

"Almonte!" he called in a brisk tone.

There was a new and angry note in his voice.

The young officer moved toward him.

"We will send Señora Dickinson and her child to Gonzales with an escort," Santa Anna said sharply.

He lifted his melancholy eyes to the woman.

"You may go, señora," he declared. "When you encounter General Houston give him my compliments and inform him that the treatment accorded the Alamo is the treatment I propose to inflict upon the remaining traitors in Texas. Tell him that I will give no quarter. Tell him—"

A hard vicious grating sound permeated his voice and he stopped abruptly with a heavy exhalation of air. A fleck of saliva struck against Mrs. Dickinson's hand. Though it was cold it seemed to burn.

"That is all," snapped Santa Anna as he deliberately averted his face and unseeingly shuffled the papers on the table before him. He gave the appearance of a man whose sensitive feelings had been hurt.

Almonte touched Mrs. Dickinson's arm gently and she turned and silently followed him out of the chamber. The attending officers watched her go with sly speculative eyes.

Santa Anna cleared his throat twice, pushed the papers away so violently that several of them floated to the floor and then scowled at the group of booted men who were standing some distance from the table. They bowed humbly. The loose rowel of a big spur clashed.

After a minute or two Almonte returned.

"Is that the end of them?" demanded Santa Anna irritably.

"There's the Negro boy," replied the young aide.

"Send him along to Gonzales with the woman," ordered the general. "Have you arranged that each Mexican be given a blanket and two dollars?"

"Yes, my general," answered Almonte. "They are pleased with your generosity."

"Good!" exclaimed Santa Anna, a faint warmth coming into his voice. "I'm glad somebody is thankful for something. These people do not understand me or my position, Almonte. That woman . . . Well, it does not matter. I shall call a general council within the hour. Let me know when Cos's scouts come in."

Almonte starting to turn stopped suddenly.

"There's a small boy in the back room," he explained. "Shall I send him along to Gonzales with the others?"

"A small boy?" repeated Santa Anna. "Oh, yes. I remember. Bring him in here. I'd like to see him."

Almonte went into the back room and returned an instant later with Charley Livingston.

Santa Anna stood up and leaned over the table to inspect the boy better. A smile lightened his sallow face.

"What is your name, hijito mío?" he asked softly.

Charley looked up into the dark pleasant eyes and felt better. He didn't remember having seen this man with the gold decorations before but it seemed to him that he must have for he had an instant feeling of knowing him. He wasn't afraid of him at all. This must be the general. The one who was married to the silly girl in the back room. He couldn't understand why the general liked her but if he did it would be well for him to accept the name she had given him. It wouldn't be proper to correct her and show that she was wrong. The general might not like that. Besides, he liked the name better than his own. It made him feel almost as though he had seen Our Lady on the Hill of Tepeyac.

"Juan Diego," he said gravely.

"What? What?" asked the general quickly. "Juan Diego? Why, what fine Spanish he speaks."

He turned to Almonte.

"Who is he?" he demanded. "Was his father killed up there? Where is his mother?"

"No one seems to know anything about him," replied the aide. "I can make inquiries . . ."

"Never mind," broke in Santa Anna hurriedly, a sly expression of satisfaction infiltrating his smile. "We will dispense with the inquiries. Dios mío! El es un picarillo. I don't want any stupid inquiries."

He reached over the table and tweaked Charley by the ear.

"You are a fine little fellow," he said happily, "and if your name is not Juan Diego I now give it to you. How do you like that? Juan Diego, eh? Juan Diego de Béxar. Isn't that good? How old are you? Nine? Ten?"

"I am ten years old," replied Charley, his eyes dropping to the embossed hilt of the general's saber where a bowknot of red, white and green ribbons was elegantly tied.

Santa Anna laughed aloud.

"A splendid boy," he declared. "And how excellently he speaks. Why, in a few years he will be ready for the Military College. Almonte, we must find some new clothes for this hombrecito. Break into a few houses and find some."

"You are going to send him to Gonzales, of course?" remarked the aide in a questioning tone that was disapprovingly sharp with doubt.

"Gonzales? Ridiculous!" exclaimed Santa Anna. "I shall send him to San Luis Potosí in the coach with the other. He is my boy now. After all, he is alone in the world. Would I . . ."

"But we don't . . ." began Almonte, his brown face flushing.

The general stopped him with a flashing look.

"You would like it at Manga de Clavo," he said to Charley. "You will play all day there and when you are larger I will give you a little uniform. I will give you plenty of oranges. Eh, Juan Diego? You would like that? Eh?"

Charley looked up soberly at the laughing general.

"I will like that," he assented.

Santa Anna bent down and gave him a resounding kiss on the forehead. Then he straightened up and faced his officers.

"I am a humane and softhearted man," he said simply as a single
tear trembled on his long lashes. "Never forget that, señores."
Concealing a scowl Almonte strode toward the outer door.

The big coach was balanced on huge leather straps and it rolled
and tumbled as the mules dragged it along the road in the direction of
the Nueces. Charley clutched fast to the looped thong that served for
arm support and watched the top of the cavalryman's boot rise and fall
beyond the open door-window. He was tired of the girl's chatter and
a little startled when she slapped him because he would not answer her
stupid questions but he was not frightened. He had got all over that.
He did not know exactly where he was going but as the general was
taking care of that he felt quite safe. He felt even safer than he had
when Mrs. Dickinson stroked his hair with her thin hand. He had not
felt so safe since his father had gone away and never returned again
and the big man with the carrot-colored sidewhiskers had taken David
to his house and Belita and Enriqueta had rolled up all the pots and
pans in the bedclothes and hurried off with them and Captain Dickinson
had put him on the horse and ridden into Bexar with him. He couldn't
understand all of it but he had understood more than they thought.
That was a frightened boy, that Charley Livingston, but now that he
was Juan Diego he wouldn't be frightened any more. He was a new
boy now and he didn't belong to Texas any more. He belonged to the
general and he was going south to the general's big house. There would
be plenty of Mexican boys to play with there and he had always preferred to play with them. He liked the way they talked and the way
they thought. They were different from the gringo boys. They grew
out of the ground, in a way, while the gringo boys did not seem to
belong where they were. He couldn't explain it exactly to himself but
he knew how he felt about it. When he was with the gringo boys he
didn't feel like them and when he was with the Mexican boys he did
feel like them. That was part of the secret between him and old
wrinkled Juan Diego, the loco Indian. Now he *was* Juan Diego and he
would not have to pretend to be Charley Livingston any longer. That
was good.

All the same there was something at the bottom of his mind that
might have troubled him if he had stared at it too fixedly. It lay there
like a curious stone in clear water as a reminder but he kept away from
it and was conscious of it only when his thoughts veered too close to
the attack on the Alamo. And as yet he would not circumscribe that.
His mind grew numb before it and realized it only in sharp little
fragmentary recognitions that stabbed like splinters of glass. The man
with the red mask. The disappearance of Mrs. Dickinson. Captain
Dickinson's body. The sound of the guns. These things hurt him but

he avoided them without too much effort by confining himself to what was immediately passing and what was to come. It was easy. It was like a game. He had played it as far back as he could remember. When his father knocked the lamp over and set the kitchen on fire and then beat Belita because she screamed he pretended that he had not seen or heard it and went right on playing with the broken pieces of the pottery jar. It was something like that. He shut the bad things out. He shut them out because they hurt him and by ignoring them they did not exist. When they came too close to him he moved away. That was all. It was only gringo boys who showed when they were hurt. Mexican or Indian boys didn't.

The coach lurched and squealed and the girl went on chattering. She was wearing a velvet dress that was too big for her and her active hands stuck out of the sleeves like a bird's claws. At her feet was the little dog that she called Dulce. It had already spread its tiny hind legs twice and voided on the matting of the floor and once it had nipped Charley on the ankle. "Do you want to do that?" the girl asked, pointing to the stain of urine. He continued to look out the window. "You can if you want to," she said. He maintained his silence. "If I wanted to I would," she declared. The cavalryman's boot rose and fell. "I'd pull my skirts up and squat right there and do it," she boasted. Beyond the cavalryman's horse was browny-white earth and gray-green bushes. "Do you want to see me do it?" the girl persisted. He shook his head but would not turn his face. Presently she slapped him on the back of his neck. "Idiota," she said. "You are an idiot."

He was hungry but he would not ask the girl to open the basket that was beside her on the scuffed leather seat. To do that would be to engage in conversation with her and to speak to her would be surrendering something that he had determined not to surrender. He had established his attitude toward her in the back room of the Múzquiz house and he meant to stick to it. It wasn't that he actively disliked her. She talked too much, that was all. She was like a parakeet. Chattering all the time. And trying to put her hands on him. Perhaps her marriage to the general had made her slightly loca. He couldn't understand why the general liked her. The coach rose mightily and collapsed over a washed-out place in the road and the girl screamed and fell against him and clutched him by the front of his shirt. The basket slid off the seat and hit the dog who immediately set up a shrill yipping.

"Let go," said Charley, endeavoring to extricate himself from the clutching hands that had already torn his shirt.

The girl half-lay across him and did not move. Her head was twisted sideways and she was looking out and up.

"Look! Look, idiota!" she cried, extending her arm and pointing.

"The smoke! Do you see the smoke? The general, my husband, is burning all those wicked gringos."

His eyes followed her directing finger and he saw against the noon blue of the sky a dark column like a monstrous feather that waved in a short arc from side to side. At first he comprehended neither what she said nor what he saw and he continued to thrust her away. Under the velvet dress her body seemed hard and immovable and he did not like the musklike reek that came from it. He thought that she smelt like a cat. She would not stir and finally he gave up the attempt to move her and began to consider the huge swaying column of smoke. The lax wind detached small portions of it from near the top and they turned and disappeared like puffballs. The main trunk appeared to palpitate as though it was drawing up into itself a pulsing energy from its invisible source. What a great . . . Suddenly the meaning of the girl's words plunged into his consciousness like a shining knife and he understood that this column of smoke rose from the piled bodies of many men, most of whom he had seen and a few he had known. Colonel Travis was there and Captain Dickinson and Captain Crockett and . . . The course of the coach altered and the column of smoke slid across the horizon and out of sight. The girl, still chattering, removed the weight of her body from him and arranged herself on the seat, her feet up and the narrow sharp heels of her slippers pressing against his small thigh. He couldn't hear a word she was saying. He wasn't hungry any more. He watched the top of the cavalryman's boot rise and fall beyond the open door-window and tried not to think at all. It was time for his game. There was something he would have to avoid. The coach lumbered and jounced southward and a great loneliness like a gray cloud flowed up on all sides and engulfed him. He was lost in it. Suddenly, strangely, for the first time in his life, he began to cry. He cried very quietly, concealing his face from the girl and pretending that the light hurt his eyes.

Book One

LAS GOLONDRINAS

Las Golondrinas

BOUT six o'clock in the morning Don Isidro Núñez de Haro y Peralta, draped in a pale-blue silk dressing gown decorated with silver-threaded frogs, came to the arched window of his sleeping room and glanced down into the wide plaza of Las Golondrinas. Being full-blooded the chill morning air did not affect him at all. His own particular world was already awake and across the sun-dried bricks below him passed uninterruptedly the visible evidence of its completeness in itself. Don Isidro observed the movement with lazy and ambiguous attentiveness while behind him the Indian youth, Chepe, directed the filling of the great metal pot with hot water and prepared shaving materials. The imminent and anticipated occurrences of the day would be unique enough in themselves to justify a complete bath. It would not be sufficient, as was usual, to have his feet washed by Pedrito and his face scraped by Chepe. Not, no lo quiera Dios, on a day when one's only daughter, the slender María Catalina, was to be married and El General, Antonio López de Santa Anna himself, was to halt for refreshment and to offer felicitations on his way to the great camp at San Luis Potosí.

Don Isidro presented an impressive figure as he stood like a monolith in his open window with one large hairy hand resting on the elaborately designed iron grille that served for guard. He stood six feet six inches tall in his dark-blue morocco slippers (purchased by his agent in Cartagena) and his long face with its heavy protruding underlip had a Hapsburg touch. He was about fifty years old but his high bush of thick black hair and his silky side whiskers had no touch of gray in them. Time had been kind to him and except for the long slightly furrowed white scar that ran diagonally across his right temple it had left no particular mark to show that Don Isidro had lived strenuously. As he gazed across the plaza and observed the morning activities of his numberless overseers, guards, specialists and peons he appeared to be both attentive and deliberately aloof. Chepe, who worshiped him as other Indios worship Our Lady of Guadalupe, saw in Don Isidro a primitive force and an end in itself. He was like the god who lived in the cave in the mountains above Tepic. As the lean young Indian, a snake-eyed Yaqui who had been captured and brought east-

63

ward years before and who, to the amazement of all his companions, possessed the added value of speaking the English language, polished the large glittering razor, he stared at the broad back and capacious buttocks of his master and comprehended intuitively the profound reservoir of self-assurance that was contained in the man. Don Isidro was muy fuerte. Like one of the tigers in the stone hills to the west.

Don Isidro was both conscious and unconscious of his strength. He accepted it as he accepted the clear October air he was drawing in through his powerful nostrils. He was like a king in a kingdom all his own, and although matters might not be moving as serenely as they did in the days of the Spanish viceroys he felt himself as yet untouched by the so-called new order of things. Less than a league from the great gate of his hacienda the ancient Camino Real, the King's Highway, passed, and along it creaked and clattered heavy coaches and horsemen forwarding the multifarious businesses of the Republic; but, as yet, the Republic had not intruded upon Las Golondrinas. It stayed outside the gates and did not pass the armed guards who slouched against the high yellow walls wrapped to the nose in tattered sarapes and smoked their black tobacco wrapped in cornhusks. One paid for this isolation, of course, but so, too, had one paid in the time of the viceroys. There was always a tribute of sorts to be vomited forth when one was a ruler. Don Isidro paid his, paid it twice, in fact, once to the zealous representatives of the Republic and again to the equally zealous representatives of the Church, and, as a result, laws that might have applied to him were never invoked at all.

Las Golondrinas was a principality in itself. The lands of the hacienda—the innumerable leagues they covered were unknown to Don Isidro himself—stretched as far as the eye could see into the blue distances where the mountain ranges jagged the horizon and some seven thousand human beings populated its villages, fields, cleft valleys and rolling hills. Don Isidro was father, patron, judge, executioner, protector and God Himself to all of them. He, with his jefe, the principal overseer, and the priest in the hacienda church, ruled in a sort of supreme triumvirate but Don Isidro's was the final decision. Even the priest was willing to admit that. The bishop had explained everything to him for the better glory of God and the priest was accordingly wisely politic. When Don Isidro was younger he had been more conscious of his temporal power and once in those intoxicating days he had remarked humorously to his wife, "Sometimes I even talk back to God." Doña Ágata, profoundly religious and niece to the bishop of Puebla, had turned a hawk-shaped shocked face toward him. Now that he was older it never occurred to him to say things like that. They were taken for granted.

Life intensified below him as he rested a hand on the iron grille and gazed remotely across the teeming plaza. There was noise and varying movement there. High-saddled horses bearing vaqueros wearing heavy embossed silver rowels stepped daintily like gentle-born ladies from Spain, their thin necks arched and sensitive; shaggy midget burros with gray noses and white-ringed clownlike eyes clicked over the hard bricks half-buried with enormous loads; a pack of mangy curs yapped as it scurried from the sweetish-sour-smelling peons' quarters built against the wall to the still-closed door of the tienda; a six-span ox team lumbered through the great central gate dragging a toplofty two-wheeled cart piled high with hemp. The horns of the oxen were lashed to crossbars of wood attached to the center pole and the driver, a little pockmarked Cora, endeavored to hasten the sluggish beasts by alternately biting their tails viciously and yelling "Arre! Arre!" From the door of the tinacal near the solid-studded outer portal the mayordomo peered and saw the sun rise over the tiled front of the casa grande. Behind him the horsehide vats of bubbling white pulque fermented beneath the colored paper decorations in the dark sour air. These tawdry festoons had kept the evil spirits away all night and provided a good brew for the day's festivities. The mayordomo was a mestizo named Timoteo and as he had killed seven men (five in the line of duty and two in love affairs) he boasted five silver and two gold bands on the grip of the huge pistol that swung from his thigh.

Don Isidro saw all this and did not see it. He heard the interwoven orchestra of noises: the shrill voices of half-naked children, the squealing of litters of shoats being driven toward the great ovens around the kitchen patio, the bleating of unmilked goats, the rhythmical clapping of hands as the squatting Indian women slapped into paper-thin circles the mountainous piles of tortillas, the clatter of hoofs and the screaming of solid wooden wheels, and yet he did not hear them. It was a pattern, a familiar design in living, and as long as it followed its accustomed grooves it did not impinge upon his alertness. He accepted it as he accepted the cold breath he drew into his lungs. But should there be a divagation, an alien sound or an unexpected color, then all his immobilized awareness would leap toward it and both he and the foreign element would know that he saw and heard with an intensity that was cruel and complete. And having seen and heard, his reaction and disposal of the extraneous intrusion would be immediate and stark.

This unconscious discipline made it possible for him to be in two places at once—where he was standing and in his own mind. And at the moment he was mostly in his own mind as he stood with veiled eyes and heard remotely but reassuringly the mounting tumult of his awakened kingdom. His heavy underlip thrust out farther than ever but even Chepe could not tell by that that Don Isidro's mind had been lassoed by a reata that reached far back into the past. It reached back to a cold church in Seville and a muddy bank by the Guadalquivir. And it reached forward, too, to the marriage of his daughter. It stretched across thirty years, this tough twisted rope of memory, and yet as Don Isidro stood by his window and watched without watching a flock of fattened turkeys, white and paunchily majestic, like Orléans kings, like half a hundred Louis-Philippes, scolding their way across the plaza, it did not seem to him like a full generation. Why, it was only yesterday that his hunting knife had slid into Don Francisco's throat and the brown-legged Gitana had run screaming along the muddy bank of the river. But yesterday was the year 1816.

Don Isidro lifted his large hand and rubbed a finger absently across the white scar that furrowed his temple. Chepe said, "The hot water is ready, patrón," but the big man did not turn. Yesterday was the year 1816 and today was the year 1846. Pues sí! It was so, indeed. It was October in the year 1846 and Mariano Salas was acting president of the Republic. And General Antonio López de Santa Anna, benémerito de la Patria, the immortal savior of the Republic, the hero of Tamaulipas, was in his leather-slung coach rolling along the Camino Real toward Las Golondrinas. This was not like yesterday and yet today, if matters proceeded as they should, would be the completion of yesterday. Youth, friendship, passion, death, a vow to God. It was these things . . . yes . . . a completion. Chepe kicked the great metal pot with his sandal. "The hot water is ready, patrón," he repeated. Still Don Isidro did not turn. The great circle of Time was achieving its completion, end meeting end, and after today the ever-abiding weight of a sacred vow would be lifted from shoulders that had never bowed. This was good. It would leave the road free, oh, not for other vows, never that again, but for a carefree disposal of an untethered will. The reata would be cut. It was regrettable that the bishop of Puebla would not arrive before noon. There was the story to tell and the approbation of the Church to receive. Hilario, wise, wrinkled, sly-eyed old Hilario, was just the man for that. It was an excellent thing to have a bishop in one's family. It was like having the grace of God in one's own strongbox. Don Isidro turned slowly and started to unfasten his dressing gown while Chepe circled the steaming metal pot and hurried toward him, his guaraches scuffing on the polished floor.

In another part of the casa grande, some hours later, María Catalina sat up in her great bed and drank with repeated sips from the bowl of hot chocolate she held in both hands while her mother stared soberly through the tightly closed window. Unlike Don Isidro, who possessed strange ideas totally at variance with the fashionable medical opinion of Mexico City, the women of his household feared and shunned fresh air on a brisk morning with the same horror that St. Anthony feared and shunned the devil. The girl, just past her seventeenth year, was slight in build, almost birdlike, waxen-skinned, gray-eyed and crowned with a turbulence of dark hair that dwarfed her pointed face. Without anxiety or excitement, indeed, without any emotion whatsoever, she observed the angular back of her mother and sipped the bowl of chocolate. Doña Ágata was thinking rapidly as she gazed down into the bleak inner patio, sacred to the women, where the round central fountain basin, bone-dry and flecked with the first falling leaves, gaped like an old crone's gray toothless mouth. Her high-bridged insolent nose and black eyebrows nearly meeting above two small piercing jet-black eyes gave her the semblance of a watchful hawk searching for a prey that was not in sight. She was exasperated. She did not understand her daughter, never had understood her and never would understand. As she complained to her sister, Doña Marta, who lived in the beautiful city of Puebla where the men did not smell of horse dung, "It is exactly like having a wax image in the house. Mother of God, she is no different than the little figures sold before the cathedral in the Grand Plaza." And now, on her wedding day, María Catalina exhibited no more excitement over the imminent event than she did over her bowl of chocolate . . . and, certainly, she was not exhilarated by that. True enough, there was little about Don Alejandro's appearance or habits to arouse enthusiasm in the breast of a young girl but Doña Ágata was convinced that if Don Juan of Austria should rise from the dead and come to Las Golondrinas as a suitor María Catalina's absolute lack of reaction would be the same. It was true, further, that a properly raised young lady was not supposed to know much about her prospective husband before the marriage, but even so . . . well, one was married only once in a lifetime (at least, in a family that could boast seven bishops in its long illustrious line) and there should be *some* excitement about it. Not for the public eye, of course . . . that was vulgar . . . but before one's mother . . . Doña Ágata recalled with an actual tightening of her body the faraway morning when she stood by the barred window in Puebla and listened for the horse's hoofs that would herald the arrival of Don Isidro. Pious and exemplary as she had been, the clatter of those hoofs had sent little devils running up and down her thighs. She turned abruptly and walked over to the charcoal brazier that stood near the carved foot of the bed. The heat fanning out from it made the almost hermetically sealed room quite comfortable. She said:

"Chuchita will bring all the new dresses and spread them out for you on the bed."

"Thank you, my mother," replied María Catalina in a light uninterested voice.

She set the bowl of chocolate down carefully on the French guéridon beside her bed. Then she wiped her mouth with the handkerchief that lay on the lace pillow, pulled down the sleeves of her sleeping gown and rested back against the dark wood of the bed head. She observed her mother with calm blank eyes. Doña Ágata wished she had brought one of her small black cigars with her. She always thought more calmly when she was puffing tobacco. She yanked down her lace jacket and cleared her throat.

"This is the most important day in your life, my child," she said.

"I know, my mother," the girl answered.

"You must not be nervous," continued Doña Ágata.

"I am not nervous," said María Catalina. "Why should I be nervous?"

The mother pursed her lips. What was it the hacienda priest had suggested?

"It is true that your actual acquaintance with Dan Alejandro is brief," she began.

"I have seen Don Alejandro three times," announced the girl.

Doña Ágata raised her bold black eyebrows.

"As often as that?" she exclaimed . . . and then nodded. "Oh, yes. You saw him here when you were six years old. I remember now. He was a handsome youth of nineteen, then. You saw him again in Mexico City when you were twelve. That was in . . . in . . ."

"Eighteen-forty," supplied María Catalina.

"Yes, 1840," agreed Doña Ágata. "Don Alejandro came to Mexico as an aide to Calderón de la Barca, the Spanish ambassador. He was very handsome in his uniform."

She yanked at her lace jacket again. That priest had suggested . . .

"And for the third time you saw him when he arrived yesterday at noon," she said.

"Yes, my mother," replied María Catalina.

She raised a thin hand and stifled the beginning of a yawn.

"He was not quite himself yesterday," remarked Doña Ágata. "The inconveniences of the long coach journey had somewhat discommoded him."

"He had imbibed too much *tequila* in the coach," said the girl.

"Naturally he was somewhat excited," declared Doña Ágata. "He had traveled a great distance. He was anxious to see you. The . . ."

"He was intoxicated last night, too," announced María Catalina wearily.

Doña Ágata stared at her daughter.

"Who told you that?" she demanded.

"Chuchita," replied the girl. "She said that he tried to pinch her on the back of the leg when he was mounting the stairs and that he dropped the candle and fell down and Chepe and Pedrito . . ."

"What silliness!" exclaimed Doña Ágata. "I shall explain to that girl that no flies enter a closed mouth. Don Alejandro was in an extremely exalted frame of mind last evening. He was wearied from travel, too. Perhaps he was unwise to attempt to emulate your good father in drinking toasts to all the Spanish viceroys since Antonio de Mendoza."

She paced across the room to the closed window and back again. That priest . . .

"Don Alejandro is a very handsome man," she declared firmly.

María Catalina said nothing.

"Do you not think that Don Alejandro is a very handsome man?" demanded Doña Ágata.

"I have no thoughts on the subject," answered the girl equably. "Would that not be rather forward on my part?"

Doña Ágata opened her mouth and shut it. She was inclined to say, "For the love of God . . ." but refrained. After all, Don Alejandro did look very much like a toad in tight pantaloons and to assert that he was handsome was to exhibit the ultimate in Christian charity. She had never liked him from the first moment she had laid eyes on him and that had been eleven years ago when, a young Spanish cadet on leave to make his grand tour, he had arrived at Las Golondrinas as the guest of Don Isidro. She had heard of him even before that, as far back, indeed, as the day, little less than a year after her marriage, when, lying exhausted in her great bed after the difficult delivery of her daughter, Don Isidro had leaned above the red mite of humanity that was his first child and said, "Thy future, chiquirrita, is already written in the stars. Thy husband, Don Alejandro de la Barca y Padilla, attends thee in the great city of Seville." He had said that not so much to the thinly bleating infant as to her, Doña Ágata, and she, hands pressed against her bandaged torn womb, had heard vaguely and hardly understood. Afterward, she had been mildly surprised to observe with what complacency Don Isidro accepted the fact that his first-born was a girl. Most men of his station would have regarded the production of a puny girl as a deliberate affront from a careless wife. Not so Don Isidro. Indeed, there were moments when it seemed to Doña Ágata that her husband had actually *willed* a girl. She suspected it but she could not know for it was not among her privileges to ask such questions. Don Isidro had made that plain on the evening of their marriage.

Her duty was to acquiesce and this she did with the hereditary dignity of a Gayoso de Lemos. Don Isidro was the autocrat and she was his obedient adjunct. It never occurred to her to protest when, upon first seeing Don Alejandro, she conceived a scornful dislike for him. It never occurred to her to betray her dislike of the squat young Spaniard to anyone, not even her exalted uncle, the bishop. Don Isidro had selected this toadlike youth for his son-in-law and that was enough. Why he had selected him, or when, or even how he had first encountered him in Spain, were complete mysteries to her but she never stepped across the semiceremonious relationship between herself and her husband in search of answers. Don Isidro would explain when he chose to explain and if he never explained at all that was quite in accordance with his character. Curiously enough, she felt no loneliness. Things were as they were and that was all there was to it. Loneliness was always a lack of something and one could never lack what one had never possessed. In other words, she had known and accepted her place in Don Isidro's life from the beginning. She had slept with him and borne his children, María Catalina and, three years later, young Lorenzo, now a cadet in the Military College at Chapultepec Castle. She had been quite aware of but loftily ignored the existence of her husband's two mistresses, one in Mexico City and the other less than a league away on the hacienda. She had graced the dinner table, ordered the domestic affairs of the casa grande, observed the feast days, prayed regularly and zealously, admonished her children and given them good council and been faithful to Don Isidro. What uncertainties she had she kept to herself. For instance, she had never made up her mind whether she loved Don Isidro or not. She had been sexually excited by him during the first three years of her marriage and his heavy step along the corridor had set free waves of anticipatory ecstasy in her blood; but after the birth of Lorenzo the current had slowed and when Don Isidro no longer came to her, or came at long intervals as a glum duty, she did not feel angry, disappointed or frustrated. She merely said an extra prayer, rolled over and went to sleep.

Another uncertainty was María Catalina. Did she love her? She hoped so but she could not say. She was as baffled here as she was in her personal relationship with Don Isidro. The girl was so entirely lacking in responsiveness, her kisses were so obedient and cold, her docility (the priest had said that it was God's mark of goodness) was so frighteningly complete; all this lifeless and flawless perfection of demeanor awakened unrevealed dubieties in Doña Ágata's mind. Of course, María Catalina was only seventeen years old but even so: at seventeen one was not a child. It might be so in colder northern climes but not here in Mexico where the flesh ripened so quickly and young men loitered beneath barred windows and sang their disturbing songs. Doña Ágata knew very well what budding girls chattered about when they were left together. There was no least hint of that in María Catalina. She played Mozart upon the pianoforte, embroidered, cared for her small family of turkeys, tended her little flower garden, sang in a thin husky voice and occasionally, under persuasion, read a book. At other times she just sat and watched the colored world of Las Golondrinas pass like a fluctuating panorama before her calm eyes. She said, "Yes, my mother" and "No, my father," in sweet complaisant tones. She had no friends, no confidantes, no playmates. If she ever thought about anything she kept it to herself. There were moments when Doña Ágata was almost convinced that María Catalina possessed neither brains nor emotion. There was this matter of Don Alejandro, for instance. The girl accepted the fact that she was to be married to him as composedly as she accepted the fact that she would have a bowl of chocolate for breakfast every morning. It was unnatural, Doña Ágata often thought to herself, and yet it was as it should be. Of course, María Catalina had always known that she was destined to be the wife of the squat little Spaniard. It had been settled from the day of her birth and perhaps that had something to do with her acquiescence. When one began to breathe one continued to breathe and thought no more about it. All the same . . . Doña Ágata felt that something was wrong and because she could not place a discerning finger upon it she was irritated.

If she was uncertain of her affection for Don Isidro and María Catalina and their emotional response to her she was very sure of the relationship between herself and young Lorenzo. She loved the dark thin fastidious fourteen-year-old boy with an intensity that sometimes startled her and she knew, because she could feel it like a magnetic wave, the profundity of his adoration for her. He was her only son and in him she saw all the virtues that her early dreams of perfect manhood had pictured in solitary hours during those secluded years in Puebla when she saw the world pass by beyond a barred window. It had been a cruel wrench, like the loss of one's right arm, when, two years before, Don Isidro had sent the boy to the Military College just outside Mexico City. The colors had blown out of Las Golondrinas and Doña Ágata had realized that she was growing old. She had lost her son and she suspected that he would never come back. But after some months he had returned on a short leave of absence and to her great joy (a joy carefully restrained from all eyes) Lorenzo had been just the same as ever. His neat little uniform failed to conceal him. He was gentle, gravely affectionate, attentive and subdued. He preferred to remain at home rather than ride the broad acres with his father. Since that first visit he had returned several times to the huge hacienda and so far as Doña Ágata could perceive (and she had an instinct for this delicate sort of observation) Lorenzo remained Lorenzo. Proximity to the capital and life with a group of boys from twelve to sixteen years of age had not changed him at all. Even the new discipline of military routine had failed to shift his demeanor. He continued to be her son and that, she felt, was as it should be although she knew that Don Isidro confidently expected the boy, as he approached man's status, to be *his* son. It was the way of the world. Mothers were supposed to lose their sons at the age of fourteen (if not before) and fathers were supposed to find them. As for daughters . . .

Doña Ágata stood at the foot of the bed and stared at María Catalina.

"Yes, yes," she said. "But naturally."

Would that not be rather forward on my part? It was barely possible that this girl was wiser than she appeared to be. Certainly she avoided any affirmations or negations and slid dexterously around opinions that might lead to argument. Doña Ágata glanced sharply at the reclining figure and saw nothing but a calm attentiveness. That priest . . . The mother cleared her throat.

"There are many responsibilities in marriage," she said.

María Catalina said nothing.

"Children, for instance," continued Doña Ágata, a faint flush creeping over her sharp-featured face.

"Yes, my mother," admitted the girl.

Could it be possible that at seventeen this child was so ignorant or was the hacienda priest an idiot? Doña Ágata felt like an idiot herself but she plunged on with a waspish insistence.

"It is not true that children are found behind maguey plants," she declared.

The ghost of a smile haunted María Catalina's face for an instant.

"No, my mother," she admitted. "They come out of here."

She laid her hand on her flat belly.

"And when one is married . . ." floundered Doña Ágata. "When the husband loves . . . when . . ."

"I understand," broke in the girl.

Doña Ágata yanked at her lace jacket and peered questioningly at her daughter.

"I have seen the dogs in the plaza," explained María Catalina.

Doña Ágata was stunned and a great feeling of shame flowed through her spare body. For some obscure reason the mention of dogs raised a vivid image of Don Alejandro before her mind's eye. It was true and an emotion of sorrow for her daughter followed the shame. She suddenly saw the girl as a pitiful sacrifice to some obscure decision on the part of Don Isidro. What *had* happened during those years before she met her husband? There was something that stank in this arbitrary disposition of a life that could not (or would not speak for itself. A great wave of tenderness for this unreciprocative girl surged through Doña Ágata. She said:

"Are you content?"

María Catalina twisted in the bed and her lean thighs lifted like the blades of a scissors. Doña Ágata regretted her question as soon as she asked it for it seemed to her to be a vague criticism of Don Isidro's decision, and then, fleetingly, she was relieved for her common sense told her what the girl would say. María Catalina remained true to form. She said:

"It is as my father desires. I am content to be his daughter."

The old exasperation ruffled Doña Ágata's mind again. Dale! she would never understand this daughter. She could understand obedience for she had practiced it all her life; she could understand humility and deference and abstinence from argument for these things had been bred in her by her own family; she could even understand acceptance for that was the lot of woman; but she would never, never understand her daughter. She was too removed from any reality to seem human. If there was a spark in her it was so concealed that even the most inquisitive eye could not discern it. Yes . . . a wax image. She had been like that since she first toddled across the stones of the inner patio. No one had ever heard her cry, no, not even when she had fallen down and bumped her nose. She had never desired anything; she had never exhibited jealousy over her toys; she had never ardently begged for a new dress; she had never stared at herself in the mirror. Well . . . Doña Ágata repressed a sigh and turned as fat Chuchita waddled into the room, spread-legged, bearing the bright heap of new dresses.

The bishop of Puebla was a lean, sharp-faced little man with a high nose, sly black eyes and a thin lipless slit of a mouth that appeared to be drawn by pucker strings. His scant white hair glistened like silk and the pink texture of his skull glowed through it like a woman's round breast seen through gauze. A faint likeness to his niece, Doña Ágata, was perceptible but it was ghostly and faraway and softened by the blurriness of comfortable old age. At the moment he was sitting beside a table in the chamber that had been assigned to him and eating nuts and sipping a small glass of dark port wine. Don Isidro sat opposite him and near the door stood the hacienda priest, Padre Flores, his hands folded over his paunch and a worshipful expression on his wide stupid face. Both the bishop and Don Isidro desired to discuss different topics and both wanted the priest to go away. The bishop was eager to discuss the war with the United States (hostilities had been going on for some six months) and the triumphant reappearance of Santa Anna on the Mexican scene. Don Isidro was determined to narrate certain passages in his past life and so make a sort of unofficial confession. Padre Flores wanted to be blessed again by the bishop.

The prelate thrust out a gray.tiny tongue, licked his lipless mouth and set down the port glass.

"Excellent," he exclaimed in a husky surprised voice. "Really now . . . It recalls the Douro . . ."

"I am happy that it pleases you," said Don Isidro heavily. "My dear and most holy uncle, I want . . ."

The priest emitted a palpably artificial sneeze.

The bishop turned his shining head.

"There you are, my son," he admitted grudgingly and then facing Don Isidro he said, "There were many troops moving north. At times I feared my coach would be unable to make its way through the baggage trains. Such an uproar! It wearied me more than the journey. I can tell you, my dear nephew, that at my age, seventy-four, no less, for I was born in 'seventy-two, a long trip over vile roads in a bouncing vehicle is not calculated to improve either one's health or disposition. But, come, tell me . . ."

Padre Flores sneezed again.

"Take that damned snorting out of here!" bellowed Don Isidro in a sudden explosion of impatience.

The priest slipped around the door like a large fat hare and disappeared.

"Don Isidro, Don Isidro," murmured the bishop in a reproachful voice although his bright little eyes were filled with suppressed laughter.

Don Isidro sighed resignedly and crossed one long leg over the other. His big silver spurs clicked against the table leg. He understood that he would have to keep his confession (if that was the word for it) to himself until he had satisfied the bishop's curiosity concerning other matters. It was easy to guess what those matters were.

"Come, tell me," repeated the prelate, opening and shutting his eyes very rapidly as though that would loosen Don Isidro's tongue, "what are your ideas about this war?"

Don Isidro pulled at his protruding underlip.

"I haven't thought much about it," he replied slowly. "I haven't been in Mexico City for a year. I have been minding my own business. You probably know more about it than I do."

The bishop grimaced as though he had tasted something sour.

"I know that we are paying through the nose for a mirage," he said grimly. "But first, do you think we are justified in opposing a power like the United States? Do you think we can possibly win?"

Don Isidro's mind was but half on the subject. He fumbled about for words.

"Win?" he remarked vaguely. "Well, why not? We outnumber the Yanqui army by thousands. We have the generals. We are a fighting people. We . . ."

The bishop raised his hand impatiently and the large square jewel in his ring blinked like a suspicious eye.

"My dear nephew," he said wearily, "let us not sum up what we have and are. The government manifestoes can do that better than you can. Let us sum up what *they* have and are. Do you know?"

He leaned back, picked up a nut and smashed it with a metal cracker shaped like a wolf's head. The meat fell into the lap of his robe and he brushed it to the floor.

Don Isidro looked puzzled.

"It is very plain that you have not been in Mexico City for a year," continued the bishop. "That is unwise. It is also plain that you lack information. That may be fatal. Do you know that the American troops now control a full third of our country? Do you know that General Taylor's line of invasion across the states of Coahuila, Nuevo León and Tamaulipas stretches from Saltillo and Monterrey to Tampico and the Gulf? Do you know that Frémont has captured Sonoma and planted his Bear flag in California? Do you know that Commodore Sloat has captured Monterey on the Pacific coast and that General Kearny has occupied Santa Fé?"

"I don't know half of those names," admitted Don Isidro. "Is it really as bad as that?"

The bishop closed his eyes and shook his head despondently.

"It is worse," he declared. "It is worse . . . and you sit here in your private fortress and imagine the world will go on as it has in the past. My poor nephew. We have lost every battle in which we engaged. Palo Alto. Resaca de la Palma. Monterrey. We . . ."

"Ah," exclaimed Don Isidro, grasping eagerly at a slight straw of justification that he imagined he heard in the conversation. "That is simple. The bulk of our forces has not met the Yanquis yet. We were not organized for the war. We did not possess a unified command. Taylor invaded us without warning or a declaration. We require a little time to . . ."

"Time, indeed!" broke in the bishop contemptuously. "That is all that we think of . . . time. Well, while we take time and organize great armies do you think Taylor will sit quietly in Saltillo? Will he do us that favor? No! He will be in San Luis Potosí in a month."

"Santa Anna will be in San Luis Potosí in a week," announced Don Isidro triumphantly.

His strong face creased into a smile.

The bishop looked very stern.

"Ah, Santa Anna!" he said.

"Why, yes," insisted Don Isidro. "As a matter of fact, he will be here in an hour or so. He has kindly consented to break his march at my door and attend the wedding. The wed—"

His mind dove back into the subject that crowded his consciousness.

"My uncle . . ." he began hastily.

But the bishop forestalled him.

"Santa Anna," he repeated in a cryptic tone. "We will speak of him presently. I am now discussing the war. Everything in order, if you please. We are doing badly, Don Isidro. Very badly. And the Salas government is worse than corrupt. It is weak. It is helpless. It has been jockeyed into calling for the election of delegates to a new congress in December. That will mean a majority of ultraliberals, libertines and antiecclesiastics. Scoundrels ready to rob left and right to fight a war that they cannot win. There! I have said it. We cannot win this war."

"I cannot agree to that," said Don Isidro stubbornly.

The bishop raised his eyebrows and poured himself another glass of port.

"Does the Church affirm that we cannot win this war?" demanded the hacendado.

The bishop ignored him.

"You don't know Mexico City," he declared. "It is like a hornet's nest. There is no unity there at all. Every time you see three men with their heads together over a bottle of wine you may be sure that some new conspiracy is being planned. How can you expect a solid front against an enemy when the elements that should compose it are green with hatred and jealousy of one another?"

The indignation suddenly left his voice and he smiled wryly.

"Well," he said piously, "God's will be done. We shall know by this time next year if the road we have chosen is the one we should have chosen or not. It may be that God will bless our arms, for the Americans are an irreligious and blasphemous folk. But until it happens I must doubt it."

A small sigh escaped his lipless mouth.

"I am sorry to hear that Mexico City is so divided," remarked Don Isidro. "I repeat, I have been minding my own business. I have been approached for money and I have given it. However, I have considered it wise to keep out of sight. When one is not recalled to mind one is safe. That is one excuse for my ignorance. Ampudia offered me a colonelcy but I refused it. The governor of Querétaro demanded five hundred peons from me to fill up his ranks and I sent a hundred worthless fellows."

"In other words, you are clever enough to see that this is not your war," said the bishop.

Don Isidro plucked at his lip.

"I wouldn't say that," he answered with drawling deliberation. "True enough, I like to be left alone. I don't bother with the Republic and I don't want it to bother with me. Why should it? I am self-sufficient here and I bother no . . ."

"Feudal as ever," broke in the bishop, smiling.

"It is not a bad way of life," admitted Don Isidro. "But still I would not say that this war is not my war. I wouldn't give a centavo for all of Texas and California which the Americans desire so badly but if the war comes too close to me . . ."

"Did I understand you to say that Santa Anna is coming here today?" interrupted the bishop suddenly as his mind flew back to a previous declaration.

Don Isidro nodded.

"Why, yes," he replied and then felt confused. "My uncle," he added, "if you feel that you shouldn't . . ."

The bishop calmly sipped his wine.

"It will not disconcert me to see him," he said tranquilly. "I have seen him before and I shall see him again. Isn't it impossible to live in Mexico without seeing him sooner or later? He comes and goes like the . . . like the vómito. Tell me, what do you think of him? When did you last encounter him?"

Don Isidro thought for a moment.

"I saw him last at the funeral of his first wife," he said. "That was in August, 1844. He was—"

"Yes, yes, yes," the bishop interjected. "And within six weeks of Doña Inés' obsequies he married a fifteen-year-old girl."

Doña María Dolores Tosta," acknowledged Don Isidro indifferently. "A charming girl with beautiful . . . Well, it doesn't matter. He was then at the apex of his power as president-dictator but already there were signs that the foundations of the edifice were crumbling. A remarkable man, Santa Anna. It was through his kindness that my son, Lorenzo, was admitted to the Military College. Santa Anna has written to me from exile several times. And now, I think . . ."

"His return from Cuba was rather a surprise," declared the bishop, fixing his bright little eyes firmly upon Don Isidro's face. "Oh, the Santanistas expected it and preached it but the Paredes administration fought it to the end. A curious turnabout, eh? Here was a man exiled in June, 1845, by an indignant revolutionary public because he turned his presidential office into a dictatorship returning in August,

1846 (only fourteen months later, mind you), as the representative of federal principles and to the cheers of the populace. Truly, we are a volatile people."

"The spell of Santa Anna is strong," remarked Don Isidro sententiously.

"Have you fallen beneath it?" inquired the bishop softly. "I believe that there is some talk intimating that our Hero has been listening to the persuasions of Yanqui plotters. They even go so far as to say that he has entered into an agreement with Washington to—"

"I don't believe it," said Don Isidro bluntly.

"Oh, I do, I do," declared the bishop, laughing. "Santa Anna would not run true to form unless he was conspiring and preparing to betray somebody. Let us hope that it is the Yanqui plotters he intends to betray this time."

Don Isidro looked a little sulky.

"I have always found him to be a gentleman," he said stoutly.

"Every man finds what he pleases in Santa Anna," admitted the bishop gravely although his eyes were twinkling. "He is all things to all men. Even an enemy, if you like. Tell me, what do you think of him as a man?"

"He has good qualities," insisted Don Isidro.

"And bad," added the bishop.

"He has great natural ability," continued Don Isidro.

"He has no moral or intellectual training," put in the bishop.

"He has initiative," announced the hacendado.

"He has no fixed purpose or definite objective," capped the prelate.

"He has energy."

"But he is handicapped with grave defects."

Both men looked at each other and burst out laughing.

"So endeth the litany of Santa Anna," remarked the bishop. "He must be an extraordinary man or we would not talk about him so much. Well, enough of him. It is very plain that we differ on the war and practically everything connected with it. But, you shall see. A few months more and you shall see."

"There is no reason why this war can't be won," said Don Isidro doggedly.

"That shall be as God wills," declared the bishop piously. "Despite the outrageous onslaughts on the Church by the so-called liberals the True Faith will triumph in the end."

Don Isidro looked up quickly.

"Santa Anna has never been an enemy of the Church," he said.

The bishop pursed his thin lips.

"Why, no," insisted Don Isidro. "In 1834 the clergy coupled his name with the cause of religion. The bishops supported him. He put Bishop Portugal of Michoacán in his cabinet. In 1841 the Church was with him again. It raised money for him. And now . . ."

"We have used Santa Anna," declared the bishop smoothly, "and Santa Anna—shall we say?—has used us. Many a rotten reed has supported a holy shrine. But these are matters that concern the archbishop of Mexico. I am but an humble gleaner in my Master's cornfield. The toil is arduous."

Don Isidro, who was becoming bored, thought, You are a sly old fox. But the True Church is greater than you are and . . . a vow is a vow. Ah, yes. The time for confession seemed to have come. He leaned forward and opened his mouth but before he spoke the bishop, settling back in his chair, anticipated him.

"Yes, yes, yes," he said. "We have got nowhere. Which, perhaps, is as it should be. Now what is this matter that so consumes you that I am fearful you will burst out in flames any minute?"

It was nearly noon and Don Alejandro de la Barca y Padilla sat on the edge of his high bed with his head held between two fat hands. He was clad in a flowered woolen nightshirt and a velvet sleeping cap lurched like an uneasy crown on his bullet-shaped skull. Truly, Don Isidro's liquors were strong. He had sat up until all hours of the morning emptying bottle after bottle with his future father-in-law and the overseer and now it seemed to him that some invisible demon was endeavoring to split his cranium into two equal halves with a dull ax. His tongue, which was really too big for his mouth, anyway, appeared to have the shape and taste of a saddlebag. Guay! What strong liquors! He raised his head carefully and peered out at the day through bleary eyes. The light hurt and he shut his lids tightly. There was somebody tapping at the door but he did not care. His tongue would have to shrink before he could speak. The high sun, flooding through the long window, fell full on his face and illuminated for nobody to see a square froglike physiognomy with eyes too far apart, nose too small and mouth too large. The fact that his neck was too short added to the Batrachian similarity. When he stood up, as he did after a moment while resting one hand heavily on the bed, it could be seen that his legs, also, were too short. However, they were heavy and beneath the goatlike hair that adorned them flexed powerful muscles. It was the continued knocking that brought him reluctantly to his feet. "Diablo! Demonio! Diantre!" he mumbled as he stumped across the room, fumbled at the gilded knob, pulled the tall door back and entered into the dusk of the tiled corridor.

It was Chuchita with a large container of hot water.

Don Alejandro brightened considerably and when she passed

him with an expressionless sidelong glance he attempted to lean
against her and nearly fell flat on his face. Diablo! Recovering himself
he lumbered after her, legs somewhat straddled and long nightshirt
bulging in the draft before him. He had a vague memory of Chuchita.
Where was it, now? Last night? On the stairs? Oh licor divino. Quite
suddenly he felt better. The dull ax was diminishing its strokes and
his thick legs had recovered their equilibrium. En verdad, she was an
attractive plump little chicken. Softly broad in the bottom and with
such a straight back. When she bent over to put the container on the
wooden stand he could see the little jumping muscles in her calves.
They were like restless fish in a tight net. She was short and square
and almost the color of red clay. There was a sweetish smell about her
that filled his nostrils, a frank seminal odor like the damp soil about
a spring in the mountains. It pleased him. Always amorous after a
drinking bout when his stupefied flesh was returning to life he felt
himself rekindled again by this pervasive odor that was like an elixir.
Truly now, the pale fatigued women of his own class in Seville could
not be compared with this sturdy girl who set her feet so flatly when
she walked. One had to go to the gypsies . . . He lurched against the
girl's red petticoat and thrust his arm about her white chemisette.
Under his fat hand her small high firm breasts seemed to leap.

Chuchita half-turned, her big silver earrings swinging like bells
and her smoky black eyes entirely devoid of any expression.

"What . . . what . . . what's your name?" Don Alejandro stuttered as his grasp tightened.

His tongue still troubled him. It would take half a bottle of wine
to shrink it back to its normal size.

"María de Jesús," replied the girl calmly and respectfully without
moving. "They call me Chuchita."

"Chu . . . Chuchita, eh?" he repeated, pressing his belly against
her hip. "That is good. Very good. Chuchita, I think that I will take
you back to Spain with me."

He was feeling decidedly better now. A woman or another bottle
always accelerated his recovery from a night's debauch. Liquor was
divine. Women were divine. Any women. From duquesas to criadas
they were all the same. They all did it the same way. Some were better
than others. That was all.

"I will buy you a pair of yellow shoes with silver buckles," he
declared, smiling as he fumbled for the nipple of her breast. "You
will like that. I shall insist that you be retained as the personal maid
to my wife. We shall . . ."

Chuchita's smoky black eyes stared across his shoulder at the
open door.

"The señor don is ready," she said.

For an instant Don Alejandro failed to realize that she was not speaking to him and then something in his befuddled brain caused him to turn his head.

The lean young Yaqui Indian, Chepe, was standing in the doorway with two large open razors neatly crossed on a towel resting on his two hands.

Don Alejandro disengaged his arm and backed away from the girl.

"Cómo!" he exploded. "Do they not teach you to knock at doors in this damned country?"

"The door was open, Señor Don Alejandro," replied Chepe, his black snakelike eyes fixed unblinkingly on the other's slightly flushed face.

Grumbling, the squat figure in the flowered woolen nightshirt took several steps toward his disordered bed.

Chepe's eyes slid from Don Alejandro to Chuchita.

"The young mistress has asked for you," he informed her softly. Without a word or a side glance she left the chamber.

"Señor Don Alejandro, the patrón sent me to . . ." began Chepe advancing into the room.

Don Alejandro, who had reached his bed and sat down heavily upon it like a man who did not intend to get up again for a long time, lifted his hand impatiently. He stared from the glittering razor blades to the Indian's inscrutable face as he spoke. He said:

"Don Isidro is too kind. I have my own razors. Inform him that I always shave myself."

He glowered truculently at Chepe.

"Yes, Señor Don Alejandro," said the Indian as he turned to pass through the door.

The Spaniard watched him go and just as he was about to disappear in the corridor he called after him.

"Mozo!" he bawled. "Bring me a pitcher of pulque."

"Yes, Señor Don Alejandro," replied Chepe.

An instant later the man on the bed found himself staring at a closed door.

Don Alejandro sat for some time without moving. Then he scratched his stubbly cheek, glanced over at the container of cooling water, scowled and spat on the floor. Pulling up his nightshirt he scratched his muscular thigh. Then he swung his legs into the bed, drew the blanket up to his breast, put his arms under his head and stared intently at the ceiling. Gradually his eyes began to blink, to close for longer and longer periods, and when, some fifteen minutes later, one of the boys from the tinacal arrived with a pitcher of brown pottery brimming with fresh pulque, he was sound asleep. The boy knocked for several minutes, opened the door a trifle, peeped in and then passed carefully down the corridor and followed a flight of descending stairs that brought him to the kitchen patio. His grandmother, who labored there at one of the big mound-shaped ovens, was very fond of pulque.

The bishop of Puebla leaned back in his comfortable chair, clasped his hands over his lean stomach and smiled at his nephew.

"Come. I repeat," he said, "you will consume yourself with the fires of impatience. What is it, now?"

"Am I as transparent as that?" inquired Don Isidro soberly.

The bishop said nothing but closed his eyes and put his hands together, palm touching palm. He was ready to listen and his attitude seemed to suggest that he had heard everything and that nothing could surprise him and that his understanding and mercy, direct virtues from God, were infinite. All the same Don Isidro was aware that behind the thin curtains of his pale lids were two sharp wise little eyes that sparkled more with worldly wisdom than heavenly benevolence. The hacendado cleared his throat.

"Why, yes," he said with an exaggerated casualness, "I have an old story to tell and an explanation to make."

He relapsed into a ruminative silence and after a moment the bishop opened one eye.

"Is it about Doña María Catalina?" he asked softly.

"Yes, in a way," admitted Don Isidro.

"Is it about her marriage?" continued the bishop.

Don Isidro nodded.

"Proceed," said the bishop and he closed the open eye.

"You have met Don Alejandro," declared Don Isidro.

The bishop made a faint grimace as though the ghost of a bad odor had reached his nostrils.

"He called upon me in Puebla," he said precisely. "He stayed five minutes and brought me messages from Spain. That was six years ago."

"He is young," explained Don Isidro as though the bishop had asked a question, "and he has not quite found himself yet. Perhaps he has been somewhat spoilt . . . an only child, you know, with no father and the head of the family. But the blood is good and while he is not as blessed in this world's goods as I would desire him to be he has great prospects. In the diplomatic service. I am a considerate man, my uncle, and, I hope, an indulgent father. I . . ."

His voice trailed off into silence and he poured himself a glass of port wine. The bishop did not open his eyes. Young! he was thinking

Why, the little swine is at least thirty. Don Isidro drank the beryl-hued liquid at a single draught and put the glass back on the table.

"In the natural course of events I would never have selected Don Alejandro for a son-in-law," he said desperately. "But I have no choice in the matter. No choice at all."

The bishop suddenly opened both eyes and stared sharply at his nephew. It was a trick he had learned when he was a priest in Guadalajara.

"There is no reason why it shouldn't work out, though," went on Don Isidro. "After all, one can adjust one's self to the inevitable and even make it bearable."

"What *are* you talking about?" demanded the bishop in a weary voice.

His nephew was as indirect as a political cleric.

Don Isidro smiled, then frowned and finally shook his head as though this would toss his thoughts into order.

"I am awkward in explanation, my uncle," he said. "But I have a story to tell that concerns María Catalina and Don Alejandro and concerned both of them before they were born. Permit me to tell it in my own way."

The bishop sighed and shut his eyes again.

"In 1816," began Don Isidro, settling back in his chair and speaking in almost a monotone, "I went to Spain to complete my education. I was twenty years old and quite educated enough to assume my station, such as it was, in the social life of Mexico City and here at Las Golondrinas; but my father wanted me out of the country for specific reasons, not the least of which was my own safety. You will recall, my dear uncle, that those were the turbulent years of rebellion against the government and Spain. The insurgent forces of the defrocked priests, Hidalgo y Costilla and Morelos y Pavón, had been destroyed and the leaders executed but the country was overrun with rebel bands and adherents of the so-called Constitution of 1814. Mexico was a nest of angry hornets. There were conspirators everywhere and that new word 'independence,' which had filtered in from the United States, could be heard in the darkest alleys. My father was a fervent and loyal subject of Ferdinand VII and he regarded as monsters those subversive fellows tainted with the absurd democratic principles of our northern neighbors who preached rebellion against Spain and the formation of a Mexican Republic He belonged to Latin culture and he believed in it. He saw in this disaffection the destruction of his whole way of life and the brutalization of our civilization, the oldest in the New World, to the level of the peon and—"

"I know all this," remarked the Bishop mildly.

"That is what he thought," continued Don Isidro, ignoring the interruption. "I thought so, too. And I expressed myself so forcibly on the subject that it frightened my father. I was his only son and as Las Golondrinas, the houses in Puebla and the estates outside of Jalapa would all come to me he desired to preserve me for the future, so to speak. When I divulged my plan to raise a mounted company of my own from the peons on the hacienda and set out into the hills after the rebel Francisco de Paula, he decided on a drastic action. He would send me to Spain for a year or two where I could move in less savage circles and outgrow my youthful belligerence. So in June, much against my will, I sailed from Vera Cruz to San Cristóbal de la Habana in Cuba and there took ship for Spain."

The bishop could not repress a yawn. The port wine had made him sleepy and the room was warm.

"I am explaining all this so that you will understand that it was a dissatisfied, passionate-minded, reckless young man who arrived in Cadiz in July, 1816," explained Don Isidro in an apologetic tone. "Perhaps it will make plainer to you what happened after and even afford a thread of extenuation. Passion in itself is a terrible thing. It destroys both reason and religious instruction. But when one is young and hot-blooded and ignorant and dissatisfied . . ."

He paused and observed his uncle expectantly.

"Go on," said the bishop.

"I went to Seville," explained Don Isidro. "I was the house guest of Don Francisco de la Barca y Quiroga, a young man some three years my elder and a distant kinsman on my mother's side. We became fond of each other and we went everywhere together during the first weeks after my arrival in Seville. We visited Marchena and Triana and Morón and Aguilar and Córdoba and Minas and even traveled as far as Málaga; but it was Seville itself that I loved best. Seville with its sense of the past, its memorials, its gay parties, its festivals, its processions, its beautiful women and its gallant men. Seville, where a young man's first duty, as it was his first thought, was to fall in love and . . ."

The bishop cleared his throat.

"I was a young man," insisted Don Isidro somewhat defensively, "and I acted as a young man would act. I was neither a plaster saint nor an apprentice priest. Neither was Don Francisco. His wife was six months gone with child and he did not like to look at her. Fat anyway, Doña María Cristina was becoming enormous. For this reason he passed most of his evenings away from home in my company. But not all of them and toward the end . . . the end hardly any at all."

Don Isidro paused and regarded his uncle. The bishop seemed to be asleep but the slight flutter of his eyeballs behind the closed lids informed Don Isidro that this was not so. "Go on," the expressionless face appeared to say. "You will speak less self-consciously to closed eyes." The grating of the confessional. I do not see you, my son. Speak on. You are talking to God. I am only the Ear.

"Close to the river Guadalquivir in Seville," resumed Don Isidro, "there was a poor quarter inhabited mostly by gitanos in those days, a craze of alleys stinking of onions and human excrement. I don't remember how I discovered it, perhaps through the guidance of one of the youthful roisterers who sometimes accompanied me on my nocturnal rambles. It was a place where one drank and gambled and whored and danced and sometimes fought. There were burdels and small restaurants, bodegones, and . . ."

"Spare the details," murmured the bishop.

"It was in one of these eating places that I first saw Seda," declared Don Isidro almost angrily. "She . . ."

"Seda?" questioned the bishop softly.

"Her skin was so smooth and soft," explained Don Isidro. "It was like silk. When you laid your hand on it . . ."

"Yes, yes," broke in the bishop hastily. "Seda. Silk. Very well."

He opened one eye, glanced at his nephew for an instant like a small inquisitive parrot, repressed a vague smile and shut out the material world again. There were moments when Don Isidro, for all his fifty years, looked no more than thirty and this was one of them. His long face and protruding underlip had softened and there were touches of color in his brown leathery cheeks. Memory was a dangerous thing. It could frighten a man or make him young again.

"Seda was not like the other gitanas," said Don Isidro, a withdrawn expression suffusing his eyes as his mind took the long step back into the past. "She was the daughter of the proprietor and though she brought food and porrones of wine to the table and sometimes danced while her father played the violin she refused her body to the persistent young men. There was a fierce pride in her that enhanced her beauty. And she was beautiful, my uncle, very beautiful. Her eyes were large and dark and her mouth small and red as the petals of crushed roses and her hair black as night and wild as a storm in the mountains. Her body was lean and perfect and the color of rich goat's cream and always clean. When she danced her bare feet flashed like little flames and her haunches rose and fell like the graceful sailing boats in the bay of Cadiz. 'Ah! Ah!' she would cry as she clapped her hands together and danced and her red skirt would swirl about her cream-colored legs like darting tongues from a log fire in the evening."

The bishop opened both eyes now and regarded his nephew with an extraordinary attentiveness. This was a new Don Isidro, one he had never encountered before and had never dreamt existed, and while it did not surprise him (he was incapable of being surprised), it interested him. Don Isidro had been young and passionate, then, and full of bad poetry and thirty years after he could feel the far glow of it. Why, he was as romantic as Ignacio Rodríguez Galván. It was a new aspect to the bishop and as such he would file it in his mind where he retained all those hints and betrayals that made up his understanding of his nephew. Don Isidro, oblivious of the observation, continued to live in the past with the impulses of a boy of twenty, his face increasingly flushed and a rapt expression in his eyes.

"I loved her," he declared. "I loved her, my uncle. My passion for her was not an immediate desire that would be satisfied with the fulfillment but a . . ."

The bishop, who was about to close his eyes again, having completed his scrutiny, decided not to and lifted a thin hand.

"Did your father know this?" he inquired. "Did your friends in Seville know? Surely, you didn't intend—"

"Wait," broke in Don Isidro. "No one knew. No, no, I never thought of marriage. What in the name of God has love to do with marriage, anyway? You know and I know. That is why we fix strong bars on our daughters' windows. We never guard our children against marriage; we guard them against love. I loved Seda. I desired her. But it was her soul I desired as well as her body, that inexpressible wholeness that was her flesh and her mind and her very being. I avoided my friends, even Don Francisco, so that I could pass every evening in her father's eating place where the oil was bad and the wine tasted of granite and the bread was moldy but where she would come to the table in her red petticoat, her hips and breasts trembling when she walked, and smile in that secret way that the gitanas, who see more of the future than we do, have. We smiled. We conversed. Our eyes embraced. I implored her to meet me outside but she refused. Oh, gently, our eyes still embracing. So it went. Evening after evening. I think now that she understood from the first the depths of my frantic passion for her and was sorry for me. Perhaps a little frightened. That was not what she desired at all. I thought that afterward, long afterward, but then, at the moment, I was incapable of thinking. I existed in a sort of glowing trance that was a dream world set down in the midst of the real world. The real world was all about me, cobbled streets and stone houses, churches, restaurants, gardens, reception rooms crowded with ugly women, rain, blue skies, trees and sunshine, but it was drab and lifeless compared to the magic world in which I seemed to walk."

The bishop's eyes were closed again and his lips moved as though he was speaking confidentially to himself.

"One evening when I was sitting alone at the little corner table that had been tacitly recognized as my own," said Don Isidro with some difficulty, as though he was approaching a portion of his story that he feared, "the door opened and when I raised my eyes I saw Don Francisco standing on the lintel and smiling at me. Have I described Don Francisco to you, my uncle? He was three years older than I and considerably shorter. But he was very strong. Wide-shouldered, thin-hipped, muscular-thighed. He was not bad-looking, either. Olive-colored, slant-eyed, broad-mouthed. When he smiled his teeth glistened. He was filled with life and divinely reckless. He had fought against the French in 1813 and achieved a great reputation for bravery. He exuded confidence and authority. Well, there he was standing in the doorway and smiling at me with that friendly yet mocking air that he displayed to all his companions and which had once amused me. I was angry and I made no attempt to conceal it. He belonged to the real world and I did not want to be reminded of it. Besides, I was intensely averse to being spied upon or followed, even by my friends, and I was certain that Don Francisco had followed me. It was not chance that brought him to this wretched eating place. When he came over and drew up a stool and seated himself opposite me I must have shown my resentment, for he laughed loudly and began to click through his teeth. 'Come, come!' he cried. 'You give me the face of a Guadarrama goat. After all, I am your host and it is my duty to oversee your welfare and protect you from the evil eye.' 'You followed me,' I declared with some bitterness. He acknowledged that. 'And a pretty chase you led me,' he said. 'I've stepped in dung, slipped on cabbage leaves, bumped my head on a stone cornice and been baptized by a chamberpot emptied from an upper window. I've jostled a wench, knocked down a garlic-stinking patrol and kicked a donkey in the behind.' 'It didn't occur to you that I desired no company?' I asked. 'Frankly, it didn't,' he answered, opening his eyes very wide. 'Your old friends miss you, Don Isidro. I miss you. What, in the name of the Holy Nails of Jesucristo, brings you to this foul, obscene, stinking, sour dog's hole of a bodegón? Are you planning an insurrection against our most blessed nincompoop, Ferdinand VII, because he kicked the Cortes down the palace stairs? Are you a Freemason? Come, tell . . . Oho! . . . Oho!' At that moment Seda stepped up to the table with a bowl of lentils and Don Francisco, who was no fool, understood everything in a flash. I remember all this as clearly, my uncle, as though I were reading from an old family book. He looked at her and nodded approvingly. He reached forward and slapped her boldly on the buttocks. 'Don't . . .' I began and then stopped for fear of making a fool of myself. I waited to see what *she* would do. Smash him on the head with the bowl of lentils, perhaps, or snatch the

knife from her garter and slice his face with it. I was as simple a
bobo as that, my uncle. She merely smiled at Don Francisco and went
away."

Don Isidro moved abruptly in his chair and his spurs jangled
against the table leg. The bishop did not open his eyes. Outside there
sounded a mingled shouting of men and the creaking rumble of heavy
wheels.

"Don Francisco went straight to the heart of the matter," resumed the hacendado. "He pointed out that I was ill and that there
was an easy cure for this malady. 'Give her father a piece of gold and
then grab her by the neck and haul her upstairs,' he said. I could only
look at him. 'If there are too many chinches up there," he went on,
'I'll get young Federico and Juan and Esteban and, Dios mío, we'll
carry her any place you like. After all, she is only a gitana.' I sprang
to my feet. 'No, no!' I cried. 'You do not understand. I will not . . .'
I couldn't bear his mocking smile and without saying another word
I hurried to the door. When I glanced back he was eating my lentil-
and ordering wine from Seda's father. It was with this glimpse of his
flushed smiling face and open mouth and the cringing figure of the
gitano that I stumbled off into the darkness."

Don Isidro stopped dead at that point and for a time it appeared
as though he was not going to continue his story at all. He poured
himself a glass of port wine and drank it. He fumbled in a heavy
beaten-silver box on the table and produced a small cigar which he
placed between his teeth and started to chew. He changed his position
and then changed it back again. He coughed heavily and scratched
the white cicatrice on his temple. The flush disappeared from his
cheeks and the rapt expression from his eyes. During this interlude
of busy silence the bishop did not move.

"From that night everything changed," declared Don Isidro
gruffly as he took up his narrative again. "I continued to frequent the
eating place but as often as not Seda was not there. This was unusual
but I did not mark it at the time. I was still walking in a dream world
that was quite removed from the real although a mist that I could not
explain was falling across it. At home or, rather, in the home of Don
Francisco there was a mist, too, and there the actual world impinged
sufficiently on me to make me notice it. I saw Don Francisco at the
noon meal and that was about all. He was as smiling, as friendly, as
mocking as ever but he did not urge me to accompany him on his
nocturnal rounds as he had never failed to do in the past. I considered this thoughtfulness on his part and was accordingly grateful
to him for it. He never spoke of Seda and this pleased me, too. But,
all the same, I found myself liking him less and less and this irritated
me when I thought of it for I could adduce no valid reason for such

a shift. Doña María Cristina did not add to the gaiety of the noon meal, either. Fat, pregnant, white as cream cheese and constantly reproachful to her husband, who contemptuously ignored her, she was more of an ordeal than an expectant mother. Good women can be so dull, my uncle. It was with relief, then, that I hurried away from Don Francisco's house to my unsatisfactory evenings in the little eating house. Of course, I did not go there all the time. There were hours when I walked without seeing where I walked or leaned on the parapet of a bridge and watched the muddy river flow by on its sluggish way to the Gulf of Lebrija. I was a man devoured by a constant urge and incapable of fulfilling it."

He glanced unseeingly over the bishop's head at the veined ivory Christ on the black wooden cross that hung on the wall.

"That does not sound like me, does it?" he asked. "I, too, have that feeling. It is another man that I am describing, a fool, a dunce, a youth possessed. Well, he is dead. He is of no interest but one may discuss him as one would discuss a half-forgotten journey that had no meaning. Listen. One gray afternoon I went to the eating house early, in the hope, I suppose, of finding Seda there. I had not seen her for three evenings and a frightful feeling of calamity filled my mind. Young men are like that, my uncle. A touch, a smile, the mere presence of the one beloved is enough to arouse the happiest emotions, the highest optimism, the most joyous anticipations; but the absence of the beloved, especially the unexplained absence, the unawareness of where she may be, gives birth to fear, foreboding and mental torture. A thousand horrible pictures flit through the mind. All is black and white in love. So it was with me. I had not seen Seda for three days and now in the middle of the afternoon she was not where my possessive mind demanded that she should be. You will wonder why I did not ask her father where she was. I will tell you. I was afraid. I was afraid to find out where she was and I was frantic to find her. Can you make any sense of that, my uncle? I sat down at my usual table and ordered a porrón of wine. Her father, to whom I had not spoken ten words in all the weeks that I had frequented the eating house, came over to me. He was a tall gitano with gray hair and flickering black eyes. He was chewing a ripe olive and he spat the stone out on the floor. He stood looking down at me. 'Señor Don Isidro,' he said. 'This is useless.' I heard him but I did not comprehend. 'This is useless,' he repeated. I did not reply. 'Maldita sea!' he exclaimed with a liberty that would have brought a blow if I had been myself and not a hollowed reed marrowed with one desire. 'It is time to make an end. You are attracting the watch to my door and giving me a bad name. You and the other. I will no longer let this pass, no, not for three gold pieces. There is danger here. Go, then, to such and such a place . . .' and he described a small posada a mile or so beyond the city limits on the bank of the Guadalquivir which I knew as a place where the young hidalgos took their mistresses and sometimes the wives of their friends, 'and see what you will see. Much good may it do you. Oh, the devil!' He stamped away from my table like a man who had done something terrible and must conceal his fright by noise. I think that it was some minutes before that part of me which could reason fully understood what he had said and then I rose very quietly to my feet, as though an invisible hand was lifting me by the elbow, and passed out of the eating house. Within an hour I was at the posada. It was a low brown building raised close to the water and with a narrow strip of muddy soil pitted with hoof marks before it. I remember a few stakes with boats tied to them and the deepening twilight that plunged the farther shore in violet shadow. I remember, too, the young moon, crescent-horned, like a silver shaving in the mauve heavens. There was a light carriage, a sort of birlocho, before the inn and one gray horse that looked familiar. I stood opposite the door meditating whether or not to enter when it opened (it opened almost immediately as though Fate had already planned this moment) and they came out. Don Francisco had his arm about Seda's waist and her face was up-turned gazing into his. At that moment, my uncle, I ceased to be young and I ceased to be a man. I became a beast, a wronged tiger, a desperate lion."

The bishop sighed but did not open his eyes.

"Don Francisco saw me and his face turned white," went on Don Isidro. "It was like a sheet of parchment in the deepening twilight. He thrust Seda aside and pulled out the revolving pistol he always carried when he went into the country. My rage paralyzed me and I could not move as he prepared the pistol, raised it, cocked it and fired. The ball creased my forehead and flung me sideways but now I could move. Blood streamed into my eyes as I drew my hunting knife and ran to meet him. He ran as eagerly as I with his knife in his hand but when we met in the midst of that damp brown hoof-pocked soil it was my knife that plunged to the guard into his thick white throat. The blood came out black and he fell down and gurgled like a burst wineskin for a minute and died. Seda ran screaming down the bank of the river."

"Oh, Blessed Jesús! Oh, My God!" murmured the bishop in a low voice but he uttered the words without any surprise.

Don Isidro drew a deep breath and shook his head like a bewildered lion.

"Why did I kill him?" he asked almost plaintively. "Why did he desire to kill me? We were friends. I do not know. It was so and that was all there was to it. The moment my knife entered his throat I no longer loved or desired Seda. The moment he died I knew that he wa right and that we must not place too much value upon a woman's virtue. He had followed the custom of his class and if I had been wise I would have done the same. My imagination betrayed me."

"The absence of God from your heart betrayed you," said the bishop soberly.

He had opened his eyes and was regarding his nephew much as one would regard a strange animal in a zoo.

"Perhaps so," replied Don Isidro. "Call it what you will, my uncle. The Church gives you such authority."

"But you killed in self-defense," proclaimed the bishop anxiously. "You killed to preserve your own life."

Don Isidro was silent for a moment.

"Why, yes," he said finally. "Call it that, too."

"Proceed," commanded the bishop reluctantly. "There is more to this, is there not?"

"There is more," assented Don Isidro gloomily, "but it is difficult to explain. I remember walking back to Seville. I remember prowling through the streets, passing Don Francisco's house and seeing the candles shine through the bars, pausing at the doors of eating houses and then moving on again, saluting the patrol, standing at corners and watching the night. An intolerable feeling of guilt permeated me and I had the sensation of being set apart from the rest of the human race. I think I even meditated making away with myself, perhaps jumping into the river. But as I walked and walked the chaotic streets the mad tension of my mind lessened and I began to consider other people, my father and mother, Doña María Cristina and her unborn child. How would this affect them? What could I do now? I came to a small ·church and I went in and leaned against a pillar. It was dark and damp there and deserted but to one side of the altar was a cluster of votive candles blinking weakly in the draft before a small plaster figure of Our Lady. I fixed my eyes upon it and watched the little petals of flame for a long time. It was still in the church, attentive, a sort of waiting hush. My uncle, I am sorry to admit that I was never zealous in my faith but I always believed in God and the invulnerability and mercy of His Church. I may have ignored but I never doubted. At that moment in the stillness of the church with the candles faintly glowing before my eyes I felt a new calmness suffuse my thoughts and quite suddenly I knew what to do. It was no miracle that happened to me. It was no light from heaven or still small Voice of God. Our Lady did not open her lips and speak to me. I merely remembered what I was most proud of in my short life. It was my word. I had never broken a promise or a vow. It was the one virtue that I had cultivated in my twenty years and it was the only thing that I could offer to the spirit of Don Francisco in expiation of my crime. I reasoned about it, my uncle. I reasoned for a long time and it must have been midnight when I lighted twenty candles and knelt before the Blessed Image of Our Lady and made my vow. It seemed to flow into my mind of its own volition. I swore that if Don Francisco's posthumous child were a boy I would marry him to my first daughter and if the child were a girl I would marry her to my first son."

"Oh!" ejaculated the bishop as though at last he had heard the fact for which he had waited so long. He closed his eyes and resumed the appearance of one asleep.

"It sounds like a little thing now that I speak of it aloud," continued Don Isidro. "It sounds like a foolish and boastful thing, too, for I was neither married nor had any prospects of marriage. But it was not meant as a little thing. At that time in the church I saw my vow as a means of tying myself to Don Francisco's memory. How could I forget him when my marriage to be and my child to come were inextricably connected with his child to be? Do you see, my uncle? I knew I would be married someday and I knew that I would have children. I was pledging myself to at least twenty years of memory and regret. It has been thirty years."

"You should have gone to a father of the Church and confessed and accepted his advice," murmured the bishop.

Don Isidro's heavy underlip protruded a trifle as he stared at his uncle.

"How could you know what to do?" insisted the bishop. "You sinned in taking this decision upon yourself as you sinned in slaying Don Francisco. This vow was taken without sanctification. You, the guilty penitent, arrogated to yourself an authority that was not placed in you. The Church is very jealous of its authority. I must speak to the archbishop about this."

"The vow was made," said Don Isidro firmly. "And I have never broken my word."

The bishop sighed.

"No one knows of this?" he asked finally.

"No one," replied Don Isidro. "At that time there were many unsolved killings in Spain. There were insurrections, assassinations, burnings, a kind of undeclared civil war over the greater part of the kingdom. Don Francisco was an uncompromising adherent of Ferdinand VII and it was believed that he had been killed by some zealous assassin of the so-called liberal element. Seda and her father fled from Seville, probably fearing to be sacrificed as scapegoats. So far as I know they were never heard of again. Doña María Cristina, when her time came and in spite of her grief, gave birth to a strong well-knit boy."

"Don Alejandro," said the bishop.

"Don Alejandro," repeated Don Isidro. "I returned to Mexico in 1817 but I never lost touch with Doña María Cristina. We corresponded regularly and once or twice when I revisited Spain I saw her and renewed an old friendly relationship. Of course, she spoke often of Don Francisco, extolling his virtues and the great career that was destroyed by his sudden death. He had become a saint in her calendar. I think she was slightly daft and when she died a few years ago it must have been a relief to all her family. I have heard that she weighed three hundred and twenty pounds when they sealed her in her coffin. You know the rest, my uncle. There was my father's death, then my mother's, my marriage to your niece in 1828, the birth of María Catalina in 1829 and the birth of Lorenzo in 1832. I lived an active life and no ghosts haunted me."

"Humph!" grunted the bishop. "This Don Alejandro, now. You saw him often?"

Don Isidro shook his head.

"I saw him when I went to Spain," he explained. "He passed a summer with me here at Las Golondrinas in 1835, the year before Santa Anna's defeat at San Jacinto. Again in 1840 he came to Mexico with the Spanish ambassador and remained for nearly a year. And this time."

He paused and pursed his lips.

"Do you like him?" inquired the bishop gently.

"I detest him," replied Don Isidro frankly.

"That's what I thought," admitted the bishop.

He lifted his thin hand and scratched his scant white hair.

"What do you want me to do?" he asked presently. "Tell you that your vow is not valid?"

Don Isidro lifted a large hand with liver-colored spots on the back of it in a gesture of dissent.

"Have I not explained that I have never broken a vow to God or man?" he asked with some spirit. "To do so even once and for actual cause would destroy me to myself. I want your approval."

The bishop moved testily as though there was a flea in his sotana.

"You cannot bully the Church even if you are my nephew," he declared. "I neither approve nor disapprove. You have left me no choice. Your vow, foolish in itself, has obviously become an integral part of your curious self-centered pattern. It is like a keystone. To knock it away would precipitate a collapse for which I should not care to be responsible. But there is nothing holy in your vow, Don Isidro. It is much less a promise to God than a promise to yourself. Have you considered María Catalina's feelings in this matter?"

Suddenly his sly black eyes were very bright.

"María Catalina always does as I desire," replied Don Isidro slowly, "and this obedience gives her pleasure. She has always known that she was destined to marry Don Alejandro and I doubt that she has any particular feelings at all."

The bishop opened his thin mouth and then shut it without a word. It was as though he had decisively closed a book that he knew his nephew would not understand.

"If Don Alejandro does not make her a good husband," continued Don Isidro in a raised voice, "I will thrash him within an inch of his life."

"I see," remarked the bishop dryly. "The vow is fulfilled at the marriage altar. After that . . ."

"After that I am free," broke in Don Isidro. "The second after the ceremony I am free. Free of vows, and there will never be another one, and released from a thirty years' incubus."

"In other words, you absolve yourself, my nephew," said the bishop.

"I do not see it that way," insisted Don Isidro.

The bishop yawned and hastily placed his hand over his mouth.

"I must think about this," he declared. "We will discuss it again. You wouldn't consider postponing the marriage?"

Don Isidro said nothing. He merely looked stubbornly at the forlorn figure of Christ over the bishop's head on the wall.

"I thought not," went on the bishop, hardly waiting for an answer. "Your pride is greater than your reason. I think I will speak with Doña Ágata."

As though that would do any good. All the same, there was a half-conceived intent to prevent the marriage that was to take place so few hours away. It was growing in his mind like a mushroom in a warm cellar. And it was growing less for the sake of María Catalina, who, so far as he recalled, exhibited no more life than an obedient lizard, than it was to prove to Don Isidro that even *his* vows could be thwarted by the Church. Don Isidro was altogether too final and determined to be allowed such a victory. It smacked too much of permitting a man to shrive himself. The bishop groaned as he rose somewhat stiffly to his feet, an old man who wanted to nap and felt that he had a task to do. Don Isidro stood up, too.

Before either could speak again the customary tumult of the plaza beyond the window was quickened by several blaring trumpets, an increasing rumble of coach wheels, scattered shouting and a many-hoofed tapping of horses' feet on hard earth.

"It must be the general!" exclaimed Don Isidro, hurriedly stalking toward the door.

The bishop made a grimace and sat down again.

"Qué sinvergüenza!" he mumbled to himself without indicating whether he meant the rascal to be Don Isidro or the general.

General Santa Anna had already descended from his coach when Don Isidro reached the plaza and he was carefully directing the removal of several crates of gamecocks from a second coach that stood behind his own. He greeted the hacendado with a glittering smile and turned back to the restless birds whose heads with the flat jewels of their evil eyes thrust through the slats of the crates. As Don Isidro hurried forward he observed with interest the physical appearance of this curious man who had been alternately savior and devil of Mexico. He saw before him a middle-sized man, now in his fifty-second year, dressed in a blue and red general's uniform plentifully besprinkled with gold leaf. The famous peg leg was painted black. Santa Anna smiled and gesticulated with his cane as he directed the careful removal of the crates and the half dozen young staff officers tumbled over their sabers and ran into one another in their anxiety to please him. Men will always alternately hate and love him, thought Don Isidro as he advanced with outstretched hand. "Now they love him."

"I have brought you Cola de Plata, Don Isidro," declared Santa Anna abruptly as he shook the hacendado's hand warmly. "It is like giving you a piece of my heart, my dear friend."

"Cola de Plata?" said Don Isidro in equal bewilderment at the name and at being called "my dear friend."

"He is my favorite fighting cock," explained the general. "He comes to you fresh from fifteen victories in the pits of Jalapa. And would you believe it, he has never been gashed."

"It is very generous of you, Señor Presidente," replied Don Isidro, who was one of the few Mexican gentlemen who detested cockfighting and did not have a single bird on his estates.

"It is the least that I could do," said Santa Anna. "It is a most inadequate return, a mere friendly gesture, in return for the sixty thousand pesos you are contributing to the campaign."

His large dark eyes, slightly bloodshot, twinkled as he observed the other's face.

"Sixty thou . . ." began Don Isidro angrily and then discretion caught his tongue.

He bowed formally over the general's hand.

"It is the least that I could do . . . for my invaded country," he said precisely.

He was furious at what he regarded as a holdup, so furious that the plaza blurred before his eyes, the halted coaches with their tired mules, the scurrying officers, the troopers on horseback that crowded by the gate and the body of men on the road all mingling in a dancing picture of senseless movement and color. But an inner wisdom held all this chaos in check and he gave no sign of his anger as he turned toward the door to the casa grande with an inviting gesture of the hand toward Santa Anna. There was repressed admiration in the yellowish sallow face of the general as he acknowledged the invitation and stumped along beside the hacendado, striking the metal tip of his cane against the hard clay-filled earth.

"A wedding is always an event of joy to me," he said affably. "Dios mio! I made the coachmen whip their mules nearly to death in my anxiety to be here. It will give me great pleasure to drink a toast to the bride."

He peered sideways at Don Isidro's face and clutched him familiarly by the arm.

"This is a great day of happiness for you," he went on. "Who is the groom, my dear friend? A young Spaniard? Was he not at the Spanish Embassy during Bustamente's time? And your daughter— Doña María Catalina? How happy she must be! I understand that your illustrious uncle, the bishop of Puebla, is here. Did he arrive this morning? The journey must have been arduous for such an old man. Is he resting now?"

He wants to show me that he knows everything, thought Don Isidro. His idea of friendliness is a display of omniscience. Well, that may serve for ignorant Indians but it does not impress me. Of course, he asked right and left before he left Mexico City and of course he was reminded of what he had set down in his notebook by some young officer as his coach approached the gate of Las Golondrinas. He probably has a list of every proprietor between Mexico City and San Luis Potosí and exactly how much each is capable of disgorging to pay for his campaign against the Yanquis. Sixty thousand pesos. Sixty thousand devils! Don Isidro became aware of a young officer who was pressing close behind the general and endeavoring to attract his attention. Santa Anna interrupted his stream of questions and turned half-frowning but when he saw the youth who was very neat and straight his face relaxed into a smile.

"Oh, yes," he said. "Eh, Juanillo? What is it? Micheltorena has all the orders concerning the quartering of the men."

"The surprise, general," explained the young officer. "You have not forgotten . . . ?"

"Oh!" exclaimed Santa Anna stopping dead in his tracks.

He glanced at Don Isidro, his teeth flashing brightly in his ochre-hued face. Then he turned to the second coach that was some distance away.

"Tobalito," he called. "Tobalito. Is there not another gamecock in the coach for Don Isidro?"

Christ burn all the gamecocks, thought the hacendado angrily, but when instead of a fighting bird in a crate a slender boy jumped down from the coach and walked rapidly toward him a proud exultation filled his heart and he spread his arms wide in greeting.

"Lorenzo!" he exclaimed.

His son broke into a run and in an instant was enveloped in his arms. Don Isidro kissed the boy on both cheeks and then on the forehead and thrust him back holding him by both shoulders. Santa Anna and the young officer stood by smiling. An unexpected feeling of tenderness and pride flowed through the father as he pressed the thin nervous shoulders and observed the narrow intelligent face and large affectionate eyes of his son. He was almost a man. The cadet uniform and jaunty cap emphasized both his youth and the maturity he was approaching. How pleased Doña Ágata would be! Don Isidro did not trust himself to regard the boy further but pushed him gently away.

"Seek thy mother," he said. "She will be overjoyed to see thee."

Lorenzo, whose few mumbled words of greeting to his father had passed unheeded by all, glanced questioningly at the young offi er and receiving a friendly nod of acquiescence sped into the casa grande. Don Isidro cleared his throat as he ushered Santa Anna up the few steps. He could not but feel grateful to the general for this thoughtful and well-meant surprise. There were many sides to this erratic man. But . . . sixty thousand pesos . . .

"You are very thoughtful, Señor Presidente," he said with some warmth.

"I thought you would like to see the boy," remarked Santa Anna, hopping nimbly up the steps with the aid of his cane. "Of course, I cannot take him on to San Luis Potosí. But a few days here . . ."

He turned to the young officer who was standing doubtfully at the foot of the steps.

"You may come with me, Juanillo," he said amiably. "I'm sure that Don Isidro will want to talk to you."

For the first time the hacendado observed the youthful lieutenant with some attention and discovered that he was spare of figure, thin-faced with large hazel eyes and not even remotely Spanish or Indian in appearance. Don Isidro blinked his eyes. He had seen that type before but never in the Mexican army. Germans, yes. French, too. But never that type. He turned his puzzled glance to Santa Anna. The general, who was about to enter the open door where Chepe stood at stolid attention, answered Don Isidro's questioning look with the flourish of a gold-braided arm.

"Don Juan de Béxar," he explained. "Lieutenant and personal aide and my protégé."

"Don Juan de Béxar," repeated Don Isidro in a puzzled tone.

Santa Anna burst into a laugh.

"Don Juan Diego de Béxar," he corrected himself. "I ought to know for I named him myself. It is a story for the dinner table. I hope you have some good wines here. My throat is as parched as the desert."

He stepped through the door and Don Isidro, still glancing sideways at the young officer, followed him. He would take his oath that Don Juan Diego de Béxar was a Yanqui of the gentler class.

The long dining table, covered with a fine lace cloth from Salamanca and glittering with old silver, was a pool of neutrality about which cautiously fenced a group of figures wearing dissembling masks. From his post near the long window where he stood with two young aides Juan Diego de Béxar observed these disguised personalities endeavoring to impress one another and not betray themselves at the same time. He had seen more than one table like this, in Vera Cruz, in Jalisco, in Mexico City. It was thoroughly Mexican. No one believed his neighbor and everybody was suspect. Eyes were always watchful and sharp with distrust. It was so here with the difference that there was more finesse and a cleverer dissembling. Don Isidro, who sat at the head of the table in a high-backed chair carved with his arms, exhibited a lofty amiability but his glance was keen and devoid of friendliness whenever he fixed it on the general. Santa Anna was a very paragon of graciousness but he, too, was dissembling. It was, as Juan Diego knew, an affected graciousness, an histrionic accomplishment that he had perfected in the political gatherings of Mexico City and Vera Cruz. He was waiting and watching for something, as he always waited and watched for something, but what it was no one would know until it happened. He studied men and ferreted out their weaknesses and played with them as a sly cat plays with a mouse. When the time came he pounced. The little withered bishop of Puebla, who constantly cast imploring glances at the hawk-nosed Doña Ágata, was obviously devoured by a desire to broach something to her that he had no opportunity to broach and this frustration had put him in such an inward boil that he refused to eat at all. Of all those present he was the one who seemed most likely to erupt. Young Lorenzo, his eyes fixed on the open window, seemed like a young eagle meditating a sudden flight through it. He, at least, was no part of the emotional masquerade. The others, the wedding guests, in their tight antelope-skin breeches and embroidered jackets, their brocaded gowns and elaborate coiffures, were bewildered and uneasy. There were coils within coils here and even so youthful an observer as Juan Diego could sense them. It didn't look like a merry wedding party at all. Where, for that matter, were the prospective bride and the man she was to marry? Neither was present. Oh, there had been excuses but the sound of them had been forced and false. The girl, María Catalína (and Juan Diego pictured her as short and fat and lardish in complexion), was engaged in dressing for the ceremony, and Don Alejandro, the Spanish husband to be, was suffering from a headache. It didn't sound right. Juan Diego knew it and so did the general. Juan Diego didn't care but the general did. He liked to look at women. Juan Diego knew that, too.

The bishop ol Puebla sniffed disdainfully at the spicy aroma of mole that rose from the table and turned his discontented little face toward Santa Anna.

"You are quite certain of victory, general," he said dryly.

Santa Anna glanced quickly at the prelate and smiled. Deliberately he scooped up a little mole sauce with a folded tortilla.

"Why not?" he asked amiably, his mouth full. "I am nearer my sources of supplies than the Americans and I shall have twenty thousand men at San Luis Potosí within three months."

"From Durango and Zacatecas?" inquired the bishop mildly.

The general's eyes flickered under his half-closed lids as he swabbed his plate.

"No," he said equably. "Nor from Michoacán, either. I know that I am disliked in those districts. But in San Luis Potosí and Guanajuato and Jalisco and Vera Cruz and Hidalgo and Tamaulipas and Sinaloa the story will be different. I shall have plenty of men."

"You will need plenty of money too," said the bishop.

"I shall raise it," declared Santa Anna confidently. "The government will forward it. I shall issue drafts in my own name, if necessary. The Congress will vote forced loans. I will establish local collections."

He paused and glanced smilingly at Don Isidro.

"The Mexican people are a patriotic people," he said. "They will make sacrifices willingly for the Republic. Is that not so, Don Isidro?"

"They will do what they can," answered the hacendado shortly.

The bishop shut his eyes.

"You are a miracle worker, general," he murmured. "Anybody who can raise and equip an army of size in a country that is half in revolt against him is a miracle worker."

"It will be no miracle," said Santa Anna dryly. "I shall have your help and the help of Don Isidro and the help of a hundred others as generous and patriotic as the both of you are."

Juan Diego, standing by the window, repressed a smile at the momentary expressions that flitted across the faces of the bishop and the hacendado.

Don Isidro turned his big head.

"Chepe!" he bawled. "Is the champagne cold? Serve it, you fool, serve it."

The stolid-faced Indian hurried around the table.

The bishop opened his eyes and observed the general carefully, much as a visitor to Mexico City might stand in the Zócalo and study the façade of the cathedral.

"Your confidence encourages all of us," he said in a flat voice.

There was a murmur of assent from the uneasy guests about the glistening lace cloth.

The general reached for another tortilla.

"I'll have a little more mole," he announced pleasantly. "Your cook is a treasure, Don Isidro. The spices are in perfect proportion. I am almost tempted to take your man with me to San Luis Potosí."

The bishop returned to the attack.

"It will be an unfortunate day for you, my general," he said maliciously, "if you should have the misfortune to fall into the hands of the Yanquis again."

"That is a chance that one must take in war," replied Santa Anna equably. "However, I do not think it will happen. It is more likely that I shall have their General Taylor before the winter is over."

The bishop closed his eyes.

"Yes," he said. "I tremble to think of what might happen. Up there they have not forgotten the Alamo or the fate of Fannin's men."

There was a deathly pause about the table and Juan Diego heard Don Isidro suddenly suck in his breath. Santa Anna's heavy lips drew in to a straight line.

"I appreciate the fatherly concern of your Grace for me," he said dryly.

He turned his head and shot a glance at the three young aides by the window. Then he addressed himself to Don Isidro.

"I will tell you a story," he began. "When I arrived in Washington after the disastrous campaign of San Jacinto, Mr. Forsyth, then secretary of state, called upon me and requested that I go with him and see General Jackson, then confined to his quarters. I did. The American president asked me why I permitted the execution of the Texians of Fannin's command, and at the Alamo. Beginning with the last action I explained that it was not expected of any commander to restrain his troops when a place was taken by storm, and still less so when the disproportion of the forces of the besiegers and the besieged was so great as to make a successful defense altogether hopeless—that in such a case, to protract the defense was a wanton sacrifice of the lives of the assailants—and unjustifiable. I explained, too, that scenes equally sanguinary were enacted by the troops under the command of the Duke of Wellington at the storming of San Sebastián, Ciudad Riego, and Badajoz. To be brief, I had precedent. The Texians who defended the Alamo did not exceed one hundred and fifty men, with almost no artillery, against between four and five thousand Mexicans, with artillery. Seven different times I summoned the besieged to surrender and offered them quarter, which I would have taken the risk and responsibility of granting, but they refused and fought to the last. I was justified in what I did because the men of the Alamo, knowing that their cause was lost, were no better than murderers. As to the shooting of Fannin's men, I explained that the campaign of Texas had been commenced under a special act of the Mexican Congress providing that no prisoners should be made. I added that if the law was a sanguinary one then the odium should attach to the legislature which passed it and not to the military commander who obeyed and executed it. I pointed out, too, that the men of Texas were outlaw Mexicans fighting against their own government and, as such, traitors liable to the penalty of death."

"Did General Jackson express himself as satisfied with your explanation, my general?" demanded the bishop.

Santa Anna still addressed himself to Don Isidro.

"General Jackson," he said, "declared that I had satisfied him on those points."

The bishop coughed violently and reached for a goblet of wine.

Juan Diego continued to observe the diners. There was no doubt about it; they were all at cross-purposes. They were saying one thing while thinking about another. Take the bishop of Puebla, for instance. It was obvious that he entertained no affection for the general but it was not the general alone that made him so disagreeable. There was something else, something that caused him to gaze imploringly at Doña Ágata from time to time and to stare disapprovingly at Don Isidro. As for Don Isidro, he studiously avoided the bishop's eyes and acknowledged the prelate's presence only when the irritated little man seemed about to address Doña Ágata. Then he would leap in with some remark or question that would divert the bishop from the lady of Las Golondrinas. It was curious. The general, Juan Diego knew, was a trifle vexed because he had not seen the bride to be. Santa Anna loved to look at women if they were fair. Don Isidro would have to pay for that.

"The Alamo reminds me of something," the general was saying. "I promised to tell you about Juanillo. He was . . ."

Juan Diego heard himself referred to and a flush mantled his thin cheeks. They were all glancing at him now and their eyes seemed like a host of crawling beetles. As the general, who loved to extend and enlarge a story, continued to speak, an array of ghosts and faraway happenings passed through the dining hall. "The prisoners of the Alamo . . . this orphan . . . I adopted . . ." The voice of Santa Anna flowed on and on. Juan Diego seemed to hear a distant sound of guns firing

and somewhere a man without a face ran through sulphurous smoke.
He glanced at the two young aides, who were smirking at him, and
then looked out the window. He detached himself from them as easily
as he detached himself from the boy of the Alamo. These were recognitions that he could refuse or put away or pretend not to notice. After a
while they ceased to exist. He had always possessed that queer power
of erasing by ignoring, of shutting his mind fast against anything he
did not want to know. The raised voice of the bishop, a high-plucked
string, cut through the general's tale. "I wonder how he will react
when he meets his own in the north?" Who? Oh, me. Well . . . He
continued to look out the window and watch the Indians drape paper
festoons to newly planted poles. There was a squad of soldiers squatting in the courtyard now. He observed their new uniforms carefully.
The rest of the vanguard must have come up. The dark vivid faces
turned in the sunlight, disks of curiosity. One of the young aides
nudged him sharply and he swung about on his heel. The general, having completed his story, was addressing him.

"Juanillo," he said, baring his gold-flecked teeth in a sudden smile,
"Don Isidro is kind enough to let us have thirty horses. Will you go
down to the corral and pick them out? Take Tobalito with you. He has
a fine eye for good horseflesh."

He turned to the hacendado.

"Don Isidro," he continued in a silky voice, "the Republic is
proud of you. Your generosity will not be forgotten."

Don Isidro's large face was brick-red with rage but he acknowledged the general's words with a graceful inclination of the head.

"Thank you, my general," he replied. "All that I have is at the
disposal of the Republic."

The bishop cleared his throat with a loud cough.

He has wonderful control, thought Juan Diego as he moved toward the door. Well, he has paid for not producing his daughter at
dinner. Thirty horses. A stiff price for something that possibly he
could not control. The high door closed behind Juan Diego and he
walked rapidly down a long corridor hung with faded Spanish tapestry.

When the young officer, accompanied by Tobalito and followed
by half a dozen Lancers, turned into the open gate of the huge corral
he saw that already a number of the hacendado's vaqueros were cutting horses out from the frightened mass of half-broken animals that
were stampeding by the white wall. Tobalito spat over his horse's head.

"Jesús mil veces!" he said without emphasis. "What jacos! They
are assembling wrecks, not horses, for the general. There isn't an animal there that a third-rate picador from the worst bull ring in Mexico
would venture to ride. It would fall in pieces under him."

Juan Diego shrugged his shoulders.

It was true. The horses cut out from the others and being isolated in a corner near the gate were the sorriest-looking group of bony nags that he had ever seen. Well, perhaps Don Isidro had a sense of humor. If he had to be plucked by the general he would be plucked of what he least desired. It might not be patriotism but it was human nature. All Mexico seemed to fight its wars this way. Wretched horses, spoiled provisions, dodged taxes, reluctant and inadequate gifts, constant desertions, jealousy, inertia, procrastination, lack of discipline, big words and little actions, this was the turmoil behind the colored façade of the young Republic. What could the general do? What order could he establish in this colossal disorder? Juan Diego's face was grave as he studied the growing mass of selected horses.

"There must be better animals than these," he said. "Let us ride over to the caballeriza."

The low whitewashed stables extended along one side of the corral and when Juan Diego reined in his pony before them he received a surprise. There was only one horse there. It had just been led out from an open door by a squat man in an overdecorated green riding outfit while a quiet Indian, whom Juan Diego recognized as Don Isidro's personal servant, Chepe, stood stolidly by and watched. Tobalito burst into a short laugh.

"Don Isidro is a wise man," he declared. "He has hidden his best horses."

"Not all of them," replied Juan Diego in a hushed voice. He was staring at the animal before him. Never in his life had he seen such beauty among the mounts of Vera Cruz or the Plateau. His eyes ran over the short intelligent head, the sensitive mouth with its small tight underlip, the large pink nostrils, the flashing eyes with their long black lashes, the prominent forehead, the little pointing ears, the arched throat, the deep strong breast, the short wide back, the muscular thighs, the light legs and the hoofs like polished iron. This, he knew although he had never seen one before, was of pure Arabian breed. What a horse for the general to ride into Monterrey at the head of his victorious troops! Tobalito, his jaw dropped, had been studying the horse, too.

"Cáspita!" he exploded. "If we could find thirty like this one our cavalry would be across the Rio Grande in a week. We would be in Washington in a month. You, there!"

He bawled at the Indian.

"Where are the rest of this breed?"

The Indian shifted snaky black eyes from the horse to Tobalito and then came slowly forward,

"There are no others," he said. "This is Simún, the horse of Don

Alejandro. He brought it from Spain with him. It is his own, Señor Sargento."

"We will take it anyway," asserted Tobalito, turning to Juan Diego.

The young officer shook his head.

"Our orders are to accept thirty of Don Isidro's horses," he said, but there was disappointment in his voice.

"When the general sees this animal he won't care if it is the private property of the Virgin Mary," grumbled Tobalito.

The squat man in green, who was dragging the horse forward by a rope halter, turned truculent frog's eyes at the two mounted men. The minute he did so the Arabian stretched forth a graceful neck and nipped viciously at his ear. Bright drops of blood fell on the green jacket.

"Ah, ah, you putrefying bastard!" screamed the injured man, dropping the halter and retreating several steps toward the stable door. Simún, dancing slightly and with head outstretched, followed him like a boxer. The man grabbed up a slab of wood that lay near and lifting it with both hands brought it down heavily on the animal's head. The horse screamed and kicked violently. The man scampered awkwardly through the stable door and disappeared. During this brief interval of violence the Indian had stood absolutely still but now he stepped toward the frightened Arabian and grasped the halter firmly in a dark hand. Simún attempted to throw back his head, then whinnied plaintively and thrust his nose along the Indian's neck. In an instant he was quiet. The Indian raised his free hand and wiped a smear of blood from the glistening cocoa-colored forehead.

"Is that Don Alejandro?" demanded Juan Diego in an indignant voice.

The Indian started to lead the horse toward the stable.

"Yes, Señor Teniente," he replied. "That is Don Alejandro de la Barca y Padilla of Seville."

"The bridegroom," said Tobalito ironically. "Is he as popular with his bride as he is with his horse?"

A faint light filled the Indian's eyes for a second.

"I do not know, Señor Sargento," he replied formally.

"All the same, we should take that horse," grumbled Tobalito.

Juan Diego lifted his hand.

"I will speak to the general about the animal," he said with emphasis.

The sargento observed that the Señor Tentiente was angry.

Hoofbeats caused them to turn in their saddles. It was one of the aides who had been in attendance at the dinner, Ezequiel Oropesa, a youth just graduated from the Military College at Chapultepec.

"Orders, Don Juan Diego," he said brightly. "You are to set out immediately with the horses and join the forward baggage train and turn them over to the blacksmiths. The train passed here about two hours ago. You should overtake it on the road to Celaya."

Tobalito blew his nose dexterously by placing a dirty thumb against a hairy nostril and whooshing mightily.

"Any smith who tries to shoe those horses will find the hoofs coming off in his hands," he declared.

He grinned at the young officer.

"You'll miss the wedding fiesta," he added cheerfully.

"So will you," answered Juan Diego. "You're the expert on horseflesh."

He turned to Ezequiel Oropesa.

"Inform the general that I will start as soon as the animals are haltered," he said. "I'll take Tobalito and a guard of eight Lancers. Am I to return?"

"Oh, yes," replied the youthful aide. "That is, if you can get back before morning."

He broke into a gentle laugh.

"I envy you," he avowed. "Enjoying the nice dusty road while I suffer here in the shade drinking fresh pulque."

"May it poison you," grumbled Tobalito with the freedom of an old regular army sergeant. "May every drop of it bring out black spots on your pretty face."

Juan Diego turned his pony.

"Come along," he said. "Don't frighten the boy with such curses. You'll have him wetting his pants."

Ezequiel Oropesa drew his index finger across his throat with a frightful grimace.

The bishop of Puebla could not sleep. Before, during and after dinner he had endeavored to seclude Doña Ágata for a moment and speak to her of this shocking vow that Don Isidro was fulfilling. Every attempt had been frustrated. Whenever he approached his niece there was the hacendado with some imperative diversion that could not be ignored. He must consult with the hacienda priest, that fat rabbit. He must listen to the interminable and intolerable conversation of the general. He must speak with becoming unction to the constantly arriving guests, many of whom were props and pillars of the Church in this damned district. It was maddening.

Now that he was lying on the couch in the high-ceilinged chamber that had been assigned to him and the sleep that he enjoyed every afternoon failed for once to materialize he bethought himself of ways to circumvent Don Isidro's evident determination to keep him and Doña Ágata apart until after the wedding. He lay back on the couch and studied the whitewashed ceiling while he listened. There was a far-away murmur of noise from the great plaza where, he supposed, they were arranging decorations for the ceremony. It sounded like the surf off Sacrificio. The faint sound of a bugle echoed eerily and he assumed that more troops were arriving or passing on their way to the north. This idiotic war! The slap of straw sandals in the corridor outside the door caused him to raise a peevish head. They paused at the door for an instant and then passed on. Probably one of Don Isidro's Indians peering through the keyhole to see that he was safe in his cage. A sudden rage convulsed him and he sat upright, swinging his feet to the tiled floor.

No, no, this would never do. The archbishop should be informed about this matter. No hacendado, no matter how rich he was or how many peons he ruled, could assume the prerogatives of God. The pride of Don Isidro was swollen too big and it should be deflated. It was an absolute danger to the omniscience of the Church for such a man to make himself so big. The Church had enough troubles as it was . . . what with those secret Masonic orders, the Freethinkers, the damned Republican Liberals and the hosts of Indians who saw the very features of their pagan deities in the faces of Jesus Christ and the Holy Mary. The bishop stood up and walked wearily to the window. It was barred.

He looked down into the desolateness of a deserted patio where the dry central fountain was flecked with fallen leaves. Autumn was in the air and it made all things sad. Time, thought the bishop (who was feeling sorry for himself), is almost as old as I am. He toyed with the thought for a moment and then thrust it aside. Let it wait. Let it wait for another ten years. The small face of María Catalina flashed into his mind for an instant and then disappeared. "This intemperate nephew of mine must be taught a lesson," he said aloud to the silent room. Pride in the Face of God was the ultimate sin. It was for that that Lucifer and his minions were cast headlong from heaven. They hung heads downward in the terrible void. A vow! A vow, indeed!

The bishop turned and stared at the closed door to his chamber. Where were all these swollen people? The general, for instance. Well, the general had finally started out for his big coach where he kept his boxes of papers. It stood on the shady side of the courtyard with the six mules still harnessed to it. They rested with drooping heads, occasionally switching their thin tails at the buzzing flies and making the chains jingle lightly. The chattering young officers in their new boots had clustered about the dark door to the tinacal. They would be drunk before evening. Don Isidro? He was probably everywhere. But Doña Ágata was either in her chamber or with María Catalina. As a matter of fact . . . She was his blood niece and there was no reason why he could not visit her in her own quarters. It did not matter if it did put Don Isidro in a rage. Don Isidro was *not* God. The bishop walked slowly toward the door. He would talk to Doña Ágata about this blasphemous procedure and halt this marriage until the archbishop decided what was right and what was wrong. The bishop turned the knob and yanked at the door. It was locked.

For a moment he stared at the dark wood.

"Que sinvergüenza!" he exclaimed bitterly and turned helplessly toward his couch. And there was no doubt whom he meant this time.

Torches were blazing all about the great courtyard when Juan Diego wearily turned his pony in at the solid-studded outer portal where four drunken guards weakly waved him on. Behind him Tobalito and the eight Lancers, covered with dust and indignantly sober, slouched in their saddles and snapped their leather thongs at the mass of peons and soldiers that blocked the way to the casa grande. There was a smell of roasting meat, gunpowder, blood and sour liquor in the night air.

"Ah, the chivos!" Tobalito cried in an envious rage. "They drink themselves into insensibility while we ride until our arses are red masses of blisters!"

He lashed out at a yellow-faced Indian with his thong and cut him across the cheek.

"That's enough!" snapped Juan Diego.

He slipped from the saddle and handed the reins to the sargento.

"Take care of the horses," he ordered, "and then spend the rest of the night as you like."

Without turning to see if his command was being obeyed he started to push and thread his way through the great mass of revelers and stolid-faced Indians. In the center of the courtyard a huge bonfire was blazing and he directed his steps toward it. The sour stench of unwashed men was all about him and once or twice he was forced to step over prostrate figures who lay in their own vomit. He skirted two soldiers who were yanking a shrilly bleating Indian girl with a torn chemise back and forth. When he was within a few paces of the hot breath of the bonfire he was seized abruptly by the arm and turning he looked into the flushed and smiling face of young Ezequiel Oropesa.

"What a night!" cried the exuberant aide. "We've had pulque, mezcal, tequila, French wines, Yanqui whisky, Spanish brandy and only the Mother of God knows what else. The general has discovered a delectable Otomí wench. The bridegroom fell down twice on the way to the church. Somebody forgot the bishop and left him locked in his room until the ceremony was over. He is in a yellow fury. Two men have been knifed and I understand a dozen duels have been arranged.

But the bride . . . ah, válgame Dios! . . . she is like a little picture out of heaven. She is as still as a burro on a rainy day. She—"

He interrupted himself with a monumental hiccup.

Juan Diego continued to push his way through the swaying mass of soldiers and peons while the babbling aide skipped along beside him.

"They roasted a dozen steers," he continued, "and a heap of geese and chickens as high as the big pyramid at San Juan Teotihuacán. Have you seen the Indian dancers? They're over there now."

He flung his hand out vaguely toward the casa grande.

"When I marry," he added, "I'm going to have a hacienda wedding."

"You'd better have a hacienda first," said Juan Diego dryly.

"I'll marry the daughter of a hacendado," declared Ezequiel Oropesa.

He burst into loud laughter at his own feeble witticism.

Juan Diego skirted the bonfire and struck off in the direction of the tiled façade of the casa grande. There was a great mob of people here and it took him some time to force his way to the forerank which formed a wide semicircle before the lighted front of the long building. In a cleared space lighted by torches the Indians were dancing and beyond them, raised some steps from the ground and directly before the open doors of the casa grande, sat a group of observers in high-backed leather chairs. Juan Diego recognized the big head and jutting underjaw of Don Isidro. He did not see the general anywhere. Perhaps the Otomí wench had drawn him away from the illustrious guests.

The Indians were performing a gourd dance. Juan Diego watched while the performers, dressed in short skirts ornamented with tin coils and colored ribbons and with heads covered by elaborate paper crowns trimmed with rooster feathers, executed the short running steps to the thudding of a small drum, the tinkling of a jarana and the buzzing rattle of the gourds attached to their hands, knees and chests. A stand-ard-bearer balancing a pole ornamented with leaves and flowers fol-lowed the dancers, repeating their steps with sedate gravity. Yellow light shifted on the dark faces and shot in sparks from tiny mirrors and metal designs hanging from the snakeskin belts. At intervals a sharp dry sound of clapping hands mingled with the beat of the music and the rattlesnake buzz of the gourds.

"Those fellows are from Tzintzuntzán," remarked young Eze-quiel Oropesa.

Juan Diego nodded. He was faintly surprised that the aide was still with him and after a moment he turned to speak to him. But Ezequiel Oropesa was no longer there. The crowd of observers had swallowed him up. Juan Diego directed his attention to the dancers again but his interest was not in them. Tzintzuntzán. That was the ancient city on the shores of Lake Pátzcuaro. It was in the mountains southwest of there that he had drunk the black-red wine of San Lorenzo. The old Tarascan had handed it to him in a pottery goblet striped in black and red. The colors of strength. Of manhood. At Janitzio he had seen the idols in the caves under the Church of San Jerónimo. Tzintzuntzán. Pátzcuaro. Janitzio. Uruápam. Paracho. The Michoacán names were like music.

Some one tapped him lightly on the arm and he looked down into the face of Don Isidro's son, Lorenzo. The slim boy with the large smiling eyes was looking up at him with an affection that was embarrassing. He hardly knew the lad. From Mexico City they had traveled north together, sometimes riding in the same coach, sometimes on horseback together, talking of this and that, of the imminent campaign (which Lorenzo would never see), of cadet life at the Military College, of the size and splendor of Las Golondrinas, of all the little things that engross the minds of young men, but Juan Diego, instinctively, had maintained an attitude that was aloof and somewhat chill. Some frigid monitor inside himself prevented him from giving himself to anybody. Except the general. He had given himself long ago to the general and without even thinking about it. The general had come forcefully into his life and taken charge of it at a moment when he was incapable of choosing, and presently it had seemed as though he had always been there, watching, directing, consistently affectionate, an idol and a second father. Manga de Clavo, El Encero, Chapultepec, the abrupt mountains and semitropical valleys of Michoacán, Vera Cruz under the blistering summer heat, in all these places he had moved in the shadow of the general, listening to him, worshiping him as a boy worships a strong and flamboyant personality, turning a deaf ear to insidious scandal and adverse criticism. If, during the last year or so, certain questions concerning Santa Anna had lifted snakelike heads in his mind he had ignored them or thrust them aside as unworthy lapses in the fidelity he owed to the only man who loved him. He was sure of that love and because he was sure of it he could ignore everything that tended to destroy it.

He turned to Lorenzo with a questioning glance.

"My father desires you to join him and his guests," said the boy. "He is sorry you were not present at the ceremonies. He would like to present you to my sister."

So Don Isidro had seen him in the mass of spectators. The old hacendado had the eyes of a hawk. Turning from the dancers he followed Lorenzo across the lighted space to the open platform that stretched along the front of the casa grande. There were many people here sitting in the high-backed leather chairs whom he did not know but he saw the head and shoulders of Don Isidro rising like a bluff above the others. When he mounted the few steps he recognized one or two of the general's young aides, Doña Ágata, sitting stiffly with lifted eagle-beak, and General Micheltorena, chief of staff to Santa Anna. Don Isidro grasped him warmly by the hand.

"It is regrettable that the exigencies of war took you away from us this afternoon and evening, Señor Teniente," he said with a grim smile. "I trust that you delivered all my horses safely to their . . . er . . . destination?"

"Yes, Don Isidro," replied Juan Diego. "I caught up with the baggage train well this side of Celaya. Your horses are being shod now."

"For cavalry mounts?" inquired Don Isidro ironically.

Juan Diego smiled.

"No, Don Isidro," he said, "I believe they will be attached to provision wagons."

The hacendado grunted. He extended a big hand.

"I believe you have been presented to my wife, Doña Ágata," he declared.

Juan Diego bowed over the thin hard hand that was extended to him.

"And my son-in-law, Don Alejandro de la Barca y Padilla," Don Isidro continued.

A froglike face and two bleary eyes were lifted to the young man's gaze and then insolently averted. Don Alejandro was very drunk.

"And my daughter," concluded the hacendado shortly.

Juan Diego looked down into two long gray eyes in a small pointed face and found himself holding a hand that seemed no larger than a bird's claw.

"You are welcome, Señor Teniente," said a light uninterested voice.

The hand the young man was holding was cool and if it were not for the slight pulse jumping in the wrist it would have seemed dead. There was a remoteness here that suddenly antagonized Juan Diego. He released the hand abruptly and stepped back.

"Chepe!" bawled Don Isidro. "Chepe! Are you asleep, baboso! Fetch the Señor Teniente a goblet of champagne."

He twisted his great head toward Juan Diego who was now standing behind his chair.

"Our hero, el Señor Presidente," he said deliberately, "has retired early. The night air of Las Golondrinas is not good for his lungs."

He burst into a loud laugh like a donkey's bray.

Juan Diego accepted the cut-glass goblet of warm champagne from the silent figure that loomed beside him and raised it to his lips.

"The general has tropical blood in his veins," he said calmly. "He is happy only in the state of Vera Cruz."

"He's got more than tropical blood in his veins," began Don Isidro, and then, as though he had gone too far, he added, "Well, well. Autumn is here. The winds from the mountains . . . Ah, you will like this!"

He was referring to a new dance that was starting in the lighted space before the guests and not autumn or the winds from the mountains. Juan Diego sipped from his goblet and watched.

A procession of dancers, leaning heavily on rough canes, were crawling along with bent knees in a large semicircle. They were crowned with wide-brimmed hats from which hung varicolored ribbons. Their faces were covered with clay masks representing very old men. Strands of ixtle, representing long white hair, swayed about the unchanging features. Huanengos of coarse cloth embroidered with cross-stitch designs in red thread covered most of the dancers' bodies. It did not need a loud burst of anticipatory laughter from the crowd of observers in the courtyard to tell Juan Diego what was happening. This was "Los Viejitos," the dance of the little old men. It originated in the state of Michoacan. And once again the young man's thoughts darted back to that South Pacific state where he had drunk the wine of San Lorenzo. The dancers moved around, the leader almost upright and the line behind him diminishing in height until the last old man almost had his chin on the ground. They wabbled, staggered, tapped their canes, almost fell and recovered themselves, attempted a Mexican clog, tried to jump and zigzagged while the spectators roared with joy. Finally, extremely tired, they went off carrying their canes across their shoulders in the absurd bravado of senility.

During the dance Juan Diego occasionally shifted his eyes from the performers to the guests seated around him. Don Isidro, leaning forward, a goblet clasped in his hand, had lowered his heavy underlip in an expression of pleasure. A stout old lady near him nearly burst her corset with laughter. General Micheltorena was shaking with amusement. Doña Ágata was struggling to preserve her gravity but she could not suppress the thin smile that curled under her high-bridged nose. Don Alejandro, collapsed in his chair, had fallen asleep and was beginning to snore. The face of Doña María Catalina was an expressionless white spot in the depths of the big leather sillón. Juan Diego decided that he liked neither of them. One was a cipher and the other was a . . . Spaniard. Chepe came forward to replenish his glass but he waved him away. He did not feel like drinking . . . and perhaps that was because he had seen so many drunken men. When the last old man had disappeared around the fringes of the crowd Don Isidro rose to his feet.

"This will go on all night," he said to those around him, "but it need not keep us up. Come, Chepe! Pedrito! Candles for my guests. This has been a long day and we need rest."

Little lights flickered inside the open doors of the casa grande.

Juan Diego turned doubtfully. He did not know where he was supposed to sleep but he was determined that it should not be inside the big house. Not even if Don Isidro asked him. He would search about the plaza and perhaps he would encounter Ezequiel Oropesa. He turned to go and yet he lingered. He knew that he should bid a ceremonious good night to Don Isidro and his immediate family but the hacendado had already clumped off through the open door, a lapse of courtesy so unusual that it betrayed the fact that his calm was but a pretense and an inner agitation was compelling him to think only of himself. Even Juan Diego, who had never seen the man before this day, could understand that. Don Isidro reached some climactic point in life today, he thought, and he is both relieved and angry. It was more than the sixty thousand pesos and the thirty horses . . . although, God knew, they were bad enough. It was something that touched deep into his very soul. Two house servants assisted the recumbent Don Alejandro to his feet and guided him toward the yawning door. Juan Diego's face expressed disgust as he watched the squat figure trip over the threshold. Instinctively he turned toward the high-backed leather chair where Doña María Catalina had been sitting. It was empty. She had disappeared as silently as a shadow. The young officer smiled sourly. All young girls were little fools. Of course she couldn't wait. She would hurry to the bridal chamber to strip herself, smear perfume over her body and don the lacy French nightgown that had been saved for this tremendous occasion. Perhaps the spectacle would bring Don Alejandro back to life. Perhaps it wouldn't. Obeying a vague impulse he descended the steps to the hard earth of the plaza and stood looking across the crowded expanse where the bonfire and torches still flared brightly. He felt tired now, exhausted inside and weary of people. Yet he was not sleepy. He had ridden far and long, his thighs were stiff, his throat was dry and the rims of his eyes burned. He wished that he hadn't refused the second goblet of champagne. Well, he would try to find Ezequiel Oropesa. He stepped forward and found himself walking beside General Micheltorena. The chief of staff's face was flushed and he was smiling in a high good humor.

"You look half-dead, Juanillo," he said. "Haven't you been assigned a bed yet? I understood the aides . . . Well, well, the general neglects his boys sometimes . . . when more important duties occupy his mind. I believe she is an Otomí girl. Quite delectable. For a man who is more than fifty . . ."

He broke off and began to hum a light zarzuela melody.

"I thought of looking for Ezequiel Oro—" began Juan Diego.

"It has been a pleasant interlude, this halt at Las Golondrinas," declared Micheltorena. "The marriage, the fiesta, the food, the drink . . . really an interlude. Nevertheless, I hate to think of the men's heads in the morning. What's that? Young Oropesa? Oh, yes. The Military School boy. You'll probably find him behind some wall with a willing lady. If you're looking for a woman, Juanillo—"

"I'm not looking for a woman," broke in Juan Diego swiftly. "I don't care for women. The devil take every one of them. I'm looking for a bed."

Micheltorena opened his eyes very wide.

"Dios mío!" he said softly. "A St. Anthony brought up in the shadow of Santa Anna. This is wonderful . . . and unbelieveable. What's the matter with women?"

"They're animals," answered Juan Diego briefly.

The chief of staff began to shake with laughter.

"Most men thank God, Jesus Christ, the Virgin Mary and the Holy Ghost for that," he said. "If they weren't animals . . . Well, well. If you want a bed . . . by yourself . . . there are several I am sure will be unoccupied in my quarters. I'm in that empty storehouse near the tinacal. The odors should put you to sleep in five seconds. Will you join me?"

"You are very kind, my general," replied Juan Diego.

They had passed the bonfire and were walking toward the great hacienda gate. The chief of staff took another long look at the young man.

"Is it true that you have never touched a woman?" he asked in an awed voice.

"I don't like them," said Juan Diego.

"How old are you?" persisted Micheltorena.

"Twenty," said the young officer shortly.

They walked along in silence for a minute.

"Ave María Purísima!" exclaimed the chief of staff, raising his eyes to the night sky. "Does Santa Anna know this?"

Juan Diego was irritated. He merely shrugged his shoulders in response.

"Why?" demanded the senior officer indignantly.

Why, indeed. The memory of a swaying coach and a girl in a velvet dress that was much too large for her flowed into Juan Diego's mind. Idiota. You are an idiot. Do you want to see me do it? The little dog's name was Dulce. The girl had fallen against him. He thought that she smelt like a cat. She . . . Did women give themselves to drunken men? Willingly? His nose wrinkled and he shook his head.

"I don't like women," he repeated.

He was angry and he made no attempt to keep the indignation out of his voice. The chief of staff's hand slid softly under his elbow.

"Do you like men?" he asked softly.

Juan Diego carefully detached his arm and stepped away from Micheltorena. He was shaking with rage.

"No," he said deliberately. "They are greater animals than women. If you will excuse me I will try to find Ezequiel Oropesa."

He turned and started to walk toward the peons' quarters built along the farther side of the plaza. Micheltorena stopped and watched him go.

"Juanillo," he called in a low voice. "You will find a bed waiting for you in the storehouse near the tinacal."

Juan Diego continued to walk without answering or turning back.

Long after midnight the great bonfire in the center of the plaza had died down into a glowing heap of wood embers and most of the torches had sputtered into darkness. The crowds of Indians and soldiers who had thronged the vast square had vanished and only a few softly talking groups and a number of prostrate figures in odd corners and along the front before the peons' quarters remained as exhausted reminders of the fiesta. Even the dogs, who had been busy barking and growling all evening, had slunk away to rest in preparation for the morning howling that would express their hunger and the fact that the farm hands were departing for the fields. There were no lights in the windows of the casa grande. Las Golondrinas seemed to have run down. In one spot alone was there life. And that was in the tinacal near the gate where the maguey juice was fermenting in the horsehide vats. Timoteo, the mayordomo, stood in the doorway and kept a sharp eye on his laborers while he listened to the young officer's slow footsteps. The young officer had been walking back and forth for at least an hour and the Indian blood in the mestizo mayordomo recognized that walk as one of restlessness and tired irritation. It was possible that the young officer thought too much. Life was always complicated for blancos. They lacked the sense of fatality that was a part of the Indian's equanimity. Timoteo spat on the ground, shifted his big pistol with the silver and gold bands on it and scratched his groin where he had a fine colony of ladillas.

Juan Diego had not found Ezequiel Oropesa nor a place to sleep. As a matter of fact, he had not tried very hard. He had reached that stage of weariness, both physical and mental, where the idea of slumber was repugnant to him. He had discovered long ago that he needed what he called a white mind to lie down and immediately drift off into quiet insensibility; lacking that he must keep moving until his weariness became so great that he could lie down anywhere and inexorable nature would pull his eyelids shut. In the past he could make his mind white by deliberately putting out of it anything that troubled him or pretending so strongly that it did not exist that it really did not exist. It was the old art of defense of his boyhood. Just why he could not summon it up now puzzled and irritated him. Assuredly there was nothing at Las Golondrinas that concerned him. He was no part of it and certainly it was no part of him. Yet a troubled sense of foreboding filled his mind and because he did not know what it was he was angry and wakeful. He could not ascribe this mixed emotion to the long journey with the wretched horses or the fact that he had missed most of the fiesta. These were little things and did not matter. Neither was he apprehensive about the military campaign toward which he was slowly traveling. That was something he anticipated because he believed in the justice of his cause and detested the avariciousness of the United States whose troops had invaded his country although Mexico had persisted in no more than claiming what was undeniably her own. The Americans wanted Texas, the lands to the west, and all of California. They were a rough and ruthless people who sang hymns to liberty while they reached out and grasped what was not theirs to grasp. They were like the Jews. They considered themselves the Chosen People and mouthed big words about their manifest destiny. Did they think that nobody else had a manifest destiny except them? No, it was not the potential campaign that troubled his mind.

Neither could it be anything that had happened at Las Golondrinas. He had met a few people and most of them he did not like but none of them impinged directly on his personal life. Don Isidro had impressed him but only as the Pyramid of Cholula might impress an Egyptian from the Nile Valley. He was solid but there was nothing extraordinary about him. The fact that he had been disturbed during dinner and while watching the Indian dances aroused curiosity, to be sure, but it was a detached curiosity. As for Don Alejandro, he was a detestable sapo, a toad, but there were many of them in Vera Cruz, in Jalapa, in Puebla, in Mexico City, and none of them had caused the young officer a second thought. "What have I to do with Don Alejandro," he asked himself, "or he with me?" Doña Ágata was a hawk-beaked figure in two dimensions. Lorenzo, the boy, with his constant silent proffers of friendship, was like a well-kept house dog. The bishop of Puebla did not seem human at all. He was merely the visible gesture of a Power that was both divine and unscrupulous. And Doña María Catalina . . . why, she was no more than a blob of whiteness in the glow of wood flame, a minus quantity in the process of living. That was what all women were, anyway. The young aides, the company officers, Ezequiel Oropesa, the soft-speaking Micheltorena, the other generals, the lines of infantry and cavalry, all of whose faces ran together into a smear that was familiar and inhuman, even Santa Anna himself, now possibly sleeping beside some Otomí girl, all these were an accepted part of his existence and hardly calculated to arouse any dubious impulses in him. "There is no reason why I cannot sleep," Juan Diego said aloud as he walked at a slow pace across the plaza. "No reason at all." He was like a cat before a thunderstorm, he thought, like a mountain lion who senses the approach of hunters when they are a dozen miles away, like the Indians at Janitzio who do not like strangers and start to sniff the air a day before they arrive. He drew in his breath sharply. Was that it? Was he anticipating something? Was there a vague prophecy in the atmosphere of Las Golondrinas? Anda! He was beginning to think like a Tarahumara medicine man. He was overtired. That was it. He was overtired. Yet he really didn't believe it at all.

He reached the end of the plaza before the casa grande and stood for a moment with lifted head staring at the tile designs on the broad wall. Above them a bright wheel of stars twinkled in the deep black-blue of the night sky. He could not see the moon though its light lay like a transparent veil across the packed earth. Two sentries in the oblong of shadow by the door moved slowly but they did not challenge him. He turned and walked along aimlessly until he came to an arched entrance to an inner court and after a moment's hesitation passed under the mutilated coat of arms. The inner court was absolutely bare. He cut across it toward a covered way over which a portion of the house was built. It did not occur to him that this might be forbidden territory or that he might be stopped by a bullet fired by some nervous guard. His footsteps echoed lonelily under the covered way. Reaching its end he emerged into a fairly small patio bounded by narrow pillars supporting the projecting upper floors of the casa grande. In the center was a dry fountain flecked with fallen leaves and on its low rim he sat down and glanced without curiosity at the shadowy porticoes.

Suddenly he felt depressed, vaguely disappointed. He was like a man who had half-hoped for something, knowing in his heart that it would not happen and yet disturbed because some miracle had not out-reached the accepted actuality. The depressing part of it was that he had no idea what he had desired. He sat for a long time without moving and presently the moon lifted a white face above the secluded well in which he sat and flooded the enclosed space with a milky glow. He thought of himself as caught in the searching brightness, very small, defenseless, a minute specimen, an insecto, a bug. Perhaps a great eye was peering down at him through some enlarging glass and wondering with mild contempt why he existed at all. Why did he? Now that he was twenty years old it was time to ask that question. But who could answer it? The bishop? The general? He passed his hand fretfully over his forehead. Perhaps this was the depression and unrest that preceded illness. Yet, physically, he felt well enough. He had never been sick in his life.

The sudden crash of a violently opened door brought him quivering to his feet. For an instant he thought a gun had been fired at him and then from the shadow of the portico opposite a slim figure in a clinging robe darted into the bright moonlight. As she approached he saw that her solitary garment was blue and studded with little golden designs. A flood of dark hair poured over her shoulders. Her face was a white mask. He found himself striding toward her with the surprising conviction that this was what he had been expecting all the time. It was like a prepared event. Words formed in his mind. *A cloud came down from the high air and from it stepped Our Lady in a garment of blue terciopelo with stars of bright gold all over it.* An odor, sharp, unforgettable, of gardenias momentarily suffused the air of the patio and then, miraculously, like two clouds coming together, she was in his arms, clutching his neck, and he looked down into the distended eyes of Don Isidro's daughter.

"What . . . !" he began in a stifled voice.

She did not appear to see him. She merely flung her bare arm backward in a violent gesture and he lifted his head to see a squat figure in a flowered woolen nightshirt lurching toward them with outspread hands. A square froglike face with eyes too far apart, nose too small and mouth too large, was raised to the moonlight. From it came a baying sound. Juan Diego acted automatically as he thrust the girl aside and plunged toward the advancing man. A rage that turned the white placid light to red flame possessed him as instinctively he struck with the whole power of his body and heard his clenched fist smack like a pistol shot on the square chin of the other. The man in the nightshirt fell heavily like a stunned bull and rolled over on his stomach, his short hairy legs kicking out of the long robe.

Juan Diego, staggering forward from the violence of his own blow, recovered his balance and started to turn. He was immediately seized by two strong arms that pinioned his own and a sharp commanding voice spoke over his shoulders.

"Chepe! Pedrito!" it snapped. "Carry Don Alejandro to his chamber. Chuchita! Accompany Doña María Catalina to her mother's quarters."

The young officer became aware that there were other figures in the patio and the unnecessary flicker of lighted candles. He struggled helplessly in the ironlike clasp that imprisoned his arms. The red flames flickered and died out of the moonlight.

"Don Isidro . . ." he said in an indignant voice. "I am quite . . ."

"Do not speak," ordered the man who was holding him. "Turn now. We will walk this way."

Juan Diego was propelled across the patio, through the covered way, along the inner court and under the arched entrance with its mutilated coat of arms to the great plaza. It was not until they had reached the spot where the bonfire had burned that the young man felt himself released. He turned with some anger. Don Isidro, clad in a silk dressing gown and shod with dark-blue morocco slippers, stood looking down at him with a perfectly expressionless face.

"Don Isidro," said the young officer, "if you will permit me to explain . . . I saw that your daughter . . ."

"I saw everything," broke in the hacendado. "I understand everything. But it should not have been you. You had no business in that patio. Do you think that I was not watching? This is an affair that concerns my family . . . and me."

Blood rushed into Juan Diego's head.

"It should have concerned you long ago, then," he said deliberately.

The heavy underlip of Don Isidro thrust outward. He continued to look fixedly at the young man.

"I am my own adviser," he declared coldly. "You have pushed yourself into a situation that has nothing to do with you. I do not like that. I must—"

"I was protecting your daughter from a drunken brute," interrupted Juan Diego bitterly. "Perhaps I should have stood aside. Perhaps . . ."

Don Isidro's hand fell heavily on his shoulder.

"My daughter would have been protected," he said roughly.

"I was confused," explained the young officer, suddenly disgusted with Don Isidro, with María Catalina, with himself. "I was not aware that heaven was watching over your daughter at that moment. I did not see you, Don Isidro. I saw a man attempting to assault a woman and I struck him down. Perhaps it is not the custom at Las Golondrinas . . . but I would do it again."

"I do not mind the blow," said Don Isidro mildly. "It should have been me who struck it."

He lifted his hand from the young man's shoulder.

"You do not understand these things," he said in the same mild voice. "It must be your Yanqui blood. Now I must ask you . . ."

"I am as Mexican as you are," Juan Diego burst out.

"Perhaps you are more Mexican than I am," said Don Isidro. "But that does not matter. Señor Teniente, I cannot have you on my lands in the morning. There will be enough gossip as it is without your . . . heroic figure to increase it. Also, it would be embarrassing for my daughter to encounter you again. It is probable, too, that Don Alejandro would shoot you on sight. Will you leave tonight?"

"I am not afraid . . ." began Juan Diego hotly.

Don Isidro lifted his hand.

"No," he said. "You are not afraid. Will you leave tonight?"

For a minute the two men stared into each other's eyes.

"Yes," answered the young officer. "I will ride on and join the forward baggage train. If you will explain to the general . . ."

"I will explain everything," promised Don Isidro.

Unexpectedly he extended his hand.

"Farewell," he said. "May God go with you on your journey."

Juan Diego took the big hand.

"Farewell," he said.

He started to walk at a rapid pace across the plaza toward the massive outer gate. Don Isidro stood watching him go until he disappeared beyond the sleepy guards. Timoteo, the mayordomo, leaned by the tinacal door and watched, too. Dios mío, he thought, that young man never sleeps. Don Isidro swung around and moved slowly toward the casa grande, a grim and perplexed expression spreading over his broad features. He wondered if the bishop of Puebla was sound asleep.

Book Two

BUENA VISTA

Buena Vista

JUAN DIEGO DE BÉXAR had ridden several yards ahead of Santa Anna and his staff, a score of brightly plumaged birds in feathered hats, and now, coming to a sharp outcrop of rock which slanted upward to some seven feet, he dismounted wearily, flung the braided reins over the head of his wiry little horse and climbed up the prowlike mass, spurs clicking and boots slipping, and gazed out before him. He was like a spectator in a huge theater gallery and before him, like a vast set scene, spread the undisciplined terrain that would be the battlefield. His tired back ached and for a second he clasped both hands over his hot eyes. They felt as though they were full of gravel. Then, winking vigorously, he concentrated his vision. What he saw was lonely and bleak. He was staring down a valley some two miles wide along which ran the dirt road to Saltillo. To the west of this road and flowing from south to north was a deep-bedded stream. The valley, flanked on both sides by ranges of the dark-green pine-covered Sierra Madre Mountains, narrowed like a funnel to a gap which Juan Diego already knew from his map was La Angostura, the Narrow Pass. About a mile and a half beyond it would be the hacienda of San Juan de la Buena Vista. On the west the ground, rising toward the mountains a mile distant, was slashed by deep barrancas so worn by centuries of spring torrents tumbling down fissures from the snow-capped peaks that the young man, though a novice at war, realized that it would be practically impassable for artillery or mass cavalry. A few reckless horsemen might thread the dangerous maze but he doubted it. To the east, the side of the road he was on, the mountains appeared closer and from their base the broken surface declined gradually to the ribbon of the highway. However, it was cut by three big ravines. The entire complex of ridges, plateaus and gorges, Juan Diego saw, was badly disposed for an action in large force. It was too bad that Santa Anna had not caught up with the Americans at Agua Nueva. But they had fallen back leaving nothing behind them but blazing wagons filled with stale bread as hard as stone, spoiled pork and a quantity of corn.

However, it was not the surrounding countryside (which seemed to his tired eyes to have been crazily furrowed by some unbelievable giant's plowshare) that retained the young man's attention for long. It was La Angostura, the Narrow Pass.

From where he stood, and even without the field glass which he held loosely in his hand, he could see clearly the defile bounded on one side by a slender ridge that formed a natural parapet and on the other by the deep-bedded stream which here had several small tributaries emptying into it. There was life there, the bright brown slash of newly piled breastworks on the right of the road, a faint glitter where the February morning sun, weak and constantly threatened by clouds, reflected from the guns of a battery and a constant fluctuation of tiny figures that looked like dolls but were men. Juan Diego was looking for the first time at detachments of Taylor's American army. By shifting his gaze a trifle he could see that the ridge to the left and slightly in the rear of the pass was crested with dark oblongs of massed men, presumably regiments in company order. Farther back, almost at the base of the mountains, were other oblongs. And even as he stared at them, noting that as the sun rose the black masses were touched to blue, a puff of dust ran along one of the ridges and in it he saw midget batteries drawn by midget horses moving like toys. The tiny legs of the animals moved mechanically and the caissons bobbed up and down like little boxes on strings. A moment later he saw the guns being unlimbered and the midget horses moving to the rear. It was very like a puppet show.

He had not known what it would be like to see the enemy for the first time and he was relieved to realize that it created no change in him whatsoever. At least, he could feel none. This pleased him although it aroused no virtuous emotion of bravery. He was tired, terribly tired, he knew that, for he had not slept for twenty hours, and that might be the reason for his lack of reaction, but, so far as he could feel at this moment, the sight of Taylor's Americans aroused no more emotion in him than the distant spectacle of a religious festival procession on some feast day. One stopped and looked and was curious. Then one went on. It was so here except that he was not going on. He had expected to tremble and he did not tremble. He had expected to be exhilarated and he was not exhilarated. He was merely tired. He did not even think of the Americans as human beings, men like himself with lives to preserve or throw away, men with lethal weapons in their hands and curses or cheers on their lips; they were too small for that. They were like dolls, like toy soldiers made of lead, like little pieces in a game. He half-expected a great hand to reach out of the desolate sky and lift an oblong up and set it down in another place. Men, indeed. It was difficult to believe that the infinitesimal needles they carried in their hands were muskets that could deal death; it was even harder to admit that the squat little guns (about the size of firecrackers) could vom-

destruction. These men and weapons were too far away to be real. And Juan Diego in his divine simplicity was tempted to believe that war was merely a game in which the emotions played no part.

He had expected, as well (perhaps the bishop of Puebla was responsible for that), to be shaken or, at least, disturbed by the simple fact of gazing upon a multitude of men in whose veins, presumably, ran the same sort of blood as his own. They were Americans and he was the child of Americans. True enough, he did not feel like an American or as he believed an American should feel and the few men, officials, commercial agents, one or two travelers, from north of the Rio Grande whom he had encountered in Mexico City during his infrequent trips from Manga de Clavo had repelled him for reasons that were vague but absolute. Without pondering the matter he had decided that these sly traders and negotiators were exceptions. They were not representative. When he encountered Americans in the mass, he half-feared, the submerged urges possibly in his blood would rise to the surface, drawn there by he knew not what, emanations, say, or the invisible hands of his own prenatal past pulling him back to it. The bishop again. He had not looked forward to such an emotional disturbance for he felt himself to be a Mexican in everything and he had never thought of the blood. He desired to remain a Mexican, too. He possessed no curiosity at all about the sprawling Republic to the north and he conceived it, when he thought about it, as no more than a grasping and ruthlessly encroaching civilization that was intellectually mediocre, morally hypocritical and always materialistic. These things he had been told, of course, for he barely remembered the United States. There was a vague, almost indecipherable, picture of it somewhere in the back of his mind but it was like a badly focused faded daguerreotype. It was buried beneath layers of later memories and experiences.

Well, nothing had happened. He was soberly grateful at the thought.

Recalling the field glass in his hand he lifted it to his eye. The lens brought everything closer. Now he could count the guns in the road at La Angostura. There were eight of them and around each one he could see the gun crews clustered in separate groups and the swabs lifted like wallpaperers' paste brushes. Some distance to the rear an officer on horseback was levelling a field glass and it seemed to Juan Diego that this unknown atomy in a blue jacket, his mustaches drooping beneath his lifted hand, was looking directly at him. Half-aware of mounting noise from the south, a rolling sort of shuffling thunder threaded by an intermittent buzzing hum like plucked strings, he continued to look at this American officer and the American officer appeared to be looking as attentively at him. Of course, he does not see me, he thought, and then, why should he not see me? I see him. At least, I see a figure on a horse. A big doll. What does he see? A figure standing on a rock and looking at him? Another big doll? It is curious. And Juan Diego reflected that perhaps he, too, was a mechanical puppet from that American officer's distant vantage point. Indeed, he thought, that figure in the blue coat does not see as much of the suggestion of life as I do for his impatient horse is moving and I am still. He had forgotten the bright clot of Santa Anna and his befeathered staff in the shallow hollow behind him. Yes, they were all dolls, little unhuman atomies moved by invisible fingers in some mysterious game whose rules were a secret between the unknown players. Did the helpless figurines know or care who won or lost?

The chill day was approaching noon and the shadows lessened. Clouds, gray-blue and pregnant with rain, hovered over the Sierra Madre Mountains. The air rustled with sound but not with wind, the cockerellike crow of a bugle in the near distance, that increasing rumble that now resembled distant thunder or huge boulders rolling into deep ravines, the interrupted buzzing like a vast swarm of lost bees veering, circling, approaching and receding. The atmosphere was full of voices that could not be heard by the ear but which were unmistakably there, discovered by some subtle sensitivity in the nerves. The game suddenly became gigantic. The pieces were increasing in size. Juan Diego continued to observe the American officer. The American officer continued to regard him. Then, suddenly, the blue figure moved. He lowered his field glass and leaned forward in the saddle, his saber abruptly sparking as it shifted with his movement and momentarily caught the sun. He was saying something to a little doll who had detached himself from a gun crew and run back to him. A minute later there was movement, a scurrying about, the disappearance of a swab and a frozen instant. At the same moment that Juan Diego, from his eminence, saw the rapid puff of dirty yellow smoke he heard the unexpected report. It was heavy and lonesome in the high air. And then . . . ptht! The brief sound like the echo of a hawk's wing just above him that followed the report was swallowed in loud outcries and the hysterical trampling of horses' hoofs. Juan Diego turned hastily. A cannon ball had landed in the midst of Santa Anna and his staff and a horse was down. The young man slid down the prowlike rock, grabbed his mount by the bridle and ran awkwardly toward the shallow hollow.

The general's horse, a fine beast of Arabian origin that he had brought from Manga de Clavo, had been struck square in the rump and blood, still steaming manure and smashed flesh and bone had spattered the legs of the other mounts, who were rolling their eyes, squealing and dancing about. Santa Anna sat on the ground clutching the stump where his leg had been amputated and cursing with that rare fluency he shared with the léperos of the capital. His dark face possessed an unwholesome grayish undertinge and his eyes protruded with anguish.

Juan Diego pushed through a group of officers who had dismounted and gathered in an alarmed semicircle about their commander and when he reached the forerank he paused and glanced downward. The blood from the dying horse was running like a purple rivulet into the slight declension where Santa Anna sat and his white duster, worn over his uniform, was soaked with it.

The general stopped swearing and glanced up at the young man.

"Help me," he ordered, extending his hand. "These dolts will stand about and do nothing at all. Jesucristo, but my stump hurts. I landed square on it. Did you draw that shot by sticking your cursed head a league into the air? Well, well. Never mind. Help me up."

Juan Diego drew Santa Anna to his one leg and the general, placing an arm about the youth's neck, began to hop toward a new horse that was being brought toward him by a frightened groom.

"Bestir yourselves," shouted the commander furiously at his staff. "You, Genaro Miranda, shoot that poor beast in the brain. Por Dios! They are like a crowd of old women. I call them my lechuzas of Ometusco. No streets there."

Grumbling, scolding, designating unmentionable obscenities for the mothers of the entire staff, he permitted Juan Diego and the groom to lift him into the saddle. Once there he straightened and his anger, fell away from him like a soiled cloak disengaged by the wind. Juan Diego, glancing upward, his hand caressing the silky neck of the new horse, felt anew the disarming charm that emanated from this paradoxical man who rode after Destiny as a hunter rides after the fox. Santa Anna looking into his ward's young eyes smiled slightly and then the cruel lines deepened about his mouth.

"Come, come," he said gruffly, "if we are going to drive el General Zacarías Sastre all the way to Tennessee it is time we started. You, Juan Diego, ride back along the lines and say to the divisional commanders that it is my wish that they hurry. Be off, now. Miranda, find Van der Linden and bring him to me. Vázquez . . ."

"You were not hurt, general?" asked Juan Diego in a low voice. Santa Anna glanced at him impatiently.

"No, you fool," he snapped. "I merely bruised my stump. Now, off with you. Vázquez . . ."

Juan Diego turned toward his horse.

On one of the ridges less than a quarter mile from La Angostura and about parallel with that pass Major General Zachary Taylor, commander of the American forces, sat on his favorite horse, Old Whitey, and watched the result of the cannon shot. As usual, he perched, or, rather, squatted, with both legs dangling over one side of the animal, a short, heavily-built man with a lined weathered face resting on a double chin and disordered uncut gray hair. Crowned with an old oil cap and garmented in a dirty green coat and a frightful pair of trousers that apparently had not been washed or pressed since Andrew Jackson was president he resembled nothing so much as an untidy backwoodsman in straitened circumstances. Beside him General John E. Wool, his blue tunic neatly buttoned and his fringed epaulets glittering, bestrode his gray horse with dignity and a short distance away a small group of staff officers and aides, some of them with the bandbox-newness of West Point yet to be rubbed away, soothed their restless mounts, conversed with one another and fixed attentive (and sometimes faintly ironical) eyes on their superiors.

"A square hit, by Jehoshaphat!" exclaimed Taylor. "There's a horse down."

He had just returned from Saltillo, whither he had gone the day before to inspect the defenses and to requisition supply wagons, and had passed some time riding along the lines to observe how Wool had placed the little army. On the whole, he was satisfied. Wool's dispositions had been simple and practically forced by the conformation of the terrain. If one chose to stand and fight here (which Wool would not . . . his desire was to fall back on Saltillo) this was the thing to do. The funnel of the valley at La Angostura, the narrowest point, was plugged by Major John M. Washington's battery of eight guns, the Fourth Artillery. It was from this battery that the cannon shot had been discharged. Flanking Washington, on the ridges that overlooked the road, were the First and Second Illinois regiments and behind them to the north and east, cresting the ridges and plateaus, was the rest of the American army, somewhat less than five thousand strong. The Texas Volunteers, the Second Kentucky, the Arkansas and Kentucky regiments of cavalry, the Indiana Brigade, the Mississippi Rifles, the First and Second Dragoons, the Light Batteries of Sherman and Bragg, all of them waited drawn up in order, their packs piled to the rear or in the wagons far back on the Saltillo road, while the two generals observed the result of the single cannon shot. Yes, the dispositions were satisfactory. The right, naturally protected by a labyrinth of deeply eroded ravines, was safe enough unless the Mexicans had wings. It was the left that would bear watching and see hard fighting.

"There's an officer down, too," remarked Wool, whose field glass was lifted to his eye.

"Let us hope that it is old Peg-Leg himself," grumbled Taylor.

He turned his head and stared belligerently along his own lines. The creases at the sides of his mouth dragged his face down into a mask of grimness.

"They're riding off," said General Wool, his field glass still lifted. "They're turning down one of the barrancas. They're out of sight."

Taylor, who had been studying his limited lines, suddenly snorted.

"God damn it!" he exploded. "What does Scott want me to do? He has robbed me of my best troops and my best officers and expects me to rot at Monterrey as commander of a minor holding force while he pushes up from Vera Cruz to the capital with all flags flying and gathers all the laurels."

Several staff officers, well aware of the general's feelings toward Scott, smiled discreetly at one another. There was some commiseration in the smiles for it was true that Scott, as senior officer, had robbed Taylor of Generals Worth, Patterson and Twiggs and the greater part of his trained troops for the Vera Cruz venture.

Taylor glared at Wool.

"Scott isn't conducting a field campaign," he asserted in a rough voice, "he's conducting a presidential campaign."

Wool cleared his throat. He wanted to say several things. He wanted to say, So are you. He wanted to say, Scott, who is your superior officer, explicitly ordered you to abandon Saltillo with your weakened force and fall back to Monterrey but here you are at the pass of La Angostura with five thousand men, many of them undisciplined volunteers, and there is Santa Anna riding up to meet you with perhaps twenty thousand men. He wanted to say, Your own recklessness and rancor brought you here and your own recklessness and rancor must extricate you. He wanted to say, As soon as you cleared the Rio Grande and established yourself well to the southern side of it your job was done. Reason might have told you that you could never reach Mexico City from the north. Why, it is three hundred miles across bleak desert alone to San Luis Potosí. The way to Mexico City is ·along the same route that Cortés took in 1519 and that is Scott's way. For once, Old Fuss and Feathers is right. But, being a politic man, he said none of these things. Instead, he remarked:

"Look at the dust along those ridges. Santa Anna must be coming up in great force."

Taylor took the field glass and clapped it to his eye.

"They've passed Encantada," he said. "If Santa Anna is half the man I think he is he will be deploying in battle order by early afternoon. We must keep an eye on his damned Lancers. My volunteers are liable to run like sheep before them. Have the Rangers any ideas about his guns?"

Wool shook his head.

"McCulloch saw only his picket lines at La Encarnación yesterday evening," he answered. "He had not brought his guns up. McCulloch estimated the extent of the campfires and he guesses fifteen or twenty thousand—"

"I know," broke in Taylor. "Half of them are ragamuffins who never marched in step before. But nothing about guns, eh? Well, we shall find out soon enough."

He cleared his throat and spat over the horse's head.

"Do you think the volunteers will hold?" he asked abruptly.

Wool shrugged his neat shoulders.

"They should be well-supported," he answered carefully.

Personally, although not a West Point man himself (neither were Taylor and Scott, for that matter), he detested the volunteers and regarded them as a mob of drunken thieving hoodlums. He suspected that they would skedaddle at the first whiff of grapeshot. After all, it was not Arista who was before them now. And thinking momentarily of the volunteers and the excesses they had committed at Matamoros and Saltillo his thought, in a process natural enough to him, swung to Taylor. The general was no hoodlum, to be sure, and neither was he of the type that indulged in any excesses beyond profanity, but Wool, a New Yorker, saw in him nothing more than a haphazard old Indian fighter who had never commanded a real army in a real battle before the two days' actions divided into Palo Alto and Resaca de la Palma. He was unfit and untrained in the art of commanding large bodies of troops composed of infantry, artillery and cavalry and that was all there was to it. He might have personality (Wool did not like this particular type) but it belonged on the border and not in the drawing rooms of New York and Philadelphia and Washington. Wool was frankly dubious of the outcome of the impending action (it seemed slapdash and not planned at all to him) but he was civil enough to keep his doubts to himself. Another general, the preening Pillow, perhaps, who had gone to join Scott, would have written to Washington. Escaping his momentary reverie Wool became aware of Taylor's sharp quizzical eyes fixed unblinkingly on his face and he could not suppress the slight flush that flowed up his cheeks. Angrily he looked away at the visible streaks of dust stirred into lapsing waves above invisible roads a mile or two to the south. Yes, Santa Anna was approaching in great force. That distant hum was the music of regimental bands.

Taylor's mouth loosened in a sly smile and he was about to say something when a loud halloo echoed from a nearby rock.

"There's a man coming in under a white flag," shouted a voice.

One of the staff officers trotted toward the observer.

Taylor scratched his gray unshaven chin and glanced knowingly at Wool.

"The usual demand, I presume," he said flatly. "Santa Anna is quite punctilious. Quite the West Pointer in manner."

He turned to the officers behind him and indicated a young brevet second lieutenant who was mounted on a magnificent black horse.

"You . . . er . . ." he began and then realized that he had not met this subaltern before.

"Brevet Second Lieutenant David Livingston, sir," exclaimed the young officer, riding forward and saluting smartly. He sat beautifully in his saddle.

"Texan?" queried the general.

"By adoption, sir," replied the second lieutenant, smiling. "I am just down from West Point."

"Oh," said Taylor.

He regarded the square young face for a moment and then flapped his hand toward the road.

"Get along," he said, "and escort that fellow to me."

The young officer rode off and Taylor followed him with his eyes.

"Another West Pointer," he remarked morosely.

"Yes, general," admitted Wool. "He was on Patterson's staff but applied to remain here in the north."

"I'm surprised that anybody desired to remain in the north," declared Taylor mildly. "The sun shines brighter in Vera Cruz. Well, well, let us see what this overdressed gentleman from Santa Anna desires."

Juan Diego loosened his reins and allowed his horse to pick its delicate precise way downward through the sliding shale toward the road. He judged by the height of the pale sun that it was close to noon. Then it was time for him to be hungry. He could not recall when he had last eaten (was it at the Paso de Piñones that morning?) or what it had been (cold frijoles like dark mud? Tortillas from some camp-woman's fire?) but he was sure that he must have eaten at some time or other in the last dozen hours. Even so, it was curious that it was time to eat again and he was not hungry. He was not even thirsty. And it was not excitement that had bereft him of his appetite. He was not excited. He had been startled and slightly sickened when the cannon ball had killed the general's horse and he had been concerned for the general's safety but he had not been excited. The blood had not rushed through his veins in that fine delirium that was supposed to be excitement and was sometimes suppressed fear. In spite of the cannon ball the Americans were still dolls. His horse turned carefully, half-circling a large rock, and Juan Diego saw before him a long wide gully that sloped gently to the road. It was filled now with some fifteen hundred booted men and as many horses. These were the Húzares who had ridden in the van of Pedro de Ampudia's Light Division as an escort to Santa Anna and his staff. Most of them were dismounted and sitting about in groups on the ground or on rocks, conversing, smoking cigarrillos, dozing or examining their weapons. They were crack troops and skillful horsemen who had been picked for recklessness and bravery. Lolling about now in their new uniforms (for Santa Anna had favored them) they appeared to be entirely unconcerned about impending events. They were veterans who had fought before and would fight again and with the wisdom of old campaigners they rested while they could and ate when there was any food and drew their belts tighter when there wasn't any and did not trouble their heads about the future. That was a problem for the senior officers. In other words, they were old-fashioned fatalists. At this moment they were tired. They had traveled thirty-five miles from Encarnación in ten hours over wretched roads or no roads at all and while, being mounted, they were not so badly off as the plodding infantry they were wise enough to take full advantage of the halt. To Juan Diego they looked like great relaxed cats.

The young man guided his horse through these squatting, sitting or recumbent figures, who either remained where they were or reluctantly moved aside while they grumbled at being disturbed, and rode down the gulley toward the road. He passed an opening to his left and through it saw a portion of the advance wagon train and several wood fires about which clustered groups of camp-women busily cooking. Their skirts were kilted up and he saw more than one sturdy pair of brown calves. The pungent smell of frying chilies reached his nostrils. He gave the women no thought, for, unlike most of the officers young or old, he had nothing to do with them. After all, they were an integral part of the army and could be acknowledged as such and then put out of mind. One did not think about the axle of a wagon until it was broken and one need not think about the women until they were forced into one's personal pattern. So far Juan Diego had escaped this intrusion. Yet the women were all too visible. The flash of their skirts and eyes and teeth was everywhere behind the lines. They had other uses, too, besides that of bedmates on chilly nights; they foraged, cooked, sewed and did most of the camp work. It was only the mistresses of the senior officers who did no manual labor but passed their days in wagons, coaches or tents plastering scented French powder on their unwashed bodies and gossiping about one another. Santa Anna, himself, had brought half a dozen buxom wenches with full-blown breasts along with him and Juan Diego supposed that they were established somewhere in the vicinity with the general's crates of gamecocks. The young man, if he had stopped to think about it, would have seen nothing questionable in such an arrangement. It was a part of the great pattern of war as it was practiced in Latin America.

Reaching the road well out of cannon shot of the American guns he set out southward in search of the divisional commanders. He had not ridden half a mile before he came upon Pedro de Ampudia's Light Division. It had already broken ranks and was awaiting orders. Ampudia, a short, dark, cruel-faced man who had been thrashed by Taylor at Monterrey, was standing at one side of the road and conversing with his staff officers. He looked up expectantly as Juan Diego reined his horse to a halt.

"I expected Micheltorena," he said gruffly. "What is it, Señor Teniente?"

Juan Diego explained Santa Anna's desire for speed. Ampudia spat on the ground.

"Hurry?" he demanded. "I am here, am I not? I have no commissary. My men have not eaten since two o'clock this morning. It is difficult to fight on empty bellies. Tell the general that."

The young man pointed out that his orders were to visit all the divisional commanders and that it would be some time before he could return to the general.

"Very well," said Ampudia in a disagreeable tone. "I will ride forward and talk to the general myself. If you encounter any provision wagons tell the sutlers that my men have not eaten. Even a few biscuits . . ."

He turned away and then swung back again.

"Oh, Señor Teniente," he called. "When you see General Lombardini tell him that I have already dispatched Mejia's brigade to the Yanqui right. He will want to know."

"The Yanqui right is impregnable," declared Juan Diego before he thought.

Ampudia lifted bloodshot bull eyes and inspected the young man.

"The generals will draw the conclusions, Señor Teniente," he said dryly.

Juan Diego flushed and rode on. He could hear a regimental band playing in the near distance now and the brassy quickstep was caught up in the convolutions of the pine-clad hills and multiplied endlessly. It appeared to him that he was entering a vast semicircle of music that was interpenetrated with the click of hoofs, the jangle of chains, the rumbling of heavy wheels and the measured thud of thousands of tramping feet. It took him some time to pass through the arrested Light Division and then for a mile he had a clear road before him and he took advantage of it by spurring his horse to a canter. Then he was halted by a battalion of Sappers and a battery of three sixteen-pounders. The guns grumbled, screeched and wheezed as the artilleros lashed the exhausted horses to the semblance of a gallop that continually degenerated into a walk. "Arre borrico!" shouted the artillerymen. "Arre borrico! Jesús mil veces! Arre borrico!" How tired those beasts are, thought Juan Diego. This is a tired army. It should rest for a day. It has traveled two hundred and fifty miles in twenty-five days across the most desolate desert in the vilest weather and it deserves to sleep. And he thought with a shudder of that long travail and the stony trail that was marked by so many dead. There were corpses all the way back to San Luis Potosí. The blare of the regimental band was closer now and with its proximity the spreading sound waves seemed to withdraw and gather into a nucleus, a compact core of sound that could be circumscribed. He rode on, lifting his hand in greeting to the Sappers. The music approached him steadily and when he turned a sharp curve in the highway he cantered right into it. It was the band leading F. Pacheco's division.

This body of men, mostly raw recruits, was the uncertain factor in Santa Anna's army. They were badly drilled and a large portion of them, the so-called Corps of Guanajuato, had received practically no instruction at all. They had just been picked up and dumped into the army and then thrashed for not obeying orders that they could not understand. There wasn't one in a hundred who could read his own name. As Juan Diego posted himself by the side of the road and watched the vanguard stumbling past he saw that the majority of these men in clumsy infantry shakos and tight pants (a good proportion were without any uniforms and wearing the ordinary cotton trousers and shirts of the peon covered by a dirty sarape) were boys of seventeen or eighteen. Their drawn faces and glazed eyes betrayed their utter weariness. They were not accustomed to long marches and their ill-fitting boots, or, in many cases, worn-out sandals, obviously made walking a torture. Yet there was spirit to them. They tried to sing to the music and made awkward conflicting attempts to close ranks when the officers shouted and slapped them with the flats of their swords and they carried the standards with pride. But weakness of flesh was stronger than determination of spirit and even as Juan Diego looked he saw boys dropping from the lines and collapsing by the roadside. They simply rolled over on their backs and faced the noonday sun with one arm flung across their eyes. Their bruised bloody toes thrust upward like scarlet cockscombs.

Pacheco was riding with the second section of his division and when he came abreast Juan Diego rode out to him and delivered Santa Anna's hurry-up message.

Pacheco bowed despondently.

"I'll do my best," he said, "but the hot griddles of hell couldn't make these men step faster."

Suddenly his face tightened.

"The general does not propose an assault today!" he exclaimed with some trepidation.

"I believe he does, Señor General," answered Juan Diego.

"Oh, Jesús mío!" moaned Pacheco.

The young man worked his way through the suffering recruits and his face was very sober as he proceeded down the road. The music (now behind him) that had sounded so lively had suddenly become transformed into a sort of hurried devil's dirge. It seemed to him that these boys were being driven like a flock of goats toward their graves which were already dug on the slopes about La Angostura. There they could lie down and sleep at last. They, at least, were not dolls although, curiously enough, they appeared to be acting like dolls now, mindlessly moving forward without any will of their own and so dulled by a great weariness that they cared not where they went. But dolls did not bleed. Their dark glazed protesting eyes and the blood on their sandals proved they were not dolls. Perhaps the Americans were not dolls, either. Perhaps if he gazed into their eyes and heard their voices he would find out that they were men very much like himself and Santa Anna and the boys of Pacheco's division.

Five minutes after he passed through the last stragglers from the raw recruit regiments he came upon a battery of five twelve-pounders. It was halted in the middle of the road for one of the lead horses on the first gun had fallen down and broken a hind leg. There was some confusion and shouting while an officer knelt down and inspected the prostrate beast. The guns, caissons and eight long springless ammunition wagons drawn by mules that were stalled behind the motionless twelve-pounder wanted to get on but the road was too narrow here for them to make a detour. This occasioned the shouting. Finally the officer stood up and indicated the unfortunate animal to a sergeant. The sergeant, a fat Indian with Mongolian features, methodically seated himself on the horse's nose, and, drawing a large knife with a three-inch blade from the sheath attached to his belt, plunged it into the beast's jugular vein and drew it around under the jaws. The bulging muscles of the sergeant's arm flexed under his cotton shirt sleeve as he nearly decapitated the horse. The first gush of dark blood rose like a small fountain and then collapsed. It was the second animal that Juan Diego had seen killed within three hours and the two deaths seemed like an awful portend of what was to come. There was no life inherent in these hills; they were the birthplace of death. The young man was inclined to ask why the crippled horse had not been shot and then it occurred to him that perhaps Santa Anna, who was wise in little things if not in great, had issued orders that the troops move up as silently as possible. But, in that case, why was Pacheco's band playing? He didn't know.

He waited ten minutes while the dead beast was unharnessed and dragged to the side of the road and a spare horse was brought up from the rear of the ammunition wagons and strapped into place. The guns began to rumble along and Juan Diego cantered down the highway. Already the forerank of a dense column of men was in sight and when he came up with it he saw that it was Manuel María Lombardini's division. Lombardini himself was leading it. Juan Diego had met him before in Mexico City and he disliked him exceedingly. Lombardini was a swarthy-faced strutting fellow with heavy mustaches and goatee (a favorite adornment of Mexican generals) whose excessive volubility, everybody admitted, was a screen to hide his colossal ignorance. He was one of those stuffed figures who achieve prominence by so ardently proclaiming their virtues that the paralyzed listener becomes too weary to observe their flaws. There was a fairly well-authenticated rumor that he was exceedingly jealous of Santa Anna. Juan Diego caught his eye and saluted. Lombardini scratched his nose and rolled his eyes.

"Ho, ho," he said. "Our general's delightful foster son. How are you, Señor Teniente? Aren't you riding in the wrong direction? The powder is over there."

He extended his arm in the general direction of La Angostura.

"I am the bearer of a message to you, Señor General Lombardini," replied Juan Diego civilly enough. "General Santa Anna desires that all the divisional commanders hurry forward their troops as rapidly as possible. He—"

"He is not going to engage today," interjected Lombardini hastily as he glanced up at the sky. "It is past noon now. How can we reach our positions before three or four o'clock? The men must eat . . . if there is anything to eat. Who in the name of the devil of Zacatecas ever heard of beginning an action at four o'clock on a February afternoon? Neither you, nor I, señor. It is my opinion—"

"I believe the general will engage," insisted Juan Diego firmly. "I have that impression, Señor General. Also, Señor General Ampudia desired me to inform your Excellency that he has dispatched Mejia's brigade to the Yanqui right."

"To the— Oh, yes," exclaimed Lombardini. "Yes, yes, yes. That is excellent. Turn their right. Throw them back toward Saltillo. Take Saltillo the day after tomorrow. Be in Monterrey in three days. And then the Rio Grande, Texas, who knows? Tenne . . . Tenne . . . I suggested that movement, Señor Teniente. One had but to look at the map— Yes, yes, yes. But to engage in the late afternoon! Every man will have to carry a lantern in his hand. Jicotercal! Jicotercal!"

He turned to bawl at one of his officers after a quick nod of dismissal to Juan Diego and the young man rode slowly down the lines. These were better troops than the boys of Pacheco's division. They were older and in better physical condition and they marched easily and with confidence. They had seen action before, smelt powder and heard the beelike hum of bullets. It was encouraging to observe how excellently they had endured the long and grueling advance from San Luis Potosí. The young man thought, These are the men who should have had the regimental band. They deserve it. As a matter of fact, there were several regimental bands with Lombardini's division but their instruments were piled in carts and they were marching along without any equipment. They were saving their wind for the victory. Juan Diego smiled at the brown faces, dark eyes and white teeth as he proceeded on his way and the troopers smiled back, seeing a young staff officer who seemed to be radiating confidence. All is going well, they thought. One burly sergeant shouted, "On to Texas!" and some scattered cheering greeted the cry. I must remind the general of this division, decided the young man, for they are dependable. All the same, he mused, it is regrettable that Lombardini commands it. If occasion arises he will sacrifice all of them for his own glory.

A battery of five eight-pounders bounced past and Juan Diego made way for it while he observed the emaciated horses with pity and concern. Their ribs stood out in relief like the slats in a wooden fence and the spreading sores under the harness straps were an ugly burning red. The riders on the lead horses lashed them violently and roweled their lacerated withers with a constant ferocity that was terrifying. It was obvious that the artilleros saw in these unfortunate beasts nothing more than mechanisms for rapid locomotion. The young man leaned forward instinctively and patted the neck of his wiry little mount and the animal as though recognizing the difference in his status from that of the artillery horses turned his head sideways and softly whinnied.

More troops came into view, a long smear of men marching in free order to a hum of voices singing the popular song "Adiós." The dust rose in billows about their legs. This was J. M. Ortega's division, made up partly of recruits and tropas de línea, regulars of the line. Like all of the others, the heavy marks of the long march were stamped on their.drawn faces. It was curious how the signs of exhaustion differed on the varying physiognomies. On some the features were pulled together as though by a drawstring and on others the mouths sagged open and the component parts of what had once been faces appeared to be sluggishly struggling away from one another. Ortega, a glum-faced man as sparing of words as Lombardini was prolific with them, listened to Juan Diego's explanation of Santa Anna's desire without comment and then muttered a few words to his aides. They rode back along the lines with the young man and presently he observed a sort of deliberate acceleration in the movement of the troops. The funny part of it was that while their legs manifestly moved more rapidly the companies appeared to be actually progressing no faster. They were working harder to maintain the same rate of speed.

Leaving Ortega's division behind, Juan Diego almost immediately found himself engulfed in a huge crawling snakelike baggage train. Covered wagons, open carts, spare horses, burros, rolling blacksmith shops, sutlers' canvas-topped vehicles, coaches crammed with women, dogs, parrots and even a few monkeys, crowded the road from side to side. The air was clamorous with shouts, barking, whips that snapped like pistol shots, clanking of chains, rumblings, squeakings and creakings. Juan Diego noticed that, while the ammunition wagons were piled high with boxes, the provision wagons contained little. Most of these latter were crowded with sick or exhausted men who took no interest at all in what was happening around them. Stragglers by the score limped along beside the horses clutching at harness straps for support. An occasional span of oxen bowed beneath the heavy wooden yoke retarded the slow syruplike movement of the baggage train and aroused angry obscene comments from the drivers who sought to pass. For a brief time Juan Diego sought to thread his way through this agglomeration of vehicles that might be called the great intestine of the army but it was impossible. He was blocked, cursed and thrust aside until he gave up, withdrew to one side of the road, dismounted and seated himself on a rock. For nearly an hour the reluctant river of hoofs and wheels oozed slowly past and the young man watched it go and considered the lack of food with grave eyes. Santa Anna would have to capture Taylor's supplies or his army would be in a perilous predicament. Well, perhaps they would all be dining inside Saltillo tomorrow. And then Monterrey. And then . . .

Several hundred yards after the baggage train rode squadrons of cavalry, many with tall lances from which fluttered bright pennons. There was something jaunty and gay about these mounted men in their bright uniforms and feathered hats and with their heavy sabers clinking against the iron stirrups. There was élan and dash and confidence there and the spectacle revivified Juan Diego's spirits as he climbed to the saddle and trotted toward the approaching riders. A Mexican on horseback was something to look at and thousands of Mexicans on horseback was something to remember. These were the squadrons of A. Torrejón and Juvera and next to the Húzares they were the delight of Santa Anna's militant heart. They were the men who would descend like a furious torrent on the American guns, saber the gunners and tear open great gaps in the enemy lines. Their proud dancing horses, better cared for than any Juan Diego had seen, seemed resistless and the sun, now past the meridian, appeared to touch with gold and red glints the polished spearheads of the lifted lances. Suddenly Juan Diego felt happy. Those hundreds of trotting hoofs beat a sweet music in his ears. The fluttering pennons and feathers and raised standards reminded him of the jigging foam-flecked waves off San Juan de Ulúa.

He conveyed Santa Anna's message to Torrejón, whose white teeth glittered in acknowledgment beneath his big mustache.

"We shall be there in time, Señor Teniente," he called as his stallion pranced like an Indian dancer.

"Vaya usted con Dios," exclaimed Juan Diego impulsively.

"Ya nos veremos," responded Torrejón, laughing.

They were off in spumy breakers of dust, riding in fours, almost filling the narrow road from side to side.

The cavalry! Ah, the cavalry! The centaurs of the storm who always broke the squares!

Juan Diego, still flushed with pleasure, rode past a ruined wall and the gutted remains of an old stone building (possibly a depository for corn) and found himself in Agua Nueva. Fires were still burning and the stench of spoiled pork, biscuits, corn and smoldering wagons permeated the foul air. It was here that Santa Anna, by a forced march across the twenty miles of flat sterile plain, the Plan de la Guerra, from Encarnación the day before, had hoped to catch Taylor napping. Taylor, forewarned by his scouts, had set fire to Agua Nueva and fallen back to the pass at La Angostura. Juan Diego recalled that Santa Anna had been in a fury, stamping his feet and shouting "Se fueron! Se fueron!" he had immediately issued orders for Vicente Miñón's cavalry to make a sweep around to the east, cross the Sierra Madre Mountains through the Palomas Pass and intercept the Americans before they could reach Saltillo. He had not even allowed the cavalrymen to water their horses or fill their canteens. Juan Diego supposed that somewhere beyond the ridges and moving almost parallel with the Saltillo Road were Miñón's squadrons. What sort of night had they passed in the hills?

The young man halted his horse near a blazing wagon about which crouched half a dozen stragglers warming themselves and scratching for lice and was listening to their illiterate gabble when the familiar rumble of hoofs caused him to lift his head. An oblong block of cavalry was bearing down on him and he saw that it was General Manuel Andrade's Presidial troopers, the rearguard of the army. This was all, then. He had missed Santiago Blanco's division but he presumed that it had come up, or was coming up, through some of the connecting ravines and gorges to the left of the road.

Andrade, who had made much of the young man at San Luis Potosí—possibly because he was one of Santa Anna's protégés, expressed delight at the encounter and Juan Diego swung in beside him. It was after one o'clock in the afternoon now and the cavalrymen ate as they rode, gnawing hard biscuit and washing the dry crumbs down with gulps of water from their canteens. They cursed the food and compared it to boot soles but their grumbling was only dissimulation. They desired to disguise their anticipation of the action that lay ahead. Even Andrade betrayed himself.

"I hope the general has decided to give the order to attack this afternoon," he declared to Juan Diego. "We have our second wind, so to speak, and are prepared to sweep the Yanquis right into the Rio Grande."

"General Lombardini expresses the opinion that it is too late in the day to attack," remarked the young man.

Andrade spat violently.

"Lombardini!" he said scornfully. "What does the general say?"

"I believe he will attack," replied Juan Diego.

A rapt smile lighted the cavalry general's swart features.

"Then everything is all right," he cried joyously.

The hoofs hammered along the hard dirt; the pennons waved; the spurs and sabers rattled and clanked. Juan Diego felt happier than ever. He was riding with the cavalry and that was another way of saying that he was riding with the gods. He had completely forgotten the dolls.

Brevet Second Lieutenant David Livingston rode slightly ahead of the Mexican emissary as he mounted the slope toward General Taylor. It was the first time he had been particularly noticed by the commander and a modest but pleasant appreciation of his fleeting importance swelled his chest and caused him to sit somewhat stiffly in the saddle. This was not because he was vain or desired unduly to be noticed; it was because he wanted to be useful, to be of service. He was ambitious, to be sure, but if he was ever to wear a general's stars he hoped to win them by merit and not through favoritism. In other words, he would not solicit the influence of a senator (and his own foster father was one) or dance attendance on the wives of colonels or brigadier generals. At twenty-four some young officers were like that. And he was a very young officer, not in years, perhaps, for he had entered the Academy late, but certainly in point of service. He had received his diploma after the actions at Palo Alto and Resaca de la Palma.

The excitement of his transition from cadet life to a commission in the regular army was still quivering in his mind. How vividly he remembered the gabble of talk at the Point after the battles and the sensation created in the corps of cadets by the reported capture of Captains Thornton and Hardee with their companies and the fall of Lieutenant Mason in the conflict. The rules and regulations of the

Academy were temporarily disregarded; wave after wave of cheering made a pandemonium of the two barracks; boisterous laughing and shouting and racing about confounded the instructors; tattoo and taps were ignored; and the next day the entire body of young men had petitioned the government for immediate active service. The war, though expected, had come like a thunderbolt. Future captaincies, colonelcies and generalships haunted the halls of the stone buildings on the Hudson and more than one young cadet who could raise no more than the faintest down on his upper lip saw himself seated on a white horse and with extended arm directing the climax of some great battle.

He was not so optimistic. After graduation he had traveled south with three classmates, Thomas J. Jackson, Archie Botts and Clarenden Wilson, to Washington, of course, for Washington was the fount of commissions and promotions and assignments to duty. The capital was a Babel of conflicting voices and authorities but the consensus seemed to be that Taylor, the glorious Taylor, would be in Mexico City by the Fourth of July. Few spoke of Winfield Scott except to suggest that he was a superannuated old fogey. It was in Washington, through his foster father, that he met Mr. Jefferson Davis, a lean-faced handsome man of thirty-eight who was a Member of Congress. Mr. Davis, who was a West Point graduate, had just accepted the colonelcy of a volunteer regiment. He liked Mr. Davis very much. He liked Mrs. Madison, whom he saw at a White House levee. He liked the President, who did not speak to him. In fact, he liked everybody.

After his short furlough with his foster parents he received his orders from the War Department and one fine autumn morning he embarked at Memphis on the New Orleans boat. Several older officers, also on their way to join Taylor's army, gravely warned him against scorpions, tarantulas, centipedes, alacráns and rattlesnakes but when he informed them that he had passed part of his youth in Texas they moved on to more innocent victims. At New Orleans he had boarded the steamer for Brazos Santiago and there, in that crowded plague spot, he caught his first glimpse of the real side of war, rows of wounded men, terribly emaciated, yellow-faced, many delirious, lying on the sand in the hot sun while the flies buzzed about their mouths. An awareness of what he was about to face crept through his stocky young body. From Brazos Santiago, restless and impatient, he tramped the nine miles to the mouth of the Rio Grande where he was lucky enough to get immediate passage on a river steamer going up to Camargo. The trip took two days and when he arrived at his destination he learned that Taylor had taken Monterrey. Certainly the old man was moving fast.

Major General Robert Patterson had his headquarters at Camargo, which was being used as the central port of supplies for Taylor, and to this officer he reported. That was in October. Since then, nearly five months, he had fulfilled all the duties assigned to him as a junior aide-de-camp but he had seen absolutely no fighting. He had not even heard a gun fired except for a night squabble among some drunken volunteers in Monterrey who suddenly decided to have a little war of their own. But he had seen destroyed buildings, plenty of wounded men and some dead. These sights gave him something to think about but they did not deter him from his ardent desire to see action. It was for the sake of action that he requested Patterson's permission to remain in the north when that officer prepared to join Scott before Vera Cruz. Patterson had shrugged his shoulders and acquiesced. "If you want to stay with the old man, you may," he said, "that is, if the old man will take you. But you won't see anything. Everything that is going to happen is going to happen in the south. Taylor's job is to sit on his tail in Monterrey and guard the river." He did not believe it. Taylor was not that sort of general. In other words, he was a Taylor man. And this in spite of the fact that the commander paid no attention to him. He paid no attention to him now as he rode up in advance of the messenger from Santa Anna. As a matter of fact, nobody at all looked at him or his slightly swelling chest. They were all scrutinizing the Mexican officer. This individual, a short big-bellied man with Germanic features, reined his horse in before the spick-and-span General Wool and saluted smartly.

"Señor General Taylor," he said in guttural English.

"This is General Taylor, sir," replied Wool hastily, indicating the commander who still sat sideways on Old Whitey as though he was in a rocking chair.

The messenger looked bewildered.

"Excuse me, Señor General," he said stiffly to Taylor. "I am Pedro Van der Linden, surgeon general of the Mexican army, and I bring you a communication from Señor General Don Antonio López de Santa Anna."

He proffered a square paper that had been folded once and sealed at the two open corners.

"He's a German," declared Taylor to Wool, blandly ignoring the outstretched missive. "They are like the Irish. You will find them in all the armies of the world."

The messenger's eyes grew hard.

"I am a Mexican citizen, Señor General Taylor," he insisted in a strangled sort of voice.

"Truculent fellows. Damn 'em all!" muttered Taylor.

He took the paper without ceremony, ripped it open with a rather soiled thumb and read the contents. Then he lifted his head, pushed

back his oil cap with a furious hand, glared at the Mexican officer
and turned to Wool.

"By God!" he exclaimed. "Listen to this!"

In a rapid voice he read:

Camp at Encantada, February 22, 1847.

You are surrounded by 20,000 men and cannot in any human probability
avoid suffering a rout and being cut to pieces with your troops, but as
you deserve consideration and particular esteem, I wish to save you from
a catástrophe, and for that purpose give you this notice in order that you
may surrender at discretion, and the assurance that you will be treated with
the consideration belonging to the Mexican character, to which end you will
be granted an hour's time to make up your mind, to commence from the
moment when my flag of truce arrives in your camp. With this view, I
assure you of my particular consideration.

God and Liberty!

Antonio López de Santa Anna.

To General Taylor,
Commanding United States Forces.

Finishing the communication Taylor raised a flushed indignant
face to Wool. The group of staff officers who had ridden closer to
listen preserved poker-blank faces but there was a suppressed twinkle
in more than one eye. Brevet Second Lieutenant David Livingston
wanted to swear in the florid manner of McCulloch's Texas Rangers.
Wool looked uneasy and tugged at his gauntlet.

"Why, the impertinent patronizing pisspot!" Taylor cried. " 'As
you deserve consideration,' hey? He wants to save me from a 'catastrophe,' eh? By God, I'll 'catastrophe' him! I'll drive him into the
Gulf of Mexico and throw his wooden leg in after him. Bliss! Bliss,
bring the writing case!"

The commander's favorite aide rode forward with the oblong
leather box.

Opening the box and resting it on the pommel of his saddle he
prepared to write.

"What shall I set down, general?" he asked.

Taylor's immediate dictation was so forceful and profane that
several of the staff officers, unable longer to contain themselves, burst
out laughing. Van der Linden, his puffy cheeks a violent red, stared
fixedly before him at nothing at all. Wool took his gauntlet off and put
it back on again.

"No, no, general," expostulated Major Bliss with the liberty of
an old friend, restraining a smile and shaking his head from side to
side in gentle reproof. "The ceremonies must be observed. Wait! . . .
How is this?"

He began to write rapidly.

"There are too many ceremonies," grumbled Taylor. "This is not a cotillion. This is a war."

"There!" exclaimed Bliss, lifting the paper upon which he had just written and shaking it. "Short and succinct. Listen. This should do."

He read out:

Headquarters Army of Occupation near Buena Vista,
February 22, 1847.

Sir In reply to your note of this date, summoning me to surrender my forces at discretion, I beg leave to say that I decline acceding to your request.

With high respect, I am, sir, your obedient servant,

Z. Taylor,
Major General United States Army.

Señor General D. Antonio López de Santa Anna,
Commander-in-Chief, Encantada.

"'I beg to say,'" repeated Taylor in a mincing voice. "It sounds like dancing-school correspondence. Well, well, if you like. It is a matter of complete indifference to me. Washington and Sherman and Bragg will dispatch stiffer messages, I hope. Here. Hand it over with the quill. I'll sign it."

He wrote his signature slowly and deliberately, shaping the Z with particular care.

A minute or two later Don Pedro Van der Linden, following Brevet Second Lieutenant David Livingston, rode down to La Angostura and was there permitted to go on his solitary way along the Saltillo Road toward the Mexican lines.

Juan Diego, returned from his long ride and refreshed by a hasty meal of cold tortillas and pork, stood in the opening of the tent and watched the staff council with great interest. At times, it was good to be privileged. One could stand modestly to one side in the very heart of things and see the decisions being made. Behind him a group of saddle horses pawed the hard ground and several mozos de cuadra loafed about in dejected attitudes. They had received no food and they were terribly hungry. The tent, a large affair of striped canvas, had been raised in a hollow like a shallow bowl about a hundred yards to the rear of the exposed height where Santa Anna's horse had been killed. It was crowded. The general had just finished devouring a skinny boiled chicken and the square camp table behind which he sat in his personal leather chair was covered with cracked bones, biscuit crumbs and several half-empty bottles of aguardiente. His sallow face was slightly flushed and his rather mournful eyes were enlivened by the infrequent sparkle that snapped in them during moments of crisis. It was not often that Juan Diego saw him so but when he did he, like everybody else, experienced or, rather, shared the quickening of blood in the veins and the agitation of mind that was so compelling a part of Santa Anna's persuasion. The general was a paradox and as such he was inexplicable. When in repose his melancholy and rather attractive features suggested nothing so much as a brooding scholar but when he was plunged in dangerous and risky action he became transformed into a veritable tiger. His face was distorted, two demons gleamed out of his large eyes and he appeared like a man possessed. He could be urbane, kindly, aloof and speculative and he could be savage, cruel, uncontrolled and devoid of consideration. But in either case the prevailing power of his extraordinarily magnetic personality was never in doubt. The contradictions in his character were infinite and even Juan Diego, who had been his charge for ten years although there were long intervals when he did not see him, could not predict what he would do from one moment to the next.

Around the camp table, facing the general like schoolboys, were Ampudia, Lombardini, Pacheco, Ortega, Blanco and Torrejón. Their expressions varied. Ampudia, Pacheco, Ortega and Blanco appeared alarmed. They scraped their boots along the ground while their spurs jingled and their fingers fidgeted with their sword sashes. Lombardini, stroking his goatee with long yellow fingers, was obviously trying to ape the general's convinced manner. Torrejón alone seemed serene and anticipatory. He stood with a half-smile on his face and bright attentive eyes. Santa Anna, pushing the debris of food to one side, spread out a map on the table while his glance rapidly flickered from face to face.

"It is after three o'clock, Señor General," Ortega was saying in a defensive tone.

"I do not care if it is after six o'clock," replied the general in his warm flexible voice.

As always he took a dry pleasure in snubbing his inferiors in rank.

"It will be dusk in an hour," pointed out Pacheco mildly.

"It will not," contradicted Santa Anna flatly. "Besides, men have fought in the dusk before. Have you never heard of night attacks?"

He bowed his head over the map and silver hints of his fifty-three years (his birthday had passed unnoticed the day before) veined his thick black hair.

"If we could be sure of their strength . . ." began Lombardini portentously.

"I am," broke in the general, glancing up testily. "Do not forget the letter from Scott to Taylor which my scouts intercepted in January. Do I have to explain to you again that Scott ordered this miserable Taylor to send all his command except six thousand men to the coast to join the Vera Cruz expedition? Do you know how many effectives Taylor has left? I will tell you. About five thousand. About five thousand and less than a thousand of them are regulars. The rest are volunteers, farm boys who will run like rabbits when they see our lances. What the devil . . . !"

"All the same . . . four o'clock in the afternoon . . ." mumbled Pacheco, looking at Ortega for approval. "If things are as you say they are, Señor General, we can as easily attack in the morning. A little rest . . ."

"Mañana! Mañana! Tomorrow! Tomorrow!" exploded Santa Anna. "That is the curse of this country. Let us have a siesta while the city burns down! No, I say. Shall we sit here twiddling our fingers while Taylor withdraws his forces to Saltillo? Permit me to inform you, señores, that I do not propose to waste time. We will finish Taylor off here and now. Ampudia will then take three divisions to the Rio Grande and hold the northern gate while I go to Vera Cruz and give Scott a warm welcome. I will have all Vera Cruz, Puebla and Oaxaca on the back of his neck. A blow here, you see, to be followed by a blow there. The Americans will sue for peace within three months."

"But . . ." stuttered Lombardini, who had composed a speech in his mind and had now forgotten it.

"That word is not in my vocabulary, Señor General," snapped Santa Anna insolently.

Lombardini's face darkened. "We who do not know the general's commitments sometimes need it to express our ignorance," he declared in a choked voice.

Angry blood rushed into the general's cheeks.

There had been many rumors that Santa Anna had negotiated with an emissary from the president of the United States in Cuba prior to his arrival in Vera Cruz on August sixteenth of the previous year. Else, argued the sly gossipers, how could he have passed the American blockade which had rendered useless all the Mexican ports on the Gulf of Mexico? The ships had let him through and it naturally followed that they had let him through for a price. After all, the Americans were not philanthropists. Was that price the betrayal of his country? Had he agreed to put up a show of action, fight a few bloodless battles and then consent to a peace that would hand over California and Texas to the gringos? Juan Diego had heard these rumors for he could not avoid them. They were everywhere from San

Juan de Ulúa to the plaza in Mexico City. But the young man had observed no least sign of any double-dealing on the part of Santa Anna from that day in August when he had returned to Manga de Clavo to this hour in the front lines before La Angostura and he had been near him practically all of the time. The return had been like a return from Elba. The general had issued his manifesto and traveled over the old rising trail to the capital accompanied by an increasing enthusiasm that spread like fire before him. When he entered Mexico City on September fifteenth the National Theater resumed its old name of the Santa Anna Theater, statues and busts of the "hero of Tamaulipas" were exhumed from hiding places and crowds paraded the streets yelling vivas for the general and mueras for the Monarchists. The old exile was back and once again a paragon of all the virtues. Salas, the acting president, and Gómez Farías, the leader of the Puros, met him and escorted him to the National Palace. It had been a triumph. Juan Diego was certain that if there had been treachery in the heart of Santa Anna the tumultuous reception he had received and the obvious temper of the Mexican people had burned it clean away or else it had been a treachery calculated to betray the gullible American negotiators who apparently labored under the misconception that everybody in Mexico could be bought.

The general stared fixedly at Lombardini for a moment and it was plain to see that he was controlling his anger by an intense effort. Lombardini, already shocked at his own temerity, fussed with the hilt of his saber and tried to look at though he had just made an innocent joke. The general, exhibiting a self-discipline that was astonishing to Juan Diego, and deciding to ignore the innuendo in Lombardini's remark, put his finger on the map.

"Let us continue our warfare with the Americans," he said smoothly, emphasizing the last word. "Ampudia!"

Ampudia stepped forward hastily, butting against the camp table and nearly knocking it over. He had been staring at Lombardini with round eyes and open mouth.

"Yes, yes, Señor General," he said.

"Do you see this plateau?" asked Santa Anna.

On the map he indicated a blank space somewhat forward and rather to the left of the crosses that marked the American positions. It was bounded on the east by the near slopes of the Sierra Madre Mountains and inclined toward the Saltillo Road in a series of long ravines. Between the mountains and these ravines was a respectable-sized table of high ground that dominated the valley. Most of the generals had already studied it through their field glasses.

"Yes, yes, Señor General," repeated Ampudia, leaning forward and inadvertently belching.

"It is this plateau that we must take this afternoon," declared Santa Anna. "It overlooks the American lines and from it we can flank the pass."

"Mejia is already moving to the American right," announced Lombardini whose chameleon nature had recovered its aplomb.

"A stupid gesture but harmless," said Santa Anna reasonably. "The American right is impregnable. However, Mejia may draw some of their fire and every ball they waste is our gain."

He turned again to Ampudia, who stood leaning over and studying the map.

"Now, then," he continued, "do you see this mountain slope at the southeastern edge of the plateau? I want you to take it. We'll jump from there straight upon the plateau."

He thought for a moment and then lifted his eyes.

"Take four battalions of your Light Division," he said. "That ought to be enough. Baneneli will act as your second in command. Send back runners with news of your progress. Keep constantly in touch with me. My future moves will be governed by circumstances . . . your circumstances. Por Dios! Fight! That is all."

Ampudia raised his puzzled face in the dead silence that followed the general's orders.

"The hour of attack, Señor General?" he asked in a hoarse voice.

"Now!" snapped Santa Anna.

Ampudia drew himself up, saluted and passed out of the tent to a great jangling of elaborate spurs.

Juan Diego, making way for him, sucked in his breath sharply.

The ball was about to commence.

From a vantage point to the rear of La Angostura Brevet Second Lieutenant David Livingston had watched the divisions of Santa Anna come up the Saltillo Road, wheel and take their places in an arc that spread much farther to the left than it did to the right. The compact bodies of men were heralded first by dense clouds of dust, then bands could be heard playing, after that raised standards and lances came into view, and, finally, the troops appeared, moving at an accelerated pace and looking very much like the arrays of toy lead soldiers in the windows of novelty shops on Nassau Street in New York City. These miniature men, seen at a distance slightly out of cannon-shot range, were garmented in a variety of uniforms, many of them gaudy in hue and plumed with feathered hats, and the general aspect was more festive than warlike. If there was a sluggishness in their progress the young officer was too much the novice in appraising men to observe it. They seemed all right from a distance and the martial blare of the regimental bands gave them a semblance of confidence that disturbed Livingston. There seemed to be a great many of them, too, and that was not reassuring. Yet the American officer was not frightened. After all, he reasoned to himself, these marching men are not Americans and therefore they can be defeated. Three times already have they run before us and this will make the fourth time. The sun was sliding toward the west as he watched and shadows lengthened on the ridges and plateaus. If Santa Anna was going to start anything he had better start now. Assuredly, time was fleeting. It was not usual to open a battle in the late afternoon. Indeed, it was possible that they would sleep on their arms this night and engage in the morning.

He was mistaken.

Just beyond cannon shot the Mexican troops began to deploy to the left and right of the Saltillo Road, the bright hues of their uniforms and bobbing standards making rich streaks against the green-brown background. To the American left the movement was particularly noticeable. Small bodies of men, apparently in loose company order, appeared and disappeared and appeared again as they worked their way through the ravines and arroyos, the scrub pines and boulders, and up toward the plateau. The little figures darted along like beetles with tiny shining horns. Almost simultaneously with the beginning of this leftward movement Livingston heard the click and hum of action to his immediate left and half-turning in the saddle he saw detachments of Americans moving outward in an arc toward the base of the Sierra Madre Mountains that bounded the far side of the large plateau. Squads of them passed so close to him that his nervous horse became restive and began to stamp the hard turf. As they hurried past, their boots clattering on the rocks and the insignia on their stiff headgear winking, he recognized them. There was a portion of Colonel Humphrey Marshall's regiment, dismounted and carrying rifles; riflemen from Yell's Arkansas regiment and the Indiana brigade; the Second and Third regiments, commanded by Major Gorman; and the dismounted squadrons of Captains Milam and Johnson Price of the Kentucky cavalry. Old Rough and Ready was moving fast to meet any threat to his left. So far not a shot had been fired. The men passed swiftly, talking cheerfully, calling to one another, the cavalrymen joking broadly about the new places where they would get calluses now that they had left their horses behind and the infantrymen grinning with pleasure at the thought. They appeared confident and even anxious for action.

A thudding of hoofs echoed about Livingston and he suddenly found himself in the midst of the general and his staff. Taylor, flanked by Wool and Bliss, was still on Old Whitey but for once he was sitting properly in the saddle. He glanced at the young officer from beneath his shaggy eyebrows.

"You have an excellent position here, Mr. . . . er . . . Livingston," he said without smiling.

Before the brevet second lieutenant could reply he turned to Major William Bliss.

"My compliments to Colonel McKee," he directed, "and request him to move his Second Kentucky out to our right and block that flanking threat. He'd better take a section of Mr. Bragg's battery with him. There's no real danger there but you can never prophesy what Santa Anna will attempt."

Bliss began to scribble the order.

"It's on this plateau and in those ravines that we will fight," Taylor added.

He didn't seem pleased at all as he studied the three large ravines slicing into the upper table of land.

A young officer named Cousins reined in a fine bay mare beside Livingston. The brevet second lieutenant remembered him from the Point, a plump self-sufficient young man with shaggy sandy hair that overlapped his stiff collar and restless china-blue eyes always on the alert for feminine visitors.

"It looks as though the ball is about to commence," remarked Cousins in a cheerful voice.

Livingston observed the advancing troops with an intent eye. They had spread out in ragged open order and were moving rapidly across the plateau toward the fringe of pine trees that stretched like a flounce on the bottom of the green skirt of the mountain range. The Mexicans had already reached the shelter of the trees and were beginning to ascend the slope, for their arms and bright uniforms could be seen through the branches. An unexpected tightness began to spread through Livingston's bowels.

"Yes," he said in a careful voice. "I wish I was over there."

Cousins glanced at him speculatively and smiled.

"This is your first action?" he asked.

Livingston nodded, his eyes still following the advancing men.

"I was at Resaca and Palo Alto," explained Cousins happily. "I missed Monterrey. Dispatch duty. You do feel funny the first time. I wasn't afraid but I couldn't stop shaking. I nearly pissed in my pants. It was the excitement, I guess. I remember you from the Academy," he ended abruptly.

"I don't feel funny," said Livingston. "I remember you, too. You went out in 'forty-four, didn't you?"

Cousins started to sing softly:

> "Oh, Benny Havens, oh,
> Oh, Benny Havens, oh,
> We'll sing our reminiscences
> Of Benny Havens, oh."

"What?" he ejaculated, interrupting himself. "Oh, yes. 'Forty-four. Dear old 'Forty-four and all the rest of it. Lieutenant, you'd better begin to feel funny. If you don't . . ."

A heavy explosion blotted out his words.

All heads turned toward the Saltillo Road down at their right. The Mexicans had moved a battery forward there and were beginning to shell Marshall's advancing men. Their range was bad and the missiles (for after the first shot the guns opened up rapidly) whooshed over the heads of the Americans and landed in the boulders and pine trees beyond.

"Shrapnel," said Cousins. "They can't even see what they're firing at down in that road."

The heavy spitting of the guns changed everything and Livingston found himself trembling and inclined to duck at every explosion although the shells fell nowhere near him. He *did* feel funny. The tightness had increased in his bowels and the hot blood seemed to run up his neck into his face. He had not felt like this since he had suffered from stage fright when as a schoolboy he had been forced into amateur threatricals. His hands felt moist as he closed one tightly on the reins and clutched his belt with the other.

"Wasn't George McClellan in your class?" inquired Cousins calmly.

"The little fellow? Yes," replied Livingston, controlling his teeth with difficulty.

"Did you come down with him?" persisted the other.

"No," said Livingston. "He's in the Engineers."

"I know," remarked Cousins. "I believe he's with Patterson now. Going to the fine show at Vera Cruz."

The angry coughing of the Mexican battery continued.

"They've got too much elevation," said Cousins, squinting as he stared toward the road. "Their artillery has always been miserable."

He began to whistle "Benny Havens, Oh" again.

Livingston looked toward Taylor. The general, slouched in his saddle and with his old oil cap pulled over one eye, was chewing on an unlighted cheroot as he watched Marshall's men picking their way toward the green flounce of low trees. The hubbub in the Saltillo Road didn't seem to interest him at all. General Wool, still looking as though he had just emerged from a bandbox, sat very straight, his back like a ramrod and his horse's reins held slackly in a gauntleted hand. Livingston observed that the New Yorker, from Newburgh, too, so near West Point, appeared abnormally serious. There was silence for a full minute among the men on horseback. The hoarse coughing of the guns cut it into almost equal lengths. Then a scattering of flat reports echoed from the base of the mountains at the edge of the plateau. The Americans and Mexicans, coming within range of each other, were engaging with rifles and muskets. The flat reports increased and swelled into a sort of chatter.

Taylor, spitting the cheroot out with a grunt, extended his hand to Bliss and the major placed a field glass in it.

"They outnumber us like the devil," grumbled the general as he focused on the mountain range at the southeastern corner of the plateau.

"There must be four thousand men on that slope," remarked Wool.

Livingston peered anxiously after the advancing men. Though dusk was falling the action was as plain as any one of the moving dioramas he had seen in New York City. The Mexicans, pushing up the steep wooded side of the range, were endeavoring to outflank the Americans and the Americans, accelerating their pace, were spreading to the left as they advanced with the purpose of forestalling this attempt. The rattle of small-arms fire increased in volume; the repeated flashes of the rifles and muskets were distinct in the darkening air; a low blanket of smoke was rising above the trees; an acrid stink of gunpowder floated across the plateau. This, thought Livingston, is the sound and smell of war.

Taylor lowered his field glass.

"Mr. Cousins," he called.

The plump young man turned his bay mare and saluted.

"Sir," he said.

"My compliments to Major Washington," directed the general, "and request him to move two of his pieces up the plateau toward the mountain."

Cousins kicked his heels into his horse and rode off.

Taylor turned to Wool.

"Our peg-leg friend will try to extend along the ridge if we fail to keep him from the summit," he explained. "Perhaps the guns will put a little speed in the legs of Marshall's men."

"They're moving as fast as they can," said Wool, staring into the twilight. "If Santa Anna turns our flank we shall have to fall back on Saltillo, general. The volunteers are undependable."

Taylor's mouth closed like a trap and with an impatient movement he pushed the old oil cap to the back of his grizzled head.

Livingston, deserted by Cousins, continued to stare at the developing action before him. The agitation that had possessed him was dying away and he began to feel irritable and useless, the way he used to feel at a game when he was not permitted to take part in it. It was impossible to control completely the trembling of his hands but he did his best, clutching tightly to reins and belt. It was not fear. He was not afraid at all. Perhaps he had been afraid of being afraid and perhaps now he was afraid that this quivering of the flesh and heightened bloodstain in the cheeks would be mistaken by the others, the general, for instance, for fear. It wasn't. It was something else altogether and part of it was a desire for action. Why hadn't Taylor sent him down to Major Washington? Or ordered him forward with Marshall's men? Anything would be better than sitting here in the dwindling light and watching other men moving forward with a purpose. But that was a stupid and impulsive way to reason. The Academy had trained him for other duties besides rushing into action with a body of semitrained volunteers. They all had their places and their purposes and waiting for orders that never seemed to come was a part of the strategy of war. When the general needed him he would be there and ready. That was *his* purpose and he would have to be satisfied with it. Taylor was not turning brevet second lieutenants into heroes today.

For the next half hour he spoke to nobody and nobody spoke to him. He submerged his irritation in an absorbed observance of what was going on. The Mexican troops continued to scale the steep slope of the range. He could see them moving above the mid-height line, filtering through the pine trees and around the rocks, firing, pausing to reload and ram the charge home and firing again, jumping, hoisting one another to stone shelves. They were like a horde of agile monkeys. The Americans farther to the left, bulkier in build, larger men than their nimble antagonists, climbed, too. The action was developing into a race for the high crests. The constant rattle of rifle and musket fire merged with distant shouting. A flag was bobbing through the trees. Two guns from Washington's battery unlimbered some distance to Livingston's left and the caissons clattered off to the rear. The gunners sprang to their places, the rammer with his nine-foot swab poised near the muzzle. A third gun bounced up, its wheels bounding up and down and the heavy hoofs of the horses pounding up a cloud of dust. It passed the unlimbered guns and halted almost in the center of the plateau. A body of men arrived at a dogtrot and spread out in support of the guns. Livingston recognized it as the Second Indiana, Colonel Bowles commanding. The three American guns began to throw occasional shrapnel against the upper slope of the mountain, their wheels bounding into the air with every explosion. From the Saltillo Road the Mexican battery still coughed hoarsely at intervals. The din was growing.

Suddenly Livingston found Cousins beside him again.

"What an awful waste of gunpowder," said the plump young man. "I don't believe a man has been hit yet."

Livingston did not answer and Cousins, who obviously did not expect a response, started to sing in a low voice. The words threaded the sound of the firing:

> "Wild roved an Indian girl,
> Bright Alfarata,
> Where sweep the waters of . . ."

It grew darker and the flashes from rifles and muskets spurted and spun out like small fireworks on the farther slope. A queer unreality seemed to flow up from the earth and envelop everything in a strange clarified mauve light. It was growing colder, that quick cold that comes with the setting of the sun and bites into the bones, and Livingston was sorry that his greatcoat was not rolled at the back of his saddle. He sat tense on his horse and watched the action with the restrained excitement of a spectator at a circus. The trembling in his limbs had ceased altogether and he felt as sure of himself as he had on the parade ground at West Point. Surer, as a matter of fact. A cold exhilaration flowed through him and he knew that he had stifled any chaotic impulses that the first gunfire might have started. Was this the baptism of fire? Was it as easy as this? Wavering figures approached. A half dozen men stumbling back across the plateau, some limping with rifles for crutches, others carrying their hastly bandaged arms as though they were nursing babies and one being borne by two companions. They passed like unreal pictures out of some book. The blood on their bandages was black in the twilight.

> ". . . the blue Juniata."

"Mr. Cousins."

It was the voice of the general again. Lieutenant Cousins was apparently a favorite. Livingston, still watching the small group of wounded pass, heard Taylor's unperturbed voice explaining the orders to the plump young man.

"Bliss," the general was saying, "you had better write this out as I give it to Mr. Cousins. Lieutenant, you are to seek out Captains Milam and Pennington—they're about a quarter mile to our rear—request them to dismount their men and pass through that narrow gorge almost in line to our left. Once through they are to swing south and ascend the range from the rear. If they move quickly enough they may keep Santa Anna from the crests."

"I think that it is too late for that, general," declared Wool.

"We'll see," said Taylor placidly.

"The Mexicans are more than halfway up that range," persisted Wool. "How do you expect our detachments to pass the gorge and climb the entire height before—"

"We'll see," repeated Taylor.

Livingston saw the sharp disapproving lines on Wool's face as Cousins, accepting the scribbled order from Bliss, hurriedly rode off. There were contemptuous expressions, also, on the faces of the two or three West Point men attached to Taylor's staff and Livingston sensed that they regarded the general's order as belated. It was something he should have thought of at least two hours before. But he hadn't. And that, Livingston reflected, was tantamount to indicating that he was not a West Point man. His foresight, the Academy officers declared, was not so good as his hindsight. Well, perhaps it was so. However, one thing was certain and that was that the men in the ranks set great store by the general and that his presence was always a visible tonic to their fighting ability. Few West Point men could claim such devotion.

Within twenty minutes after the departure of Cousins actual twilight had fallen and night itself was steadily flowing like a black river up the ravines and across the plateau. The skirmishing forces, both American and Mexican, were blotted into the dark background and their positions could be determined only by the flashes of the guns and rifles and muskets. The cold became intense and a high wind dashed splatters of rain into the faces of the staff observers. The men sat hunched in their saddles, gloomy, dispirited and weary. They were hungry and they wanted to stretch their legs. Livingston felt the exhilaration flowing out of him like water out of a canteen. He had straddled his horse for hours·and it seemed like a lifetime. The high band of his cap with its pancake top and stiff visor tightened about his head and he began to feel cramps in his thighs. He was meditating dismounting and walking up and down the ground for a while when a sharp exclamation from Wool diverted his attention from himself.

"Look, general," the New Yorker cried. "They've reached the crest."

A ragged line of yellow spurts of fire ran along the summit of the Sierra Madre.

Taylor cleared his throat.

"Yes, General Wool," he answered. "Santa Anna is faster than I gave him credit for being. However, he has not turned our position."

There was a glum silence for several minutes and Livingston became aware that the firing was dwindling away. Washington's guns and the Mexican battery had stopped altogether and the flat reports of the rifles and muskets were occasional and scattered. A Mexican signal gun bellowed three times at minute intervals somewhere to the south and Taylor, as though waiting for it, turned his horse.

"We will ride down, gentlemen," he said. "The action is broken off for the night."

Livingston followed with the others. The chill rain, now a steady drizzle, had soaked his jacket and wet his saddle. As the horses picked their way down a narrow gully to the Saltillo Road he could hear Taylor directing certain precautions to Wool. The dismounted men of Milam and Pennington were to be recalled. Marshall's force was to sleep on its arms where it was. There were to be no fires. Pickets were to be thrown out far enough to keep in touch with the Mexican pickets.

"I shall ride to Saltillo," continued Taylor. "I'll take Davis's Mississippians and May's dragoons with me. There are a number of things I want to see to there."

Wool murmured something about the enemy being seen in force beyond Saltillo.

"I believe it is a detachment of cavalry," explained the general. "It will probably try to cut our lines of communication between Saltillo and Monterrey. I'll see to that."

They reached the dark muddy road.

Wool inquired if his presence would be required in Saltillo.

"No," replied Taylor. "You'll have to remain here. If Santa Anna attacks at daybreak do your damnedest to hold him. I'll come up as fast as I can."

He turned his head to the group of officers who were following him.

"Is Lieutenant Cousins there?" he asked, peering through the darkness.

"No, sir," answered Livingston. "He has not returned."

"Who's that?" demanded Taylor sharply. "Oh, Mr. Livingston. Well, Mr. Livingston, you may ride into Saltillo with me."

"Thank you, sir," said Livingston happily.

The rain drummed on the taut canvas of the tent and Juan Diego, wrapped in a blue and red blanket, lay flat on his back on a heap of damp straw and tried to go to sleep. God was witness that he needed it. His body ached with weariness and his eyes felt like two burnt holes clotted with dry sand; but a tight aggravation of the nerves heated him like a fever and kept him awake. He couldn't stop thinking, if the jumble of conflicting images pouring endlessly through his mind could be called thoughts. Perhaps they weren't. Perhaps they were just the agglomeration of impressions that refused to submerge in his mind, fragmentary bits like splinters of colored glass that danced and clashed on the vexed surface and would not sink. It was no use to ask why his mind should continue to function when he wanted it to rest dormant. He lacked the intensive will power to suppress these jagged bits, to empty his consciousness as veteran soldiers lying down to rest should always do, as the Húzares, for instance, were doing in the ravine not a hundred yards away from his tent. He could visualize them recumbent in the rain or under the parked wagons or in small shelters of branches and cloth wrapped in blankets with their brown high-smelling women beside them and he was sure that they were sleeping. Yes, the love-making was over and they were sleeping. Even Santa Anna, his conferences concluded, was sleeping in his pabellón of striped yellow and green while his horses locked their legs and slumbered standing. The lean grey dogs were sleeping, too. It was the art of the old campaigner to empty the mind like a woman emptying a jug and sleep without dreams.

Juan Diego groaned and squeezed his eyelids tightly together. He had come a long way since that day late in January when he clattered out of San Luis Potosí in a bright new uniform and a special scarf with Santa Anna's picked vanguard. A sudden gust of wind shook the tent poles and he groaned again as the rain sounded like flung handfuls of pebbles against the canvas. Ah, the damned rain! The damned eternal pounding freezing rain! It had been like that on the long march to the north. They had endured all sorts of weather from drenching downpours of congealing rain and snow and sleet to burning suns that nearly fried the flesh. Broken pictures of that month of hardship and horror whirled through his refractory mind. It had started auspiciously enough. Regimental bands playing and standards flying while the townfolk of San Luis Potosí waved sombreros and shouted encouragement. On to Saltillo! On to the Rio Grande! On to Texas! Santa Anna and his plump doxies in a coach like a chariot drawn by eight mules and five pack animals following loaded with crates of evil-eyed gamecocks. The overlarge brilliantly arrayed staff on blooded horses and the chattering horde of soldaderas in bright-colored petticoats. The endless lines of troops, regiment after regiment, the favored in new habiliments and the rest looking like pelafustanes, like ragamuffins, on foot and horse, and the white-topped wagon trains and the heavy guns and the bumping caissons and the farriers' carts and the trumpets and the drums. "Adiós." They all sang it. For a day or two. Then the green vegetation dwindled from the slopes, disappeared, and they found themselves in the northern desert. Ah, that desert! It was cold at first and then it turned so hot that the sweat poured in streams down the unwashed bodies of the gasping soldiers. The stink was frightful. After that came the terrible calm. It was neither hot nor cold. The wind was dead and the animals whinnied

and trembled and rolled their eyes as though they knew and feared
what was coming. They marched in a vacuum. It was on the tenth
day that the rushing black clouds dashed up from nowhere. There
was a lurid white streak in the north. And then the crash and fury of
the storm as it burst with unbelievable intensity. The lashing ice-cold
cutting whips of rain that rapidly turned to driving sleet and snow.
Heads bowed they plowed into it. They were caught in the freezing
clutch of the "blue whistler." It cost Santa Anna four hundred men
in sick and dead. About that time the desertions commenced, men
slipping away in the darkness and vanishing forever and others falling
in feigned disability to the ground and being whipped to their feet by
the cursing sargentos. On to Saltillo! On to the Rio Grande! On to
Texas! The bulk of them pushed doggedly northward, through water-
less terrain, through cactus and Spanish bayonet, through rocks and
fissured plains. It was like the land of death. Well, it was over now.
They had traveled more than two hundred miles from the church of
Nuestra Senora del Carmen in San Luis Potosí to the Sierra Madre
heights where Ampudia's troops were sleeping on their arms in the
rain at this moment.

Juan Diego's revolving consciousness centered upon the present
and he endeavored to think coherently about what had happened during the afternoon and what would happen tomorrow. Or was it today?
Santa Anna had been jubilant. He had successfully extended his right
to the crests of the range where it could look down on the American
left and from where it could turn that left in the morning. "They
haven't enough men," he had told Lombardini, laughing and showing
his strong white gold-flecked teeth. "They have no reserves. I'll be
behind them by noon tomorrow. Miñón's cavalry will cut them off
from Monterrey. We'll have their wagon train in time for the midday meal. We'll all be eating American pork before sunset." He had
whistled and slapped his chief of staff, Micheltorena, on the back and
even Lombardini had smiled in anticipation. A vision of hot meat
danced before his eyes. Santa Anna, exuberant, was irresistible.

The rain beat against the canvas like rapid fingers on war drums
and Juan Diego rolled sideways until his face was half-covered with
the damp sour-smelling straw. He began to yawn but still he could
not sleep. Yes, Ampudia was on the heights. They were sleeping up
there now in the darkness and rain under the shelter of the trees and
rocks. In the morning . . . The plateau was the objective. Plateau
Pork. The steady percussion of the rain began to have a mesmerizing
effect on Juan Diego but he did not dare to think that he might be
going to sleep. To think of it would be to stay awake. The good sol
dier didn't think of anything. He was a good animal. He just shut his
eyes and went on to . . . They didn't seem like dolls any more. To

close. The cannon and musketry fire had changed all that. The horses. Dead horses. Santa Anna's stump. Terciopelo. What? Wait. His body seemed to settle itself of its own accord into the straw. The edge of the blanket fell over his face. His mouth opened in a long shuddering yawn. Darkness. Dark. In a trance between sleep and wakefulness he felt the tension flowing out of his body and the rising of amorphous shapes behind his closed eyelids. Nuestra Señora. María Santísima. They swelled, diminished and coiled like figures of pearl-gray smoke. There was a little light in the distance no larger than the eye of an ox. As it approached it grew in circumference until it was a wide circle. There was a shape in the circle and it turned its head and looked steadfastly at him. Odor of gardenias. It was a woman and her garment was of blue terciopelo with bright stars of gold all over it. Where . . . morena. Ah. In a dream he recognized the waxen-skinned pointed face with the gray eyes and turbulence of dark hair. Don Isidro's daughter . . . María Catalina . . . María Cata . . .

Juan Diego slept the deep sleep of exhaustion.

David Livingston sat at a rickety table in the drinking room of the Cantina del Río in Saltillo and observed with some disgust the cup of viscous chocolate that had been set before him by the three hundred pound patrona. She had sworn before God, Jesus Christ, the Virgin Mary and all the saints in heaven that she did not possess a gota of alcoholic beverage in the place. He suspected that this astounding lack was due solely to General Taylor's rigid orders concerning the serving of liquor to men in uniform and that if someone familiar to the patrona were to ask he would be served. It made him a little angry. Behind him at the larger table the quintet of volunteer officers continued to discourse in loud voices, certainly not enlivened by lukewarm chocolate, about Taylor's plans for the next day. They constantly interrupted one another. As a 'regular' the volunteers bored him to death. The majority of them, he believed, were lawless loud-mouthed rascals who thought that a temporary uniform exempted them from every law, both civil and moral. True enough, the officers were a little better but their pigheadedness, ignorance, disciplinary incompetence and fear of their own men made them equally responsible for the outrages committed by the privates. Drunken, brawling, insolent, the volunteers were the living embodiment of a moral pestilence. They were bullies, thieves, rapists and murderers. They would leave their mark on Mexico for a hundred years. Of course, there were exceptions. Colonel Davis, for instance. But then, Davis was a West Point man and had fought as a regular in the Black Hawk War. Why had he thrown away his career in the army so many years before and then gone in for politics? Livingston wondered about that. It had been pleasant to encounter him again on this night ride to Saltillo.

The patrona waddled over and indicated his congealing chocolate with a dirty finger.

"Quiere usted un poco más?" she asked.

Livingston looked up at her black mustache and shaking chins with puzzled eyes.

"What's that?" he demanded.

"Quiere usted un poco más?" repeated the patrona.

"I don't understand," said Livingston.

Muttering to herself she turned slowly like a barge in narrow waters and lumbered back to the door that led to the kitchen.

"She's puttin' the devil's curse on ye, lootenant," called one of the volunteer officers from the large table.

Livingston did not turn his head. He heard a jabber of voices behind him and someone saying something about the regular army. Then the officer who had called to him said in a loud voice, "Who th' hell cares? High and mighty in a stiff collar, hey? Like a chiny pisspot painted with red flowers."

The devil take them. Livingston impatiently pushed his cup away and as he did so the door to the street opened and let in a slanting fury of rain and First Lieutenant Cousins. The newcomer was wet and smiling and he had one hand concealed behind him. He started to walk toward Livingston.

"Is that another one, Claiborne?" asked the volunteer officer loudly and burst into a guffaw of laughter.

The smile was erased from the face of Cousins and without halting he shifted his direction and approached the large table.

"Are you here with special permits, gentlemen?" he asked in a quiet voice. "Are your companies stationed in the town?"

"Now look here, lootenant . . ." began the vocal volunteer officer in a bullying tone.

"Officers in town without the general's express permission must return to the camp at Buena Vista," declared Cousins calmly. "Let me see your passes."

"Say, look here!" exploded the volunteer officer, pushing back his chair and rising to his feet.

"Now, now, Jack," said one of his companions hurriedly, putting his hand on the irate officer's arm. "We don't want no trouble. We don't—"

"Start marching, misters, or I'll take your names," snapped Cousins.

There was a scraping of chairs and the quintet, muttering angrily clumped across the room and out into the rainy night.

Livingston had not turned but there was a slight smile on his lips as Cousins dragged a chair up to his table and sat down opposite him.

"Texas scum," said the plump young man serenely.

He smiled and blinked his blue eyes happily.

"They told me at headquarters I would find you here," he explained. "Look at this!"

He raised his hand and put a bottle of whisky on the table.

"Liquor!" exclaimed Livingston in mock disbelief. "Don't you know that it is forbidden in Saltillo?"

"Really?" murmured Cousins.

"You'll get fifty lashes for that," warned Livingston.

"Let's get some glasses," said Cousins.

"General Taylor has forbidden liquor," continued Livingston.

"What General Taylor doesn't know won't hurt General Taylor," responded Cousins, grinning. "But if you insist, St. Anthony, I'll destroy the vile stuff. Curse it anyway for a mocker and an enrager."

He made as though to dash the bottle on the floor.

Livingston turned hastily toward the kitchen door.

"Glasses!" he bawled to the patrona. "Glasses! What do you call 'em? Vasos! Glasses!"

"A linguist," remarked Cousins admiringly.

Facing the plump young man again Livingston chuckled with pleasure. He liked this man. This man recalled to him the two barracks at West Point, the parade ground, the smell of June in the air, the lordly sweep of the Hudson and the red-cheeked girls of Highland Falls and Newburgh.

"Did you catch up with your Kentuckians?" he asked.

"Who? Oh, yes. Milan and Pennington's companies, yes," answered Cousins. "Yes, indeed. They were a good way up the range, within rifle shot of the Mexicans on the summit, in fact, when I caught up with them. Well, they're down. Down in the gorge, I mean. I suppose I should have reported to Wool but my mission was from Taylor and the fleshpots of Saltillo called me and . . ."

"Fleshpots!" exclaimed Livingston sourly.

"Isn't it awful?" asked Cousins quickly. "Mud, dung and stink. It's the capital of Coahuila, a mile above sea level and boasts twenty thousand inhabitants, but I'd swap it for the smallest hamlet in Orange County. Monterrey wasn't so bad, though."

There was a reminiscent smile on his face as he stroked the back of his thick sandy hair.

"Good old Monterrey," he continued. "The mountains in the sun, the dark green of the aguacates, the palmettoes like ladies' open fans, the date palms like feather dusters, the golden oranges and blushing pomegranates and murmuring streams and creamy pools of lilies . . . Ah . . ."

He opened his blue eyes very wide in mock surprise at Livingston. "How's that?" he asked briskly. "Wouldn't you say that I was the James G. Percival of the American army?"

"I presume there was a young lady at Monterrey," remarked Livingston dryly.

"Very smart of you," murmured Cousins.

Suddenly he slapped the table with his open hand.

"By the way, where's your fleshpot with the glasses?" he demanded. "Vasos, Señora Gran Barriga! How did you get here, Livingston? I'd pictured you sleeping in a wet tent behind Angostura."

"I rode in with General Taylor and Colonel Davis," explained Livingston. "After we reached headquarters the general dismissed me for the night and the colonel suggested that I come here. What there is . . ."

"Oh, Davis will probably drop in here after he has consulted with Taylor and bedded down his Mississippians," said Cousins. "He likes the place. There's a dish that the fleshpot makes . . . a kind of pork stew. Davis must be interested in you. Had you met him before?"

"Yes. In Washington," admitted Livingston. "I . . ."

"Oh, there you are," crowed Cousins as the fat patrona shuffled up to the table with two glasses. "Un millón de gracias. Nothing stingy about me. Prenda mía! Mi alma! Si supieras lo que te quiero! Me amas tú?"

"Chiflado!" grumbled the patrona hoarsely as she waddled away.

"What did you say?" inquired Cousins of Livingston, uncorking the bottle and pouring two generous slugs of whisky. "Washington? Don't tell me that you are a secret son of James K. Polk."

Livingston laughed and shook his head.

"No," he replied. "I'm the foster son of Senator Alphonsus Ewing of Tennessee. It was through him that I met Mr. . . . Colonel Davis."

Cousins took a long swallow from his glass and studied Livingston over the rim of it.

"A senator's foster son," he said with reverence. "The adopted child of Cicero. Does he have any influence with the War Department?"

"I'm sure I don't know," answered Livingston. "Why? Do you want a star on your shoulder?"

"Not now," said the other. "I'd like a soft post in Washington, though, after this brawl is over. There's a lot of pretty women there and I dance beautifully."

Livingston picked up his glass and sipped from it. The raw whisky went down his throat like barbed wire.

"He was the general's son-in-law," remarked Cousins inconsequently.

"My foster father?" laughed Livingston. "Oh, no. He . . ."

"Don't be an idiot," said Cousins. "I refer to Colonel Davis. He was the general's son-in-law."

Livingston set his glass down with some surprise.

"What?" he exclaimed.

"I said that Jefferson Davis was the son-in-law of Zachary Taylor," explained Cousins patiently. "Didn't you know that?"

Livingston shook his head.

"Well, I'll tell you what I know," volunteered Cousins. "It's as good a subject of conversation on a dreary night as any. But another drink first."

He reached for the bottle and poured himself a half glass of whisky.

"I picked up most of this at Wool's headquarters," he began. "They're great gossipers there and the general was fair game. It all started in 1832 just after the Black Hawk War. Taylor was a colonel then and Davis was a damned handsome young lieutenant. Tall, you know, slim, very aristocratic. The sort that could hand a lady in to dinner in such a way that the other men looked like clumsy donkeys. Sarah Taylor, our general's daughter, was eighteen, charming if not beautiful and reputed to be the best dancer in Kentucky. Well, Sarah and Davis met and fell violently in love with each other. But Taylor would have none of it. I don't suppose that he personally disliked Davis at first but he didn't want Sarah to be an army wife and undergo all the hardships that her sister Ann, married to an army surgeon named Wood, was suffering. And it is a hell of an existence, too. Here you are today and there you are tomorrow and *you* know what the pay of a lieutenant is. Wait, Livingston, until you are a colonel before you marry. Where was I? Oh. Wool says that Taylor declared to Stephen Kearny, 'I'll be damned if another daughter of mine shall marry into the army. I know enough of the family life of officers.' But Davis wasn't taking 'no' for an answer. The engagement, if it can be called such, dragged on for three years and Taylor did everything in his power to break it up. Of course, he gradually conceived a personal hatred for the young officer. Who wouldn't? And you must have heard how 'sot' the general is in his ways. There isn't an ounce of romance in him. I'll take another drink."

He carefully poured himself another huge hooker of whisky and drank down half of it before he resumed his story. Livingston, still toying with his first drink, listened with great interest.

"Now then," continued Cousins, leaning back in his chair and unbuttoning his jacket. "To cut it short, sometime in 1835 Davis resigned his commission in the army and met Sarah at the home of her aunt near Louisville. Both knew what they wanted to do and they did it. They got married."

He paused, finished his third drink and presented a somewhat flushed face to Livingston.

"Come on now," he insisted. "You're begging the . . . the bottle. Didn't the senator ever tell you that it was always time for another drink?"

Livingston obediently poured himself a half glassful of whisky.

"I'm interested," he said. "Go on. Did the general and Davis make it up between them? They seem . . ."

"Wait," ordered Cousins, waving his hand. "Listen to this. Less than three months after the marriage Sarah Taylor Davis died of malaria."

"Good Lord," said Livingston softly.

So that was the reason for the eternal shadow in the handsome face of Jefferson Davis.

"They buried her in West Feliciana Parish, Louisiana," added Cousins. "It nearly killed Davis. He withdrew from the social world altogether for eight long years and now that he has come out into the light of day again he is an altogether different man. His old friends told Wool that."

"How did it affect Taylor?" asked Livingston, although his thoughts were all concerned with the younger man.

Cousins shrugged his shoulders.

"Who knows?" he said. "Taylor is a grim man at heart. He conceals his emotions. He is an ambitious man, too. Wool says that he met Davis for the first time since the death of Sarah on a river steamer to New Orleans in 'forty-five. Davis was on his way to marry his second wife, Miss Varina Howell of Natchez. The two men shook hands."

Livingston took a large swallow of his whisky. It was still like barbed wire but it was more endurable and the warmth that gradually permeated his body was welcome and pleasant. It might be raining in the dark streets of Saltillo but here in the Cantina del Río with its mingled odor of onions, peppers and meat stews it was comfortable and conducive to reverie. Such mighty matters as battles were far away. He took a second swallow from the glass. He thought that he understood Jefferson Davis better now from the telling of this story. Men were always shaped in maturity from the tragedies of youth. Sometimes it set them apart, endowing them with an understanding or a determination or an urge that was unique in themselves and would carry them to high solitary places. Sometimes it made them actually *look* different. Davis . . .

"Let's sing," said Cousins suddenly.

Livingston glanced with some surprise at the flushed face opposite him.

"Sing," he said vaguely.

"We're getting into a rut," declared Cousins. "Here, my moody broody friend."

He rose solemnly to his feet and lifted a newly filled glass.

"I give you 'Niagara Falls,' " he announced gravely. " 'Niagara Falls,' sir. Sung with great success in all the finest theaters of the country by Mr. Winchell and now rendered even better by First Lieutenant Seymour Cousins, the boy baritone of Highland Falls."

Animatedly he began:

"From Buffalo, my labor done,
For curiosity and fun,
I took the cars, the morning run,
    To go to Niagara Falls, sirs.
The morn was cold, the snow fell fast,
Old Boreas blew a piping blast,
With two horse pow'r set off at last,
We'd passengers of ev'ry cast.
There was Mister and Missis Frost and son,
A charming lady of fifty-one,
Whose volubility of tongue
Reminded me of a Chinese gong."

"Join in, Livingston," he called and swept into the refrain.

"Oh, rumbling, tumbling, tearing away,
Wallowing, bellowing, wet with spray,
Like Aunt Deborah's washing day,
    This trip to Niagara Falls."

Livingston didn't join in but he was suddenly convinced that he was having the best time of his life. His smile widened to a grin, then broke into a chuckle and finally he was laughing aloud as he bobbed his head delightedly to the tripping melody. With happy unconsciousness he filled his glass again. Cousins, raising his voice, plunged into the second verse:

"The driver did his horses crack,
Going to Niagara Falls;
At length we arrived in time to dine,
    The Cataract Hotel is fine, sirs.
We'd flesh and fish of ev'ry kind
And Negro waiters to stand behind;

> The landlord he procured a guide,
> Who took us down to the water-side,
> Where we rocked and pitched in the foaming tide,
> As through the surge our boat did glide,
> But the snow kept drifting o'er the track,
> Which made our travelling rather slack.

The patrona came to the kitchen door and stared with popeyed disbelief at the caroling officer. Livingston took a long drink and laughed harder than ever. It really was quite warm and comfortable now. His feet began to dance under the table.

> Oh, rumbling, tumbling, tearing away,
> Wallowing, bellowing, wet with spray,
> Like Aunt Deborah's washing day,
> This trip to Niagara Falls.

Stopping just long enough to empty his glass and set it down Cousins continued to warble lustily:

> Midst foaming billows at length we land,
> On cakes of rocky ice and stand,
> We all got safely upon the strand,
>   Going to Niagara Falls, sirs.
> We gazed upon the English Falls,
> Tumbling over nature's walls,
> The noise of which your heart appalls,
> Just like the thousand thunder squalls;
> A redcoat sentry bid us stand,
> A broth of a boy from Paddy's land,
> With bayonet fixed and pen in hand
> To sign our names did us command.

There was a scraping sound as the street door opened but Livingston was unconscious of it. Even the cold gust of damp air that swirled across the room and lapped at the back of his neck did not disturb him. He was too engrossed in humming an obligato to Cousins' valiant chorus.

> Oh, rumbling, tumbling, tearing away,
> Wallowing, bellowing, wet with spray,
> Like Aunt Deborah's washing day,
>   This trip to Niagara Falls.

Superbly Cousins attacked the fourth verse:

> Stuck fast in mud with sad turmoil,
> Some lost a shoe amidst the toil,
> At length we reach'd the topmost soil,
>   That leads to Niagara Falls, sirs.

The rival cataracts in view,
Roaring and rushing ever new,
Goat Island stands betwixt the two,
The English Falls they call Horseshoe;
Near Table Rock we all descend,
Down winding steps that never end,
The ladies our aid we had to lend,
Each begging the other her pace to mend.

Oh, rumbling, tumbling . . .

"Oh, Gemini," said Cousins and sat down abruptly.

"Bravo!" called a voice near the door and Livingston turned in time to see Colonel Davis walking up to the table.

"Don't stand up, gentlemen," directed Davis hastily as the two young men started to rise. "You are in excellent voice, Lieutenant Cousins. Castle Garden's loss is the army's gain."

Cousins grinned sheepishly at his glass and then immediately recovered with an aplomb that seemed peculiar to himself.

"Yes, sir," he said. "I understand that Tedesco and Marini burst into tears at the mention of my name. Will you have a drink, sir? Is there anything new?"

Davis shook his head to both questions.

"I've just left General Taylor," he said. "There's a Mexican cavalry force in our rear but that's all. It must have come through the Palomas Pass. The general has dispatched orders to General Marshall at Rinconada Pass and Colonel Morgan at Cerralvo to bring up their men, Marshall's to Buena Vista and Morgan's to Monterrey. That's all. I'm to leave two companies of my Mississippians here and the rest of us will ride back to La Angostura in the morning. You lads had better get some sleep."

His eyes shifted to the bottle of whisky and away again.

"What do you think about tomorrow, sir?" inquired Livingston.

"I'm afraid of the volunteers," replied the colonel frankly, "and I'm certain that I shouldn't admit it at all. After all, my men are volunteers. But . . . Well, I think that our artillery will hold them. Bragg and Sherman and Washington are good officers. And we can always look for a certain lack of co-ordination amongst the enemy elements. They're better at guerrilla tactics than a pitched battle."

"They outnumber us heavily," remarked Cousins.

"I know it," acknowledged Davis calmly. "But then, you must remember that we have never fought a war in which we haven't been outnumbered and we have won every one of them."

"Has the general a plan of action?" asked Cousins.

"That's for the general to say," replied Davis dryly. "We'll find out in the morning."

He turned toward the kitchen door.

"Oh, Señora Adelita," he called.

"Adelita," repeated Cousins admiringly. "Prenda mía. Mi alma."

Smiling, Davis glanced at Livingston.

"Señora Adelita concocts an excellent stew," he explained. "It is a relief from army food. Will you share a plate with me?"

"Pork?" demanded Cousins before Livingston could answer.

"Chicken," said Davis.

"I'll stay," announced Cousins as though the invitation had been extended to him. "But where on earth did she get the chicken? I thought the volunteers had wrung every neck between here and the Rio Grande."

"It is not so bad as that," said Davis. "And Señora Adelita has her own secrets. You'll like this stew, Lieutenant Livingston. There's onions and raisins and nuts in it."

"I wouldn't dream of refusing it," affirmed Livingston.

"Dinner at midnight," declared Cousins happily, "and no cursed patrol to order us back to quarters. I could almost take another drink in honor of this occasion."

"Take it with your stew," advised Davis. "Your head will feel better in the morning."

The slow steps of the patrona shuffled across the floor.

Juan Diego, waking early in the morning, felt much better than he had the night before. The few hours of heavy slumber had refreshed his sinewy young body and though there was a painful stiffness in his limbs and his smart uniform was soggy with damp and astoundingly wrinkled he bounced out of his tent in an exhilarated and expectant frame of mind, the very epitome of a spry junior staff officer. If he had had any dreams or visions while he slept he had forgotten them. The rain had stopped and while the sky was filled with lowering clouds there was yet a sort of clarified sharpness in the air that made the terrain, the plateau, the mountains, and the road, stand out distinct and clear. It was like looking through a newly cleaned window at a newly washed world. Humming to himself he ran across the ridge of land that separated him from Santa Anna's pabellón. It was like a buzzing beehive.

The general had evidently just returned from a tour of inspection, early as it was, for his white and brown horse with its high elaborately decorated saddle and red leather stirrup shoes pawed the ground impatiently before the tent and tossed its long taffy-colored mane in an attempt to get free from the restraining hand of the Indian palafrenero.

Santa Anna was leaning over the camp table and thrusting a brown blunt finger at various spots on the unrolled map. He was talking rapidly and appeared to be in excellent humor. He is sure of himself today, thought the young man as he stood just outside the open flaps of the pabellón and waited to be noticed. Several junior officers, in high collars, plumed hats and reeking with French perfume, also waiting to be noticed, clustered about him. After all, he was the general's protégé. He learned that during the night Ampudia's infantry on the heights had been reinforced. Santa Anna's objective was unmistakably the plateau that now spread before them like a hand with ravines for the spaces between the outstretched fingers. Would they attempt to force the pass at La Angostura?

"Look for yourself, Señor Teniente," said one of the junior officers, handing him a field glass.

Juan Diego adjusted the instrument to his eye and studied the narrow defile. He saw immediately that the Americans had worked hard during the night. A new ditch with a traverse on its right had been dug before the unlimbered battery and behind the ditch a breastwork running from the guns to the sunken stream had been raised. It protected a dense body of men whose long bayonets flickered in the early morning light.

"It's going to be a hard nut to crack," he said in a judicious voice as he handed the field glass back to its owner.

At that moment Santa Anna walked out of his tent clutching Lombardini by the arm and followed by a score of general officers and aides in varied uniform. There was a vast jingling of sabers and spurs and bobbing of white plumes.

"No, no, no," the general was saying in a good-natured voice. "Mejia is entirely wasted on the Yanqui right. It would take a division of monkeys to force those gullies. Micheltorena! Micheltorena!"

The chief of staff pushed forward.

"Send an order to Mejia to withdraw from our left, cross the road a mile back and come up on our right," ordered Santa Anna.

He saw Juan Diego and smiled.

"You slept too long to be sleeping alone, Señor Teniente," he remarked dryly.

One or two of the younger officers tittered.

"Now, I never sleep alone," continued Santa Anna, "but I was in the saddle long before sunrise."

"My general, I swear to you that I slept alone," said Juan Diego cheerfully.

He had observed the playful expression in the general's eyes.

"Really?" inquired Santa Anna in mock amazement. "Very well. I shall have to beg the archbishop of Mexico to give you a church."

"He wouldn't sleep alone then," declared one of the junior officers boldly.

Santa Anna clapped his hands together.

"Come!" he exclaimed. "It is time to begin the music if we intend to dine at Buena Vista. You have my orders. Away now!"

The generals, including Lombardini, and staff officers moved off hurriedly in various directions toward their horses. There was a stamping of hoofs, a creaking of saddles and the clicking of swords and spurs. Santa Anna stood for a moment staring across the plateau and ravines to the near distance where the American troops could already be seen in motion, their bayonets glinting dully and one or two guns hauled by straining horses bucketing along the farther ridge. A few scattered rifle shots sounded from the heights. As always in repose when he forgot that he was observed Santa Anna presented a sad contemplative face to the slowly warming morning air. Juan Diego had never figured out whether this melancholy suggestion was merely the natural lines of the general's features or the unconscious betrayal of a remote inner temperament. There was a dream in that face but whether it was a good dream or a bad dream remained Santa Anna's own secret. What did he desire and what had he missed? He would never tell and it was possible that no one would ever find out. As though conscious that he was being studied, Santa Anna suddenly turned toward Juan Diego.

"You will find something to eat at the little table, Juan Diego," he said, indicating the open entrance to the pabellón.

"I hadn't thought of food," replied the young man. "Isn't there a message I can . . ."

"Eat," broke in Santa Anna. "You will have enough messages to carry before this day is over."

He approached and put his arm about Juan Diego's shoulder.

"I have them," he declared triumphantly, as he urged the youth toward the tent. "Taylor will never forget this day as long as he lives. Listen to those trumpets. Ah qué alegría! Eat now, eat. Then remain here. If I want you I will send for you."

He thrust Juan Diego into the pabellón.

"I'm not hungry . . ." began the young man—but Santa Anna had gone.

Trumpets started to peal in all directions like a circling flight of great musical birds rising joyfully into the rain-cooled air.

Juan Diego gazed with distaste at the cold food on the table and then turned his back on it and walked out of the pabellón into the pearl-gray morning. How could he stay under cover at a moment like this? He could hear the scraping sound of feet, hoofs and wheels; it made a noise like a great sprawling beast, and it aroused an irritated impa-

tience in his mind. It seemed to him that everybody was on the move
except himself and he was so concerned about it that he did not notice
the equal impatience of the other young aides in reserve who were sitting down on rocks and ammunition boxes and jumping up again for
no visible reason and striding to and fro, the fringes of their sword
sashes fluttering behind them. He moved away from them to the edge
of the ridge that bordered the nearer of the three larger ravines and
watched the methodical movements of the troops as they seemed to
drift like low slow clouds of color to their appointed positions, their
standards ruffling in the light breeze. Along the Saltillo Road to the
left he could see the dense mass of Blanco's division, its left supported
by the Húzares. It was spreading lethargically, bits of it floating off
here and there and coming to rest like feathers on various small
heights. To the right of Blanco and directly before and below Juan
Diego in the nearest ravine was Pacheco's division and to the right of
that on raised ground and closer to the mountain range where Ampudia's men were engaged already with the American left were Lombardini's men. In the rear and even farther to the right Ortega's division was being held in reserve. At the base of the mountain a battery
of eight-pounders, Ballarta's, most likely, was wheeling into position.
Santa Anna's purpose was simple and plain. Blanco's division was to
force the pass at La Angostura and the divisions of Pacheco and Lombardini, assisted, if need be, by Ortega's reserve and certainly by
Ampudia's men on the mountain, were to roll back the American left,
making the plateau the heart of the action. If these twin objects could
be accomplished the Americans would have to retreat on Buena Vista
and even Saltillo and a hurried retreat could be slashed to pieces by the
Mexican cavalry. The result would be nothing less than a complete
rout.

The young officer gazed down at Pacheco's raw recruits and saw
the priests in vivid chasubles running along the moving lines and administering absolution. The regimental bands were brassily playing the
eternal "Adiós." Standards fluttered everywhere. It was astonishing
what excellent order these sketchily trained lads kept and Juan Diego
judged that a night's rest and the mob excitement of the morning had
stiffened their determination and made them feel like veterans. They
moved steadily up the ravine and would eventually debouch on the
plateau some distance ahead of Lombardini's better-trained soldiers.
The haphazard musketry fire from the mountain was suddenly
drowned by rapid explosions from the left and Juan Diego, turning
his head, saw that Blanco's division, marching in close-company order
along the Saltillo Road, was being shelled by the guns at La Angostura.
The Americans were throwing spherical case shot into it and their gunners appeared to be good, for several times in succession Juan Diego

saw rents torn in the ranks of the marching troops and eddies of disorder as they re-formed and continued onward. The shelling did not stop them. They pushed along the gray-yellow road at a regular pace, their standard bravely flying and the even taps of drums marking the pace.

"They are marching straight into the American grape," said a guttural voice and Juan Diego glanced around to see the German surgeon general, Van der Linden, standing near him with an upraised field glass.

"How else will they break through, Señor Médico Mayor?" asked the young officer. "There is the river to their left."

"Pouf!" exclaimed the potbellied doctor. "We should hammer the pass with our biggest guns first. Reduce it to bits. Then take it with the bayonet. In Europe we understand these matters better. We know how to make artillery work for us. There! You see?"

The battery at La Angostura had opened with grape and the steel hail was ravaging the front ranks of Blanco's men. Suddenly spellbound, Juan Diego stood and watched the Mexican troopers spin and fall in heaps, the indescribable confusion that swept away all order, and then a hasty melting of the mass of men as the survivors scurried to the sides of the road and disappeared in hollows and behind rocks. Van der Linden was saying something but he did not hear him. Several of the young aides were crowding around and exclaiming in loud startled voices but he did not hear them either. This was death and he was seeing it en masse for the first time. It made him feel as though he had run a long distance and was winded. His lips were dry. For no reason at all a man without a face, with nothing but a red reeking mask, ran across the air and disappeared in the smoke. He was going to be dizzy. And then as suddenly as it came the abnormal sensation vanished and he was cool, collected and clear-eyed. He could see everything. He could see that Blanco's division was off the road and that along it lay heaps of stained clothes that sometimes twitched. He turned to the surgeon general to make some remark, any remark that would prove he was calm, but Van der Linden was running across the ridge toward the hobbled horses.

"The Americans are good artilleryists," he said judiciously to the aides who clustered near him.

"Jesucristo!" exclaimed one of them, a thin yellow youth with a pockmarked face. "Did you see them fall? How quickly they die!"

"There is one crawling to the side of the road," said another. "Ah! He has fallen down again. He is vomiting."

"You will see more than that before the day is over," remarked Juan Diego in a matter-of-fact voice.

The young aides glanced at him with some respect.

I am not frightened, thought Juan Diego. I will not let myself be frightened. I have seen bulls and dogs and tigers and horses killed and why should it frighten me to see a man die? Besides, I can see it and put it out of my mind. I can look the other way just as I am looking the other way now although my eyes are fixed on the shapeless bundles of clothes in the road. I see what is happening but it does not affect me. The first shock is all. After that, it is merely repetition. See, I am neither frightened nor stirred. It pleased him to be able to reason so. It pleased him to think that he was so detached and he made it a matter of pride to accept everything that happened as though he had foreseen and expected it.

"Pacheco is coming out of the ravine," exclaimed the pockmarked aide, extending his arm and pointing.

Juan Diego turned his head from the road and looked across the uneven terrain. It was true. The recruits were ascending from the ravine and forming across the ridge. At the same time the young officer observed an American battery of three pieces coming forward rapidly with a line regiment moving in support. The American guns unlimbered and opened fire on the advancing Mexicans and almost immediately the battery at the base of the mountain began to throw shells into the blue-jacketed line regiment. The din mounted as the musketry joined its thwacking repetition to the reverberating belch of the cannon and the mountain walls flung back the dissonant echoes. Pacheco's men continued to pour out of the ravine, those behind pushing against those ahead, and the long irregular line spread across the ridge. Elements of it thrust tentatively forward, urged by angry officers with flailing swords, but Juan Diego could see that they were taking heavy punishment. The American grape and canister swept through them and whole platoons seemed to disappear in the smoke and dust. The lines sagged, broke and reassembled before the quick orange flash of the guns and there were moments when they were entirely invisible in the whirling upchurned clouds of clods and flying earth. The terrible stink of gunpowder drifted across the ravines. It became impossible to see clearly or make out exactly what was happening in the confusion on the near edge of the plateau and Juan Diego, half-forgetting his pose of calmness, leaned forward anxiously, hands clenched, like a runner about to leap forward in a race.

A sharp blow on the shoulder that nearly knocked him into the ravine brought him angrily out of his watchful trance and he turned quickly to see Santa Anna's black-painted peg leg thrusting at him like a gun barrel. The general, a white duster covering his uniform and a wide hat of woven straw on his head, was flourishing his whip and shouting to Micheltorena, who was riding directly behind him.

"Lombardini!" he bawled in a loud voice. "Where in the name of

Jesucristo and His Holy Nails is Lombardini? Pacheco is going to break at any minute."

"He is coming up as fast as he can," answered Micheltorena in a worried voice. "I can see his standards now."

"He's wounded," called a voice and Juan Diego saw that the level space on the ridge before the pabellón was filled with a prancing mass of mounted officers.

A breathless runner was hastily pushed forward.

"General Lombardini is hit, Excelencia," he stammered. "He has turned the command over to General Perez. The division is coming up, Excelencia."

"There they are now, general," broke in Micheltorena.

To the right and rear near the mountain base several waves of troops could be seen trotting and scrambling over the uneven ground toward the edge of the plateau where Pacheco's hard-pressed men were crumbling away like a wall of loose sand before a relentless wave. They were flanked by Lancers.

"They are five minutes late," shouted Santa Anna in a hoarse voice. "That is just the time between victory and defeat. Ah, the devil smother Lombardini! I hope his wound is fatal."

Even as he spoke, the fragments of Pacheco's disordered lines broke before the concentrated cannon and musket fire and dived back into the ravine. Through the smoke and dust Juan Diego saw the confused stream of men darting like a startled swarm of ants before the constant onslaught of the Americans and he knew instinctively that no power of discipline could halt their headlong flight. Pacheco's scared boys were definitely out of the battle. The three American guns were being moved forward, too, and now they were so near that Juan Diego could see the open mouths of the straining horses and the blackened gunners dragging on the hand spikes and wheel spokes. The entire American left was fluctuating with advancing troops. Blue-jacketed pygmies with white bandoleers and tall-banded caps swarmed over the ridges and behind them the drifting smoke clouds revealed and concealed bodies of mounted men galloping obliquely across the plateau. The firing was loud and incessant and beneath it echoed that shrill sustained undertone that could be nothing but the shouting from hundreds of mouths. From the Saltillo Road now came only the infrequent crash of a gun. But on the mountainside the rattle of musketry was redoubled as Ampudia's Light Corps from its advantageous height fusilladed the Americans who still clung to the lower slope.

Juan Diego felt somebody tapping his shoulder and looked up to find Santa Anna leaning from his saddle. There were beads of perspiration on the general's sallow face.

"Find your horse, Juanillo," he ordered gruffly. "Where is it? Mount, you young idiot, before you're caught in that stampede."

Already a few pasty-faced recruits, their shirttails flapping behind them, were darting up out of the nearer ravine and racing across the ridge. They dodged nimbly through the mass of mounted officers and disappeared in the direction of the parked wagon trains. Juan Diego turned after them but before he had taken more than two or three steps in the direction of the horse hobbled behind his tent a loud exclamation from Micheltorena arrested him.

"Cáspita!" cried the chief of staff, hastily handing his field glass to Santa Anna. "Look! Look! They are turning back!"

Juan Diego whirled and stared with the rest. Through the tattered curtains of smoke an astonishing event was taking place. A large body of the troops supporting the American guns had halted its advance, broken off the action, and, moving quickly to the right, was withdrawing from the plateau. There was no explanation for this tactic, for the Americans had been easily driving Pacheco's routed boys before them and in a few minutes would have taken the farther lip of the ravine. The intent group of officers clustered about Santa Anna observed this inexplicable retreat at the moment of imminent victory with amazement and relieved pleasure. Santa Anna handed the field glass back to Micheltorena.

"I do not need it," he said. "God has given back to us that lost five minutes."

Suddenly he burst out laughing and whacked the stump of his leg with delight. He winced at the pain but kept on laughing. Then he rode off hastily to the right followed by a dozen members of his staff. Juan Diego, hardly hearing him go, continued to watch the action on the plateau. Something was beginning to jump inside his breast and he thought that it must be his heart.

The first wave of Lombardini's division, flanked by cavalry, passed through the fleeing fragments of Pacheco's boys and reached the plateau edge where they opened a steady and disciplined fire on those Americans who had not left their advanced positions. At the same time Ballarta's eight-gun battery near the mountain redoubled its destructive fire and gaps began to appear in the enemy ranks. Two of the three forward American guns were limbered up and dragged back into the smoke and confusion. The other, all its horses killed, was abandoned. There was a perceptible wavering on the American left and with it came a mounting confidence in the Mexican lines that spread like a contagion through the dust-dimmed stinking air until it reached the ridge where Juan Diego and the young aides stood. It seemed to Juan Diego that he could smell victory in the reeking atmosphere, that it had always been there and that it was like the odor of growth in a tropic springtime. He forgot the rout of Pacheco's untrained recruits as he saw Lombardini's division, now commanded by Francisco Perez, pushing rapidly forward and maintaining a close grim progress in the face of the galling American fire. Men were falling but the lines never faltered. They moved like Fate.

The gunfire of the Americans became furious, sounding like the eruptions and screams of a cornered beast, and their grape slashed through Lombardini's men like deadly invisible scythes but the Mexicans pushed on like an army of determined beetles with metal horns leaving behind them windrows of dead and wounded. Disordered lines of Yanqui cavalry trotted rapidly to their own rear baring the ragged left flank of their infantry and through the billowing clouds of smoke and dust and upflung clods Juan Diego could see that this flank was being steadily turned. It was almost like a swinging gate. Perez was driving a long tongue of men, horse and foot, between the Americans and the mountain range. His cavalry, pennons fluttering and lances gleaming dully, was skirting the heads of the ravines and pursuing the crumbling blocks of blue-coated invaders. Ampudia's Light Corps suddenly appeared through the trees as it poured down the mountain side and joined the cavalry. And now, precipitately, in a flash, as it were, the Americans were running like swarms of hysterical ants whose hill has been kicked to pieces and Juan Diego saw that the gringo left was definitely broken, was smashed to disparate bits, was visibly melting away as Lombardini's division with its covering cavalry and Ampudia's Light Corps accelerated its triumphant advance parallel with the mountain range.

Juan Diego was only vaguely aware of the exultant shouting about him and he did not dare to glance around for fear of betraying the fact that he was no longer cool and collected. So much had happened in so short a time that the aplomb he had maintained after the first shock of mental dizziness had been shattered as though by a high wind. He wanted to cry out as the others were crying out but he was certain that if he did he would not be able to stop. He was trembling again but it was not because of what he was seeing or the bitter taste of gunpowder on his dry lips or the harsh irritation of his eyeballs where it felt as though sand had been rubbed or the deafening noises that beat upon his eardrums; he was trembling with nothing less than an ecstasy that seemed to snatch him up into an understanding of the gigantic forces that shaped men. The rolling gunfire issued from mouths that were more than the mouths of guns and the glitter on the bayonets became a signature that was more than the sun on steel. He could not encompass his own swelling emotion but he could see it in Santa Anna's face as the general, accompanied by his staff, galloped

past him in a flurry of hoofs calling out, "We have them! Their left
is smashed! They're running like rabbits!"

At that moment the general assumed a colossal stature in Juan
Diego's mind. He was no longer a human being but an impulse, a
gathering to himself, as it were, of the indomitable will of the thousands of men who were advancing like a torrent on the broken and
bewildered Americans. This was what set him apart from the other
commanding officers, from Lombardini, from Ampudia, from Pacheco.
He *became* victory and for the glorious instant he could not be doubted.
It might be true, as some affirmed, that in defeat he *became* defeat, too,
but Juan Diego doubted that. In defeat the general merely laid plans
for a future victory. He resigned himself to nothing and at climactic
moments such as this he transcended himself. That was why his soldiers would follow him again and again. He was the inspired flamboy-
ance of the Latin soul personified.

The pockmarked aide, in a paroxysm of joy, flung his arms about
Juan Diego and embraced him violently. Juan Diego instinctively
pushed him away.

"You will see more than that before the day is over," he said for
the second time, struggling mightily to keep the tremolo out of his
voice.

Some miles below Agua Nueva three riders bearing important
dispatches from Gómez Farías in Mexico City lashed their fresh horses
to greater speed. They could hear the cannonading to the north and it
sounded to them like a low thunder in the mass of mounting hills.

"It sounds like a battle," said one of the riders.

"The general had better conserve his troops," responded the larger
of the other two sourly. "He may have need of them in Mexico City."

"If the Polkos start to dance," added the third rider.

They continued to whip their horses and the flying hoofs struck
sparks from the rocky road.

David Livingston, riding from Saltillo with Taylor and his aides,
heard the rapid firing of the guns and in a common impulse with the
others urged his horse to a gallop. Behind him Colonel May and his
four companies of dragoons thundered to a gallop, too, and still farther
back Colonel Jefferson Davis and his subalterns barked speed at the
eight companies of Mississippi Rifles. They passed the hacienda of
Buena Vista and a large parked section of the wagon train, its cylin-
drical white tops bright against the dark-green trees and tobacco-brown
earth. They did not respond to the fluttering hands of greeting. The
nearing mountain range held their eyes, for on the southern slope they
could see sudden flashes and these sudden flashes (like exploding

lights) were spreading northward and steadily descending. Cousins, who was riding beside Livingston, seemed to lose all his bounce and buoyancy. His underlip was drawn in and his eyebrows met in a scowling frown.

"By Christ!" he exclaimed violently. "It looks as though Wool has let them flank his left."

His mare rocked under him like a small boat in breakers.

Taylor turned his head.

"Lieutenant Livingston," he called. "Kindly ask Colonel Davis to ride forward.

The young officer reined in his horse abruptly and a few minutes later Davis was beside him.

"What is it?" asked the older man, frowning. "Has Wool messed matters up?"

Livingston conveyed his message and the two hurried forward to overtake Taylor.

The general was exhibiting a little anger.

"Colonel Davis," he said, waving his hand toward the mountain, "it looks very much as though Santa Anna has partially flanked our left. That gunfire is far too advanced to suit me."

"Wool must have miscalculated," exclaimed Davis.

"I don't know what Wool has done," said Taylor. "We'll find out when we get there. But I know what *you* must do, colonel. Cut in by the first ravine we come to with your Mississippians and mount the plateau as far to our left as you can. You'd better take a piece from Bragg's battery with you. Stop that flanking movement!"

His voice rose in a grim command.

Davis saluted and galloped back toward his men.

Taylor turned to Major Bliss and began to talk to him in a low rapid voice.

Cousins was muttering and swearing.

"This is what happens when you use fancy New York generals," he declared to Livingston. "Wool is all right when he hasn't any responsibility. If he paid more attention to his flanks and less to his uniform . . . God damn it, this is a pretty beginning for the day!"

Livingston watched the steadily moving flashes on the mountainside.

"Santa Anna is trying to cut us off from Saltillo," he remarked in a concerned voice.

"Of course he is," snapped Cousins. "You don't think Santy Anny is a fool, do you?"

Livingston did not answer.

The Mississippians began to pass at a fast trot holding their muskets high and cheering as they went. Davis waved a gloved hand as he rode by in their midst.

"They don't look bad for volunteers, that's a fact," said Cousins reluctantly.

It was a little after nine o'clock when Taylor turned from the road into a shallow ravine some distance behind Washington's battery, which could be heard blasting away with dogged persistency, and rode up toward the plateau. No sooner had he emerged on the height than a pale and frantic-faced Wool dashed up to him.

"General Taylor," stammered Wool. "General, we are whipped!"

"Sir, that is for me to decide," replied Taylor, his heavy eyebrows moving together like two caterpillars. "What has happened?"

His eyes, almost closed, like those of a sea captain accustomed to far distances, peered through the smoke and dust at the confused field.

"Washington's battery is holding at La Angostura all right," explained Wool, endeavoring to speak calmly, "but our left is beaten back. The volunteers are running like rabbits, God damn them! Near Washington down there is all that remains of my line as it was occupied this morning. I told you yesterday—"

Taylor lifted his brown hand.

"Just a moment, sir," he said in a sharp metallic voice. "I will receive your report of this action. Be brief. We have no time to lose. We will argue the tactics after the day is over."

Livingston, sitting tensely on his horse some three feet from the two generals, understood why Taylor was the commander. There was a solidity about the old man, and at sixty-three he was old, that was like a veritable tower of strength. One might question his tactics, his military knowledge, his manners and even his tact but one could not question his solidity. He was like an old bulldog, centered on four strong legs and single-willed in his purpose. That was why the soldiers liked him. That was why they called him Old Zach and Old Rough and Ready. They understood him and they believed in him and they would follow him straight to the burning gates of hell. He was no mincing general in a new uniform overlarded with decorations but Old Zach Taylor in a shapeless hat and a dirt-stained coat. That was what the soldiers saw and felt. Of course, there was another side, too, the politician, as clever a one as the frontier school had produced, but at this moment that side was not in existence. It was put away for the time being like the single dress uniform in the packing box in Monterrey. There was nothing on the plateau by La Angostura but solidity.

Wool had flushed a deep red and drawn himself up in the saddle.

"Yes, general," he said to Taylor. "Our right is secure. An enemy force that tried to breach the pass by the Saltillo Road has been repulsed with heavy casualties. Observing that the enemy had reinforced his

troops on the mountainside during the night I sent forward part of the
Second Illinois to support Marshall but the main body of the Mexicans
assaulted the plateau through the ravines leading up to it. I sent General
Lane with the Second Indiana to hold them. They were covered by
Captain O'Brien and three of Washington's guns. I—"

"That's enough," broke in Taylor rudely. "General Wool, ride to
the extreme left and try to rally those men. Give them the flat of your
sword if they won't turn. Be off, now."

Neglecting to salute, Wool pivoted his horse and galloped away
over the uneven ground.

Livingston, staring across the plateau, could make no sense out of
the turbulent scene. The heavy smoke of the guns, the thick dust rising
in billows, blocks of troops who seemed to move aimlessly, men running here and there like hysterical ants whose hills had been destroyed,
all this, added to the noise of bellowing guns, the crackle of firearms
and the confused shouting, beat in upon the officer's mind and senses
until he felt himself in the midst of a phantasmagoria peopled by
lunatics. The meaning was beyond him and he marveled that Taylor
could understand anything at all about it. The textbooks and lectures of
West Point might have been theoretically exact but how in the name
of the devil was one to apply their lessons to this entangled scene where
thousands of conflicting human equations did all sorts of mad things
that were not even mentioned in the textbooks? Yet Taylor seemed to
comprehend something as he moved slowly across the plateau followed
by his staff. The old man suddenly possessed a dozen eyes that saw on
all sides.

The troops were beginning to see him, too. Rough voices called to
him, officers waved their sabers and an invisible communication that
was as swift as Benjamin Franklin's electricity spurted in all directions
from the unkempt figure on Old Whitey. It had a galvanizing effect,
for sagging lines were stiffening, cannon fire increasing, and a renewed
doggedness was permeating the combativeness of the infantry. Livingston realized that faith was half the strength in battle and that it
was the leader who personified faith. Solidity. That was it. That was
what Taylor had to offer and that was what the troops needed. Even
the volunteers could react to that.

They had reached a point where they could see Davis and his
Mississippians. They had moved out to the American left and were
slowly advancing up the ascent down which the Mexican infantry,
flanked by cavalry and followed by reserves, was steadily moving. For
the moment the air was clear and Livingston, slouching in his saddle
beside Cousins and behind Taylor, could see everything as though it
was brightly painted on a panorama. The great disparity between the
two opposing forces was unpleasantly plain. "By God, there must be at

least four thousand of those Mexicans!" exclaimed Cousins. The Mississippians pushed on deliberately holding their fire although the Mexican infantry was clattering away with its muskets at long range. Behind Davis the one gun from Bragg's battery began to spit shrapnel. It reminded Livingston of an angry watchdog. Between the two forces lay one of those ravines that sliced the sides of the plateau and it was not until the Americans reached the edge of it that they opened fire. The Mexicans on the other side halted their advance and Livingston could see men falling in their foreranks. "O Kentucky! The hunters of Kentucky!" bellowed Cousins. "Watch 'em go down!" They aren't Kentuckians, thought Livingston, they're Mississippians. And damned good ones, too. The Mexican cavalry, endeavoring to cover the infantry, descended into the ravine and as though this was a signal Davis's troops, cheering loudly, descended themselves and clambered up the farther bank, firing point-blank at sixty yards into the disorganized ranks of the enemy infantry. The Mexican fire slackened, the front disintegrated, gave way and began to fall back on the reserves. "We've got 'em!" declared Cousins to Livingston. "We've got 'em on the run now!" Livingston was peering through the rising smoke. "Their cavalry!" he exclaimed. "It went into the ravine. It . . ." Even as he spoke horses' heads began to appear in the rear of Davis's riflemen. The Mississippians, as though prepared for this further show of force, countermarched rapidly and poured a heavy fire into the ravine. A minute or so later the Mexican cavalry could be seen rapidly emerging from the farther end and retiring on their own men. The entire episode was like a little set scene.

"Davis is a damned good man," declared Cousins fervently.

Taylor turned his head.

"He is an able commander, lieutenant," he said dryly, his face pinched and remote in expression.

Livingston wondered if he was thinking of his lost daughter.

While this action was taking place a large force of Mexican Lancers, their spear blades glistening and pennons fluttering, continued to pass along the split ground at the foot of the mountains until they had reached a point about a half mile beyond Davis, where they turned to trot toward the Saltillo Road. This obvious attempt to cut the Americans off from Saltillo was observed immediately by Taylor and he ordered the four companies of Dragoons, who were in rest behind him, to proceed at full speed to the support of the enfeebled left wing of the Americans. They crossed the plateau rapidly and took positions in the rear of the Mississippians. Livingston now saw that the endangered flank was protected by Yell, Marshall and Davis's troops with the fresh Dragoons moving in to the right of Marshall. Groups of troops who had broken and fled earlier were reassembling and moving back into the line and a few guns were bucketing across the difficult terrain in support. It began to look decidedly better and Livingston was elated to discover that he could see some reason in what was going on. It seemed more like an applied lesson from a West Point textbook. Don't let your wings be turned and don't let yourself be cut off from your base of supplies, etc. The elementary lessons in battle tactics.

Suddenly the roar of heavy guns reverberated from the Mexican right near the mountain and Cousins clapped his field glass to his eye.

"Sixteen-pounders, sir," he said breathlessly to Taylor. "How in the devil did Santy Anny get 'em across those ravines and ridges!"

"They must have been hauled by hand," answered Taylor briefly. "Santa Anna is no fool."

He extended his hand for the field glass and peered through it for a moment.

"Yes, by God," he said. "That's the San Patricio battalion."

"There's a rope waiting for every one of them," declared Cousins grimly.

Livingston stared through the smoke but could not see the traitors. It was difficult for him to believe that Americans would desert their colors and fight on the side of the enemy. Yet there they were, Roman Catholic Irish most of them, who had been seduced by the Mexican priests about the time of the action at Monterrey and were now killing their own flesh and blood.

The heavy battery raked the plateau from the mountain to the Saltillo Road but the infantry supporting it was suffering severely from the fire of Bragg and Sherman's batteries. They began to retire. The action was accelerated now and Livingston lost all sense of reason in it again. He could not see clearly. Smoke and dust obscured the air. Vague lines disappeared into declivities and reappeared. There was a turmoil of couriers dashing up and dashing away again. He could hear Taylor's dry voice constantly giving orders. To the battery commanders. To Bragg and Sherman and O'Brien. A worried Wool popped out of the rolling smoke and back. Commands were sped to Lane and Hardin and McKee and Bissell. Guns dragged by lean horses cleft the dark curtain of flying particles. Livingston's eardrums throbbed to the sustained roar that was like the unending roll on a gigantic drum, a drum as big as the plateau itself. By God, this was a battle! All that had gone before was a feeble indication. This was the real thing.

Cousins cried out suddenly.

"It is nothing," said Taylor, removing his shapeless old hat, studying it for an instant and then putting it back on his head.

A bullet had gone clean through the crown.

Oh, then. Livingston looked up into the air with surprise. *That* was the reason for the sibilant little whispers that he had thought existed only in his eardrums, a reaction from the continuous thunder of sound.

Suddenly, like a prepared event, the enormous pall of smoke momentarily lifted before a great gust of rain-filled wind and he saw the rear of the plateau with its backdrop of mountains, a huge set stage. Long lines of enemy cavalry and infantry stretched along it. The front had shifted. The American left had swung back like a door and an impressive portion of Santa Anna's forces were facing the Saltillo Road. The Americans were fighting with their backs to it. The curtain of smoke descended. Taylor turned in the saddle.

"Lieutenant Livingston," he called.

The young officer urged his horse forward.

"I want you to ride down to Major Washington," directed the general. "Inform him that the enemy is moving down our left with the intention of cutting the Saltillo Road between Buena Vista and his position. Tell him that if he hears firing behind him he is to pay no attenton to it. He is to hold his position and not shift any of his guns."

Livingston jerked the head of his horse about and descended into the nearest ravine leading to the road. It was sheltered here and a first-aid station had taken advantage of the fact and set up its equipment. Four doctors were working busily over a dozen blood-smeared figures and there was a queer sour smell in the air. As Livingston rode past he heard one of the doctors shout, "God damn it, Prescott, stop cleaning that knife in the dirt! Wipe it on your pants." The ravine opened on the road some hundred yards behind Washington's position. Livingston, turning here, guided his mount around two dead horses who lay with their legs stuck up in the air and approached the mass of stinking smoke that enveloped the guns. The earth seemed to be shaking here. Major Washington was sitting on an empty canister box biting a cud off his plug of chewing tobacco. He got up and received the young officer's message with a grunt.

"Christ!" he said. "I can hear firing in all directions. Tell General Taylor I'll hold my position all right and that I haven't got enough guns left to shift any of 'em. Wool took three more'n an hour ago."

Livingston watched the blackened cannoneers load, fire and swab their pieces for a few minutes, and then, his eardrums aching from the detonations, turned his horse and rode back to the mouth of the ravine. There was a fresh taste of rain in the air and dark clouds were climbing rapidly in the sky. He passed the first-aid station, mounted to the plateau and found Taylor and his staff only a short distance from where he had left them. They had ascended a broad knobby outcropping of rocky ground and were staring intently across the ravine-slashed plateau. For the moment the atmosphere was fairly free of smoke and Livingston, edging his horse in beside Cousins' stocky little animal, felt again like a spectator at a monstrous show. The Mexican lines now stretched along the farther rim of the plateau as far as the eye could see, their banners waving and their muskets constantly flashing. From all appearances they had penetrated as far as the hacienda of Buena Vista and heavy firing from that direction gave warning that an action was going on there. It did not seem to trouble Taylor. He acknowledged Livingston's report of Washington's situation with a brief nod and continued to peer through his field glass at the plateau. There, some five hundred yards in the rear of the ravine where the Mississippians had met and fought off the Mexicans earlier in the morning, a great ragged V of American troops had been formed. Cousins rapidly acquainted Livingston with the situation.

"You're going to see something now, my boy," he declared. "Santa Anna is forming to attempt a break-through to the Saltillo Road. See those men? They're Davis's Mississippi Rifles, the Second Indiana and the Third Indiana. One of Sherman's twelve-pound howitzers is supporting them."

His voice raised to a shout.

"There *they* are!" he yelled.

Livingston saw a long wall of horses moving at a hand gallop. The Mexican Lancers, at least fifteen hundred of them formed in close column of squadrons, riding knee to knee, their flags and pennons well-dressed and flying, moved down the slope toward the American V with all the picturesque discipline of well-trained troops. It was like a review on an impossible parade ground. The rich uniforms and the elegant caparisons of the horses merged into a varicolored machine that seemed to be resistless. As the cavalry approached the infantry Taylor and his staff became an immobilized group of frozen figures. Livingston felt his heart beating as though he had run a long distance. Inwardly he braced himself for a terrific shock. He was barely aware of it but the firing on other parts of the plateau had ceased and thousands of grimy men who had been indistinguishable actors now became spectators waiting for a tremendous climax. It did not occur. The hand gallop of the Mexican Lancers dwindled to a walk instead of accelerating into a furious headlong charge and finally ended in a halt. At this moment the Americans opened a crackling fire with rifles and muskets, Sherman's howitzer began to bellow, and in an incredibly short space of time the leading squadrons were torn to pieces, men and horses going down in heaps, and what remained of the Lancers retreated in hasty disorder toward the mountains.

Cousins whooped with joy.

"They can't face it, general!" he shouted. "Sherman's spherical case is too much for them! Oh, Jesus, did you see them skedaddle!"

He reached over and flung his arm around Livingston's neck, almost pulling him out of the saddle.

Taylor suddenly came to life, issuing a series of orders that sent young aides and couriers riding off in all directions.

Artillery fire was resumed on the plateau. May's cavalry, Roane and Gorman's volunteers and Reynolds with two of his guns assailed the disordered Mexican right; Bragg rattled forward with three field pieces, unlimbered and began to throw round shot and shrapnel at close range; and Davis and Lane and Sherman, sensing the kill, urged their men across the uneven ground. The tide of battle had turned and though the Mexican heavy guns poured a desperate infilading fire into the Americans they could not stop them. Round shot, spherical case, canister, grape and musket and rifle balls tore into the intermingled cavalry and infantry, men and horses, muskets and lances, flags and guidons all hopelessly confused. Upon all this turmoil the heavens opened and it began to rain, a heavy pelting rain heralded by sharp claps of thunder that seemed like gigantic echoes of the cannon fire. It became difficult to see through the slanting downpour and Livingston had the sensation of looking through badly fashioned glass. Forms were distorted; the mountains seemed to sway; the ravines became long palpitating scars; the gunpowder smoke was beaten in thick layers close to the earth. Out of this watery chaos appeared Wool.

"General Taylor," he said, remembering to salute this time, "there's a white flag flying near the Mexican heavy battery southeast of the plateau. A Mexican officer there has transmitted a message to our advanced line. It is to the effect that General Santa Anna wants to know what *you* want."

"What I . . ." began Taylor.

He took off his shapeless hat and shook the rain out of it. Large drops flowed down his face and his thin gray hair hung in lank pointed locks over his forehead.

"Why, God damn . . ." he began again and then impatiently wiped the water out of his eyes.

"Go over there, Wool," he said, "and see what Santa Anna proposes. Order those guns to stop firing until we find out what all this is about."

Wool disappeared into the crazy-glass of rain.

"Do you suppose he wants a truce, sir?" demanded Cousins in a surprised voice.

Taylor looked grimly at the young officer.

"We'll know when we find out," he replied shortly.

The group sat stolidly, shoulders hunched against the storm, and waited. In a few minutes the firing slackened and gradually came to a stop. There was no sound except the whirring of the rain and the constant booming of a Mexican battery near the mountain. Cousins muttered something about there being one fellow who didn't believe in truces but no one acknowledged his remark. Livingston moved uncomfortably, his sodden saddle creaking beneath him. The silence suddenly became unreal to him, like a suspension of living in the necessity of life. After what seemed a lifetime Wool appeared, a vexed look on his face.

"There was no one there," he explained to Taylor. "Their battery continued its fire. I don't know . . ."

Taylor slapped his hand heavily on Old Whitey's soaking neck.

"He's diddled us!" he said. "That was a trick to extricate his cavalry from our gunfire. I suppose they're all beyond the ravines now."

Wool nodded his head.

"They've reached their own reserves," he admitted, "and an eight-gun battery has come up closer to the plateau."

"He's a damned monkey for unfair tricks," exploded Cousins indignantly. "I marvel that . . ."

Taylor settled his bedraggled hat on his head.

"We'll move on to another position," he said. "We can't see a thing here."

They walked their horses forward through the pelting rain. Blocks of figures moved mistily in the distance before them. A scattered firing began and steadily increased in volume. Somewhere to the left there sounded the creak, squeak and rattle of gun caissons. Livingston, wiping his wet sleeve across his eyes, felt tired and hungry. He wondered vaguely what time it was and decided that it was long after noon. Battles, it appeared, were endless. This would go on forever and then it would decide nothing. A courier, stumbling along on foot, met them and made a hurried report to Taylor. His horse had fallen and broken its leg. He'd shot the poor beast. Godamighty, there was going to be hell to pay on the plateau. As if there hadn't been enough . . . A heavy column of fresh Mexican reserves, mostly infantry, was advancing and its vanguard had already reached the higher ground. It looked like several divisions. There was nothing to stop it. Could the General —Taylor, cutting the man short, immediately dispatched orders to Hardin, Bissell and McKee, who were well in advance of the artillery, to throw their volunteer regiments against the advancing column and push it back toward the mountains. The courier received a spare horse and galloped away.

Messengers continued to arrive, report and hasten off again. The bellowing of the bigger guns merged into an uninterrupted roar and the nerve-racking obbligato of musketry and rifle fire shifted and returned, rose in volume and dwindled to a desperate twanging like plucked loosened wires. The rain slackened and the visibility increased.

Taylor, reaching a spot that served him as observation post, reined in Old Whitey and his aides grouped themselves about him in a tight semicircle. From where they now paused with loosened reins on their horses they could see what was happening with some distinctness. The plateau was filling with troops again. Livingston, close to Taylor, discovered that by some miraculous means a field glass was in his hand and he immediately placed it to his eye. The rainfall that had clarified the atmosphere by beating down the dust and swallowing the smoke seemed to have clarified his mind, too. He could make sense of what he was seeing. Beyond heaps of head horses and splintered caissons he could see the Mexican columns, several of them, engaged by Hardin's regiment. The musketry fire was intense, flickering lines of flame running along the opposing fronts, and presently the head of one of the enemy columns dipped for safety into a long deep ravine that slashed all the way to the Saltillo Road. Bissell and McKee's regiments moved forward in good order and after a hot exchange of balls swept out of sight into the ravine, too. O'Brien and Thomas's guns, which had come up, opened with grape on the Mexican columns but they continued to advance, their vanguard rising from the ravine and proceeding along its both sides while pouring a withering fire down into the invisible Americans. With only three guns blazing away on the plateau and the volunteers caught in the ravine it began to look very serious.

Somebody snatched the field glass out of Livingston's hand.

"That's mine, damn it all!" exclaimed Cousins. "Where did you get—Jesus! They must be pulverizing those poor buggers of Illinois and Kentucky volunteers."

He turned to Taylor.

"General . . . sir . . . let me . . ." he began in an excited voice.

But Taylor had kicked Old Whitey in the haunch and was moving away. His staff streamed after him.

The little group of horsemen, following the commander, rode deliberately into the outer fringe of the fighting and Livingston could hear the tiny whispers of musket balls over his head. *Psst. Psst.* And sometimes the *tzing* of a spent shot. He resisted the inclination continually to duck his head, reasoning that by the time he heard the sound the bullet had passed. Taylor was disturbed and angry. The young officer could see that. Old Zach was worried at the plight of the volunteers and the absence of any supports on the plateau. He was continually sending messengers to the troops to the left of the plateau, urging them to speed up and to the artillery and cavalry who must cross ridges and ravines with jaded horses. Something had got out of hand here but just what it was Livingston could not say. Cousins, however, was vocal enough. "The old man should have stayed on the defensive," he declared jerkily. "He never should have thrown those green volunteers forward without supports. They're as ignorant as my arse." Livingston, maintaining his seat with difficulty in his wet slippery saddle, saved his breath.

Taylor suddenly pitched sideways and a cry of alarm escaped Major Bliss, who was riding beside him.

The general recovered himself immediately.

"It's nothing, Bliss," he said testily. "Let's get on."

In rapid succession two balls had passed through his clothing, one through his left sleeve above the elbow between the arm and the body and the other through the breast of his coat, cutting through the lining and coming out at a buttonhole.

"We'd better . . ." started Major Bliss concernedly but got no further when Taylor turned a taut angry face toward him. The old man was in a fury but he was as solid as ever. He knew what he was doing and he meant to finish it. He might not have the polish and theory of a West Point man but he was a leader and that was all that counted at this moment. The blackened rain-soaked cannoneers of O'Brien and Thomas knew it as they rammed their charges home, fired, swabbed their guns and reloaded again. The tide of Mexicans continued to advance toward the three barking guns and the musketry fire and screaming from the long ravine made a terrible music; the situation seemed impossible, three guns against an unending flood of infantry and a trapped body of badly trained men in a ravine whose farther end was already blocked by Mexican Lancers; but confidence and determination were riding with Taylor and all who saw him knew it. Old Zach would work it out in some way. And even as Livingston thought this he heard behind him the roar of Washington's guns and knew that the battery holding the pass at La Angostura was shelling the mouth of the ravine opening on the Saltillo Road, blowing it clear so that the trapped volunteers could escape the murderous cross-fire that way and seek shelter behind the spitting guns.

Almost simultaneously with this reassuring thunder Livingston saw Bragg's battery, his men whipping hell out of their exhausted horses, reach the plateau, rumble into place and unlimber. They were in the very nick of time, for O'Brien and Thomas, now working but two guns and with all their horses dead and their ammunition practically exhausted, appeared about to be swallowed up by the charging floods of Mexican infantry. Taylor wheeled and galloped toward Bragg, followed by his staff. The battery captain, his face streaked black with powder, glanced up with a crooked grin.

"What are you using, captain, grape or canister?" called the General.

"Canister, general," shouted Bragg.

"Single or double?" demanded Taylor.

"Single," came the answer.

"Well, double-shot your guns and give 'em hell!" ordered Taylor, spots of red showing in his weathered cheeks.

Just as Bragg began firing, Sherman's battery, his gasping winded horses stumbling in their traces, topped the rise to the plateau. A moment later Davis's Mississippians and the Indiana regiments poured from north and left across the end of the plateau and went in to support for the artillery. To Livingston all this reinforcement appearing so suddenly and at the most crucial moment and in the right place seemed like a miracle. Bragg's first discharge of canister caused the Mexicans to hesitate, his second and third drove them back in disorder. The Mississippians poured a galling fire into the enemy right flank and in a few minutes the masses of infantry that had been advancing so triumphantly crumbled into a horde of frightened men fleeing pell-mell toward the mountains.

For the next hour Livingston, moving from place to place on the plateau with Taylor and his staff, observed a chase and a rout. Bragg would limber up, move forward and go into battery again and blast the disordered retreating Mexicans with canister. The Mississippians and Indiana regiments, in strong support, advanced with him, their muskets and rifles spurting a continual flame. Dead bodies, horses, lances, shakos, muskets, ammunition boxes, knapsacks, water canteens, coats, swords and flags littered the damp broken ground. The rain had stopped completely and an early dusk was falling. A sickening stench of gunpowder, burned flesh, piss, vomit, blood and rotting wetness rose like a swamp miasma from the plateau.

The couriers continued to ride in to Taylor with reports of what was happening on other parts of the disputed ground. The volunteers in the ravine had escaped and were now behind the protection of Washington's guns but the slaughter had been terrific. Hardin and McKee were dead and so, too, was Lieutenant Colonel Henry Clay, Jr., the son of the statesman. The Mexican cavalry that had attempted to cut the Saltillo Road between Saltillo and the hacienda of Buena Vista had been beaten back by guns of the First and Third Artillery and a company of Illinois volunteers. Colonel Jefferson Davis had been hit in the heel by a Mexican ball and was being treated in a first-aid tent near the road. His Mississippians were now commanded by Major Bradford. Taylor listened to the couriers without a change of expression. He had exhibited neither triumph nor despair during the long frantic day, nothing but anger. In the growing twilight Livingston, his weary legs barely able to clutch the slippery hide of his horse, listened to the diminishing gunfire and wondered if this was really victory. First Lieutenant Cousins seemed anxious to tell him.

"We're exactly where we were this morning," he said disgustedly.

"Santa Anna still holds his positions on the mountain. We'll have the same thing to do tomorrow."

Tomorrow? Livingston turned his head and peered through the dusk at the talkative young officer.

"Do you mean we shall have to fight this battle all over again?" he demanded.

Cousins started to whistle "Benny Havens, Oh" and stopped.

"That's war," he replied cheerfully. "And Christ alone knows if we can stand another day like this."

Livingston groaned inwardly.

Santa Anna had been closeted for twenty minutes in his tent with the three riders from Mexico City and Juan Diego, with several young aides in overlarded uniforms, sat on empty boxes in the deep dusk by the lowered flap of the door and waited. No one had anything to say. The young officer had the feeling that he had passed through heaven and hell during the long turbulent day. He had walked on the heights of triumph and descended into the depths of defeat. He had seen the cavalry and infantry go forth in magnificent order and he had watched them come back in tattered and disorganized fragments. He had heard the wailing of the women and the shouting of the Lancers, the blare of the bands, the beating of the drums, the brassy cries of the bugles, and, above all this, the constant reverberation of the big guns. He had looked into black smoke and opaque rain. His mind was filled with contradictory pictures, splintered bits like broken mirrors, men riding and rushing into action, banners and guidons waving, men falling, men retreating, men recovering and turning, men lying dead with their blank faces lifted to the dark clouds. All of it merged until he was incapable of detaching one action from another, of saying this happened here and that happened there, it was at this hour or that hour, this was when Ampudia drove down from the mountain and that was when Torrejón's clattering lines of cavalry, their bright pennons fluttering from the long lances, had ridden all the way around the Yanqui left. He hardly remembered exactly what he had done himself during the day, what messages he had delivered, what places he had visited. It was all too jumbled, too inextricably intertangled. The one dominant fact in his mind was that the Yanqui lines had not been broken, that Santa Anna was not in Saltillo and that the American provision trains were not in the hands of the Mexican commissary. It meant, too, that all must be attempted again the next day.

It was cold and he looked sideways to see what his companions were doing.

The pockmarked aide, who had pursued him like his shadow all day, was sitting with clasped hands between his legs.

"What are you thinking about, Señor Teniente?" asked Juan Diego softly.

The pockmarked aide looked up and scowled.

"I was thinking how nice it would be to be eating a fine turkey mole before a wood fire in my father's house in Pachuca," he said angrily.

"You are from Hidalgo," remarked Juan Diego.

"I am Mariano Aviraneta of Pachuca," explained the pockmarked aide, "and I am the bastard child of a burro to be here."

Juan Diego recalled how enthusiastic Mariano Aviraneta had been during the first part of the day.

"We will finish it tomorrow," he said without confidence. "The Yanquis have suffered worse than we have and we outnumber them."

"Guay!" muttered the other. "I wish I was in Pachuca."

A lone gun boomed in the growing darkness, a grim reminder of the thunders that had so recently died away.

"It is simple," persisted Juan Diego. "We have shown ourselves to be a match for the Yanquis. See, we are still here. Tomorrow we will drive them into the hills. We will—"

"I am hungry," broke in Mariano Aviraneta. "I am hungry and you talk about fighting tomorrow."

He stood up abruptly and walked away.

Juan Diego wondered why he was talking at all. He knew no more than the young men about him what would happen tomorrow. *Was* there any food left? And if there wasn't could the men and horses stand another day's fighting? He suddenly remembered that he had not eaten all day. The general had ordered him to eat that morning but the cold food in the tent had disgusted him and he had walked away from it. He had not felt hungry. He was not hungry now. And he didn't feel tired. He was exhausted with reaction from the confused mass of fragmentary memories of the day that still spun crazily in his head but he was not tired. He got up, too, and began to walk back and forth before the closed entrance to the general's pabellón. The other aides watched him for a moment in silence and then returned their eyes to the lower distance where in the darkness the bright fires of the Americans were increasing like a bed of flickering flowers.

The cloth covering to the general's pabellón was thrust aside and many boots scratched on rock as a dozen men came out. Juan Diego paused in his walk. He recognized the general, the three messengers from Mexico City, Ampudia, Ortega and Pacheco.

"Very well, then," Santa Anna said in a thick weary voice. "If that is the opinion of all then it must be done. If Gómez Farías cannot stamp out . . ."

He stopped and peered about him.

"Who is there?" he called. "Is that you, Juanillo?"

Juan Diego stepped into the light that shone from the tent. He saw that the general's eyes were bloodshot and his lips puffy. Ortega and Pacheco were sullen and scowling. The three strange messengers from the capital presented the blank faces of political underlings.

"Juanillo," said Santa Anna, grasping the young officer by the arm. "Are you too exhausted to ride? It seems I am no longer . . . Well, well, let it go. Juanillo, I want you to skirt the mountain range in a northerly direction and find Torrejón. Tell him to fall back with his cavalry to Agua Nueva. Tell him . . . Well, that is all. Just tell him that. Inform him that I will meet him at Agua Nueva. Ortega!"

The general, releasing the young man's arm, turned.

"My general," said Juan Diego quickly. "Aren't we going to hold our old positions here? Surely, in the morning—"

"Will you be off!" shouted Santa Anna irritably. "Por Dios! It seems we are all tactical commanders in this army. Ortega!"

It was apparent that the general was on the verge of one of his nervous rages.

Juan Diego moved off into the darkness and slid down the declivity to where the horses were tethered. He mounted a small mare which he recognized as belonging to Santa Anna and set off in the general direction in which he supposed he was to go. He did not have the slightest idea where Torrejón's cavalry might be but he remembered that earlier in the day mounted troops had penetrated as far as the hacienda of Buena Vista and it was possible that he would encounter Torrejón somewhere near there. Keeping well to his right of the plateau and taking advantage of the constant gorges and ravines he proceeded along the foot of the mountain. His horse occasionally stumbled and once or twice he had to make lengthy detours to avoid slashes in the rocky ground too precipitous for his mount. It was dark and it was lonely. There were strange noises that might be anything from a dislodged stone crashing into the low brush to a Yanqui picket with a cocked rifle. The stench of the battle seemed to have settled into the hollows. Once, when his horse stumbled, he glanced down and thought that what he saw was a human body. Why had that man died here? Was he Mexican or American? He supposed that they would be finding forgotten bodies in odd places for months to come. Some would never be found but would rot to pieces and become a part of the indifferent earth. Brighter flowers would grow there and that would be all.

The thin light of a moon swathed in semitransparent clouds vaguely lighted the way and with devilish ingenuity transformed rocks and bushes into crouching men. It was getting terribly cold and a sharp insistent wind cut like a knife into Juan Diego's flesh. The horse scraped and clattered, making a monstrous noise that must be heard as far as Saltillo. Juan Diego crouched in the saddle and endeavored to stop his body from trembling. It was the cold that made one feel drowsy. It congealed the blood and dulled the senses and weighed upon the eyelids. To keep thinking. That was it. He guided the horse around a huge boulder that must have fallen from high up on the mountain. It looked like a gun caisson. Perhaps the shelling had dislodged it. The very sound of cannon fire could start avalanches. To think. Well, there was the general. One who knew him had but to look at him and see that things had not gone right. The demon that was in him had risen to the surface and was peering out of his bloodshot eyes. But with all its fury it was a calculating demon and was watching everybody and everything and measuring, measuring and planning and studying and . . . and understanding. Demon or no demon, it was impossible to question the general's courage. He could face anything without flinching. Even bad news from Mexico City. Those three messengers. Well, the general would know what to do. It was a lie that he ever *became* defeat. He always found a way out of it as he had found a way out of the debacle of San Jacinto. He would return in triumph as he had returned more than once before and the doors of the National Palace in the capital would swing open before him. Defeat . . . Juan Diego shook his head. Why was he thinging of defeat? There had been no defeat. There had been nothing more than a long-drawn-out bloody inconclusive action. Tomorrow . . . tomorrow . . . tomorrow . . . Por Dios! He was dozing. He straightened up in the saddle and rode along for a while, his eyes on the vague trail. Many horses had passed this way. There was fresh dung. There was a lance thrust into a bush, its soaked guidon hanging limp in spite of the wind. It was frozen. That was it. It was frozen. To his right he could see faraway fires burning. The Yanquis . . . the . . . the . . . the . . .

His horse had stopped and he opened his eyes to discover that he was surrounded by a shadowy group of men who were leaning toward him from their saddles. The bridle of his mount was tightly clutched in a big hairy hand.

"Git down, sonny," drawled a deep voice. "We want to git a good look at our little manikins."

Juan Diego automatically slid to the ground.

Rough hands ran over his body, relieving him of his pistol, knife and sword.

"It's a little Mex all right," said another voice. "What nice shiny boots. Prob'ly from Santy Anny's staff. Th' rest of 'em mostly go barefoot."

"Th' little bastard!" piped a high voice. "We don't have to bring 'em *all* back do we, capt'n? Let's cut out his liver and eat it."

"Shet up, Higbee," ordered the deep voice. "These fellers don't speak no English. It's all quién sabe with 'em."

Juan Diego was wide-awake now. He saw that he was surrounded by a group of mounted men, one or two of them had dismounted, who wore no recognizable uniforms but were clad in outlandish civilian garb. The hats ranged from Panamas to slouch and the jackets and breeches thrust into big riding boots were various shades of black, gray and brown. Colt revolvers and big ugly-looking knives swung from their belts and every man carried a rifle. Something tugged in the back of Juan Diego's mind. Texians. Of course. They were Texians. Texas Rangers. He had heard of them around many a campfire during the last three months. A feeling of fatality icily suffused him and he glanced up stubbornly at the bearded faces. Let them do what they would. At least, they would not see him cringe. Apparently he had fallen asleep in the saddle and ridden right into the midst of them. Let the wine of San Lorenzo sustain him now. He would speak no word until his trial was finished.

One of the dismounted men struck him heavily in the face. He staggered and recovered his balance.

"What's yore name, you God-damned Mex?" his assailant demanded.

Juan Diego compressed his lips tightly and stared unseeingly into the other's eyes.

"He don't want to answer," piped the high voice. "Hit 'im agin, capt'n."

"Shet up, Higbee," growled the man addressed as captain. "I'm in command here."

He grabbed Juan Diego by the shoulders and shook him violently.

"Don't you speak English?" he bawled. "Christ Awmighty, I'm askin' you what yore God-damned name is!"

Juan Diego maintained his silence.

The captain slapped his face and turned away.

"Rope 'im up, boys," he said. "And let's find some more."

Great bonfires were burning on both sides of the road that passed by the hacienda of Buena Vista and by their light Livingston could see the debris of the fighting that had taken place here late in the afternoon. The rutted road and uneven countryside were littered with equipment, lances, boxes, muskets, headgear, dead horses and men's bodies. The thick wall of the hacienda was pitted by shot. Livingston turned his horse in by the gate and was accosted by a grimy noncommissioned officer with a yellow handkerchief wrapped about his head for protection. A squad of ragged weary men filled the gateway.

"Lieutenant Livingston," explained the young officer to the sergeant. "Is Colonel Yell here? I have a message . . ."

"He's here all right," replied the sergeant grimly. "You'll find him in what's left of th' old grain-storage house lying alongside Captain Porter and Adjutant Vaughn. We're waitin' fer wagons to take the bodies into Saltillo."

"He was killed?" asked Livingston quickly.

"Yes, sir," answered the man in the yellow handkerchief. "All of 'em was killed. We'd a got him into town before this but we was usin' the wagons fer the wounded. Just cleared out over a hundred of 'em."

"It was pretty hot here, then," remarked Livingston for want of anything better to say.

He was neither surprised nor shocked. In the face of the inevitable all words were futile.

"Jesus Christ, sir, it was terrible," declared the sergeant earnestly. "We was in position near the spring when the Mex Lancers come down on us like bats out o' hell. Captain Porter yelled to us to hold our fire until the buggers was near. Then we let' em have it. They rid right into us an' it was just a gang fight. Sabers agin lances and fists agin jaws. You couldn't see fer the dust. Jesus Christ! They pushed us right back to the wall here and then the Arkansas men on the flat roofs give 'em such a shower of musket balls that they bust up. Part of 'em went back toward the mountains and the others went around to th' west. Hollering all the time they was. Hot, you say, mister? I never hope to see it agin."

"Two guns come up an' give 'em what-for, too," interrupted a lanky private with a big boil beside his nose.

"That was Reynolds," said the sergeant. "They's over thirty Mex bodies out there yit. Do we have to bury 'em, too, sir? I never been in a fight before."

"I saw them," replied Livingston shortly. "Your officers will tell you what to do. Who is in com—"

A trampling of horses and rough voices interrupted him and he drew his mare to one side just in time to permit a dozen riders, Texans from the grotesque appearance of the costumes, to trot through the gate into the courtyard. In the glare of the nearest bonfire he could see that they were escorting prisoners, men probably picked up in dark gullies or found wandering haphazardly behind the American lines. These unfortunate fellows were trotting and stumbling along on foot in the midst of the horses, their hands pinioned behind them and ropes running from their necks to the saddle pommels of the mounted men. There were six or seven of them. They passed swiftly but not before Livingston observed a grizzled officer in a Lancer's uniform bleeding from an ugly cut on the side of his head and a slim young man with a grim set face and puzzled wide-set hazel eyes. The young man lifted his head as he was half-pulled by and stared vaguely for an instant at Livingston. The American officer, impelled by an impulse that was spontaneous and unexplainable, hastily averted his glance.

"The' Rangers bin roundin' 'em up fer the last two hours," said the sergeant, staring after the hurrying group. "Real devils with 'em, they are. Don't like 'em at all. Clout 'em on the head with their sabers every chance they git."

"That's right, sargint," agreed the lanky private. "I reckon them Rangers ain't fergit Goliad and th' Alamo."

"Well, 'tain't none o' my pudden," remarked the sergeant. "I ain't got nothin' agin 'em. I'm from Kentucky."

"I'll ride up to the big house," said Livingston abruptly. "I suppose headquarters is still there?"

"Colonel Marshall's there, lootenant," answered the sergeant.

Livingston urged his horse across the vast courtyard lined with deserted peons' quarters and dismounted before the open door of the case grande. His face was set and frowning as though he were trying to discover what it was that was plucking at his mind. It wouldn't come. Colonel Marshall had left, presumably to seek out General Taylor who was supposed to have ridden on to Saltillo, and so Livingston delivered his message (one concerning the hurried removal of all wounded from Buena Vista, which might form the center of the next day's fighting) to the unknown captain in charge at the hacienda. The harassed captain nodded briefly and began to bawl for teamsters. Livingston, uncertain whether to ride on to Saltillo or not, walked out into the courtyard and stood beside the drooping head of his mare for several minutes with a puzzled expression on his face. He was trying to remember something that would not come back to him. What made it more perplexing and irritating was that he could not orient this urge or even tell what had aroused it. It was something but whether it was in the past or the present, in Mexico or in the States, he could not say. It was close behind the baffling veil of his memory, though; if he knew how he could stretch out his will and easily encompass it; but he didn't know how. He would have to look for a sign.

Still puzzled and brooding, he turned without thinking and walked through the great entrance of the casa grande that led to the inner court where an uneasy line of unfed saddle horses were haltered to the adobe pillars that supported the second story. He walked along the black and white tiled arcade, his spurs jingling, until he came to the rear entrance that presumably led into the kitchen patio. Here a dozen guards were loitering about a fire over which one young soldier was heating a stew that appeared to be made from a skinned degutted rabbit, black corn and peppers.

"Prisoners in there, lieutenant," said one of the guards as Livingston paused and stared into the kitchen patio where several fires were burning.

"I see," said the young officer vaguely.

He glanced about the square enclosure for a moment and then stepped past the guards and walked over to one of the fires. A dozen barefooted Indians, one or two with bloodstained bandages around their heads, were crouched about the flame warming their hands and scratching for lice. They lifted expressionless black eyes to Livingston's face, studied him briefly and then looked away. There was a sort of stolid hopelessness about them, a passive fatalism that was disturbing. They stank and their dark leathery skins were ingrained with years of dirt and yet they preserved an aloofness that came close to a withdrawn dignity, a rightfulness of being that belong to them alone and to nobody else. Livingston wondered what they thought about and how they saw the world about them. He knew that he could never find out. He was outside of them and would always be outside of them, a man from another existence of which they knew nothing and desired to know nothing. He turned away, invisibly drawn by the uncomfortable urge within him, and moved toward another fire.

There were officers here, a tall lean Lancer with an abnormally narrow face, a short squat fellow in a dirty white tunic with a bold Semitic nose and a thin ragged mustache and goatee, the grizzled officer with the livid cut on the side of his head, and the slim young man with the puzzled eyes. Again the feeling that there was something that he should remember, nay, that he *must* remember, surged back into Livingston's mind and he stood for a long time looking at the prisoners, his eyes flitting from face to face and finding nothing but a tired antagonism, withdrawn but steadfast. The lean Lancer looked beyond him, his narrow face like an ax blade waiting for the arm that would swing it; the squat fellow raised pudgy fingers toward his goatee and then dropped them as though the effort was not worth the result; the grizzled officer with the ugly cut sat with closed eyes oblivious to everything; and the slim young man in the shining boots appeared to watch and not watch with a contained arrogance that was calculated and sustained. This was the enemy.

Far back in his consciousness a perplexing question like a small dog scratching at a closed door irritated Livingston's mind: Why was this the enemy? Who had made them so? Was it the Congress in Washington? Was it President Polk? Was it the Mexican people? Was it the people of Texas? But the question went away and his mind, that had not opened the door and let it in, filled with other images. He stood stubbornly in the firelight endeavoring to discover what he was seeking, what he must remember. It pulled him far back. San Felipe? Yes.

He saw a brown street and a dead woman and a red-faced man much the worse for liquor. Think hard. Dive back. Seek. Yes. Men on horses. Men with guns. Belita. Enriqueta. Charley. Charley. The names came fast now. The forgotten past flooded in upon him and he saw the dry streets of San Felipe where the powdered dust rose like a smoke about the horses' hoofs and the heavy-wheeled creaking wagons and the sleeping Indians in the shadowy corners and fat Belita bowed over the brasero while she turned the tortillas and pimply Enriqueta in the stained cotton dress and the flushed face of his father as he tipped the mezcal bottle to his mouth and Mr. Alphonsus Ewing smacking his long lips and pushing back his flowing curls and declaiming on the virtues of Tennessee. And Charley . . . Charley!

He knew.

He walked around the fire to the slim young man and stood looking down on him. Wide-set hazel eyes met his with a startled admission.

"You are my brother Charley," said Livingston in a voice hampered by the thickness in his throat. "That's who you are. You're Charley."

The young man in the Mexican uniform stood up.

"You're not dead. You're Charley," said Livingston.

He caught him by the arm and began to walk with him toward the entrance that led out of the kitchen patio. The group of Indians watched them pass with black obsidian eyes on which the firelight flickered. At the entrance the soldiers looked up from their cooking and a sergeant made a half-gesture with his hand.

"You got authority to take that man, lootenant?" he asked. "Old McCulloch warned us to be mighty careful with 'em."

"It's all right," said Livingston and marveled at the evenness of his voice.

The sergeant looked doubtful and then turned back to the concoction of stewed rabbit. His shoulders seemed to say, Oh, what the hell . . .

Livingston, still holding the young man tightly by the arm, cut across the courtyard to the door where he had left his mare. The horse, cold and hungry, whinnied gently. Livingston thrust his free arm through the hanging reins and proceeded toward the outer gate of the hacienda facing the Saltillo Road. The unknown captain, bawling indignantly for teamsters, brushed against him but did not see him. Beyond the gate Livingston, continuing the clutching grasp on the young man's arm and followed by his mare, picked his way through the debris to a spot some hundred feet south of the bonfires. Here he released the young man and stepped back to study his face by the soft light of the distant flames. Both men looked at each other for a long time and both recognized the similarity of their features, and, more than that, the common blood that stared out of their eyes and inexorably accepted each other.

"I thought you were dead, Charley," said Livingston in a low voice.

"David. David, I remember you," said the young man, speaking for the first time in English but with a decided accent.

"You were killed at the Alamo," insisted Livingston. "They told Mr. Ewing. There was proof. They buried your body at . . ."

"It was another boy," said the other. "I remember him. A big boy from . . . from Nacogdoches, I think. No. I went to Mexico. I went to Mexico to live."

Livingston cleared his throat.

"Are you . . . all right?" he asked huskily.

"Yes, I am all right," answered his brother. "And you, David?"

"Oh, yes."

Livingston laughed jerkily and touched the other's arm.

"It's all pretty sudden, isn't it?" he asked foolishly. "I mean . . . like this . . . with everything . . ."

"It is like a miracle," said his brother solemnly.

They lapsed into silence for a moment and the mare pawed restlessly.

"Well," declared Livingston, "I think we'd better ride on to Saltillo. Have you got a horse? Of course not. I'll get you one. Or else . . . I'll explain everything to Colonel Davis . . . he's a good fellow . . . and get you out of that uniform . . . did they force you to wear it? . . . of course . . . there'll be some sort of legal . . . I mean . . . well, it'll be fine to have you back again . . . I'm sure Senator Ewing . . ."

He paused in his floundering speech as he sensed a cold stiffening in the slender figure before him. His brother's eyes were cold and fixed in expression.

"What is it?" he demanded. "Don't you want . . . why, for God's sake . . ."

"As a Mexican officer of junior grade I suppose I can be exchanged," said the other deliberately. "You must know that we captured many of your men."

"Good God, Charley!" exclaimed Livingston, staring in amazement at his brother. "You don't *mean* to say that you want to live down there? Don't you want to live in a civilized country . . . in the United States . . . in your own country?"

"No!" said his brother with a finality that was beyond argument.

Livingston tried to repress the anger that was rising within him.

"We've just found each other," he said desperately. "It was a miracle. You said that. I know that a lot of terrible things have hap-

pened to you. I know that they've brought you up down there not to
know your own country and how good it is. You haven't had a chance
to know how big the United States is. But you'll find out. I'll send you
to Washington where Senator Ewing will look after you. Maybe he'll
get you into West Point. Why, Charley, you must be twenty years old,
at least."

"I am not a citizen of the United States," declared his brother.
"I am a citizen of the Republic of Mexico. I don't want to be a citizen
of the United States."

"Look here . . ." began Livingston in a loud voice and then he
caught himself. "Gosh, Charley, we always used to fight. Remember?
We wouldn't be together ten minutes before we started pummeling each
other. Let's not fight now. Let's . . ."

"We've been fighting each other all day," broke in the other
heatedly, "and we damned near licked you, too."

"Licked!" exclaimed Livingston. "Now, look here. Well, never
mind. We'll talk of all these things when we aren't so tired. You look
awful tired, Charley. You need sleep. A lot of it. Let's get going to
Saltillo. We'll fix everything up there and straighten out things tomorrow. My God, but it's good to see you again. It makes me feel as
though I had a family of my own at last. Do you remember fat old
Belita and her . . ."

"If you want to take me to Saltillo as a prisoner of war you can
do so," said his brother. "I can apply for exchange there as well as
here."

Livingston rubbed his hand across his scrubby chin.

"You *have* changed," he declared. "You have forgotten completely
that you are an American. You . . ."

"I was a Texan when Texas was a part of Mexico," broke in the
other. "Do you remember that our father would let us speak nothing
but Spanish? It was our language. It . . ."

"We were born in Massachusetts," said Livingston.

"What does it matter where we were born?" exclaimed his
brother. "My country is where my heart is. But if you want reason I
will give you reason. I stand upon the principle of rightful sovereignty.
Texas was ours before there was a United States. It was part of the
old Spanish possessions and when we freed ourselves from Spain we
freed Texas with us. You have no right here. You are strangers. Your
civilization is not our civilization."

Livingston's eyebrows drew together in a puzzled frown.

"That is not true," he said. "We come as deliverers. The free
Republic of Texas chose to unite with us and we . . ."

"Texas is and was nothing but a revolted province," exclaimed
the other heatedly. "It is our problem. In your delirious ambition you

aspire to plant your unclean flag, the emblem of treason, ingratitude and injustice, on our free soil."

"The population of Texas desired annexation," declared Livingston.

"Your barbarians came in and begged land from us and we gave it to them and then they fomented a rebellion," said his brother earnestly. "There isn't a Mexican in Texas who wants to live under your flag."

Livingston shook his head.

"Charley," he said, "they have filled you with poison. You cannot see. Burke said, 'Nobody will be argued into slavery.'"

"Slavery!" flashed his brother. "Tell that to your Negroes in the cotton fields. All that you want is another slave state. There is no slavery in Mexico. We are all free, white, brown and black. How do you dare to invent such arguments? You are warring upon an innocent neighbor. You bring havoc into our own country. You want Texas and all the lands through California so that you can spread out at our expense. That is the real reason. Everything else is trumped up, including the old American claims. You are invaders. You are fighting on Mexican soil. Your hands are not clean."

"Jesus Christ!" exploded Livingston, completely losing his temper. "What are you saying? Have you ever thought of responsibility and progress? Mexico is not a republic, it is a chaos. It is a land of anarchy. I am sorry for the common people but I have no sympathy for the leaders. They are all plunderers and thieves. We bring free institutions, freedom, democracy, equality . . ."

"Yes, I know. Manifest destiny," sneered the other. "I have heard it before. A holy excuse to justify the invasion of a sovereign people."

"You are not a soverign people," shouted Livingston. "You are the backwash of the foundered Spanish Empire. There isn't a peon in your country that isn't worse off than the lowliest slave in our southern states. You're a bunch of murderers. You're—"

He stopped abruptly and fairly gasped for breath. A feeling of frustration and shame and loneliness swept away his anger and a gnawing desire to repossess his brother filled his heart. The miracle of meeting was transformed into an inevitable event and now he saw nothing unusual in it at all. Surprise was swallowed up in desire and a flood of affectionate memories filled his mind. He looked into the distant face of his brother and refused to see a stranger there. He put his arm about the taut stubborn shoulders and laughed shakily. What in hell did the United States or Mexico matter? They were names, divisions, plans, colored segments on a map. The heart knew no boundaries and the soul was above all differences. *This is my brother. This is my flesh*

and blood. We issued bloodstained and helpless from the same womb.
He clasped his brother to him tightly and fumbled for words.

"We must not talk this way to each other," he said. "Everything
will work itself out if we do not talk this way to each other. How you
have grown! I recognized our mother's eyes in you. Do you remember
her? She wasn't very happy, was she? She didn't like Texas. She
wanted . . ."

He paused and glanced back at the bonfires blazing before the
gates to the hacienda of Buena Vista. They were sad beacons. They
were the forlorn lights of death sending up their snapping sparks into
the deep night like little souls springing toward heaven. He was sad,
too. He was sad and tired and he did not know what to say. Words
were futile. They were so many prattling little misrepresentations of
what the heart desired to say. He pressed his brother closer to him and
continued to laugh.

"We always fight," he said. "Always . . . always . . . It is the
Livingston blood in us. Independent. We were always independent.
Do you remember how father went to Bexar? No, no, you were too
young. I think he knew he was going to die but because people told
him not to go, told him he was too old, he just went."

His brother seemed to be yielding to his fast embrace.

"We have a million things to talk about," he went on persuasively.
"Each of us has a lost decade to explain to the other. Each . . ."

"David," said the other in a low voice.

They stared deeply into each other's eyes and Livingston's arm
dropped from his brother's shoulder.

"Yes," he answered. "What is it, Charley?"

"We are two strangers," declared the other in a tone of pity and
regret. "We belong to two different worlds. Oh, it *has* been a miracle
that we should encounter each other again and know that we both lived.
But we cannot live together. I cannot live in your world any more than
you can live in mine. Your very language is alien on my tongue. You
do not even speak mine. Don't you see? Perhaps this is the fault of
evil men on the face of the earth—that we who are brothers in blood
cannot be brothers in spirit. I do not know. I am not versed in these
things. I love you and yet I cannot be a part of you. You love me and
yet you cannot understand the virtues in my world. Neither one of us
is to blame personally for the great gulf that separates us. *Something*
is to blame . . . but what it is neither of us can see. It will take a
lifetime to find it out but perhaps it will not be our lifetime. I know
that I belong to Mexico as you know that you belong to the United
States. How can we, then, belong to each other? Do you see? I do not
speak very clearly in your language . . . but do you see? I must go back
to my own as you must stay with your own. Now . . . will you return

me to the prisoners back there or take me on to Saltillo where I may hope for an exchange?"

Livingston, deeply moved, ran his tongue over his dry lips. A dark and helpless fatality rose up in him and he could not fight against it. He had never pictured the world in which he lived like this before, a world in which brothers could be separated by more than distance and ignorance. They could be separated by awareness, too.

"What do you want me to do?" he asked almost in a whisper.

"I am your prisoner," said his brother.

Livingston thought for a moment and then he disengaged the reins of his horse from his arm and extended them to the other.

"Here, Charley," he said in a determined voice. "Take my horse and ride into your own lines."

His brother took the reins but stood looking at him without mounting.

"Go on," ordered Livingston. "Go on, Charley. I know what I am doing. You are right. We will meet again . . . if not soon, then later. Go, now, and keep a sharp eye out for any pickets or wandering squads hunting for prisoners."

The other swung to the saddle.

"Keep well to your left," directed Livingston in a matter-of-fact manner. "I doubt that you will run into any of our men as late as this. It is after midnight. It is less than two miles to your own lines. Go on, I say."

The mare turned.

"We'll meet again, David," said his brother in a stifled voice.

Livingston lifted his hand in salute as the mare tightened her haunches and sprang forward.

Juan Diego rode in a bewildered dream through the darkness. He rode recklessly, making no attempt to cling to the shadowy side of the mountains, but following the beaten trails now lighted by the cold glow of the moon. A picket, at some distance, challenged him once and there was the loud report of a rifle. He did not even turn his head. Low shrubbery crashed beneath his horse's hoofs, dislodged stones clattered against his stirrups, and then again he was on the hard-beaten trail making a sound like an Indian drum. He passed well to the left of the plateau where he could see bobbing lanterns like little witch fires and smell the stinking aftermath of heavy fighting, an odor he would never forget as long as he lived. Ahead of him the Mexican campfires glowed against the sky, a long crescent of misty illuminated bubbles in the damp air. It was almost time to encounter his own pickets.

The meeting with his brother had become a part of his waking dream. He knew that it had happened and yet it seemed as though it had unexpectedly been fashioned out of a vision. It was both real and unreal. The figure of David standing there in the glow of the bonfire, with drawn brows and puzzled eyes and grim mouth, was as solid as the stony earth over which the mare was fleeing and yet all that had happened had been like an hallucination. But, then, a dozen occurrences during the past eighteen hours had been like hallucinations. War turned the world upside down until the impossible became real and the real became impossible. Reason ceased to exist. Since everything in war was unreal, it seemed quite natural that he should encounter his brother, that he should discover the vast abyss that stretched between them and that he should be galloping back to his own lines through the moon-bathed night. It was all a part of the extraordinary impossibility become possible that was war. One accepted everything and lost everything.

Even love. He knew that he loved his brother the moment he recognized him and yet he had not thought of him for years. He knew that he loved him and yet he could leave him after that momentary meeting without a single regret. He had not even asked one question about his brother's life during all that decade that they had existed apart from each other, one thinking the other dead and the other not thinking at all. It was monstrous and yet it was natural. Perhaps a time would come when the strangeness of all this would pierce his fatalistic armor and rouse him to wonder. But not yet. Not while two armies lay almost within gunshot range of each other under the frozen stars. Not while the dawn was so few hours away, the dawn with its renewed artillery fire and its thundering squadrons of cavalry.

Cavalry! Of course. He had been dispatched hours earlier to find Torrejón and order him to fall back on Agua Nueva. He was to have found Torrejón somewhere on the road to the hacienda of Buena Vista but he had been all the way to that American stronghold and seen no Mexicans except prisoners. Where was Torrejón? It was possible that some other messenger had found him and delivered Santa Anna's message. The general, who was no fool, often sent half a dozen couriers with the same important order. But . . . Agua Nueva. Why Agua Nueva? That was moving backward instead of forward. Perhaps the general desired Torrejón to re-equip his men. That must be it. See, thought Juan Diego, I have put my brother out of my mind already. I am a soldier again, thinking only of war. He mounted a rise and the Mexican campfires blazed in a great arc before his eyes.

But where were the pickets? He would have to tell the general that he had met no pickets. That was probably due to the neglect of Micheltorena.

He rode through the outer ring of campfires nervously alert for a sudden challenge. None came. He reined in his horse and looked about him. There were no men here, no tents here, no horses, no wagons, no piles of ammunition, nothing but disordered debris, empty boxes, stray equipment, bloody rags, broken objects, all the disordered waste that a great host leaves when it hurriedly departs for new places. The general's pabellón was gone. The flags were gone. Juan Diego stared wildly about him with unbelieving eyes. There was no army here at all. It was as though the earth had opened up and swallowed it. There was not even a sound of it, nothing but an oppressive silence through which the deserted campfires sputtered and crackled. A conviction that fairly sickened his stomach possessed the young officer. Those messengers from Mexico City . . . The glum faces of the generals . . . Santa Anna's bloodshot eyes . . . Yes. Yes. Yes. Oh, God, thought Juan Diego, this is the most shameful betrayal of all. In another day we would have been in Saltillo. In another day we would have had the Yanqui baggage trains, pork and all. In another day . . . He touched a spur to the mare and it quivered all over as it broke into a canter across the deserted camp.

He rode for some time, filled with bitter thoughts, shame, and his first distrust of the general. *In victory he became victory; in defeat he became defeat.* But it had not been a defeat. It had been a repulse and a drawn battle. In the pits of Jalapa two gamecocks, one cut, perhaps, were always thrown in for a second round. He had seen a bullfighter who had been tossed over the barrera return to the ring and kill the bull. Why . . . Taylor was still at Buena Vista. Taylor . . . and David . . . As he rode along he heard a faint sound, a cry or a wail, to his right and he turned the mare toward it. In a few minutes he was by a fire where a man in a ragged sergeant's coat lay stretched out, his head pillowed in a woman's lap. The man's hands were interlaced over his stomach and blood flowed from between the fingers. The woman, her black hair fallen over her face, was weeping and occasionally calling out like a dog in pain. Juan Diego dismounted and walked up to them.

"What is it?" he asked in a harsh voice. "What has happened? Where is the army?"

The woman said nothing but kept on crying. The man opened his eyes and his blue lips moved.

"If I . . . let go . . . my hands," gasped the sergeant, "my guts . . . will come . . . out."

Juan Diego shook the woman viciously by the shoulder.

"You," he said. "Look up. Stop howling. What has happened?"

She pulled her black hair tighter over her face and continued to wail.

"Agua Nueva . . ." said the sergeant with difficulty. "All there
. . . or beyond . . ."

Blood began to bubble out of his mouth. The woman wiped it
away with her hair. She peered up at Juan Diego.

"They went away," she cried in a shrill voice. "Ay de mí! They
went away with all the horses and wagons and guns. They took the
wounded in litters, four men to each litter, but they would not take
my man."

She began to cry again in a loud hoarse terrible voice. The sergeant's hands separated over his stomach and a portion of intestine
began to ooze through the black wound. He was dead.

Juan Diego stood looking down at the couple for a full minute
and then he swung himself into the saddle and turned the mare's head
toward Agua Nueva.

Around the silent camp the deserted fires burned forlornly.

Book Three

PUEBLA

Puebla

About ten o'clock in the morning Don Isidro stepped out of his house so beautifully decorated with Talavera tiles and set off in the direction of the cathedral. He had decided to visit his uncle, the bishop, and as the day was fair and sunny it was a pleasure to walk. It gave him an opportunity to think and he had plenty to think about these days. Puebla, he decided as he inhaled the fresh air, was never so charming as on a fine clear April day when the gentle breeze was like wine and the snow-crowned peaks, Popoca-tépetl and Ixtaccíhuatl to the west, Malinche to the north and Orizaba to the east, visibly guarded the plain where glittered in many colors the jewel of the angels. If one's life had to be bounded by a city (God forbid!) there was no better place on earth than Puebla de los Ángeles. It was not Las Golondrinas, not his little absolute kingdom, to be sure, and his decisions were not final here; but neither was it like Mexico City, a simmering volcano of cabals, conspiracies, betrayals and pronunciamientos that erupted periodically and carried off in a lava-flow of violence both the innocent and the guilty. Mother Church was regnant in Puebla and his uncle, the bishop, the visible embodiment of that invisible power, was vicar of the Poblanos. That made it easier for Don Isidro. It made it easier in so far as he was indubitably the black shadow of his uncle, his authorized reflection, so to speak, and that was as near as he could come to the incontestable reality that he felt himself to be at Las Golondrinas.

There he was an absolute monarch and there he would be on this cool April morning if it were not for Doña Ágata. It was her fright that had forced him to pack the coaches and long line of burros and set out for Puebla early in March. An hysteria had seized her. She had been certain that the Americans would arrive any day and, according to her information, gleaned, perhaps, from the hacienda priest, the Americans were horned monsters. They were barbarians who branded captured Mexicans with red-hot irons and sent them into the States to serve as slaves on southern plantations. They impaled babies on bayonets and paraded them through the streets of captured towns. They raped all the women from thirteen years of age to seventy. They robbed and murdered and butchered the livestock and burned the

houses and poisoned the wells. Don Isidro didn't believe all that but
when the news of the action at Buena Vista trickled through about the
last of February and several days later he learned that Santa Anna
was back in San Luis Potosí with a few American guns and standards
and claiming a great victory he grew dubious. If the general had won
a battle why was he and his army nearly three hundred miles south
of it while the Americans, according to all accounts, were still in
Saltillo? Why wasn't the general in Texas? What had happened to the
campaign? Where was Santa Anna's twenty thousand? Was it possible that the bishop was right, after all? Being sensible-minded, Don
Isidro admitted the gravity of these questions and while he did not
believe that the Americans would push as far south as Las Golondrinas he weakened sufficiently to his wife's fearsome prophecies to
remove to Puebla. One, he reasoned, should always provide for con-
tingencies.

But had he?

As a matter of fact, it seemed to him now that he had jumped
precipitately from a frying pan under which there was no fire to a
place that already smelled the heat of an approaching conflagration.
Taylor, so far as he knew, was nowhere near Las Golondrinas, or San
Luis Potosí, for that matter, but it was very certain that the Americans were in Vera Cruz (they had occupied the port on March
twenty-ninth) and already some distance beyond it along the mounting National Highway. Conflicting rumors of a disastrous engagement at Cerro Gordo were spreading through the streets and houses
and cantinas of Puebla. It was to discover the precise truth behind
these rumors that he was on his way to the bishop. The bishop knew
everything. Sometimes it seemed that he knew what had happened
almost before it happened. He would be sure to know about this Cerro
Gordo business. Don Isidro, striding along the neat flat flagstones of
the street over which thrust the tin pipes that carried off rain water
from house roofs, gazed up at the bright mathematical tile design on
the front of the building he was passing and thrust his heavy underlip
out in a mild scowl. He had plenty to think about. No, it looked very
much as though he had fled from the Americans only to fly into the
Americans' arms. It was a stupid effort and he might just as well have
stayed where he was and concerned himself with those young bulls
that he was raising for the summer novilladas in Mexico City. Yet
it was so unusual for the customarily repressed Doña Ágata to insist
that he felt no lessening in himself for yielding. Both the insistence
and the yielding, in a way, were unprecedented precedents that established nothing but the disjointed articulation of the time. Everything
was breaking apart. It almost seemed as though a world was bursting
like an old ship on black alien rocks. Still, the sun continued to shine

in Puebla and that was something. One could preserve a sort of balance while the sun shone and the ominous cracking sounds were far away.

The two timid beggars at the corner observed the large caballero in buckskin pantaloons tight at the hips and flaring around the bunchy calves and extended their hands apologetically as they softly chanted their litany for alms. Don Isidro passed majestically with an automatic, "Dios los ampare, hermanitos." He lifted his eyes to the two dark towers of the cathedral and saw the yellowish encrusted domes that topped them clear-cut against the deep-blue sky. Each raised a globe and cross to the Glory of God. There was something else to think about. Yes, God was insuperably installed in Puebla. He was housed in churches and chapels and monasteries and convents. He was served by priests and monks and nuns and friars. Bells tolled and chimed constantly and when the Elevation of the Host was silverly announced from the cathedral men, women and children, and sometimes the donkeys, fell to their knees in the plaza and adjacent streets and remained so until the Holy Office was completed. Clerics in religious habits and shovel hats abounded in the thoroughfares, walking with rapt faces, smiling and discoursing, scowling and intent or frankly begging with outstretched palms in the name of Our Lady. Sacred images in wood painted blue and gold and bright red were paraded from church portal to church portal. All the intense and possessive machinery of Rome was visible here in a higher degree than in any other city in Mexico. It truly was something to think about. At Las Golondrinas there was only the one little church and the subservient rabbitlike priest. But Puebla . . . Don Isidro rather doubted the legend that when the Indians were unsuccessfully struggling to hoist the heavy bells to the towers of the cathedral the Angels of the Lord came down and helped them but he thought that it was a clever idea, as clever as the stories of Our Lady of Guadalupe and Our Lady of the Remedies, and a fit legend for a sacred city. After all, myth and actuality were inextricably mingled into each other in the Holy Body of the Church and it was futile and stupid to try to separate one from the other. They mingled to make a divine essence that was all spirit and yet contained in it all flesh and that was a mystery beyond human understanding. The fact that a friar had lice did not lessen the sanctity of the Veil. However, Don Isidro was not in a religious mood as he passed a side door of the cathedral and meditated whether or not to go in and light a candle. He decided against it and moved on toward the plaza. The bishop would be at his villa, anyway. And Doña Ágata and María Catalina might be in the cathedral. Doña Ágata was forever lighting candles.

As he approached the plaza where the market was in full activity his thoughts reverted somewhat reluctantly to his daughter. In a moment of disconcerting frankness the day after her marriage he had acknowledged his guilt toward her although neither to her nor to Doña Ágata directly. The acknowledgment had been stamped indelibly on his grim face at midday when he had confronted a surly fuzzy-minded Don Alejandro and unsmilingly suggested that as Doña María Catalina's health was suddenly impaired it might be advisable for her husband to make an immediate and indefinite visit to Mexico City. Don Alejandro, observing his father-in-law's uncompromising visage through one good eye (the other was closed and the color and size of a ripe plum), had ungraciously acquiesced. Don Isidro, catching a flash of his own face in a nearby mirror, recognized the angry acknowledgment of his guilt toward his daughter and was plunged straightway into a condition of uncertainty that remained with him to this very moment when he crossed the round stones toward the humming plaza of Puebla. He was guilty and yet he could not blame himself. Inevitable circumstances, he doggedly argued to what might be his conscience, had placed him in this predicament. He had made a vow and he had fulfilled a vow and that was justice to himself although it might be injustice to others. There were moments when he wanted to explain all this to Doña Ágata and María Catalina, to explain that a vow was a vow just as an earthquake was an earthquake or a west wind was a west wind, that an oath never broken was a tower of mental and spiritual strength, that a word given and never recalled was a vindication of man's integrity as he visualized it, but the opportune instant never seemed to arrive as precisely as it should and his instinctive feeling that explanations were admissions and therefore a sign of weakness prevented him from speaking. It was sometimes painful in the hard metal armor of his pride. Yet he lurked there and acted himself with the skill of long habit.

Days passed. Don Alejandro wrote several threatening letters from Mexico City but the hacendado forwarded orders and money drafts to his agent there and the agent, a clever and understanding man, did what was necessary and silenced, at least for the time being, the disgraced husband. Young Lorenzo went back to the Military College at Chapultepec and Doña Ágata presented red-rimmed eyes over the dinner table for a week. And to the casual unsuspecting eye María Catalina continued as unresponsive and placid as before her unconsummated marriage.

Yet she was not the same. Don Isidro was too unversed in the subtle emanations spreading from a young girl's personality to make them explicit even to himself but he felt it and inwardly resented it for it laid an onus upon him that he did not like to feel he deserved. He wanted relationships to remain as they had been before the marriage.

His emotional life had been simple and crude and once violent and it pleased him to assert that it was over and done with. It belonged to a growing state and now he had grown. Having reached that point of time when the follies of youth, the uncertainties of passion, the uneven responsibilities of intimate relationships and the hazards of clashing personalities should (as he saw it) no longer disturb his self-centered empery and tranquil existence, he was angrily averse to the threat of undesired complications. He was fifty years old and he did not want the carefully arranged mold of life he had perfected for himself broken by outside blows. María Catalina, without saying a word or visibly changing her obedient status, had become such a threat. For the first time he saw her as an individual, a personality in her own right and with rights of her own, but he could not explain why or how this illumination had come to him. And that perturbed him. She was no longer a piece of furniture in his household that could be moved where he chose and whose particular care belonged to Doña Ágata. He didn't know what he was going to do about her and he did not want to prophesy even to himself. Neither did he know what he would do to Don Alejandro. Time would make all that clear to him, he thought, and was a little truculent at having to depend on time and not himself.

As he plunged into the noisy activity of the plaza, dodging a line of mules with their tails put up in leather bags, he was disturbed by diverse matters, by his hasty removal from Las Golondrinas, by the war that was beginning to look ominous, by his daughter whom he could not understand, by the very hectic and unpredictable atmosphere that permeated all Mexico. He suspected that the hitherto stable pattern of his life was being shifted and he did not like it at all. All these diverse matters were adjoints to this nefarious purpose, tying together in some manner that was beyond his comprehension. He had not yet reached the point where he could say "My day and way are done" but he was approaching it and the new feeling that he had responsibilities as well as privileges was a signpost on the way.

Don Isidro moved under the arcades into the great square of the plaza, passing the dulce sellers displaying their sponge cakes, figs, dates and candied fruits and the hawkers of toys. A motley array of wax, wood and rag dolls and puppet groups fashioned from prepared linen stared after him with unblinking painted eyes. If he had not been so immersed in his own disturbing thoughts he would have stopped to examine some of these amusing little groups for he was fond of them and possessed a number at Las Golondrinas. For instance, there was one composed of three figures—a drunken man, his lolling neck too weak to support his head; next, his mother, comically enraged at him and about to belabor him with a tiny stick; and, last, a frightened daughter-in-law clutching at the mother's arm. Another trio represented an alcalde administering a lecture to a husband with a shamed bowed head while the wife, on the other side of the official from the husband, is smiling to feel the alcalde's hand on her knee. Don Isidro passed them all with veiled eyes. Behind him, too, he left the merchants of crockery squatting in the shade beside their piles of plates, dishes, cups, bowls, water jars, coarse and fine mattings and willow baskets ranging in size from three inches in diameter to three and a half feet. Around him the hubbub of barter was deafening as hucksters and customers followed the immemorial method of bargaining, the prospective purchaser indignantly marching off when informed of the price demanded and the huckster, after making sure that the prospective purchaser meant it, shouting "Niño! Niño!" after him and offering a more reasonable price. Often, a determined customer would march off half a dozen times before the price was lowered to his satisfaction. This was going on all over the market. Don Isidro advanced like a strong swimmer into this clashing surf of noises, shouts, bells, arguments, singsong and clatter.

He passed great piles of corn, yellow, blue and black, on outspread mattings, heaps of large onions as white as snow, wild green tomatoes and overflowing baskets of soup greens. He passed half-naked tortilla women sitting on their haunches before their charcoal stoves and snatching dirty cloths from woven containers to display the cooked masa. He passed displays of cabbages, radishes, turnips, squashes, peas, carrots, boiled and sweetened sweet potatoes and crooked mammoth pods of okra. He passed pile after pile of peppers of all shapes and sizes and colors: the dark red chile ancho and the green chile poblano, the shriveled red chile pasilla, the long black chile negro, the dark chile mulato, the long red chile carrizo, the squat dark green chile jalapeño, the small green chile serrano, the seed-rattling little chile cascabel, the long brown chile piquín and the mouth-burning dark red chilpotle. He passed pears and peaches and apples and cherries and mameys and apricots and zapotes and avocados and mushrooms. He passed oranges and limes and muskmelons and watermelons and goat's cheese and eggs and chocolate and wooden spoons. Near the fountain in the center of the plaza he stepped by rows of earthen and iron cooking untensils, squawking chickens, grumbling turkeys, cooing pigeons, mounds of white chalky lime, woven hats, huaraches, piles of beans, bananas, plantains, coconuts and pineapples. Across the rickety awnings he could see the Governor's palace and he wondered what Isunza was thinking and doing with the threat of invasion so steadily approaching his bright city. Well, the bishop would know about that. He accelerated his stride and turned somewhat eastward as he left the din of the market behind him.

Puebla, he had to admit, appeared to be its normal self. Life continued in its usual noisy unwashed grooves. The clerics crowded the streets and the Poblana market girls, blacked-eyed, hair combed over the ears from which dangled huge silver earrings, wearing their white chemisettes half-covered with gray rebozos and short red petticoats fastened about the waist with silver bands and fringed with yellow, were as attractive as ever. The Indians crouched at the corners in the shade with their blankets raised to their noses and their sombreros tipped over their eyes. The water carriers passed with their ten-gallon jugs strapped fore and aft. Fat women plodded along, legs slightly spread, babies dangling on their hips and containers of provisions resting on their bowed backs and supported by straps around their foreheads. A few caballeros, lured out by the sunshine or business that could not be put off until tomorrow, sporting short jackets, pantaloons of buckskin, blue cloth or velvet slashed down the sides and ornamented with buttons, lace or embroidery trotted along the streets on small wiry horses. Jackasses brayed and dogs barked. A mingled odor of spice, melons, dung, fresh flowers, urine, and unbathed bodies was carried along by the breeze. One's nostrils caught it in whiffs and then it was gone again. It was the familiar Puebla and if there was trepidation at the heart of it it did not make itself manifest to Don Isidro. It was only when he reached the eastern corner of the plaza and was about to turn into the highway that ran to the suburbs that he came face to face with an ominous hint.

A half dozen mounted troopers, dusty, exhausted and slouching in their saddles, had halted their horses in the shade of a clump of poplar trees and were conversing volubly with a rapidly gathering crowd of Poblanos. Their brown hands flashed in gesticulation. Don Isidro recognized the stained wrinkled uniforms, their bright colors pathetically subdued, as those of the Lancers of Chalchicomula. For a moment he was tempted to push his way through the mass of curious jabbering onlookers and question the soldiers but before he could do so the horsemen kicked their heels into the haunches of their animals and started off toward the plaza. As they passed close to the hacendado, saddles creaking and bit chains clinking, he observed the sweaty winded appearance of the horses and the grim drawn lines on the troopers' faces. Instinctively he raised his head and sniffed the air. There was a new odor there or perhaps he imagined it. It was more than the reek of tired horses. It was faint, acrid, bloodish-sweet and without ever having experienced it before he recognized it instantly as the smell of war. It had come to Puebla, then. It was here at last. An alarmed expression spread over Don Isidro's face, his heavy underlip thrust out glumly and he accelerated his long stride as he left the city behind him and approached the bishop's red-brick villa.

The bishop was receiving visitors in his library and more waited impatiently in the gloom of the stone-tiled hall where the masklike faces of long-dead clerics peered through smoke-darkened varnish. Don Isidro, therefore, after leaving his name with the harassed young priest by the door passed on through the house and into the small garden where he seated himself on a pink-stone bench inset with blue and white tiles. Against the farther wall the espadañas were in bloom and a plump padre marched up and down the gravel walk peering with weak eyes at an open book that he held in his hand and mumbling softly to himself. The padre had a long nose that trembled sensitively with the moving of his lips. It was quiet, almost too quiet, in the garden. The customary subdued lisp of the fountain was silent and the usual birds that chattered about the espaliered fruit trees had sought other hunting grounds. Don Isidro crossed his hands on his stomach, sighed and closed his eyes. The thought flitted through his head that he was growing old but it vanished almost as rapidly as it came. It was like the flash of a fish glimpsed in translucent water. The sun, mounting to the midday, pressed balmily against his legs and he wondered somewhat testily why he could not relax as he always had relaxed on a cool sunny day. A scraping sound on the path reached his ears and he supposed it was the plump padre until he sensed someone sitting down beside him and opened his eyes to see the bishop.

Don Isidro struggled to his feet and sat down again.

"I slipped out through the garden door," explained the bishop, smiling slightly. "Let them stew in there for a bit. One of Isunza's aides is waiting. I'll keep him long enough to make sure that he misses his dinner."

He studied Don Isidro's face with his sharp little eyes.

"What is it?" he asked. "Did you walk out here? If the information you seek is what I think, it is quite true. It must be all over the city by this time."

Don Isidro cleared his throat.

"I bring you greetings and affection from my family," he said formally and then his lower lip thrust out. "We have been defeated?"

"Decidedly," answered the bishop tranquilly. "At the pass of the Cerro Gordo."

His observant eyes fastened on the meandering padre who had accelerated his mumbling and was crossing himself constantly.

"Brother Eugenio is fencing with the devil again," he remarked dryly. "He must have had bad dreams last night. Do you know, he comes to me and confesses his dreams?"

Don Isidro was not interested in Brother Eugenio.

"Well, what happened?" he demanded with suppressed impatience. "What are the particulars of the action? You have had reports?"

"I can give you a minute or two only," said the bishop, pursing his bloodless lips and tugging at his ear with a bony forefinger and thumb. "There are half a dozen people waiting in there to report or beg favors. Yes, I have had reports. They are not complete, Don Isidro, but here is the story as I have patched it together."

He yielded to his old habit of closing his eyes as though he could marshal his facts better by shutting out the visible world.

"The Americans began their advance from Vera Cruz on April eighth," he said. "On the eleventh they reached the National Bridge. During this thirty-seven-mile march through torrid country nothing was done to harass or stop them because nothing could be done. We had neither the men and equipment nor the time to raise fortifications or barricades close to the coast. Besides, La Viga, who commanded this district, is a zote, a numskull, and his superior, Canalizo, is a windbag. Santa Anna, coming down from Jalapa, hit upon the pass at the Cerro Gordo, which as you probably don't know, is on his own land, as the appropriate place to make a stand. He may be a windbag, too, but he is not a numskull. Strongly fortifying the heights overlooking the road by the Cerro Gordo he rested his right on a ravine with almost perpendicular sides several hundred feet high and his left on the Cerro Gordo which rises more than nine hundred feet above the river. His entire line faced hills along which extended for miles the Vera Cruz-Jalapa road, the only road possible for artillery. Vázquez of the Ingenieros informs me that it was a good position and should have held."

He opened his eyes and glanced inquiringly at his nephew.

"I know the Cerro Gordo," declared Don Isidro for want of something better to say. "It's about sixty miles from the coast and would seem to have been an excellent place to make a stand. What happened? Didn't the general have sufficient forces?"

"He must have had at least twelve thousand men," said the bishop.

"Then, in the name of Heaven—" began Don Isidro with some excitement.

"Wait," interrupted the bishop. "There are more elements necessary for success in warfare than men. I am an apostle of peace but I have wit enough to know that. For instance, generals. For instance, a plan. For instance, morale. That last, the most important of all, Santa Anna did not have, True, he had men. True, he had a sort of plan ... although, according to Vázquez, it was based too much on assumption and vitiated by a disregard of particulars. For instance, there was a forward hill called La Atalaya which the engineers argued should be fortified and strongly held. Santa Anna sent twenty-five men to it. Robles, believing the Americans could turn the main position, wanted fortifications on the extreme left. Santa Anna said, 'No.' Santa Anna said that a rabbit couldn't get through. Santa Anna, as usual, was too cocksure."

"The morale of the troops must have been bad," remarked Don Isidro gloomily. "But why? What—"

"Why?" repeated the bishop quickly. "Ah, I have been hearing about that all morning. Their morale was bad from a complexity of causes. The narrow camp was too crowded with cottages, tents, huts and market booths and the result was a confusion that made everybody irritable. Swarms of insects kept the men awake all night. The water supply was insufficient and the pulque was so green that it gave those who drank it diarrhea. A sort of cholera swept the camp and the exposure brought on lung troubles. There wasn't enough to eat. But worst of all was the hopeless feeling about the Americans. The men from the north recalled how they had been forced to turn their backs on the Americans at Palo Alto, the Resaca, Monterrey and La Angostura and the men from the south had seen Vera Cruz and San Juan de Ulúa capitulate. In short, they regarded the Americans as invincible. And it didn't help any when Santa Anna began shooting captured deserters. According to Vázquez, even the officers talked privately about disaster. All the tinder of a panic was there. Only the spark was needed."

Don Isidro groaned.

"Go on," he said. "I suppose I might as well hear about the spark."

The bishop made a slight gesture of impatience.

"We are not an objective people," he declared. "We do not scrutinize; we feel. Our impulses are always our undoing. Discipline, Don Isidro, we lack discipline. The story of the Cerro Gordo appears to be a story of the lack of discipline, of leadership, of will. Certainly, we had the troops . . ."

His voice trailed off into silence and he observed the marching figure of the padre with some distaste.

"The story?" he said after a moment. "It is like most of our stories. The Americans attacked and we resisted but not enough. They took two tactically important hills and a height. They did what our generals had declared impossible, turned our left. We trusted to the fact that there was no road there. They hacked a road through the chaparral. They outshot us, outmaneuvered us, outfought us. We broke and ran. They killed a thousand of us, captured three thousand prisoners including several generals, more than four thousand stand of arms, about forty cannon, a large amount of ammunition, most of the army funds and . . . Santa Anna's wooden leg."

He erupted into a short laugh.

"Isn't that good?" he demanded. "Santa Anna's wooden leg!"

Don Isidro refused the levity.

"It is terrible," he said somberly. "Some sort of infernal luck seems to go with the Americans. What are we going to do now? Do you think . . .?"

The bishop became grave.

"Perhaps the Americans are too unimaginative to accept defeat," he answered. "Perhaps we are too volatile to achieve victory. What are we going to do? Well, what would you do?"

"At Jalapa . . ." began Don Isidro.

"The Americans are in Jalapa," interrupted his uncle.

"We must fight again," said Don Isidro heavily. "Surely, Santa Anna will make a stand at La Hoya. The pass is more than a mile long and the road runs between steep mountains. Santa Anna can . . ."

"You don't understand," explained the bishop patiently. "The Americans are beyond La Hoya. Santa Anna ran away. His troops are streaming along the National Highway and all the side tracks and mountain paths. The vanguard of the fugitives is passing through Puebla now. It is a rout."

Don Isidro fingered his heavy underlip.

"Then . . ." he stuttered. "Oh . . . but . . . the Americans will enter the city."

"Of course they will," said the bishop. "They will enter the city. They will pass through the city. They will go through San Martín. They will pass Ixtaccíhuatl and Popocatépetl and cross the Río Frío. They will reach the Valley of Mexico. Why? Because there is nothing to stop them. Nothing at all. Except a moral reason. And Texas and California are worth more to them than moral reasons. They are practical men."

Don Isidro half-heard him. He clenched his big fists.

"We must make a stand," he asserted. "Where is Santa Anna? What is Isunza doing? We can fight a battle at Ojo de Agua or Nopalucan. The city is full of men and if, as you say, troops are passing through . . ."

"Vázquez tells me Santa Anna is at Orizaba," said the bishop sharply. "I have no doubt but that he will arrive here in due time. He always does. He will ask for money and for men. He will not get either."

"If he organizes quickly . . ." began Isidro and then the meaning of the bishop's last words struck him like a bolt of lightning.

"What's that?" he cried in a loud voice. "What did you say?"

"We've had enough of General Santa Anna," said the bishop. "That is what I say."

Don Isidro glanced with angry perplexity at his uncle.

"Who is there to take his place?" he inquired in a shaking voice. The bishop turned his irritated fox-face to the sunny sky.

"He would bleed us white if he could," he said. "I beg you to recall what happened in Mexico City. Forced loans from the Church, eh? Well, they found little enough in my strongboxes. I was fore-warned and when the troops came the funds of the bishopric of Puebla were safely hidden elsewhere. Oh, I saw to it that a few pesos were left. Just enough to drive the officials wild. The sacrilege . . ."

"That was the work of Gómez Farías!" exclaimed Don Isidro. "That was the work of a government that has ceased to exist. Have you forgotten that when Santa Anna returned from the . . . er . . . action at La Angostura he found the capital in a state of insurrection and put down that insurrection and took over the presidency and saw that the obnoxious laws were repealed? After all . . ."

"The Church paid him two million five hundred thousand pesos for that," broke in the bishop.

"The Church raised that much money in the name of patriotism to carry on the war," declared Don Isidro. "Why, there wasn't a priest in Mexico who didn't bless the name of Santa Anna in March."

"Well, it is April now," said the bishop baldly. "Besides, you do not understand. Santa Anna bled us when he passed through Puebla and he will try to bleed us again when he returns. He will not succeed. This is a city of peace. The Poblanos do not want to fight. We shall make such arrangements with the Americans as we please and Santa Anna can retreat to the capital and make his stand there . . . if he can raise enough troops."

Don Isidro stood up in amazement and then immediately sat down again.

"Are you informing me that Puebla will put up no defense against these gringo invaders?" he asked in a precise voice.

"That is exactly what I am informing you," replied the bishop. "This is a City of God."

"And Mexico?" demanded Don Isidro in the same precise voice. The bishop shrugged his shoulders.

"Mexico is in the hands of God," he answered.

The two men sat and stared at each other for a half minute.

"No one loves Mexico, the Mexican people, more than I do, more than the Church does," declared the bishop calmly, "but wisdom always should be a part of love. We should not lose sight of the larger good when we are faced by the smaller vexation. My people are simple people and they are weary of violent struggle. The políticos in Mexico City made this war and they can finish this war. It was not made in Puebla. I do not say that we are waging an unjust war, for we are fighting invaders and that is always just. We are fighting imperialistic buccaneers. But I do say that it is not the duty of Puebla to offer resistance. Do you imagine we want our holy monuments bombarded, our people slain, our communal life smashed? No, my dear nephew, Puebla will not fight. I shall see to that."

"It is the duty of every Mexican patriot to fight to the last man," exploded Don Isidro. "We should raise barricades in the streets, fortify the houses, hold the Americans until a new army, an overwhelming army, is raised in the valley."

"It sounds very noble," remarked the bishop, "but it won't work out. The army would split and the parts would fight against each other; the generals would conspire and the políticos would defraud."

"It seems that we were more united under the viceroys than we are now," said Don Isidro bitterly.

"It is quite possible," agreed the bishop tranquilly. "A strong hand has its virtues."

"Submitting without a struggle is no evidence of strength," declared Don Isidro roughly. "I shall go to Isunza and ask him to resist."

The bishop smiled slightly.

"You may do what you please, Don Isidro," he said in a friendly voice. "You will merely waste your time. As I am wasting my time now."

He stood up.

"Don't let the American advance worry you too much," he continued. "They are not quite savages."

"I shall go to Isunza," repeated Don Isidro stubbornly as he rose heavily from the bench.

"Is there any more information I can give you?" asked the bishop politely. "I'm afraid you will have to wait for particulars of the fighting at the Cerro Gordo. Well . . ."

He took a step toward his side door.

"How is María Catalina?" he asked perfunctorily.

"Isunza will *have* to do something," declared Don Isidro. "It is impossible that he should . . ."

Anger bereft him of speech. The bishop moved down the path toward his villa.

"Visit me any time," he said cordially. "Come tomorrow. Or this evening. God bless you, my son."

His purple robe disappeared through the narrow portal.

Don Isidro stalked toward the house door and bumped violently into the strolling padre, knocking the book out of his hand.

"Por Dios . . . !" he began and then skirted the stooping figure in grim silence. He was repressing an almost uncontrollable desire to kick the padre right in the middle of his broad backside.

He was so angry as he walked along the road to the city that he hardly observed the gathering traffic flowing toward the plaza. The jingle of chains, bridle bits, spurs and sabers sounded musically in the clear air and the soft pounding of horses' hoofs in the gray dirt made a muffled drumlike undertone. He heard it as at a distance. Without being conscious of looking he was aware that these mounted men were cavalrymen, fragments from the Húzares, the Fifth of Morelia and the Ninth of Coraceros. There were men on foot, too, but they were like trees or bushes to him. He pushed brusquely by them as he had always pushed by pedestrians all his life . . . without care or excuse. He was angry and he was sufficiently detached to be aware of his anger and to wonder at it. He could not attribute all this inner rage to the fact that the serenity of his existence had been destroyed. No, it was more than that now . . . though that had been enough to begin with. It was Mexico. It was the pusillanimity of men. It was the dubious prospect. It was the damned criminality of it all. It was . . .

He bumped heavily against a burro and cursed inwardly.

Could it be patriotism, an awakened sense of the wrongs perpetrated against his land, say, that was boiling up within him and rousing his fury? He had never considered patriotism as a passion in itself but rather as a lip service for foreigners, a necessary intimation of one's honored place in time. One did not emphasize it for that would have been vulgar. It was indicated, insinuated, suggested as something that should be taken for granted. That, perhaps, was because it had never presented itself to him as a burning issue at Las Golondrinas and in Mexico City it had seemed to be no more than the angry shouts or crafty gestures of conflicting politicians and ambitious generals. It had slightly sickened him, then. He had been safe and removed at Las Golondrinas and patriotism there, now that he thought of it, was merely fidelity to himself. It had been fidelity to himself as far back as he could remember. Yes, even in those distant days when he had desired to raise a company of peons and ride off into the hills after the rebel Francisco de Paula. He had reacted then as youths of his caste reacted. It was not so much patriotism, not so much a profound affection for Ferdinand VII and the regime of the viceroys, as it was a desire to maintain his own culture and way of life, his privileged place in time, that roused him to such a pitch that his alarmed father had sent him to Spain. No, that was not patriotism. And after the battle of La Angostura (which he was convinced was a defeat) his irritation had not been patriotism. He had been merely inconvenienced by his wife's fear and hysteria and the moil and trouble of transferring a household through the difficult terrain to Puebla. It was the indignities that he had endured. It was a feeling, he imagined, that the padre back there in the garden would have experienced if he had actually kicked him in his backside.

But, then. Yes . . . no. At La Angostura, or Buena Vista, or whatever the history books would call it, the Mexican soldiers had fought and according to all secondhand tales they had fought well. At least, they had stopped the Americans dead in their tracks. Or had the Americans stopped *them* dead in their tracks? It was all mixed up. It didn't matter, though. What did matter was that the Mexicans had fought . . . and fought well. Now, the bishop and his cuadrilla of bootlickers proposed to hand Puebla over to the Americans without firing a gun. That was it! That was what put him in a rage. It was the shoddy acquiescence in defeat, the calculated surrender, the shameful understood *bargain* and not defeat in itself that put him in a rage. If that was patriotism, why, it was patriotism. It was pride, too. It was the pride of keeping a vow, or doing what one said one would do, of facing the worst without flinching, of being consistent. The Republic had accepted this war; the soldiers had marched forth singing "Adiós"; the populace had cheered and breathed defiance against the gringos; the Church had put its hand down into its pocket and produced funds to carry on the campaign. Let them all stand up to it, then. Let them stand up to it. Let them stop thinking about their precious skins and their concealed money boxes and their personal jealousies and . . . stand . . . up . . . to . . . it!

If he was to be made uncomfortable there might as well be a worthy reason for it. And if there was a worthy reason the rest of them (and that included the Church, by God!) should accept their responsibilities and face the music whether it was a triumphal march or a funeral dirge. One did not mix politics and war. Or religion, either. War was like a sponge. It sucked up everything into itself and that was all that there was to it. One did not postpone a war in order to fight an election. The enemy would not co-operate. Por Diós! There *was* an election coming along in May. A presidential election. Don Isidro groaned. Was that the reason that the bishop . . . ? These old manipulators . . . ! But, no. What good would it do Santa Anna's candidacy to hand Puebla over to the Americans? What benefit would the Church acquire by defeating Santa Anna? He was the only general in Mexico who even attempted to fight a battle. It would be instructive to know more about the man. Curious personality. Oh, undoubtedly an opportunist. But . . . "City of God," indeed! "Not the duty of Puebla to offer . . ." His rage flared up again as he swung sturdily into the sunlit streets.

I'll go straight to Isunza, he thought. I'll tell the bag of fat that he has sworn a certain oath to the Republic and that it is his duty to fortify the city, barricade the roads and put men with muskets behind

the barricades. He can do it. Look, troops are pouring into the plaza
now. There must be hundreds of them. Isunza must do that. We'll
fight. I'll fight with the rest of them. Then it won't matter whether
the Americans take Puebla or not. At least, we shall have fought. We
shall have kept our vow and God will take care of the consequences.
Then . . . Suddenly a new Mexico danced in his mind, a Mexico of
of united citizenry, of one oath, of combined will and purpose, of
. . . As though directed by an invisible guide he turned his large head
and saw a row of Indians sitting with their backs against a rose-pink
wall, their sombreros tipped over their eyes, their blankets raised
across their mouths. Not even the excitement of scores of fugitive
soldiers hurrying along the streets could rouse them from their detached and somnolent observation. They were like the hills beyond
the city, like the mountains, like Malinche, Orizaba, Ixtaccíhuatl and
Popocatépetl, immovable and stubborn and distantly contemptuous.
What did it matter to them if the Americans entered the city? Nothing had mattered to them since Cortés with his frightening horses had
passed this way and gone on to Cholula where the temple to Quet-
zalcóatl was raised. Nevertheless . . . He would go to Isunza anyway
and tell him that Puebla must fight. It was something he could not
say with any degree of firmness to his uncle, the bishop, but he could
say it to Isunza. That bag of fat!

He was back in the plaza now and it seemed to him that the busy
market had suddenly blossomed uniforms like some magic garden
instantly sprouting colored flowers. They were everywhere, and, the
anger that had sustained him so long suddenly dwindling in strength
he began to turn his head right and left with some curiosity. Yes
there were all sorts there. The battalion insignia flashed in the sun
Atlixco. Libertad. Zacapoaxtla. Jalapa. Coatepec. Teziutlán. How
small most of them seemed. Such little fellows. Grabbing fruit from
the piles and devouring tortillas, each at a single gulp, one after the
other. They were thirsty, too. The cantinas would be crowded tonight
Some knifeplay, perhaps. Where were . . . Oh. There are some officer
now. They look cool enough. Standing on the corner and looking a
the Governor's Palace. Isunza. Now? No. He'll be in conference al
day. I'll send Chepe toward evening. Appointment. "Don Isidro Núñe
de Haro y Peralta requests the pleasure . . ." Hello. There is . . . h
. . . yes . . . With flurried steps he pushed through gesticulatin;
jabbering marketers toward a young officer who was weighing a melo
in his hand.

"I am glad to see you again, Señor Teniente," he said, raising hi
voice above the hubbub.

The young man glanced up, faintly flushing, and a quick flas
of surprise lit his eyes.

"Don Isidro!" he exclaimed, extending the hand with the melon in it and then tossing the fruit to the huckster.

"Of all the men in the world you are the one I wanted most to encounter at this very moment," declared the hacendado solemnly as he clasped the other's hand.

The young officer looked so puzzled that Don Isidro broke into a rumbling chuckle.

"I didn't know it until I actually saw you," he continued, thrusting his arm inside the young man's and urging him toward the corner by the cathedral, "but it is so. You have just come from the Cerro Gordo? Where is General Santa Anna? What is going to happen? I am curious about a dozen matters that only you can answer. Where is your headquarters? Have you found a place to sleep?"

The young officer walked along with him willingly enough.

"Where shall I start?" he asked, laughing. "Do you want . . . ?"

"You are right, Don Juan Diego," said Don Isidro. "There should be order in everything, eh? After all, one has but one mouth. Have you found a place to sleep? Perhaps you have friends here?"

"I have just arrived," responded Juan Diego. "No, I have not found a place. There are plenty of posadas. Or the barracks. It will be . . ."

"The posadas and the barracks are full of fleas," declared Don Isidro positively. "I hope you will do me the honor of being my guest."

"Oh, but . . ." began Juan Diego. "I could not think . . . The inconvenience . . ."

"Nonsense!" broke in the hacendado. "I have no guests at the moment. There are plenty of chambers."

He looked sharply at the young man.

"I came down from Las Golondrinas with just Doña Ágata, my daughter and three criados," he explained carefully.

"If you are sure . . ." said Juan Diego. "It would be a pleasure."

"Good!" exclaimed Don Isidro heartily. "I shall have the pleasure, or I intend to cross-examine you to distraction. You see, there is complete selfishness in my invitation. It was a happy chance encountering you. Have you any luggage? I suppose . . ."

"The little I had is still at the Cerro Gordo, so far as I know," replied Juan Diego gravely.

The half-smile on Don Isidro's face was abruptly erased.

"Yes," he said flatly, "the Cerro Gordo. Well . . . You must have seen a lot of action since we last met. La Angostura. Vera Cruz. The Cerro Gordo. Well, later we will . . ."

"I was not at Vera Cruz," explained the young officer. "The others . . . yes."

He exhaled his breath sharply.

"I know," muttered Don Isidro. "Oh, the devil. Well. We turn at this corner. My house is a short way down. I . . ."

He brushed by two timid figures with extended hands.

"Dios los ampare, hermanitos," he said automatically.

Anxiety shriveled his eyelids as he glanced at Juan Diego.

"It was bad," he ventured glumly.

The young officer acknowledged with a brief nod the statement that was not a question. He looks older, thought Don Isidro. His face is thinner. But the tan suits him. It would be hard for anyone to tell that he is not a full-blooded Mexican. Full-blooded . . . ? I mean the Spanish type, of course. He will have much to tell me. It is time I began to learn.

"You were with the general all of the time, of course," he remarked.

"Yes, Don Isidro," replied Juan Diego. "Until yesterday."

"I shall have much to ask you," said the hacendado. "I have just been visiting my uncle, the bishop. I gather from him . . ."

He compressed his lips as he felt the anger rising within him again.

"Well," he went on after a moment, "we will talk of these things later. You look tired. You give me an excellent excuse to open a flask of old port. Do you like it? The English say it gives them gout but that is because they drink until it has no place to go except their legs."

Juan Diego laughed.

"I like all good wines," he said. "But I am not tired. I was tired. I was tired until I rode into the city an hour ago and then quite suddenly the weariness vanished. Perhaps it was the sight of so many people at their peaceful pursuits and the sun shining and the bells from the cathedral ringing and the men sitting along the walls and—"

He stopped speaking as Don Isidro halted and turned him toward a large studded door.

"Yes, yes, I know," interrupted the hacendado. "It is here. I live here. Yes, you came from a world of weariness into one of peaceful movement. I know. Will you step in?"

Juan Diego appeared suddenly frightened.

"You are quite sure that I will not be intruding?" he asked in a rather breathless voice. "I can just as easily—"

"Step in, step in," ordered Don Isidro in a peremptory manner. "I am honored to welcome you as my guest. It will give my wife and daughter great pleasure to see you."

Juan Diego squared his shoulders and stepped through the just opened doorway. Chepe's dark immobile face lighted with pleased surprise as he closed the heavy oblong of thick wood and followed his master and the unexpected guest.

It was long after the midday meal and the little group still sat about the uncleared table. Juan Diego, feeling as though the contents of his mind had been dumped out like a pile of varicolored shells from a basket and turned over and examined one by one by the meticulous and exhaustive Don Isidro, glanced from face to face and was not surprised to find them so familiar. He had encountered this puzzle before. Strange faces flowed by constantly and one barely noticed them or noticed them and turned away and then one would fix the attention by its familiarity. One recognized it although one had never seen it before. There was no explanation for this. It was so here. Of course, of the four seated at the table he had seen three before and two under extraordinary circumstances but that did not explain why they were more familiar to him than most of the young staff officers with whom he had lived for months. All through the long meal while Don Isidro had plucked from him all that he knew or thought about the action at the Cerro Gordo and the plans of the general he had been increasingly aware of this familiarity, this sensation of being with people he had always known. And that was curious, for he knew little or nothing about them. Yet he *did* know something. Don Isidro's large face and jutting underlip and half-worried, half-angry curiosity were as transparent as the hawklike alarmed countenance of Doña Ágata, and Doña Concha, whom he had never seen before and whose status in the family was a mystery to him, was as simpática in all her comforting largeness as Doña María Catalina was in her slender awareness and quiet attentiveness. Even the shuffling sound of Chepe's sandals fitted into an acceptance that he felt had been tacitly admitted on all sides.

Doña María Catalina. His one vivid memory of her had been almost like an invisible bar across the street door when he had turned with Don Isidro and for an instant a sudden fright had tempted him to whirl and run away as fast as he could. He had dreamt of her more than once during the weeks and months that had lapsed since he had held her momentarily in his arms at Las Golondrinas. He had dreamt of her without willing it, without volition, without any consciousness of her in his waking mind. Sometimes she had been Our Lady of Guadalupe garmented in a blue robe and shining with golden stars and again she had been merely herself, a slight figure running across the moonlit patio, always running toward him and never reaching him. He never tried to explain these dreams. He had put them out of his mind on waking as he put out of his mind all the vague visions and unsought images that floated through his relaxed slumber. Doña María Catalina meant nothing to him. She was no more than a fugitive impression that had been caught up in the wide nets of his fancy. Like a peculiar blue of a certain hand-woven sash he had seen once at the market at Milpa Alta. And yet he had been afraid at the opening

door. Afraid of what? Surely not of her whom he hardly knew. And
yet . . . "It would be embarrassing for my daughter to encounter you
again . . ." Had Don Isidro forgotten? He had said nothing about
their last meeting in the patio at Las Golondrinas. He had been like
an old friend; pleasure shone in his eyes; the grasp of his hand had
been an unmistakable welcome. The very walls had seemed to melt
before Juan Diego and he had found himself surrounded by smiling
faces.

It was strange. In a way it was like coming home; and now as he
answered Don Isidro's endless series of questions he wondered why
he had hesitated at the door in sudden fright at the thought of entering. What had he expected? Whatever it was he knew that he had
not encountered it. It had not been evident in Doña Ágata's slight
wiry figure, high-bridged nose and piercing black eyes. Why, she had
fairly sucked him into the high-ceilinged reception room where the
barred windows overhung the quiet street and anticipated Don Isidro
in ordering Chepe to bring wine and fruit. Doña Concha had greeted
him with a smile so large that it seemed to dwarf her great body to
normal size. And when, some time later, Doña María Catalina had
quietly entered the room and greeted him without surprise, welcomed
him with a formality delicately touched with an unexpected friendliness, he experienced the warm sensation of *belonging* in a milieu he
had not known existed until that minute. He would have liked to
taste it quietly for a while, to have relished it slowly and with becoming meditation but Don Isidro gave no time for that. He wanted to
know all about the Cerro Gordo.

So throughout the meal (and what he ate or whether he ate, Juan
Diego never knew) he had described what he had seen on that unfortunate day, the savage fighting at El Telégrafo and the tower of
the Cerro Gordo after the hill of Atalaya had been lost, the break-
through of the Americans and their encircling movement to the Jalapa
Road and the disorganized rout of Santa Anna's hysterical troops. It
wasn't the tactics that mattered, he had explained, it was the lack of
will, the absence of faith, that had defeated the Mexicans. Oh, their
arms had been bad—old French muskets; the supplies had been scant,
the water poisonous, the leaders, always excepting the general, mediocre, all that was true; but it was the will, the faith in one's invulnerability that broke like a reed at the first encounter, that explained the
disastrous action at the Cerro Gordo. What did the actual movements
and clashes matter, or what regiments and squadrons had fought
bravely or broken and run, or what particular hill was lost, or what
individual general had misunderstood his orders or not given any at
all? These things happened in every battle and to describe one was to

describe them all. Chance was always the victorious general in battles.
Chance was not with the Mexican arms. They had not willed it.

Don Isidro was less interested in all this than in what Canalizo or
Pinzón or Alcorta or La Viga or Rangel had done. Juan Diego who
didn't know himself, tried to explain. He used silver casters and tiny
porcelain cups and knives and forks to diagram the maneuvers of the
two days and the others had bowed their heads above the white napery
and striven to see massed bodies of men and unlimbered guns in the
inanimate table objects. It was funny to think that the silver salt caster
was Arteaga's brigade. But where *was* Arteaga's brigade on April
eighteenth? Had it come up at all? Was it that body of troops that had
broken in confusion near Santa Anna's headquarters and not gone
into action but fled toward Jalapa? He didn't know. The participants
in a battle knew little or nothing about it until they read in the history
books the descriptions by men who had never been there. If one could
only station one's self in the clouds above a battlefield and have a
strong field-glass . . .

Across the uncleared table he heard Don Isidro asking about the
general.

"He is at Orizaba," he replied mechanically. "He should be here in
three or four days."

Then he realized that they were all curious about Santa Anna's
reactions and movements after his army had disintegrated.

"When the general saw that the day was lost he left the National
Highway at a point near the Cerro del Telégrafo with a small escort,
of which I was one," he explained. "We descended the barranca by a
narrow path, leaving the screaming and gunfire behind us, crossed the
stream and with some difficulty gained the opposite height. There we
found Generals Ampudia and Rangel and Colonel Ramiro, and the
general ordered them to collect the dispersed troops and march them
to the rear. Then we rode toward Encero where the general intended
to get a new wooden leg—the one he had irritated his stump severely
and the extra he had brought with him was lost with his personal baggage train. We never got there. Less than a mile from the hacienda we
were fired on by American cavalry already speeding up the road toward
Jalapa and so we turned off into the path leading to the hacienda of
Tuzamápam. The general was exhausted, hungry and very low in
spirits. He complained constantly of the pain in his stump. We stopped
several times to give him some rest and at one place we encountered a
priest and asked him if he knew where we could procure a fresh horse
for the general. The priest spat on the ground and replied that he
knew where there were several fresh horses but the general would have
to find them out for himself. I wanted—"

"That was a priest?" broke in Don Isidro.

"It was a priest or a friar," replied Juan Diego. "A fellow in a brown habit. After that . . ."

"They've deserted him, then," said Don Isidro grimly.

"We reached the Hacienda of Tuzamápam about five o'clock in the evening," continued Juan Diego. "There were two corporals of the Eleventh there with the money chest of their corps and the general was so pleased to see honest soldiers that he kissed them on both cheeks. About six o'clock—"

"Was there really cash in the money chest?" demanded Don Isidro.

"All the cash of the Eleventh Corps," answered Juan Diego. "About six o'clock—"

"Those two corporals ought to be stuffed and set upon the altar of Our Lady of Guadalupe," declared Don Isidro. "This is the most marvelous thing that has happened in Mexico since Our Lady appeared to your illustrious namesake on the Hill of Tepeyac."

"About six o'clock," went on Juan Diego, suppressing a smile that he did not feel was quite appropriate at the moment, "Major Domo and a small party rode in. They brought bad news of the dispersal of the various army corps, the loss of the wagon trains and heavy guns and the complete lack of all authority. It was a gruesome tale and it did not make the general feel any better. However, he was too tired to talk and so we all lay down and tried to refresh ourselves with a little sleep. But that was not to be. Before midnight Major Domo roused us and told us that his sentries reported mounted troops in the vicinity and that they must be Americans. The devils seemed to be everywhere. The general decided that there was nothing to do but push on. We had decided to fashion a litter for him but there was no time for it. So we got him on his horse and started down the path toward the Hacienda del Volador, a soldier with a lighted lantern leading the way on foot. It was bitterly cold and the rocky path was dangerous and slippery. More than once I thought my horse would fall and I could hear the general groaning every time his mount slid or stumbled. We reached Volador after sunrise, a procession of scarecrows on exhausted animals. We slept."

He paused to gaze on their attentive faces and saw the brown hand of Chepe slide over his shoulder with a tilted bottle. The red wine lisped into his glass.

"When we awakened shortly before ten o'clock," he continued, "the sun was shining and tortillas had been made. All of us felt better but the most miraculous change was in the general. He who had gone to sleep exhausted, in pain, desperate in mind and prospect awoke rested, determined, bubbling with plans for recouping all that had been lost and voicing schemes for a guerrilla warfare that would force the

Americans back into the vómito. If you could have witnessed the change . . ."

"Yes, yes," said Don Isidro gravely. "General Santa Anna plunges from the heights to the depths and then leaps back again in the twinkling of an eye."

"He is a man of violent emotions and great sensitivity," explained Juan Diego carefully.

Don Isidro appeared about to say something and then thought better of it.

"Go on, my friend," he urged gently. "You have still to get the general from El Volador to Orizaba."

"We fashioned a litter," resumed Juan Diego, "and left El Volador before noon. For the next twenty-four hours, with infrequent stops for rest, we crossed mountain spurs, dipped into deep ravines, followed rocky byways and circled precipices. One of the horses fell down a rocky shelf and we had to kill it. There were places where the general had to descend from the litter and stumble along on foot. It was cold. We were hungry. But we were cheerful and that was because the general's optimistic demeanor buoyed us up. He is a great leader, Don Isidro. Whatever they may say about him he is a great leader. It was late morning when we reached Huatusco and as we were uncertain of our reception there the general sent Major Domo into the town. The entire ayuntamiento came back with him to greet us and escort the general to the subprefect's residence for breakfast. We made a triumphal entrance and in the plaza the general spoke a few words to the cheering populace. He reminded them how General Valencia, when pursued by the enemies of independence, hid in a cave near Huatusco and never lost faith in the eventual triumph of his cause and swore that it was the same with him, that from the town he would emerge and lead the Mexican people to the victory that the justice of Heaven would not deny them. He was wildly cheered by the citizens."

He paused again as though expecting some comment from his auditors but none came. Don Isidro slid his wineglass to and fro and stared almost sullenly at the oscillating liquid; Doña Ágata and Doña Concha gazed earnestly at him; and Doña María Catalina smiled almost imperceptibly into his serious eyes. Suddenly he felt confused and hastily resumed his story.

"The general passed the day writing dispatches for Mexico City, consulting with the town officials and resting," he said. "During the afternoon and evening stray detachments of troops began to come in and by the next morning there were more than a thousand men in Huatusco. The general became a veritable fountain of optimism; the people were enthusiastic; the soldiers, recovered from their fiery trial, exhibited an admirable discipline and resoluteness that . . ."

He began to feel stilted and stopped.

"Drink some wine," said Don Isidro, "and then tell us how the general got to Orizaba."

Juan Diego drained his entire glass without thinking.

"Oh, we left Huatusco during the morning," he explained hurriedly, "and reached Orizaba toward evening. We were met outside the city by a delegation including Don José Joaquín Pesado, Don Manuel Tornel, General León and General García Terán. They had a landau with them and the general was driven in it through the streets to Señor Tornel's house. Everything went beautifully. Cheers. Shouts of confidence. The brigade officers came in a body and paid their respects."

"And now the general is at Orizaba collecting and reorganizing his army," added Don Isidro quickly. "I see. I see. All is not quite lost, then. May I ask if you are on a special mission? Confidential, perhaps?"

"A mission, yes," replied Juan Diego. "I am instructed to report to the governor and request him to raise all the reinforcements he can . . ."

Don Isidro snorted loudly.

"The bishop is your man," he said dryly, "but I doubt very much that you will get any satisfaction out of him. There are complications here, my young friend."

Some time later Juan Diego stood by the barred window in the small chamber that was to be his own for as long as he liked and glanced down into a patio. Except for one corner, which was shaded by a willow tree against whose trunk was a sort of rustic bench, the sunny oblong expanse was a mass of glowing flowers, roses, sweet peas, marguerites (with here and there a dahlia) and pinks. The profusion of roses was astonishing, their bright reds, whites and yellows flaming everywhere. Sometime he would have to explore the patio, smell the roses and sit under the willow tree and pretend there was no such thing as war. But not now. It was the hour of the siesta and while his mind did not feel tired his body was relaxing in a blissful lassitude. He sat down in a nearby chair and drew off his boots. Then he walked over to the canopied bed and stretched himself along the blue and yellow coverlet. He lay looking up at the embroidered designs above him and did not see them at all.

It was curious, the things that could happen to a man without him willing them at all. Don Isidro was the last person on earth he had expected to meet in Puebla. And Doña María Catalina . . . He smiled and shut his eyes. It amused him to remember that when he had first seen her at Las Golondrinas he had experienced a feeling of dislike, almost of contempt for her. But he had not really seen her at all at Las Golondrinas. She had been merely a fragile shape with a white blob for a face, something less than human in the yellow flare of the torches and the bonfire. It was only later . . . Suddenly his hands, lying lax at his sides, tingled with the softness of her flesh beneath the blue sleeping gown. Automatically, he clenched them. She was human all right. And now that he had gazed frankly into her unshadowed face he knew that she was beautiful as well. Human and beautiful . . . and familiar. That was it, too. She had been familiar. She was like a woman whom he had seen many times before . . . and knew . . . and . . .Yet he could not remember a word she had said at the dining table. Had she said anything? It didn't matter. She had existed, familiar and long known and an assured portion of his intimacy with life.

He threw his arm over his head and blinked at the canopy above him. It was curious. Was it possible that he had merged her in his imagination with Our Lady of Guadalupe, with that Blessed Virgin who had walked through all his dreams and waking visions since he had been ten years old? He had never explained Our Lady to himself. He had never had to. She had come always without his willing it, watching over his sleep and moving invisibly beside him during the day, a summons and a protection and a shining light to follow. She had come in her garment of blue terciopelo all glittering with golden stars and with the odor of gardenias rising like the music of scent about her. It was so, he thought, that she came to all Indians. And now she came to him with the features of Doña María Catalina. There was a mystic significance here that he could not unravel. Perhaps that was why, without knowing it, he had been frightened at the thought of seeing Don Isidro's daughter again. An inner spell was conquering his mind and he knew now that it would be futile to fight against it. Doña María . . .

For some inexplicable reason his memory flashed abruptly back to his meeting with his brother at the Hacienda of Buena Vista. What . . . He scowled at the design above him . . . What had the meeting with David to do with Doña María Catalina? Or with anything, for that matter? He had never told the general about that encounter. He had never told him that he had been captured by the Yanquis, and then, miraculously (for it seemed miraculous now), set free by his brother. He had kept it to himself as he might keep a shameful thing to himself. And yet he knew that there had been nothing shameful about it. When he had caught up with Santa Anna's rear guard at Agua Nueva that sad night and seen the long disorderly lines of Mexican troops retreating into the darkness, deserted by their commander (for Santa Anna was miles ahead in his coach, intent only on reaching San Luis Potosí and then Mexico City) he had been filled with the grief and fury of humiliated disappointment. And when he had rejoined the general in the capital he had been brimming with chagrin and pricked by his first distrust of the man he loved. Perhaps that was why he had said nothing about David at the time. Yet he knew that this was not true, for when the general had explained the reason for the retreat after an inconclusive battle and he had been convinced that lack of provisions and ammunition combined with the revolutionary chaos in Mexico City had made no other choice possible he had still said nothing. No, the reasons for his silence lay deeper than he could fathom.

Yet the meeting with David had something to do with Doña María Catalina. He had not known it at the time but now, lying on the blue and yellow coverlet with the faint odor of the roses flowing in through the barred windows, he admitted the mysterious fact and sought vaguely, sleepily, for an explanation. It would not come. It was just behind his prescience but it would not come. David stood for something and Doña María stood for something but what these things were he could not say. It was too simple to say that one was the United States and the other was Mexico. It was very much more than that. That was too obvious, a simplification that satisfied and explained nothing. He swung his legs off the bed and sat up. My mind is as uneasy as an untamed monkey in a cage, he thought, and it is better for the monkey to go to sleep. See, it is the hour of the siesta and everybody else is asleep. I am becoming as wakeful as a . . . as a Yanqui. He stood up and walked over to the window and inhaled the odor of the flowers. Was it the early afternoon heat that caused them to suspire so? They spread their scent so far and yet they did not move. They were static in the windless air, no visible movement and yet such invisible traveling. Like the mind that flowed like an odor and permeated strange places. Like Doña María Catalina who did not seem to move at all and yet was everywhere. Oh, he must talk to her. Oh, he must find out . . . He was sleepy and yet he continued to stand by the window, gazing down into the patio and inhaling the odor of the colored roses.

About five o'clock in the afternoon Juan Diego and Don Isidro pushed their way through the gesticulating crowd before the Governor's Palace and mounted the steps to the open doors. Both were in a grim mood. Don Isidro had explained that Isunza, the governor, was a puppet of the Church who had been put into office in place of Ibarra, a stronger man with some rags of independence and honor left. "Don't expect anything from Isunza," warned the hacendado. "He does not speak for himself. Or for Puebla. He is the mouthpiece of the Church and if the bishop, my worthy uncle, has not instructed him what to say he will merely say nothing at great length." "But General Santa Anna is still commander in chief of the Mexican armies," insisted Juan Diego. "If he gives orders to raise supplies and reinforcements in

Puebla the governor is by law forced to accede." Don Isidro snorted like an old bull. "That is what I mean to tell him," he declared, "but what good do you think it will do? You are simplicity itself if you imagine that anything can be accomplished here in Mexico without the assistance of the Church. We are a cursed people . . . cursed with religion, among other things. But do your duty, say what you have to say to the governor and then I will arrange for you to see the bishop. If he has slept well and had a good breakfast . . ." His voice died away.

There was so much confusion at the doors that the couple were not challenged by the guards. They passed into the lower hall, weaving their way around knots of men who seemed engaged in angry argument. More than one sotana was in evidence. "I advise you not to listen," warned Don Isidro. "Most of these fellows are merchants who do not want their places of business blown up or sacked. They are ready, nay, anxious to sell out the Republic for a few chests of onyx beads or a warehouse of cotton or tobacco or Tlaxcalan pottery." He seized Juan Diego by the arm suddenly. "My disgust is turning me into a patriot," he asserted, surprise in his voice. Juan Diego shook his head as though to clear it from unpleasant fumes. "There are a lot of priests here," he said. "The bishop is a good general," replied Don Isidro. "He knows how to dispose his forces." They mounted marble stairs, passed beneath dark faded portraits of forgotton governors and came up to the entrance of Isunza's reception chamber.

Here the door was open, too. A babble of voices like a heavy upflung surf splashed into their faces as they crossed the threshold and walked toward the long table where the governor sat. Don Isidro moved in a straight line, unceremoniously shoving men right and left, and Juan Diego moved directly in his wake, ignoring the exasperated exclamations aroused by his burly companion. The governor was fat, pale-yellow in complexion and exceedingly nervous. Juan Diego thought that he looked like a plump gopher blown up to enormous proportions but still retaining all of his timidity. It would not have been surprising to see him pop suddenly into some protecting hole and completely disappear from sight. Don Isidro reached the table, swept away a slight little man before it and leaned over.

"Señor Gobernador," he said in a loud voice. "I present a messenger from General Santa Anna, the Señor Teniente Juan—"

"I cannot receive him now," broke in Isunza in a high tenor voice that shook with irritation. "He must arrange an appointment with my secretary. In two or three days, maybe."

"This is no time for formality, Señor Gobernador!" exclaimed Don Isidro. "Are you aware—"

"You must leave the chamber," ordered Isunza. "You and your companion. This is not right, Don Isidro. Our friendship does not—"

"Friendship!" boomed the hacendado. "Who in the name of Jesucristo is speaking about friendship? I bring you an urgent messenger from General Santa Anna. He carries certain orders with him. He—"

"I do not recognize the authority of General Santa Anna," declared Isunza flatly. "I am waiting for instructions from Mexico City. Will you be so kind, Don Isidro . . ."

"Whose orders do you recognize?" demanded Don Isidro insolently. "Those of my uncle, the bishop? Or those of the Yanqui generals? Is it true that you have sent representatives to Jalapa? Come now . . ."

Isunza rose to his feet, his yellow cheeks shaking.

"Captain Huerta!" he called in a shrill voice. "Eject these men from the chamber. Throw them out into the street. This is unbear—"

"And what will my uncle say to that?" asked Don Isidro evenly. "He may not like my opinions but he likes me."

Isunza sat down.

"I cannot receive the messenger from General Santa Anna now," he said sullenly. "If the messenger has a written order and he wants to leave it . . ."

Juan Diego unbuttoned his tunic and took a folded paper from his inner pocket. He placed it on the table before Isunza.

"There it is, Señor Gobernador," he said crisply. "It is an order for supplies, ammunition, money and reinforcements. It is also an order to fortify the city and hold out at all costs until the general reaches here with . . ."

Isunza picked up the paper and threw it back on the table.

"Dios mío!" he exclaimed. "What supplies? What ammunition? What money? What reinforcements? Has General Santa Anna lost his senses? We have none of these things. Puebla is not a fortress. It is a city without defenses. It is—"

"We can made it a fortress," interrupted Don Isidro. "We can build defenses. We can fight at Ojo de Agua. We . . ."

There was a murmur of voices, a loud laugh and then a bold voice declared, "Don Isidro thinks he is the Cid." The hacendado whirled around.

"Who was that?" he asked sharply. "Who is the dog that barks so loudly behind a man's back? Let him show his teeth to my face. Let him—"

Isunza hammered despairingly on the table.

"Don Isidro, Don Isidro!" he squealed. "I have had enough of this. This is a meeting of the city fathers and as you have never stooped so low as to become one of them your place is not here. You and the messenger must go."

He inspected Juan Diego briefly with small angry eyes half-concealed in cheeks like corn-meal dough.

"I have your dispatch from General Santa Anna," he said. "I will read it. I will consider it. Come back in another day and I will give you my decision."

"Does that mean that you will do nothing before the Yanquis get here?" asked Don Isidro.

"I will consider everything," declared the governor, ignoring the hacendado's angry question. "Come back in a day, Señor . . . Señor . . . Yes, yes, come back in a day. Captain Huerta, show these gentlemen to the door. Now . . . if you will excuse me . . ."

Before he could take more than a step forward Juan Diego grasped Don Isidro by the arm.

"Come, my friend," he said. "There is nothing more to be accomplished here. I have fulfilled my mission. The general will receive the answer when he rides into Puebla."

"I would like to tell the Señor Gobernador . . ." began Don Isidro.

"I beg you to come," pleaded Juan Diego.

Without a word the hacendado turned and strode heavily across the polished floor. Faces, dark, yellow, brown, moved and shifted before and behind him. Juan Diego, following, thought he saw expressions of concern and admiration in some of these faces but by far the greater part of them were either indifferent or antagonistic. They stepped into the hall, passed beneath the faded portraits, descended the marble stairs and crossed the lower hall and reached the outer doors without saying a word. Here Don Isidro stopped and drew in a deep breath of air.

"I am not politic," he said querulously and then he smiled.

"You see," he went on as they left the pavement behind them and plunged into the plaza. "I have no patience with these fellows. These are the worms that are turned up by the plow of the Republic. You delivered your message. Well, that was right. But the answer to it will not come from Isunza. It will come from the bishop. In my anger this morning I was fool enough to think that I could go to Isunza and rouse him sufficiently to stand up to the bishop. Well, well, for the moment I had forgotten what he looked like—an evil spirit of the vómito. There is nothing to be done in that direction. We will go to the bishop, you and I, and talk to *him*. That is all we can do."

Suddenly Juan Diego chuckled.

"If I go to the bishop with you will you promise to restrain your anger?" he asked.

Don Isidro looked sharply at the young officer, scowled and then permitted a faint smile to flit across his mouth.

"I am not patient," he said. "Well . . ."

He walked along in silence for a moment.

"I am not accustomed to being spoken to in that manner," he declared mildly.

A beggar's open palm flashed beneath his nose and he paused to search for a coin and slip it into the cupped fingers.

"I imagine that I must accustom myself to many things I would not suffer in the past," he said in a slow puzzled voice. "Even, perhaps, at Las Golondrinas. Everything is changing. The world is getting smaller."

He rubbed the white scar on his temple as he looked up at the façade of the cathedral. Juan Diego walked silently beside him.

"It is impossible to be God when you have to stop and think," the hacendado remarked in a low tone and the young man wondered what he meant.

"My hastiness was not fair to you," the older man went on. "I should have been more politic before Isunza. I forgot momentarily that ceremony is four-fifths of success in life. You see, I never had any need for it. But now . . . Yes, Juan Diego, I promise to restrain my anger before the bishop."

The young man flushed.

"I was merely making a bad joke," he said self-consciously.

"It wasn't such a bad joke," replied Don Isidro.

Late that evening the two men sat at the deserted dinner table eating morronas and drinking aguardiente. This, although Juan Diego did not know it, was unusual in two ways. Don Isidro, hitherto, had scorned morronas, those little round cakes made from flour, lard and spices, and his after-dinner refreshment always had been port wine from the Douro or French champagne. Aguardiente, he claimed, was as crude and common as the Republic. It was not as common as pulque but it had no pedigree and all the things that mattered, liquor, women and horses, particularly, had pedigrees. Yet, against his better judgment, he discovered that he liked aguardiente. He drank steadily and deliberately as though it was a duty and a ceremonial. Juan Diego, drinking much less, began to feel the heat of the liquor. He listened lazily while Don Isidro ate, drank and talked.

"Yes, Señor Teniente," he said, "if we knew a little more we would know all. But I think I know enough to tell which way the wind is blowing. You saw Isunza, that yellow son of a Vera Cruz nocharniega and a sick mule, and you must have realized that he is nothing more than a mask, a false face for the sly power behind him. It is the

Church, my friend. It is the Roman Catholic Church in Mexico. And Puebla is the Holy City of the Church. Do you think the bishop wants a cannon ball in one of the towers of his blessed cathedral?"

"The bishop knows we are at war," declared Juan Diego, "and the miter is backing the war."

"Who knows what the miter is doing?" Don Isidro asked. "Are we in the confidence of the archbishop? The miter is doing exactly what it thinks most profits the miter. That is all. The miter doesn't give a damn for the Republic or Texas or the lands of California. Oh, it would like to control all of them but not at the expense of its wealth and prestige in Mexico. I know more about these things than you do, Señor Teniente. Perhaps the truth does not occur to me immediately and perhaps my anger gets in the way sometimes but sooner or later I can smell out a bad smell. You tell me that the miter is backing the war. Very well. I tell you that the miter backed the war as long as it thought the Church had a chance to take over completely and that Santa Anna would be destroyed in the process. That is what I think now. The Church favored the war because it hoped Santa Anna would devour himself. It doesn't know at this moment whether he has or he hasn't. It doesn't know whether or not he can raise another army. It doesn't know what power he has left in Mexico City. The ecclesiastical cabildo is watching and waiting. The—"

"He *is* raising another army," broke in Juan Diego. "He has the brigade of Antonio de León. He . . ."

Don Isidro raised his hand.

"He is an astonishing man," he said heavily, "but the Church is an astonishing organization. It moves on principle. It has no heart. What can Santa Anna do for the Church? What can the Americans do for the Church? Do you know . . ."

His voice dropped and he leaned forward.

"Do you know," he repeated, "I believe the Church is already discussing these matters with the Americans. The Church . . ."

"That is treason!" exclaimed Juan Diego.

Don Isidro broke into a deep chuckle.

"I shouldn't laugh," he said, "but I do. Treason? What an idealistic young man you are! Treason is committed by unsuccessful men. Do not forget that the Church is not a national institution. It belongs to all countries and it desires all countries to belong to it. If an emissary of the United States can convince the Church that resistance is dangerous and that the invading Americans will guarantee the freedom and property of the miter I am very certain that the Church will listen."

"It is abominable!" burst out Juan Diego.

"It is common sense," said Don Isidro. "Since my outburst before Isunza I have been thinking about these things. Do you know what I

believe now? I believe that the Church is working for a peace of negotiation. I believe that the Church is now working against Santa Anna
as the chief obstacle. I believe that the Church arranged with the
ayuntamientos of Jalapa, Perote, Puebla and, yes, Mexico City, that
those places offer no resistance to the advancing Americans."

Juan Diego stared with amazement at the hacendado.

"It cannot be as bad as that," he said in a choked voice.

"Drink some more aguardiente," advised Don Isidro, pouring
himself another glass. "What else is there to think?" he went on. "The
guns of the Americans are rumbling up the National Highway. Their
cavalry has been seen as near as Perote. Is anybody opposing them?
Have you seen any efforts to fortify Puebla? Are there any barricades
in the streets? Are supplies pouring in? No, no, Señor Teniente."

His voice was raised and firm.

"We are a lost people," he affirmed, "but you are more lost than I
am because you have ideals. This is a business war, Señor Teniente.
There are no ideals concerned in this war. The Americans want something that we have and we do not want to give it to them. But if we
discover that we cannot stand our ground we will make the best bargain we can. The Americans call it Manifest Destiny, which is another
way of saying that they are big enough and determined enough to take
California and Texas away from us and if they cannot do it by means
of an absurd legal bluff they will do it with the bayonet. Our Most
Holy Mother Church does not intend to lose either way. That is, if by
some miracle we should win, the Church will win with us; if, as seems
very possible now, we lose, the Church will win with the Americans."

"We are fighting for our own lands," said Juan Diego slowly.
"We are fighting *on* our own lands."

Don Isidro shrugged his big shoulders.

"If you fight in Puebla," he declared dryly, "you will be fighting
alone. Puebla will not fight. I am sure of that. Puebla will open her
doors to the Americans and the Poblanos will raise their prices and
make as much as they can out of the occupation."

"The general will have something to say about that!" exclaimed
Juan Diego fiercely.

"I have no doubt but that he will say a lot," answered Don Isidro.
"What interests me is to see what he will *do*."

He crumbled a morrona between his fingers.

"Tomorrow," he continued, "we will call on my uncle, the bishop.
If he feels like talking he will—"

Suddenly he stopped and stared at the young man.

"I have talked a great deal, haven't I?" he asked without smiling.
"Perhaps it is the aguardiente. I never liked it before. Well, let us
dismiss the war until tomorrow. Shall we? It is late and . . . There

is something I have wanted to say to you for some hours now, something, thank God, that has nothing to do with the war or the Church or General Santa Anna. It is something between you and me."

Juan Diego looked his surprise.

"What have I . . ." he began.

"Do you remember when we last spoke to each other at Las Golondrinas?" asked Don Isidro deliberately. "I see that you do. I must ask your pardon . . ."

He hesitated and cleared his throat as though the words were sticking in it.

"I must ask your pardon," he went on doggedly, "for a discourteous attitude on my part. I realize—"

"Don Isidro," broke in Juan Diego quickly, "you do not have to say these things to me. I would rather—"

"Let me say it," insisted the hacendado gloomily. "I am not quite so sure of myself as I was on the evening of my daughter's marriage. It will do me good to say it. I make my excuses to you, Señor Teniente. You see . . . I . . . ah . . . am beginning to understand that a man does not always dispose . . . I mean . . ."

"I have forgotten everything that happened that night," said Juan Diego firmly.

"I do not believe that," remarked Don Isidro calmly.

His hesitation vanished as he gazed speculatively at the aguardiente flask.

"There is a lot of fire there," he said, smiling.

Then he reached over and placed his hand on the young man's wrist.

"There is a lot of fire in you, too," he said. "But it does not come out. It is hidden under too many layers of control. Is that your Yanqui blood? You must show more flame, Juan Diego. It is bad for you to keep this fire under too much control. It will consume you inside and that would be bad. Be angry often. Fall in love. Do anything but do not remain static inside of yourself. No, I am not drunk. Oh, a little, perhaps . . . but not much. Do you understand me?"

Juan Diego did not feel like smiling.

"I think I understand you," he replied.

"Here we are, an old man and a young man," continued Don Isidro, "sitting and talking, eating and drinking, dropping one subject for another without reason, and . . . But let the fire out, my friend, let the fire out."

"I will," promised Juan Diego, summoning up the smile he did not feel.

"I believe you will," said Don Isidro seriously. "If all Mexico would let the fire out there would be no gringos on our soil today. Come now, shall we have another glass of this potent liquid before we bid each other good night? Come, let me pour it."

He raised the flask and poured carefully while Juan Diego sat and observed his heavy head, the white scar on his temple and the determined push of his underlip. He was beginning to feel a great affection for Don Isidro.

He awoke early and surprisingly clearheaded. Through his open window the fresh spring air flowed in and brought him the scent of morning roses from which the dew had not yet been sucked up by the bright day. He lay blinking at the light and endeavored lazily to assemble his impressions and put them into some sort of tidy order. Here he was in Don Isidro's house in Puebla and there was the general laboring mightily at Orizaba to forge an army out of splintered fragments and resume the fighting of a war that had stopped dead in its tracks. That was his first impression and he imagined he should build on that and see where it led him. But it wouldn't work that way. His second impression had nothing to do with the war, with the attitude of Puebla or Isunza or the bishop toward the general and his plans; it had to do with Doña María Catalina. He was beginning to see her clearly now and somehow that pleased him. He could shut his eyes and visualize her face and it came easily, not in the likeness of Our Lady but in that of a girl who has her secrets and desires. Last night at the dinner table he had looked at her frequently and there were moments when it seemed to him that her mild reserve became transparent and he could look through it as one looks through a glass mask and see the *real* face, the *real* person, behind. Then, at a word directed to her by Doña Ágata or Don Isidro or Doña Concha (who he had discovered was her companion or dueña), the mask would grow opaque and she would disappear into the mystery of herself. It had become like a little game, a secret game shared between the two of them, to catch these brief revelations. I should be thinking of the great problem the general has before him and how best to help him, he thought as he blinked at the bright light filling the room, yes, that is what I should be thinking. The bishop . . . Suddenly he remembered Don Alejandro and the glow shivered and darkened. That . . . that *toad!* For a minute or two he lay still and permitted his mind to reconstruct that last evening at Las Golondrinas but he found nothing new in it. He could see it all as clearly as though it were happening at this instant but there was nothing to add. Don Alej— Probably, he was in Mexico City. It was safe enough there.

There came a rap at the door and Chepe entered with a pitcher of hot water.

"Good morning, Chepe," said Juan Diego, sitting up in bed.

"Good morning, Señor Teniente," replied the Indian, putting the pitcher down and turning with a faint light kindling in his eyes. "Shall I bring the Señor Teniente a cup of hot chocolate?"

The young man swung lustily out of bed.

"No, Chepe, no," he answered. "I will join Don Isidro later downstairs."

"The patrón will not come down until near noon," said the Indian.

He moved toward the door, his guaraches scuffing on the tiles.

"Chepe," called Juan Diego.

The Indian stopped.

"Chepe," demanded the young man, feeling his cheeks fill with color and furious at the sensation, "Is Don Alejandro in Mexico City?"

"Yes, Señor Teniente," said the Indian.

He stood waiting for a moment and then as Juan Diego did not speak he walked toward the corridor. At the door he turned.

"It is very pleasant in the patio this morning," he said.

Juan Diego stood looking reflectively at him as he disappeared from view.

When he had finished washing and dressing the young man stepped to the window and looked down. The flowers, faintly fluttered by a slight breeze, appeared to be struggling to rise from their roots. Juan Diego turned around, walked across the chamber, stepped into the hall, closed the door, went downstairs and followed a corridor that opened into the patio.

It was beautiful.

He moved slowly along the flagstoned path, pausing to admire the roses that seemed to bend toward him from all sides and when he arrived at the rustic bench beneath the willow tree he was not surprised to see Doña María Catalina sitting there. She was arranging a number of cut roses in a pottery vase from Talavera. Near her, holding a woven basket in which there were yet more roses, was the plump figure of Doña Concha. He stood looking down at the luxuriant black hair of the girl and wondering what to say. Perhaps a cough was the thing.

"Will you sit by me, Señor Teniente?" asked Doña María Catalina without lifting her head.

He laughed and looked at the empty portion of the bench covered with rose twigs.

"Permit me," he said and stretched forth his hand but before he could sweep the twigs away she had done it herself. She uttered a little cry and held up her forefinger. A large thorn was embedded in it. For the first time she raised wide hurt gray eyes. He exclaimed with sympathy and took her by the wrist and pulled the thorn out. A tiny bead of bright blood took its place. Quite suddenly he was transfixed, mes-

merized by this small drop of red that had come from the heart of the
girl, and stood without moving, staring down, holding Doña María
Catalina's wrist in a tight grasp, knowing and not knowing that what
he was doing was something no strange man had ever done to her
before. He could feel a small even pulse beating beneath his fingers.
The drop of blood gave the illusion of growing, of swelling to enormous proportions as though it was being brought closer and closer to
his eye until it covered the pupil and shut out all the rest of the world.
Then, in a flash, it was no more than a tiny bead of crimson. He
glanced up, startled and confused. Doña Concha was staring at him
strangely, he thought, and Doña María Catalina was deliberately withdrawing her hand from his grasp, not hastily or with visible disapproval but naturally, without surprise or second thought.

"It is nothing," she said. "I prick myself three or four times a
day, Señor Teniente. Will you sit down now?"

He looked carefully along the bench and then sat down.

"It is so beautiful out here," he said inanely.

She nodded and stretched her hand toward Doña Concha.

"The rest of the roses," she demanded. "Now cut me some yellow
ones, tiíta."

The fat dueña waddled away with her basket and Doña María
Catalina appeared absorbed in arranging her flowers. She was half-
turned from Juan Diego, her head slanting forward and her hair
swinging about her cheeks, but he could see the soft curve of her chin
and the whiteness of the even teeth clutching the full lower lip. Presently she raised her head with a sharp gesture that threw back her hair
and looked directly at him.

"There," she said. "I will wait for more roses."

She inspected him frankly for a moment and then smiled.

"Señor Teniente," she continued, "I am happy to see you here this
morning. It gives me an opportunity to thank you for the help you
gave me that night at Las Golondrinas."

He was suddenly confused.

"I don't remember anything—" he began quickly, but she interrupted him.

"I do," she declared. "I remember it very well."

"I remember it, too," he said immediately, "but I cannot—"

"I am very direct," she broke in calmly. "I am not an expert in
the oblique language of the ladies of Mexico City. I have no false
modesty and I cannot pretend to be interested in things that do not
interest me. That is why most people find me unresponsive and
tiresome."

He was surprised at this language and shook his head.

"I don't find you tiresome, Doña María Catalina," he said.

"I don't believe you do," she replied serenely. "You will observe, Señor Teniente, that I am not shy, either."

"No," he remarked, smiling. "I can now see that you are not shy."

She laughed and put the pottery vase down on the ground beside her.

"I am very quiet," she said reflectively, "but that is because I seldom can think of anything worth saying. I am certain that people talk too much. You must have heard them in the drawing rooms of the capital gabbling like geese for the mere sake of the sound. I am not like that. I can exist for days without saying a word. I know that this worries my mother, who expects me to exclaim over trifles, a new dress, a bracelet or a rare stone from the mines, or to gossip with her or to express surprise or joy over what she may say. I cannot do that. There are moments when I am sure that she considers me an idiot. But it is the way I am fashioned."

She paused and regarded him in a questioning manner.

"I am glad you have told me this," he remarked, endeavoring to adopt a light tone. "Hereafter I will discuss only weighty topics with you, those that are worthy of words."

"I am too ignorant for that," she declared quickly. "And that is not what I meant. No, I want you to understand me a little. Do you know why?"

He shook his head.

"It is because I like you, Señor Teniente," she announced deliberately.

He flushed to the roots of his dark hair and immediately felt like a fool. It was the first time in his life that a woman had ever told him in so many words that she liked him and it was something he had feared and avoided all his life. An instinctive repulsion had guarded him from women and the only one to whom he had surrendered his affections had been the general's first wife, Doña Inés. But she had been both mother and protecting goddess to him and he hardly thought of her as a woman. As for Doña María Catalina, he remembered his vague unwilled dreams of her and the confused fear he had experienced when he first crossed the threshold of this house in Puebla and he found now that he could no longer dismiss these emotions as a fugitive impression caught up in the net of his fancy. They were much more than that. The moment she made her candid avowal everything crystallized in his consciousness. He had always wanted to see her. He had always wanted to talk with her. He had always wanted her to like him. He had come into the patio hoping and expecting to find her. And now it seemed as natural as the sunlight falling on the wall or the roses gleaming upon their little bushes or the slowly moving figure of Doña Concha moving beyond the web of branches.

"I am glad of that, Doña María Catalina," he said earnestly, meeting her level gray-eyed glance with relief and pleasure.

"Tell me, Señor Teniente," demanded the girl suddenly, "has my father ever spoken to you of that night at Las Golondrinas?"

"Yes," he replied. "Last night. Only a few words. I . . ."

"Did you tell him also that you had forgotten?" she asked.

Juan Diego could not repress a self-conscious smile.

"Yes," he admitted, "I did."

She did not smile. She placed her hand upon his wrist in a brief gesture and then removed it.

"You must always tell the truth," she said, as though she was speaking to a child. "To say that one forgets when one does not forget is either infantile or cowardly."

"I thought it was the thing to do," he mumbled.

Suddenly she laughed, a high trill that caused Doña Concha to half-turn in the garden.

"You look like a boy whose knuckles have been rapped by his schoolmaster," she said. "I beg you, Señor Teniente, do not look like that. And never consider the thing to do when you speak with my father and me. We are somewhat alike although we do not seem so. My father has never spoken to me of that night and I have never spoken to him of it, either. That is because we are both independent. But there are moments when I think we are beginning to understand each other without words. Señor Teniente, my father is changing. My mother does not know it but I do. I think you can help him but you must be very sure never to let him know that you are helping him."

"He seems to me like a man who reaches his conclusions in his own way and at his own time," pointed out Juan Diego.

"In his own way, perhaps," agreed the girl soberly, "but not always at his own time."

Doña Concha came plodding toward them with her basket filled with yellow roses. She handed over the flowers and sat down, puffing on the end of the bench.

"Have you been amusing the Señor Teniente with stories?" she asked after she had regained her breath.

"Riddles," replied Doña María Catalina, thrusting roses into the pottery vase which she had picked up again.

"Riddles?" repeated Doña Concha. "I like riddles. Ask me one sobrina."

"Very well," answered the girl. "What shall we have for the mid day meal?"

"Eh! Eh! That is no riddle," exclaimed the dueña. "We are going to have a picadillo with almonds."

She shut her eyes and leaned back against the bench.

Juan Diego watched Doña María Catalina's busy hands shifting back and forth in the sunlight and it seemed to him that they revealed the most graceful motions he had ever seen. They were small hands, almost transparently white, but there was no suggestion of weakness in them. It was so with all of her body, small, to be sure, what the French would call petite, but assured, co-ordinated and resilient. She was no fragile porcelain figure although she might give that impression from a distance. Instead, she was firm and compact with reserves of energy that he could sense flowing through her faintly perfumed flesh. He sat lazily beside her (for she appeared to have returned into her customary silence) and watched her crowd the roses into the vase. Each movement delighted him. The bend of her arm, the inclination of her neck, the twist of her body, these gestures reminded him of music. And like music, too, was the faint rustle of her petticoats, the scrape of her heel on the gravel and the tinkle of her half dozen silver bracelets.

There was an entire absence of self-consciousness about her that delighted him as much as it surprised him. She was not like the young women he had fled from in Mexico City, those painted and pouting young women with embarrassing eyes who stood behind barred windows and listened to the serenaders and sometimes flung down a rose or a ribbon. Or the women who rode in open carriages in the Paseo, bareheaded, in dinner dress, presenting the backs of their hands and twiddling their fingers at their passing friends. These women, who flirted outrageously whether married or single, had not actually frightened Juan Diego but they *had* aroused in him a wariness that was instinctive and whose deep roots he had never troubled to examine. But Doña María Catalina was a rare discovery. Her lack of surprise pleased him almost as much as her lack of self-consciousness. And the forthrightness of her manner unembellished by all those artful coynesses that composed the stock in trade of most privileged young women who had nothing in life to do but adorn themselves was as fresh as a gourd of spring water. The curious part of it was that he was so little surprised at the discovery of these unexpected qualities in her. The moment they had appeared they seemed as natural as the daylight. If anything, he was surprised at his lack of surprise.

She finished arranging the vase of roses, nudged Doña Concha to rouse her from the verge of a nap, and rose to her feet. Juan Diego observed that she wore small buckled Spanish shoes and white cashmere stockings.

"It is time for me to go, Señor Teniente," she said as the young man scrambled to his feet. "Adiós . . . until this noon."

"I'll carry the vase, Doña María Catalina," he volunteered, extending his hands.

"No," she replied. "Remain here. Doña Concha will carry the vase."

She smiled, turned and walked toward the house door, a small erect figure in wide-flowing skirts, followed by the waddling dueña. Juan Diego watched them until both disappeared and then he sat down again on the bench. The sun was warm on the knees of his military breeches. He sat for a minute smiling softly to himself and thinking of nothing at all. Then he glanced about the patio. It was really the most beautiful place in the world and the silence, now faintly broken by the sound of invisible bees, made it even more beautiful. It would be pleasant to sit here all day and do nothing at all but dream beneath the willow and watch the roses sway softly in the gentle breeze. Yet he knew that the temptation to do so was something that must be put aside and denied. Too many Mexicans yielded to the same temptation. To sit in the sun. To dream. To pull one's sombrero over one's face and sleep. Mañana. That was the word the general hated. It was the people who sat in the sun who said it. Mañana. We will do it tomorrow. And tomorrow never came. Perhaps it was dangerous to live in too beautiful a world. It left nothing to fight for.

A faint scowl spread across his face. Oh, there was plenty to fight for, all right. And he remembered that Don Isidro and he were to visit the bishop this afternoon. He had little faith of changing the bishop's mind on anything whatsoever and his only hope appeared to be that the bishop had not quite made up his mind. If that were so, some word that he might say might have some influence. He thought of the invulnerability of the bishop sitting in the library of his villa with the rows of books in Latin all about him and the soft-stepping priests bowing their tonsured heads like so many grajos picking up crumbs, and the sunlight in the patio did not seem so fine, after all. If Isunza was an echo of the bishop, as Don Isidro had intimated, then seeing the bishop would be nothing more than a waste of time. But the gesture must be made. He had promised the general that he would spread the word about the required reinforcements. He had seen the governor and now he would see the bishop. Surely, among them all there must be one with some vision.

He rose from the bench and walked slowly along the narrow flagged path toward the house door. My God, what a curious world he thought, so beautiful and so wretched at the same time. At the door he paused and bent over and picked up a yellow rose that lay exactly on the lintel. He walked slowly up the stairs to his chamber, swinging the flower by its cut stem. That was a strange thing. It must have fallen from the vase. But . . . Chepe was just finishing putting his room in order and he slipped around the door and disappeared as the young officer crossed to the window. Juan Diego gazed at the peaceful scene

for a moment and then turned and laid the rose on the high Spanish
tocador that stood against the wall. He moved over to the canopied
bed and sank upon it, putting his folded arms under his head and
letting his booted legs dangle toward the floor. He shut his eyes tightly
and drew in a long breath. He remembered now that he had not read a
newspaper in days. What was happening? Where was the general?
Where, for that matter, were the Americans? He would remember to
ask Don Isidro to secure a copy of the *Monitor del Pueblo*. It was this
damnable waiting . . . He heard the soft slap of sandals and supposed
that Chepe had entered the room to put something in its place. This
waiting. Yes. One waited for weeks and then fought for a day. And
then one waited for more weeks and piled up ammunition and supplies
for another day's fighting. The slap of Chepe's sandals died at the door.
Gone. The invisible Indian. He opened his eyes and stared straight
upward at the canopied top of the bed. He couldn't stay here all morning. Perhaps Don Isidro had left his chamber and gone down to the
library. He unfolded his arms and swung himself to a sitting position.
He might as well go down. If the hacendado was not there he would
browse among the books. There might be . . . Hello. He stood up
smiling. The rose that he had laid on the tocador now stood in a little
blue glazed vase. Chepe. He walked over to the flower and bent over it
and inhaled its delicate odor. There was water in the vase. He thought,
it is very still and peaceful around the rose. When he bent to inhale its
odor again he imagined that he could smell the faint perfume of Doña
María Catalina's hand. Then he went downstairs to the library. Don
Isidro was not there and he picked up a book of verse by Fernando
Calderón y Beltrán and began to read it.

As they approached the bishop's villa Don Isidro slackened his
pace.

"It won't do any good to make speeches," he said to Juan Diego.
"The bishop stopped listening to speeches forty years ago. I must warn
you that he carries little pellets of cotton about with him and whenever
he is bored he pops them into his ears. He is nearly always bored."

"I am not going to make a speech," declared the young officer
gloomily. "I shall try to explain to the bishop that it is to the advantage
of the Church for Mexico to maintain a stout defense against the
Americans."

"If you can convince him . . ." remarked the hacendado doubtfully.

They turned in at the open door of the red-brick villa and after
waiting no more than a moment or two were admitted to the library.
The bishop of Puebla was sitting behind a long table covered with
books, manuscripts and a carafe of water. American-made spectacles,

apparently just removed from his nose, were clutched in his right hand. He made a grimace when he saw his nephew and observed Juan Diego with some interest.

"Good afternoon, my nephew," he said immediately. "I understand that you visited the governor yesterday and lost your temper."

"It was a momentary weakness," replied Don Isidro. "I had forgotten what a nonentity Isunza was and the sight of him upset my stomach."

The bishop scratched his chin impatiently.

"Yes, yes," he said. "You do not like Isunza. Well, you do not have to like Isunza. What is it now? This, I take it, is the emissary of General Santa Anna."

"Don Juan Diego de Béxar," proclaimed Don Isidro. "He was the bearer of a dispatch to the governor. But it appears—"

"I am sure the governor is giving full consideration to any communications from the general . . . and president," broke in the bishop.

He studied the young officer with small sharp insolent eyes.

"What is it, Señor Teniente?" he asked blandly. "Do you carry a communication for me, too, from the . . ."

"I bring you no particular communication, Ilustrísimo Señor Obispo," said Juan Diego carefully, "but the general advised me to speak to anybody I thought might strengthen the defensive spirit of Puebla."

"Yes, yes," murmured the prelate. "And you have come to speak to me about it. Is that right? My son, I am not concerned with military matters. My province is spiritual. It is the souls of my—"

"The defensive spirit is in your province, then," broke in Don Isidro.

"Are you interrupting?" asked the bishop mildly, without looking at the hacendado.

"Ilustrísimo señor," said Juan Diego earnestly, "it is true that the general has suffered a defeat at Cerro Gordo. But it is also true that he is reorganizing his forces and means to make a stand before or within Puebla. To do this he will need the complete support of the Poblanos. He is struggling solely for the glory and safety of the Republic. He is fighting for the Church, the integrity of our lands and the common man. He is facing a formidable invader who—"

"Wait a minute, Señor Teniente," exclaimed the bishop, fumbling in the sash that circled his waist. "You are about to make a speech and I do not like speeches. Let us converse, my young friend, let us converse. The general has been facing a formidable invader for years. He faced him on the San Jacinto. He faced him at Buena Vista. He faced him at the Cerro Gordo. And every time he ended by turning his back on him. That is not good, young man. One does not win a war by constant defeats. What does the general plan now? To make a stand a

Puebla until the city is a mass of rubble and then turn his back again? It is a curious way of fighting a campaign, although, as I said before, I am not concerned with military matters and know little about them."

"We've *got* to fight," exclaimed Juan Diego desperately. "You've *got* to fight. Don Isidro must fight. Every man in Puebla must carry a musket to the barricades. Our cause is just!"

"I hear disturbing things about the Americans," said the bishop. "Is it true that their cavalry men can hew a man asunder with one stroke of the saber? Is it true that their horses are gigantic and incredibly swift? Is it true that their artillery is unspeakably terrible? Is it true that their bullets split into fifty pieces and every piece fatal? Is it—"

"You speak like Moctezuma when he heard the runners describe Cortés and his army!" cried Juan Diego indignantly. "There is no truth in any of those rumors. The Americans are soldiers like ourselves. We killed plenty of them at Buena Vista. We broke their lines there. It is true that they are better equipped but it is also true that their hearts are not in this war. We can hold them if we have the heart to hold them. Every mile they travel along the National Highway stretches their line of supplies. We can cut that line to pieces. We can hold them before Puebla until new armies of our own come down from Mexico City. Put aside your personal dislike of the general—"

"I have no personal dislikes," broke in the bishop sharply. "All men are the children of God to me . . . except those who through arrogance or invincible ignorance or unrepented sin are lost and fulminating in outer darkness. What do you desire me to do, Señor Teniente? Preach on the street corners like Peter the Hermit? Tell my people to go out and die for the general? Do you believe for one moment that we can hold Puebla against the strong forces of the Americans?"

"Yes, I do," declared Juan Diego. "I think we can hold the Americans long enough for Mexico City to put itself in invulnerable defense. I think the turning point of the war is here in Puebla. I think—"

The bishop waved his hand impatiently.

"Very well, very well," he said. "You think, you think . . . That is very good. I am glad that you think. But be good enough to remember that the rest of us think, too."

He stopped abruptly and observed both men keenly.

"I do not say that Puebla will not be defended," he declared, after a moment. "Neither do I say that it will. That is a matter for the governor, the prefect and the comandante general to decide between them. They know what supplies there are and what strength is at our disposition. If, in their judgment, the prospects are good for a successful defense I have no doubt but that the city will fight. If these prospects are *not* good . . ."

He fluttered his thin bloodless hand in the air.

"When does the general expect to enter the city?" he asked suddenly in a businesslike voice.

"I don't know," replied Juan Diego. "In a few days, perhaps. He is organizing at—"

"At Orizaba," broke in the bishop. "I know. Well, when the general is here we . . . I mean the city government . . . will talk with him. Now, then . . ."

He looked meaningly at the door.

Don Isidro, who had stood stolidly without saying a word since the bishop had accused him of interrupting, growled in his throat like an old watchdog. Juan Diego stepped forward and leaned across the long table.

"Señor Obispo," he said, "you are a patriot. The glory of Mexico is the glory of the Church. It has been ten years since Mexico and the Church lost the province of Texas. The deserted missions there call out to their mother, the Church. The missions of California call, too. You cannot desert them. The sound of their bells would sound like regret in your mind for the rest of your life. If you open the gates of Puebla to the Americans you are throwing away a part of the rightful heritage of the Church. Those valleys and deserts and mountains and forests are baptized in the blood of the mission fathers. Remember the blood. Listen to the bells."

He stopped and Don Isidro could see tears glistening in the young officer's eyes.

The bishop coughed, a faint little croak like a faraway frog.

"Señor Teniente," he said in a subdued voice, "there is much sadness in the world. We who are old know that. Our only refuge is in God and this is especially true when we are the weak and are attacked by the strong. It is easy to say that we can die, for, after all, that is the inevitable end of all of us so far as this feeble envelope of flesh is concerned. But our immortal souls do not die. They fly to heaven. The blood of the mission fathers and the sound of the mission bells are not forgotten. The blood shines in our eyes forever and the bells ring in our ears as long as the sun rises and sets over those deserted missions. The dead helping hands of the mission fathers will never disappear from Texas or California. They will be there as long as the land is there. My son, the Church throws nothing away, not even the weak bodies of its children."

A creak at the door interrupted him. It was the plump padre whom Don Isidro had been inclined to kick in the backside the day before.

"What is it, Brother Eugenio?" asked the bishop sharply.

"The messenger with the manifesto from the govern—" began the padre.

"That's enough!" exclaimed the bishop. "Tell him to wait. I will see him in a moment."

The birdlike prelate rose nimbly to his feet as the padre slid through the door. He came around the table and put his arm about Juan Diego's shoulders, looking up with a half-smile into the young officer's face.

"You are an eloquent young man," he remarked with good humor. "I shall consider all that you have said and I am sure that the governor will do all he can to satisfy General Santa Anna. We are not as unpatriotic as we may seem. I wouldn't be surprised if Isunza sends for you tomorrow. Go, now, with my blessing, Señor Teniente."

As he led them toward the door he turned to Don Isidro.

"You are developing self-control . . . as well as patriotism, my nephew," he remarked humorously. "This, I believe, is the first time I have seen you silent since I first had the pleasure of meeting you. Ask Doña Ágata and Doña María Catalina to remember me in their prayers. They are well?"

"They are well," mumbled Don Isidro.

"I am happy to know that," said the bishop. "Very happy, indeed. Farewell, then. Farewell. I shall hope to see you again in a few days."

He stood smiling at the door as they passed through.

It was not until they were some distance from the red-brick villa that the hacendado spoke.

"So Isunza is concocting a manifesto," he said soberly. "Now, what can that be? And the bishop must give it his approval. Well . . ."

Juan Diego walked along with his eyes turned toward the roadway.

"What are you thinking about, Señor Teniente?" demanded Don Isidro.

The young officer looked up.

"I was thinking that patriotism is sometimes born from difficulty and frustration," he said slowly. "When the sun shines it is only a shadow and a lip service; when it is darkest it becomes a reality, a burning urge, a positive strength that keeps the mind sane. It . . ."

He gave up the explanation and returned to his inspection of the ground.

Don Isidro swung along tugging at his heavy underlip.

"Yes," he said after a moment, "I understand. There is that way of looking at it, too. It is only when we are in danger of losing something that we become aware of its value. Yes."

For some strange reason his thoughts reverted to his daughter.

The two men strode along in silence the rest of the way to Don Isidro's house in Puebla. The sun shone brightly.

It was late evening again and, as before, Don Isidro and Juan Diego sat in the hacendado's dining room drinking aguardiente. It seemed to be the only thing to do in the evening in Puebla, for the heaters were closed, there was no entertaining, and the humbler

cantinas, which would have remained open if there had been an earthquake or a simultaneous eruption of the neighboring volcanos, were
hardly the place for landowners and staff officers. Beside this isolation
from the outside world there was the isolation in the house itself. Doña
Ágata and Doña María Catalina, with Doña Concha, always left the
dining room early and retired to their own quarters, leaving the men
free to do what they liked. Just what the women did, sleep or sew or
gossip, was something Juan Diego hardly hoped ever to find out. In
spite of the greater freedom of intercourse under the Republic the
average Mexican gentleman let his friends' women severely alone and
did not trouble his mind, at least publicly, about them. The influence
of the Moor was still implicit in the Spanish code of honor.

As a matter of fact, Don Isidro was interesting enough in himself
to repay Juan Diego fairly for any curiosity he might have about either
Doña Ágata or Doña María Catalina. The hacendado, it seemed to the
young observer, was not blessed with too many brains but he possessed
a *design* that was well worth tracing. He was like a monument that
had endured for a long time and had been, or was being, thrown out of
balance by a sinking of foundations. He was barely conscious of this,
as yet, but there were moments when he was startled by something he
could not divine, a force that was disturbing his gravity and upsetting
his equanimity and it was obvious that he did not like it at all. This
evening, while he continued to drink aguardiente to an excess that Juan
Diego had not believed possible, it was obvious that in his mind he was
struggling toward something he sensed but could not quite capture. It
developed that certain things Juan Diego had said during the interview
with the bishop and immediately after were the cause of this struggle.
It was made more difficult by the fact that Don Isidro was on the
verge of drunkenness, something so unusual in a man of his station
as to betray a personal crisis.

"You spoke very well," he said to the young officer. "Very well,
indeed. When you told my uncle about the valleys and deserts being
baptized in the blood of the mission fathers I liked that. And the sound
of the mission bells. That was good, too. Do you know, Señor Teniente,
for the last hour I have been hearing the sound of the little church
bell at Las Golondrinas? Isn't that curious? I swear to God I never
thought of it in my life before. Yet there it rings . . . and rings . . .
it is just like music. Let me help you to another glass of this liquor. It
is very good. Don't you think so? We make it at Las Golondrinas."

"No, no," protested Juan Diego hastily. "I've had more than I can
carry safely now. I'll have an awful head in the morning."

Don Isidro screwed up his face as he carefully poured himself a
brimming glass of aguardiente.

"Nonsense," he said. "Aguardiente never leaves you with a head.
It is an excellent liquor. No. But what was I saying? The bells. Yes.

There are a lot of bells in Mexico. I wouldn't be surprised if there were more bells in Mexico than in all of the United States. That is good. Don't you think so? If we stop and listen the bells will remind us of so many things—"

He stopped abruptly and sat motionless with a scowling visage staring vacantly at Juan Diego. An old clock ticked away in a corner and its sound seemed to grow progressively louder as nothing was said. The young officer studied the hacendado's face at leisure and then cleared his throat.

"What are you thinking, Don Isidro?" he asked.

The older man held his hamlike hand up in an awkward gesture.

"I was thinking that there was so much to love in Mexico," he answered in a grave voice that was touched with surprise. "Oh, not my leagues of land and dependents and privileges, although I love them too, but a thousand other things beyond and above them and all around them. It all comes rushing in upon me as though it was the spirit of the aguardiente, the purple mountains and green valleys and bone-white deserts and burning southern beaches, the ancient cities and monuments and endless trails and woods and rocky paths, the names like music, like the bells, the orchards of Jalapa and the silver mines of Pachuca, the ruins of Mitla and Yucatán and the fathomless faces of the Indians of Michoacán, Ixtaccíhuatl and Popocatépetl, the shrine at Guadalupe and the great ahuehuete trees at Atzcapotzalco and the Sanctuary of Los Remedios at San Bartolo Naucalpán and the ruins of the Casa of Cortéz at Cuernavaca and the pyramids of San Juan Teotihuacán and the maguey fields and the bulls and the flowers and the fruits and the rain and . . ."

He hiccoughed loudly and knocked his glass over and then peered in a bewildered fashion at Juan Diego across the candles.

"Por Dios!" he said as he righted the upset glass and tremblingly refilled it from the bottle, "I am as drunk as a priest. But do you understand, Señor Teniente? Everything I can think of in Mexico I love. Except certain men. Oh, excepting them, certainly. Excepting generals and politicians and priests and such vermin. I love everything else. Señor Teniente . . . pardon me . . . did you suggest . . . what? . . . Is this patriotism? Is it patriotism because I am beginning to think about them and . . ."

He paused and twisted up his face in a ferocious attempt at thought.

"And . . . and . . ." he floundered, "and finding them all parts of something that is big and contains all of them and is . . . is . . . in my blood and brain . . . is in this hand . . ."

He held it up and discovering a glass in it immediately quaffed it off.

"Is that . . . is this . . . pat . . . pat . . . ?" he struggled.

"That is patriotism," affirmed Juan Diego solemnly.

Don Isidro sighed and blinked his eyes.

"I can think well enough," he said slowly and carefully. "Sometimes my tongue gets too big for my mouth but I can think well enough. Come . . . er . . . Señ . . . Señ . . . let me pour you another glass of this excellent 'guardiente. Is very good. Is very good for the mi . . . mi . . . mind."

Juan Diego watched him fill the glass until it ran over on the table and accepted it when it was pushed toward him. He knew that Don Isidro had passed the verge of drunkenness and yet this drunkenness seemed to have a curious purpose of its own. In an odd way it released a certain emotionalism in the hacendado and caused him to say things he never would have said, even if he had thought them, while sober. It was good, then, for Don Isidro to drink. It was good that these things were happening to him. It was possible that he would forget all of them when he woke up in the morning . . . but Juan Diego did not think so. They had come out into the open at last and they would remain there, a conscious part of his mind in the difficult days that lay ahead. They would furnish him a strength that he would need if the worst, which seemed so probable now, was to happen. The young officer lifted the glass and drained half of it. The fiery liquid coursed down his gullet and hit his stomach like a hot coal.

"That is patriotism," he repeated in a loud tone.

Don Isidro nodded vigorously.

"You may not know it, Señor Teniente," he said thickly, "but that is patriotism."

He leaned back in the chair, blinked once or twice and fell asleep.

Juan Diego picked up the glass of aguardiente and inspected the liquid with great solemnity. Then he drank it off. Chepe entered the dining room softly with two bottles. He put them on the table, picked up the empty ones, glanced casually at his master and went out. The young officer watched him go without saying a word. He had learned that evening that Chepe could speak a fair English and the revelation had astonished him. Imagine it! A Yaqui! Don Isidro himself didn't know where . . . The clock in the corner began to tick with tremendous force. It was like a hammer hitting a big spike. Juan Diego was tempted to get up and stop it for fear it might awaken the hacendado but a loud snore from that quarter restrained him. It was obvious that Don Isidro slept as heavily as he drank. The young officer relaxed in the leather-backed chair and entertained himself by watching the candle flames sputter and tilt. There were ten of them in the two candelabra and most of them were burned down to an inch or two of the round containers.

I'll sit here until the first one flickers out, thought the young officer. Then I'll go to bed.

He sighed. It had not been an eventful day but it had offered him
more than one unusual moment. He wondered if Don Isidro knew that
he had spoken for some time with Doña María Catalina. He wondered,
too, if the girl would be in the garden in the morning. Perhaps she
went there every morning to gather roses or breathe the fresh air
before the day got too hot or to sew or . . . He should have mentioned the fact that he had met Doña María Catalina in the garden to
Don Isidro. It would have been so simple. A chance word or a stray
sentence. Well, he would do it tomorrow. The prospect of visiting the
bishop, with its incidental excitement, had probably driven the matter
out of his mind. That bishop. What a meager little sharp-eyed fellow
he was! It was impossible either to like or dislike him. He was outside
one's personal circle where likes or dislikes counted. He was a force,
something that was not quite human and yet dealt wholly in human
elements. *The Church throws nothing away, not even the weak bodies
of its children.* Oh, was that so? The thought idly occurred to him that
it was on the flowery expanse of the Alameda in Mexico City that the
Inquisition victims were burned. The colored processions leading the
stunned victims to their death passed with arrogant pomp through the
silent streets of the city. The clock ticked and Don Isidro snored. Juan
Diego began to feel drowsy. Where were the candle flames now? One
of them was very near the container, almost ready to expire in its little
lake of melted wax. Well, he would wait until it was out. He supposed
that Chepe would look after Don Isidro. Chepe was a faithful servant.
Could speak English. Yes, they had talked and thought this day. Don
Isidro was finding out that he was not God. It *could* be put that way.
It could be . . . The amazing thing about Doña María Catalina was
her lack of surprise . . . or self-consciousness . . . or . . . There.
The candle flame had blinked out.

Apparently Don Isidro was right. Aguardiente left one without a
head the next morning. Juan Diego never felt fresher as he completed
his morning ablutions, drank the huge cup of chocolate that Chepe
brought him, learned from that taciturn servant that the hacendado had
awakened and gone to bed about four o'clock in the morning, and ran
down the stairs and along the familiar corridor to the door opening into
the patio. It was another beautiful day with the softness of spring in
the air. Puebla in the morning was very like Paradise. Especially . . .
Yes, she was there. He could see the flash of her wide white skirt
beneath the willow tree. It was a habit, then. She was not arranging
roses this morning but sewing with tiny colored threads at some long
panel of cloth. Doña Concha sat beside her placidly eating nuts. Both
women glanced up in the most natural manner as Juan Diego halted
before them.

"Good morning, Señor Teniente," said Doña María Catalina in her fresh flutelike voice.

"Good morning, Doña María Catalina," returned Juan Diego. "Good morning, Doña Concha."

The companion revealed a double row of large white teeth.

The girl drew her skirt closer to her in an inviting gesture.

"Will you sit, Señor Teniente?" she remarked, smiling slightly. "There are no rose thorns this morning."

"There may be some lost needles," said Doña Concha. "My young lady is always losing them."

Juan Diego sat down and the subtle perfume of the girl suddenly assailed his nostrils. When she moved he could hear the faint shifting of her garments. Her hand moved rapidly with the needle.

"Do you rise early every morning, Doña María Catalina?" he asked, for want of anything better to say.

"Not always," she replied. "But lately I have been going to an early Mass in the cathedral with my mother. It is very pleasant, then. I enjoy the little walk through the streets. Later, when the sun is too high and too hot, I avoid it."

He noticed that her skin was almost transparently pale.

"I like the sun," he said. "Part of my youth was spent in a tropical climate. We are well-baked in the state of Vera Cruz."

She observed him frankly over the lifted needle.

"Yes," she remarked. "I can see it in your face. The little wrinkles around your eyes were made by the sun. You look as cooked as a tortilla."

He laughed at that.

"I have been in other places as well as the south," he said.

She continued to sew for a minute without saying anything and he leaned lazily back on the bench watching her dexterously moving fingers. Doña Concha cracked a nut loudly. The faint buzz of bees sounded from the roses. A bell began to ring at regular intervals from the near distance. It was all so familiar and comfortable. He drew in his breath with an audible sound of contentment. For the moment war and the thoughts of war were very far away. Presently Doña María Catalina lifted her head.

"Tell me about yourself," she commanded gravely. "You are not of Mexican blood, are you? I know that. Where were you born, Señor Teniente?"

He stirred uneasily.

"Far to the north," he replied shortly. "In a state whose name you cannot pronounce. It is called Massachusetts. I do not remember it very well."

She made no comment and after a moment he went on:

"My father and mother brought me to Texas when I was very

young. My mother died. My father was killed. The general adopted me when I was ten years old. Since then I have been a Mexican. That is all."

She smiled over her sewing.

"That is a very short story," she said. "I desire more than that."

He cast about in his mind for details but all of them seemed to run together. Ah . . . Manga de Clavo . . .

"It was on the general's hacienda between Vera Cruz and Jalapa that I became a Mexican," he declared. "It was beautiful there and every time I return to it I feel my faith in this country that adopted me renewed. I remember Doña Inés, the first wife of the general, with love and thanks. She was my second mother, my real mother, the mother of my mind and heart. She . . ."

Now that he had started it came easily and he desired the girl to understand what those boyhood years on the hacienda meant to him.

"I seemed to exist in an eternal summer at Manga de Clavo," he said. "I was washed and well-fed and taught to read and write and handle figures. I learned to ride and farm and swim. I was taught the history of Mexico. I could go down to Vera Cruz on the coast where the sun burned so terribly and the insects shrilled and the fever vapors rose from the swamps. I saw the baroque churches and the zopilotes perching on the towers and the business houses and the French and English merchants and the religious processions. Or I could go upward to Jalapa where the air was cool and wander through the endless gardens of convolvulus and acacia trees and roses and palma Christi and ferns and mango trees and banana plants. But it was the hacienda that I loved the most, the hacienda with its comfortable house, its herds of cattle and sheep, its prize gamecocks and its constant visitors. And Doña Inés. And her daughter, Guadalupe. The general was not there during my first year at Manga de Clavo for that was the time of the San Jacinto campaign and he was a prisoner of the Yanquis. So Doña Inés and the hacienda priest were my sole teachers. The priest taught me to read and write but Doña Inés taught me to live. She showed me a way that I had never dreamt of and which became a part of my mind and blood. There was a great peace at Manga de Clavo but it did not last. The general came home and for a time all seemed well and then the war with the French broke out. That was in 1838. The general went away again and when they brought him back he had lost his leg. Those were sad months on the hacienda."

He stopped, somewhat surprised at his own verbosity and ready to laugh and dismiss these memories of Manga de Clavo; but Doña María Catalina's eyes were fixed steadfastly upon his face and she had ceased to sew. He was amazed and pleased to discover that she was interested. The church bell was still ringing and Doña Concha continued to crack nuts.

"They were sad months," said the girl in a prompting voice.

"The general was extremely ill for a long time," explained Juan Diego. "But he had become a national hero. Delegations came down from the capital and one day he was carried away in a litter and later we heard that he had been made provisional president of the Republic. A boy of thirteen does not know much and there are few to tell him what is happening. It was so with me at Manga de Clavo. I know that there was a period of rebellion and unrest, that once, I think it was in 1839, Doña Inés went to Mexico City to get the general, that for a time he was military commandant of the state of Vera Cruz and that he remained on the hacienda for various periods. I was growing up and he was kind enough to make a companion of me. We rode together often and sometimes he talked of matters that were far above my head. But he was always kind, always generous, always warm in affection and always eager to meet my boyish wishes. My little world revolved about him and any memories that I might have retained of Texas or the place of my birth faded into dim shadows. One loves the good things that are about one and after a time one becomes part of them. I became part of Manga de Clavo, part of the general and Doña Inés, part of the state of Vera Cruz, part of the Republic. It was natural and it must have been what I wanted. As a matter of fact, my few memories of Texas (for Massachusetts was no more than a dream) had not been too pleasing—hardship, hunger, neglect, bloodshed and a crude way of life that revolted the instincts within me. I had always desired something else and I knew that I had found it at Manga de Clavo."

He paused again and stared in a puzzled manner at the nearer roses, large yellow ones, as though he was trying to see something in their petals that was invisible to the ordinary eye. After a moment he gave it up.

"There was the rebellion of September, 1841," he announced finally. "I remember that very well, for in October we, Doña Inés and I, went to Mexico City to see the general inaugurated as provisional president of the Republic. It was the first time I had been in the capital. I was fifteen years old. I went everywhere and saw everything. I haunted the cathedral and studied the Aztec calendar stone cemented into its façade. I reveled in the noisy streets, watching the caballeros canter by, the platoons of Lancers, the gold-fringed coaches and the dirty léperos. I rode with Doña Inés on the Paseo along the Viga canal and saw the ladies in crinolines and the charros and the barefoot Indians selling orchids and gardenias and calla lilies. I attended the theater with the general and sat in the presidential box surrounded by generals in full-dress uniforms. I strolled in the Alameda and visited the cockpits and the bull ring and watched the dancers at San Agustín de las Cuevas and appeared at formal dinners and stayed up too late and learned to drink French wines and like them. You see, I was the president's protégé, his adopted son, and, as such, a curiosity to be shown off. I did not mind. The simplicities of life at Manga de Clavo were buried beneath the heavy brocade of existence in Mexico City. What boy would not enjoy it? And yet I think I had a nagging doubt of all this ostentation at the time. I think I knew that too much of it was not good for me and that I was too young to know where to draw the line. I needed a mentor. I found one. It was the general himself. One night, after a state dinner, he took me into one of his offices and sat down and put his arm around my shoulder. 'Juanillo,' he said, 'you have learned a lot about pleasure. Now it is time for you to learn about endurance and strength and—' "

Juan Diego broke off his narrative in a confused manner and a horrified feeling of having gone too far beset him. What, in the name of Heaven, had led him to this? Why, he could not . . . He cleared his throat and laughed self-consciously.

"When I was sixteen . . ." he began doggedly.

"Wait!" said the girl, placing her hand over his wrist. "I want to know about this strength . . . and endurance . . ."

"It is nothing," he mumbled. "Some Indian ceremonies. I think you will be interested in the Military School because your brother . . ."

"I'll hear about the Indian ceremonies," said Doña María Catalina in a voice that was surprisingly determined. "Come, Señor Teniente. There is no escape for you."

He knew it. It was inevitable because it had come so powerfully into his mind. It was there to tell and he must tell it. Suddenly it seemed quite right that he should tell it. Very well, then.

"The general told me that he had been speaking with an old Tarascan from Michoacán," he said carefully. "Where he had met him I do not know. But at that time the general was meeting everybody and endeavoring to strengthen his political hold on the various states by respecting their customs and showing his willingness to accept their advice. He had never been strong in Michoacán for they are a distant people there and he felt that a personal gesture toward them might be wise. The old Tarascan said, 'Señor Presidente, give me your adopted son. In Michoacán we will make a man of him.' It tempted the general and he asked me if I was willing to go, pointing out that, in a way, I would be a hostage for him and a sign to the Indians of his confidence. 'It is possible that you will undergo some hardship,' he said, 'but it will be good for you and for me. The Tarascans will say that the presidente has sent his son to them. It will be a gesture of friendship and faith. I know the Indians. I know that they will teach you what I did not know until I lost my leg at Vera Cruz. Will you go?' I think I was already tired of the eternal fiesta that was my life in Mexico City. I said that I would go. In the autumn of 1842 I went."

He paused and glanced at Doña María Catalina to see if she was weary of his narrative. She was not looking at him now. She was looking at the yellow roses with her lips slightly apart and her hands lay in the curve of her skirt like two still fallen gardenias. Doña Concha was trying to crack nuts without making any sound. The bells had stopped.

"It was pleasant in the valleys of Michoacán," resumed Juan Diego. "I lived the life of an Indian youth in the dwelling of the old Tarascan and I was instructed in many things that were new and strange to me. But all this was a prologue, a mild preparation for what was to be the climax of my training and initiation into the hard art of living. There came a day when I, together with a score of Tarascan boys, was ordered to wrap a few tortillas in a cloth and follow one of the wise men of Tzintzuntzán from the shores of Lake Pátzcuaro to a place in the mountains to the southwest. We walked for several days and when our tortillas were eaten we tightened our belts and existed on spring water. It was then that I first heard the words. Hill dwellers came down to the trail and pointed at us and said, 'They are going to drink of the wine of San Lorenzo.' We walked until our legs ached and the sun burnt the backs of our necks and our chests seemed about to burst with our hasty breathing. Always we heard that whisper, 'They are going to drink of the wine of San Lorenzo.' How long we traveled on foot I do not know. It may have been a week or ten days. But at last we came to a high defile in the mountains and passed through it and mounted and reached a great hollow where there was a long house without windows and roofed with green reeds. In this house, where there was no light nor fire, we lay on mats with a jug of cold water beside us and listened to strange wise men, some of them a hundred years old, who spoke to us of the difficulties and pains of living and the need for strength and endurance if we were to exist in the treacherous world. They spoke to us for three days and nights. Then we were ready to endure the ordeal and drink the wine. We were led from the darkness of the long house into the sunlit meadow before it and there we saw three young red bulls tethered to strong posts. The wise men came to us with skin bags and ordered us to thrust our hands in and we did and drew them forth clutching handfuls of long thorns hardened by fire."

He could not tell her everything. He paused to choose his words carefully.

"The wise men explained what we were to do and it seems to me now that we were under a spell and had no other will than the will of the wise men, for we did it without hesitation. We drove the long thorns through our cheeks and through the palms of our hands and through the flat portion of our feet behind the third toe and through the ends of our tongues . . ."

Doña Concha uttered a cry of horror but the girl remained silent and did not remove her steady glance from Juan Diego's face. No, he could not tell her everything. He could not tell her how they drove the thorns through the foreskins of their genitals.

"I think the thorns were smeared with a poison," he said, "for they burned like flame and we staggered and fell against each other and were almost blind with the agony. 'This is pain,' the wise men said. 'No matter what you may suffer in the years to come it will never be as bad as this. You will always be able to say that you have suffered a worse pain in the mountains of Michoacán and this will be a strength to you until the days of your deaths.' Some of the boys screamed like wounded animals and others fell senseless on the ground. They were removed to the long house and not permitted to drink of the wine of San Lorenzo. The rest of us, covered with blood and sweat and tears, were pushed toward the tethered bulls. The wise men plunged stone knives into the throats of the animals and they fell to their knees, coughing and snorting through their nostrils. The black-red blood gushed out and the Tarascan wise men caught it in pottery goblets striped in black and red and put them to our swollen lips and we drank the hot sweet coagulating liquid. 'This is strength,' they said. 'This is manhood.' Again some of us fell to the ground but those of us who were still on our feet were led to a smaller house walled with green branches interwoven with bright flowers and there we lay on fresh mats for a day and a night. Of this period I remember only strange visions, forms walking in circles of colored light, voices, music and the soft touch of hands. When I regained consciousness and the thorns had been removed from my flesh, all pain had left me and my old Tarascan guardian was bending over me. 'You are a man now, Juan Diego,' he said. 'You are a man because you understand pain and endurance and the virtue of strength. Tell that to your foster father. Tell the presidente that having had the strength to endure this you have the strength to face and endure anything that the evil spirits in the world may inflict upon you.' We made the long journey back to Tzintzuntzán and we were not weary. I returned to Mexico City but I had no appetite for the gay life there. It seemed too silly and a waste of time. I desired discipline and a reason for my existence. I told the general about this and he was delighted. Together we decided what course I was to pursue and in the spring of 1843 I entered the Military College at Chapultepec as a cadet."

It was difficult for him to realize that all this had happened little more than three years ago and he paused instinctively to wonder at the swift passage of time. It flew like an eagle on broad steadily moving wings. Doña María Catalina picked up her sewing from her lap and bent her head over it as she thrust the needle in at random.

"I understand now," she said inconsequentially.

He looked at her questioningly.

"I mean," she continued, a faint flush creeping up her cheeks, "that I understand why the rose thorn in my finger startled you so yesterday."

He nodded.

"Yes," he admitted. "It must have been . . ."

Doña Concha cracked a nut loudly.

"These Indian tortures," she declared disgustedly. "They give me nightmares."

She ate the nut noisily and spat out a bit of the shell.

"Tell me, Señor Teniente," she went on. "You must have been at the Military College when Don Lorenzo first entered."

"I was," acknowledged Juan Diego, "but I do not remember him very well. We were in different battalions."

Doña María Catalina handed her sewing to her companion.

"I don't feel like needlework," she said impatiently. "I have pricked myself three times. How long were you at the college, Señor Teniente?"

"Two years," replied Juan Diego. "It was a period of hard work, few pleasures and some anguish. In August, 1844, Doña Inés died and I was desolate. I had lost my mother. She was only thirty-three when she died but she had lived long enough for all Mexico to adore her. She was a woman of the coast, simple and affectionate in action, belonging to Manga de Clavo rather than the capital. There she was about her duties in the morning dew and under the stars still in flight in the warm coastal dawn; with hands hardened by the milking of cows; clothed in cheap cloth; with mind strong to manage mayordomos or peons; often mounted in her sidesaddle on her favorite horse. The general remarried soon after her death. It was shortly after that that Fate turned her back on him and I sometimes think that if he had followed Doña Inés's advice his path would have been different and less arduous. But he didn't and his way was hard. The revolution broke out in the autumn of 1844, the general was defeated and from June, 1845, until August, 1846, he lived in exile in Cuba. For a time I was left undisturbed at the Military College but the political enemies of the general eventually smoked me out. I was dismissed and I went to live with Señor José Julián Gutiérrez, the general's manager of estates, at Manga de Clavo. I remained there until I went down to Vera Cruz to meet the general on his return from exile. We met affectionately, he attached me to his staff and . . . and that is all."

He observed Doña María Catalina with a smile and then diverted his attention to several bees that were buzzing about the yellow roses.

"I know you better now," said the girl simply.

Juan Diego laughed self-consciously.

"I am not a good storyteller," he remarked. "Are you?"

"I prefer to read them . . . or listen to them," she replied. "There are things that you have not told me. But I will find them out."

This pleased him very much.

"You have but to ask," he said lightly.

The sun was high now, not hot but bright, and moving his hand along the bench he could feel the warmth in the dark wood. There was a steady buzz among the roses and from some distance he could hear the musical call of a water seller. He felt lazy, relaxed and slightly hungry. He wondered vaguely if there was anything more pleasant in life than sitting in a rose-scented patio in the sun beside Doña María Catalina, in a crisp white gown, while the day wheeled slowly by. It was like stealing a bright span out of the long traverse of time and making it a comfortable shell that closed one from the thousand imperious calls of duty and cares. What more did she want to know? And what more could he tell her? It was surprising how easily he could talk to her, easier, in fact, than he could talk to Don Isidro or anybody he could think of at the moment. That was because there was a sympathy between them. He could feel it like a fine invisible warmth, a summer-feeling, like the touch of earth, comfortable, communicative without speech and almost caressing. He shut his eyes in the pleasure of it. After a moment he heard the soft shift and rustle of her garments. She was standing up and smiling at him. Hastily he rose to his feet.

"I thought you were dozing," she said. "I meant to slip away and let you sleep."

"I am not sleepy," he declared. "I am merely happy. Do stay a little longer."

She shook her head.

"I have little duties to perform," she answered, "and if I stayed a little longer my little duties would not be done."

She was laughing at him as she left the patio.

Shortly before the noon meal when Juan Diego was standing before the mirror in his chamber with a pair of scissors in one hand and a comb in the other there came an urgent rap at the door. The young officer, who had been trimming his hair, put the comb and scissors down hastily and turned.

"Come in," he called.

It was Chepe.

"The patrón begs you to come to the library," he said, his white teeth flashing in the first smile that Juan Diego had ever seen on his dark face.

The young man ran his hand swiftly over his trimmed locks. For the last day or so he had been particularly scrupulous about his appearance.

"I'll come right along," he said.

When he entered the library he was surprised to find young Lorenzo surrounded by the entire family. He had almost forgotten that Don Isidro's son existed, but there he was, turned out neatly in his cadet uniform, his mother's arm about his slender shoulders and his sister holding fast to his hand. There was no arguing the obvious. Lorenzo was a fine-looking boy and now that he was approaching his fifteenth year a faint shadow of down was darkening his upper lip. But his eyes were still limpid and naïve, the eyes of a boy who had yet to experience any of the perplexing problems of love or life. Through some curious instinct, thought Juan Diego, he guards himself from manhood. Perhaps he is right. He is safer that way. The young officer advanced with his hand extended.

"I am pleased to see you, Don Lorenzo," he said with a shade of reserve. "How did you leave Mexico City?"

Lorenzo released himself from his sister's clasp long enough to put his thin hand in Juan Diego's palm.

"The capital is full of excitement, Señor Teniente," he replied, revealing his white teeth in a warm smile. "I bring you greetings from an old friend, the Señor Teniente Don Ezequiel Oropesa."

"Ezeq . . ." began Juan Diego and then he nodded.

"Oh, yes," he added. "Oropesa. He was on the general's staff at San Luis Potosí. The poor fellow. He wanted to go on the Buena Vista campaign but we left him at San Luis Potosí counting goats."

"Goats?" said Lorenzo in a puzzled voice.

"So the capital . . ." began Juan Diego.

"The capital is the den of the devil," broke in Don Isidro in an indignant voice. "It seems . . ."

"It is full of rumors, of course," explained Lorenzo to Juan Diego. "All sorts of stories are spread abroad. These things always happen before a presidential election. Of course, you know—"

"Yes, yes, Don Lorenzo," interrupted Juan Diego. "What are these rumors and stories, then?"

The boy is attempting to speak like a man, he thought. Well, let him. With what affection his mother and his sister regard him. I did not know there was so much color in her cheeks.

"Oh, all sorts of stories and rumors," exclaimed Lorenzo, laughing. "Some have it that General Santa Anna has fled to Guatemala. Others say that he had arranged to surrender the city to the Americans.

And, of course, to hear them, there is another revolution brewing, this time a revolt to be headed by General Valencia. Well . . ."

"There is no love lost between the general and Gabriel Valencia," remarked Juan Diego soberly. "Is that fellow conspiring again? What does Anaya think?"

"The provisional president, I understand, leans toward General Valencia," declared Lorenzo. "They do not understand in the capital why the general has been so unsuccessful. They think—"

"They think too much," broke in Juan Diego rudely. "If they would stop thinking and do something the state of the Republic might be better. Why don't they concern themselves with sending arms and supplies and men to the general?"

"I agree," said Don Isidro stoutly. "They talk too much in the capital, Lorenzo. It is the curse of this Republic that you cannot turn your back without expecting a knife in it."

"I'm sure that the general will arrange everything when he arrives in Mexico City," affirmed the boy, somewhat shaken in his readiness of speech. "Of course, at Chapultepec all we get are rumors. I told you that."

"That's enough politics," protested Doña Ágata. "It is all very well for you men to sit up all night discussing them but I am not going to have Lorenzo's time wasted that way. Come along, now."

She began to lead her son toward the dining room. Don Isidro took no notice of the somewhat unusual asperity in his wife's voice but followed smiling. Juan Diego found himself walking beside Doña María Catalina. For some reason he felt quite lifted to hear himself associated with the hacendado as a man. You men. Well . . . He glanced down sideways at the girl but her eyes were fixed fondly on the back of her brother's head. There was no doubt about it. He was a fine boy. I shall have to know him better, thought Juan Diego. I have not paid enough attention to him.

"Lorenzo," called Don Isidro, "the Señor Teniente and myself are calling on the governor this afternoon. Perhaps you would like to accompany us?"

He turned his big head toward Juan Diego.

"It will do no harm," he said. "I think that it will interest the boy."

"Of course," agreed the young officer immediately. "It will give him an idea of the situation here in Puebla."

Don Isidro shrugged his shoulders.

"The situation. Yes," he remarked gloomily. "Yes, indeed. The situation. If his eyes were closed in the capital they will be opened wide enough here."

"My eyes are always open, my father," said Lorenzo, laughing.

The boy laughs a lot, thought Juan Diego. That is good. I like boys who laugh.

The two men, followed closely by young Lorenzo, were admitted immediately to the governor's presence when they called at the palace late in the afternoon. While passing through the door Don Isidro shook his big head.

"I don't like this," he grumbled to Juan Diego. "Isunza must have reached a decision."

Isunza sat behind his long table with an artificial smile spread across his yellow face. He was smoking a Cuban cigarro.

"Are you in communication with the general, Señor Teniente?" he asked the young officer abruptly.

"I am not, Señor Gobernador," replied Juan Diego. "My instructions are to wait for him here in Puebla and report such patriotic activities as I may observe."

"Patriotic, yes," said Isunza, looking sideways at Don Isidro. "That is very good. The safety of the country . . . I know. The ayuntamiento has considered these matters. It has decided that discretion is part of the safety of the country. Reason prohibits vain sacrifices. Civilians are not called upon to play the role of heroes. Puebla . . ."

He interrupted himself in order to heave a long sigh and roll his eyes upward toward the decorated ceiling.

"Puebla," he went on, "can only await with resignation the terrible blow with which Providence chooses to afflict us."

Juan Diego stared steadily at the governor.

"Does this mean that the city will offer no defense?" he asked.

Isunza ruffled a pile of papers on the table.

"You know what happened at the Cerro Gordo," he said. "You were there. The same army that defeated the general at the Cerro Gordo is moving up the National Highway. There were plenty of men at Cerro Gordo, plenty of fortifications. There are no fortifications at Puebla and very few men."

He spread his arms in a helpless gesture.

"What can we do?" he asked sadly.

"We can fight," burst in Don Isidro, speaking for the first time. Isunza carefully ignored him.

"What can we do?" he repeated to Juan Diego. "Do you not see that reason prohibits vain sacrifices?"

"There are plenty of men," replied the young officer. "The general will arrive with reinforcements and guns. If we can hold the Americans for a week it will give the capital time to put itself in a state of defense. This war is not over, Señor Gobernador. It has just begun. The Americans are not superhuman. I have seen them. They—"

"No, no," broke in Isunza. "You are right. The Americans are *not* superhuman. They are men like us and with the good will of men like us. They are not bad fellows at all. Certain misconceptions have been spread about them. They are very willing to negotiate if we will meet them halfway. Here . . ."

He fumbled among his papers and drew forth a sheet that appeared to be newly printed.

"Here," he repeated. "Here is a manifesto by the American general— Scott, is that his name? Permit me to read it to you. See, it is printed in two languages, English and Spanish. You will see . . ."

He began to read in a rapid voice.

" 'It is my duty, Mexicans, to make known certain facts that are purposely concealed from you. For the sake not only of ourselves but of the whole American continent and of republican institutions, we of the United States made every effort consistent with honor to adjust our difficulties with Mexico, but the patriotic Herrera was thrown from power, and the new government, ignoring your interests in order to further the monarchical designs, compelled my nation to take up arms. Like you, we hoped that good would result from the overthrow of Paredes, and therefore we permitted Santa Anna to return; but, again like you, perhaps, we were mistaken as to his intentions. What has followed, you know. Your troops, whose devotion and valor we admire, have been badly led, and even betrayed or deceived; and he has not only rewarded those who waged civil war at Mexico, but insulted the brave defenders of Vera Cruz. Recently the battle at Cerro Gordo showed what you may expect from him. Everywhere generals long supported in idleness by the nation have exhibited a lack of honor or skill, while the dead or wounded soldiers, abandoned on the field, have not been given by their leaders even the poor recompense of a grave. The clergy and all other peaceable and useful citizens have been, and still are, taxed, menaced and sacrificed, whereas criminals go unpunished. Can this be called liberty? The Mexicans, I am sure, have the courage to admit mistakes that involve no dishonor, and to adopt for the future a policy of peace, of liberty and of harmony with their brethren of the United States. My troops, as your bishops and priests will testify, have not committed the outrages alleged against us for the purpose of exciting your anger. We adore the same God as you, and many of our people and of our army are Roman Catholics. We punish crime and reward merit; we respect property—especially that of the Church—and we seek your friendship. Abandon prejudice, then; cease to be victims of the ambitious; act as a great American nation. If, however, the war must go on, my country will send—should they be needed—one hundred thousand men, and settle the pending difficulties in a decisive manner. Guerrilla warfare, should it be persisted in, would lead to reprisals, and you could not blame us for your sufferings. I have set out for Puebla and Mexico, and shall certainly reach those places; but my desire is peace, friendship, union. It is for you to choose between these and war.' "

He paused and looked up.

"Are you afraid of a piece of paper?" demanded Juan Diego hotly.

"Especially when General Scott's style seems to be the same as the bishop's!" added Don Isidro.

The parchment-yellow skin of Isunza's face wrinkled as he glanced distastefully at the hacendado.

"Your most sanctified uncle will be pleased to hear that," he said heavily.

"The devil take . . ." began Don Isidro and then he thought better of it.

Juan Diego had stepped forward and picked up a copy of the manifesto, which he turned over and over in his hand.

"This is a bad thing," he declared gravely. "Its circulation should not be permitted in the city. It insults us. Have you taken steps, Señor Gobernador, to see that all copies of this defeatist rag have been confiscated and destroyed?"

"I do not need any directions concerning the duties of my office from a second lieutenant," replied Isunza rudely.

Juan Diego flushed and bowed formally.

"You mentioned the word 'negotiate,' I believe, Señor Gobernador," he said. "Shall I inform the general that that is your decision?"

"I'll inform the general of my decisions myself," snapped Isunza.

The artificial smile had splintered into a rising ill humor. The governor snatched the manifesto from the young officer's hand and flung it down on his table.

"I believe that is all," he said insolently. "I have other appointments, Señor Teniente. If you will be so good . . ."

Don Isidro turned with great deliberation to his son, who had stood by observing the conversation with large amazed eyes.

"Lorenzo," declared the hacendado. "I want you to take a long look at the governor of Puebla. You see before you one of the reasons for the unfortunate predicament of our country. You see . . ."

Isunza fairly shook with rage.

"Don Isidro," he stammered, "I'll put you in the deepest dungeon in the fortress of Loreto. I'll keep you there until your feet rot off. I'll have the guards break every rib in your carcass. I'll . . ."

The hacendado turned and walked with stamping feet toward the door.

Juan Diego hesitated an instant and then bowed slightly to the governor.

"I bid you good afternoon, señor," he said.

Isunza did not answer him but continued to scowl at the broad back of Don Isidro.

The two men and the boy did not speak until they reached the plaza before the Governor's Palace. The late afternoon sun lengthened the shadows and in the darkest corners the somnolent Indians still squatted, their sombreros tipped over their eyes and their blankets drawn up over their mouths. It was quiet except for the clicking hoofs of a couple of burros picking their way across the cobbles and almost invisible beneath the high piles of straw baskets they were carrying. A stray water seller sat on the ground picking out the dirt from between his toes.

"You must be more careful with the governor," remarked Juan Diego somewhat tentatively. "It is quite possible . . ."

Don Isidro snapped his fingers.

"He is nothing," he said gloomily. "He will complain to my uncle and my uncle will smile behind his hand and agree with me. I do not fear Isunza."

They crossed the plaza toward the shaded front of the cathedral. An Indian woman, carrying vegetables in a knotted blanket that was supported by her forehead, passed them with a small naked child clinging upside-down to her hip. She uttered a greeting in a soft guttural voice. Through the open door of the cathedral came the sound of violins and a bass viol. The peacefulness seemed unreal to Juan Diego, an affront, in a way, to the vexed thoughts that were troubling his mind.

"It is too calm," he said suddenly, waving his hand toward the sleepy plaza and the stolid front of the cathedral. "The world is not like this any more. It is like a dream that was dreamt long ago and that is not right. It is time for all of us to wake up."

Don Isidro glanced briefly at the young officer.

"You mean that we live in the past too much," he remarked without any particular interest.

"I mean that we try to preserve the past too much," explained Juan Diego. "The world is not like that today. This is an era of change and progress. We should—"

"Wherever the Church is strong the dream is deep," declared Don Isidro sententiously. "I suppose the most backward countries in the world are the most religious. Well . . ."

He glanced in at the open door of the cathedral as they walked slowly by it.

"What are we going to do now?" he asked presently.

Juan Diego shook his head in perplexity.

"What can we do, Don Isidro?" he counterquestioned. "The situation is plain enough. They mean to hand Puebla over to the Americans. I shall spend the evening drawing up a report for the general. That is all I can do. If I knew enough of the leading citizens . . ."

"I know most of them," said the hacendado. "I can go around and talk to them but it won't do any good to put our desires on patriotic grounds. If we could convince them that a stout defense of Puebla would benefit their money-boxes they might fight. But . . ."

He sucked his upper lip into his enveloping underlip and looked doubtful.

"Perhaps the general will arouse them when he gets here," declared young Lorenzo in a hopeful voice. "He is very persuasive, you know. And he possesses the power, too. He is the governor's superior, isn't he?"

"Theoretically he is," replied Don Isidro. "Well, we shall see what we shall see."

They turned the corner by the cathedral.

"We will do what we can until the very end," said Juan Diego. "We can do that . . . and we can pray for a miracle."

Nuestra Señora de Guadalupe . . . pray for us . . .

Juan Diego ate little and slept badly that night. He excused himself early from sitting over the aguardiente bottle with Don Isidro and the hacendado, who seemed depressed and quite willing to be left alone, waved his big hand in a friendly farewell. In the canopied bed the young officer tossed from left to right, pounded the pillows on the oblong bolster and endeavored to force sleep by squeezing his eyelids together tightly. It wouldn't work. The old trick of emptying his mind failed him and long after midnight a confused procession of images and faces continued to dance arbitrarily across his consciousness. Don Isidro, scowling and looking thoughtful. The general, angry and puffing out his lips like an adder's throat. Víbora sudafricana. He remembered the picture from a book at Manga de Clavo. Isunza, yellow-faced, a great toad. The bishop, small, sharp-faced, with tiny jumping black eyes like beads on a snapped string. Sometimes the faces would dance in a row and then again they would draw together and merge into one large mask that flew toward him, swelling as it came, and then receded until it was no bigger than a silver peso. This continued for some time and then he found himself not in the bed but in a long dark house where a pile of fagots was burning. The smoke filled the enclosure and tickled his nose and made his eyes water. He was lying on a mat and there was a hole in the roof of the long house and through it he could see a round white phosphorescent ball that he supposed was the moon. After a moment the ball began to move and he knew it was not the moon. It entered the long house and moved along the ceiling to the wall and down the wall and across the packed earth toward him. It dragged a long body behind it and the body slithered and sucked as it approached him. He could see now that it was a great snake with the head of a man, an anaconda, perhaps, but such an anaconda as had never crawled through South American jungles. It writhed toward him with a scraping rustling, an ominous kissing sound, its dark-blue scales palpitating to the motion of its ringed muscles. He could smell the fetid odor of it as it came close and presently he felt its weight on his legs, heavy, crushing, as it began to move up his body. With an effort he raised his head and stared into the human face of the monster and saw the pale illuminated features of his brother David. He screamed and woke up and found himself covered with perspiration.

For a long time he lay bewildered and attempting without success to reason out this dream. An Indian could tell him, for they had an elaborate system for ferreting the meanings out of visions. They would know what the anaconda stood for and why it had the head of his brother. They would know, too, why he had been afraid of David in his dream. David. David Livingston. Why, he had hardly thought of him since that dark night at Buena Vista and yet he knew that he carried David about within him wherever he went. There was an affection between them whose only obvious reason was their common blood but there was something else, too, something that was more than blood and outreached reason. He tried to picture David's face in the darkness but failed and found that curious for he had seen him plainly enough in his nightmare. There was a part of the mind that could not be coerced, he decided, a part that was independent of will and manifested itself as it pleased. It could be controlled no more than one could control one's dreams. Well, he had not been very kind to David. He had been abrupt and cold and even savage, refusing him when he offered himself and fighting against imaginary fetters. But David had been as adamant. Yes, it didn't seem so important now. When they met again, thought Juan Diego gazing upward at the shadowy canopy, he, at least, would be more reasonable. He would listen to David and David would listen to him. When they met again. One thing was certain. David was no anaconda.

The oblong of window was lightening and he decided that it was futile to lie there in bed when he could not sleep. He watched the window for a while and his thoughts revolved about the moon and the stars and the sun. He had been taught that all of them influenced man's destiny but he did not have much faith in such theories. Man influenced man's destiny. In his own case . . . Well, there was the general . . . There was no doubt about that. And Don Isidro? . . . and David? . . . and Doña María Catalina? . . . Their names leaped so quickly into his consciousness that he supposed they must all be influences of a sort. But just what, he could not tell . . . as yet. They had appeared and reappeared and that meant something. Some reason must have caused him to enter that inner patio at Las Golondrinas late at night. Some directive force must have brought him into the plaza of Puebla just when Don Isidro was crossing it. Some mysterious power must have carried him to the hacienda of Buena Vista the dolorous night that David came to look at the prisoners. Was this what they called Destiny? And he began to visualize Destiny as a hill—the Cerro del Destino—to which all men were brought at climactic moments in their lives. Either they recognized it or they didn't. Either they accepted it or they didn't. Perhaps he had been brought to his Cerro del Destino and had not recognized it. Or perhaps he had yet to be brought to it. He would have to wait and see. He put his bare feet out of the bed and stood up in the darkness, the ample folds of the nightshirt Don Isidro had loaned him falling like a tent to the floor. He walked over to the tocador and felt for the rose in the blue glazed vase that had stood there for two days. It was gone. Dead, probably. Chepe must have removed it. Well . . . He pulled the voluminous shirt over his head and dropped it beside him. The night air felt good on his naked body. He observed that the window was a square of pallid predawn light now and he began to dress slowly, drawing his clothes on with great deliberation and pausing over each button. He shaved with cold water, soaked his hair and combed it several times. Then he adjusted his belt, picked up his military hat and walked silently down the stairs and through the corridor to the door that led into the patio.

He heard a snail crunch beneath the heel of his boot as he followed the flagstone path to the bench beneath the willow. The sky was a bright dark blue and the stars had disappeared. He sat down, crossed his legs and leaned his head against the tree . . . and fell asleep . . .

. . . A faint tickling sensation . . . He raised his hand to brush his nose and opened his eyes at the same time to bright sunlight. Doña María Catalina was just withdrawing a rose from his face and he heard her quick laughter before he recognized her. He rose hastily and awkwardly to his feet and stuttered a greeting. She sat down and looked up at him still laughing.

"Were you here on this bench all night, Señor Teniente?" she asked. "It is barely eight o'clock now."

"I couldn't sleep," he explained. "I came out early. I . . ."

"You can sleep fast enough," she broke in. "Even Doña Concha's shouting could not wake you. Could it, tiíta?"

The dueña, who was standing behind the girl, merely shook her head and smiled broadly.

Juan Diego was wide-awake now. He ran his hand over his hair and straightened his belt.

"I was fairly caught," he confessed. "I must have looked terrible with my head on one side and my mouth wide open. But I didn't come out here to sleep. I came out because I couldn't sleep. Apparently the morning air was what I needed. I hope that your night was undisturbed'."

"Your mouth wasn't open," she said. "Oh, yes, I slept well enough. I always do. Come and sit here by me and talk to me. You see, I have no roses to arrange or sewing to do this morning. I came empty-handed so that I could give you my undivided attention."

He sat down intensely pleased. It seemed to him that she had told him in her own way that she had come into the patio particularly to see him.

"Talk about what?" he asked humorously. "It seems to me that I did nothing but talk yesterday. I did nothing but talk about myself. It is your turn to talk about yourself."

"I thought you would say that," she replied. "It would be the natural thing, wouldn't it? Tiíta, tell the Señor Teniente all about me."

Doña Concha looked surprised and seated herself on the other side of the girl.

"Go on," urged Doña María Catalina. "Tell him everything. Tell him how well I play the pianoforte or what a good gardener I am or how well I sew or how many turkeys I raised last year or how well I ride a horse or how frightened I am of firearms. Leave nothing out, tiíta, not even the fact that sometimes I read books."

"There is no reason to tell him," said Doña Concha in a good-humored tone. "He has already heard it all."

Juan Diego chuckled.

"You sound very accomplished," he remarked with the same feeling of ease and familiarity that he would have felt toward Doña Inés or her daughter, Guadalupe, with whom he had played at Manga de Clavo. "But all these things are outward shows. Tell me about *you*."

"She is bad-tempered sometimes," declared Doña Concha.

"That is hard to believe," said Juan Diego.

"Ah, Señor Teniente, I have known her to go an entire day without saying a word," asserted the dueña.

"That is not bad temper, Doña Concha," explained the young officer. "That is merely reserve."

"What is it?" asked the fat woman. "Reserve? Then, burros have it often."

"It is true that there are days when I do not care to talk," said the girl, "but that will be hard for the Señor Teniente to believe."

"I have never heard you talk so much as you do to the Señor Teniente," declared Doña Concha.

Bright spots of color appeared in Doña María Catalina's cheeks.

"Perhaps no one listens so well," she said deliberately.

"It is my military training," explained Juan Diego hastily and laughed.

But the girl did not laugh.

"I was a quiet child," she explained soberly. "I was never demonstrative in affection because I realized at a very early age that it was not a part of my nature. I was content to sit and look. I did not like to be touched, either. It made me uncomfortable. My Indian nurses were like that, too. I did what I was ordered to do without comment because I knew that it would avail me nothing to protest. You see, I knew my father. I think discipline, a scolding or a slap, would have destroyed the tiny sense of dignity that made me a personality to myself. Therefore, I was docile, well-behaved, always complaisant. But I was never shy or frightened or uneasy."

"Were you ever lonely?" asked Juan Diego.

She shook her head slightly.

"I don't know," she said. "I don't think so. I passed most of my life at Las Golondrinas and there were children there if I had desired to see them. What is loneliness? Is it the lack of companionship? If that is so, I was not lonely. I enjoyed solitude but that is another thing. I enjoyed being by myself. I was not unhappy."

"But when you grew older . . . when . . ." started the young officer hesitantly.

She glanced at him out of her level gray eyes.

"Are you thinking of my marriage?" she asked calmly. "I will tell you about that."

Doña Concha moved uneasily on the bench and muttered to herself.

"I knew that I was going to marry Don Alejandro when I was six years old," said Doña María Catalina steadily. "That is as far back as I can remember. There are certain things in life that become inevitable, like one's birthday or the first of the year or the place where one lives or rain in November, and the prospect of my marriage to Don Alejandro was like that. My father talked of it and my father was like God. My mother accepted it. The hacienda priest favored it. What could I do? I grew up in the belief that it was a part of my life and that nothing I could do would change it. I might just as well wish the shape of my nose different. Not that I ever thought that way about it. Now do you understand?"

"I think I do," replied Juan Diego soberly. "You were an unconscious fatalist."

"I don't know what that means," she said. "Fatalista . . . what is that word? As to a personal liking or dislike of Don Alejandro, that never entered my mind, either. One is foolish to dislike or like the inevitable. It makes no difference. There was no one else whom I liked, I mean outside of my own family, for I saw very few people, very few young men, and those that I did see knew I was betrothed to Don Alejandro. I can't say that I experienced any excitement over the marriage . . . but neither did I feel any grief. I simply didn't know what it meant and what it entailed."

He wanted to say, But you found out. The words failed him. In a moment he didn't need to say it.

"I found out the minute he . . . he touched me," she added in a low voice that shook perceptibly.

Juan Diego straightened in a fierce anger that he felt throbbing through all his body. The world, he was convinced, had been grossly unfair to Doña María Catalina. Don Isidro had committed a crime. The whole system of arranged marriages was an intolerable farce bristling like a hedgehog with tragic and cruel quills. It was not the way of love. Love was free and unforced and traveled where it desired and nothing that man might do could obstruct its way. It should be so for Doña María Catalina. But what way out was there for her? What could she do now that the Church had blessed this unnatural union? *I can kill Don Alejandro,* he thought fiercely to himself. But would he ever see her again if he committed such a crime? And suddenly it occurred to him that it would be unendurable if he never saw her again. She had become a part of his world now, like the sun and the moon and the stars, and to see her no more would be too much like death. The rustle of her gown and the scent of her body, faint like gardenias, like the gardenias of Our Lady of Guadalupe, and the fullness of her lips and the dark luxuriance of her hair and the calm light in her long gray eyes, all these things were *in* him, an integral portion of his being, and to lose them would be to lose the sun and the moon and the stars. This surrender and acceptance and necessity rushed over him now like an invisible wave and he was speechless.

She was gazing at him and her slight breast rose and fell in quickened movements. She half-started to rise from the bench and then sank back on it again.

"Doña Concha," she said, "perhaps we will gather roses, after all." The stout dueña rose reluctantly to her feet.

"We have no knife, Marquita," she said. "I will go in the house and get one."

"No, no," said the girl hurriedly. "Never mind the roses. Sit down again."

Bewildered, Doña Concha resumed her seat on the bench.

"Tell me, Señor Teniente," asked Doña María Catalina after a moment, "have you heard from General Santa Anna?"

"Who?" demanded Juan Diego stupidly. "Oh, the general. No. I have not heard from him."

Except for the trembling of his hands he felt calm again.

"He will ride into the city one of these days," he added in a casual tone.

Doña Concha cleared her throat loudly.

"Don Isidro says that he must be coming on his hands and knees," she said, "he is taking so much time about it."

Both Doña María Catalina and Juan Diego laughed in sudden relief.

"Go," ordered the girl. "Get the knife, tiíta. We will cut some roses."

"If you will make up your mind . . ." grumbled the dueña, rising again to her feet.

A thin black shadow fell across them and Doña María Catalina and Juan Diego looked up quickly to see Chepe standing before them.

"What is it, Chepe?" asked the girl.

"The patrona is in the library," he explained. "She is asking for the Doña María Catalina."

The girl rose quickly.

"I must go, then," she said to Juan Diego.

"The patrona has her prayerbook in her hand," added the Indian.

Doña María Catalina smiled and ran with light steps toward the door, followed more slowly by the waddling figure of Doña Concha and the lean Chepe. Juan Diego watched them go with sober eyes. He felt that there was a secret bond between him and the girl—they had recognized it simultaneously during that moment of silence just before she had first spoken of the roses to Doña Concha—and he wondered how this would affect his relationship with Don Isidro. He should have told the hacendado about these meetings with Doña María Catalina in the patio, told him casually as though they were natural encounters occasioned by chance, but somehow he had not done so. Each time he had hesitated and the apt moment had been lost. Or had he hesitated? Might it not be that some inner check had kept him silent, some fear, perhaps, that if he did tell the hacendado he would no longer find the girl under the willow tree? Then, again, it might be that both Doña Ágata and Don Isidro knew about these meetings. He could not imagine Doña María Catalina concealing anything from her mother and father if they asked any questions. "Did you see anybody in the patio this morning?" "Yes, my mother, I saw the Señor Teniente." "And yesterday morning?" "I saw the Señor Teniente." "And the morning before that?" "I saw the Señor Teniente." Now that he thought of it that way it seemed worse than ever. After all, she was a young married woman. He *would* have to say something to Don Isidro.

Married. He scowled and began to draw a haphazard design with
the toe of his boot. Well, she had told him all about that. No woman
in the world, at least, in the Mexican world, had ever been so honest
and frank as she had been and that had meant that there was something more between them than a mere friendly acquaintanceship of a
few days' standing. Mexican women did not usually open their hearts
that way. At least, he thought not. After all, there was very little that
he knew about women. When she spoke . . . when she said, "I found
out the minute he . . . he touched me," it had aroused a demon within
him and he had shaken with an anger that had left him speechless. She
knew that. She had seen it. It had surprised him as much as he supposed it had surprised her. And then he had known how dear and
necessary she had become to him and how the thought of her being
married to Don Alejandro was like a knife thrust into his side. "Ay
Dios!" he said aloud. Matters should never have reached this point between them, for now he had placed himself in a predicament for which
there was no solution. What could he do? And what could she do?
They were caught in a coil from which there seemed to be no escape.
He could go away, to be sure, but how would he explain to Don Isidro
that he must leave his house when Don Isidro knew that he must remain in Puebla until the general came? "Ay Dios!" he said again.

He was perplexed and unhappy now and he supposed he would be
perplexed and unhappy for the rest of his life. There was one word
that he would not say, that he would not admit into his consciousness,
although he suspected that it was tapping already at the back of his
mind. Out, word! It is not so. He slapped the hard bench with his hand
and got up and started to walk toward the house door. He was oblivious of the roses and the sunlight. He was determined on one thing.
He must speak to Don Isidro and tell him about these meetings in the
patio. That was the honest thing to do. Nearing the door he walked
more slowly. Still, he should wait for the opportune moment. It was
senseless to rush in and babble as though he had committed some indis-
cretion. After all, he had not taken Doña María Catalina into consideration. Perhaps it would be wiser if he waited until the morning and
asked her what she thought about it. It was a poor excuse for procrastination but he hugged it to himself as he passed through the door and
into the cool dark corridor.

The midday meal concluded, Don Isidro, instead of enjoying a
siesta as was his habit, decided to call on one or two of his business
acquaintances. "If they are sleeping," he declared, "I will awaken them
by putting montsrous fleas in their ears." Doña Ágata and Doña María
Catalina retired to their quarters. Young Lorenzo was left alone with
Juan Diego. It was an opportunity for which the young officer had

been waiting for some time and he immediately took advantage of it. He watched impatiently while Chepe and Chuchita cleared the table and then he broached the subject that had been troubling his mind for the last two days.

"Tell me, Lorenzo," he said, "did you, by any chance, see Don Alejandro in Mexico City?"

The boy's face darkened and a scowl that was more like a pout spread across it.

"Yes, Señor Teniente," he replied. "I saw Don Alejandro several times. I saw him riding in the Paseo on his beautiful horse. I saw him again in the entourage of General Valencia when the general made a formal visit to Presidente Anaya. We acted as a guard of honor that day. And once he came to see me at the Military College."

Juan Diego looked his surprise.

"He came to see you?" he repeated.

"He came with a letter for my father," explained Lorenzo. "He wanted me to forward it in a letter of my own. I told him that all correspondence with my father was conducted through his agent in the Calle de Vergara. He said that the agent did not forward his letters."

"Yes," said Juan Diego.

"I refused to accept the letter," went on the boy. "He was very angry and threatened to beat me."

"What happened then?" asked the young officer.

"Nothing," said Lorenzo. "I left the guardroom and after a while he went away."

There was a pause while Juan Diego traced a vague design with his finger on the tablecloth. Lorenzo stared at him expectantly.

"I think he is a dangerous man," remarked the young officer at last.

"He is a very bad man!" exclaimed Lorenzo. "Oh, I heard about him, too. He pretends to be a Moderado although he is not a citizen of the Republic at all. He is a Spaniard and one of the older boys at the Military College told me that he was working for the Monarchists. He hates the general and desires to see him superseded by General Valencia. He is very cruel, too."

"Cruel. Yes," said Juan Diego reflectively. "You spoke of his beautiful horse. Does he still . . ."

"It is the horse that he had at Las Golondrinas," broke in Lorenzo. "Simún. That is the horse's name. Don Alejandro brought it with him from Spain."

"Yes," nodded Juan Diego. "I remember the horse. You are right. He is very beautiful. And full of spirit."

He paused and regarded Lorenzo carefully.

"You really think that Don Alejandro is conspiring against the general?" he demanded.

"Yes, I do," cried Lorenzo. "I am sure of it. I know that the commandant at Chapultepec ordered me not to receive him again and the commandant is a Santanista. Will you speak to the general about Don Alejandro, Señor Teniente? Would it be possible to have him sent back to Spain?"

"I don't know, Lorenzo," answered Juan Diego. "It is possible. But we must have proof first."

The boy swelled to the "we."

"I will try to get it," he declared earnestly. "When I return to the capital I will try to get it."

"I would keep away from Don Alejandro," warned the young officer dryly. "If there is anything to be found out the general will attend to that. He still has his friends in Mexico City. There are methods for this sort of thing."

He hesitated and eyed Lorenzo thoughtfully.

"Do you know where Don Alejandro lives?" he asked finally.

The boy shook his head.

"No," he replied. "But my father's agent will know. My father sends money through his agent to Don Alejandro."

He looked in a puzzled manner at Juan Diego.

"Why does he do that?" he asked plaintively.

"I don't know," replied the young officer shortly.

"My sister hates that man," said Lorenzo in a low tense voice.

Juan Diego's lips were drawn into a straight grim line. He knew more than Lorenzo about this hatred, but, for some reason that he could not explain to himself, he did not want to discuss Doña María Catalina and her feelings with the boy.

"Yes, yes," he exclaimed, putting up his hand. "We must not discuss these matters. It would be a lack of courtesy on my part, Lorenzo . . ."

The boy glanced questioningly at the young officer.

"Lorenzo," repeated Juan Diego, "I think it would be wise if we kept this little conversation to ourselves. Shall we be allies? You will tell me what gossip you may hear of Don Alejandro and I will see that the general is warned about him. We will tell nobody else, not even Doña María Catalina or Doña Ágata or Don Isidro, about it. Does that suit you?"

"Oh, yes!" cried the boy. "We will form a confederation of two. I'd like that very much."

"Good!" exclaimed Juan Diego, pushing back his chair and standing up. "And now would you like to walk with me in the plaza? We will purchase a great basket of fruit and . . ."

Lorenzo knocked his chair over as he jumped up.

"That will be fine," he declared enthusiastically. "I do not think the fruit sellers will be out now. But we can walk. It will not be too hot."

He ran ahead of Juan Diego to find his cadet cap.

It was close to eleven o'clock in the evening when Chepe knocked on Don Isidro's bedroom door and informed him that the bishop was waiting downstairs in the library. The hacendado looked disbelievingly at the Indian for a moment and then drew on the short jacket he had just discarded and stalked heavily down the long flight. The bishop was turning over the leaves of a book of verse by Fernando Calderón y Beltrán.

"I am glad to see that you have taken up poetry," said the prelate as he indicated the volume.

"I don't read poetry, my dear uncle, and you know it," replied Don Isidro. "Somebody took the book from the shelves and forgot to put it back."

"Doña María Catalina, probably," remarked the bishop.

Don Isidro shrugged his shoulders.

"You pay late visits," he said without any warmth in his voice.

The old man glanced keenly at his nephew for a moment and then sank back in the leather chair with a sigh of comfort.

"I am very busy, Don Isidro," he explained mildly. "Besides, I wanted to see you alone. Is your young friend with the . . . er . . . remarkable name somewhere about?"

The hacendado sat on the edge of the table and gazed down on the little figure below him.

"He is in his chamber, I believe," he replied. "He didn't sleep well last night so he retired early. Why do you ask? Do you want to see him?"

"No, no," cried the bishop. "I wish particularly not to see him. I want to see you alone. I don't want to startle anybody. Why didn't your young friend sleep well? Has he a bad conscience?"

"I don't know," answered Don Isidro. "Why don't you ask him? There must be a good many bad consciences in Puebla tonight."

The bishop smiled and shut his eyes.

"I don't doubt it," he said. "I don't doubt it at all. There are a great many evil men in the world. I do all that I can to reason with them but they have deaf ears."

Don Isidro snorted.

"Did you say anything?" asked the bishop, opening his eyes.

"No," said the hacendado shortly.

"It must have been mice," remarked the prelate.

He shut his eyes again.

"How is my dear Doña Ágata?" he asked after a moment.

"Very well," replied Don Isidro.

"And Doña María Catalina?"

"Very well, also."

The bishop sighed,

"I am very glad to hear that," he said. "Tell them that I always remember them in my prayers."

The hacendado was silent.

"My dear nephew," the bishop went on, opening his eyes and inspecting the other from head to foot. "This is remarkable. I find you practically bereft of speech and that is something that no one who knows you would ever expect. Are you ill?"

"I never felt better in my life," answered Don Isidro. "I thought, as you came at this unusual hour to find me alone, that you had something particular to communicate to me. I am merely waiting."

"Merely waiting," repeated the bishop. "There is so much of that in life. Yes, yes. And so few of us wait patiently. I am glad that you are feeling well. At your time of life one must walk more cautiously. The seasons . . ."

"At my time of life!" exploded Don Isidro. "I can ride a horse, rope a steer, shoot a gun, run a mile and drink a litro of aguardiente with any baby-faced charro from Mexico City. If you call fifty-one . . ."

The bishop laughed aloud, a shrill high whinny, and held up his thin little hand.

"That is better," he said. "I recognize you now, Don Isidro. No, you are not ill. I am glad of that. You are merely angry at me."

The hacendado resumed his silence and the bishop sighed for the second time.

"I am sorry for those of my children who do not understand that I am always watching over them," continued the prelate in a resigned voice. "What I do I do for them and the glory of God. If I see farther than they that is because I have been given wisdom and have access to knowledge that is denied them. I know why you are angry with me, Don Isidro, but I bear this cross with equanimity for I know, too, that the day will come when you will admit that I was right and you were wrong. But I didn't come here to discuss these matters with you. I came to give you a friendly warning concerning Doña Ágata and Doña María Catalina."

Don Isidro lifted his head abruptly.

"What's that?" he said sharply. "What do you mean?"

The bishop leaned forward in his chair.

"Puebla," he announced deliberately, watching the hacendado

closely as he spoke, "will be a different place in a very short time. I
know that the Americans are not the monsters they are reported to be
but I realize, also, that they have another attitude toward women than
our own. There was some trouble in Monterrey and Saltillo. The
Americans are more free in their expressions and some of them, volunteers, I understand, with little experience of military discipline, are
liable to be . . . er . . . importunate. I suggest, therefore, that you send
Doña Ágata and Doña María Catalina away for a time."

He paused to see how Don Isidro would take this suggestion.

The hacendado did not move. He sat on the table staring down
at his uncle intently.

"You are suggesting that the Americans, or some among them,
will assault our women," he said slowly. "Is that what you have come
here so late in the evening to tell me?"

"No, no, no!" expostulated the bishop. "I am suggesting nothing
of the sort. The Americans are not Visigoths or Vandals. It is merely
that their customs differ from our own and that they think nothing of
speaking to a woman whom they do not know. You would not like it if
some foolish young soldier should accost Doña María Catalina when
she left the cathedral, for instance. You—"

"I would knock the man down," interrupted Don Isidro grimly.

"There! You see," pointed out the prelate. "And then what would
happen to you? You might be arrested and thrown into prison. If you
injured or killed the man you might even be executed. I don't suppose
you would consider leaving Puebla?"

"No," said the hacendado shortly.

"No," repeated the bishop. "And yet you can do no good here."

"You would like to be rid of me," remarked Don Isidro. "However, I will not go. No Americans are going to drive me from my
home. I fled from them once at the request of your niece but I will not
do it again. Por dios! Am I a fox to be driven from place to place by
a pack of foreign dogs? No! I will stay and see these Americans and
show them that there is one Mexican who can hold up his head and
show no fear."

The bishop sighed.

"That is very brave," he said, "but it means absolutely nothing.
I shall pray that you do not get into trouble. But surely you will not
refuse to send the women away?"

Don Isidro thrust out his heavy underlip and thought for a
moment.

"No," he said at last, "I will not refuse that. As a matter of fact,
I would rather that my wife and daughter did not see the Americans
. . . if they get to Puebla. However, it is still possible that we will fight.
We have not heard from Santa Anna yet."

The bishop made an impatient gesture with his hands.

"Even if we fight . . . which we will not . . . there will be reason for sending the women away," he declared. "Have you ever heard of American artillery? It is very good. It reduced Vera Cruz and it can reduce Puebla. I have had reliable reports of the bombardment of Vera Cruz. The picture was not pretty. Burning roofs; toppling houses; flying fragments of pavement; doors, windows and furniture choking the streets; bells ringing by themselves; ear-deafening explosions; steeples lurching in the air; the earth shaking; crowds of screaming women rushing about; gaping wounds and sudden death. I heard that after the second day there was only one bakeshop left undestroyed in the city. That is what it is, Don Isidro, to be bombarded by American artillery. Would you like to have Doña Ágata and Doña María Catalina go through that horror? I am certain that my niece would lose her senses."

"I will send the women away," said Don Isidro.

"Good. You are wise, my nephew," declared the bishop, standing up. "I knew you would see reason. My one regret is that you will not go away yourself. Where will you send them?"

"Doña Ágata's sister, Doña Marta, is at Apizaco with her children," explained the hacendado. "I can send them there."

"Ah, yes, Doña Marta," said the bishop. "That is good. Apizaco is not quite so far away as I would wish but it is off the National Highway. I see no reason why the Americans should want to go there. Send them to Apizaco then and see that they remain there until the peace is signed."

"The peace!" exclaimed Don Isidro indignantly. "What peace? I know of no peace unless you or the archbishop has been negotiating with the Americans. The peace will be signed when we have driven the invader from our soil."

"That is one way of looking at it," replied the bishop amiably as he moved toward the door. "By the way, I would lose no time if I were you in sending the women away."

"I will pack them off tomorrow," said the hacendado, slipping from the table and following his uncle. "Why do you say that? Do you expect something to happen soon?"

The bishop spread his hands in a gesture of uncertainty.

"One never knows what will happen," he answered. "Only God knows that. However, it is wise to be prepared. Don't follow me to the door. Chepe, whom I see in the corridor, can let me out and put up the bars. Farewell, my nephew. I am glad to find you so reasonable."

"Farewell," said Don Isidro.

He stood by the library table listening to the creak of the door and the rattle of the bar and chains. He felt lonely and depressed and somehow hunted. It was regrettable that he had not remained at Las Golondrinas where he could order all as he pleased; in Puebla he was less than nothing, a mere cipher in the vast sum of things. It was getting so that he could not call his own roof his own. How the times had changed since those faraway days when he boasted of talking back to God. He would never do that again. He had discovered that the earth did not belong to him but that he belonged to the earth. Or that he had more of a responsibility to the earth, the earth upon which he dwelt, than it had for him. He had a responsibility toward other men, as well, a responsibility that shaped his own life as much as it did theirs. He had not thought enough about other men in the days that had passed. Indeed, he had not thought enough about his own family. Doña María Catalina, for instance. He would have to know her better. He walked slowly toward the stairs that led upward to his bedchamber but he did not feel like sleeping. For a moment he was tempted to rap at Juan Diego's door and rouse him and talk to him for a little while. The young officer was well worth talking to. Then he thought better of it. Let him sleep. He would have enough wakeful nights after the general came. When the campaign started. He climbed the stairs slowly and methodically and turned down the corridor toward Doña Ágata's quarters. She might be surprised to see him at this hour but he had things to tell her. At the door to her room he paused for a minute before he rapped. He liked the silence of the house.

The sky was overcast when Juan Diego entered the patio and a fresh wind that rippled the roses blew coldly against his face. There was rain in the air. The break in the fine weather seemed almost symbolic. There was a break, too, in the sun-shot anticipation that warmed him each morning and sent him hurrying from his chamber to the bench under the willow. It manifested itself as a sense of guilt, a disturbing conviction that he was committing a clandestine act. He *should* inform Don Isidro about these meetings. He had intended to do so the evening before but when the moment came, that moment after dinner when he sat with the hacendado in the quietude of the dining room and drank aguardiente, he had funked it and pleaded weariness and gone early to his chamber. He had excused his cowardice to himself by arguing that he had Doña María Catalina to consider and must consult her first. But that was weakness and he knew it. He was afraid of the consequences. He was afraid that Don Isidro would thrust out his underlip in disapproval and tell him that he should not see Doña María Catalina alone (for Doña Concha hardly counted) so often. He was afraid, too, of the growing intimacy that was flowering from these meetings and especially so after the emotional tumult that had shaken him yesterday. Where was all this leading and what would be the

result of it? He would have to do something about it. For the sake of
all of them. The fire was beginning to burn too brightly and it should
be extinguished while it was yet possible to do so. He had thought
about it, anxiously, sorrowfully, while he was dressing and now he
was convinced that he must speak to Doña María Catalina. He did not
know how he could word it but perhaps she would help him. She was
so understanding and wise in her straightforward way. Before Heaven,
he had never encountered anybody like her before on the face of the
earth. Simpática. Ah, she was more than that. She was his alter ego,
his second self, a part of him now. But what foolishness. He was
stupid to think like that. There was nothing . . .

She was not sitting on the bench when he reached it and for a
moment he was bitterly disappointed. Then it occurred to him that he
was early and that there was no reason why she should be there at this
hour. Why, it could be hardly more than eight o'clock and did she not
go to church each morning with her mother? Why should he be disappointed? Yet he was as he sat down and listened to the rustling of
the wind in the willow overhead. He had half-expected her to rush out
ahead of time, too. And that was a silly way to feel. He was taking too
much for granted. Already he was expecting a response from her that
he knew would be dangerous for both of them. He would have to
watch himself more carefully and not assume that she was experiencing
the same emotions that he alternately felt and endeavored to suppress.
Suddenly it occurred to him that maybe she was not coming down to
the patio at all and something like a cold hand folded softly about his
heart. Well . . . why not? She had made no promises and a single long
glance was not a pledge. It was possible that his imagination was running away with him. And then he saw the flash of her skirt as she
came through the door and a silly sort of happiness flowed through all
his limbs. He knew she would come.

Surprisingly enough, she was alone. He watched the door carefully but no round-bodied Doña Concha emerged from it. She was
alone. All alone. It was the first time in his life he had ever seen her
alone and she seemed to take on an added beauty. She came toward
him holding her wide skirt slightly lifted in both hands and he could
see the white flash of her stockings and the small soft curve of her
breasts. He was almost dizzy to discover that she had breasts and the
reality of her body impinged upon his awakened senses like a great
discovery. She was small but not so small as he had thought. Even the
great clumsy skirt could not hide the sway of her hips as she walked.
It made him self-conscious to be so aware of the white flesh that was
moving beneath the colored garments and he averted his face. What in
the devil was the matter with him anyway? A little pulse began to beat
like a midget drum in his temple.

She came directly to him and sat down beside him. When he glanced at her he saw that her face was unexpectedly grave and he instantly assumed that he was the cause of it.

"What is it?" he asked with a sinking sensation. "What has . . ."

"I am going away," she said directly. "My mother, Doña Concha and I are going to Apizaco. They are packing the coach now."

He looked at her with amazement and then his expression changed to one of guilt. He might have known . . .

"Did Don Isidro—" he began.

"The bishop came last night," she broke in. "He advised my father to send all the women away from Puebla. My mother has just told me. That is all."

A feeling of relief swept over him and then it was immediately superseded by one of emptiness. What would Puebla be like without her?

"Apicazo," he said. "Have you friends in Apizaco?"

"My aunt," she explained. "My aunt Marta. She lives in this house when we are not here. She has a small holding in Apizaco. I don't want to go away."

She brought out the last sentence with vehemence.

"I am not afraid of the Americans," she continued. "I do not believe that they are ogres. I can take care of myself. But what can I do? My mother is filled with fears and continues to treat me like a child."

"Is Don Isidro going to Apizaco?" inquired Juan Diego.

"Of course not," she replied. "Why should he go to Apizaco? Why should anybody go to Apizaco for that matter?"

She was flushed and indignant and this gave him a glimpse of a spirit she had never shown before. He knew now that beneath the usual composure and quietness of her demeanor unexpected fires were burning. The knowledge pleased and excited him.

"It is probably the wisest course to take," he said judiciously.

She stared at him brightly.

"Señor Teniente," she declared, "you speak like an old man. I wonder that you did not become a priest."

He had to laugh at that.

"Wisdom is not the prerogative of old men and priests," he explained as though he was speaking to a child. "It is free to all who take advantage of it."

"Chállese!" she exclaimed rudely.

"What did you say?" he asked in amazement.

"Chállese!" she repeated and burst out laughing at his shocked expression.

"I have heard Chepe say .that to Chuchita," she explained. "Be sides, I am angry and you do talk like an old man. There is no reason why I should not remain here."

"If there should be fighting . . ." he began.

"Do you believe there will be fighting?" she demanded.

"I hope there will be," he answered grimly.

They were silent for a moment.

"It is not a good day," she said finally. "The sky is too gray. I am sure that it will rain all the way to Apizaco and it smells in the coach. I shall be lonely at Apizaco."

There was a note of brooding in her voice. She stared unseeingly at the roses.

"And that is curious," she added, after a moment. "I never felt lonely before."

He didn't quite know what to say. He wanted to put his hand on hers and feel the warmth of it. There it rested, close to his knee, on the brown worn bench, half-closed, the fingers small and tapering and a silver Indian bracelet banding the thin wrist. Quite suddenly, as though she was aware of his desire, she removed her hand and began to fumble at the necklace around her throat.

"I shall miss you terribly, Doña María Catalina," he said in a low voice.

She started to speak and then thought better of it and for a moment he thought she was going to cry. There was the shadow of tears in her eyes.

"I must go," she said in a husky voice. "They are waiting for me. I just slipped out to tell you because I did not want you to think . . . to think that I did not want to come."

He stood up silently and offered her his hand. She put her own in it but did not rise for a moment. He could feel the tiny pulse beating in her wrist. He felt as though he was holding a small bird.

Then she stood up and faced him.

"Farewell, Señor Teniente," she said composedly. "May luck be with you wherever you go."

"Farewell, Doña María Catalina," he replied. "Vaya usted con Dios."

She started to walk slowly away but had not gone far when she broke into a swift little run, her skirt ballooning about her and her white stockings flashing in the sunless light. In a moment she had disappeared through the door.

He sat down on the bench again. Well, it had happened as quickly as that. He hoped he had been as reserved as he should be. There was no need to speak to Don Isidro now. Everything was solved and the danger had been taken care of by a force outside himself. But he felt no relief, nothing but an endless regret, a despairing sensation of frustration. Now that she, was gone he could think of half a dozen things he might have said to her and which might have sent her away with a better memory of him. He was an incoherent fool at best but he had been particularly idiotic with her. The warm touch of her fingers still tingled in the palm of his hand and he half-lifted it and looked at it as though he might see an impress of her there. Then he dropped his hand limply to his knee and sat motionless while a sharp tide of desolation washed over him and left him cold under the gray sky. He was staring into his own tragedy now and the word that he had refused to admit into his mind was echoing loudly in his ears. Amor. Amor. Amor. Its reiteration was like a bell. He could not lie to himself. He could not pretend to himself any longer. I love her, he thought, I love her. There is no answer to this. The time for questions and answers has gone by. I love her.

The scraping of heavy feet caused him to lift his head and he saw Don Isidro approaching along the flagstoned path. It was the first time he had ever seen him in the patio. So many first times today. The hacendado lowered himself carefully to the bench and placed his big hands on his knees.

"It is a filthy day" declared Don Isidro glancing up at the gray sky. "I hope it rains like the devil when the procession starts."

"Procession?" echoed Juan Diego in a questioning tone.

Don Isidro looked at him curiously.

"Yes," he said. "There is to be a procession for peace this afternoon. Shall we go and see it?"

"If you like," replied the young officer indifferently.

Don Isidro fixed his eyes on a rosebush and puffed out his underlip.

"There is nothing else to do," he remarked. "I am sending the women away today."

Juan Diego said nothing.

"They're going to Apizaco," the hacendado continued. "It's just as well to be prepared for all eventualities. Besides, I thing that Doña Ágata will be easier in her mind there."

"Of course," responded the young officer.

Don Isidro sighed and scratched the scar on his forehead.

"Her sister's there," he added inconsequentially.

The fresh breeze ruffled through his side whiskers and he held out his hand.

"There's rain in the air all right," he said. "Well, it won't do us any harm."

"No," remarked Juan Diego. "It won't do us any harm."

Don Isidro twisted on the bench and cleared his throat.

"You will miss your morning cara a cara with my daughter," he said mildly.

For an instant the young officer did not grasp what he was saying and then a feeling of confusion caused his cheeks to flame with color. He had known all the time, then. He had been aware of these meetings and he had said nothing about them. More than that, he had permitted them to continue.

"We chanced to meet . . ." mumbled Juan Diego at last and then stopped.

Why should he prevaricate? Excepting, perhaps, for the first time there had been no chance in it at all. They had met consciously and in the same place and nearly always at the same time. If Don Isidro knew it he knew everything. And if he knew everything and had not interfered then it naturally followed that he approved everything. But did it? Did Don Isidro have any idea of what these meetings had meant to him? The hacendado had never mentioned the name of Don Alejandro and what he thought of him, in what light he viewed him as the husband of Doña María Catalina, remained a mystery. For an instant Juan Diego was tempted to blurt out the truth and declare frankly his affection for Doña María Catalina and then he thought better of it. The time had not come yet.

"I enjoyed conversing with Doña María Catalina very much," he said at last.

"I am sure of it," replied Don Isidro, "and I am sure that she enjoyed conversing with you. I . . ."

He seemed embarrassed for a moment and then recovered himself and went on.

"She does not lead too lively a life," he said. "I could wish that she had more to entertain her. Perhaps I have not considered her as much as I should have. I might have talked to her oftener but habits are tough harnesses and an old horse does not break free from them easily. Still . . . I am glad that you were here to divert her for a while."

"She is very intelligent and sensitive," declared Juan Diego.

"Is she?" asked the hacendado. "I am glad to hear that."

He fumbled in the pocket of his jacket and drew forth a thin black cigarro which he thrust in his mouth and began to chew.

"The bishop paid me a visit last night," he said.

Apparently the subject of Doña María Catalina was dismissed.

"I know," replied Juan Diego. "Your daughter told me."

"Yes," continued the other. "He came as usual with words of wisdom. I think that he wanted me to leave Puebla, too. He is afraid that I will make a one-man assault on the Americans."

He laughed shortly and the cigarro flew out of his mouth and landed on the path. He looked at it morosely for a moment.

"The bishop is a sly little man," he said, "but he shows good sense frequently enough."

"I suppose he does," agreed Juan Diego. "At least, he is always aware of what will benefit the Church."

"That is exactly it," exclaimed Don Isidro. "From that point of view he is consistent. But is he always aware of what will benefit Mexico? Of course, the Church comes first. Ever since the partial separation of church and state in 1833 we have had a state within a state and I sometimes wonder which is more powerful, the Republic or the Church. If the Church was fighting this war with all its might I would be sanguine of victory. As it is . . ."

He spread his hands in a gesture of hopelessness.

"We are a poor priest-ridden country," he remarked gloomily.

Suddenly he turned and faced Juan Diego with sharp eyes.

"What do you really think of Santa Anna?" he asked. "Can you put your natural affection for him aside and view him objectively? If you can, what do you think of him?"

The young officer hesitated for a long time.

"That is a difficult question to answer," he said slowly. "I don't think that I can put my natural affection aside. It is too much a part of me. But I can see certain aspects in the general's personality and methods now that I never thought of looking for in the past and which I do not like to consider. When I was a boy I thought that he was always right but sometimes misunderstood by his countrymen. I am not as simple as that now. I know that the general has his flaws and that his nature is unstable. I have never admitted this before to anybody, Don Isidro, not even myself, but it seems to me that lately I have begun to see a great many things that were before me all the time but which I did not recognize. The general is ambitious and sometimes he puts his ambition before his duty. He is a natural conspirator. But I believe with all my heart that he loves Mexico and I believe, too, that he is the only man in the Republic today capable of carrying on a war against the Americans. He is our only hope and when he is destroyed the war is lost. Who else is there?"

Don Isidro nodded.

"I am inclined to agree with you," he admitted, "although I have more doubts of the general's honesty than you have. He *is* our only hope. If the Church and the Republic would get solidly behind him I think we could drive the Americans out of our country although we might not be able to hold Texas or California. After all, what is our enemy? Some ten or twelve thousand men, a long, long way from their own land. Potentially we could raise an army of fifty thousand soldiers and we could drag this war out until the weight of opinion in the United States made the Washington government withdraw their troops. You see, I have been thinking a lot about this lately. I think you're to blame for that."

Juan Diego nodded absently. He was still thinking about Santa Anna, trying to disentangle the man from his fond memories of him but he found it difficult. He was like a youth who, being told that his father was a stern reprobate, would respond, "My father is the kindest man in the world." Yet he could realize that there were two sides to it.

"I think that the Republic has something to do with the general's character," he said with a puzzled frown. "I mean that the thirty years of it, of revolution, of conspiracy, of unrest resulted in a forced habit of dog eat dog. No one reaches the presidential chair in Mexico without making enemies. One must protect one's self against enemies and the only way to do it is to plot, outtrick and even assassinate. We are a nation of individualists and we cannot bow our stubborn necks easily to authority, not even the authority that we set up ourselves."

"Yes," agreed Don Isidro. "In other words, we are either only half-civilized or too civilized. We are too volatile. Our blood runs too hot. Freedom intoxicates us. When the old viceroys ruled we were subdued by fear and tradition. Under the Republic we lost our fear of our leaders and we had no tradition. Even an Indian could aspire to the presidency. The viceroy was appointed by the king and that was all there was to it. He represented nothing but authority. The president is theoretically chosen by the qualified voters and he represents a party. In other words, he must compromise, insinuate and conspire to hold his dominancy. Sometimes he becomes a dictator and then he is merely aping the viceroys. I think that most of us in our secret hearts prefer the dictator."

"Yet the Americans have had a republic for seventy years and there has been no revolution, no bloody conspiracies or upset governments," remarked Juan Diego.

"Do you know why?" asked Don Isidro. "No? I will tell you. The Americans have always had an outlet for their unrest. It is all the lands from the Atlantic seaboard to the Pacific Ocean. When they became uneasy or restless they could strike toward the west building new homes and cities and clearing virgin lands. They exhausted and renewed their energy in that way. They didn't need to kill each other. They could kill Indians. Do you know, I believe there are more Indians in Mexico today than in all of the United States? Why, they outnumber the whites. In spite of what the lying Anglo-Saxon histories say, we never tried to destroy them. We live beside them. They form a part of the population of our largest and oldest cities. We never drove them away. How many Indians will you find in New York City or Boston or Philadelphia? And when the Americans decided that there were no more lands to the west to exploit and so em-

ploy their excess energies they solved that lack by invading our lands.
It was as simple as that. They spread and spread all the time. Besides,
they are not a Latin people."

He ceased speaking and stood up.

"Do you believe that the Americans are animated solely by
greed?" inquired Juan Diego, rising too.

"What else can you call it?" demanded the hacendado. "Oh, they
call it other things for they are a great race when it comes to justify-
ing themselves. They are like the Jews. They consider themselves a
Chosen People. Liberty is their private property and they will thrust
it down your throat whether you want it or not. Democracy, which
does not exist in their country, is always on their lips. They will make
you pay lip service to it if they have to do it with a howitzer."

"They were walking toward the door of the house now.

"I think they are moved by more than greed," said Juan Diego.
Don Isidro glanced quickly at the young officer.

"I'd like to know what it is, then," he announced gruffly.

"That's the trouble," pointed out Juan Diego swiftly. "We don't
know them and they don't know us."

"Do they want to know us?" asked Don Isidro.

"Do we want to know them?" countered the young man.

The hacendado grunted.

"If we would meet without guns in our hands we might get somewhere," persisted Juan Diego.

Don Isidro laughed shortly.

"If we do," he said, "they will have the shirts off our backs before the introductions are completed."

Juan Diego shook his head as they passed into the house.

The streets beside the cathedral were covered with cloth awnings
stretched on poles when Don Isidro, Juan Diego and Lorenzo came
into the plaza. A great mob of people, most of them in their finest
clothes, pushed back and forth, bought dulces and fresh fruit drinks
from the hawkers, shouted and hurled imprecations at the burros and
horses that bumped against them. It was more like a holiday than the
hour for a solemn procession of peace.

"The bishop's crowning achievement," remarked Don Isidro as he
slapped a crowding donkey ferociously on the haunch.

The front of the cathedral above the center door was hung with
old tapestries that swelled and sank back under the pressure of the
wind. The sky was still gray and lowering.

Juan Diego glanced over the fluctuating sea of brown faces and
bobbing sombreros and noticed that there appeared to be hundreds of
able-bodied men there. Not one of them was in uniform. There was no

anxiety in their faces. They laughed and joked, gobbled sweetmeats and tortillas, slipped in and out of the cantinas and ogled the young women in their bright red petticoats. Why, there were enough of them to make up a regiment. Yet not one of them wanted to fight and the young officer suspected that not more than one in ten of them knew, or cared, what the war was about. The war was something that the government carried on and the general public avoided as far as possible. He wondered if this was true of all wars, that those who were caught fought while the great bulk of the population remained apathetic and endeavored to carry on life as usual. It seemed to him that there was more excitement over an internal revolution than there was over this struggle against an invader.

"I think the procession is coming now," exclaimed Lorenzo loudly as he rose on tiptoe and tried to look over the shoulders of the moving crowd.

A sound of chanting could be heard in the near distance and as it grew louder the crowd packed closely along the road and craned their necks in its direction. Sombreros began to disappear as men snatched them from their heads and when the van of the parading column appeared it moved like a slow river between banks of black hair. Here and there devout women fell on their knees and fumbled at the beads that hung from their throats. Four boys in white lace surplices marched first, swinging censers from which coiled thin spirals of blue smoke. A scent of incense gradually suffused the air. Then came a sort of litter or platform covered by a shaky canopy. It was borne by six friars in ragged robes who marched flatfooted, slapping their sandals on the cobbles. On the platform, obviously fastened in place by ropes and sometimes tipping at an awkward angle, stood a small figure of Our Lady elaborately garmented in heavy brocade covered by glittering stones. Juan Diego wondered if any of these stones were real and doubted it. Our Lady stared out blankly over the heads of the crowd with round black-painted eyes. The red smear of her mouth seemed to smirk at the cathedral. As the young officer watched this battered doll being carried past while a thousand heads bowed like wheat before a passing wind he sensed anew the curious power of the Church over its communicants. It seemed to him like a sort of idolatry. The Virgin of Puebla was not as famous as Nuestra Señora de los Remedios, that little alabaster puppet with the broken nose and one eye which Don Hernan Cortés found in the knapsack of one of his soldiers after the noche triste and presented to his routed troopers as an image sent from heaven, or the miraculous tilma of the Indian, Juan Diego, hanging enshrined with gold in the church of Guadalupe, but it was potent enough to sway the minds and hearts of thousands of people. It could be manipulated to signify peace or war, anything, in fact, that the bishop wanted it to indicate. Now, when the Republic was invaded and armed men were needed, it was signifying peace.

Behind the platform came a mass of priests in bright vestments, snowy albs and gold-embroidered stoles. They were of all sizes and shapes but not one of them seemed to have ever suffered any privation. Their cheeks and bellies were too round for that. They marched along, droning their chant and casting bold speculative eyes at the spectators. The dull light cast a leaden glow on their tonsures and white supplicating hands. Behind them came a number of nuns muffled to the eyes and then a vast number of monks and friars in shovel hats and dark garments. The chanting rose in volume as they passed under the swelling tapestries into the cathedral and the sound of their shuffling sandals was like the sound of the sea on a shelving beach.

"I don't see the bishop," said Juan Diego in a low voice.

"The bishop is no fool," answered Don Isidro loudly. "He is probably at his villa eating a good chicken. Look at this, will you, my friend? The monkeys have arrived."

A large concourse of army officers and municipal administrators was passing, gaudy in uniforms, crested with plumes and glittering with epaulets. At their head waddled Governor Isunza, a tun-belly of a man with the pride of a gamecock. Don Isidro burst into a loud guffaw and the Governor swung his big yellow face sideways and glared angrily at the source of the laughter.

"Dios mío!" exclaimed the hacendado stridently. "Our Lady has accomplished one miracle today. The governor is sober."

Somebody in the crowd near Don Isidro squealed with laughter and Isunza averted his face swiftly and waddled into the cathedral.

The procession was followed by a horde of Indians in white cotton pants and dirty shirts. They crowded after the officials and as Juan Diego watched them disappear through the huge open doors, their bare unwashed feet and spread toes looking unreal in the sunless light, he wondered what they made of it all. Did they have the faintest idea why they were here, except to see a show, and what was the reason for this demonstration? He doubted it. They were the great incoherent bedrock upon which the unstable edifice of the Republic was built and yet they had little or nothing to do with it. They worked like animals for a few coins or scraped the ground for their little patch of corn and beans or slept in the sun and let the world go by and that was all they knew about the Republic. They paid lip service to Our Lady and continued the customs they had followed under their own ancient gods. Who knew them? Yet they would have to be understood and taken into account if the Republic was to have a firm foundation. Here was a subject to discuss with Don Isidro sometime.

"Shall we go into the cathedral?" asked Don Isidro.

He was already moving toward the portal with Lorenzo, and Juan Diego followed them.

He had never been in the vast building before and now he was amazed to see how much larger it seemed inside than outside. Heavy stone columns in clusters of four rose to the vault and all of them were covered with rich damask. Darkened oil paintings, some huge, hung from the walls and from the heavy frames peered the painted eyes of Jesus Christ and his saints. There was gold work everywhere and one altar seemed to be fashioned solely from colored Puebla onyx. Clusters of candles lit the gloom and on the central altar, where the priests were officiating, there appeared to be at least a thousand dancing flames. The two men and the boy stood for a few minutes inhaling the mingled odor of incense, unwashed bodies and fetid breath and listening to the violins, chanting voices and tiny ringing bells. Then Don Isidro turned and pushed his way through the mass of people toward the door and Juan Diego and Lorenzo silently followed him. Outside the hacendado drew a deep breath.

"The fresh air is good after all the stink," he said.

They walked along aimlessly under the awnings.

"I have been thinking about the Indians, Don Isidro, and what the war means to them," remarked the young officer.

"It doesn't mean anything to them," said the hacendado. "Give them a jug of pulque and a few tortillas and they are satisfied."

"I can't believe that," dissented Juan Diego. "After all, they must know that the Republic—"

"The Republic is only a name to them," interrupted Don Isidro confidently. "An Indian doesn't think of himself as a Mexican, as a citizen of a large country; he thinks of himself as the native of a certain village. For a copper he'll go out and kill a man from the next village and think nothing of it at all, or if he does think of it he'll merely say that he killed a stranger, a foreigner. The Indian is a tribal man, a village man, not a nationalist or a republican. He wants a chief and that is enough for him. I have six thousand Indians on my lands at Las Golondrinas."

"They can be educated . . ." began Juan Diego.

"Educated? Oh, the devil!" exclaimed Don Isidro. "Leave that to the priests. If you educated them enough we'd all be murdered in our beds."

"Oh, come!" said the young officer, laughing. "They are not as bad as that. I know plenty of good Indians and some who have reached high stations in life. General Alvarado—"

"Yes, yes, yes," broke in Don Isidro. "Of course. There are a lot of exceptions. But there are at least two million that are not exceptions. The Indian is a problem that will not be solved in our time. I refuse to trouble my head about them. They are dirty, lazy, thievish, ignorant and superstitious. Come along. We'll walk out to the Alameda."

Juan Diego fell into step with him and they walked along the middle of the road. Don Isidro, he thought, was too intolerant. One couldn't dismiss the Indians like that. If they were dirty, that was because they had never been taught the virtues of or given the means of being clean. If they were lazy, it was because they had no objective or ambition. If they were thievish, perhaps it was because they lacked so much and had no way of honestly getting anything. If they were ignorant, it was because they had no teachers. As for superstition, that might be another wisdom of their own. What was superstition, anyway? It might even be genuflecting before a doll with a broken nose and one eye. It was curious how he was beginning to think about the Indians. He had hardly given them a thought since he left the Tarascans in Michoacán. The Tarascans. The wine . . . Instinctively he glanced at the palms of his hands. There was not a mark there.

Suddenly it began to rain, a cold spitting rain that pricked their faces and got into their eyes.

"Curse it!" said Don Isidro, turning. "We'd better go back to the house. Now why didn't it rain while those fellows in sotanas were strutting along to the cathedral. I saw them caught in a downpour once. They picked up their skirts and ran like a bunch of old ladies to the nearest cantina."

"Ladies? Cantinas?" exclaimed Juan Diego, laughing.

"Like a bunch of old whores," amended the hacendado.

Lorenzo chuckled audibly and his father looked at him with a thunderous expression.

"You are not supposed to listen all the time," he snapped.

There were people scurrying for shelter on all sides and it was with some difficulty that the trio pushed their way to the street that led toward the house. Once there they were in a deserted thoroughfare and they strode rapidly along it to the tiled front of the familiar dwelling. Chepe, who had apparently been on the watch, let them in immediately

"Oh, you are back," said Don Isidro. "Was everything all right at Apizaco?"

"Yes, patrón," replied the Indian. "I have brought a letter for you."

"Put it on the table in the library," directed the hacendado.

He took off his hat and jacket and threw them on the hall bench

"The house feels empty when the women are gone," he remarked glumly. "Well, God willing, it will not be for long. Lorenzo, go up stairs and change your clothes."

The boy went obediently.

"I shall go up, too," said Juan Diego. "I'll rejoin you in the library in half an hour or so."

The house *did* feel empty as he mounted the stairs.

The two weeks following the departure of the women was a period of despondency and irritation to Juan Diego and one of stubborn but hopeless activity for Don Isidro. The hacendado, methodical and merciless in his systematic canvassing of the business and social elements in the city, carried his argument for a stout defense of Puebla into every private home and office. He pleaded, cajoled, argued, threatened and painted fearsome pictures of what would happen if the Americans took over control. He was listened to in sullen silence. Counterarguments were thrust at him and he found himself incapable of destroying them. He did not know enough. The business element pointed out that the cotton factories were no longer operating, that thousands of workers had no employment, that prices were rising while supplies dwindled and that the average laborer in Puebla was more interested in filling the bellies of his family and himself than in dying for glory on hastily raised barricades. They had heard about those American guns and they did not mean to become targets for them. They had heard, also, that the American wagon trains were piled with provisions of all sorts, pork and corn meal and fruits, and that the officers paid good money for everything they took. But, most often of all, the business, as well as the social, elements pointed out to Don Isidro that the Church, which ruled all in the city, had called for no defense. That was the argument before which the hacendado was helpless and furious. When he returned after his futile sorties among the Poblanos and reported the extent of his failure to Juan Diego over brimming glasses of aguardiente he was exhausted but dogged. It was more than a matter of pride for him to go on. It was a matter of principle. It was as though he was making up for the years he had not thought about the future of Mexico at all. Whenever he did win some stray adherent (and occasionally he did, for there were a few dreamers in Puebla) he was overjoyed. There was Don Pompilio de Lebrón, for instance, who had his cooperage factory near the road to Atlixco. He weighed three hundred pounds, but, Don Isidro swore, his soul was as great as his body. Don Pompilio offered to march out alone with the hacendado and meet the Americans face to face. "We will make the Yanquis run!" he swore and he and the hacendado got uproariously drunk fighting the imaginary battle. It was impossible infants like this that made all the blacker the general scene. They were like brief sparks momentarily illuminating some mammoth cave.

Juan Diego's despondency and irritation were due to his helplessness. He could not even argue with stubborn people for he did not know them and they never would have listened to him. All he could do was listen to Don Isidro and wait, wait, wait for the general. So he drank more aguardiente than was good for him, under the pretext that he was keeping his host company, ate little, slept badly, missed Doña María Catalina damnably, avoided the little rose-scented patio and prayed feverishly for the quick arrival of the general. He still felt that Santa Anna could do something with the Poblanos. It was possible that he would lash them into activity and if he brought enough troops with him he might even hold the city against the Americans for a time. But he must come quickly. All sorts of rumors were flying about the towers of Puebla concerning the advance of the enemy. He had occupied the fortress of Perote. He was at Tepeyahualco. He was at San Juan de los Llanos. He was at Virreyes. He was as close as Ojo de Agua. The young officer visualized the American column like a long inevitable snake slithering inexorably up the National Highway with fixed bayonets for scales. Where, where, was Santa Anna? Where were the troops he had brought together at Orizaba? The two men asked these questions each evening as they sat late in the dining room while Chepe brought fresh bottles but they never answered them. The faint doubts of the general that had assailed Juan Diego's mind first on the deserted battlefield of Buena Vista deepened and he had a new source of despondency and irritation. Where was the general? What kind of war was this? What, in the name of God, was going to happen to Mexico? They drank their aguardiente and waited to find out.

Santa Anna rode into Puebla on May eleventh at the head of two thousand cavalrymen.

It was young Lorenzo who brought the news to Juan Diego and Don Isidro, rushing into the house from a ramble about the plaza and shouting the information before he discovered in what room the two men might be. Juan Diego, who had been standing by the window in his own chamber gazing down reflectively at the deserted patio, heard the boy's shrill voice, recognized the unexpected excitement in it and ran hastily down the stairway. Don Isidro came lumbering out of the dining room, flanked by a glittering-eyed Chepe.

"What's this? What's this?" the hacendado called. "Stop dancing Lorenzo, and explain what you have seen."

"The general," vociferated the boy. "The general. General Santa Anna. He has just ridden into the plaza with hundreds of cavalrymen. They're hobbling their horses there now. And I heard music on the road. Drums and trumpets. I heard . . ."

Before he finished speaking Juan Diego and Don Isidro were out of the house and running toward the corner by the cathedral. From doors on all sides men and women spurted, tumbling over one another in their hurry and knocking children down right and left, gathering in density where the thoroughfare opened into the plaza and finally coagulating into a mass of flesh like a palpitating wall some distance beyond the long lines of horses. A few scattered huzzas could be heard but for the most part it was a surprisingly silent crowd for a mass assembly of Mexicans. Don Isidro's rocky shoulders did their battering-ram job, as usual, and Juan Diego and Lorenzo followed like two skiffs in the wake of a sailing vessel, ignoring the protests and villification heaped upon them by the pushed and insulted.

The horses were tired. They stood with their heads drooping low and a moist film of sweat over their rough haunches. The heavy stirrups swung slowly as they twitched their tails against the black flies and occasionally tossed their full-maned heads and necks. The cavalrymen, lounging beside them, were tired, too, their eyes dark-circled and black patches of sweat smearing the armpits of their tunics. The air reeked with fresh dung, the sour smell of unwashed men, greased leather and alcoholic fumes, horse-piss and the clayey odor of uncleaned boots. And something else, too, something that was indefinable and yet plain enough. It was the smell of war, the same smell that Don Isidro had inhaled that day on his way to the bishop's villa after the first discouraging news of the Cerro Gordo action.

They pushed their way past the exhausted animals toward the group of mounted officers before the entrance to the Governor's Palace. Santa Anna was leaning sideways and speaking vehemently to a clot of civilians who looked sullen and perturbed. The general's sallow face was puffy and his lips seemed swollen. Juan Diego saw that he was tired and angry. The long black-painted peg of his wooden leg aimed like a rifle barrel at the closed door of the palace. He held a sheet of paper in his right hand which he shook viciously at the silent civilians. His voice, harsh and biting as a whiplash, rose and fell. Juan Diego, now followed by Don Isidro and Lorenzo, edged past the restless horses and came to a halt near the tossing head of the general's mount. Santa Anna glanced down.

"Ah, Juanillo!" he exclaimed with no pleasure in his voice. "There you are. What devil has possessed this obscene son of a diseased ramera, this pox-scarred bastard who calls himself governor of Puebla, this dog of the Isunza family, this . . . this . . ."

He shook the sheet of paper in the young officers' fase.

"Instructions in which the ayuntamiento advise the Poblanos what to do when the Americans take over the city," he shouted. "It is all decided. Isunza has made up his mind to go to bed with Scott. The municipal council will hold the chamber pot for them. Ah, that is so, is it? Where is this old whore of a governor? We will talk to him.

León, Terán, Alcorta, we will talk to this grandson of a Guatemalan monkey."

Juan Diego laid his hand on the general's knee.

"We have done all that we could do, my general," he said breathlessly. "The Poblanos will not fight. The governor and the bishop . . ."

"How much money have they raised?" demanded Santa Anna. "How many troops have they recruited? How much ammunition has been gathered? I need horses. How many have been found. How—"

"Puebla has done nothing," broke in Don Isidro with his big voice.

Santa Anna looked vaguely at him.

"Now that you are here the city will have to prepare a defense" added Juan Diego hastily.

"Defense? What defense?" stormed the general. "The defense should have been prepared days ago. The Americans are less than twenty-four hours' march behind me. They may be at the gates by tomorrow. Am I supposed to be a man of miracles?"

"Not since the Cerro Gordo," called a voice from the crowd.

Santa Anna whirled furiously in his saddle.

"Help me down, Juanillo!" he called. "Help me down so that I may thrust my sword through the guts of that fellow. León, Terán, Alcorta, dismount. We will pay a visit to this governor who is hiding in his wretched palace. We will talk to him."

He dismounted with some difficulty and began to stump through the crowd toward the palace steps. The three officers he had called by name followed him and Juan Diego, Don Isidro and Lorenzo pressed close after them. The crowd parted silently, drawing away from the seven men as though it feared to catch some contagious disease. Enthusiasm, perhaps, thought Juan Diego. But the general is going about it in the wrong way. He cannot work them into a fighting spirit by blustering and calling them names. He is too angry to be wise, now. The group mounted the steps to the closed door of the palace, the heavy rowels of their spurs scraping on the stone and the high heels of their boots clacking. A fat gentleman on the top step waddled importantly toward Santa Anna but Alcorta, the cavalry general, thrust him aside so roughly that he staggered and nearly fell. Don Isidro observed that it was Don Pompilio de Lebrón, one of the general's few adherents in Puebla.

Neither Juan Diego nor Don Isidro was surprised to discover the bishop seated at a corner of the governor's large table, his little face and sharp speculative eyes turned toward the dust-covered officers. Isunza, his yellow visage like perspiring corn-meal masa, sat in his customary high-backed chair playing nervously with a large muzzle-load-

ing pistol that dated back to the days of Iturbide. Behind him, in a half
circle, stood the various city officials. Juan Diego was faintly amazed
at the variety of faces. *There* was the rat, the fox, the monkey, the hog.

"Ah, Señor Gobernador!" cried Santa Anna, stalking forward,
his peg leg striking like a gavel on the tiled floor. "I observe you have
issued instructions directing the Poblanos how to receive the Americans. Upon what authority, Señor Gobernador, do you take over federal powers? Have you received orders from Mexico City, Señor
Gobernador? Where is your tongue, Señor Gobernador? Let me hear
what you have to say, Señor Gobernador."

"It is my duty, Señor General, to protect the best interests of
Puebla," replied Isunza sullenly. "My people—"

"Your people!" screamed Santa Anna. "Ah, bribón! What have
you done to your people? You have destroyed their valor, their spirit,
their soul. You have sat here like a great bag of fat and done nothing
while I have labored night and day to build an army and shape it into a
wall of defense against the invader. I sleep two or three hours in every
twenty-four. I ride from town to town calling upon true patriots to
come forth with their weapons and stand beside me to repel the Americans. My duty is to sacrifice myself and I know how to fulfill it. What
is your duty, Señor Gobernador? Is it to open the gates of Puebla to
the accursed Yanquis? What! I come to you with four thousand brave
men and I find the city organizing reception committees for General
Scott. Ah, no, Señor Gobernador. I will not permit that. I will have
something to say about that. I have orders to issue and I will see that
they are obeyed if I have to hang all traitors and cowards to the
willows in the Alameda."

He paused to recover himself and immediately the metallic voice
of the bishop cut in like a knife of sound.

"Has the government in Mexico City delegated to you the necessary powers for hanging all of us?" he inquired.

Santa Anna glanced at him contemptuously.

"Ah, there you are," he said rudely. "You are so small that I did
not see you. The Congress in Mexico City voted me unlimited powers
on April twentieth. Surely you knew that. You seem to know everything before it happens."

He returned his angry glance to Isunza.

"There has been nothing but indifference and neglect in Puebla,
Señor Gobernador," he declared. "I have a medicine for that. I demand
a loan of thirty thousand pesos from the city. I demand all the horses
in the city. I demand a draft of five thousand men capable of bearing
arms. I demand twenty cannon and five hundred bags of gunpowder
and all the round shot, canister and shrapnel in the forts of Loreto and
Guadalupe. I demand that this be furnished me by sunset tomorrow."

Isunza's jaw had dropped almost to his chest. He stood up, clawing the air before him as though it were dense with smoke.

"What do you say, Señor General?" he stuttered. "All this is impossible. Where will the ayuntamiento find thirty . . . thirty thousand pesos? Or five thousand men? Or twenty cannon? Or such an amount of ammunition? Such things do not exist in Puebla. You took everything from us when you passed through on your way to the Cerro Gordo. You took everything and you lost everything. You . . . you say that you know how to sacrifice yourself. You also know how to sacrifice *us*. On behalf of the ayuntamiento I refuse your demands, Señor General, for the reason that it is impossible to fulfill them."

For a moment the two men stood glowering at each other and then Santa Anna pivoted slowly on his wooden leg.

"Alcorta," he called roughly and as the cavalry general stepped forward he extended his hand toward him. "Alcorta," he repeated, "listen to me carefully. Select one hundred men and divide them into squads of ten, each under a sergeant. They are to go out and scour the city and lands adjacent to it and bring back to the plaza every horse they find. Tell them to be exhaustive in their search, for it is possible that the Poblanos will endeavor to hide their animals. Go, Alcorta. Start the search this very minute."

The cavalry general saluted and went out, his spurs and heavy saber rattling to his long steps.

The bishop drew his small bony hand across his tight little mouth.

"Señor General," he said mildly, "there are a few poor folk who depend on their horses to bring produce to the market. I hope—"

"Good!" broke in Santa Anna. "We will take their produce, too."

The bishop shut his eyes.

"León!" snapped Santa Anna. "Take a hundred men and some carts to the forts of Loreto and Guadalupe and remove from the powder rooms all ammunition of any sort that you may find. Count the guns there and report to me. I will have them removed when the caissons come in this evening."

"How are we to defend Puebla with dismantled forts?" demanded Isunza in a trembling voice. "Señor General, you—"

"Defend Puebla?" cried Santa Anna. "Ah, do you think of that now? It is late in the day, Señor Gobernador. You should have planned for that three weeks ago. I am not going to defend your wretched city, Señor Gobernador. I will make my stand on the plateau."

"Yes, yes," murmured the bishop, his eyes still shut. "There is to be a presidential election on May fifteenth. The Señor General will want to be close to the capital."

Santa Anna's bloodshot eyes inspected the prelate for a moment.

"You are the source of all discord here," he said with surprising calmness.

Then he turned to General León.

"Go, León," he ordered. "And see to it that nothing is hidden from you. If there are any soldiers in the forts bring them back with you. Direct that the streets and cantinas be combed for deserters and skulkers from the army of Vera Cruz and the Cerro Gordo."

León saluted and left the chamber.

"I will cashier every officer of the Vera Cruz garrison that I find hiding here," declared Santa Anna to Isunza.

He spoke without passion and Juan Diego, who had been standing motionless behind him with Don Isidro and Lorenzo, observed that his anger had ebbed and a sly calculating look was spreading across his face. He was studying both the governor and the bishop with half-closed eyes now. The politician was devouring the hero. It had been this way often before, the immediate almost hysterical anger raging up like a quick fire of paper and then dying down with astonishing suddenness, almost as though two men struggled within the general—one impulsive and regardless of consequences and the other crafty and careful, the eventual victor nearly always being the second, but now Juan Diego could not view this swift shift with the same objective curiosity he had felt in the past. His own feelings ran too deep for that. He had desired violently that Puebla be defended and he had hoped against hope, even against all reason, that the general would find some way, no matter how desperate, of making a stand and showing the Americans that there was plenty of fight left in the Mexican people. Even another lost battle would have meant something. But it was evident that the general was not going to fight. He had other plans. Juan Diego wondered if the bishop's remark about the presidential election had anything to do with those plans. Did the general mean to withdraw to the very capital itself before he ordered the firing of another gun? It seemed disgraceful. And suddenly a wave of bitterness against the general flowed through the young officer so fiercely that his cheeks flushed with the strength of it. He glanced guiltily at Don Isidro and found the hacendado's eyes fixed on his face. An invisible spark of understanding and despair leapt between them.

"Señor Gobernador," said Santa Anna, placing both hands on the table and leaning toward the sullen yellow-faced official, "there is that little matter of thirty thousand pesos to discuss. I shall need it. It will help me to buy muskets from Guatemala and powder from British Honduras. The mills of Morelia, of Guanajuato and Santa Fé must be paid. It costs money to defend one's country, but what of that? No sacrifice is too great for the true patriot. Why, I, myself . . ."

"There isn't thirty thousand pesos in all Puebla," declared Isunza with a great attempt at calmness.

"This is a rich city," pointed out the general.

"The men with money have departed from the city," insisted Isunza, "or they have sent their gold away. What do you want me to do? Take the few coppers from the Indians in the market?"

Santa Anna's eyes roved over the ayuntamiento, the town councilors, who still stood behind the governor in a semicircle like an array of tongueless dummies.

"I recognize a number of substantial men here," he said with sardonic good humor. "I know that all of them are good patriots."

"Señor General," said a short spare man with dirty white hair, "we have no money. Plenty of debts, yes. Thirty thousand pesos of debts, perhaps. But no money. No—"

"By sunset tomorrow," broke in Santa Anna sharply.

His eyes flickered toward the static figure of the bishop.

"There are plenty of gold objects in the churches," he said flatly. "I have seen the altars glisten with them."

"You cannot rob God," declared the prelate in a low voice.

Santa Anna seemed surprised and hurt.

"A forced loan for the safety of the Republic is not robbery," he answered mildly. "I am sure that God who is benevolent will take that into account."

"You do not speak for God," said the bishop. "God has already spoken for you. 'Render therefore unto Caesar the things which are Caesar's: and unto God the things which are God's'."

Santa Anna turned abruptly.

"I will return at sunset tomorrow, Señor Gobernador," he announced briskly. "I shall expect you to have the loan ready for me then. If it fails I will make up the difference with the gold objects from the churches. I regret to do this but when the safety of the Republic is at stake I cannot weaken. Come, Terán."

He started to stump his way toward the door.

"My general . . ." called Juan Diego, hurrying after him.

There were a hundred and one things the young officer wanted to say but he could not find words for them. He had the desperate feeling that Santa Anna, who had been his father, his friend, his advisor, was lost to him. This man, whom he had seen evince anger or scowl or be suave so often before, now seemed to exhibit rage or equanimity in another way. A sinister quality had been added. The gestures were the same and so were the words but the magnetism had shifted into evil channels. Yet might not this feeling be the result of the long wait in Puebla and the consequent sickness in his own soul? Juan Diego did not know. He knew only that he was filled to the brim with doubt and disappointment and that it was through the gray veil of these emotions that he saw and heard the general. There was urgent need for illumination or readjustment here.

Santa Anna halted and surveyed the young man.

"Ah, Juanillo," he said. "Come along with me. I am rather bare of aides. There is plenty for you to do."

Juan Diego had not meant to leave Don Isidro so abruptly and he turned with a helpless expression on his face toward the hacendado. Don Isidro nodded slightly and raised his hand with the palm toward his face and the young officer, for the first time in his life, followed the general reluctantly.

The three days that ensued formed a period of desperate gestures, doubts and growing panic for Juan Diego. Scouts brought in the information that the first American brigades were in Nopalucán, some thirty-five miles from Puebla. They were marching in easy stages, conserving their energy and keeping their artillery with them. The strange names of the generals were repeated in the cantinas and open markets —Scott, Worth, Quitman. Santa Anna continued to drive his small staff at a furious gait, raving all the time at the indifference of the Poblanos and the treasonable cowardice of the ayuntamiento. His squads rounded up decrepit horses, mules, burros, anything on four legs that could bear so much as a filled powder bag. The farmers and peddlers cursed and the shovel-hatted priests passed among them with pious expressions and ironical comments about the general. Some ammunition and a few guns were secured from the forts of Loreto and Guadalupe. The recruiting of five thousand men degenerated into a travesty, Isunza furnishing less than two hundred and most of these vagabonds who had drifted into Puebla before the advancing Americans. Provisions disappeared miraculously from the market and Santa Anna's commissary was hard put to it to feed the grumbling troops barracked in the city. During this period Juan Diego saw Don Isidro but a few fugitive times while he was speeding about on the unending series of missions for the general. These missions were all concerned with money and nearly every one of them was a failure. The wealthy landowner or merchant to be seen had left Puebla for the capital or his country seat or his money-boxes were empty or he was barricaded in his house. Santa Anna's dream of thirty thousand pesos dissipated rapidly before the sullen refusal of the Poblanos and in the end he secured less than a third of that sum. Thereupon he seized the gold liturgical objects from the churches. He had signed his own death warrant in Puebla.

It was early on the morning of May fourteenth that Juan Diego saw Don Isidro for the last time. Scouts had brought in the news that the American vanguard was at Amozoc, a manufacturing town no more than ten miles from the city. Santa Anna immediately dispatched his infantry and artillery along the San Martín Road toward the capital and mounted his two thousand cavalrymen to effect a diversion on the American flank. The long lines of clattering horses were passing through the plaza when Juan Diego, who was riding with Alcorta's staff, saw Don Isidro standing forlornly by the cathedral, his heavy underlip thrust out, staring gloomily at the slouching riders and their tall lances. The young officer dismounted hastily, threw the reins to the horseman riding beside him and ran over to the hacendado.

"Don Isidro!" he cried. "You are out early."

The older man clasped his hand.

"Chepe informed me that the troops were leaving the city," he replied. "I wanted to see you before you went. What has happened? Are the Americans . . ."

"They are practically at the gates," explained Juan Diego soberly. "Yes, we are withdrawing. The infantry and artillery have gone already with General León and his staff. The cavalry . . ."

He broke off and glanced at the jingling line of horsemen.

"They look very fine," said Don Isidro heavily.

He put his hand on the young officer's shoulder.

"I have a feeling that I won't see you again," he continued. "By this time tomorrow you will be well on your way to Mexico City. Do you remember our last parting? It wasn't under happy circumstances but I say to you now what I said to you then: Farewell. May God go with you on your journey."

Juan Diego recalled that moonlit night at Los Golondrinas when he had parted from a man whom he hardly knew and was silent. Time had moved since then and the world seemed smaller.

"There is one favor I would like to request from you," went on Don Isidro with some diffidence. "You will be in Mexico City and there may be fighting there before the year is out. Lorenzo will be there, too. He has just received a message from General Monterde, superintendent of the Military College, ordering him to return to Chapultepec. My good friend, if things become too serious and you have the opportunity will you keep an eye on the boy? I don't mean—"

"Of course I will!" broke in Juan Diego swiftly. "I will do all that I can for him."

Don Isidro was silent for a moment.

"Good," he said finally.

"Are you going to remain in Puebla?" asked Juan Diego.

The hacendado nodded briefly.

"Yes," he answered. "I might as well be here as anywhere else. I tried to run from war once and I appeared to have run right into it.

Puebla will be as safe under the Americans as it has been under Isunza
. . . or Santa Anna. The bishop will see to that. I may even send for
Doña Ágata and my daughter."

He eyed the passing files of cavalry morosely.

"Well . . ." began Juan Diego uncertainly.

He scuffed his booted foot along the cobbles and cleared his
throat.

"You had better go," remarked Don Isidro quickly. "God willing,
I will see you again. I consider you like a second son. Farewell, then.
May God go with you on your journey."

"Farewell!" cried Juan Diego and ran out toward the moving
lines of horses with eyes half-blinded by unexpected moisture. He
didn't want to look back. As he waited for one of the occasional led
horses that would carry him forward to Alcorta's staff he felt a great
sadness welling up within him. It was beginning to seem like the end
of the world, of *a* world, anyway. He secured a spare pinto, swung to
the saddlecloth and forced the animal rapidly along the clattering lines.
He rode easily without stirrups as the Indians at Manga de Clavo had
taught him long ago. He did not know what lay before him and at the
moment he did not care. It was what lay behind him that counted.

Juan Diego was riding his own horse with Alcorta's staff, now
joined by Santa Anna and his personal aides, when the columns of
cavalry reached the heights of Chachapa overlooking Amozoc. The
town, famed throughout Mexico for its spurs, bridle bits and saddles,
lay beneath them in the sunlight and its few streets were crowded with
American troops. In the suburbs and beyond the town halted regiments, obviously resting, darkened the roads and green fields. Juan
Diego remembered how like dolls the enemy had seemed to him when
he first saw them at La Angostura. But they did not seem like dolls
now. He knew them for what they were. As he peered through his
field glass he could see that many of them were shaving, washing their
heads or their clothes or cleaning and polishing their weapons. For the
triumphal entry, thought the officer bitterly. That is it. They are so
God-damned sure of themselves! But why shouldn't they be? That was
it. Why shouldn't they be? They were having it all their own way.
Even as he peered his ears caught the long roll of divisional drums and
he knew that the Americans had spotted the cavalry above them. Hundreds of little figures now began to run like ants and the sound of distant shouting rose above the continuous and incessant thudding of the
drums. Juan Diego slipped the field glass into its leather case and
speeded his horse toward the vanishing staff.

Santa Anna and Alcorta were riding fast and the squadron of
cavalry thundered after them, their swift-moving varicolored array of

regimental tunics blurring beneath the dancing pennons and glittering lance spikes. The wind whistled in Juan Diego's ears as he galloped and the exhilaration that he always felt when he was with the cavalry started his pulses beating but he felt no thrill of imminent action. He felt that he knew what would happen. And it did. They rode parallel with the Americans on the road and downward for a time but there was no attempt at a charge that might have cut up the enemy infantry. Once they came within artillery range and an American battery threw a few shells at them, two or three horses went down and Santa Anna inclined away from the challenge. He kept to the left of the road, passed beyond Amozoc and then turned off squarely to the north with his two miles of cavalry streaming behind him. That was all. Juan Diego turned a perspiring and disappointed face toward the captain riding beside him.

"Was there any reason for this?" he demanded.

The captain, who was fat and uncomfortable upon his horse, gasped his answer.

"Dios mío!" he said. "Did you see them? The general must have been misinformed by his scouts. He expected to find a vanguard and there must be two divisions in Amozoc. I'm satisfied to be where I am."

Juan Diego said nothing.

They rode toward La Malinche, dismounted for rest in a wood slashed by barrancas and well-nigh impassable because of thickets and after a fatiguing circuit of some nine leagues arrived when twilight was falling at the gates of Puebla. A small crowd, gathered at the garita, watched them pass and a few voices raised some scattered viva for Santa Anna. The general addressed a few words to these loiterers but Juan Diego did not hear them. Even the exhilaration of being with the cavalry could not sustain his sinking spirits. The day was darkening over Puebla as they rode through it and this deepening shadow seemed symbolic to the young officer. The shadows were deepening over all Mexico, over the Hill of Tepeyac where Our Lady of Guadalupe had willed roses out of the porphyry rock, over the hidden hollow in the mountains of Michoacán where the boys drank the wine of San Lorenzo, over Las Golondrinas and Manga de Clavo and the deserted field of Buena Vista and Mexico City itself, toward which their horses' heads were now turned.

It was quite dark when they rode out of Puebla toward San Martín.

Shortly before noon Don Isidro, with his usual disregard for anybody who blocked his way, thrust himself unceremoniously through the crowds that lined the space before the cathedral and secured a for most place from which to view the entrance of the American troops into Puebla. He was not astonished at what he saw, for his knowledge of the Poblanos was intimate enough to forewarn him that their curiosity and cupidity would far outweigh any sentiments of anger, disappointment and patriotism that might be lurking in the backs of their minds. The ideal thing, of course, would have been to see a deserted city, a city with closed doors and shuttered windows and barricaded shops and empty streets, with nothing moving but the flags of the Republic waving from their poles, a veritable stone graveyard, in fact, through which the isolated invaders might pass with the heavy feeling that they were unwelcome trespassers; but the grand plaza was the very reverse of the ideal thing and what Don Isidro did see was a shifting and noisy panorama that had the color and élan of a joyful fiesta. All the eighty thousand inhabitants of Puebla seemed to have poured out of their houses for this occasion. They crowded the roadways and sang, laughed and shouted. Scores of hucksters with fruits, fresh drinks, chickens, tortillas, cheap jewelry and knickknacks pushed their way along crying their wares. There were flags flying, flags of the Republic, but there were American flags as well, crude Stars and Stripes hastily fashioned from whatever strips of colored cloth had been at hand. The general hubbub swelled continually into a roar. Discordant musical instruments squawked and thudded from cantinas and porticoes. Dogs barked and donkeys brayed. The shrill voices of Indian women rose and fell. Puebla, instead of appearing like a lost or surrendered city, had all the appearance of a liberated community.

Don Isidro stood four-square, so to speak, as solidly settled on his two strong legs as the cathedral on its deep foundations, and stared about him with a perfectly expressionless face. This was neither more nor less than he had expected. The Church and the city government had done their work well. The civil population of Puebla was no more at war with the United States, he supposed, than the civil population of Boston, Massachusetts, was at war with Mexico. Indeed, it was becoming a problem to find out who was fighting whom. The bishop, certainly, was not fighting anybody. And the general was hurrying to the capital not to fight the Americans, for there weren't any there, but to fight recalcitrant elements in his own government. The whole war was being conducted like a badly assembled play written by some amateur who constantly changed the plot. At least, it seemed that way. Don Isidro blinked his eyes as an insistent peddler drove a tray into the small of his back. He resisted an impulse to turn and knock the rascal down. Yes, *he* knew what the war was about. And Juan Diego knew, too. But did anybody else? It was being fought to preserve one's integrity and the integrity of one's country and that was patriotism. And here were the people of Puebla showing their integrity, which was another word for their patriotism, by offering dulces to the enemy and applauding his triumphal entry into the city. *I think that the turning point of the war is here in Puebla.* Juan Diego had said that to the bishop. Well, here was the turning point, then. Though why Buena Vista had not been the turning point, or, for that matter, Monterrey, or Vera Cruz or Cerro Gordo, was beyond the hacendado's wit. It seemed to him now that in every place Destiny had turned her back on the Republic. Whose fault was it? Who was to blame? Was it the government or the generals or these thousands of people laughing and whistling in the grand plaza? A people, it appeared needed more than justice on its side to be strong. It needed the will as well. "None of us have loved Mexico enough," grumbled Don Isidro aloud and then he glanced about him angrily to see if anybody had overheard him. He saw many faces but not one was interested in him.

And now the shouting rose in volume at one end of the vast square and the crowd rippled and split apart as though a great wedge was being slowly driven into it. The Americans were entering the grand plaza to drumtaps and Don Isidro was about to see the almost legendary enemy for the first time. He moved forward with the pushing mass of Poblanos and presently he saw some twoscore horsemen picking their way across the cobbles. They were big men, all right, but what impressed him immediately as it did the majority of the crowd, was the size of the horses. They dwarfed the average Mexican mount and though the hacendado had seen big animals, even possessed a few at Las Golondrinas, he had never observed twoscore of them at one time. There was something magical about them, something that gave him the impression of fiction, of folktales, of enlarged stories told by ancient storytellers in the market. It gave an aspect of invincibility to the Americans that Don Isidro did not believe they really possessed. Still, he was serious as he regarded the officers, noting the subdued quality of their uniforms, so unlike the flamboyant regimentals and staff brocades of his own commanders, their matter-of-fact postures and, above all, their appearance of confidence. That tall fellow with the white hair and little side whiskers would be General Worth, he supposed. He seemed almost sleepy as he rode along but from beneath his heavy brows keen eyes watched the turbulent sea of heads in straw woven sombreros. The clattering horses progressed slowly and steadily across the grand plaza cleaving a pathway along which moved a regiment of infantry, an oblong block of men in rather disorderly alignment carrying muskets with fixed bayonets.

Don Isidro stared with some amazement at these troops of the line.

There was nothing frightening about them at all. For the most part, they were little men, no larger than the Mexicans, as a whole though now and then a tall gangling fellow with a prominent Adam's apple would loom at least a head above the rest. They marched easily, paying little or no attention to the drumtaps, and constantly called out to the spectators in very bad Spanish. " 'Guardiente? Habla pulque? Habla cigarro?" The crowd laughed and shouted back. It seemed almost unbelievable to Don Isidro that these men, or men like them, were the victors of Resaca de la Palma, Monterrey, Buena Vista, Vera Cruz and Cerro Gordo. In what way did they differ from the average Mexican trooper? Their uniforms were not so bright and there was a workmanlike glitter to their weapons that the French muskets of the Mexicans sometimes lacked, but, considered en masse, there was little difference. At least, at a first inspection. They marched raggedly, constantly called out in the most unmilitary manner, often ignored the despairing shouted orders of their officers, burst into song, lost step and otherwise displayed what Don Isidro thought was their Yanqui independence. A European general would have fallen off his horse in either scornful laughter or an apoplectic seizure at the sight of them.

Yet Don Isidro had heard too much about them to laugh. He sought for the secret of their strength in their faces and there were moments when he thought he had found it. There was no fatalism there. There was none of the uninspired stolidity of the Indian or the insolent abruptness of the Spaniard. Instead, there was good humor, a somewhat swaggering equality of demeanor, an easy confidence, an inclination toward clowning, an al fresco air and an abundance of animal spirits that translated the hard actuality of war into a sort of dangerous carnival. It was possible that there were darker shadings that did not catch the hacendado's eye at the moment, sickness, rancor, thievishness, bad discipline, drunkenness, malingering, but if there were they had been gilded momentarily by the May sun that was illuminating this triumphal entrance into the City of the Angels. These men were in the best of spirits and being so they emanated an atmosphere of confidence and insuperability that increased the grim foreboding in Don Isidro's mind and caused his heavy underjaw to thrust out more desperately than ever.

The regiment passed, wheeled in the direction of the Governor's Palace, broke ranks and stacked arms. It was followed by a battery of two six-pounder field pieces and two twelve-pounder howitzers. The artillery horses were lean but large and as the ironbound wheels of the caissons and gun carriages rumbled across the plaza Don Isidro watched them with grave eyes. The cannoneers, who seemed to go in rather strongly for whiskers, bounced on their wooden seats, grumbled and flashed tobacco-yellow teeth at the crowd. The men on the off horses slapped the straining haunches of their animals and apostrophized them in language that would have petrified any Mexican señorita with a knowledge of English. The guns seemed to Don Isidro to be the first really ominous aspects of the day, the sullen reminders that this was no carnival but the calculated occupation of a city. Their blunt snouts, the brasswork and chains in the harnesses, the black-headed swabs lying in their rests, the closed caissons, the inevitably rolling wheels, the rumble, the bounce, the snap of whips, the guttural shouts, all these things composed an ensemble that was grim in portent and menacing in appearance. These were the chariots of death and destruction and they brought the smell and chaos of war closer to Don Isidro than the slim malignancy of the bayonets or the unimpressive barrels of the muskets and rifles. It seemed to the hacendado that he could smell again that stink of war he had experienced a month before when the fragments of Mexican Lancers had ridden into Puebla after Cerro Gordo. It was like an aura about the passing guns.

More infantry passed, squadrons of cavalry, additional batteries, a small siege train, and, finally, the white tops of provision wagons. Don Isidro maintained his post before the cathedral and watched them enter the plaza, move through it, turn down side streets, enter public buildings and break ranks. He watched the invading soldiers hurry into cantinas and crowd about the peddlers and tortilla women. He watched the Poblanos scream and laugh and strike the Americans on the back and thrust fruit into their hands. He watched the street walkers appear stealthily at corners. He watched the priests move about with smiling faces as though they were a welcoming committee. He watched the booted officers, in dress uniforms and carrying swords, mount the steps of the Governor's Palace. He saw smiles and fraternizing on all sides and heard laughter and singing and shouting. People pushed past him, jostled him, clapped him on the shoulder and he made no effort to avoid them. He felt that he was the loneliest man in the world and that this Puebla that he had known for so many years was an alien city. It was no longer a part of Mexico. Presently his eyes were caught by signs of activity on the balcony that formed part of the façade of the Governor's Palace and after a moment he saw the American flag ripple out from a staff and spread its alternate stripes to the May breeze. This seemed the last touch of all, the sign and signature of the disgrace of a great people misled by little men, of the triumph of opportunism over justice and honor, of manifest destiny over manifest right, of imperialism over weakness. His cheeks felt damp and he raised his hands to them with some surprise. For the first time in his life he felt the tears falling from his eyes.

Book Four

CIUDAD DE MEXICO

Ciudad De Mexico

DURING the summer Juan Diego had plenty of opportunity to observe the political chaos and consequent inefficiency of the Republic in the very shadow of the invader. The panorama, sometimes like a bad dream and always like a hasty and patchwork improvisation, moved jerkily and hysterically before his eyes throughout June, July and August until he lost all hope of victory or an honorable peace. He suspected everybody now, including the general, and it seemed to him that there was not an honest or capable man in office, either civil or military, in all Mexico. A terrible thought assailed him. Were these conniving men, who put their petty jealousies and rapacious lusts before the welfare of the nation, worthy to possess and administer such potential sources of wealth and civilization as Texas and California? Man owed a duty to the earth and if he did not perform it he was not worthy of his inheritance. This seemed to him suspiciously like an approach to the American credo of Manifest Destiny and he sought to put it out of his mind. A few bad men could not destroy the rights of a multitude. However, events brought the thought back to him again and again. The despairing pictures of the frantic summer emphasized it until his one refuge was the faith that the Republic could be cleansed and made worthy of its inheritance, those great sparsely populated lands to the north. But the Republic needed guidance; it needed men of good will; it needed an understanding neighbor; it needed selflessness and patriotism and a common ideal. Who, or what, would furnish forth these virtues?

The panorama gave no answer. Its pictures and impressions merely increased the young officer's despair. Being on Santa Anna's staff he could view and hear everything from a privileged point of vantage although there were some things that he could not see but only guess at. The general had his secrets which he did not breathe even to his pillow. The uncertainties had begun on May eighteenth when Santa Anna and his ragtag-and-bobtail army occupied Ayotla, less than fifteen miles from the capital. Three perspiring politicians, Manuel Baranda, Ignacio Trigueros and J. F. Ramírez, hurried out to meet him and persuade him that the Moderado, Anaya, should remain in office as substitute president while he remained in the field with his troops.

317

Santa Anna agreed and wrote a letter to that effect. The next day, repudiating his hasty decision, he entered the city with his soldiers. Juan Diego knew the reason why. Tornel, that intriguing follower of the general, and one or two others had convinced Santa Anna that a handful of enemies in the capital were seeking to eliminate him as a power in the Republic. That was enough. The general flew into one of his furies and acted with his usual regardlessness of consequences.

The panorama moved rapidly now, agitated by unseen hands and conflicting rumors. Mexico City was a hornet's nest of underhand activities. Almonte was plotting to be president; Valencia aspired to the chief military command; Arista was plotting; Ampudia was plotting; Gómez Farías was plotting; Bravo was plotting; Olaguíbel was plotting. The Puros, opposition party to the Moderados, were organizing a revolution. The number of intrigues was estimated at twenty million by one exaggerating publicist. Into this buzzing nest came the general. He sought to draw the poisoned stings by reassuming the executive power and as a first gesture he restored the freedom of the press. It responded by exclaiming, "The man of Angostura, of Cerro Gordo, of Amozoc, weary of destroying Mexicans on the field of battle, comes home tranquilly to find repose in the presidential chair." Santa Anna, disconcerted by the opposition, resigned again.

Then the panorama shifted. The Puros postponed their revolution and some of them came over to the general, who was sulking like Achilles in his tent. The dissident Valencia went to San Luis Potosí to assume command of the Army of the North. Almonte was clapped into prison as a conspirator. Arista and Ampudia were banished from Mexico City. Bravo retired from his post. And Santa Anna made a volte-face and withdrew his resignation. The *Monitor Republicano*, paraphrasing his manifesto, bawled, "Mexicans, I shall be with you always—to the consummation of your ruin," and added, "What a life of sacrifice is the general's; a sacrifice to take the power, to resign, to resume; ultimate final; ultimate more final; ultimate most final; ultimate the very finalest. But let him cheer up. He is not alone in making sacrifices. For twenty-five years the Mexican people have been sacrificing themselves, all of them, in the hope that certain persons would do good to the country." Yet the general had triumphed again. There was no doubt of that.

The panorama continued to unroll. Detested by a large group, disliked by a larger, and distrusted by practically everybody the general maintained his power, if not his prestige, by a combination of good luck, audacity and cunning. The opposition was too split to oppose him; the Congress failed week after week to form a quorum which left him a virtual dictator; and the selfish interests accepted him as the spearhead of their designs. He ignored, but watched carefully, the prelates and the Monarchists who went on plotting against him and he suppressed, or choked, the fulminating newspapers. He balanced his government on the point of the bayonet. He had a job to do. He swore this again and again to his political henchmen, his generals, Juan Diego, anybody who would listen. He swore it in the face of ominous rumors, the most constant being that he was negotiating secretly with the Americans for a certain sum, some said a million pesos, and that for this fortune he was to endeavor to persuade the Congress to accept dictated peace terms while Scott advanced slowly into the Valley of Mexico.

If this was so his actions did not bear it out. Once firmly in power he began to arm, provision and fortify the capital with his usual fury. He called loudly for troops from the various states and the governors refused to send them, arguing that success in the field would enable Santa Anna to overthrow the democratic principles of the Republic. He swore at the damned fools and went on organizing. Cannon were brought in from neighboring garrison posts. More were cast from the bells of the churches and the antiquated ordnance at Chapultepec. New muskets were purchased, some from British firms quite willing to see the Americans in difficulties in Mexico. Arms were seized from private homes. Vast quantities of gunpowder were shipped from Morelia, Guanajuato and Santa Fé. Government establishments and private factories clanged away at mortars, bayonets, lance blades and projectiles. And some supplies were obtained even from New Orleans by way of Campeche. In spite of the recalcitrancy of the states outside the Federal District troops began to crowd the streets of Mexico City, the National Guards, five hundred from Querétaro, two hundred Irish Roman Catholic deserters from the American army, the Army of the South commanded by the Indian, Alvarez, a few thousand National Guards and irregulars under Canalizo, and, eventually, in July, the Army of the North commanded by the ambitious Valencia.

The panorama moved at an accelerated speed. Santa Anna started to fortify the city for a defensive campaign. He put the technical direction under General Mora, Manuel Robles and Juan Cano and pushed them vigorously. He impressed laborers wherever he could obtain them, depopulating villages, robbing haciendas, emptying jails and clearing the streets of léperos. Stockades, breastworks, parapets and gun emplacements began to rise like monstrous warts about the city. The Old Peñón, a rocky hill near the Puebla road some seven miles from Mexico City bristled like the Rock of Gibralter. Trenches were dug and meadows were inundated. Juan Diego watched all this with a mounting excitement that was shared by the populace but he did not share their confidence. It bloomed suddenly like a tropic flower. A new sort of courage seemed to animate the people in the streets and they jabbered less of past defeats than future triumphs. The mere sight of a fortified hill appeared to double their optimism. Contemptuous rumors concerning the Americans spread through the markets and cantinas. Scott had forced his troops to fight at Cerro Gordo by opening a battery on them from the rear. His men were constantly deserting and the American president, Polk, aghast at the expense of the invasion, would send no more reinforcements. The guerrillas were cutting the American line of supplies from Vera Cruz to Puebla. A sort of Dutch courage inflated the population of Mexico City and for the moment internal conflicts were forgotten. The general and Valencia dined together and all was well with the world. The Eleventh Infantry, headed by its music of twenty-five pieces, paraded along the Paseo and the war was won.

Juan Diego could not go as far as this. He had seen the Americans.

The inevitable panorama blossomed with new pictures. On the ninth of August a sixteen-pounder boomed from Chapultepec and the people of the city knew that Scott (who was an evil man because he had no saint's name, there being no St. Winfield in the calendar) and his army had set out from Puebla for the Valley of Mexico. The long roll of drums echoed through the streets, military bands strutted and blared and fountains of rockets flung a fiery rain high in the air. "Blinded by pride the enemy have set out for the capital," proclaimed Santa Anna. "For this, Mexicans, I congratulate myself and you." He was all confidence again and so were his people. Vivas greeted him from balconies and housetops as he rode like Napoleon on a white horse out to the Old Peñón with all his troops, regiment after regiment with standards waving and bayonets gleaming, for a grand review. The green fields blossomed with white tents and bands crashed into patriotic airs. The soldiers quickstepped gallantly while the priests in rich vestments pronounced benediction after benediction. It was another apotheosis of the general but whether it was the sixth or the seventh nobody stopped to figure out. That night the *Diario* cried, "*Ecce Homo!* Behold the illustrious champion of 1821, the hero of 1829, the genius of 1838!" Maybe this was the fourth apotheosis.

Watch the panorama! The Americans could not be seen, except by fast-riding scouts, but their progress was heralded each morning in the streets. They were at San Martín. They were crossing the Texmelucán. They had halted at Río Frío. They had reached the rocky summit, ten thousand five hundred feet above sea level, where they could gaze down into the smiling Valley of Mexico. Was it cold up there, Americanos? Are you coming down to see us? Well, let them come. We have something waiting for them that they will not digest easily . . . lead fotheir bellies . . . bayonets for their guts. And the Americans came down. Guns, batteries, baggage and all, they came down. The sound of their horses was like a rushing stream. On the eleventh of August their vanguards were at San Isidro and Ayotla. That was all right. Just wait until they reached the Old Peñón. *There* was a nut they could not crack.

Juan Diego was not so sure. He had been present a number of times when the dust-covered scouts reported to the general and he did not like the color of the information. It appeared that the thirteen thousand trees cut down for barricades had not obstructed the enemy advance at all. It also appeared that the people along the route, instead of conducting an irregular warfare against the invaders, had welcomed them with smiles and even assisted them in clearing the roads. Çanalizo, with six hundred men, had fled from San Martín the moment he saw an American uniform. The yellow-faced Governor Isunza had flatly refused all assistance. These were straws showing which way the wind was blowing and the wind seemed to have a cutting edge. Yet the inhabitants of Mexico City continued to talk big. They shook a great figurative fist at the Americans. Wait! they exclaimed. It will not be long before you feel the hot breath of the guns mounted on the Old Peñón.

But the panorama unrolled persistently and regardless of the desires of the people and the plans of the general. At one moment the invaders were advancing toward the Old Peñón as they had been expected to do (Wait! Wait!) and threatening the village of Mexicaltzingo and at another moment they were not there at all. Where were they, then? Where in the devil were the Americans who should be dying in swarms before the Old Peñón? They were at Chalco. They were at Chimalpa. They were at Ayocingo. They were at Tuiscingo. San Gregorio. And then it dawned upon the disconcerted populace and the generals and the soldiers. They had been diddled. Scott had refused battle at the fortified rocky hill, merely making a feint at it, and then rendered it useless by bypassing it and marching his army along a seemingly impossible mud-choked road almost washed out by the torrential afternoon rains that wound southward around Lakes Chalco and Xochimilco. He had marched his troops twenty-five miles in a day and a half. He had moved his supply wagons and heavy guns along his reputedly impassable route. He had beaten off a brief attack by the irregulars of Alvarez. And by the eighteenth his whole army was camped in and around San Agustín some ten miles to the south of Mexico City. In two days he had placed himself on the weakest side of the capital.

The panorama showed tints of gray. Juan Diego, passing through the streets on the afternoon of the eighteenth, found them empty.

There were no cheers for the bewildered troops who were being hastily transferred from the Old Peñón to the new southern front. The balconies and housetops were vacant and the windows were shuttered and barred. There were no skyrockets or bands playing or flags flying. All the somber and oppressive atmosphere of a beleaguered city hung like a thundercloud over the capital. Behind closed doors and in dimly lighted cantinas the whispering began and in a day or two it was all over the city. Santa Anna was an incompetent fool. Why had he massed the bulk of his troops and guns at the Old Peñón where Scott could nullify them all merely by marching south on a road that the stupid engineers had declared to be impracticable? Disappointed malcontents talked of La Angostura again. Hadn't that idiot of a Santa Anna marched off into the northern deserts when the Americans were moving against Vera Cruz? And what had the coward done at Cerro Gordo? And, listen. It was reported on the most reliable authority that one of the outposts had seized a treasonable communication from the general to Scott.

Juan Diego heard it all and he did not know what to think. There were curious aspects . . .

Then the panorama glowed frighteningly with the violent hues of blood and flame. The general maintained a composure that was admirable and informed his staff officers that he would just as soon fight to the south of the city as to the east. He ordered the erection of defenses at the bridge over the Churubusco River four miles from the capital and on the lands of the great feudal hacienda of San Antonio two and a quarter miles beyond. He occupied Mexicaltzingo on the left, placed the brigade of Pérez at Coyoacán in the center and Valencia with fifty-five hundred picked troops at San Ángel on the right. Between this uneven arc of fighting men and the Americans at San Agustín extended a huge pedregal, or lava bed, covered with fissures, caves, jagged spikes of rock and concealed pitfalls masked by stunted trees and clumps of bushes. Now let the Americans try to break through. He was ready for them, he told Valencia, and that general, squat, broad-shouldered, bull-necked and suggesting an orangutan from Borneo, flickered his tiny blue eyes and grunted. He had his own ideas too, for he considered himself the superior general. He had observed a round hill some three miles in advance of San Ángel and near a hacienda called Padierna and it had taken his fancy. It was closer to the American lines and it would make a fine stage for his masterful role in the imminent fighting. By the morning of the nineteenth he was there with five guns in battery and Santa Anna's angry authorization to do as he damned well pleased and take the responsibility for it.

That afternoon Scott struck. The bloody tints of the panorama deepened and then were obscured by rolling clouds of smoke. The fighting continued until nightfall and when the gunfire ceased the Americans were behind the outflanked and isolated Valencia and in the Indian village of San Gerónimo, while Santa Anna, who had hurried from San Antonio through Coyoacán and San Ángel, was camped with Pérez's brigade and seven or eight hundred cavalry and artillery three-quarters of a mile behind these Americans. A storm burst and torrents of chilling rain fell on Mexicans and Americans alike all through the night. It did not cool the general's fury. He understood immediately how completely the swollen-headed Valencia had been caught and he gave expression to his anger in voluble curses. "Valencia is an ambitious, insubordinate sot!" he screamed at the aides offering excuses. "He deserves to have his brains blown out, and I will not expose my men to the storm for him. Let him spike his guns, make the ammunition useless, and retreat." But Valencia could not retreat. He stood on the flank of his isolated round hill and swore to heaven that the traitor, Santa Anna, had betrayed him.

In the morning fog that followed the rain the Americans crept forward and took their positions and put their firearms in order. At six o'clock, as the skies cleared, they struck on both front and rear and Valencia with his picked troops was lost. The Mexican Lancers gave way almost immediately and threw the infantry into extreme disorder. All was confusion on the slopes of the round hill as foot soldiers, horses, artillery, mules, camp-women and laborers mingled in a frantic mass that fled over the breastworks pell-mell. The American field commander, Persifor Smith, took out his watch and glanced at it. "It has taken just seventeen minutes," he remarked. The booty included two guns that Santa Anna had captured at La Angostura.

This was the fatal beginning of a bloody and desperate day and Juan Diego, ordered against his will to remain in the National Palace and handle the requisitions for kegs of gunpowder as they poured in, saw none of the monstrous panorama. But he could hear the constant thunder of the guns and he could imagine the rest. He could imagine, too, the sensations of the stunned populace as they heard this dreadful music so close to their southern garitas and saw the litters bearing bloody bodies carried through the streets. Bad news travels fast and it flowed into the National Palace all day, borne by exhausted scouts, smoke-grimed runners, stuttering quartermaster officers and flurried army doctors who did not know where to put their wounded. When the sun set the bridge and town and convent of Churubusco had been taken by the Americans; they were in Los Portales, in San Antonio, in Mixcoac, in Coyoacán and San Angel; and the entire southern defenses of the capital had been overrun and occupied. It was a dolorous night in the city. Wounded and hysterical soldiers roamed the streets, crying out at the slightest alarm, "Here come the Yanquis!" There were loud sounds of weeping in many houses and in the cantinas men drank themselves into insensibility to forget the horrors of the day. The dead-wagons rattled constantly across the cobbles. There were no lights. Santa Anna, seated in his office in the National Palace, summed up his losses while his sallow face turned the color of wet clay. He had lost more than four thousand killed and wounded and more than twenty-five hundred taken prisoner, including eight generals, besides horses, cannon, muskets, great stocks of ammunition and other supplies, in other words, at least a third of his effectives. He was tired. He expected the Americans to breach the garitas in the morning and was faintly surprised that they were not marching down the Calle de Corpus Cristi at this moment. He would have to think quickly. By midmorning everybody in Mexico City knew what he had thought and what he had done. He had sent General Mora to Scott with a proposal for a truce and the American general had countered by acceding to a short armistice.

The lurid colors faded out of the panorama and for two weeks, while hastily appointed Mexican commissioners explored with Nicholas P. Trist, the representative of the American secretary of state, James Buchanan, the possibilities of a peace, Santa Anna worked like a beaver to reorganize his shattered army. Men talked at Atzcapozalco and Tacubaya and the general collected missing soldiers, reconstituted companies, regiments, brigades and army corps, punished delinquents and cashiered disaffected officers. The populace recovered gradually from its stunned condition and the old voices of discontent and hatred were raised once more. Gamboa, a minor politician, formally charged Santa Anna with treason. Valencia, who had escaped from the debacle of his troops still considering himself a second Napolcon, combined with Olaguíbel and pronounced against the general. The conniving heads of Paredes and Almonte and Canalizo popped up again. The hornet's nest was buzzing with an angrier vindictiveness than ever before and the greater good, the paramount necessity for cohesion, for a unified attitude, was ignored while petty jealousies were aired and every politician sought to better himself at anybody's expense.

Meanwhile the commissioners talked. Trist, on behalf of the United States, demanded all of Texas, New Mexico and the whole of California. The Mexican representatives, coached by the general, offered upper California and Texas to the line of the Nueces. There was some discussion that the lands between the Nueces and the Rio Grande might be made into a buffer state watched over by some neutral European power. Trist spoke of money. He suggested that the armistice be extended so that Washington could be consulted concerning the disputed territories. But Santa Anna had his ear to the ground and he heard a new and menacing rumble. The volatile Mexicans were forgetting their constant defeats and snorting fire and brimstone again. What! Give up their sacred territories! Permit the general to sweep away republican institutions and establish himself as dictator for life with the aid of American gold! The governor of Querétaro declared that any sale of territory would be the signal for a general secession. Gómez Farías pointed out that negotiations not shared in by the Congress were treasonable and the Congress would not assemble to vote on such a dangerous proposition. The Valencia-Olaguíbel coalition loomed menacingly. Those states which had refused to support the war now denounced Santa Anna for trying to end it. Anything, anything at all, even destruction was better than a peace dictated and signed by the general. And the general was no fool.

On the sixth of September the Mexican commissioners presented Trist with counterproposals they knew he would reject and the next day the armistice was at an end.

Juan Diego sat on a long bench in one of the corridors of the National Palace and waited, with half a dozen other aides, for any messages that the general might desire delivered. He was silent and moody and not even the chatter of Ezequiel Oropesa, whom he had not seen since those faraway days in San Luis Potosí before the battle at Buena Vista, could rouse him from the gloomy condition of mind that he suffered like a disease. The panorama of the past few months had convinced him that the war was lost, that Texas, New Mexico and California were lost and that the Republic was in evil hands. He had no faith in the powers of the general to perform miracles and nothing less than miracles could save the honor of Mexico. He couldn't even understand why the soldiers continued to fight and die for a cause that was so moribund. In Puebla he had been fiery for a struggle to the last ditch, for that went with integrity, but now he had seen the last ditch and it looked too much like a common grave. He thought often of Puebla, wondering if Don Isidro was still there and drinking as much aguardiente as ever, if the bishop still walked in his garden, if all the roses had fallen from the little bushes in the patio and if Doña María Catalina was happy in Apizaco. Even the thought of her failed to raise his spirits, for it seemed more like the memory of someone lost than it did like a thought. Puebla and all it contained (and had contained) was a hundred years and a million miles away. It might just as well be on the moon. So much had happened between May and September, so much to change a man and stifle his dreams and destroy his illusions. He regretted that he had no one with whom to converse for it was impossible to talk with the general and none of the aides appeared to have a brain in their heads. If he could only talk to somebody . . . and he knew that he was thinking of Don Isidro and his daughter . . . he might make some sense out of this gray-toned imbroglio.

He did not feel that he had lost his patriotism but he suspected that he needed more than that now. He needed the sustaining strength to see wickedness done and evil men triumph and still have faith in the eventual goodness of Mankind. It was really simple when he put it to himself that way but that was just the beginning. Where did the mind go from there? If he had the bluff cynicism of Don Isidro (and he wondered sometimes if he had weakened it) or the unentangled straightforwardness of Doña María Catalina or even the ignorant boyish optimism of young Lorenzo he might be able to satisfy himself, or, at least, achieve some sort of inner equanimity that would make it possible for him to go on with a confident air. Lorenzo. He had visited the boy two or three times during the summer at the Military College (where only the youngsters were left, for the older classmen had been inducted into the army) and found him full of spirits and following the course of the war with a curious logic of his own. It was Lorenzo's simple idea that the Republic should keep on fighting until the last man was killed and then it would not matter. He had the vaguest idea of what the war was about and did not seem to want it explained to him. That complicated matters too much. Juan Diego supposed that this was what might be called pure patriotism and an application of the American Decatur's, "My country right or wrong." It did not suit the young officer. He didn't know what did suit him and that was what troubled his mind. He had lost his faith in certain things and he had found nothing to replace it. It seemed to him that he was wandering haphazardly in a negative world where nothing much made sense and there was no guiding star to follow. That was it. For the moment he was lost. He would have to find someone to set him right, by argument, by illumination, by example, by a chance remark, perhaps, and then he could orient himself again. But it would not be the general. He was sure of that.

An orderly beckoned and he rose and followed him into Santa Anna's big office.

The general was standing behind his table, upon which lay a large map, and finishing some remarks to General Andrade.

". . . proceed to Los Morales," he ended and lifting his head from the map saw the young officer.

"Ah, Juanillo," he said and then to Andrade, "That is all, general."

The cavalry officer saluted and withdrew. Santa Anna whistled through his teeth as he bowed above the map again and traced certain lines with the tip of his finger. Then he sat down. Juan Diego observed his confident face and marveled at the resiliency of the man. He rose from the ashes of defeat like a phoenix and no one would ever suspect the depths of despair and uncertainty through which he must have passed. He was like a professional gambler whose expression did not change as his gold was raked across the green baize. He glanced up suddenly, an old trick of his and caught the young officer's speculative appraisal. He smiled.

"Juanillo," he said, "you are looking pale and thin. Are you sick? Perhaps you would like to go—"

"I'm all right," interposed Juan Diego quickly. "I am not sick at all. Did you ask for me?"

The general shuffled among the papers under the map and picked up a single sheet.

"Tornel has discovered your man, Juanillo," he explained. "Your ... what's his name? ... oh, yes ... Don Alejandro de la Barca y Padilla ... Dios mío! ... the one you warned me about before—"

"Yes, yes!" broke in the young officer eagerly. "What about him? What did Tornel—"

"Kindly allow me to finish," ordered Santa Anna good-naturedly. "I have a report on the fellow here. Let's see. Hmmm. Not a Mexican. A Spaniard. He was seen often with Valencia before the action by Padierna. Well, that's enough to damn him straightaway. Why I didn't wring Valencia's neck. Hmmm. During the last ten days he has been acting peculiarly, visiting all the jails and frequenting those cheap pulquerías patronized by the léperos. What the devil ... ! A Barca y Padilla, too. He lives at twenty-six, Calle de San Ildefonso. Here, take the report. I suggest that if you have nothing to do this evening you look him up and find out what he is up to. Follow him. See where he goes. Tornel is too busy to do anything about it."

Juan Diego took the paper, folded it and put it in his pocket.

"He is probably conspiring," he declared a little too loudly.

Santa Anna put his tongue in his cheek.

"Everybody is conspiring, Juanillo," he said tranquilly. "Everybody except you and me."

He slapped the map on his table.

"Scott will attack in the morning," he announced flatly, "but I am ready for him."

A feeling of despair swept through the young officer. In his ears he could hear the roll of the dead-wagons again and the screams of the wounded.

"God be with us!" he exclaimed involuntarily.

The general stared at him in a disapproving manner.

"Never mind God," he said harshly. "Leave God to the archbishop. What is the matter with you, Juanillo? You are acting more like a novice priest than ever. Do you want me to take that uniform off and put a sotana on you? I think I can handle Scott without God. My scouts tell me he has about eight thousand effective men. Well, I have twenty thousand."

Suddenly he became excited and jumped to his feet.

"Look!" he cried, dragging the map across the table. "See here. I have arranged everything. Scott will undoubtedly try to seize Chapultepec and the Belén Causeway. Now, observe. I have posted León's and Rangel's brigades at El Molino del Rey. There. The best of Pérez's brigade is garrisoned at the Casa Mata. Ramírez's men occupy the intermediate space. Four guns a little in front of the bend here. Two divisions of horse under Alvarez and Andrade at Los Morales. Reserves of infantry and artillery in the rear. Do you see? Here. And all the guns on Chapultepec made ready, mines laid on the slopes and the powder magazines full. Do you think that Scott with his miserable exhausted eight thousand can break through all that?"

He glanced up triumphantly at the young officer but the old magic failed to work.

"It looks formidable," he said, "and if Scott attacks where you think he—"

"He's bound to," asserted Santa Anna. "Where else can he move from his present positions? He knows he must reduce Chapultepec before he can take the city. He . . ."

Suddenly the name repeated twice struck a sharp note in Juan Diego's mind.

"Chapultepec!" he exclaimed. "Do you mean there will be fighting at Chapultepec? What about the boys? Have they been removed?"

"The boys," echoed the general. "Oh, you mean the cadets in the Military College. Por dios! I completely forgot them. I'll issue an order to Bravo to have them removed. Here . . . no. I'll see Bravo later in the day. Get along now and try to shorten that long face of yours. We'll all be toasting victory tomorrow night."

"Will you need me this evening?" inquired Juan Diego as he turned toward the door.

"What? No," replied Santa Anna, sitting down behind his table and drawing the map toward him. "If you want to investigate that Spanish fellow, go ahead. Send one of the aides in to me. I want to send a message to Alvarez."

"You won't forget the boys at Chapultepec," Juan Diego reminded him, hesitating at the threshold.

"No, no, no!" cried Santa Anna.

The young officer observed the bowed head with its unruly gray-black hair for an instant and then passed into the corridor. By the bench he paused and looked down at the grinning Ezequiel Oropesa.

"I'm sure you'd like a nice horseback ride to Los Morales," he said. "The general wants to see you."

Ezequiel muttered an uncomplimentary reference to Juan Diego's mother, grandmother and great-grandmother and got up and marched into Santa Anna's office. Half-smiling the young officer passed through corridors and inner gardens and eventually reached the Grand Plaza where before the cathedral a large crowd of people was assembled. There had been a procession in which the image of Our Lady of Guadalupe had been borne through the streets. It was strange how the clergy had quite suddenly come over to the general again. They preached on the street corners against the heretical invaders and saw to it that the church bells clanged continuously. What had happened to cause this change of heart was a mystery but Juan Diego doubted the sincerity of it. His experiences with the bishop and Isunza in Puebla had cured him forever of any faith in the patriotism of the Church. And yet might it not be that the Church, like himself, required something more than patriotism? That was a new thought and something upon which to cogitate. He stood for a few moments and watched the shifting crowd, women passing into the cathedral and soldiers in ill-fitting uniforms slouching around the great square. A squadron of clattering cavalry passed swiftly in the direction of the Alameda and the Garita de San Cosme and he followed them with his eyes until their fluttering pennons disappeared in the narrow streets. The cavalry was always gallant. Presently he began to walk slowly toward the single room he occupied in the Calle de Santa Clara. He had decided to change into civilian garb for his evening's investigation and the thought that he might encounter Don Alejandro aroused a queer sort of savage pleasure in him. He would know what to do when he met that toad again. He would follow Don Isidro's advice and let the fire out.

It was after eight o'clock in the evening when Juan Diego set out from his room in the Calle de Santa Clara for twenty-six, Calle de San Ildefonso. The air was clear but cold and in the heavens above Mexico City the great wheel of stars glittered and twinkled. As he walked along with his dark cloak held closely about him the young officer observed that there was a lot of movement in the streets, people passing to and fro and the rumbling of voices from cantinas and fondas, occasional saddle horses and once or twice a small coach that rattled loudly over the cobbles. The city was wide-awake and wondering what would happen on the morrow. Juan Diego continued along the Calle de Tacuba to the end of the block and then turned up the Calle de Santo Domingo to the Calle de la Encarnación. Here he turned again and passed the dark bulk of the Church of the Incarnation. There was a faint glow from the high windows and a subdued sound of chanting. He crossed the Calle de Santa Catalina and proceeded down the Calle de San Ildefonso. He walked more slowly. Now that he was here he did not quite know what to do. What reason

could he give for accosting Don Alejandro? He was not seeking a
fight although the prospect of giving the Spaniard a good beating had
its attractive features. But that would solve nothing. What he desired
was some knowledge that Don Alejandro was engaged in actions inim-
ical to the Republic, conspiring, say, or enciting to violence, something
that would take him out of Doña María Catalina's life for a long time
and possibly forever. He didn't delude himself about his purpose. It
was not patriotism that was stirring him. It was Don Isidro's daughter
and the imperative fact that he loved her. He admitted that freely to
himself now. He loved her. His love had been a despair when he left
Puebla and it was still a despair but now he was clutching at the
vaguest possibilities. Like mirages they lightened the dark horizon occasionally and although he dismissed them for the witch fires they were
he could not quite ignore them. Hope was a persistent weed that sprang
up in the rockiest soil.

It never occurred to him that Don Alejandro might be guiltless
of any wrongdoing, that he was merely a stupid and brutal Spaniard
who associated with léperos and jailbirds because he liked them. No,
the man was a scoundrel and being a scoundrel must be mixed up with
criminals and engaged in criminal activities. He had seen the mark of
the scoundrel stamped on his froglike face that day at the stables at
Las Golondrinas when he had beaten his Arabian horse. The thing to
do, then, was to ferret out what the toad was up to and report to the
general and the general would act quickly and mercilessly as he always
did. There must be no violence, then, no hint that would put Don
Alejandro on his guard or cause him to disappear in this vast labyrinth
that was Mexico City. Watchfulness was the method by which he
might be caught, watchfulness until he was caught red-handed at his
guilty activities. The little that Juan Diego had to go on seemed sufficient to justify his suspicions. Young Lorenzo had seen him in the
entourage of Valencia when Valencia was conspiring against the general. One of the boys in the Military College had heard that he was
working for the Monarchists although he pretended to be a Moderado.
Might he not be a Spanish agent, one of those fellows who sought to
increase the discontent in the Republic until it blew up in a monstrous
revolution? And Tornel's spies had reported that he was associating
with the beggars and criminal elements in the city, those jackals of
léperos who came out of their dark lairs to murder and pillage whenever the government broke down. He was visiting the jails, too, and
that was curious. Yes, there were enough suspicious circumstances to
warrant a close examination of Don Alejandro de la Barca y Padilla.
But how was he to set about it? The young officer had no experience
as a secret agent and now he regretted that he had not brought one of
Tornel's men with him. He supposed that the first thing to do was to
locate the house in which Don Alejandro lived. There was a small can-

tina, the Four Roses of Xochimilco, near the corner of the Calle de San Pedro y San Pablo and he went in there.

It was a low smoky place insufficiently lighted with half a dozen tables huddled together and a crowd of men about each table. The sour smell of pulque and stronger liquors permeated an atmosphere shot through with the stink of garlic and the pungent odor of peppers. It was not until Juan Diego had pushed his way well into the room that he recognized the types slouching over the wet tables and was immediately sorry he had come in at all. The conversation had stopped abruptly and a score of bold inquisitive eyes were carefully inspecting him from head to foot, observing the neatness of his costume and the fine material in his cloak and his well-washed hands and carefully combed hair. If these men were not léperos they were close to it. He paused indecisively and was about to turn and walk out when a dirty hand grasped his cloak.

"Here is a chair, señor," said a guttural voice. "Make a place for the señor there. The señor will buy us a drink, no?"

There was a scraping and some movement and he found himself wedged between a fat fellow whose nose was half-eaten away by a running sore and a little mestizo with black oily hair.

"Yes, I will buy a drink," announced Juan Diego. "Where is the mozo?"

The putrid stench of the fat fellow filled his nose until his head swam.

"Patrón!" called the mestizo. "Come quickly. Here is real money. A gentleman who rides in the Paseo. I have seen him often."

Inwardly Juan Diego cursed the half-breed. He had never ridden in the Paseo in his life but it would never do to deny it now. They were all looking at him and he had the feeling that he was being studied by a cage of wild beasts.

A stout man wearing a red sash and with the lean narrow face of a Northern Italian pushed past the tables and came up to him. This, he supposed, was the patrón.

"What is it?" demanded the stout man. "What does the señor desire? We have very good aguardiente."

"Aguardiente!" cried the mestizo. "That is it! Excellent aguardiente! The señor is a generous man. I have seen him on his own horse in the Paseo. Perhaps he will buy a whole bottle. Ask him, patrón, ask him."

The stout man glanced contemptuously at the half-breed.

"Shut up, Servando Herrera, you bastard son of an Otomí wench and a mule driver," he shouted. "You thief, the police are looking for you in Pachuca where you stole the shawl from your grandmother and exchanged it for a demiliter of pulque. Do you want a glass of aguardiente, señor?"

The last sentence was directed at Juan Diego and he nodded.

"Bring three glasses," he said. "One for each of us."

"The señor is the son of a general," exclaimed the mestizo. "He lives on a great estate near Tacubaya. I have seen him often."

All this while the fat fellow with the rotting nose was staring with unblinking eyes at the young officer and not saying a word. At regular intervals he belched gently and a miasma of sour stomach gas was wafted across the table. At the other tables the interrupted conversation was being resumed in low voices.

"Do not believe the patrón," went on the mestizo confidentially. "It is his idea of humor. I was never in Pachuca in my life. I come from the south. Do you know Chilpancingo? I was born there. I served with the lancers at the Cerro Gordo where I was wounded three times. That is why I am no longer with——"

"He is a liar," broke in the patrón, who had just returned with the drinks. "He was in jail for robbing a bakeshop when they fought at Cerro Gordo."

He waited while Juan Diego extracted his purse and counted out the money for the three glasses of aguardiente. The mestizo leaned on the young officer's shoulder and watched with greedy eyes.

"You have plenty of money," he said. "You are a great hacendado. I have seen you in a box at the Teatro Santa Anna. Give me a peso, señor. Give me a few coppers."

Juan Diego pushed a coin toward him and the half-breed snapped it up and concealed it somewhere in his ragged clothes. Then he drained down his aguardiente in one gulp.

"Perhaps the señor will buy another," he chattered. "What is a peso to a man so rich as the señor? Give me another peso, for the love of God. I am starving, illustrious son of a general, and my heart is bad. Sometimes it stops. Sometimes——"

"Be silent, cochino!" bawled the fat fellow suddenly. "You give me a pain in my ear."

During this brief outbreak he never removed his glance from Juan Diego's face.

"The señor is a stranger here," he said after a moment in a hollow husky voice. "The Four Roses of Xochimilco is honored by the señor's presence."

He had not touched his glass of aguardiente.

"I merely dropped in to inquire about an address," replied Juan Diego without thinking. "Perhaps you can direct me? Twenty-six, Calle de San Ildefonso?"

The fat fellow stared at him for a full minute while at measured intervals he emitted three belches. Then he raised his voice in a disconcerting shout.

"Don Alejandro!" he called. "Don Alejandro! Here is a caballero
inquiring for twenty-six, Calle de San Ildefonso."

A cold chill ran down Juan Diego's spine and he half-rose from
his chair.

"No, no," he protested. "I didn't want . . ."

Then he sank back speechless in his seat.

From a far corner of the room a squat figure in a green velvet
suit had emerged and was making his way leisurely toward the table.
There was no mistaking the froglike face with eyes set too far apart,
the small nose and the large mouth, the short neck and the solid little
legs. This was the man whom he had hated without knowing for
eleven months. This was the man he had knocked down in the inner
courtyard at Las Golondrinas. This was Don Isidro's son-in-law. This
was the husband of Doña María Catalina. He was not afraid of him
but he regretted the stupidity that was bringing them face to face.
Like the general, he would have to think quickly.

"What is it?" asked Don Alejandro in a thick voice. "Why are
you shouting, Mateo Báez?"

"Here is a señor who is inquiring about twenty six, Calle de San
Ildefonso," replied the fat fellow calmly. "He has just bought me a
glass of aguardiente and he gave Servando Herrera a peso."

Don Alejandro stared vacantly at the young officer for a moment
and shook his head.

"I do not know him," he said.

"Somebody told me that there was a chamber for hire at that
address," explained Juan Diego quickly. "I understood . . ."

"Twenty-six, Calle de San Ildefonso is a private dwelling," declared Don Alejandro. "It is my house. I do not rent rooms. I do not
believe that anybody told you that there was a chamber for hire there."

Sparks of cunning began to flash in his eyes.

"Who are you?" he demanded. "What is your name, señor, and
why were you looking for my house?"

"I was not looking for your house," expostulated the young officer, "and my name is my business. I was told—"

"Are you one of Tornel's agents?" persisted Don Alejandro. "If
you would like to search my house I will accompany you there."

"I am not an agent," said Juan Diego steadily. "I regret this mistake. I must have been misinformed."

He controlled a desire to jump up and smash his fist into the froglike face and picked up his glass of aguardiente and drank half of it.
Don Alejandro stood looking down at him with sly eyes and wrinkled
forehead. It was plain that he did not recognize him and it was equally
plain that his suspicious nature was seeking intensely to find a reason
in the young man's presence. He pursed his lips obscenely.

"I have nothing to hide," he said, the words stumbling over his big tongue. "I am merely a visitor to Mexico City. If you are an agent of Tornel go back and tell him that. Ask him why he has had me followed for the last week. I can complain to the Spanish chargé-d'affaires, Señor Ramón Lozano, about that."

"I am not an agent," repeated Juan Diego irritably. "Señor Don Alejandro . . . whatever your name is . . . you are annoying me. I say once and for all that I have no interest in you and the more I look at you the less I desire your acquaintance."

Damn it all, he thought to himself, if he wants to quarrel I am quite ready for him. It does not matter now. He has seen me and my usefulness as an investigator of his activities is destroyed. But Don Alejandro did not seem disposed to quarrel. He wiped the hairy back of his hand across his prominent lips and ignored the insulting note in the young man's words.

"Barca y Padilla," he said softly. "That is my name. I live at twenty-six, Calle de Ildefonso and Señor Tornel can always find me there."

He turned slowly.

"I will remember your face, señor," he added. "I will not forget you."

Juan Diego watched him edge his way through the crowded tables to his seat in the far corner of the room and then finished drinking his glass of aguardiente. The fat fellow with the rotting nose, whom Don Alejandro had addressed as Mateo Báez, sat before his untouched glass gently belching and staring with unblinking eyes across the table. Juan Diego rose to leave.

"Just one more peso, señor," babbled the mestizo seizing the back of his cloak. "Just one more. I remember you, señor. I have seen you walking into the National Palace as though you owned it. You are a great man with plenty of money. See, señor, my hand shakes from an old heart trouble. I have two little daughters and not a rag to put on their backs. Señor, for the love of God . . ."

Juan Diego snatched his cloak away and passed through a dead silence out of the Four Roses of Xochimilco into the Calle de San Ildefonso. He was furious at himself for what had happened and now that he was under the night stars he could think of a dozen things that he should have done. He should have worn ragged clothes and gone unshaven, for one thing. He should never have mentioned Don Alejandro's address. He should have kept his mouth shut and listened. What a lucky chance he had missed! There he was in the very cantina apparently frequented by Don Alejandro with a perfect opportunity to sit and see who conversed with him and he had spoilt it all by blurting out the one thing he should have kept to himself. The general would enjoy that. The only thing he could think of now was to ask Santa Anna to have Tornel put some unknown clever agent on the Spaniard's trail. Disgusted and disappointed he walked rapidly toward his own room in the Calle de Santa Clara hardly noticing the ammunition carts that lean mules were dragging through the streets.

In the first dim light of the morning the Americans launched their first attack for possession of Mexico City and it was over by seven o'clock. Amazingly enough, Juan Diego, sleeping heavily and with closed windows, had not been roused by the firing although it was little more than two miles away and it was not until he reported at the National Palace some time after eight o'clock that he heard the details of the action. Ezequiel Oropesa, who had been on his feet or in the saddle all night, and half a dozen other young aides were vociferous with their information. Allowing for their enlargements Juan Diego gathered that the general had suffered another defeat but one with its redeeming features. It appeared that the Americans had lost heavily and gained only a few dilapidated buildings that were of no use to anybody. They had captured El Molino del Rey and blown up the Casa Mata. The young officer knew both these places well. El Molino del Rey, the King's Mill, was a congeries of connected buildings rather more than half a mile west of Chapultepec that had been used as a foundry for bronze cannon and the Casa Mata was an old powder magazine about half a mile northwest of the Mill.

"The Americans attacked as soon as they could see the white walls of the Mill," explained Ezequiel Oropesa. "We held our fire. They advanced, thinking we had abandoned the buildings, and then we opened on them with canister and musket balls. Dios mío, were they surprised! We broke their column and nearly a third of them bolted. I tell you, Juanillo, they ran like rabbits. Lieutenant Colonel Echegaray came down from Chapultepec with the Third Ligero and then we went after them hell-bent-for-leather and cut them down with our sabers."

"I thought you were at Los Morales," interrupted Juan Diego.

"I was, damn you!" replied Ezequiel Oropesa, "but I got all the details from those who saw it. I am using the editorial 'we.' "

"Well, what happened after that?" demanded the young officer.

"I'll tell you," said a large aide with gloomy Indian features and his arm in a sling. "The Americans came back. They came back with cannister and rifle balls and bayonets and captured our guns, penetrated into the Mill and forced their way to the azoteas. General León got a bullet in his side and Balderas was shot. They cleared us out of there in a hurry because our God-damned reserves didn't come up."

"And the Casa Mata?" inquired Juan Diego.

"I was there," said a third aide taking up the story. "Pérez was in command. The Americans attempted a frontal assault without artillery and we picked them off as easily as you pick off birds in a mass hunt. I saw half a dozen of their officers go down. They got under the walls and behind the embankment of the ditch and the magueys and tried to pick us off, too. I can hear those balls whistling about my head yet. After a while, their muskets got fouled and their ammunition gave out. Then they withdrew and skedaddled across the uneven ground toward the Mill. We felt pretty good . . . until their batteries moved up and began to shell us. They blew hell out of the Casa Mata and we got out of there as fast as we could."

"And the cavalry!" exclaimed Juan Diego. "Where was the cavalry all this time?"

"At Los Morales," declared the large aide with his arm in a sling. "Ask Oropesa. He was there."

"Alvarez is not a cavalry officer," said Ezequiel Oropesa. "He's a thickhead of an Indian. He tried to advance with his division but it broke and fell back on Andrade's men. There was some cannon fire and then all of them fled."

"Leaving the field to the Americans," added Juan Diego.

"What did they get?" demanded Oropesa. "Some old dilapidated buildings and an empty powder magazine. And they paid heavily for it, too."

"We lost two generals," said the large aide gloomily.

The lines of a map suddenly sprang into Juan Diego's mind.

"You idiots!" he snapped. "Do you think Scott is such a fool as to throw his men away for a few old buildings? Can't you see what he has done?"

"He probably thought there were cannon in the Mill," insisted Ezequiel Oropesa. "Jesuscristo! There was nothing there but a few old molds."

"He got what he wanted," declared Juan Diego dryly. "He has cleared the way for a direct assault on Chapultepec."

He turned on his heel and walked into the general's office.

Santa Anna was sitting behind his table with a weary expression on his face. He glanced up without comment as the young officer entered. He was covered with dust and his riding boot, thrust out from beneath the table, had lost its usual luster.

"Good morning, my general," said Juan Diego formally.

"Good morning, Juanillo," replied Santa Anna in a tired voice. "I feel like the devil. I have been up all night. You have heard about the action this morning?"

"Yes, I have," answered the young officer. "From Oropesa and some of the aides. I'm sorry I slept through it. It was . . . unfortunate."

Santa Anna ran his hand through his heavy hair.

"If my generals would co-operate better and the cavalry would come up to expectations things might go better," he said glumly, "but," he continued, brightening, "it might have been worse. Scott undoubtedly meant to accomplish more than he did and he failed. I think his strength is diminishing. If we can hold out for another fortnight . . ."

He paused and shook his head, relapsing into a weariness that seemed to be both mental and physical. How old is he? thought Juan Diego, fifty-three? He looks sixty now. How can he go on in the way he does? He possesses an inner demon that will not let him rest. He must know that the war is lost . . . but perhaps he is struggling for better peace terms. He is too old . . . but how old was Scott? Sixty-three? Age didn't matter. It was the demon in the man that mattered.

"Is there anything particular that you want to see me about, Juanillo?" asked the general. "I have a thousand and one things to oversee: a staff meeting, consultations, the redistribution of troops. . . . I don't know when I will sleep. Perhaps never."

He *is* tired, thought the young officer. He has lost his flair. At this moment he is at a low ebb . . . but something will happen, some word, some attitude of one of the generals and he will be his flamboyant self again, breathing fire and fury, coercing and driving weaker wills before him, exuding a confidence and strengthening weakening wills. He is like that.

"Yes," replied Juan Diego, "I want to report about last evening."

And he narrated his adventure in the Four Roses of Xochimilco. Santa Anna could not resist a smile.

"You'll never make a secret agent, Juanillo," he remarked. "However, I'll set Tornel on the trail again. There are a few léperos on his payroll. I am beginning to be interested in your man . . . what's his name? . . . Barca? . . . Where did you first run across him?"

"I heard about him in Puebla," explained the young officer vaguely.

"Well . . ." Santa Anna made a note on a sheet of paper that lay before him. "There may be nothing in it, but we will see. Is that all?"

"Scott will try to take Chapultepec, I suppose," said Juan Diego. The general shrugged his shoulders.

"He will find it a hard nut to crack," he answered. "Bravo is in command there now and the old fellow has his points."

"The capture of the Mill puts the Americans on the sloping side of the hill," pointed out the young officer.

"It is all mined," replied the general. "However, I think Scott will try to force the southern garitas. Belén, Niño Perdido, San Antonio and La Viga. And I have prepared for that. There are marshes, inundations, ditches full of water, cut causeways and destroyed bridges. When the Americans try to get through they will run into our cross fire."

"Have the boys been removed from Chapultepec?" asked Juan Diego suddenly.

"What? The boys?" repeated Santa Anna with a puzzled air and then his face cleared. "Oh. You mean the cadets at the Military College. I think I did send a message to Bravo. Por Dios! I have so much to think about. But I'll send another to make sure."

He made a second note on the sheet of paper and looked up smiling.

"Why this concern for the cadets?" he asked amiably. "Have you an illegitimate son among them?"

"I was a cadet there once," answered the young officer.

"So you were, so you were," agreed the general. "And now get along with you. Tell one of the mozos to bring me a bottle of champagne. You'd better remain on call in the corridor. I shall have plenty of messages to send."

"You won't forget the boys," insisted Juan Diego.

"No, no, no," replied Santa Anna.

He watched the young officer disappear through the door and one of his infrequent sad smiles curved his lips. Juanillo was like a son. There was no military etiquette between them. And yet there was a steadily widening gulf that was pushing them farther and farther apart. He was no longer the boy of Manga de Clavo. The general, who had his sentimental moments, sighed and turned to greet the group of officers who came with sabers rattling into the room.

During the next three days Juan Diego caught only infrequent flashes of Santa Anna as he dashed in and out of the National Palace, hurrying to fortified points, moving regiments from one place to another and seizing provisions wherever he could find them. The city was in a trembling state of fever steadily increased by false alarms, the constant marchings and countermarchings through the streets and the continual clang of the church bells. The usual rumors were discussed eagerly in the cantinas: The Americans were on half rations. There was dissension among their generals. Scott was in a state of indecision and did not know what to do. On the eleventh of September the general celebrated the anniversary of the surrender of the Spaniards at Tampico in 1829 by a grand review and a proclamation exhorting the Mexicans to victory. Yet all these rumors and activities did not remove the emotions of weakness and confusion that sapped the stamina of the people. Juan Diego, as he sped from place to place carrying messages, could sense the taut desperation in thousands of eyes and the fatalistic premonitions that darkened a multitude of faces.

His own mind was in an angry turmoil. The fate of the city, which meant the fate of the northern territories, agitated him constantly and he clutched eagerly at any straw of optimism that might be blown his way. But they broke in his hands. He did not believe the rumors concerning Scott's army and the heroics of the general failed to exhilarate him as they had in the past. He could not forget the retreat from La Angostura, the carnage at Cerro Gordo, the empty gesture at Amozoc, the futile rages and flight from Puebla, the disasters of Padierna and Churubusco and the defeats at El Molino del Rey and the Casa Mata. He had enough perspective now to see the pattern and it was an evil one. Defeat and retreat, defeat and retreat, defeat and retreat, that was the whole story and it summed up to complete disaster. Augmenting this despair was a sorrow that was never far from the surface of his mind—the feeling that Doña María Catalina was lost to him (he did not pause to remember that he had never possessed her) and that he would never see her again. Between wherever she was, Apizaco or Puebla, and the besieged city where he labored for a failing cause stretched the black shadow of Don Alejandro. It could not be erased. He didn't know whether or not the general had spoken to Tornel about this man who was the husband of Doña María Catalina in the eyes of the powerful Church but he had heard nothing and this seemed ominous. Another thing that disturbed him was his failure to find young Lorenzo. The cadets from the Military College on Chapultepec had been removed from their exposed position (he had seen a detachment of them marching in review, their gray uniforms and blue caps bobbing along bravely) but where they were barracked he did not know. And he had been unable to visit Chapultepec. The general and his staff kept him too busy for that. All he could do was question hurrying aides who knew less than he did and rush from place to place himself delivering messages and wondering . . . and brooding . . . and cursing his own helplessness.

Lorenzo was still on Chapultepec.

When the majority of the cadets had been removed in accordance with Santa Anna's belated order a number of them begged to remain and Nicolás Bravo, the commandant, a stern old veteran of the battles for independence, had consented. There was a Spartan streak in this grizzled warrior and he saw no reason why these boys, who would be officers some day, should not experience the blood and fire of war. The best way to learn was the hard way. Besides, his garrison was undermanned. Aside from the gunners and engineers all he had to defend the rock were the Tenth Line Infantry and the Mina, Unión, Querétaro, Toluca and Patria battalions, a little more than eight hundred men. The volunteer cadets, therefore, were welcome. Lorenzo, with his simple philosophy of fighting to the last ditch, was among the first to request permission to stay. He desired action and he did not have long to wait for it.

On the morning of September twelfth he was roused by the roar of sudden gunfire and he dressed quickly and ran out to the parapet. It was a beautiful and sunshot day and from his high eyrie he could see clearly the whole Valley of Mexico below and beyond him. To the west the majestic wall of rugged mountains formed a barrier and to the east twin snow-crowned peaks stood like gigantic sentinels. The mountains descended into green hills and then leveled out into a vast plain studded with glittering lakes. Fields of ripened grain, the emerald slash of rows of maguey plants, white quintas with surrounding gardens bright with flowers and tree-lined avenues split up the broad expanse like a varicolored quilt. Immediately to the east, as finely chiseled as a cameo, glistened Mexico City, Ciudad de Mexico, its towers and azoteas shining in the sun and just below him on the west, sloping toward the ruined buildings of the captured Mill, was a grove of giant cypress trees protecting the easier approach to the old viceregal fortress. But it was not these familiar sights that caught and held the boy's excited attention but the white puffs of smoke rising from American batteries and the reverberation of their explosions.

During the night Scott had moved his pieces forward, two sixteen-pounders and an eight-inch howitzer on the road from Tacubaya to Mexico City about a thousand yards from Chapultepec, an eight-inch howitzer and a twenty-four-pounder south of the Mill and a sixteen-pounder siege gun and an eight-inch howitzer almost at the Mill itself. They were hammering away with good effect and the buildings of the Military College already were suffering direct hits. Lorenzo could hear the explosion, the almost-immediate whistle of the shell and the crash as it tore into the masonry. The Mexican gunners were replying and every time one of their missiles sent the sandbags flying from the American parapets the little garrison cheered loudly.

The cannon duel continued all day.

It was the first time Lorenzo had been under direct fire and for a time it seemed to him like some monstrous fiesta in which the rockets went wild. The deafening roar, the blossoming balloons of smoke that merged into a gray fog, the crash and clatter of falling bricks and stones, and the ear-splitting replies of his own gunners joined in a wild music that shook him from the toes of his boots to the black locks on his head. This was war and for a long time he leaned over the high parapet clutching the antiquated musket that had been given him and waiting and praying for an assault that he could meet with a stubborn defense. Beside him boys as young as he waited, their lips trembling and a mazed look in their wide eyes. But nothing happened. The guns bellowed, shells exploded in the air, fragments of the buildings blew away with a loud clatter and that was all. But eventually it was too much. Two of the guns were disabled and a gunner was killed. A corner of one of the buildings was on fire. A feeling of helplessness swept over Lorenzo and he began to experience that weakening of morale that attacks cornered infantry when it can do nothing but wait. His nerves were on extreme edge now and he felt that if the bombardment did not cease he would go mad. But it went on inexorably, methodically, with an insane regularity that destroyed the will and battered at the senses. One hour . . . two hours . . . three hours . . . it would never stop. The gunners, stripped to the waist and blackened with powder, were carried along by their own exertions and the engineers, blocking off fires and replacing shattered parapets, had no time to stop and think; but the infantry, and that included the cadets, could do nothing but stand to their posts with unfired muskets in their hands and wait through a dozen eternities. It was too much.

Near noon Santa Anna rode into the rectangle below the fortress to reconnoiter and the boys, stretching their bodies across the parapets, saw a shell burst near him and cover his red pony with flying dirt. He brushed the earth from his jacket and went on conversing with one of the officers. What were they talking about? A flank attack against the American batteries? The cavalry? Where was the cavalry, anyway? The boys, eager to divert their minds from the unending cannon fire, speculated among themselves but as they knew nothing they could reach no solution. Presently the general rode off, following the causeway to the Belén garita, and the speculation died away. There was nothing to do but crouch by the parapets and listen to the roar of the howitzers and watch the buildings steadily crumble away before the impact of the American shells.

Toward evening General Bravo descended from the battered eyrie and galloped into the city to consult with Santa Anna. He realized the almost hysterical condition of his garrison and intended to demand fresh troops. He was back inside of an hour with the information that Santa Anna could see no use in sending men forward who would be destroyed on the way or demoralized after arriving. "I will provide men at the critical moment," he informed Bravo. The quick twilight fell and suddenly the bombardment stopped. It stopped so suddenly that Lorenzo, his ears still tingling with the heavy sound, could hardly believe it and had to pause with his hand supporting himself by the parapet and listen for a full minute before he was sure. And now the silence seemed as awful as the sound.

That night the garrison ate cold rations and tried without success to sleep. Double watches were posted and pickets sent into the cypress grove and a little distance beyond but they were excessive gestures. At all hours until the gray dawn began to break more than half the defenders were watching at the parapets. Lorenzo wandered from spot to spot, pausing at intervals to stare out into the darkness and listen at the gun slits. It seemed to him that the earth beneath him was breathing hoarsely like a great beast attending its hour to spring and this began to frighten him. He pictured hundreds of American soldiers creeping up the rock with knives in their hands, slipping through the aged trees in the grove, climbing over the sandbag redans and slithering like black lizards over the parapets. This sensation of mysterious movement became an obsession and he shook himself free from it only when he discovered that most of the other cadets had the same fixation. "I can hear sounds down there," a boy would exclaim in a shaking voice, and then he would say, "No; it is nothing but the breeze in the bushes." Finally he convinced himself. The Americans were resting. He could see the glow of their campfires at La Piedad and Tacubaya and El Molino del Rey and as far away as Mixcoac.

At daybreak, about half past five, the infernal music began again. For two hours the American batteries hurled shot and shell at the summit of Chapultepec and then for a half hour they poured grape, canister and shells into the cypress grove where a portion of the garrison was stationed. Lorenzo wondered how he could live through another day of this bombardment without his eardrums bursting. There was a strained look on his face and the pulses in his temples seemed to jump with the explosions. He couldn't feel the musket in his hand. The queer mingled odor of gunpowder and smashed masonry filled his nostrils and sickened him and there were moments when he felt like vomiting. He wondered vaguely how General Bravo, erect and thickset, with deep eyes and a great chin, could move so calmly from post to post or stand with folded arms while the ruins of the world rained down upon him in broken stone and jagged cornices. The sun rose, hot and attentive, and the cannonade went on.

About eight o'clock there came an abrupt lull in the firing that lasted for some minutes and then it recommenced with greater fury than ever. Lorenzo did not have to wait long to discover the reason for this interruption for startling news was being shouted from all sides of the fortress. The American infantry was moving east along the Anzures causeway from the Mill with the obvious intention of cutting off any reinforcements from the north; they were attacking the south wall, too, overrunning the redan and redoubt there and spreading onto the rising slope; and on the east they were rushing into the cypress grove and its swampy borders and driving the Mexican skirmishers from tree to tree. This, the boy realized, was the critical phase. If the Americans reached the protecting fosse and crossed it Chapultepec was lost.

A terrific explosion to one side of him caused him to turn and he saw that a gun had blown up and the dead and wounded men of its crew were sprawling about in pools of their own blood. A man's hand had been hurled almost at his feet and he thought he could see the fingers twitching. The cadet beside him, a boy not more than twelve years old and hardly strong enough to lift the heavy musket, began to vomit. Lorenzo restrained by an effort the nausea that was rising within him and turned away. Through the screaming din he heard General Bravo calling but he did not move from his place. His legs seemed paralyzed, held immovable by the pressure of sound that closed about him like a thick invisible fluid. He shut his eyes against the sun and heat and leaned his forehead on the warm rough parapet. The noise in the cypress grove below him was like the thrashing of great beasts in their death agonies.

And now he heard the voice of one of the older boys, speaking gaspingly, hurriedly, with a wild urgency. His arm was roughly shaken but he did not respond. Yet he heard everything. General Bravo had called the cadets together. He had told them that there was still a way out for them, by the Belén causeway to the east, to Mexico City, that was still open. Would he come? They were leaving now. He had better hurry. He shook his head with his eyes still closed. He couldn't go. Something inside him compelled him to stay, something settled, something definite, something that was bigger than his fright. After a moment, the older boy ran away. Lorenzo opened hs eyes carefully and through the rising smoke he saw the battlements and azoteas of Mexico City black with people. Chapultepec, wreathed in fire, had its audience.

The loud rattle of small arms along his stretch of the parapet caused him to turn his eyes hastily downward and he saw that the Americans were moving up the slope from the cypress grove, dribbling through the thinning trees and forming in open order as they came. The riddled blue flag of the Voltigeurs rippled in the sun. East of the grove another mass of men was coming. Behind them a howitzer bellowed at frequent intervals. This was *it,* then. He began to fire and reload his musket, hysterically at first and then more slowly and carefully, taking aim at the misty figures in the clouds of smoke and dust. The sickness in his stomach died away after a time and a desperate coolness flowed through his body like an icy stream. He was a machine working with a regularity that killed all emotion. He felt the barrel of his musket grow hot in his hand and blisters began to rise on his fingers. The parapet on either side of him became a ring of spurting flame.

The Americans took shelter behind rocks and stumps but the *tzing* of their bullets constantly spattered against the wall of the fortress, kicking up tiny jets of stone dust. Lorenzo crouched and raised his head only to fire. A new sound of cannon fire came from the Tacubaya causeway to the southeast and he knew that the Americans were trying to cut off the approaches from the capital. If they did that Chapultepec would be completely surrounded. The thought came to him coldly and with a sort of inevitable fatality that was untouched by any passion. If that was the way it was to be then it was to be that way. He was an automaton, firing, reloading, firing, the musket burning his hands, the stone dust flying into his eyes and almost blinding him, the sweat pouring down his face, and a great hollow of nothingness swelling inside him.

Faces danced in the smoke but they were remote and faraway, little oblongs that were blurred by the perspiration pouring into his eyes. Still, he recognized them, his father, his mother, his sister, the Señor Teniente who had been so kind to him. They were all speaking at once, the tiny black holes of their mouths opening and closing, but he could not hear what they said. They were so far away and the noise was too loud. It was like the roaring of great rapids now. It did not matter what they said. Nothing mattered. Nothing but to keep the musket firing until it exploded in his hands. That was what he was there for and that was why he had not gone away with the other cadets. That was why the boy beside him hung hooked over the parapet, his musket on the ground and the blood gushing out of his mouth.

A tumult of fierce shouting rose from the southern side of the hill and although Lorenzo could not see he guessed that the enemy had crossed the ditches there and forced their way into the walled grounds that protected the foot of the rock. This shouting was re-echoed from the western slope and staring through the heavy fog of flying clods, bits of stone and gunpowder smoke he saw running figures and knew that the Americans were trying again to storm the fosse. They were directly below him and more than once he saw a clear face start out of the debris-blackened air and the evil glitter of bayonets. They were coming fast now, headed by a storming party bearing long ladders. He worked his musket as furiously as he could, ramming the charge home and firing point-blank at the bobbing heads. He saw an officer fall and another and then another. But they continued to come like an inexorable wave, pouring over their own dead and crowding at the edge of the fosse while the ladders were thrown outward and upward.

Cadets and infantrymen crowded about him, knocking him to right and left as they reached out and sought to thrust the ladders away from the parapet wall. One ladder, gray with a column of men, toppled backward and another fell sideways into the fosse. In the chaos he shot his ramrod away and began to use his musket as a club, swinging it at the heads below him until it slipped out of his hands and disappeared in the vortex of climbing men. Weaponless he reached over the parapet with his arms outstretched. Something hit him a sharp blow on the side of the head and he started to see things in flashes, now vividly, now not at all, and then vividly again. Scores of ladders were crashing against the walls and up them came columns of grimy men who loomed like giants in the glare and smoke. They yelled and whirled their bayoneted rifles with one hand. A blue flag bobbed by the barbican. And then a resistless tide poured over him and he had just time enough to cry "God and liberty!" as he fell beneath the heavy boots.

By nine-thirty Chapultepec, the impregnable, was taken and Nicolás Bravo, tears streaming down his face, had surrendered his diamond-hilted sword to a powder-blackened American officer. But Lorenzo knew nothing about it. He lay in a corner by the parapet, a crimson bayonet wound through his throat, stone-dead.

The fighting went on through the day. After clearing out all the Mexican troops in and around Chapultepec the red sashes and green banner with its gold eagle of the Mounted Rifles and the Palmetto flag of the South Carolinians began to move along the wide avenue of the Belén causeway toward the Belén garita. Running down the center of this avenue was a stone aqueduct some fifteen feet high supported by thick masonry pillars and it was through these that the Americans advanced, driving before them a small disorganized mass of Mexican infantry. About a mile from Chapultepec a two-gun battery covered by a field redan blocked the way but one small American gun reduced it in little more than an hour. The Palmettos and the Rifles continued to advance. Before them was the garita, the gate to the city, protected on the north by the formidable Citadel and strengthened by artillery. Coming within easy range they were met by a furious storm of bullets, grape and solid shot and suffered severe casualties. For a brief while they hesitated and sought shelter behind the pillars of the aqueduct, and then two guns, a long eighteen-pounder and a twenty-four-pounder howitzer, were brought up on either side of the causeway. These blasted away at the garita, bringing down heaps of rubble and masonry on the heads of the Mexican defenders and blowing such breaches in the parapets that the position no longer remained tenable. The Mexican troops withdrew, some barricading themselves in the Citadel and others fleeing into the midst of the city, and the Rifles crowded over the half-demolished fortifications with a shout of triumph. It was just twenty minutes past one in the early afternoon when the American general, Quitman, ordered the regimental flags hoisted in the very doorway of the capital.

In the meantime another column of American troops, under General Worth, had advanced along the more northerly Verónica causeway, similar in all respects to the Belén causeway, toward the San Cosme garita. This gate did not possess such defenses as the Belén garita but they were formidable enough to cause Worth some trouble. He was opposed by a well-manned parapet, a redoubt with embrasures at the garita, several cannon, rooftops crowded with troops and some guns in the Paseo. When his men came within range they were met with a hail of bullets, canister, grape and shells. But Worth was determined. He ordered troops forward under the protection of the arches toward the southern flank of the garita and others to burrow through the continuous line of deserted buildings on the other side to attack the northern flank. A young lieutenant named Ulysses S. Grant waded several ditches at the head of a squad dragging a howitzer and saw that it was planted on the roof of a church. Artillery fire drove the Mexicans from the parapet. Americans reached the roof of a three story house where they could fire down into the redoubt. They decimated the gunners and artillery mules. A flanking movement brought Worth's men into the garita and the Mexicans fled in a panic carrying along with them some reinforcements with Santa Anna himself at their head who were coming up to support the position. By six o'clock a United States flag was flying over a second doorway to the capital and by way of warning of what was to come a few shells were dropped near the National Palace.

Santa Anna was in conference with Olaguíbel, several of his generals and half a dozen delegates from the ayuntamiento. The sound of loud voices could be heard through the heavy door, and Juan Diego on his accustomed bench in the corridor, leaned back with his booted legs stretched out straight before him and watched the scowling uniformed officers and pasty-faced civilians who were waiting to see the general. They chattered and gestured but all their gabble meant nothing at all. Now that it was over, and the young officer knew that it was over, they could go on explaining to the end of time and it would mean no more than words ever meant. The explosion of the shell in the Grand Plaza had been the final response to all words. He had been rushing hither and thither all day through the streets and he knew how the people felt. He had seen fear and hysteria and fire and dead bodies and men covered with blood and women screaming from windows and he had heard the growling of the guns coming ever closer and the slap of running feet and the hard crackle of horses' hoofs and the screech and rumble of ammunition carts and mule-hauled cannon. Under the bright sun the capital had been like a madhouse where hordes of lunatics ran aimlessly in all directions. It was a terrible sight to see the population of a great city crazed by fear and to know that no discipline could whip them back into a state of sanity.

The fall of Chapultepec had been the final blow. When the rock fell the war was lost and Mexico City lay defenseless before the invader. Oh, there might be a little desperate fighting still but it would never regain what had been lost, and that was the heart of the Republic. The general could never defend the city now that the Americans had their feet in the doorway. What could he do with demoralized troops, a populace babbling with fear, and no fortifications? And, worse than that, antagonistic elements who called themselves patriots and yet weakened the ebbing strength of the government by slandering the general and conspiring against him? Unworthy men with unworthy hearts! They had reduced the clean fury of a great cause to a petty game of politics, playing one name against another and shifting their coats with the shifts of circumstance. Opportunists, all! That was what they were. Juan Diego couldn't summon up a rage about it now. It was too late and he had brooded about it too long. He was beginning to think that the bishop of Puebla was not so far wrong as he had supposed and that men who did not rise to the majesty of a great cause did not deserve to have that cause. In other words . . . Ah, he was too tired to think but he wondered if Texas and New Mexico and California would not be better off under the Yankee flag than the tricolor of the Republic. It wasn't that he had become a defeatist at the hour when all was lost, he reassured himself, but that he was seeing things differently. He was seeing the soil and the rights of the soil and the people who lived on the soil and the rights of the people who lived on the soil and if his thought phrased itself to him long-windedly that was because he wanted to feel his way and take a long time to reach the convictions he hesitated to face. Would the people of Texas and New Mexico and California be better off under the Stars and Stripes of the United States than they would be under the constantly changing, intriguing, dishonest governments of Mexico? That was the crux of it all and because an emotional patriotism still colored his mind he feared to set his reason free and let it reach its own conclusions uninfluenced by romantic fidelities.

There was some commotion in the flock of men who crowded the corridor and he saw Ezequiel Oropesa pushing his way toward the closed door of the general's office and herding before him three disheveled boys in the gray uniforms of Military College cadets. The tiredness fell from Juan Diego in a flash and he sprang to his feet as a stabbing thought dissipated all gloomy conjectures about the Republic. Lorenzo! He supposed that Don Isidro's son was somewhere in the city but now he would make sure. He hurried forward and halted Ezequiel Oropesa.

"These boys!" he exclaimed. "They are from Chapultepec?"

Ezequiel Oropesa nodded excitedly.

"Por Dios! yes," he replied. "They fought all day yesterday like veterans. Look, this fellow has a broken collarbone. His musket . . ."

Juan Diego caught the boy by the arm.

"Lorenzo Núñez de Haro y Gayoso de Lemos," he stuttered, recalling the full rolling names, both paternal and maternal, with some difficulty. "He was one of the younger cadets. Do you know him? Where is he now?"

The boy looked puzzled for a moment and then he nodded.

"Lorenzo Núñez," he said. "Yes, Señor Teniente, I know him. He was at the parapet facing the cypress grove. He wouldn't come when the rest of us were ordered to leave the college. He must be dead . . . or a prisoner."

Juan Diego stared in amazement at the tired young face.

"But . . . but all the cadets were removed from Chapultepec," he declared. "It was the general's order. I heard—"

"No," broke in the boy. "Some of them wouldn't come away."

"There's more than a hundred missing," added Ezequiel Oropesa. "Some of them must be killed. They were firing muskets at the Americans. Let this boy tell you about the inferno—"

"Wait!" ordered Juan Diego.

He dropped his hand from the boy's arm and peered into his face.

"Are you certain that Lorenzo Núñez did not leave the college with the other cadets?" he demanded in a taut voice that caused the others to stare at him with some concern.

"I am certain, Señor Teniente," answered the boy firmly. "I was in the very last group to leave and it was I who begged Lorenzo Núñez to come with us. He would not answer me or turn his head. I recall it clearly because the cadet beside him, young Manuel Puga y Roa, was already dead."

Juan Diego stood, half-leaning forward like a frozen figure, his eyes fixed imploringly on the boy's face.

There was a moment of awkward silence like a tiny island in the choppy sea of explosive conversation that filled the corridor.

"He may be a prisoner," remarked Ezequiel Oropesa at last in a hesitant voice. "He will probably be exchanged in a few days. The Americans won't want . . ."

His voice died away before the drawn mask of Juan Diego's face and he began to push the three cadets toward the general's door.

"Come along," he said. "It is time for you to receive your medals. Though what good they will . . ."

The rest of his speech was swallowed up in the hubbub of talk.

Officers and chattering civilians collided against the motionless figure of Juan Diego but he did not appear to notice them. He was suddenly convinced that Lorenzo was dead. Before his eyes danced the eager young face with its subtle reflection of Doña María Catalina's features and in its steadfast expression he seemed to see a vague and gentle accusation. He had promised Don Isidro to watch over the boy and now this was the way he had kept that pledge. There were so many things he could have done. He could have gone to Chapultepec and taken Lorenzo away. He could have explained precisely to the general why he was concerned about the cadets and the general would have taken him away. But he had done nothing. He had left it to Santa Anna and Santa Anna, as usual, had been too late and too indefinite. *Some of them wouldn't come away.* Of course not. Not after the assault started. They were not that type of boy. They wouldn't quit under fire. They were too young to know that there was more to a cause than bravery. They should have been marched into the city a day or two before the Americans moved toward Chapultepec. Juan Diego, moving like a sleepwalker, made his way back to the bench and sat down.

It seemed to him now that this final blow was an epitome of all that had happened since Taylor reached the Rio Grande, the sacrifice of youth and bravery by the old and sly and negligent. It was all wrong. Thousands had died for a cause that had been decided before the first battle started. Conniving men whose first thoughts had been for themselves and not the future of the Republic had instigated the slaughter for selfish and mercenary reasons, campaigning not for an ideal but for power, not for the people but for their own rapacious parties. And the same thing was probably true on the other side of the Rio Grande where men hungry for land and power were directing the destinies of a great people. But with a difference. *They* were struggling to seize but the Republic was struggling to retain. *They* were endeavoring to open up a new world to pioneering thousands but the Republic was endeavoring to close a world that was barely populated at all. *They* were growing by leaps and bounds but the Republic was standing still. Where, then, did justice lie? Where did it lie when Cortés and his conquistadores destroyed the Aztec Empire? Where did it lie when the Yanqui colonists drove the Indians from their lands? Where did it lie when Mexican revolutionaries broke the power of Spain? Where did it lie when Yanqui revolutionaries broke the power of England? It was the land itself that would have to give the answer, for the land was apart and belonged only to those who could fulfill its potentialities. Did it belong to the openers or the closers, to the developers or the ignorers, to the justifiers or the deniers? They were all settlers, they were all pioneers, they were all potential builders. It was only by their acts that they could justify themselves to the land. The hours passed, the gesticulating officers and civilians came and went in the corridor, generals passed in and out, and Juan Diego sat silent, his hand half-covering his eyes, while the questions that he could glimpse but not answer spun round and round in his head.

Toward midnight the general emerged from his office.

Juan Diego struggled to his feet as Santa Anna paused before him and ran his tongue over his thick lips.

"Juanillo," said the general, "get out of that uniform and put on civilian garb. I think it is best for you to remain here. I . . ."

He paused and shook his head.

"I am evacuating the city," he went on. "The troops are already moving toward Guadalupe Hidalgo. You can come with me if you like but I think it would be best for you to stay here. You can keep your eyes open and let me know what is happening. Have you any money? You can draw from the paymaster's office. I have already left directions there concerning a number of the younger aides."

"There is no hope of holding the city?" asked Juan Diego in a low voice.

"Dios mío, no!" replied Santa Anna. "The Americans will be in the Grand Plaza by tomorrow noon. What can I hold the city with? Do you know how many men I lost today? And five generals. Yes, five. Pérez killed and Bravo, Dosamantes, Noriega and Saldaña captured. And the City Council is bawling for surrender. I . . ."

He stepped forward impulsively and put his arm around the young officer's shoulder.

"Juanillo," he continued, fastening his dark bloodshot eyes on the other's face. "It may be some time before we see each other again. I intend to carry on a guerrilla warfare as long as I have half a dozen men with muskets who will follow me. Take good care of yourself for you are as dear to me as my own children. God willing, we will meet under happier circumstances."

He started to go and then came back again.

"I have spoken of you to several members of the ayuntamiento," he explained. "They will remember your name. If you encounter any trouble go to them. But take my advice and keep as quiet as you can. Wear civilian clothes always and do not tell any Americans who may question you that you are an officer. I will try to keep in touch with you at your address."

"Very well, my general," said Juan Diego.

Santa Anna appeared about to say something more and then turned away and strode rapidly down the corridor, the peg of his artificial leg striking rapidly on the tiled floor. Juan Diego watched him go with a grave face. He expected me to be more demonstrative, he thought, and he is disappointed. But he will not show it. He will never show a weakness in front of anybody and I am one of his weaknesses. He wants affection but he will not ask for it. He is tired but he will not admit it. He is defeated but he will not even hint it to himself.

He will go on like that as long as he can walk or think for that is the way God has fashioned him, restless, ambitious, the eternal conspirator and the everlasting self-worshiper. Now I know him completely and now I know what a danger he is to Mexico. That is why I could not respond to his moment of gentleness. And yet, God knows, I bear him a sort of love that is rooted so deeply within me that no knowledge of his flaws can kill it.

The young officer turned and walked slowly along the corridor to the door leading into the inner gardens of the palace. He was wondering what he would do on the morrow, watch the entry of the Americans most likely and then . . . Ah . . . if in some way he could get to the Military College on Chapultepec. If Lorenzo was a prisoner of war . . . But, no . . . Lorenzo was not a prisoner . . . he was dead. There was no doubt of that in his mind though why he was so convinced he could not say. And then the thought occurred to him that it was the eyes of Lorenzo that convinced him. He remembered the boy's eyes when he had said that the Republic should keep on fighting until the last man was killed and then it would not matter. He had meant that. Lorenzo was dead. And Doña María Catalina had loved him so.

Dark blocks of troops were moving through the streets toward the Peralvillo garita as the young officer walked toward his room in the Calle de Santa Clara.

Although he was up and abroad comparatively early the Americans were there before him. They had filtered in through the Belén garita shortly after daybreak, occupied the Citadel and the Alameda gardens and when Juan Diego entered the Grand Plaza, quietly dressed in brown civilian garb, he found dust-covered troops on the south and west sides and a grim-looking battery in the center. He was not the solitary observer of this occupation. Hundreds of Mexicans had risen with the dawn or not gone to bed at all and now they were pushing their way through the streets that emptied into the Grand Plaza and gazing with curiosity at the long-feared invaders. They seemed, for the most part, to have forgotten their fear and hysteria of the day before. Before the National Palace a company of United States Marines with white crossbelts stood on guard and voluble bystanders informed the young officer that there had been looting during the night, léperos breaking into the home of the president after the military watch had been withdrawn and plundering the elaborately furnished chambers. From the great flagstaff flew the Stars and Stripes. On the south side of the plaza a café had been opened and a crowd of the curious before its door explained that the American general, who was wearing only one shoe, and some of his officers were inside just finishing their breakfasts. Surprisingly enough, they ate meat so early in the day.

A bright sun was rising over the cathedral. Sidewalks, housetops, balconies and windows blossomed with hundreds of faces and an approaching blare of regimental bands added a festive note to the morning. Juan Diego pushed his way through the spectators, automatically noticing that many among them were ragged villainous-faced fellows with lowering countenances, and reached a point of vantage directly before the great door to the cathedral. He could see everything from here. Curiously enough, he felt quite calm. He had slept well despite the grief he felt over Lorenzo and the disillusionment he had experienced concerning the ignominious concluding scenes of the war and he supposed that was because he had been so weary. The heart and brain could endure so much and then a sort of numb trance intervened and protected one from madness. It was with a sort of cold objectivity, then, that he examined the American soldiers who were still drawn up in battle line on the broad plaza. It seemed to him that they appeared harder and surer in military bearing than he remembered them from La Angostura. They had been bad troops when they started but now there was about them a machinelike strength that was impressive and born of experience and a bath of unforgettable flame. They had grown in stature with the months while the Mexican soldiers, for all their erratic dash and unpredictable bravery, had dwindled. They were the sort of men whom defeat would make more dogged while the Mexicans in defeat became too often like hysterical women. It was the difference in the blood, in the breed, in endurance and deep-veined confidence. Juan Diego seemed to glimpse a prophecy of the future in these long motionless lines standing beneath the glittering bayonets.

A regimental band playing "Washington's March" turned into the plaza and made its way to one side of the central entrance of the National Palace. The sun was reflected in bright shifting spots from the brass instruments. In the distance a sound of cheering cut through the air. Another band passed the cathedral. It was playing "Hail to the Chief." The wave of cheering drew nearer until it seemed to beat like an invisible wave against the cornices of the stone houses and then from the northwest angle of the square a body of mounted troops appeared and filed to the right along the west side and when on a line with the front of the cathedral turned to the left. Arms were presented, colors lowered and drums beaten. Juan Diego stared at the imposing figure in full-dress uniform, gold epaulets and snowy plumes, mounted on a heavy bay charger, who led the procession. So that was Scott. He was a monster of a man, larger than life-size and with a florid regality about him that was impressive and theatrical at the same time. His gesture of uncovering as he accepted the salutes and cheers of his men was majestic and deliberate. Santa Anna, beside him, would have seemed like a dwarf.

The crowd began to surge forward and Juan Diego, forced along with it, found himself being carried toward the long façade of the National Palace where he had passed so many uncertain days and nights. American cavalrymen with drawn sabers formed a hedge against the mass of pushing people but a constant trickle of the more adventurous passed between the horses and the young officer, somewhat to his surprise, found himself with them. He was less encompassed with perspiring bodies now and he stood somewhat apart watching Scott dismount with cumbersome dignity from his charger and pass through the puerta cochera to the broad stairway of the palace. A large group of officers, smiling and exultant, followed him. The loud voice of the commander could be heard making some proclamation to his staff as he entered the Halls of the Moctezumas and a moment or so later an aide appeared and fastened a sheet of paper to the wall. Juan Diego glanced casually at this aide for an instant and then an exclamation of amazement and joy burst from his lips. It was his brother, David.

"David! David!" he called impulsively and running forward plunged headlong into the crossed rifles of two American Marines.

"Hold on there, Mexicano!" ordered one of them. "Where do you think you're going?"

"That's my brother!" declared Juan Diego excitedly in English. "Let me through. I must speak to him."

David was already disappearing under the puerta cochera.

"There ain't nobody goin' in there without a pass," said the other Marine. "You git a pass an' we'll let you through. Where'd you learn to speak English anyway?"

"I want to see my brother," insisted Juan Diego. "He just went into the palace. Let me through."

A dozen curious onlookers were gathering about the three men and the two Marines began to look concerned and exasperated.

"Look here, Mexicano!" threatened the one who had spoken first. "If you don't want a piece of steel in your guts you'll get on your way. I told you before that nobody can go into the palace who ain't got a pass. Can you understand English as well as you can speak it?"

With an effort of self-will Juan Diego recovered his reason and desisted. He stepped back from the crossed guns.

"Very well," he said. "Where can I get a pass?"

Both Marines shook their heads. One of them looked around and observed that a strong guard was being posted under the puerta cochera.

"I dunno," he replied. "You go and ask the sergeant there. Maybe he knows."

Juan Diego passed the armed men and approached the familiar entrance. A few Mexicans who had passed the guards were gathered before the posted sheet of paper and attempting to puzzle out what was written upon it.

"I'd like to speak to the sergeant on duty," explained the young officer to a soldier who was lolling against the square pillar of the puerta cochera. He was feeling cool and matter-of-fact now that the first surprise at his one-sided encounter had subsided. After all, it had been the most natural thing in the world. He had known that sooner or later he would run across David again.

The soldier inspected Juan Diego from head to foot deliberately, squirted a long brown stream from his mouth and turned lazily.

"You wait here," he said.

Juan Diego occupied himself in reading the posted notice while he waited. It was marked "General Order No. 284" and it ran:

Headquarters of the Army.
Mexico, September 14, 1847.

1. Under the favor of God, the valor of this army after many glorious victories has hoisted the colors of our country in the capital of Mexico and on the Palace of its Government.

2. But the war is not ended. The Mexican army and Government have fled, only to watch an opportunity to return upon us with vengeance. We must then be upon our guard.

3. Companies and regiments will be kept together and all stand on the alert. Our safety is in military discipline.

4. Let there be no drunkenness, no disorders, no straggling. Stragglers will be in great danger of assassination, and marauders shall be punished by courts-martial.

5. All the rules so honorably observed by this glorious army in Puebla must be observed here. The honor of the army and the honor of our country call for the best behavior on the part of all. To win the approbation of their country, the valiant must be sober, orderly, and merciful. His noble brethren in arms will not be deaf to this hearty appeal from their commander and friend.

6. Major-General Quitman is appointed civil and military Governor of Mexico.

By command of Major-General Scott.

H. L. Scott,
Assistant Acting Adjutant General.

"What do you want?" rasped an impatient voice at Juan Diego's side and he turned from the General Order to face a plump red-faced sergeant with little blue suspicious eyes.

"I want to see Lieutenant David Livingston," he declared with some assurance. "I just saw him go into the palace."

"Are you on official business?" demanded the sergeant. "You're a Mexican, aren't you?"

"I am a Mexican," answered Juan Diego steadily, "but I know Lieutenant Livingston. Will you tell him—"

"I won't tell him anything," broke in the sergeant rudely. "If you want to communicate with the lieutenant you can write a letter to him. We don't trust any of you fellows. You'd stick a knife in our backs as soon as look at us. Get along now or I'll put you under arrest."

"It would do you no harm to take—" began Juan Diego but the sergeant interrupted him with an oath.

"Be off!" he shouted. "And keep away from these doors because we're liable to shoot first and ask questions afterwards. I saw you cowardly bastards murdering the wounded at the Mill. I'll bet you're a soldier in disguise. I'll bet . . ."

Juan Diego turned abruptly and walked away from the puerta cochera ignoring the bellowed insults of the sergeant. The Americans, he sensed, were on edge and uncertain how the populace of the capital was going to react to the occupation. They saw a potential assassin in every man who approached them. Well, he would go back to his room and write a letter to his brother and have the boy who lived on the ground floor deliver it to the palace. He pushed his way past the American battery observing with an automatically critical eye how well polished the guns were. He wondered if this was part of the artillery that had reduced Chapultepec. Chapultepec. David would make it possible for him to visit the scarred ruin of the Military College and find Lorenzo. Perhaps . . . but no. There was no time for illusions now. Nothing mattered but the realities. It would be good to talk to David again. And they would talk in a way different from their alienated meeting and parting at the hacienda of Buena Vista. David would find that he had changed, that he could face and accept the actualities and not quite forget the dream either. David had seemed so familiar as he raised his arm to fix the General Order to the pink wall. So familiar, indeed, that after the first shock of surprise it seemed quite natural, quite in the ordinary course of events, to see him there in the Grand Plaza of Mexico City. I am closer to David, he thought suddenly, than I am to the general.

He had just turned into the Calle de Plateros when he heard the sharp report of a musket and immediately after two more explosions. A man ran past him and dove into the narrow entrance of an alley. Another report sounded from a nearby housetop and then several in rapid succession from the direction of the Alameda. The street was swiftly clearing and he could hear the slamming doors and shutters on all sides. He broke into a dogtrot and turned down the Calle del Espíritu Santo. The fools, the damned fools, he thought savagely, what do they think they will gain by sniping at the Americans? Do they want Scott to blow the city to pieces? The sunny air was punctuated by sharp reports that appeared to sound from all directions now and he could hear the thudding of many boots on the streets behind him. Of course. The Americans would force their way into those houses that protected snipers and clean them out as farmers clean out rats' nests. Oh, the damned, damned fools! He jogged into his own street and just had his hand on the door of the house where he lived when he heard the blasting bellow of a cannon. If Scott raked the streets . . . He mounted the stairs to his single chamber and sat down at the table. No matter what happened he must get his message to David. If the boy below was too scared to carry it to the National Palace he would go himself. He drew the paper and pen and ink toward him and began to compose his letter while the sporadic flat reports of the invisible muskets continued outside his window.

He did not dare leave his room for fear of missing his brother. The boy below, his avariciousness for a peso outweighing his fear of the gunfire, had delivered the message, he swore, to a regular officer with epaulets who was standing in the shelter of the puerta cochera. The officer had said that it would be handed to Lieutenant Livingston. And then the boy had gone into a lurid description of what was happening in the streets. Hundreds of blanketed léperos were attacking the Americans but the Americans were driving them back and shooting them down. It was fairly safe around the National Palace where the Grand Plaza had been cleared of all people. But in the side streets the chaos was awful. The Yanquis were sweeping them with grape and canister and blowing in the front of every house from which came a musket shot. The ayuntamiento was posting notices imploring the people to desist from guerrilla tactics but it was not the people, the respectable people, who were fighting. It was the léperos, the beggars and criminals. Apparently the boy had listened well. The léperos, it seemed, were organized and murdering and pillaging in well-defined districts. More than two thousand convicts had been let out of the jails through some mysterious influence and were fighting with the léperos. The jailkeepers swore that they had received signed orders from Santa Anna to release the prisoners. Juan Diego grew thoughtful as he listened and after the boy had gone downstairs to repeat the story to his mother who was cowering in the wine cellar he walked up and down the room with impatient rapidity as he put two and two together.

This, then, was the enterprize in which Don Alejandro was engaged. There could be no doubt of it. He had been one of the organizers of the léperos and he had been seen visiting the jails. The orders to release the prisoners were probably forged. But what could be the reason for it all? What good could accrue to Don Alejandro and the unknown men he served (Valencia? Paredes? The Antisantanistas?) by arranging a treacherous attack on the Americans? And then it occurred to Juan Diego that that might be one way of occasioning the complete collapse of the Republic. What if Scott retaliated and destroyed the city? What if the government, unable to preserve any order, flung up its hands and resigned? What would happen then? What would emerge from such a debacle? A monarchy? The resumption of Spanish rule? Annexation by the United States? Or a hundred years of internal warfare? Juan Diego literally wrung his hands in anguish as the house shook with the reverberation of guns and the very foundations of Mexico City seemed to quiver beneath him. Why didn't David come? And would he come at all? Perhaps he was fighting in the streets. Perhaps he wouldn't come at all. Perhaps . . .

And then he heard quick feet running up the stairs, the door swung open and he saw his brother standing on the threshold.

"I have been waiting for you for a long time," he said abruptly and David appeared to accept the statement without surprise.

"I was in the plaza," he said breathlessly, "and returned to the palace only a half hour ago. Lieutenant Cousins gave me your letter."

The two men smiled at each other and then approached and clasped hands. It did not seem strange to either to meet so unexpectedly and Juan Diego, observing the brick-red sunburnt countenance of David, seemed for an instant to be back in San Felipe and listening at the door for his father's unsteady steps. The world was smaller than he had imagined and its linked chains ignored boundaries and years. Again a feeling of inevitability blotted out all other emotions and he accepted David's presence as he would have accepted the spectacle of Don Isidro moving ponderously through the open portal with his heavy underlip thrust out. These things happened without apparent reason but if one thought for a moment they were only a part of a natural evolution of given circumstances. He was sure now that he had always expected the Americans to occupy Mexico City and that David would be with them and that he would see David in the very shadow of the National Palace. He cleared his throat and indicated a chair to his brother but the other did not sit down. He continued to shake Juan Diego's hand gently and gaze into his face.

"I was wondering when we would meet," he said. "I thought it might be at the Cerro Gordo and I feared that. Then I thought it would be in Puebla. I'm glad that it happened this way. You've changed, Charley. You look older. What has happened?"

"Everything . . . and nothing," replied Juan Diego. "David, I want you to help me. Can you arrange for me to visit Chapultepec? There was a boy there . . . I think he is dead . . . I want—"

"A friend of yours?" questioned David quickly. "I think so. I believe the Fifteenth Infantry is at Chapultepec. But it will be dangerous going through the streets now. Those damned murderers . . ."

He waved his hand toward the window where the sharp reports of muskets and the thud of cannon still sounded.

"I know!" declared Juan Diego. "Those men are traitors who

want to destroy the Republic. They are the scourings of the city who have been organized by secret agents in the pay of evil forces."

David looked skeptical.

"We believe that Santa Anna arranged this," he said shortly.

"No, no," protested Juan Diego. "I will tell you. I know something about this rising."

And rapidly he explained his suspicions of Don Alejandro and the encounter at the Four Roses of Xochimilco. David listened attentively and when the younger man had finished he nodded his head.

"It is possible," he said. "But you need not worry about the destruction of Mexico City. General Scott is a humane man and we will run these rats to earth before the day is over."

He turned suddenly toward the door.

"Let's visit this cantina," he suggested. "Perhaps your man is there or somebody who knows him. If there is . . ."

There was a grim note in his voice.

Juan Diego snatched up his hat and followed him but on the threshold David paused and put his arm about the other's shoulders.

"I am glad to have found you again," he said with some effort and then ran down the stairs.

Juan Diego followed more slowly. It was movement that David wanted, rapid movement that would stifle all emotionalism or sublimate it into violent gestures. The younger brother could guess that. North of the Rio Grande men rarely expressed their affection for one another. They were a colder breed, more self-conscious, afraid of anything that suggested weakness, and love was a weakness. They didn't understand these things or if they did they suppressed the knowledge beneath a bluffness that was hard for the warm-blooded Mexican to comprehend. The two types simply didn't respond in the same way and neither took the trouble to find out what deep springs animated the other. There was too much ignorance here, too scornful a refusal to take the trouble to understand, too self-satisfied a dwelling in their respective caves of tradition. They needed to know one another better and they required patience and an abeyance of prejudices for that. Was David afraid that he might kiss him? That gesture of the arm must have been embarrassing.

There was a squad of a dozen men armed with rifles at the door and they fell in behind the two brothers as Juan Diego led the way toward the Four Roses of Xochimilco. The streets were deserted except for slowly moving bodies of American troops although the sporadic sound of gunfire still continued in the near distance. They passed several house fronts that had been blown in and rooms filled with smashed furniture gaped like crazy stage scenes. A man's body lay face downward across the pavement and they skirted it, stepping carefully to avoid a long splash of viscous blood. A stink of gunpowder permeated the air. When they reached the cantina it seemed untouched although the houses on either side gaped with empty window frames.

"It is here," said Juan Diego.

David tersely ordered half the squad to remain outside while the others followed him into the tavern. It was dim in the small room still crowded with tables and Juan Diego thought it was deserted until in one corner he saw a man sitting motionless with both hands resting on the wet board before him. The soldiers moved forward with leveled bayonets. The man did not stir. A sergeant reached out and grasped the motionless figure by the hair, forcing the head back.

"Jesus Christ!" he exclaimed. "This feller's dead. He ain't got no face at all!"

Juan Diego leaned down and stared into the red mask. For an instant he thought . . . But no, this man was too tall. He had a long neck, and when the sergeant released his grip on the greasy black hair the head fell sideways like a smashed melon.

"You'll never recognize him, mister," declared the noncommissioned officer.

"His pistol must have exploded," remarked David, kicking some fragments of metal that lay on the floor.

"Right in his ugly mug," added the sergeant.

Juan Diego straightened up.

"It is not Don Alejandro," he said in a shaky voice.

David glanced quickly at his brother but the younger man was turning away. Somewhere . . . Far back in Juan Diego's memory a figure with a red mask for a face was reeling through clouds of smoke, rebounding from stone walls like a chicken with its head cut off. He shut his eyes and heard the quick reverberation of cannon. Yesterday . . . but it was today. This firing that he heard was in the streets of Mexico City. This man without a face . . .

"There's no one here," said David sharply.

He was still looking at his brother.

"No . . . there's no one here," repeated Juan Diego.

The sergeant and his men, who had been prowling around the room and in the premises behind, gathered about David.

"The liquor's all gone, too," remarked the sergeant in a disgusted tone.

"Them damn Marines," said one of the soldiers.

"General Scott has issued specific orders about intoxicating beverages," pointed out David in a precise tone. He kept looking at his brother.

The soldiers grinned at one another.

Juan Diego moved toward the door.

"Come," he said sharply. "Let us get out of here."

David averted his eyes from his brother and all of them tramped out into the street. A bullet spat viciously past Juan Diego's ear and thwacked into the stone wall of the cantina.

"The bastard's in that window!" shouted one of the soldiers, pointing to the second floor of the house opposite. There was a rush of heavy boots, the crashing of a door, shouts, two loud musket reports and after a moment the sergeant and one of his men reappeared dragging a limp form between them.

"Got him through the chest," explained the sergeant triumphantly. "He had five old French muskets up there and was just about to fire again."

They dumped the body down before the two brothers. The wounded man was whistling as he breathed and he tried to turn over, clutching at the stones with dirty fingers.

"Señor . . ." he gasped. "I remember you . . . I saw . . ."

Juan Diego bent swiftly and stared into the gray face.

"I know this man," he said. "He is the mestizo I told you about. Servando Herrera; that is his name."

The mestizo coughed dryly like a goat. He tried to lift his head.

"I have seen you on your own horse in the Paseo," he babbled. "You are a great man. Give me a peso, señor. Death to the Yanquis. God and liberty."

Juan Diego knelt beside the prostrate man.

"Listen, Servando Herrera," he said. "I remember you. I saw you the other night in this cantina. I bought you a glass of aguardiente. Do you remember the man called Don Alejandro? The Spaniard? Where is he now? Is he hiding in the city?"

"Don Alejandro," repeated the mestizo. "He is a great man. He rides his own horse in the Paseo. Give me a peso, señor."

"What is he saying?" demanded David.

"Wait," said Juan Diego.

He bowed his face close to the wounded man's ear.

"Where is Don Alejandro now?" he asked slowly. "Where is he hiding? Tell me and I will give you five pesos."

"He is not here," replied Servando Herrera with difficulty. "He has gone away. He left by the Peralvillo garita after the cavalry passed through it. See, I am telling you the truth, señor. Now will you give me a peso?"

A paroxysm of coughing twisted him on the stones.

"Where has he gone?" persisted Juan Diego. "Where did Don Alejandro go?"

"He went away on his fine horse," murmured the mestizo weakly. "I do not know where he went. Mateo Báez commanded this section.

He told us first to fire on the troops of Santa Anna and then last night he told us to fire on the Americans. I am very tired, señor. I am sleepy. Give me a peso and let me go to sleep."

Suddenly he sat upright.

"I want a priest," he said in a thick voice. "Give me . . ."

He gurgled in his throat and fell grotesquely sideways, his head striking hollowly on the pavement stone. Juan Diego rose slowly to his feet.

"He's dead," he explained to David and then told him what the mestizo had said.

"It's plain enough," commented the other. "God alone knows where this Don Alejandro is now. He may be in the city, he may be dead or he may be on his way to join the guerrillas. There are bands of them all the way from here to Vera Cruz. Shall we go to the palace? I think General Scott should be informed about the rascals back of this rising. And I will speak to General Quitman concerning passes for Chapultepec."

They set off through the streets, passing the same sorry spectacle of gutted houses, demolished walls and here and there a dead body. A few timorous-looking faces peered momentarily through barred windows and then disappeared. A number of shops had been sacked and the debris from them littered the pavement and roadway. Americans with fixed bayonets on their rifles moved cautiously through the ruins. The Grand Plaza was crowded with troops and several batteries of unlimbered guns covered its every approach. The firing appeared to have slackened although occasional reports sounded from the direction of the Alameda. A gray pall of smoke rose above the city and the sun shone strangely through it with a subdued light. It was hard to believe that it was only about noon.

Before the puerta cochera of the National Palace David hesitated.

"You'd better remain here," he said self-consciously. "We might as well avoid any awkward questions."

Then he turned to the sergeant.

"Remain here, sergeant," he ordered, "and see that my . . . my friend is not molested in any way."

He hurried into the Palace.

While he waited Juan Diego studied the moving companies of American troops, the glistening guns and the long row of artillery horses and mules that stretched along one side of the plaza. He recognized again a capability that was lacking in the more disorderly massings of Mexican soldiers with their flocks of soldaderas and muttering priests. Presently his eye caught the white flash of the posted notice on the wall and walking over to it he saw that a new proclamation had

been fixed just below General Order No. 284. It was signed by Veramendi, President of the ayuntamiento, and it read:

The general in charge of the American forces which have occupied
the city this morning has informed the Ayuntamiento that if within three
hours, counted from the time this notice is posted, there is not an entire
cessation of the acts of hostility now being committed with palpable impru-
dence and to the grave prejudice of the peaceable citizens, he will proceed
with all rigor against the guilty, permitting their goods and property to be
sacked and razing the block in which are situated the houses from which
American troops are fired upon.

The sergeant watched Juan Diego read the Spanish words and a
bewildered expression spread across his face.

"Say, mister, what are you anyway?" he asked. "I hear you
speak English and I hear you talk that Mexican gibberish. You look
like a Mexican but you're a friend of the lieutenant's. Where do you
come from?"

"I was born in Massachusetts," replied Juan Diego gravely.

A glint of interest flashed in the sergeant's eyes.

"Are you in the secret service?" he asked in a hoarse whisper
although no one was near enough to hear what was being said.

Juan Diego shook his head.

"No," he said flatly.

The sergeant squinted his eyes in perplexity, rubbed his unshaven
face, scratched his head and fumbled for his twist of chewing tobacco.
He bit off a great cud with some ferocity and started to chew with
astonishing rapidity.

" 'Tain't none of my business," he said mildly.

A year ago, thought Juan Diego with some surprise, I would have
proclaimed without any hesitation or forethought at all that I was a
Mexican patriot. But this was for the sake of David. He didn't know
what David desired and until he did he would continue to be a cipher.
My friend. He had not said brother. One had to be careful in an occupied city in time of war. All the same . . .

David came through the puerta cochera with a cheerful expression
on his face. He thrust his arm through Juan Diego's and began to
walk him across the plaza.

"I didn't see General Scott," he explained. "He was closeted with
some of your City Council. But I reported to the adjutant general and
he is quite interested in your Don Alejandro and his ruffians. He tells
me that the city is pretty well under control now. There are a few
snipers holding out in the northwest corner but we'll clean them out
before night. Are you hungry? I am."

"And Chapultepec?" asked Juan Diego anxiously.

"Oh, yes," said David. "I have a pass for you. We'll go out to-morrow morning. What do you say . . ."

"Tomorrow!" exclaimed the younger brother in disappointment. "Why can't we go this afternoon?"

"Military orders," announced David succinctly. "They're counting prisoners and making inventories of supplies and they don't want any visitors. What does it matter? They're not removing any prisoners and if the boy is . . ."

He caught himself and began to whistle self-consciously between his teeth.

"The boy is dead, all right," said Juan Diego calmly.

David continued to whistle for a minute and then he pressed his brother's arm.

"Tell me about him," he demanded.

"There isn't much to tell," explained Juan Diego, frowning at the mottled smoke in the sky before them. "He is the son of a friend of mine and I promised to keep an eye on him while I was in Mexico City. I failed."

"I see," nodded David, although he sensed that what his brother had said was pretty much of an evasion. "I'm sorry. In a time of war it is difficult to do all the things one promises to do. There is no harm, though, in hoping that the boy is still alive."

"Hope is a pretty brittle reed," exclaimed Juan Diego bitterly.

Again, as he had done in the Four Roses of Xochimilco, David glanced quickly at his brother's set face. He didn't know what to say and yet he was intensely curious about Juan Diego's abrupt reactions. But he wouldn't ask questions or argue. No one got anywhere by argument and he recalled somewhat ruefully his last meeting with his brother the night after the battle of Buena Vista. He would never commit that mistake again. Now that he had found Charley he meant to retain him on any terms that he desired. As though he was conscious of this determination Juan Diego turned and smiled.

"We have a lot to talk about, David," he said, "but the time has not come for it yet."

It was good to walk along arm in arm with one's own blood.

"If you are hungry," he went on, "I believe my landlady will prepare us something to eat. Shall we try her?"

"Excellent!" declared David. "I don't feel like the officers' mess and as I have a free hour or two I would like to remain with you. Your landlady's food won't burn my throat out, will it?"

"She uses peppers," admitted Juan Diego, "but I'll warn her to control her natural instincts."

They turned into the Calle de Santa Clara.

After David left, swearing that Señora Alcalá's spiced horse meat was the best in the world, Juan Diego lay down on the couch in his chamber and put his arms over his head. He was not tired physically but he found himself fighting against a weariness of the mind that dulled the corners of his thoughts and caused them to evaporate into nothingness just when they ought to be fixed. He was aware that his brother had fought shy of any comments that might bring up the fact that theoretically they were on opposing sides and therefore enemies and he was glad of it. But he knew that this tacit avoidance of the one subject that was engrossing them both could not go on forever. They would have to face it and the sooner they faced it the better it would be for both of them. What did David desire and what did he see in the future? And what, thought Juan Diego, do I desire and what do I see in the future? He knew what he desired but he could not pierce the heavy veil of the future. He would need help for that and perhaps David would supply it. David, too, it appeared, had learned a lot in a year, the wisdom of silence, for instance, and the futility of insistence. A man reached his conclusions in his own way and when he needed help he asked for it. Well, David was coming back at six o'clock with some officer friend whom he wanted to surprise and shock with the spiced horse meat and perhaps he could indicate then that he desired help. They would not talk because there would be a stranger there but the way would be cleared for those revelations which had to come, those stumbling expressions which might become miracles and translate perplexity into illumination. They would talk tomorrow when they were alone. After they had found Lorenzo . . . Juan Diego moved uneasily on the couch. A single report in the distance warned him that bloodshed was still going on in the city. Men were still killing men. He lay there listening for another report but before it came he had passed into a light doze in which a green willow bowed above him and the odor of roses delicately assailed his nostrils. He awoke suddenly, not realizing that a shot had disturbed him, and lay staring at the ceiling.

David's friend was a plump young first lieutenant with an uncut mass of sandy hair that looked like a wig and quick blue eyes that appeared to observe and estimate everything incessantly. He looked at the walls, he looked at the ceiling, he looked at the furniture, he tested the bed by sitting down on it, he inspected the legs of the table, he peered out the window, he studied the boy who brought up the savory-smelling stew, he ran his eyes over Juan Diego from head to foot and he looked under the chair before he sat down in it. His name was Cousins. The rich spicy fumes of the dish delighted him and he mumbled compliments while he shoved bits of meat into his mouth.

"It is delicious," he declared. "Do you remember that chicken stew we had with Colonel Davis in Saltillo, David? Well, this is better."

"I can't imagine a better end for an old horse," agreed David, sopping up the dark gravy with a folded tortilla.

"No, sir," said Lieutenant Cousins ecstatically, "I can't imagine a better . . . hey, what did you say? What's that?"

He put his fork down hastily and glanced from the stew to David.

"Horse meat is really good," announced David calmly as he reached for another tortilla. "I wonder we don't eat more of it in the States."

Lieutenant Cousins pushed his plate away while a contemplative look spread across his features.

"I don't think I want any more," he said. "I'm not so hungry as I was."

"This is so much better than that chicken stew in Saltillo," insisted David as he pushed a big chunk of meat into his mouth.

Lieutenant Cousins viewed him with some distaste.

"I was trained in the cavalry," he declared. "You're a loathsome fellow, David. I hope you choke."

He got up and began to walk around the chamber.

"So this is Mexico City," he announced to nobody in particular and began to sing:

> "I'm stumpless quite since from the shot
> Of Cerro Gordo peggin',
> I left behind, to pay Gen Scott,
> My grub, and gave my leg in.
> I dare not turn to view the place
> Lest Yankee foes should find me,
> And mocking shake before my face
> The Leg I Left Behind Me."

David glanced at Juan Diego with some concern but he saw only vague smile on his brother's face. Cousins went on trolling:

> "Should Gen Taylor of my track get scent,
> Or Gen Scott beat up my quarters,
> I may as well just be content
> To go across the waters.
> But should that my fortune be,
> Fate has not quite resigned me
> For in the museum I will see
> The Leg I Left Behind Me."

"He does that on horse meat," said David to Juan Diego. "You ould see what he does on chicken."

"Curse you!" exclaimed Cousins. "I feel my stomach turning over and over like a caisson wheel."

He came back to the table and sat down.

"What I need is an alcoholic stimulant," he declared. "I take it as a sort of medicine and antidote to the genus called *hippus*. God damn it, David, you ride horses, you don't eat 'em."

Juan Diego got up and went over to a wall cupboard and produced a bottle of aguardiente and three glasses which he brought back to the table.

"A veritable Ganymede," remarked Cousins admiringly.

He swallowed the contents of a glass and began to splutter and choke. Tears ran down his plump cheeks.

"Your friend has poisoned me," he stuttered. "Send for the guard. Put lilies on my grave."

"You'll recover," said David placidly as he finished eating and pushed his plate away.

He looked from Juan Diego's smiling countenance to Cousins' flushed features and an expression of gravity crept across his face. He wanted to say something and he did not quite know how to say it. For the moment he felt the incongruity of his position, an officer of an occupying army in a surrendered city, and a sense of uneasiness beset him, a feeling that all this unthinking acceptance of one's status was too superficial and bound to miss the real significance of it all. He was where he should not be and yet inevitable circumstances had brought him to this place. He couldn't explain it to himself but it troubled him. Cousins could be at home anywhere for he lived almost boisterously inside of himself, or, at least, in the wide thoughtless shadow of his own ego. It was good to be that way. It was American. He could go around the earth and in every place that he stopped he would be American demanding American things, extolling American food and establishing American ways and quite regardless of the feelings of the natives. It took a lot of confidence to be that way . . . and a lot of ignorance. Charley, without knowing it, had taught him that much.

This was Charley's city. It was the capital of Charley's land. And knowing the unmentioned abyss that yawned between his brother and himself he could realize that there was much about it that he did not know and should know, that it had a soul and a heart that was like no other soul and heart on earth, that it possessed an integrity of *being* that was foreign to him and would be insulted by an easy superiority. Insulted . . . or silently indifferent. Why didn't Cousins, who was a good fellow at heart, see that? Was it insensitivity or just the eternal braggadocio of the Yankee? Yet he knew that if a Mexican officer had trolled a ditty filled with contemptuous references to the aging bulk of Winfield Scott, say, Cousins, here in Mexico City or back in Washing-

ton, especially in Washington, would have flown into a fury. The bald
eagle would have screamed. It was curious, the instinctive ease with
which the Yankee could be himself in a foreign land and yet resent the
strangeness of a foreigner in the States. If this insularity abroad was
true of all peoples, why was it particularly noticeable in Americans, in
Yanquis? And why, for that matter, did citizens of the United States
think of themselves as Americans, taking the name of the continent
and refusing it to those who dwelt south and north of them? They
were *all* Americans and it was time they found out about each other.
Here again Charley, without saying a word, by the mere fact of his
existence, had taught him something. To admit less would be to destroy Charley.

"I perceive words of wisdom big in your mouth," said Cousins,
staring at him with inquisitive blue eyes. "What is it, David? A dissertation on roast horse?"

David roused from his reflective attitude guiltily and shook his
head.

"No," he replied. "No dissertation. I was . . . I was wondering
if you had placed my friend Juan Diego, yet. Do you . . ."

He never knew what impulse had caused him to introduce the
subject.

Cousins poured a little aguardiente into his glass with great care
and without glancing in Juan Diego's direction.

"Of course," he said. "He is your brother."

He lifted the glass and sniffed it suspiciously before he took a sip.

"Moderation in all things," he remarked. "This should be imbibed
drop by drop with a prayer after each drop. Did you take me for a
fool, David?"

"No," answered David confusedly. "But . . . is it as plain as
that?"

"As plain as the two noses on your two faces," declared Cousins,
"and they are exactly alike. No. It is more than a likeness. It is a *feel*.
I just knew you were brothers."

"Yet we are very different," broke in Juan Diego quickly. "I
don't see how . . . I am Mexican and David . . ."

"Fiddlesticks!" interrupted Cousins. "You are no more Mexican
than I am. You only think you are. Let me offer you some of your own
aguardiente."

Juan Diego pushed his glass forward and studied Cousins' face
as the American poured the liquor. It was a perfectly blank face at the
moment although the ever-living eyes seemed to sparkle with an inward
amusement. His words, a practical dismissal of the whole subject, had
aroused conflicting conjectures. Was it as easy as that? After eleven
years' immersion in Mexican life as a Mexican was he, Juan Diego

de Béxar, so manifestly Yanqui that the first Yanqui to sit at table with him could spot him at once? Did Don Isidro and Doña María Catalina recognize him as a foreigner? What was a foreigner, anyway? And this opened a whole train of thoughts that extended across the entire horizon of his mind. Had he started with a misconception? Was he trying to be something that never existed? Was his idea of a Mexican an alien one and no part of the blood-born native south of the Rio Grande? Perhaps that explained why he was so at odds with his immediate world, so dissatisfied with the Republic and the men who conducted its affairs. Perhaps he desired to be the citizen of a Mexico that was only a dream, an ideal land of his own creation, the gigantic insubstantial child of a great wish. Where was he, then? And where was his country?

He drank the aguardiente and found it exceptionally vile.

"It's a bad bottle," he said. "I don't blame you for choking."

"I can't understand how you found out that Charley was my brother," declared David, still confused in mind and manner. "I don't think there is such a—"

"Second sight," announced Cousins tersely. "I'm a mind reader. Have some of this filthy aguardiente. Your brother keeps it to poison his brother's friends. Not that I am any friend of yours, David. A man who will inveigle an innocent soldier into devouring half a horse is completely lacking in all the qualities of friendship. Come, damn you, drink and suffer as I do."

"I don't want any," said David.

He was still puzzled.

Juan Diego glanced at his brother and saw the bewilderment and wondered briefly if it was occasioned by irritability. But it couldn't be. David was floundering toward something, too, something that included *him,* and Cousins' easy identification had either stopped or started something. Yes, they would have to talk together soon, perhaps after they found Lorenzo tomorrow, and when they talked David would be surprised to discover . . . why, to discover how close they were and how a year had shifted his younger brother's conception of things. But the moment for talking would have to come of itself. The moment . . . The voice of Cousins broke in on what was turning into a reverie.

"If you chaps continue to fall into trances," said the first lieutenant emphatically, "I shall pack up the bottle of aguardiente and return to the National Palace with it. Bad as it is, it is more companionable than you two Aztec mummies."

Juan Diego laughed in relief. Why think about the morrow? It was time enough to think of it when it came. He had always been able to put unpleasant things out of his mind. He filled his glass again.

"Why not render us another one of your excellent songs?" he said to Cousins.

The first lieutenant smiled foppishly and fluttered his eyelids.

"Are you really taken by my voice?" he inquired deprecatingly. "I know that it has some reputation in the salons of New York and Washington but I never realized that its fame had percolated into the Halls of the Montezumas. Well, if you insist. Here is a little ditty composed by an engineer sergeant when the Muse chanced upon him sitting and meditating in one of the latrines of Mixcoac. It is called 'Bucking and Gagging' and I am sure that you will observe the etherial quality of it."

He stood up.

"Silence, gentlemen," he ordered, and began to sing.

They approached Chapultepec by way of the Belén causeway and Juan Diego observed that except for the chipped aqueduct pillars all evidence of the fighting on the thirteenth had been removed. In the fields on either side of the long straight road the white tents of the American troops blossomed like monstrous flowers. A few batteries were drawn up in neat parks. Reaching the end of the causeway proper the two brothers turned slightly southwest and skirted the hill. Above them the white buildings on the terreplein gleamed in the sun. David cocked an eye up at them with pursed lips. He shook his head slightly.

"It looks more formidable than it really is," he remarked. "Height doesn't mean strength any more."

"It was never intended for a fortress," explained Juan Diego. "It was the residence of the viceroy Gálvez before it was turned into a Military College."

"You studied there, didn't you?" asked David.

Juan Diego nodded.

"Yes," he replied shortly.

They passed a smashed wall and began to climb the slope. They passed a disabled four-pounder flanked with an infantry entrenchment and turned sharply toward the northeast. The narrow road was very steep here. Juan Diego pointed westward.

"The cypress grove is over there," he informed his brother. "It was there that Montezuma had his pleasure grounds, bowers, grottoes, baths, fishponds, aviary and all the rest of it. Chapultepec was his country seat."

David nodded.

They continued to climb and after a few minutes emerged on the rectangular level space that crowned the rock. To the east an almost vertical precipice guarded the height and on the other sides of the uneven ground high parapeted walls closed in the battered buildings of the Military College. These walls, which had been strengthened by sandbags and screens of blindage, showed the effects of hard cannonading, breaches and piles of rubble appearing everywhere.

A young lieutenant greeted David familiarly and glanced at Juan Diego's pass.

"Do you want to look over the prisoners, Livingston?" he asked. "They're over there, in that building."

He pointed with a brown hand.

"We might as well," replied David. "Where are the dead?"

"Ours, you mean?" questioned the lieutenant with some surprise. "Why, most of them are down . . ."

"The Mexican dead," explained David. "I think . . ."

"Oh," said the lieutenant. "Most of them are on the terrace." Vaguely he indicated the east.

"We've buried some in the grove," he added. "Digging parties are out now."

"Thanks, Smithers," said David. "Come along, Charley. We'll look the prisoners over first."

Juan Diego felt that it was futile to see the prisoners but he moved without a word after his brother. Lorenzo was with the dead on the terrace if he had not already been buried. But David, apparently, wanted to put off the grim moment of recognition as long as he could. He doesn't know how I will react, thought the young man. Well, he needn't worry. I will do nothing to embarrass him, nothing at all.

They were stopped for a moment at the door to the building where the prisoners were kept and then permitted to enter. Another young lieutenant, who accompanied them, explained that the generals, Bravo, Noriega and Dosamantes, the Military College commandant, Monterde, the chief of engineers, Cano, and the commandant of artillery, Gamboa, were housed apart in separate quarters and that they could be seen only by special authority of General Scott or Quitman.

"We don't want to see the officers," explained David. "We're looking for a cadet, one of the boys of the—"

"That's easy, lieutenant," broke in the accompanying officer. "They're all in here."

He swung a door open and a babble of voices stopped suddenly. David and Juan Diego stepped across the lintel and stared about the large chamber with its half dozen barred windows. Some forty boys ranging from twelve to seventeen years of age, stared back in dead silence. They were dirty and many of their creased gray uniforms were torn and stained with blood. A few of them wore bandages on their hands or heads. As he walked down the center of the room glancing to right and left, Juan Diego was unpleasantly affected by the hostility and hot intentness in all these eyes that followed him so closely. Did they think . . . ?

"No," he said in a low voice to David, "I do not see him."

He walked back up the room and paused by the door.

"Do any of you boys know Lorenzo Núñez?" he asked in a raised voice.

There was complete silence.

"I am a friend of Lorenzo Núñez's father," declared Juan Diego. "I am authorized to find out what became of him."

Still no sound.

Juan Diego turned helplessly toward the door.

"Espía!" hissed a voice from a far corner.

The American lieutenant laughed.

"They're spunky little buggers," he said. "You can't do a damned thing with them. One of them nearly bit Captain Abbott's thumb off. Do you want to see any more?"

"No," announced David immediately. "That's all the cadets, isn't it? No. Thanks for your trouble, lieutenant."

Outside they moved with reluctant feet toward the terrace.

"What a damned outrage!" exclaimed David. "Why, in the name of God, do they put boys in the battle line?"

"They don't," said Juan Diego. "The boys put themselves there. Mexico will not forget the cadets of Chapultepec."

David glanced at his brother briefly and then turned away.

There were about sixty bodies on the terrace, neatly arranged in rows and with blankets drawn up over their faces. Already an offensive odor, sickly sweet and penetrating, was rising from them. It was still on the terrace and except for two privates, seated in a breach of the parapet and well to windward of the bodies, it was deserted. The blue sky above was filled with a fleet of fleecy clouds that moved slowly like odd-shaped galleons. A gentle breeze was blowing.

Juan Diego looked at the rows of blanketed figures somewhat helplessly. He would have to lift the covering from face after face until he found the one he sought. It was an unpleasant business and he did not like it. He had always avoided the dead and although he had conquered the sickness that overcame him as a boy when he saw blood he thought of it was repugnant to him. Blood was strength but it was also weakness. It was one thing when it flowed in living arteries and another when it stained the ground. It was the hieroglyphic of oblivion then, the ultimate signature that signed the decree establishing man's nothingness. And a dead body, with its chilled unnatural flesh, was too much of a grotesque caricature of life, a shameful mockery of too many hopes and desires and dreams. He did not like the dead. They were mute denials of everything he wanted.

David stood to one side and watched silently as he started down the first row, plucking the blanket from each still face, glancing at it and then covering it again. A series of differing expressions met his eyes, calmness, suffering, bared teeth, the *risus sardonicus,* something that looked like laughter, a bloody mask, intense surprise, ineffable peace, a weary cynicism. There was variety, then, even in death. But all the bodies were rotting. The faces were turning black. Toward the center of the first row he drew back a blanket, perhaps the fifteenth, stared for an instant and then rose slowly to his full stature and half-turned. David came quickly down the terrace to him.

"You have found the boy?" he asked, closing his hand about his brother's wrist.

Juan Diego tried to speak but could not. He nodded.

David gazed down into the waxen face of Lorenzo, noting the clear-cut aristocratic features, the pale bulge of the closed eyelids with their long lashes and the dark curling hair that rested lightly on the forehead. He was lying with his head resting slightly to one side as though he had moved in his sleep and his lips were slightly parted. His expression was one of faint querulousness as though he heard someone calling him and did not want to awaken. The tight collar of his uniform jacket was dark with dried blood.

"He was very young," said David in a hushed voice. "Not more than thirteen or fourteen. It's a damned shame."

"Fifteen," declared Juan Diego. "He would have been fifteen on his next birthday. He was small-boned like his sis . . ."

His speech dwindled into silence and he stood for a long time looking down at the motionless face. It was both real and unreal like familiar features seen in reflection in a bad mirror. There was a remoteness about it that was forbidding and yet it seemed on the verge of springing to life. The likeness to Doña María Catalina was there, too, but far away, diminished, a faint suggestion. Ah, this blow would be terrible for her to bear, for Doña Ágata, for Don Isidro. It would mark all three of them for the rest of their lives. He obeyed the pressure of David's hand and moved away from the body, skirting the blanketed rows of still figures and following his brother with docility to the entrance that opened upon the descending path.

"I'm sorry," said David. "I had two friends killed at the Cerro Gordo and another is lying badly wounded in Puebla. It's the hardest part of war. Sometimes I think it's harder than being killed yourself."

"Lorenzo was an only son," explained Juan Diego earnestly. "He was not a soldier at all."

"I know," replied his brother. "But more than soldiers are killed in war. That's the evil part of it."

"And more than human beings are killed in war, too," declared Juan Diego savagely.

They began their descent from the Military College. David had not relaxed his grip on his brother's wrist and Juan Diego allowed himself to be led along very much like a child. It gave him a faint sort of comfort.

"Do you mean ideals?" asked David.

"And ideas," added Juan Diego. "I mean a hundred and one things, hope, peace of mind, safety, plans for the future, stability, respect, decency, and . . . yes, ideals."

"I suppose that is partially true," remarked David slowly, "but the obverse is true, too. War sometimes establishes all those things. When we won our independence—"

"I know," interrupted Juan Diego. "I have read all about your struggle for independence. Have you read about ours?"

"I don't know much about Mexico," admitted David. "It isn't taught in our schools."

They walked along in silence for a while and then Juan Diego lifted his wrist.

"I'm all right now," he said with the hint of a smile. "Thanks for the steadying, David."

His brother laughed and released his grip.

"I suppose they'll bury him in the grove," remarked Juan Diego in a sober voice. "Well, it's as good a place as any. He'll have plenty of brave company."

The smile on David's face vanished as he nodded.

Juan Diego had written a letter to Don Isidro in which he set down all that he knew about Lorenzo's last days and death and was sealing it with red wax and a lighted candle end when he heard the step of his brother mounting the stairs. It was about five o'clock in the afternoon and the city was quiet. The occasional shots had ceased an hour or so earlier, and although assassins still prowled the streets after dark seeking such American soldiers as were foolish enough to venture out alone or by twos, the insurrection had collapsed as a threat and order was being speedily established. A few unlooted shops had opened and a scattered citizenry was poking cautious noses into the afternoon air. Armed patrols from the Army of Occupation were policing the thoroughfares. Juan Diego looked up from his table when his brother entered the chamber and flung himself on the couch.

"Cousins wanted to come but I said no," he announced. "Is the letter ready?"

"I've just sealed it," replied Juan Diego. "What news?"

"Nothing much," yawned David. "Santa Anna has been hovering

about the city, marching his men from Guadalupe and back again. There's some trouble in Puebla and scattered reports indicate that a part of the city is held by guerrillas. But we're sending a messenger through tonight with dispatches for Colonel Childs. He'll take that letter for your friend."

"Guerrillas in Puebla!" exclaimed Juan Diego with some surprise.

"It won't amount to anything," declared David confidently. "The trouble is, we left only a small garrison there and a lot of sick and wounded. If the guerrillas become too threatening we'll send a few guns back and blow hell out of them."

He was gazing intently at the back of his brother's head and now he suddenly changed his tone.

"What are you going to do, Charley?" he asked abruptly.

Juan Diego turned around in surprise.

"Do?" he repeated. "What do you mean?"

David averted his eyes to the ceiling.

"Are you going to stay here?" he demanded. "Are you going to try and join those damned guerrillas? What *are* your plans?"

"I hadn't thought," said Juan Diego, and then he corrected himself.

"Yes, I have thought," he declared, "but I haven't reached any conclusions."

For a moment he was ill at ease and he clasped his hands so tightly that his knuckles showed white.

"What are you fighting for, David?" he asked finally.

"I'm fighting because I'm in the regular army and I was sent here by my government," replied his brother promptly.

"Is that all?" persisted Juan Diego.

David twisted on the couch.

"Why, no," he said. "I'm fighting for the right of the Republic of Texas to be annexed to us if she wants to. I'm fighting because Mexico attacked us, because she does not pay her debts, because she dishonors her promises, because . . . because . . . Charley, I tried to talk about this that night at Buena Vista and we didn't get anywhere."

"I'm not going to get angry," declared Juan Diego steadily.

He studied his brother for a moment.

"Are you fighting for New Mexico and California too?" he asked finally.

"I'm fighting for victory," announced David. "If victory includes New Mexico and California, then I suppose I'm fighting for them. They are the spoils of war. Is there anything so wrong in that? What has the Republic of Mexico ever done with those lands except hold them like a little dog holds a bone that is too big for him to eat? I know what you are thinking, Charley. There are a lot of folks back home who think the same way and call this a war of conquest. But what's the matter with conquest if the conqueror brings civilization with him? How about Rome? Or England in India? How about—"

"I know," broke in Juan Diego. "I know all those arguments and they are not valid. For the last few months I have thought night and day about these things. Your talk about Manifest Destiny does not impress me at all for it can be reduced to an absurdity. Suppose every nation acted upon such an extralegal authority? Why, the whole world would be plunged in war. No nation has any right over any other nation. But . . . every nation has a duty. And that is what is important, David."

"I don't quite understand," said his brother.

"I'll try to make it clear," promised Juan Diego. "I can see it shaping in my mind now. Clearly, clearly. David, the United States, whether it knows it or not, is fighting for something much bigger than conquest."

David looked puzzled.

"We have had a republic for thirty years," explained Juan Diego, "but during all that period we have lived in a state of practical anarchy. We have uttered big words but thought only of our self-advancement, self-advancement at any cost, even at the cost of the rights of our neighbors. That is a bad way to begin. We have ignored the Indians. We have enslaved ourselves to the Church. We have deified dishonest men and murdered patriots. We have conspired and plotted and cheated. We are passionate and suspicious and too self-confident. That is one side, the dark side, of the Republic. That is the side that you in the north know the most about. But there is another side, too. We are brilliant and subtle and imbued with the graces of a civilization that make you look like clodhoppers beside us. If we fulfilled our potentialities Mexico City would be a second Athens for we respond to the arts in a way that is beyond you. We have not broken the great link with Europe. We are still in the tide of a tradition that was ancient when your oldest city was a wilderness inhabited by naked Indians. But all these graces, all these potentialities, have been nullified by one great crime on our part. It is a crime that you, blundering, pushing, boastful, money-making, ashamed of sentiment and yet reveling in sentimentalism, have never committed. It is for that reason that you have won this war. It couldn't have been otherwise. It would have been traveling backward in time, against the very laws of nature, for it to have been otherwise."

David stood up and approached his brother.

"I don't understand all this," he said in a mystified tone. "What do you mean?"

"I mean the soil," said Juan Diego. "I mean the land. The land was here before any of us were, Yanqui, Mexican or Indian. It was there as a great responsibility and a great trust and it was the duty of every people to accept that responsibility and fulfill that trust. Do you begin to see now? Here in the Republic we failed and kept on failing. We permitted evil men to divert us from what should have been our first task. But you in the United States—perhaps without knowing it, I repeat—were not diverted. You accepted the responsibility of the land and loved it. You moved westward and cities sprang up in your footsteps. You did not relinquish great expanses to the Church. You moved with the sun and the sun moved with you. We might have done that for we were here on this continent before you were. But we didn't. We groveled beneath the heel of the viceroys until we rebelled and then we fought one another for power and the land sometimes became a payment and sometimes a weapon but never a cause for its own sake. Yet for every nation the land must be everything or the nation is nothing at all. And that is what you are fighting for, a responsibility, a task, an unending duty, the exploitation and civilization of the land. You don't know it, perhaps. Perhaps you think only of material wealth, strategic holdings and new spaces for a swelling population but the duty is there all the same and you do not avoid it. I found it out in brooding over the failures of the Republic and watching our politicians and generals and prelates. Not one of them spoke of the land unselfishly and not one of them realized that the Republic belonged to the land and not the land to the Republic."

David looked down at his brother with a sort of dawning dancing light in his eyes.

"Why, Charley," he exclaimed, "you're a greater patriot than I am."

"You mustn't misunderstand me," declared Juan Diego quickly. "This does not mean that I have changed my coat. I am no traitor. It merely means that a dream has exploded. I . . ."

He paused to think for a moment and his eyes misted as he seemed to gaze inward and find little comfort there. David stood silently by his side.

"Your friend Cousins said something last night that I cannot forget," he said at last. "He told me that I only thought I was a Mexican. What did he mean? That I was pretending to myself? That I was denying one thing that was real for the sake of another that was no more than a chimera? I have been trying to find out all night and all this day. And now a new question has risen in my mind. What did Lorenzo die for? I know that it wasn't for General Santa Anna and his conception of the Republic. It wasn't for much of anything at all, I suppose, except a boy's dream. And what was it that made Don

Isidro so cynical after he had paused to think? Perhaps, I am not sure, but, perhaps, they saw a Mexico, too, the one instinctively and the other like a distant light on the horizon, that had no foundations in actuality but was waiting to be built. It was not the real Mexico. It was the Mexico of the future. So when Lieutenant Cousins tells me that I am only pretending to be a Mexican he is really saying that I am trying to live now in that Mexico of the future. Perhaps there are a lot of us who feel that way without stopping to think that wishing will never make it so."

He glanced up at his brother and laughed shortly.

"None of this makes much sense to you, does it?" he asked.

"I think I understand," said David. "You thought Mexico was one thing and you found out it was another. It took a war to make that plain to you. You have been a sort of Mexican who is very rare and is not representative of the chaos that exists today. In other words, you were born a hundred years too soon. But I don't believe Cousins thought of that at all. He doesn't think that deeply. He . . ."

"That is one way of putting it," declared Juan Diego. "And perhaps you are right about Cousins. But he caused me to think deeply. I have been walking in a dream world of my own, a world that had its birth in the fragrance and carefree days of my boyhood at Manga de Clavo when I knew little or nothing about politics and selfishness and the ambitions of little men. I loved my dream of Mexico and I was ready to die for it. I remember Don Isidro one night, pretty drunk, I'll admit, trying to tell me what he loved in Mexico and asking me if that was patriotism. It was the land, its beauty, its potentialities, that obsessed him and that was good. Although he had been one of the privileged of the earth here he thought less of his wealth or his power than he did of the land. It was good, I repeat. I still think that is the real Mexico. You have found nothing here but anarchy and bloodshed and chicanery and treachery but there are millions of silent voices here that would shout out against such evils if they knew how to shout. With men of good will to build it the Republic can become one of the most civilized nations on earth, a great light shining in the west where graciousness and the arts and fair dealing can flourish like our tropical fruits. But it will not come true in my time or yours. I can see that now. It will not come true until we remember the land and accept our responsibilities to it, until we chasten our pride and forget opportunism and remember the Indian and the little worker, until we cease to sleep in the sun and put off until tomorrow the things we should do today, until we understand our neighbors and comprehend that firmness is not arrogance and the teaching of progressive ways is not patronage with an ulterior purpose, until we open up to the world what we cannot develop ourselves, until we become a unified people with a national ideal that is free for all."

He drew a deep breath and stood up and linked his arm with David's.

"Mexico and the United .States should be like this," he said, smiling. "We are children of the same mother, the land, and we dwell side by side in one great house. We can help each other. We have things to give you, too. Why don't you try to understand us better?"

David shook his head.

"I don't know," he said. "Perhaps we are too busy trying to understand ourselves. But, Charley, why don't you come home and teach us some of these things?"

"I would make an incoherent teacher," replied his brother, disengaging his arm and sitting down again. "I must teach myself first."

He glanced suddenly at his brother.

"Do you recall when we met at the hacienda of Buena Vista?" he asked. "I talked like a child, then. So did you. I said that I belonged to Mexico and you belonged to the United States and it followed that we could not belong to each other. What foolishness! We both belong to the land and we both belong to each other. A little river cannot separate us. It is only ideas that separate people and we are the masters of our ideas. Too often it takes a long time to learn. Too often we have bad teachers."

He paused and looked around the chamber.

"Well," he said finally, "I think I have said it all, now."

David sat down on an edge of the table.

"You have not told me what you are going to do, Charley," he reminded him.

"I don't know," confessed Juan Diego. "I know what I am not going to do, though. I am not going to bear arms against the United States again. I am going to admit that the Republic has forfeited Texas and New Mexico and California through its lack of responsibility to the land, legal fictions notwithstanding. But, on the other hand, I am not going to admit that you are waging a just war for I don't think you are fighting for the just reasons. They are there in spite of you and you do not recognize them. You see, it is still all tangled up."

"I think . . ." began David and then he stopped.

He took a turn about the chamber. Juan Diego watched him with a calm eye.

"Have you any of that bad aguardiente?" demanded David. "I'd like to find out what it tastes like."

Juan Diego got up and produced the bottle from the wall cupboard. David sampled his drink cautiously and then drained it off without making a grimace.

"It isn't so bad," he said. "Take one, Charley."

Juan Diego poured himself a glass of the liquor. He felt almost happy, as though a great obstacle had been hurdled in a difficult race, and he smiled with a new affection at his brother. David, he decided, wasn't stupid but neither was he too bright. He was just what he should be . . . an elder brother. He drank a part of the contents of his glass and put it down.

"No, it isn't so bad," he admitted. "I prefer it to whisky. It is more honest."

"Do you intend to remain in Mexico City?" asked David.

"I don't know," replied Juan Diego patiently.

"Do you intend to remain in Mexico?" persisted his brother.

"Confound it, David, I don't know," repeated the other. "I suppose I will remain here. Where else should I go?"

"Is there anything holding you here . . . besides habit?" asked David with some uneasiness.

Juan Diego looked at his brother for a moment before he replied. "I am still a Mexican," he said finally.

"I mean . . ." began David and then he seized the bottle and poured himself another drink.

Juan Diego closed his eyes for an instant and her face seemed to rise up without his willing it. As he had once pictured Our Lady of Guadalupe as the soul of that dreamlike Mexico so now he pictured Doña María Catalina as the soul of it. He thought she was speaking to him across a great distance but he could not understand the words. Her lips moved and her long gray eyes were fixed intently on his face but all was in dumb show, a sort of trance that was as still as the reflection of unstirred trees in a calm lake. He could tell David about Don Isidro's daughter but he did not know how he would react to it and he feared anything that might break the cord of sympathy between them. He opened his eyes and finished his glass of aguardiente.

"There are many things that bind me here," he said mildly.

His brother seemed relieved at the indefiniteness of the response. "You know, you have told me very little about yourself," he said offhandedly. "Someday you must tell me everything, what happened to you, how you lived and all that sort of thing."

"Someday I will," agreed Juan Diego. "It is not a very exciting story."

"Nor is mine," declared David. "Nothing much happened to me. Senator Ewing took me to Tennessee, saw that I was well-enough educated, got me into West Point and here I am. If you ever want a home in the States he will provide you with one. He is an excellent old fellow."

"I'm sure of it," replied Juan Diego. "I think I remember him . . . faintly. Didn't he have long curls?"

David chuckled.

"He got rid of those when he left Texas," he answered. "He has a gray senatorial haircut now. You'd like him. He's a great friend of Senator Benton."

"What happened to Belita and her daughter?" asked Juan Diego abruptly. "You remember . . . father's housekeeper?"

Old names and faces were flowing into his mind.

"I don't know," said David. "I suppose she married the chicken butcher."

Both were silent for a minute and both were thinking of the untidy little house in San Felipe and the red-faced man who zigzagged home from the tavern after it had closed for the night. It was so far away from both of them now that it seemed like something they had read in a storybook when they were children and half-forgotten.

"Belita's daughter's name was Enriqueta," said Juan Diego.

David nodded.

They were very close together now as they gazed at each other and smiled. They possessed memories, recollections like broken bits of mirror that flashed in the deep caves of their consciousness, that were peculiar to them alone and could be shared by nobody else. Each of them knew that the conversation was finished, that the long-delayed talk had been accomplished and that there was nothing to do but wait and see what would happen. Destiny could not be coerced. It came by itself and settled things in its own way.

David walked over and looked out the window.

"I'm glad the firing has stopped," he said. "Perhaps the City Council will listen to peace proposals now. Oh, by the way, Santa Anna has resigned as president and appointed a triumvirate to direct the executive power. I heard that this morning."

"Who's in the triumvirate?" asked Juan Diego.

The name of Santa Anna aroused no emotion in him at all.

David thought for a moment.

"These damned names!" he exclaimed. "Oh, Alcorta and Herrera and the president of the supreme court."

"There isn't any president of the supreme court," said Juan Diego. "The post is vacant."

"Well, I don't know," remarked David. "They're getting somebody."

He reached for the bottle.

"Come on, Charley," he ordered. "Let's finish this and then take a walk to the Alameda."

Juan Diego agreed, smiling.

During the next few days calm gradually settled over Mexico City. Those inhabitants who had fled, some to neighboring villages and others to their haciendas, returned to their town houses; business was resumed, shops and banks opening their doors and the markets filling with shouting hucksters; churches were thronged with worshipers and gay equipages began to appear on the Paseo. Only the battered buildings and a few streets where paving stones had been torn up by the desperate léperos remained to remind the populace of war. Those and the American soldiers. It was true that an occasional murder occurred, the body of some adventurous trooper from north of the Rio Grande being found in a dark corner or a deserted alley but the active enmity of the Mexican population as a whole seemed dissipated. What they thought in their hearts remained their own secret for the Americans made no attempt to pierce beneath the surface. They demanded order and backed it up with guns, and they got it.

Rumors and dispatches brought news of what was happening in the rest of the country. All this David passed on to his brother. Santa Anna was believed to be on his way to Puebla with the remnants of his army. In the Holy City itself the American garrison was besieged by the guerrilla leader, Rea, and his forces. The National Highway all the way to Vera Cruz was infested with small bands of irregulars who wreaked such damage as they could on the lines of communication, ambushing provision wagon convoys, sniping at small detachments of Yanqui troops and even looting their own people. It was the old way of war, minus discipline, morale and standards, the way the Spanish had fought against Napoleon and the Mexicans against Spain, and it infuriated the Americans who would not forget it for a century. Juan Diego deplored this guerrilla warfare for he recognized the futility of it and saw in it nothing more than the last convulsive throes of a dying creature. The beast lashed out at friend and foe alike and the general aspect of defeat was not changed at all.

The brothers were together a lot for David's duties were light and for the most part perfunctory. Cousins occasionally accompanied them on their long tramps about the capital in the clear September weather interrupted only by the afternoon rains. They visited churches and public buildings and historical spots and gardens and David began to understand the lazy charm of Mexican life. They talked a lot. Before he was quite aware of it Juan Diego had told his brother everything about his years since the fall of the Alamo, the ineffable days at Manga de Clavo, the excitements of Mexico City, the months with the Tarascan Indians in Michoacán, the seasons at the Military College and the campaigns of Buena Vista and Cerro Gordo. And David, in turn, filled in more completely the missing portion of his days. One thing Juan Diego hesitated to discuss and that was his relationship with Doña María Catalina although he knew that he must speak of it sooner or later.

The moment came sooner than he thought. They were seated one evening under the trees in the Alameda and the sound of church bells echoed clearly through the rain-washed air. A sort of purple peace isolated them from the rest of the world. Without prompting or suggestion Juan Diego began to speak of Puebla and then of Don Isidro and his house and finally of the rose-scented patio and Doña María Catalina. It all came quite naturally and when he had finished he roused himself from a bewitched half hour and knew that he had told everything from his first meeting with Doña María Catalina at Las Golondrinas to their parting in May under the willow tree. He told it simply but he had avoided none of the implications that encrusted it like the jewels on a rare vase. David had listened silently, half-afraid to breathe for fear he would impinge on his brother's consciousness. It gave him a happy feeling for now he knew that the two of them had reached the ultimate closeness and that no matter what happened they would always be together. The bells were still ringing when they rose from the bench and started to walk back to the Calle de Santa Clara. The bells seemed full of promise to David.

The next evening they were sitting in Juan Diego's chamber speaking of the new disposition of Scott's troops (he had rebarracked them about the city in public buildings and issued orders that no private homes were to be occupied) when the younger brother held up his hand for silence.

"There is somebody coming up the stairs," he explained.

David listened and after a second he could hear the quick rustling slap of feet.

"It's not Cousins," he said in a puzzled voice. "He always thumps his boots. Perhaps it's a . . ."

Juan Diego moved swiftly to the door and flung it open while David jumped to his feet and put his hand on his pistol.

A lean Indian, dust-covered and grim-faced, stood on the threshold. The two brothers stared at him for a moment and then Juan Diego caught him by the arm and drew him into the room.

"Chepe!" he exclaimed. "Chepe! What is it? What has happened?"

The Indian spread his hands, palms upward, in a gesture that signified aid.

"You must come, Señor Teniente," he said in a quiet voice that yet throbbed with urgency. "The patrón sent me. He said, 'Ride to Mexico City, Chepe, and find the Señor Teniente and tell him to come.

Here is a paper with the place where he lives written on it. Show it to anybody who can read.' I have ridden all day."

Juan Diego pushed a chair forward and forced the Indian to sit down. A dozen terrible prospects were dancing in his mind.

"What is it?" he demanded roughly. "Tell me quickly."

"The guerrillas are in Puebla," explained Chepe. "Last night a dozen of them came to the patrón's house. They broke the door down and they took Doña María Catalina away. They—"

"Wait!" cried Juan Diego thickly.

The chamber seemed to sway about him and he placed his hand on the table for support.

"Doña María Catalina is in Apizaco," he said after a moment. "You took her there yourself, Chepe."

"She would not remain there, Señor Teniente," explained the Indian. "She returned to Puebla a week ago and the patrona returned with her. There was much looting at Apizaco. They believed they would be safer with the Americans in Puebla. But most of the Americans are sick. The garrison is small. It is barricaded in the Cuartel San José, the Loreto fort and the Guadalupe church. The guerrillas hold the rest of the city."

Juan Diego continued to stare at Chepe with stunned eyes.

"Yes," he said blankly. "They broke the door down . . . Speak in English. I want my brother to hear you."

"It was after midnight," declared Chepe in fair English. "They came with guns. They forced their way into the library and they struck the patrón on the head with a musket butt when he reached for his pistols. He fell down. Three of them held me while the rest went upstairs. I could hear the patrona and Chuchita screaming. Then they came down with Doña María Catalina and took her away. They did not take anything else away."

He paused and swiveled his black snakelike eyes from Juan Diego to David. He lifted his hands again.

"I could do nothing," he said. "They held me too tight. After they went away I tried to make the patrón stand up. But I couldn't. He was too heavy. Then the patrona and Chuchita came downstairs and all of us carried the patrón up to his bed. We bound his head. When he opened his eyes he tried to lift himself but he could not move his legs. Something had happened to them for they were like the legs of a dead man. It was then that he told me to take the horse and find you."

Juan Diego turned strained eyes to his brother.

"I must go to Puebla," he declared loudly.

"Señor Teniente," said the Indian, "I saw the leader of the guerrillas. It was Don Alejandro."

"Don . . . Don . . ." stammered Juan Diego and his brother moved swiftly toward him.

But the young man waved him away. He stood absolutely still for a moment, his hands hanging loosely at his sides while he appeared to force back the shock and fury that were struggling upward within him. A haunted expression crept over his face chiseling his features into ugly lines and he turned his head as though he was listening to some inaudible call. The blood had rushed from his lips and cheeks, and when, after the eternity of a minute, he glanced at David the older brother had the sensation that he was observed by a mask of iron. He had never seen or suspected this Charley before and it frightened him. All the gentleness, the repression, the youthful uncertainty had vanished from Juan Diego and in its place was the ageless ferocity of the cornered mountain lion. And yet he was calm. He was as cold as the snow on Popocatépetl as he sat down in a chair facing the Indian and placed a hand on his knee.

"You saw him plainly, Chepe," he said in a hard dry voice that was devoid of all emotion.

"Yes, Señor Teniente," replied the Indian. "I saw him well and I saw his horse, Simún, beyond the door. He was one of those who brought Doña María Catalina down from her chamber and he kicked the patrón as he went by and spoke to him with a mouth full of obscenities."

Juan Diego's hands slowly closed into tight fists but he made no other gesture.

"You have no idea where he . . . they went?" he asked.

"Most of the guerrillas have their secret camps between Puebla and Vera Cruz," replied Chepe. "I cannot tell you now where he went, Señor Teniente, but I can find out. The Indians have ways of finding out."

"Yes," said Juan Diego.

He lifted his face to his brother.

"When the general lost his leg in Vera Cruz," he explained, "the peons at Manga de Clavo knew it before the first messenger reached the casa grande."

He rose to his feet.

"I am ready to go with you, Chepe," he declared.

For the first time since the Indian entered the chamber David intervened.

"You can't start out tonight, Charley," he protested. "You'll never get through the pickets without being shot."

"I'll take my chance, David," announced Juan Diego. "Don Isidro has sent for me."

The words were calm and metallic.

"I know," insisted his brother, "but, all the same, you must wait for the morning. What are you going to do about horses? Look, the Indian is half-dead with fatigue now. He has been riding all day. And what can you do alone in Puebla? Do you expect to pursue a body of guerrillas and snatch the . . . the lady from them all by yourself? Let us be reasonable about this."

Juan Diego sat down again.

"Yes," he said. "Let us be reasonable. What do you suggest?"

He was cold and clearheaded in his grim determination and David was glad of that. He had the feeling that his brother would show no emotion until his task was accomplished. He was holding himself tightly in check and concentrating on one thing only and that was good. It would preserve his sanity and might bring him success. David, catching this resolute bearing from the other, thought quickly.

"I know where there are horses," said the Indian. "I left word at Buena Vista, Río Frío and San Martín. We can change at all those places."

"Good!" said David. "Now, listen, Charley. I'll get three cavalry mounts from Harney's brigade at the barracks near the National Palace and we'll start off the first thing in the morning. I'll have to see . . ."

"You are coming!" exclaimed Juan Diego.

"Of course I'm coming," declared David impatiently. "What can you do without me? When we reach Puebla I'll speak to Colonel Childs, whom I know very well, and request a squad of men. Then we'll hunt down your guerrillas with some chance of success."

He hurried over to the couch and snatched up his cap.

"What time is it?" he demanded. "After nine? I'll have to rush if I'm to get a leave of absence, passes to leave the city and horses before the men I must see disappear into their quarters. Well, I'll rout em out of their beds if I have to. Will you be ready by six in the morning?"

"By six!" cried Juan Diego. "I shan't sleep tonight. Chepe, lie down on that couch and wait for us. I'm going with you, David."

"No, no," expostulated his brother. "I can do this better without you. All you could do would be to wait at doors. And, for the love of God, Charley, try to get some sleep. We'll need all of our wits tomorrow."

"The Yanqui is right," said Chepe unexpectedly. "He has good words in his mouth."

He walked over to a corner by the door and laid down on the hard floor.

Juan Diego followed David to the head of the stairs and grasped him by the hand.

"Thanks, David," he said.

His brother clattered down the stairs without looking back and an instant later the outer door slammed.

Juan Diego came back into the chamber and sat down on the couch. He stared at the prostrate figure of the Indian for a moment. Chepe lay with his arm over his eyes, motionless except for the steady rise and fall of his chest. That was the best way. Unending time and suspense were blocked out with sleep. The frantic mind was salved and the doubts that stung like hornets were drugged for a brief span. Strength poured into the weary limbs and the heart ceased to ache in its cool bath of insensibility. Juan Diego stretched himself along the couch and put his arm over his eyes, too. But he couldn't sleep. He knew that before he lay down. He could drug the passions that threatened to tear him apart only by a powerful effort of the will, by an obsessive concentration on remaining cool because that was the sole way to accomplish what must be accomplished if he was to live. The candles burned forlornly in the chamber but he did not rise to extinguish them. Let them burn. The small light was better than complete darkness. He thought he heard the Indian move.

"Chepe?" he called softly.

"Yes, Señor Teniente," came the quick response.

"You are not asleep," he said. "Chepe, did Don Isidro receive my . . . my letter . . . about Lorenzo?"

"Yes, Señor Teniente," answered the Indian. "The patrón turned gray in the face but the patrona became an old woman."

"And . . . Doña María Catalina?" persisted Juan Diego.

"She wept for many days," said Chepe.

Juan Diego groaned inwardly. But he must not think of these things. Resolution . . . coolness . . . the pain that must be borne . . . the wine . . .

"It will not be long before six o'clock," he said, half to himself.

"No, Señor Teniente," replied the Indian.

"Are you comfortable, Chepe?" demanded Juan Diego.

"Yes, Señor Teniente," answered the Indian.

The young man kept his arm over his eyes but he could not keep her face from glowing before them. She had wept for many days. She had wept . . . When he met Don Alejandro he would shoot him squarely between the eyes. He heard the watch go through the Calle de Santa Clara calling the hour. Oh, God, it was only midnight. Six eternal everlasting hours to wait.

Book Five

CERRO DEL DESTINO

Cerro Del Destino

IT WAS shortly after six o'clock in the morning when Juan Diego, David and Chepe left Mexico City behind them and set out at a fast pace for Puebla. There had been no difficulties at the San Lázaro garita where a detachment from Twiggs's second division was on guard but David had been warned that the roads were dangerous and there were no American pickets beyond Los Reyes. The two brothers were grave and silent and Chepe, resuming the taciturnity that was his habitual manner, moved like a dark shadow a little to the rear of them. They followed the road that curved around the southern end of Lake Texcoco and the horses' hoofs drummed musically on the hard-packed earth. The lake waters glittered in the clear light and the sky, a deep blue, stretched to the mountain range that was their goal without a cloud to fleck it. The cavalry mounts, all young mares, lifted their twitching nostrils to the morning and seemed to move effortlessly in this new joy of freedom and exhilarating air. At any other time Juan Diego would have felt that joy which he always experienced when he was mounted on a swift horse on a fine morning; but now his thoughts were miles ahead of him and all his will and consciousness were stretched toward them. He was hardly aware of the clear day, the shining waters and the green lines of magueyes.

They rode through the quiet hamlet of Los Reyes, eleven miles from the capital, and saw a small detachment of American cavalry halted before a pink-brick fonda. The troopers' heads turned curiously as the trio swept by and a few scattered shouts greeted them. Beyond Los Reyes they passed fields rich with corn and beans, farmhouses, squawking chickens, lean cattle, vine-wrapped gates, small milpas, bowed figures in truck gardens, barking dogs and the wooden crosses marking the places where victims had been killed by bandits and highwaymen. No one halted them or threatened them. They saw no more soldiers. The sun, mounting the sky, glowed above them and a young breeze ruffled the trees that lined the road. War seemed a million miles away. The mountains approached steadily and when they were almost at their base Chepe called out and reined in his horse before a formidable stone gate.

"The hacienda of Buena Vista," he said. "There are fresh horses here."

"Buena Vista," echoed David. "That brings back memories."

"There's more than one Buena Vista in Mexico," remarked Juan Diego sliding from his mare.

David dismounted and started to walk up and down, stretching his legs.

"The horses are not too winded," he said, "but it's just as well."

Chepe,. riding his own mount and leading the other two, disappeared through the gate. The two brothers walked back and forth, breathing in the fresh air and listening to the musical calls of birds in the heavy foliage of the trees. They had little to say but each sensed the solidity of the other and each derived a comfort from it. When Chepe reappeared he had three sturdy small horses with him and a basket filled with cold tortillas. They ate them as they rode. The highway began to ascend rapidly and they were forced to go at a slower gait. David recalled that it was little more than a month ago that he had come this way, riding in the opposite direction, and with a certainty in his soul that bloody events had justified. He was not as certain now but he would do his damnedest for Charley. They would have to trust to luck . . . and Chepe.

They mounted slowly and steadily through the still air and a coolness wrapped about them that seemed to be the invisible breath of the mountain. The country became wild, crazy outcroppings of rock and multitudes of pine trees, and the road narrow. Ominous crosses loomed by the way. The horses plodded along with bowed heads, their hoofs scattering small pebbles, and the air seemed thin and like icy water in their lungs. They began to breathe more rapidly. David observed that Chepe was watching the bushy sides of the road like a suspicious cat and that he had loosened and brought around the new Colt's revolver he wore at his belt. Juan Diego, too, was glancing to right and left. The cracking of a branch, the sudden dislodgment of a stone, the quick whirr of some unknown bird sharpened their eyes and brought them to a nervous tension. David began to fondle the butt of his own revolver. But nothing happened. They mounted and mounted and at last they reached a deserted mesón from whose grounds the earth fell away on all sides. They had reached the summit.

Behind them, in the brilliant early-afternoon sun, lay the Valley of Mexico and before them the high valley, a mere dip in the mountain slope, of the Río Frío. Not one of them looked back at the great colored panorama of Moctezuma's Anahuac; they stared ahead into the thick pine forests and gave the reins to their tired horses and pushed on at an accelerated pace. Passing downward for a time they reached the icy stream, forded it and mounted for some distance to the farther lip of the Río Frío valley. It was after three o'clock in the afternoon and they had been traveling for nine hours but they felt no particular weariness. The knowledge that they were on the last stages of their journey and that from now on their mounts could move faster aroused a new strength in them and a new seriousness as well. Pines changed to oaks and the evergreen shrubs of laurel as the long road dipped from the lip of the Río Frío valley and a new balminess suffused the air. The horses' hoofs clicked rapidly down the slanting grade.

When they reached the Texmelucán bridge, a heavy stone structure over a precipitous gorge, Chepe called for a halt.

"New horses," he said shortly.

Raising his head he emitted a long mournful carrying howl that sounded like the despairing call of a lost hound. A minute or two later a trampling of hoofs could be heard in the thick brush that lined the road and two Indians appeared riding unsaddled horses. Chepe spoke rapidly to one of them and he turned his mount's head and disappeared in the direction from which he had come.

"He goes for another horse," explained Chepe to Juan Diego.

The young man nodded as he dismounted and started to unbuckle the saddle on the tired animal he had been riding. David was already doing the same. Presently the Indian came riding back leading a spare mount. Saddles and bridles were changed to the fresh horses and again they were off, leaving the Texmelucán bridge behind them and threading their way through great stones and crackling fragments of porphyry. The descent, fringed with pines and cedars, was steeper now and there were times when the animals slid in the loose shale but no accidents occurred. Twilight had fallen and the hollows by the roadside became impenetrable pools of darkness. At one place Chepe's quick ears caught a strange sound and he guided the brothers hurriedly into a clump of cedars. They dismounted and held their horses' heads, praying silently that the animals would not become restless or whinny. The strange sound became clicking hoofs. Peering through the trees Juan Diego and David saw a dozen mounted men riding by in single file. The big hats and bowed figures were like a frieze cut out of blackness. When the sound of the strangers had died away the trio mounted their horses and continued their descent.

"Guerrillas," said Chepe. "They live in caves by Texmelucán."

"Might Don Alejandro—" began David quickly.

"No, señor," broke in the Indian. "These are dogs who rob poor jacales. I saw Don Alejandro's men. They are fighters."

The descent leveled off before Juan Diego became aware of it. The stony road became hard earth and the trees thinned out. Cultivated fields extended on either side. A few weak lights glittered ahead.

"San Martín," declared Chepe.

San Martín proved to be a small town with a church and a convent. Both Juan Diego and David remembered it, the first from the night he had passed there with Santa Anna's forces after the withdrawal from Puebla and the second as a halt of the American troops on their way to the Valley of Mexico.

"Is it safe to ride through the place?" asked Juan Diego.

Chepe shrugged his shoulders.

"Sometimes the guerrillas are there," he replied. "I do not know. We can ride around it but I must go in for new horses."

"Again!" exclaimed David. "How far is it to Puebla now?"

"About eighteen miles," said Juan Diego.

"It is always good to have fresh horses," insisted the Indian. "A tired horse and an empty gun are bad things."

They skirted the town, dismounted and the two brothers lowered themselves into a drainage ditch while Chepe rode off with the horses. Within fifteen minutes he was back again with three rough-coated little animals who proved to be half-broken and obsessed with a desire to cut off across the fields instead of keeping on the road.

"There are no guerrillas in San Martín," announced Chepe, "but there are some Lancers there. They say that the Señor General is coming this way with many soldiers."

"Colonel Childs is going to be in a pickle if he doesn't get reinforcements," declared David in a worried voice. "I hope to God some of our men are moving up from Jalapa."

Juan Diego grunted.

They rode on, passing the Río Prieto, the black river, and soon were passing huge fields of corn and acres of beans that lay quiet under the newly risen moon. A distant gun suddenly brought them to sharp attention and instinctively they put the spurs to their restless little animals. The horses leaped and started to gallop. On their right the vague pyramid of Cholula loomed darkly in the night. More cornfields and stretches of beans sped by. In a little while they could see the yellow flash of guns at Puebla and hear the occasional boom of a howitzer and the rattle of small arms.

"It is General Rea," gasped Chepe jerkily as he controlled his horse by an effort. "He is firing at the Americans in the Cuartel de San José. He fires at them every night."

"Where is the house of Don Isidro?" asked David abruptly.

"Not far from the cathedral," answered Juan Diego. "Is that part of the city in the hands of the guerrillas, Chepe?"

"Oh, yes, Señor Teniente," replied the Indian. "They are everywhere except in the Cuartel de San José, the Tívoli promenade, the Loreto fort and the Guadalupe church."

"A regular siege," commented David. "It is worse than I imagined. What are we going to do?"

"I'm going to ride to Don Isidro's house," said Juan Diego firmly. "Perhaps you had better wait . . ."

"I've got to see Colonel Childs," declared David doggedly. "We'll need men . . ."

"You can't ride through Puebla in that uniform," said Juan Diego bluntly.

"The Cuartel de San José is on the eastern side of the town," explained Chepe. "I know a way to get to it."

"Good!" exclaimed David. "That settles it."

They were close to Puebla now and the intermittent firing was very loud. All three reined in their horses. Less than half a mile before them they could see moving lights in the darkness of the garita. The faint stench of burning wood and gunpowder reached their nostrils.

"Where shall we meet?" asked David.

Juan Diego thought for a moment.

"I don't see how you're going to get a squad of men through the lines," he said, "but if Chepe knows a back trail try it. Where we meet should depend on what we find out. But there is no time to wait for that. Look! I have it. About six miles east of Puebla on the road to Amozoc there is a trail, wide enough for horses, going north and about a quarter of a mile up that trail are the ruins of a burned hacienda building. The place is overgrown, and, so far as I know, deserted. Let us meet there about ten o'clock in the morning. Whoever arrives first will wait for the other. Is that clear?"

"I know the place," responded Chepe. "The Indians avoid it because they think it is haunted. Don Salustío Alcáraz burned up his wife and children in that house."

"Very well," agreed David. "We will meet there, then. Now, Chepe, show me the way."

Juan Diego watched the Indian and his brother leave the road and strike off through a cornfield into the darkness. For some time he heard the thrashing of the horses' hoofs and then they died away, as, apparently, they reached some hidden trail. Then the young man touched his spurs to his mount and rode directly toward Puebla.

There were about fifty armed men around the garita and several of them came forward as Juan Diego approached the gate. They were obviously irregulars for they wore misfit clothing and many of them were barefooted. Three or four sperm-oil lanterns hanging from two-wheeled carts threw shafts of light across the partially blocked entrance. A narrow lane, wide enough only for a single horse, gaped between the carts. Juan Diego rode straight toward this lane. He had made up his

mind that boldness was the only means of success. Therefore, when a
grimy hand reached out toward the bridle of his horse he struck at it
insolently with his quirt.

"Get away, cochino!" he snapped. "Get away or I'll mark your
ugly face for you. Make space there so I can get through."

"Who talks so big?" inquired an irritated voice and a young man
in uniform stepped wearily into the soft light of the lanterns. When
he lifted his pock-marked face Juan Diego immediately recognized
him. He had stumbled into luck.

"Why, Mariano Aviraneta of Pachuca!" he exclaimed. "I thought
the general hanged you for cowardice at La Angostura."

"What's that?" stuttered the young man as he came closer and
peered upward. "Who are you? Ah. Are you still alive, Señor Teniente?
I might just as well be hanged for all the good I am doing here.
Dismount, amigo, and have a glass of tequila with me."

"I'm in a devil of a hurry," declared Juan Diego. "How does one
get through your labyrinth of carts?"

"By riding through," said the other. "Have you dispatches from
the general? Is he on his way? You'll find Rea in the Governor's Palace
on the plaza."

He turned to the irregulars and began to bawl at them.

"Make a way there! Hustle your dirty carcasses, asesinos, maja-
deros, fulleros, tontos, chulos, chambones, bribones, pícaros!" he
shouted. "Here is a special messenger from the general. Jump,
gentuza!"

"Your vocabulary is extensive and magnificent," remarked Juan
Diego, laughing.

Mariano Aviraneta shook his head.

"What would you?" he said. "General Alvarez sent me on here
when Rea, who is a baboon, asked for regular officers. I pass all my
days with this riffraff who stink to heaven. You are lucky to be with
the general's staff. I am a victim of circumstances. I wish to God I'd
stayed in Pachuca where I belong."

"I know," replied Juan Diego commiseratingly. "Eating a fine
turkey mole."

"I often have that thought," declared the pockmarked officer.

The space between the carts had been widened and Juan Diego
rode through after promising to drink some tequila with Mariano
Aviraneta, whom he had not seen since the day of the fighting on the
plateau by La Angostura, as soon as he had a free moment. "Which
won't be in Puebla," he muttered to himself as his horse trotted into
the familiar streets. He judged that it was some time after nine o'clock.
A crackling of musketry fire sounded from the eastern portion of the
city but it was uneven, flaring into a sustained fusillade at moments

and then dwindling into occasional reports. Twice he heard the loud bellow of a howitzer. The thoroughfares were deserted except for groups of hurrying men and all the shops and private houses were dark, barred and apparently lifeless. Here on a lesser scale, was a replica of Mexico City a day or so before the assault on Chapultepec although, then, there had been no foreign troops in the city. There was the same darkness, the same tension, the same fear of the unknown and the same atmosphere of catastrophe and helplessness.

He passed the cathedral, imposing and silent against the night sky, and wondered if the bishop was still in Puebla, laboring, perhaps, with the Americans to preserve lives and properties. He had never cared for the bishop but now he could see that the defeatism of the little prelate was based on more than cowardice and, perhaps, selfishness. He knew the inevitable when he saw it and that was more than most patriots knew. He fought and schemed and calculated for his Holy Mother, the Church, and boundary lines meant less to him than the universality of Rome. It was an inspired obsession but it possessed its theoretical verities. Across the plaza Juan Diego could see lights burning in the windows of the Governor's Palace and the movement of men before the central door. Rea and his advisers were there planning the destruction of the besieged Americans. Isunza was at Atlixco, probably, with the rest of the Puebla government. The young man turned his horse by the cathedral and was almost at his journey's end.

The house loomed before him with painful suddenness and he viewed its familiar tiled front with somber eyes. It looked as though it was deserted for not a light was showing and it seemed withdrawn in a sort of desolate silence. As he dismounted and led his horse toward the door he remembered how agitated he had been when he first crossed the threshold. He was not agitated now. He moved in a grim calmness that nothing could shake. Whatever he found could not be worse and whatever he had to do would not be less than he had accepted already in his mind. He struck the heavy door briskly with his knuckles.

It seemed an eternity before he heard the bars being removed and the large key turning in the lock. The dark wood slid inward reluctantly four or five inches and a sliver of dim light fell across the pavement. A dark eye on the level of his top jacket button peeped out.

"Chuchita?" he demanded. "I am Juan Diego de Béxar, the Señor Teniente. What will I . . ."

There was a quick exclamation and the door opened wide.

"Enter, Señor Teniente," exclaimed the Indian girl. "Enter quickly. The patrón has been waiting for you."

"My horse," explained Juan Diego. "I can't leave it here. Some rascal will steal it. Where . . ."

"Tomás will attend to the horse," said Chuchita. "He is the boy who . . . Here he is now. Tomás, take the Señor Teniente's horse to the shed. Quickly. Enter, Señor Teniente."

Juan Diego slid past the boy into the house and stood for a moment while he heard bars and lock clicking behind him. A great wave of familiarity flowed over him. Everything was the same even to the faint odor that he remembered so well.

"The patrona is in the library," said Chuchita. "Will you come this way, Señor Teniente?"

He stepped into the room where he had sat so often and saw with some surprise a little old lady rising to greet him. For an instant he was puzzled, imagining that this, perhaps, was Doña Marta from Apizaco, and then, peering closer, he suppressed an exclamation of pity and astonishment as he recognized Doña Ágata. She was like an aged caricature of the woman he remembered. The dark hair had turned to white, the cheeks and eyes appeared to have fallen in, bringing into absurd prominence the hawklike nose, and the whole stature seemed wavery and about to collapse. He kissed the dry clawlike hand that was extended to him and did not say a word. A great horror of what grief could do to a helpless body rushed over him like a dizziness.

"God be thanked that you have come," said Doña Ágata. "I have been praying for your safety, Señor Teniente, ever since Chepe rode away."

"We traveled all day," replied Juan Diego with an effort. "Don Isidro . . . ?"

"I will take you up to him presently," she declared. "For the moment I want to speak to you. Sit here, Señor Teniente,"

He observed that her voice was firm and that she seemed quite in control of her emotions. He could not take his eyes from her as he lowered himself into the leather chair. She appeared to read his thoughts.

"You find me aged, Señor Teniente," she said calmly. "My hair has turned white. That is because I have died twice since last I saw you. I died twice and I have no more tears to shed. I died for the first time when your letter came and I knew that my son was dead. I died again two nights ago when Don Alejandro forced himself into this house and carried away my daughter. You are looking at a dead woman, Señor Teniente."

Juan Diego opened his mouth but could find no words.

"I am not mad, Señor Teniente," went on Doña Ágata. "It is merely that I have died twice. At first, I wept and wept and dashed my head against the wall and clawed my breasts until they bled and once I fell down the stairs. That was when Don Isidro showed me your letter. I cursed God, Señor Teniente. I sat on the bed in my chamber and cursed God but I knew what I was doing all the time. If Don Isidro tells you that I am mad you must not believe him. That is why I wanted to speak to you before you saw him. Do not believe him, Señor Teniente. I am not mad."

"Is Don Isidro very ill?" asked Juan Diego huskily.

"He is paralyzed," replied Doña Ágata. "He.cannot move his legs. It is because he cannot move his legs that he sent for you."

She leaned forward and grasped Juan Diego by the knee.

"You must ride after Don Alejandro, Señor Teniente," she declared earnestly. "You must kill him and bring Doña María Catalina back to me."

Her hawklike grip tightened until it hurt.

"Do you understand?" she demanded, peering into his face with bright fixed eyes. "Do you understand, Señor Teniente?"

"That is why I have come here," he answered.

Her breath, close to his face, was as sour as a cat's and the unblinking steadiness of her eyes in her fallen face disturbed him. He did not know whether she was mad or not but the terrible blows that had befallen her had so changed her that she was another being altogether. She seemed possessed by an insistence on sanity both in speech and in demeanor that betrayed a fearful suspicion in herself that she might be deranged. She did not know. The paroxysms of grief had left her like this. It was true that a part of her had died, a part that wept natural tears and raved at the unreasonable injustices of time, and nothing was left but an impulse that was an obsession. Juan Diego understood that she would never be afraid again or weep again because those emotions were in that part of her that had died. She was nothing but a glittering-eyed shell.

He didn't like to look at her. The tight rein that he had kept on his own feelings slackened before her fixed stare and he knew that if he had found her in a state of collapse with a physician attending her he would not have been so moved. He would have understood that instinctively and steeled himself to bear it and choked down his own anger and foreboding while he planned what to do. That was the duty of man in a crisis—to be strong and keep one's head while women wept and lost all control. He turned his face toward the door beyond which he could see the climbing stairs while he fought the hysteria that was rising within him. In a minute he would scream and curse. Everything that had happened and everything that he had kept at a detached distance since Chepe had brought the news to the Calle de Santa Clara was beginning to roll over him like an engulfing wave. It would sweep him away. María . . . María . . . Ah, Jesús . . . ! He stood up with clenched fists.

"I cannot talk to you, Doña Ágata," he said in a hoarse voice. "I must see Don Isidro."

Her hand, like the claw of death, had fallen from his knee as he rose and now she sat peering up at him with her head on one side.

"Yes, Señor Teniente," she replied. "He is waiting for you. You must go upstairs and see him."

He mounted the stairs without looking back and walked down the corridor and tapped at the hacendado's door. Then he opened it and walked into the bedchamber.

Don Isidro was lying bolstered up in the big bed with his hamlike hands clasped over the mound of his belly. A dozen candles burned in the room and the air was close and stank of recumbent flesh.

"You came quickly, Señor Teniente," said Don Isidro. "I knew that you would. Sit here."

Except for the grayness of his face and a white bandage over his temple he looked the same as he always had. His eyes were clear and sane. Juan Diego sat down in a chair by the bed and waited while his shaken composure steadied. This was better. The vitality of the hacendado appeared to exude from the colored blankets.

"I suppose Chepe has told you everything," remarked Don Isidro.

"Yes," replied the young man. "I have brought my brother with me. He has gone to the Cuartel San José to try and secure a squad of men. We start out in the morning."

"Yes," said the hacendado, unfolding his hands and feeling the bandage on his head. "You must move quickly. I don't think that he will hurt my daughter but it is just as well to lose no time. He is a vile dog. I cannot go with you for God has taken from me the use of my legs. You spoke of your brother. I did not know . . . Who is he?"

"He is an officer in the American army," explained Juan Diego.

"Oh," murmured Don Isidro. "Well, that should be a help. Take Chepe with you, too. He has ways of finding out in which direction Don Alejandro went."

They were speaking as quietly as though they were discussing some matter that did not touch them closely.

"You didn't recognize any of these . . . these guerrillas?" asked Juan Diego.

Don Isidro shook his head.

"Excepting Don Alejandro, no," he answered. "There were a dozen or so of them. I had the impression that they seemed to be from the hot lands, Vera Cruz, perhaps. Their faces . . . It was a terrible evening . . . after midnight. I was sitting in the library, for, since the news about Lorenzo came, I do not sleep very well. Doña Ágata . . . Have you seen her? Well. I was reading when they broke down the door and forced their way in. I reached for the pistols in the table drawer but before I could reach them one of the rascals swung his musket and hit me in the head. I did not remember anything from that instant until I recovered my senses in this bed. But Chepe told me what had happened. Don Alejandro had gone up to María's room with one of his men, forced her to dress, flung my wife into a corner and then departed with the girl. According to Chepe, she did not utter a word. Tomás, the boy who helps Chepe and who sleeps in the shed, saw them ride away in the direction of the Acajete road. I have heard nothing since."

Juan Diego's fingers closed tightly.

"Why did you ever permit your daughter to marry this man?" he demanded dully.

It hurt him to ask the question.

Don Isidro stared at his big hands for a moment and then shook his head as though he was denying something that had not been spoken.

"I will tell you why," he said almost submissively.

In a slow dogged voice he related the tale of Seda, Don Francisco and himself, of the nights in the eating house in Seville, of the murder by the posada on the bank of the Guadalquivir and the vow taken in the little church. He told it without adornment or self-extenuation and Juan Diego heard him through without interruption. Knowing Don Isidro as he did the young man could understand and deplore the fanatical possession that had moved him to such a persistent extreme. He could even find it in his heart to pity the arbitrary victim of an obsession that was greater than himself. Sometimes the strong will was caught in such coils and then its strength became its own punishment. It was such singleness of will moving beyond reason and the change of circumstance that made conquerors and martyrs, Neros and St. Sebastians, Jenghis Khans and St. Pauls. Reproaches and accusations fell like dead leaves on the stout fortresses of such determined natures. They had yet to learn that everything in life was a compromise, including God.

"It was a vow," concluded Don Isidro. "I thought that a vow could not be broken. I am not so sure now."

People might be broken but not a vow. There was an anxious expression in the hacendado's eyes as he stared at Juan Diego but the young man made no comment. What was there to say? It was far too late for words. It was the moment that he must consider.

"Why should Don Alejandro kidnap Doña María Catalina?" he asked steadily. "What does he expect to gain by it? She will never . . ."

"He has a Spanish pride in possession," said Don Isidro. "He hates me because I humiliated him once. And María is my only child . . . now. All that I have will go to her."

"What do you think he will do?" persisted Juan Diego.

Don Isidro's heavy underlip thrust out as he pondered.

"I don't know," he said at last. "Perhaps he will try to reach Cuba.

or Guatemala. He is not too fond of fighting. It is the estate that he wants. If María has a child . . . his heir . . . and hers . . ."

A slow horror peered out of the young man's eyes as he met the hacendado's perturbed glance. Don Isidro was shaken by the white mask that faced him.

"I love Doña María Catalina," declared Juan Diego with difficulty. There seemed to be a tightening iron band around his heart.

"I know that you do," answered Don Isidro. "That is why I sent for you."

His voice was low, almost conciliatory. The candles sputtered like a swarm of moths striking against a lighted window while the two men, one lying helpless and the other leaning forward with his hands clasped between his knees, stared steadily at each other. In a moment Juan Diego leaned back.

"We must plan what to do," he said in a matter-of-fact voice. "We must keep our heads. Here is what I think is best. I shall meet my brother and Chepe some miles out of the city tomorrow morning. If luck is with us my brother will have some soldiers with him. If not, we will go on just the same, riding on the assumption that Don Alejandro is somewhere between here and the coast. We will question everybody. Chepe will talk to the Indians he meets. When we come up with Don Aljandro and his band we will make such plans to rescue Doña María Catalina as seem feasible. Have you any suggestions to add, Don Isidro?"

The hacendado thought for a moment and shook his head.

"That is all that you can do," he declared. "You will go heavily armed, of course. I think that you will find Chepe of great value. He is a Yaqui and he is like a hound on the scent. Through the Indians he will discover the headquarters of every guerrilla band between here and Vera Cruz. Trust him implicitly, for he worshiped María. It is all in your hands, Juan Diego. If I could mount a horse . . . but I cannot. There is no use wasting words about it. Take my pistols. They are still in the drawer of the library table. And God go with you."

Juan Diego stood up.

"I'll see you in the morning, Don Isidro," he said. "You must rest now."

The hacendado shook his head.

"I cannot rest lying down," he replied. "But I will wait. That is all that I can do now . . . wait. Your old chamber is prepared for you. It is you who need to rest . . . for you have something to do. Good night, Señor Teniente."

"Good night, Don Isidro," said the young man.

He could feel the prostrate man's eyes following him as he left the bedchamber.

Inside the familiar room he sat down on the bed and began to draw off his boots. Everything looked the same. He had but to close his eyes and imagine that he had not left this house at all, that it was still May, that he had just finished emptying a bottle of aguardiente with Don Isidro, that he would see Doña María Catalina in the patio in the morning, that Lorenzo was laughing on the stairs and that the odor of the sleeping roses was flowing through the window. But the window was closed and there were no roses. It was September and the war was lost. It was the end of illusions and the beginning of reality. He sat, holding one boot in his hands, and staring at the wall. The way of life was hard, hardest of all for the man who tried to live in a dream, and it twisted without reason. One could not choose one's own path any more. Time did that. Time and circumstances. He put the boot down and started to remove the other. In the distance he heard a flurry of musket shots and the answering bark of a howitzer. They seemed like an ominous prophecy of that world of reality which he had to face.

He judged that it was an hour before ten o'clock at least, when he halted his horse before the burned hacienda building where Don Salustio Alcáraz had consumed his wife and children. The blackened roofless ruin stood in a mass of overgrown vines, its empty windows framing the blue sky, almost in sight of the National Highway. On all sides stretched the level cultivated plain. Juan Diego dismounted and stood holding his mount by the bridle while he waited. There had been no trouble in leaving Puebla, the guards at the garita hardly noticing him as he had ridden through with a sharp word and a smart salute. They had raised their heads momentarily from the gambling game with colored stones that occupied them and that was all. A sudden bellow from the American howitzer had sped him on his way. He had encountered nobody on the highway except a decrepit Indian sitting on a stone and staring blankly into space, a small destroyed cornfield behind him where horses appeared to have foraged. Apparently he had been visited by guerrillas.

The parting from Don Isidro had been brief and businesslike, a few words, a clasp of hands and the acceptance of the pistols, several belts of ammunition and a package of food from Chuchita. It was a relief not to see Doña Ágata, who had kept to her chamber. So far all had gone well. The young man stood by the head of his horse and waited. The thought that he might tie the animal to the thick shrubbery and sit down somewhere in the shade (for the sun was high in a cloudless sky) did not occur to him. Automatically, like a sentinel on duty, he remained motionless in the middle of the trail, his head slightly bowed, and waited. He endeavored to keep his mind clear of all forebodings. And yet it seemed to him that time was rushing by like an invisible torrent while he stood rooted in the soil like a helpless tree stump. Time was bearing Doña María Catalina farther and farther away from him every second and he could do nothing about it. He remained without movement for more than an hour while the forebodings grew in his mind like dank mushrooms. Perhaps David and Chepe had been captured by Rea's men. Perhaps the American commander had refused to permit David to continue on his way. Perhaps this was not the place. Perhaps there was another burned hacienda building. Perhaps . . . And then he heard the quick clop-clop of horses' hoofs. It was David and Chepe, David in civilian clothes and a sombrero looking intensely unlike himself and Chepe in a heavy sarape and bearing an old English Tower musket. They were alone.

David shook his head at Juan Diego's concerned glance.

"Childs will not spare a man," he said without any preliminary greeting. "He has less than five hundred effective soldiers. More than eighteen hundred are sick. But he has given me an order to impress any troops we may meet on the way. Did you find out anything from Don Isidro?"

"No," replied Juan Diego, swinging to his saddle. "Nothing that we did not know already. He thinks that some of the rascals were Veracruzanos. Shall we . . . ?"

"Chepe has been inquiring around the city," declared David quickly. "Suppose we leave our first moves to him."

The Indian had already pushed his horse past them along the trail.

"We will go this way, Señor Teniente," he said. "I talked to some men I know. They heard of a Spaniard from Mexico City who is riding with Jarauta. Jarauta has his headquarters near Jalapa."

"Jarauta!" exclaimed Juan Diego. Then he closed his lips tightly.

"Do you know him?" asked David, urging his horse forward.

"I've heard of him," replied his brother. "He's an ex-divinity student who fought for the Carlists in Spain. He is not a rogue like so many of the others. He is worse than a rogue because he knows what he is doing."

"He has many men," announced Chepe. "The Indians told me that he has many Cubanos with him."

They were riding in single file along the trail that ran northeast and then turned gradually due east. Juan Diego figured that they were traveling roughly parallel with the National Highway which would be several miles to the south of them.

"There may be a way of outwitting his many Cubanos," remarked Juan Diego in a worried voice.

He had hoped that Don Alejandro was traveling with a small band of his own.

They rode all day along back roads and half-invisible trails, stopping but once to eat cold tortillas and sliced pork, meeting no one although Chepe disappeared several times into clumps of trees in search of fugitive Indians, and long after nightfall they camped in a rocky depression that Juan Diego guessed was somewhere near El Seco, which would put them about halfway across the tierra templada between Puebla and the old fortress of Perote. They slept fitfully for it was cold, resting their heads on their saddles and keeping watch in turn. Nothing disturbed them although once Chepe swore that he could hear horses' hoofs. In the morning they pushed on, riding through what seemed to be a deserted world. Two or three times they circled villages of mud huts and fields of wheat, barley and beans but these places, which were the visible evidences of life, revealed no living figures. Apparently all the natives had fled to the distant hills or crowded into the bigger towns or joined guerrilla bands. This journeying through a dead world, dead except for hawks, a few skinny cows and occasional barking dogs, affected the nerves of the two brothers and they caught themselves frequently glancing over their shoulders suspiciously at shadows, trees and rocks. Even Chepe seemed disconcerted when he failed to find any Indian whom he could question.

Twilight was falling and it had begun to rain, a slow, miserable drizzle, when, following Chepe along a narrow lane between seemingly endless rows of maguey plants, they came out on a road and saw the dust-brown castle of Perote and the town about a half mile from it. There was plenty of life here, including an unmistakable convoy of American provision wagons, their white tops blue in the dimming light, winding over the yellow road toward the castle. The cracking of bull whips sounded like little pistol shots. David, who explained that the castle was garrisoned with American troops, decided to present his order from Colonel Childs there and see if the commandant would detach a squad of men for special service and Chepe desired to question some of the Indians in the town. Therefore they rode into Perote, finding it a decayed-looking place full of mud houses, half of them roofless, inhabited by melancholy-faced natives wrapped in dingy blankets.

After some search they discovered a dilapidated cantina and there Juan Diego dismounted, David going on to the castle and Chepe disappearing into the ruinous-looking streets. Some teamsters and a few soldiers were congregated in the drinking room and gulping down aguardiente while a red-necked fellow hoarsely bawled some doggerel above their profane insults. Juan Diego stood in the doorway for a minute or two listening to the thickly uttered words and gradually comprehending that they were part of a song that David's friend, Lieutenant Cousins, had chanted in the Calle de Santa Clara.

A poor soldier's tied up in the sun or the rain,
With a gag in his mouth till he's tortured with pain;
Why I'm blessed if the eagle we bear in our flag
In its claws shouldn't carry a buck and a gag.

The verses went on endlessly. Juan Diego moved from the door where the insistent drizzle beat against his back and sat down in a corner. Nobody noticed him.

He was cold, tired and hungry but he made no attempt to call the patrón, who stood by an inner door anxiously watching the drinkers through small obsequious black eyes. There was a fat helplessness about the cantinero that was too discouraging to divert to himself. Juan Diego, therefore, sat silent and waited. He watched the faint blur of the rain in the darkening street and listened to the sound of turning wheels and horses' hoofs as the minutes passed and once caught himself nodding in a half-doze. He straightened up abruptly and rubbed his unwashed hand across his eyes. And then he saw the lean countenance of Chepe peering in through the open door. There was an urgency in the Indian's eyes that brought him to his feet and across the splintered flooring in the tick of a second. Behind him the singing and oaths mingled with the crashing of a glass.

Chepe turned immediately and Juan Diego fell into step beside him. The rain had increased and they bowed their heads into it as they passed down the dark street sliced by a few oblongs of light from drinking places.

"What is it?" asked the young man hurriedly. "You have found out something?"

"Señor Teniente," said Chepe. "There is an agent from Jarauta here. He is gathering men for the guerrilla leader, promising them many pesos and all the loot they can find. I want you to see him. He comes from Mexico City and the men I know tell me that he arrived here two days ago with a little Spaniard and a dozen riders. He remained while they moved on toward Jalapa. Señor Teniente, my friends inform me that Jarauta has many headquarters but the most important is close to Jalapa."

"I know that country!" exclaimed Juan Diego. "But your friends . . . They did not see a woman with the little Spaniard?"

"They saw many women, Señor Teniente," replied Chepe. "The guerrillas always have their women with them. This way, Señor Teniente. Around this corner."

They moved in the rear of what appeared to be another cantina. The oblong of a high lighted window glowed before them. Chepe raised himself and stared through the dirty glass and then he beckoned to Juan Diego. The young man crept forward and supported himself with both hands on the wet sill as he looked into the room. For a moment he could distinguish nothing but strange faces shifting under the illumination of metal lamps and then to one side and no more than a yard or two from the window he saw the familiar face.

"Señor Teniente," whispered Chepe, "the agent of Jarauta is sitting at the table to the left and talking with two—"

Juan Diego stopped him with a thrust of the elbow.

"I know," he muttered. "I have seen this man before."

How could he forget that face? The round greasy features with the purplish fragment of a rotting nose took him back swiftly to the Four Roses of Xochimilco in Mexico City and once again he could smell the sour effluvia from the belching mouth of Mateo Báez. He might have guessed that where Don Alejandro went Mateo Báez would go, too. And now that he saw Mateo Báez he knew that he was on the right trail. There was no doubt now that the Spaniard and his helpless captive were with Jarauta. The sole task remaining was to find the guerrilla's hideout and rescue Doña María Catalina. As Juan Diego gazed through the stained glass at Mateo Báez, who was conversing earnestly with two doubtful-looking Indians, an emotion of extreme rage at the ugly face possessed him and instinctively he felt for the Colt's five-shot revolver that David had given him. Here was one of the vermin that infested the Republic and a bullet between the round eyes . . . But, no. He did not need Chepe's quick hand on his arm to warn him that this was not the way. He stepped back from the window just as the agent's face turned toward it.

"That man is a friend of Don Alejandro's," he said in a low voice to Chepe. "I saw him once in Mexico City. If he is recruiting for Jarauta, then all we need to do is follow him. He will lead us to Doña María Catalina."

"Señor Teniente, we do not need to follow him," replied the Indian. "I will know where all the headquarters of Jarauta are half an hour after I go into Jalapa. I will know where the patrón's daughter is kept. It is best to ride ahead of this man. How can we say how long it will be before he returns to Jarauta?"

They splashed their way back to the cantina before which they had tied their horses.

"You are right, Chepe," admitted Juan Diego, nodding. "It is best to lose no time now. But," he added grimly, "I shall have the pleasure of putting a bullet in Mateo Báez before too long."

David had not returned when they reached their horses and they stood in the rain talking quietly for fifteen minutes while they waited. Juan Diego grew doubtful about leaving the agent behind and suggested that they might catch him in the darkness and force him to tell where Doña María Catalina was being kept. They would save time that way and time was of the most imperative importance. Chepe

pointed out that Mateo Báez undoubtedly would be accompanied by at
least a half dozen of his recruits and certainly on his guard in this
town directly under the guns of the Americans. Juan Diego admitted
this and then suggested that they ambush him on the road. Again the
Indian demurred. There were too many dangers attendant on such an
exploit. The agent might travel with a dozen men. He might be killed
and that would give them no information. They were but three and it
would be wiser to find Jarauta's headquarters before they risked their
lives. Unwillingly Juan Diego agreed with the Indian. Caution was best
until the proper moment to strike came.

When David rode up with the discouraging news that the commandant at the castle could spare no men for detached service they
discussed the problem of Mateo Báez again. David approved the con-
clusion that it was wiser to let the agent alone for the time being.
"We should push on," he declared, "and not get into a brawl here.
Perote is full of drunken soldiers. But where shall we sleep? In this
hovel here?" He indicated the cantina, from which the bawling voices
of troopers and teamsters still came. "After all, we need some rest."
Chepe explained that he knew a jacal not far away on the Las Vigas
road where they could find shelter and they decided to go on in spite
of the rain. "Come on, then," said David. He slapped a bulging powder
bag attached to his saddle. "Army biscuits and pork," he explained.
"We'll sleep better with filled stomachs."

They slept badly in the jacal, for it was infested with infinitesimal
insects that penetrated their clothes and raised red rashes on their
bodies. It was with relief, therefore, that they set out in the early
morning, the rain having stopped sometime during the night, on the
descent toward Jalapa, riding through long stretches of pine trees and
with occasional vistas of the wild and rugged range of hills to their
right. They rode all day, following concealed trails that were more or
less parallel with the National Highway and making wide circuits
about inhabited places, clusters of mud huts with straw roofs, though
most of these were deserted. Still, there were increasing evidences of
life all about them, the smoke of fires, dogs barking, faraway shouts
and, once or twice, the echo of shots. Chepe's natural instincts for
masked progress proved of great value during this stage of their
journey for he led them through the loose web of roads and trails with
such skill that they saw no one and no one saw them. There were always washed-out gullies, hollows, screens of bushes and trees and
helpful hills to hide their quiet movement. They rode warily through
the pass of La Hoya, crossed wide expanses of broken lava where the
only vegetation was the deathlike fingers of gray cactus and came at
last to a wide terrain of vast haciendas. The land became bright, green

fecund, as it sloped steadily toward the low sandy plain about Vera Cruz. It was familiar territory to Juan Diego, territory that he had ridden over during his boyhood at Manga de Clavo, and he started to search about him for remembered landmarks. Late in the afternoon they saw Jalapa shining like a jewel in a case of bright emerald.

Arresting their horses in a glade of trees overrun with bougainvillaea about a mile from the city and some distance from the main-traveled road they held a brief council and decided that it was best for Chepe to go on alone and find out what he could about Jarauta and his many headquarters. He would discover his friends or, at least, other Indians, perhaps a Yaqui or two wandered far from his own lands, who would receive him with that familiar freemasonry that existed among them and tell him all that it was necessary to know. At the same time, he could find out if there were any American troops in Jalapa, for it was a link in Scott's line of supplies to the Valley of Mexico, and, perhaps, bring back some food. So Chepe disappeared, on foot for fear his horse might be seized by some armed band, and the brothers dismounted, hobbled the mounts and sat down in the glade to wait.

They refrained from discussing the subject uppermost in their minds. Instead, David expressed his disgust at the type of guerrilla warfare that the Mexicans were waging.

"It is just an outlet for lawlessness that the government has sanctioned," he declared.

"It is the only resort of helpless people," pointed out Juan Diego. "When armies are destroyed by superior forces it is the only retaliation that an invaded people have, to separate into small groups, to strike in the dark, to hide in the hills, to cut lines of supply, to kill, to burn, to destroy."

"But these fellows are bandits," objected David, waving his hand in a wide circle. "I understand that they are as bad on the natives as they are on the Americans. The desire to kill and loot is their only incentive."

"Some are honest patriots," replied Juan Diego soberly, "but a lot come from the riffraff of the Republic. The heartbreaking part of it is that the Republic cannot control its own people. We use such forces as we can find and many of them are bad. The government established definite rules for guerrilla warfare. For instance, a citizen must obtain authorization from the state or national authorities to raise volunteers and goods taken from the enemy are to be divided among the band. In way the government thought of them as irregular militia and ranked the leaders from lieutenant to colonel according to the number of men they commanded. I never approved of them for they are bound to be undisciplined and regardless of the rules and usages of war. They must live on the land and it naturally follows that when they cannot take anything from the enemy they will take it from the civilian population."

He stared up into the heavy green foliage of the tree beneath which he sat and pursed his lips.

"Besides," he added, "the activities of these men amount to nothing in the long run. They irritate but they do not scare the Americans and they cannot change the results of the military campaigns. The war is lost and all they do is extend the horrors of it."

"They're a pack of murderers!" said David savagely.

"They're another proof of the disunity of the Republic," remarked Juan Diego gloomily. "Independent bands; independent leaders, independent parties, no cohesion, no common purpose, no single goal."

He drew in a long breath and closed his eyes. David, observing his face in the green shadow, noted the drawn lines of maturity that had overspread the smooth skin and the straight grimness of the mouth that was both proud and lonely in the withdrawn isolation of his features. He has lost much and gained little, thought the older brother in a repressed surge of tenderness, and there is nothing I can do about it. But he is tough and will come through. He is tough to conceal the desperation over that girl that must be eating into his heart. He is tough to say nothing and to keep himself from constantly crying out in concern and rage. He is tough to move with coolness when he should be quivering in a fever of despairing excitement. He is tough . . . and yet he has the shyness and awkwardness and tenderness of a woman. He is younger than I am and he is older than I am. He has seen more and experienced more and endured more and understood more than I have and at the moment he is more lost than I am. And David began to wonder what it was, gift or lack, that kept him from being lost while his brother was moving through apparently impenetrable fogs. Presently he dozed.

It was twilight when Chepe returned bringing a basket of cold tortillas, some fruit and startling information that brought both brothers to their feet. He had found out where Doña María Catalin was being kept. He said it calmly and then insisted on explaining the state of Jalapa before going further with the information. David and Juan Diego listened impatiently while he informed them that there were no Americans in Jalapa at the moment although a strong body perhaps a brigade, was moving up from Vera Cruz and already was near the National Bridge, some thirty-nine miles to the east. Most of the guerrilla bands were drifting rapidly toward the bridge to obstruct this advance. Among these bands, which included those of Senobi the priest Martínez, Aburto, Mendoza and Vázquez, was that of Jarauta. Chepe's eyes narrowed and he glanced meaningly at the brothers as he mentioned Jarauta's name.

"That is all very well," broke in Juan Diego impatiently. "Jarauta is moving toward the bridge. But where is Doña María Catalina?"

Chepe stooped and picked up a few pebbles from the ground.

"Here, Señor Teniente, is Jalapa," he said, putting one of the pebbles down on the ground. "And here is a road. And here is a trail from the road. And here are many trees. And here is a cave. The guerrillas are holding the patrón's daughter in that cave."

Every time that he said "here" he put down a pebble, and studying the rough design Juan Diego decided that the cave was somewhere to the northwest of Jalapa. It was lush uninhabited country there, slashed with tree-hidden ravines and pitted with concealed hollows, hacienda lands, perhaps, but unexplored by their owners and avoided by travelers who kept to the main roads.

"You are sure of all this?" demanded David, studying the pebbles. "How far away is this cave? Is it difficult to reach?"

"Señor," said the Indian, "I was told this by an Otomí who had ridden with Jarauta and is now hiding in Jalapa. It is a night's journey from the city. The entrance to the cave is in a ravine through which flows a stream. Both ends of the ravine may be guarded. It will be difficult to reach but Jarauta is not there."

"You mean the guerrillas have no leader?" asked David quickly.

"Jarauta has taken his men with him," explained the Indian. "There are only Don Alejandro and four of his followers at the cave. The rest—"

"I have heard enough!" exclaimed Juan Diego, stumbling in his haste to reach his horse. "Come, we are wasting time. We should be riding instead of talking. For once, fortune is with us, David."

It took them a minute or two to unhobble and mount their horses and trot off on a trail that ran almost due north. Jalapa, with its precipitous streets and multitudinous gardens, lay behind them and on all sides stretched semitropical woods where orchids, gardenias and camellias grew wild. Bright-plumaged birds sang in the trees, their notes dwindling as the twilight deepened and they settled in their nests. The vast crescent backdrop of mountains began to merge into the darkening sky and a few stars glowed faintly through the incredibly clear air. It was both day and night, an overlapping of both, that infinite moment in the twenty-four hours that Juan Diego loved best, and the odor of the suspiring flowers brought back to him those earlier days when life had seemed more like a dream than a reality. Not so far below Jalapa was Manga de Clavo where he had passed the happiest days that he could remember. All this was the Mexico that was eternal, that was the potential cradle of the good life and which had been betrayed villainously by selfish and savage men. The subtle scent of gardenias was in the young man's nostrils as he rode through the twi-

light and in the changing fruit trees he seemed to see the vague figure
of Our Lady in a garment of blue terciopelo with bright stars of gold
all over it. *Framed in roses and smiling she looked out upon me and I
fell to my knees and wept.* Where did that sentence come from?

A vision of Doña María Catalina's face flashed before him, the
long gray eyes wide with fright and the mouth crumpled like a desolate
rose, and suddenly, terrifyingly, as though an unsuspected knife had
been twisted in his breast, he realized anew the shame and danger that
had closed about her with dark destroying tenacles. For an instant he
swayed in the saddle. He felt his forehead perspiring with a cold
anguish that mingled with the chilling kiss of the approaching night
and he was possessed by a terror that left his body numb while his
frantic mind urged him toward a violent and hysterical cry. But he
mustn't . . . he mustn't. He must cage his mind behind strong bars
of control if he was to accomplish anything at all. He grated his teeth
in an intense endeavor to restrain the scarlet birds of panic that flapped
so wildly against the weakening bars. To hold on . . . Calmness was
everything now. Calmness and calculated decisions. He began to repeat
the word "calmness" constantly and silently to himself and after a
few minutes the convulsion within him slackened and he felt that he
was safe. The effort left him limp. He rode like an automaton that had
no will of its own. And then a slow vindictive anger surged into his
body and straightened his back and tightened his hand on the reins and
he knew that he was beyond the whirlpool of his own emotions. He
was a set purpose like a lethal machine, a determined killer, Fate riding
on a horse. David might wonder why he was so matter-of-fact and
silent but Chepe, the Indian, would understand what intense purpose
devoured everything inside him except the potential accomplishment.
The Indians were still and concealed the fires that raged within them
and that was a part of their strength. It would be a part of his strength
too. He had not drained to the thick warm lees the wine of San Lorenzo
for nothing. He would have faith in the potency of that black blood
now. At last he knew what it was and what gave it its magic. It contained the will and faith and doggedness and singleness of purpose of
generations of uncompromising men. "When I drank it," he said to
himself, "I became the vessel of their determination." To believe that
way was its invulnerable virtue.

They traveled without pausing for two or three hours, until it
was quite dark, Juan Diego in a half-dream, David peering from right
to left and with one hand on the butt of his Colt's revolver and Chepe
like a thin obsidian statue in ragged clothing staring straight ahead
and seeming to see everything in the impenetrable blackness before
him. A cloud like a flung blanket rushed across the brightening stars
and it began to rain, a heavy drumming downpour that slashed the

treetops like swinging chains. They were soaked to the skin and the horses began to slip and shudder. After an eternity that might have been half an hour Chepe guided his horse from the increasingly rocky trail they were following into the black heart of the woods. They pressed behind him, heads bowed against the whipping branches that struck out of the dark at their faces, and in a minute or two found themselves beneath a shelving bluff that afforded them some shelter. It was wet here and stank of dead vegetation but they were safe from the full fury of the storm. They dismounted stiffly and stood, backs against the wet earth, holding their horses by the bridles.

"God Almighty, how it rains here!" exclaimed David in disgust as he mopped his face with his wet sleeve. "My boots are full of water."

"We'll have to stay here for a while," remarked Juan Diego. "We can't see where we are going and these horses are tired. It will stop raining before morning."

"Morning?" said David irritably. "Do you mean we will have to stand here until tomorrow morning?"

But he was relieved that his brother had not insisted on continuing the journey through the storm. Sensing his anxiety he had half-expected that he would.

"We will eat now," announced Chepe in a matter-of-fact voice and he passed the basket of soaked tortillas and fruit.

They stood in the darkness just outside the rushing curtain of rain munching soggy masses of half-cooked masa and biting into chirimoyas. The horses moved their wet buttocks restlessly.

Toward morning the storm slackened and though the downpour was still considerable they pulled themselves stiffly into the wet saddles and rode forward, Chepe leading with a confidence that amazed David. Without stars to guide him or familiar landmarks to indicate the way the American officer could not understand how the Indian was so sure of his direction. But when the sky vaguely lightened through the veils of rain he supposed that it was the configuration of the mountains that directed Chepe. Whatever it was, an almost miraculous eye for indications invisible to the others or that extra sense belonging to homing pigeons and wary foxes, the Indian led them along trails, through trackless woods, into gullies and around ravines with a positive speed that often left them behind. During these hours of forced traveling they encountered no one, heard no signs of life and saw no rising smoke. Except for the thrash of the rain slowly subsiding into a spattering whir and the querulous calls of birds from their hidden shelters there was nothing to remove the eerie sensation that they were moving through a world that was dead. The light increased and with it the near mountains, the surrounding trees and rocks and the tilted countryside assumed their familiar shapes. Suddenly, as suddenly as it had started the night before, the rain stopped. A warmth crept into the air and the mountain peaks to the east turned rosy as the sun, as yet invisible, climbed over the Gulf of Mexico. It was day and a multitude of birds announced it with shrill cries, melodious warblings and piercing whistles. The dead land came to life as a fresh breeze ruffled through the thick foliage and now there were little mysterious sounds everywhere. Chepe began to move more slowly and to glance from right to left as though he expected something. They came to rising ground on their left and he turned his horse toward it and climbed steadily through the trees. The brothers followed. At last he came to a spot where he halted and stretched out his arm before him.

"Señor Teniente," he said, "the ravine is there."

Juan Diego and David dismounted and, walking forward a few yards, peered over the edge of land and saw below them the tops of trees and through the heavy branches a flicker of silver where a swollen stream dashed southward over jagged rocks.

"How long is it and just where is the cave?" asked David practically. "Did your informant in Jalapa tell you?"

"Yes, señor," replied the Indian. "He made a picture of it. There," he pointed to the north, "the water comes down over the stones and the entrance is narrow and difficult. There," this time he pointed to the south, "it widens out and there is a trail. Between the two entrances the distance is not great for a man can walk it in fifteen minutes."

"It's about a mile, then," broke in Juan Diego.

"The cave is nearer to the southern end but it is not far from the center of the ravine," went on Chepe. "Between the southern end and the entrance to the cave there is a cleared space with one side closed with logs. It is there that the horses are kept. There is room for thirty or forty of them. The cave is not large and it is there that Jarauta sleeps when he is in this land. His men sleep with the horses or under the rocks near the cave."

David glanced with admiration at the Indian.

"You're as good as a topographical map," he said. "Now let us lay our plans."

He turned to Juan Diego, who had dropped to his hands and knees and was staring down into the green treetops.

"Listen, Charley," he commanded. "We can ride around and come through the southern entrance by the trail or we can tie our horses and work our way on foot through the narrow northern entrance. If there are no more than five men there it should be easy. What do you think?"

Juan Diego sat back on his haunches.

"It is possible that Don Alejandro has posted a man at each entrance," he said slowly. "In that case, those at the cave would be warned of our arrival. If we come on foot from the north they might attempt to flee on their horses to the south and in the exchange of fire who knows who might be hit? If we come on horses from the south they will have time to barricade themselves in the cave and that would mean a siege. David, I don't think we should enter the ravine either way. It is the element of surprise that is our best offense. I think we should go down the side of the ravine here, cross the stream and rush for the cave before they know what it is all about."

David peered over the edge of land.

"It's a good hundred yards down there," he declared, "and it looks awful steep. How do we get back again? It will mean carrying the young lady."

"When we are through there will be no one to dispute our progress," said Juan Diego grimly.

David glaced into his brother's narrowed eyes.

"Yes," he said calmly, "I see."

Then he turned to Chepe.

"What do you think, amigo?" he asked.

The Indian was standing facing south with a slightly bewildered expression on his face. His nostrils quivered slightly. He turned immediately when David addressed him.

"I think the Señor Teniente's plan is the best," he replied. "But what we should do we must do quickly."

"What is it?" asked Juan Diego hastily.

"There are horses to the south of us," answered the Indian.

David drew his Colt's five-shooter from the leather holster and examined it carefully. The others, observing his action, did the same, Chepe studying the weapon, which was entirely new to him, with a dubious air. Then he made sure that his long wide-bladed knife was loose in its pigskin sheath. The Tower musket he had left attached to his saddle.

"Let's start, then," said David. "We'll go down the side a dozen feet apart as quietly as we can and then rush for the cave entrance. Is the stream deep?"

"It is swollen with rain," explained Chepe, "but it is not deep. It will not come above our waists. The rocks are slippery and the current is strong."

He continued to glance toward the south with narrowed eyes.

"Señores, we must hurry," he added.

They moved toward the edge of the ravine.

"David, Chepe," exclaimed Juan Diego, pausing at the brink. "Let us understand one thing clearly. Our purpose is to rescue Doña María Catalina and we must shoot every man who stands in our way. And another thing . . . if one or two of us are hit the survivor must flee for help. He must not stop to protect the fallen. Is that plain?"

"Plain enough," replied David, lowering his feet over the broken edge. "But in what direction does the survivor flee? And where does he find help?"

"If such bad luck should happen he must travel to the south," explained Chepe. "After ten hours he will reach the National Highway. I do not know where he will find help."

"Our troops may be moving up," said David.

His voice was doubtful and he shrugged his shoulders. It didn't seem to matter much anyway for he had little respect for the fighting qualities of the guerrillas and less for their accuracy in firing. He had the feeling that if there were no more than five men down there in the ravine he could handle them alone. They were like wolves, brave only when hunting in packs and sure to show their tails when in small groups. Besides, the new Colt's five-shooters would demoralize them. The whole affair was turning into an engrossing game.

"Come along," he called cheerfully. "Let's get this over with and then find some food. I'm hungry as the devil."

They lowered themselves over the edge, each man a dozen feet from the other, and slid down the perpendicular black earth until their boots hit the first bushes and dwarf trees. Here the incline became a little easier and they moved more upright, grasping at uncovered roots, projecting lips of rock and the tough bases of the undergrowth. The rich smell of steaming soil filled their nostrils and once a small bright green snake shot from under David's hand. He uttered an exclamation and rolled heavily into a spiny bush. By the time they were well in the shadow of the tree-tops their hands were black, scratched and bleeding and their clothing was stiff with a thick clayey mud. The slender trunks became of great assistance to them and they progressed rapidly in a series of calculated falls or downward jumps from tree to tree. The roaring of the stream became loud in their ears. The precipice changed into a slanting descent like the side of a roof and great boulders, fallen from time immemorial, afforded them breathing spots of concealment. And now they could see the cave across the dashing water, really a tall split in the farther rock bluff. It was somewhat to the left of them and they slid along behind the boulders until they were opposite it. The stream was perhaps six feet wide here and the rapid current was churned into a white froth. Before the high black fissure of the cave's entrance a thin spiral of smoke from a small fire, which had apparently just been lighted, curled heavenward and a man in dirty white trousers and shirt knelt before it with his back to the rushing water. He appeared to be unarmed. To the left of him, perhaps twenty feet to the south of the cave, the bluff curved inward in a half circle and across the mouth of this widened space stretched a barrier of vine-covered logs some five feet high. Over this barrier the noses of four or five horses were thrust and Juan Diego was quick to recognize the beautiful head of Don Alejandro's Arabian Simún. The sight was like a bugle call to him and he dashed from behind the protecting boulders, his revolver in his hand, and made straight for the stream. He could hear David and Chepe panting on either side of him.

All three of them hit the water at the same time with a loud splash and an instant later they were up to their waists in the strong current that nearly swept them from their feet. The stream bed had been bitten deeply and steeply into the stony soil here and it called for a determined effort of strength to ford it. As though aware that something unusual was occurring the man by the fire half-rose and turned his head. At the same time Juan Diego fired and the man pitched face forward onto the blazing twigs and did not move again. David shouted with pleasure and Juan Diego felt a wild exhilaration flowing through his body. There were but four left now and he was less than twenty yards from the spot where he knew Doña María Catalina to be. A superhuman power appeared to lift his legs easily through the leaden weight of surging current and, throwing himself forward, he half-fell, half-bounded to the farther bank. It was as though an edging quicksand had released his legs. To his left he could hear the scrape and thud of David's boots and a yard before him on the right he saw the lean sinewy form of Chepe darting through the morning sunlight like a hurled lance. He heard shouts and David's voice rising above them in a high hysterical warning but he did not pause in his headlong dash. There were but fifteen yards of trampled fairly even ground between him and the entrance of the cave. Quick flashes of fire like yellow exploding flowers flared from the black fissure and he heard the quick *pht* of bullets over his head. He raised his Colt's revolver and pressed the trigger twice, his wrist jumping with the recoil of the weapon. At that moment he heard the drumming of hoofs, and, turning his head momentarily to the left, he saw a dozen horsemen bearing down directly upon him. He faltered in wild amazement and half-turned to call to his brother. But David was no longer there. Whirling, he continued to run toward the cave, startled, understanding nothing, intent only on reaching Doña María Catalina. Half a dozen musket balls spattered around him but he did not return the fire. There were but two shots left in his revolver and he intended them for Don Alejandro. He would reach the cave if he died in the effort.

He was halfway across the trampled ground now and it seemed to him that he must bear a charmed life for in spite of the constant explosions of the guns he was unharmed. To his left he could hear the approaching thunder of the horses' hoofs and fierce shouting. These unexpected enemies were less than a hundred feet away and driving their spurs into their mounts with the intent of riding him down. He could not retreat now if he wanted to and retreat was the last thought to enter his mind. His sole chance was the cave. If Chepe and David and he could reach the cave it would take but an instant to dispose of the men in there and then turn to meet the horsemen. There were great rocks about that fissure and they could hold it with their Colt's revolvers as Travis's Texians had held the Alamo eleven years before. He turned his head to the right to shout encouragement to the Indian and was just in time to see him fling up his arms and fall heavily forward, blood spurting from his mouth and nose. A moan of rage escaped him. But David? Where was David? He shouted his name like a battle cry. "David! David! David!" There was no response. Very well, then, he was alone. He was alone as he had always been alone at critical moments in his life. He would hold the cave all by himself. There were still two shots in the Colt's revolver and Don Isidro's pistols were tied to his belt. He tripped on a bared tree root and fell to one knee but was up again in a flash of an instant. The black split of the cave entrance was less than five yards away and as he lifted his strained face toward it he saw again the exploding yellow flowers and heard the swift lisping kiss of the bullets as they flew over his head. He would reach it. He had to reach it. His body became one aching urge as he flung himself forward. There was a noise like roaring breakers in his ears and his eyes filled with a salty liquid that partially blinded him. Everything was thrown out of perspective and the bluff with its dark split seemed to fall toward him with startling rapidity. From the darkness the froglike face of Don Alejandro glowed like a death's-head, the protruding bloodshot eyes swollen with fear and hate.

Juan Diego raised his revolver and fired point-blank at the lurid mask, not knowing or caring whether it was real or a figment of his inflamed imagination. As drowning men are reported to see everything in an instant before they lose consciousness he saw everything that he detested in life in that spectral face, shame, cowardice, rape, robbery and murder. Created by man and perpetuated by man, it was there to prove how far man had fallen into the abyss of the beast. Such creatures walked the ways of the world because others were too callous or indifferent or conniving or afraid to destroy them. Well, one, at least, would never ride the hard-packed roads again. All this surged through Juan Diego's mind before the acrid smoke rose above the barrel of his revolver. Yet the horrible features were still there, glowing against the blackness of the interior of the cave with the phosphorescence of rotting meat. He had not hit it. It was like the impalpable substance of some bodiless phantom through which bullets might tear without wreaking any damage. He fired again, his last shot, and he was less than three yards from the revolting visage now, but still it glowed before him, infernal in its invulnerability, permanent like all the evils on the earth. He flung the Colt's revolver at it and this time he thought he had struck it, for the head moved suddenly backward but not before a red glint appeared on its glowing forehead. Tugging at one of Don Isidro's pistols, the young man plunged for the black entrance. There was just a yard to go. He would make it. He would . . . As swift as a bolt of lightning he was ripped backward, whipped off his feet and slammed down on the trampled ground, his shoulders and the back of his head striking with such force that a galaxy of bright lights spun before his eyes. For a moment he was stunned and then, raising his hands, he tugged ineffectually at the dark wet lariat of woven horsetail hair that bit into his biceps. He had been lassoed by one of the mounted men. He rolled over, rose to his knees and endeavored to fight against the taut strand that stretched between him and the pommel of the rider's saddle. But it was futile. The rope ate into his flesh like an iron wire. At that instant he lost faith in God and man alike.

He sat on the ground and did not raise his head as he heard horses' hoofs trampling about him and the jingle of spurs of dismounting men. The offensive fecal odor of long-unwashed bodies assailed his nostrils from all sides and mingled with this was the scent of the wet hides of the little horses. He was like a slave or a victim sitting in the ashes with his persecutors closing in and mocking him. Glancing up at last he recognized them all, escaped convicts, murderous peons, professional bandits, the scourings of the Republic. These were evil faces but evil as the faces of certain savage animals, the hyena, the warthog, the gorilla, are evil, unthinkingly, instinctively, naturally, and not evil as was the face of Don Alejandro, consciously, sadistically and premeditatedly. These men were ignorant brutes and the evil that was in them was the result of their ignorance and that was partially the fault of the Republic, but the Spaniard was the flawed fruit of a wise old aristocracy that possessed all the advantages of time and tradition and his evil, therefore, was an abnormality such as a great goiter swinging like an eggplant beneath the chin or a bulbous eye swollen like an onion out of its socket. Juan Diego shut his eyes so that he might not see these faces, pressing the lids tightly together. He was not afraid. He was sick with a hopeless despair.

Somebody grasped him by the hair, almost ripping it out by the roots, and swung his head around until he felt his neck cracking. He opened his eyes with a suppressed cry of anguish and looked up into the lowered features of Mateo Báez. The man with the rotting nose stared at him unblinkingly for a long moment and then whistled through his few discolored teeth.

"Canario!" he exclaimed softly. "Canario!"

Straightening up he released the young man's head and after a few words to the circle of men strode away rapidly toward the cave entrance.

He must have seen me through the window at Perote, thought Juan Diego wearily, and then, no, for he would not have been surprised. He was bringing recruits to Jarauta, men to meet the advancing Americans at the National Bridge, and that is why he rode all night. It was just chance that he arrived at this precise moment . . . blind malignant chance. The young man felt numb and emptied, as though he had run a long race and lost. He glanced at the dozen heavily armed men who were clustered about him and conversing volubly. His eyes passed beyond them and he saw the body of Chepe lying motionless on the ground. There was nothing but death and dishonor in the world. But David? David must have got away. The thought roused him for an instant and then he shook his head as though somebody had spoken to him. There was nothing that David could do. He would have to travel miles before he found Americans and then it was probable that they would not aid him. He would come back too late. He would find a body and that was all. But Doña María . . .

Quick steps sounded and he twisted his head toward the cave entrance. Mateo Báez and Don Alejandro were walking toward him. He watched the Spaniard approach and noted that the man's slanting forehead was wrapped in a bloody bandage. The wide heavy face with its flat nose and protruding eyes was dark with fury. Mateo Báez's fat body in tight velvet breeches lumbered hurriedly forward. With head half-turned he was explaining something to Don Alejandro. The Spaniard pushed him aside curtly and came close to Juan Diego.

"Re Dios, yes!" he said venomously. "I recognize him now."

He bent forward for a moment and the young man saw flecks of yellow in his glassy green eyes.

"Who are you?" he shouted. "Why are you here?"

Juan Diego stared up at him without saying a word.

"I will teach you to speak, bribón!" cried Don Alejandro.

Raising his booted foot he kicked the young man furiously in the side of the head.

When he recovered consciousness Juan Diego found himself lying on his back in semidarkness. There was a buzzing of voices, distant at first and then increasing in distinctness as his senses slowly began functioning again. He tried to move his head and a stabbing pain shot through his skull above his left eye. He wanted to put his hand up there and find out what had happened to him but his arms would not move. After a moment he realized that they were bound close to his body and that his legs were tied together at the ankles and the knees. He was trussed up like a fowl. He lay relaxed staring at the obscurity above him and gradually he understood that he was in the cave. Everything came back to him in a flood of bitterness. He was helpless, trapped, the victim of an evil world and there was nothing he could do about it. Somewhere near him was Doña María Catalina and she, too, was helpless, the victim of circumstances that had been set in motion before her birth. He could do nothing for her now. With difficulty he turned his head sideways and saw muddy boots with dull spurs and brightening light where the fissure that was the entrance to the cave opened upon the trampled ground. He reversed the process, twisting his head the other way and saw several boxes, some large bags and an oblong of darkness that he took to be a hung blanket. He knew instantly that Doña María Catalina was behind that blanket and the knowledge set the pulses in his temples beating rapidly. He wondered if she knew that he was lying here on the rocky ground. If she did . . . He pictured her as he had last seen her in Puebla in May, running across the patio to the inner door of her house with her skirt ballooning about her and her white stockings flashing in the gray light and the thought brought tears into his eyes. All lost. Everything was lost. His eyes had become accustomed to the murkiness and he observed that the cave was not large but decidedly narrow, its walls slanting together as they rose some fifteen feet above him. Even with a revolver in his hand he would have no chance of fighting his way out of this knife-shaped crevice. He shut his eyes and waited for what must come.

It came almost immediately. He heard footsteps approaching him and a second later a hard hand grasped his shoulder and shook him violently. Involuntarily he opened his eyes. A long-faced mestizo with a narrow head bound in a red rag was staring down at him.

"Yes, Señor Don Alejandro," said the half-breed. "His eyes are open."

"Bring him here," ordered a surly voice. "Bring the bastard here."

Strong arms dragged Juan Diego to his feet and pushed him a few steps toward the cave entrance. Upheld by the mestizo and a tall gaunt Indian with a knife-scarred face he stood facing Don Alejandro and Mateo Báez, who were sitting on boxes. There were a half dozen men, perhaps, leaning against the rock wall of the cave. Three bodies lay in a neat row just beyond the entrance. The young man observed them without curiosity. One would be the man he shot by the fire, the other, Chepe, but who the third could be he did not know. It was not David. Don Alejandro stared at him angrily although with some bewilderment.

"You will talk now," he declared thickly, his big tongue slipping across his lips as he spoke. "You will talk or I will have your guts cut out. Who are you? What is your name?"

Juan Diego maintained a stolid silence.

"I remember you," said the Spaniard. "You were looking for me in the Four Roses of Xochimilco in Mexico City. Are you one of Tornel's agents?"

Still the young man did not reply.

"He is a Yanqui," announced Mateo Báez suddenly. "Look at his eyes. You can tell by his eyes that he is a Yanqui."

"Are you a Yanqui?" persisted Don Alejandro. "Are you a spy? Are you one of General Scott's spies?"

Juan Diego continued to observe a stubborn silence.

"Where did you find out about this cave?" went on the Spaniard. "What is your interest in me?"

He waited a second and then turned to Mateo Báez.

"Perhaps he does not speak Spanish," he said.

"Señor Don Alejandro," replied the man with the rotting nose, "he spoke perfect Spanish in the cantina."

"Ah, that is true," admitted Don Alejandro.

He stood up and came close to the young man.

"I do not understand you," he said. "What have you to do with me? Eh, desdichado, por qué no me contestas?"

Juan Diego stared into the ugly face so close to his own without saying a word. His mind was working rapidly as he sought a way to use the Spaniard's uncertainty to extricate himself. Don Alejandro was dull-witted, he knew, but Mateo Báez concealed a slyness behind his round-eyed stare that was menacing. It would have to be a good story to convince him. Even as the thoughts passed through his mind the man with the rotting nose turned to Don Alejandro, called him back and began to talk to him in a quick low voice. Juan Diego strained his ears to hear and caught the name "Don Isidro." Suddenly he was frightened. This line must be stopped at all cost. He cleared his throat. Don Alejandro came back to him with a puzzled indignant look on his face.

"Are you an agent of Don Isidro Núñez de Haro?" he demanded directly. "Do you work for his representative in Mexico City? Is that why . . . ?"

"I will speak only to Jarauta," declared Juan Diego desperately. "My business is with Jarauta."

"Oh, you have a tongue," grumbled Don Alejandro. "What is your business with Jarauta? Did you come here to murder him?"

"I will speak to Jarauta," replied Juan Diego stubbornly.

If he could convince the Spaniard that he was concerned only with the guerrilla chieftain . . .

Mateo Báez came forward and took Don Alejandro by the arm.

"I do not believe him," he said softly. "He is frightened now. I advise you to do as I suggested. If he has come here from Don Isidro she will know."

There was a moment's silence interrupted by the hawking and heavy spitting of one of the men leaning against the side of the cave and then Don Alejandro turned angrily and began to walk to the back of the narrow shadowy enclosed space. A riot of conflicting emotions surged through Juan Diego.

"My business is with Jarauta," he called despairingly. "I do not know any Don Isidro. Do you want to know my business with Jarauta? Come here and I will tell you."

Don Alejandro continued on his way as though he had not heard the young man and Mateo drew a rag from his belt and wiped the rotting purple fragment of his nose. His round unblinking eyes never left Juan Diego's face. He belched softly. The mestizo and the Indian with the narrow head tightened their grasp on the young man's arms as he strained forward. Don Alejandro disappeared behind the spread blanket.

"I am a Santanista," declared Juan Diego earnestly to Mateo Báez. "I have come to see Jarauta on the part of the general."

"You are a Yanqui liar," said the other, stuffing the rag back into his belt. "You came here with a Yanqui pistol in your hand and you killed El Escupidor. We will find out who you are."

The young man heard footsteps and he closed his eyes. Oh, Our Lady, he prayed silently to himself, give me strength to betray nothing. He opened his eyes and she stood before him, not three feet away, one hand raised to her breast and her chin lifted in the old proud way that he knew so well. A great rush of relief flowed over him as he discovered that she had not changed at all and that no harm seemed to have befallen her. She was dressed in a red Poblano skirt and a white blouse through which her small breasts pressed with young arrogance. Her face was calm and her wide gray eyes blank. For an instant they gazed at each other, her glance traveling to the discolored lump on his left temple where he had been kicked by Don Alejandro and then swiftly back to his eyes again. He opened his mouth to speak but the words would not come.

"No," she said in the low clear voice that would always bring back the patio in Puebla to him, "I have never seen this man before. I swear, by San Lorenzo, that he is not an agent from my father."

By San Lorenzo. He understood and a feeling of strength rose inevitably through his body. His limbs stiffened.

Don Alejandro looked perplexedly at Mateo Báez.

"It is possible that he belongs to that cowardly dog, Santa Anna," he grumbled. "After all, we thought he was an agent of Tornel's in Mexico City."

Mateo Báez shook his head slowly. "I do not believe it," he declared flatly.

"I am an agent of Santa Anna's" announced Juan Diego firmly. "I was on his headquarters staff. Ask anybody who knows. I tell you again that my business is with Jarauta. I have no interest in you, Don Alejandro."

An emotion of confidence like the first faint ray of dawn was breaking across his despair. It might be possible yet to save both her and himself.

"We can hold him for Jarauta," said Don Alejandro tentatively.

"I do not believe it," repeated Mateo Báez. "This man is a Yanqui and he has met your wife before. I could see it in his eyes a minute ago. He was afraid to see her again. Perhaps he is her lover."

"That is not so!" exclaimed Juan Diego as an intense desire to strangle Mateo Báez possessed him.

"I have never seen this man before," insisted Doña María Catalina for the second time.

Her voice was cool and devoid of any particular feeling.

Don Alejandro swiveled his big neckless head from his wife to Juan Diego to Mateo Báez and then back again. He was puzzled and suspicious and it made him angry. Suddenly he put his hand up to his forehead where the bloody bandage was tightly wound and a glint of fury sparkled in his protruding eyes. He stepped forward hastily.

"Ah, malvado!" he cried. "What does it matter whom you came to see? You hurled the pistol and struck me with it. You fired the shots and tried to kill me. Asesino, you came for me!"

He struck savagely and his doubled fist smashed into Juan Diego's face. The young man would have fallen had it not been for the mestizo and the Indian holding him by either arm.

"Hold him!" screamed Don Alejandro. "Do not let him fall!"

He struck again, a heavy blow on the young man's injured temple. For an instant Juan Diego was blinded and then, as through a fog, he saw the white still face of Doña María Catalina and the round unblinking stare of Mateo Báez. He opened his mouth to speak but before he could utter a word Don Alejandro struck for a third time, catching him flush in the mouth and dislodging several teeth. Convulsively, he spat forth blood and teeth, bowing his head only to have it snapped back with a fourth blow that was like the kick of a horse. He thought his neck was broken. Don Alejandro struck again, slicing his cheek open and the blood dripped down on his jacket. Again he tried to say something but the croak that issued was cut off by another blow in the mouth. Again, again and again the heavy fist smacked like a pistol shot into the torn ruin of his face and his body sagged in the tight grasp of the mestizo and the Indian. He could hear his blood dripping on the rocky ground as he bowed forward and feel it running down his shirt when the unceasing blows whipped him backward. Suddenly Don Alejandro stopped. He called in a thick guttural voice and Juan Diego spluttered as a gourdful of water was dashed into his face.

"Now, then!" cried the Spaniard. "Who are you, asesino? Will you tell me now? Who sent you here?"

The young man opened his bruised mouth to speak and Don Alejandro struck him again.

"Who sent you here?" repeated the Spaniard.

Again Juan Diego opened his mouth and again Don Alejandro struck him.

"Who sent you here?" cried the Spaniard for the third time.

"Santa Anna," gasped Juan Diego hoarsely.

"He lies," said Mateo Báez calmly.

Don Alejandro had the expression of a puzzled infuriated bull but he lashed out again and the hard fist broke Juan Diego's nose. A horrible pain like a red-hot spear pierced the young man's head as the cartilage split and warm urine ran down his thighs as he lost control of himself. He could see through but one eye now and it seemed to him that all these motionless figures about him were distorted and thrown into some monstrous focus that was unreal. Doña María Catalina's face was larger than life-size, huge and pallid and eternal like the face of Our Lady on the Hill of Tepeyac by Guadalupe and the rotting-nosed bristle-grown features of Mateo Báez reminded him of the stone mask of Huitzilipochtli, the Aztec god to whom human sacrifices were made. They were both staring at him, the Mother of Christ and the Aztec idol, with the terrible calmness of lasting things. His befuddled mind thought, These two things will be always in the world. He tried to shake his head but couldn't. Some leaden weight had been attached to it.

"Santa Anna," he croaked and hardly knew what he was saying. "I came to see Jarauta."

No sooner had he spoken than Don Alejandro struck him again and this time his insides loosened and he had the sensation that his intestines were about to drop out. He could almost picture them, pearly and pale purple with red skeins of blood all over them like the dangling entrails of the picadores' horses in the bull ring. A rushing blackness seemed to bear down upon him and it was only by an animallike exertion of will that he retained his senses. He *had* to hold on to his reason for if he did not he feared what he might say. He wanted to be sure that when he collapsed it would be into extreme insensibility. Don Alejandro was mad, he knew that now, and he must confine that madness to himself. He must never let it veer away from him. If it did . . . With his last shreds of consciousness he exerted all his will to convey a soundless message to Doña María Catalina. Be silent. Be strong. Reveal nothing. Reveal nothing or all that I am enduring is wasted. One of us must live. It is you.

He could not see her as he hung between the two men and received the unceasing blows on his shapeless face but he knew that she was there with a strength and bravery that were beautiful to think of and he remembered the sound of her voice. She remained silent to save his life as he remained silent to save hers. It was the equal exchange of love and now they belonged to each other forever. The sound of her voice. She had denied him because she loved him. She had forsworn him by San Lorenzo and in the forswearing she had bound herself to him to the end of time. By San Lorenzo. Yes . . . yes. She had remembered the story as though she had drunk of the black blood of the bull herself. She had given him strength with a single name. And now he felt that all this pain that he was enduring was less than the pain he had endured in the mountains of Michoacán when he had thrust the poisoned thorns into his young body. He had suffered that and lived and now he would suffer this . . . and live or die. It did not matter. He felt a wild sort of triumph surge through his shuddering body and the methodical heavy blows on his face appeared to lessen in the anguish they caused him. He had drained the wine of San Lorenzo until the cup was empty and he was a man. With difficulty, between the raining blows, he lifted his head and twisted his bloody features into the semblance of a smile. He could not see at all now but he knew they were looking at him and wondering what power kept him conscious. She knew. The wine . . . and the mystery behind the wine.

He raised his face proudly for the final blow that would spin him into darkness and was hardly conscious that it did not come. He thought he heard hoofs beyond the cave entrance and voices calling but he could not be sure. There were so many sounds in his ears, the ringing of the bells of Puebla, the beating of regimental drums, the far roll of artillery. And then he heard a voice, clear, incisive, authoritative, through the tumult.

"What is this?" the unseen speaker cried. "By whose order is this being done?"

Many spurs jingled in the cave.

"Who is this man?" called the voice angrily.

Juan Diego turned his blind smashed face toward the speaker.

"Padre Jarauta, this is a spy," answered an invisible Mateo Báez. "He tried to kill all of us. He came with several men but all of them ran away excepting this one and the Indian who lies dead by the stream. He will not speak. Don Alejandro was trying to make him speak."

"Don Alejandro was trying to kill him," said the voice. "God has not signified that we should murder our own people. We have taken up arms to kill Yanquis."

"This man is a Yanqui, Padre Jarauta," insisted Mateo Báez.

There was a moment's silence and Juan Diego had the sensation that keen eyes were inspecting what was left of his face. He tried to speak but the blood in his mouth choked him. He began to cough weakly.

"His own mother wouldn't recognize him," said the voice at last. "You, Febronio Quijano, you are clever at these things, take this man to the pallet, wash his face and do what you can with those cuts. See if you can open those swollen eyes. When he is conscious I will speak with him."

Juan Diego wanted to say that he was conscious but his tongue would not function. He tottered as the men who were holding his arms turned him about and started to drag him across the rocky ground.

"My wife sleeps on the pallet," said the thick voice of Don Alejandro.

"Take him to the pallet, Febronio Quijano," ordered the firm voice.

The young man tried to walk but couldn't and the mestizo and the Indian carried him between them some distance and dropped him like a sack of corn on wrinkled blankets. He had the sensation that a great bubble filled with blood was swelling rapidly on his temple and would burst any minute. He wanted to raise his hands to it but the ropes held them tightly to his sides. There was a man without a face . . . It was himself. When the first gourdful of water was dashed upon him he lost all consciousness.

His soul rose slowly through a dark abyss and a sound of lapping water filled his ears. He lay supine while the world pitched toward him like a schooner in choppy seas and for the moment he had no sensations in himself but only the vague perception of movement from without, of approaching consciousness that manifested itself in a rising wind of terror. Instinctively he raised his hands to ward off the rolling bulk that was bearing down on him and it was not until he completed the gesture that he realized he *could* move his arms. Awareness poured into him and with it a pain that ran along his limbs and curled into a hard knot of anguish in his head. His soul swooned back into darkness for an instant and then mounted like a half-drowned body to the surface of comprehension. As his mind began to function it seemed astounding to him that he was capable of making gestures. He opened and closed his fingers and finally lifted his elbows from the pallet. It was true. They had removed the ropes, then, and with this definite fact established he was fully conscious and in complete possession of his reason. He remembered everything. He thought that his eyes were open but he could not see and this aroused a chaotic fright that brought his hands up convulsively to his face. There was a wet cloth there and he snatched it away. The darkness was lightened by a glow. Tenderly he prodded the flesh about his eyes and found it swollen and hot and veined with threads of pain. But he could see his hand. The shadow of his hand was visible above his face. A great shudder of relief coursed through his body and in the momentary strength of it he turned his head sideways. It took him a minute or two to adjust his vision to the gloom and then he saw that it was night and the cave was lighted by a few candles stuck on a box near the entrance. He was lying on a low pallet in that part of the rocky fissure that had been concealed by the blanket. Apparently the crude curtain had been removed or drawn aside. But Doña María Catalina . . . *My wife sleeps on the pallet.* His eyes searched carefully down the narrow length of the cave but he could not see her anywhere. There were three men sitting in the shadow of the incline of the wall and near the candles another man was walking back and forth with his hands clasped behind him. Juan Diego watched him for some minutes, and then, finally, as though suddenly aware that eyes were fixed upon him, the patrolling figure picked up a candle and came directly to the pallet.

"You have recovered consciousness," said the man, sticking the candle on a projecting bit of rock and sitting down on the foot of the pallet. "I am Jarauta. Can you talk?"

"Yes, I can talk," replied the young man.

His voice was hoarse and his jaw ached when he moved it.

"You have an excellent constitution," declared Jarauta.

Juan Diego observed him with caution and curiosity. Jarauta was a short sturdy-looking man with a smooth olive-hued face, a large mouth, aquiline nose and intense black eyes. As he leaned over the pallet the young man saw the tonsure on his head and a heavy gold cross attached to a chain swung forward from his breast. He was dressed entirely in black, except for the narrow whorls of gold braid on his jacket. The young man recalled the few things he had heard about this mysterious ex-divinity student, oftener called padre by the Indians, who had turned guerrilla chieftain and mutilated unfortunate American troopers in the name of God with a ferocity that exceeded that of the Yaquis. He had fought for the Carlist cause in Spain with the same savagery that he now exhibited in murderous raids on American wagon trains between the coast and Perote. He was reputed to have no weakness, not even that of mercy, and to regard torture and slaughter with the cold fanaticism of the "familiars" of the Inquisition. He leaned forward now and peered into Juan Diego's pulpy face.

"Febronio Quijano has made you look almost human," he said dryly. "Who are you? Do not lie when you speak to me."

"I am known as Juan Diego de Béxar," replied the young man frankly. "I was a second lieutenant in the armies of the Republic and attached to the personal staff of General Santa Anna."

Jarauta lifted his eyebrows.

"Very well," he said. "I believe you. And now . . . what was your purpose in attacking this cave with several confederates? Do not try to give me the same excuse that you attempted to foist on Don Alejandro. You did not come here to see me and you have no business with me. If you lie I will have you shot and I will not waste time by beating you beforehand."

Juan Diego stared up into the steady eyes and then let his glance drift down the length of the cave.

"You can speak freely," declared Jarauta. "Don Alejandro and his wife are by the stream. The noseless one is on guard in the ravine. Is it true that you are the lover of Don Alejandro's wife?"

"No," answered Juan Diego shortly.

"Did you try to kill Don Alejandro?" demanded the guerrilla chieftain.

"Yes," said the young man with unexpected strength.

Jarauta pursed his lips and his lean muscular hand began to caress the cross that hung from his neck.

"You are in love with Don Alejandro's wife," he announced flatly. "You came here to carry her away."

He waited a moment but Juan Diego preserved an obstinate silence.

"She must love you greatly to endure what she endured today," went on Jarauta in a tone that was almost musing. "I did not know that there was such passion in the secular life. I do not know women. They are mysteries that are not worth explanations. I would never kill for the sake of a woman. I kill for the glory of God."

"Doña María Catalina is the grandniece of the bishop of Puebla," said Juan Diego.

Jarauta's eyes flickered and he half-smiled.

"I know that," he remarked. "She is also the wife of Don Alejandro."

"In name only," burst out the young man.

"In the name of God," declared the guerrilla chieftain gravely.

He revealed his white teeth in a momentary smile.

"Are you seeking a dispensation for murder?" he asked.

"Are there any dispensations for murder?" counterquestioned Juan Diego with some bitterness.

Jarauta settled himself more easily on the pallet his shoulder resting lightly against the young man's knee.

"I perceive that you are a man of some education," he said suavely. "It is not often that I run across one in my present occupation. Most of my men are as ignorant as beasts. They eat, sleep, steal, kill and fornicate, and, sometimes, when I order them to, they pray. They are broken pitchers but the shards are sharp enough to serve me. Even Our Lord had Simon, the Cyrenian, to bear His Cross for Him. You asked me if there were any dispensations for murder. Peter the Hermit thought so. And Cortés brought the True Faith to this country with guns and two-edged swords. God, I must believe, was with them both. But to kill for Christ is not murder. To kill for a woman *is* murder."

Juan Diego peered at Jarauta with puzzled amazement. This was not the sort of conversation he had expected when he first saw the sable-clothed leader approach his pallet and it seemed to him like an affectation. Yet the man was staring back at him without a smile on his face.

"Are you killing for Christ?" he asked without thinking.

"If the Church tells me that it is good to kill Americans then I am killing for Christ," explained the guerrilla chieftain.

"In Puebla the Church was adverse to killing Americans," said the young man.

"That was last May," declared Jarauta. "And, besides, it depends upon what you mean by the Church. Sometimes it is the miter and sometimes it isn't. Here in the state of Vera Cruz I am the Church. At least, I am the temporary custodian of its defenses. As long as there is the slightest chance of cutting off the supplies of General Scott and isolating his army on the Plateau I will do my best; when I am sure that all action is futile I will make what terms I can with the Americans and those terms will include the continued freedom of the Church in this country that was won for the True Cross more than three hundred years ago."

"You are another who is not fighting for the Republic!" exclaimed Juan Diego.

"The True Republic is the child of the True Church," announced Jarauta.

He put his hand on the young man's knee.

"You cannot understand this," he said, "because you are an American at heart. You do not have Mexican eyes and Mateo Báez, who possesses uncanny discernment, tells me that you were born north of the Rio Grande. I do not care about that. If I thought you were aiding the Americans I would shoot you myself. But I believe that you are here only for love. It is only a lover who would be as thoughtless and reckless as you have been. No, Señor Teniente, you do not understand these things. You do not understand that if the Church is not everything in the Republic then the Republic is nothing at all."

"That is medievalism," declared Juan Diego.

"Mexico is medieval," replied Jarauta calmly. "And we mean to keep it so."

"You cannot," announced the young man, raising his head by a painful effort. "You cannot. To do that you would have to hold time still and not even the Church can do that. The great wave moves on and Mexico will move with it. There will be retrogressions and progressions, victories and defeats, triumphs and eclipses of the Church, revolutions and civil wars, but the wave will flow on relentlessly for men will learn and men will understand. It may take a century but the Republic will win. It *has* to win for that is the destined future of the land."

His head sank back from the exertion and he began to cough.

"Bravo!" exclaimed Jarauta in mock pleasure. "If we lived in the time of the Inquisition it would give me infinite pleasure to break every bone in your heretic body."

He laughed shortly and patted Juan Diego's knee.

"It does not matter what you think," he said. "In a hundred years neither one of us will be alive and that faraway fantastic era must take care of itself. It wouldn't surprise me if the Holy Roman Catholic Empire of Mexico extended to the borders of Canada."

The young man merely shook his head. He couldn't understand how a man who appeared to be educated could be so stupid. Perhaps it was true that most men saw only what they wanted to see and given a little power thought they could achieve the impossible.

Jarauta stood up.

"I don't know what to do with you," he announced pensively. "I am taking the new recruits with me back to the National Bridge tonight and that leaves Don Alejandro . . ."

He paused and rubbed his chin.

"You wouldn't like to ride with me?" he asked, after a moment. "We could have excellent conversations when we had time for them."

Juan Diego shook his head ever so slightly. The pains were tormenting him again. The despairing realization of his predicament, momentarily forgotten while he had been talking with the guerrilla chieftain, filled his mind and he did not know what to do. He felt that it would be futile to ask to be set free and he knew that it was impossible for him to aid Doña María Catalina while he was so weak. All the same a prescience of faint possibilities slipped into his consciousness and he glanced up warily at Jarauta.

"How many men are you going to leave with Don Alejandro?" he asked.

The guerrilla chieftain looked down at him sharply.

"Three or four," he replied. "Why?"

Without waiting for an answer he bent over the young man.

"What is it like to love a woman?" he asked softly. "Is it like killing a man?"

"It is like gazing into the eyes of God," said Juan Diego.

Jarauta straightened his solid figure and started to caress the gold cross again.

"Yes," he said doubtfully. "Yes."

"Jarauta," called the young man sharply. "Jarauta."

The black figure stood quite still.

"Put me on a horse and take me as far as Jalapa," begged Juan Diego.

Jarauta shook his head.

"I cannot do that," he replied. "You are Don Alejandro's prisoner."

"You can do anything you want to do," insisted the other.

"No," answered Jarauta. "I cannot do that. I have spoken of this to Don Alejandro and I have made him a promise. He will probably kill you but this is none of my affair. Besides, he has promised me fifty thousand pesos for the winter campaign."

"He has not a penny to his name," declared the young man.

Jarauta shrugged his shoulders.

"He has promised to get them from his father-in-law," he explained.

"Don Isidro would never consent to such a transaction," said Juan Diego.

"He would if he knew his daughter's safety depended upon it," remarked Jarauta, turning to go.

A chill ran through the young man's prostrate figure.

"Jarauta," he cried, "why did you say that you would let me ride with you if you have made such a promise to Don Alejandro?"

"I would take both of you with me," explained the guerrilla chieftain, "and you would still be his prisoner."

"Then let me ride with you," begged the young man desperately. "At least, we would all be together."

"I will not let a woman ride with me," declared Jarauta coldly. "I do not like them near me. Now that I think of it it would be impossible. Adiós, Señor Teniente."

He began to walk toward the entrance of the cave.

"Jarauta!" called Juan Diego after him.

Without looking back the guerrilla chieftain continued on his way out of the cave.

Juan Diego lay on his back with his face turned to the stub o candle that Jarauta had neglected to take away with him and tried to think coherently. His inflamed face seemed to be full of little hot needles and the great swelling over his left temple throbbed like the throat of a frog. He could lay no plans for he did not know what was going to happen to him. Besides, he was unarmed. He wondered how weak he was and brought his knee upward to see. It responded all right and he judged that his feebleness was caused by loss of blood. He must have bled like a stuck pig during that awful beating. Suddenly he was thirsty and looked about him for water but there was none within reach. He sighed and continued to move his knees and arms. Perhaps he was not so weak, after all. Jarauta. He had the feeling that there was something he might have said to the guerrilla chieftain that would have stirred him to friendly action but he could not think what it was. Anyway, it was too late now. He could hear horses' hoofs moving outside the cave and the calls of a dozen men. Jarauta was going and it would not be long before Don Alejandro came back into the cave. He wondered if Doña María Catalina would be with him. And that round-eyed villain with the rotting nose Mateo Báez. Ah, God, to think . . . to think . . . to plan something. But what? He could see the three silent men, Indians from their stolidity, sitting in the incline of the cave and he knew that all of them were watching him secretly with the sly awareness of foxes. They were undoubtedly Don Alejandro's men. Three, then. And the Spaniard and Mateo Báez made five. He sighed again and racked his brains in search of some plan, no matter how desperate, that would extricate Doña María Catalina and himself from their perilous predicament. If he only had a knife or a pistol or any lethal weapon, no matter how small, he would feel better. But there was nothing near him except the candle stub. And the three Indians were watching.

The horses' hoofs and the calling voices died away and an ominous silence settled over the cave. The candle by him sputtered out and he lay restless and anxious in the dark shadow of the alcove. The Indians sat like forgotten idols. Why didn't somebody come in? Where was Doña María Catalina? Where was Don Alejandro? Where was Mateo Báez? Was it possible that they had all ridden away with Jarauta? The thought turned him cold and it occurred to him to rise from the pallet and stagger to the entrance of the cave and see if there was anybody by the stream. But if he did that he would be shot. He could see the muskets resting by the three Indians. Perhaps that was what Don Alejandro wanted. It was even possible that he and Mateo Báez were lurking outside the cave with guns in their hands. No, he could not leave the pallet. Not until he was stronger. His mind twisted toward Jarauta again and he was sure that he had missed something in that curious conversation, some one word that might have solved everything. Jarauta, he felt, was an egomaniac and he had not appealed to the self-created Messiah in him. But there had been no time. He had been too bewildered and surprised at Jarauta's attitude to plan anything. And his head had ached . . . it still ached . . . damnably. Where *was* . . . Ay Dios mío! Doña María Catalina, Doña María Catalina, Doña María Catalina. Love was like looking into the eyes of God. Love was everything. Vaguely, then more clearly, he heard the sound of a horse's hoofs approaching through the night, a lonely beat in the silence. Perhaps Jarauta had changed his mind. Perhaps he had returned for him. For a minute or two he lay listening acutely but he could hear nothing except a distant whirring sound that he supposed was the rushing stream. The clatter of the horse's hoofs had ceased. Yet he continued to stare from the darkness of his corner toward the long crooked entrance beyond the candles. He could see very well now although the little hot needles were still thrusting through the flesh of his face.

He stiffened as he saw a shadow emerge from the blackness of the night, cross the candles and pause for a moment to mutter something in a low voice to the three Indians. Then the figure approached him and he observed that it was a strange man bearing something white in his hand. Juan Diego lay tense and waited.

"I am Febronio Quijano," muttered the strange man quickly. "I have a cataplasma for your face. There are herb juices in it and El Amo warns you to be careful. It is not for the eyes."

He leaned over the young man and as he adjusted the oblong of damp cloth something heavy slipped from it and landed on Juan Diego's chest. It lay there for a moment and then the astonished young man put up his hand and felt the cold metal and shape of a Colt's revolver.

"Jarauta!" he exclaimed in excitement, fondling the solid grip. The guerrilla chieftain had thought twice.

Febronio Quijano pressed the cloth firmly upon his mouth.

"The wise fox sleeps," he murmured.

Juan Diego slipped the gun down between his body and his arm under his jacket. Febronio Quijano straightened up and turned just as the surly voice of Don Alejandro sounded from the entrance of the cave.

"Very well, Señor Médico," he called angrily. "Jarauta is not here. I've had enough of this nursing. Why aren't you riding with the padre?"

From the baffled thickness of his voce Juan Diego, listening carefully and staring at the vague figure beyond the candles, realized that Don Alejandro had been drinking heavily. Where was . . . ?

"El Amo sent me back with this cataplasma," replied Febronio Quijano, walking soundlessly toward the Spaniard. "I found the herbs."

"Cataplasma . . . herbs . . ." stuttered Don Alejandro. "Ah, diablo! Ride on, Señor Médico. We need no cataplasmas here."

He lurched against the box bearing the candles and knocked all of them over. In the darkness he stumbled and swore as he floundered along the narrow cave toward the pallet. One of the three Indians picked up a candle and lighted it and Juan Diego saw that Febronio Quijano had vanished and the three guards were settling themselves in the very entrance of the cave. Don Alejandro approached with staggering difficulty and stood some distance from the young man. He was breathing like a winded horse.

"Cataplasma," he repeated. "We want no cataplasmas. To-morrow . . ."

His speech erupted in a loud racking hiccup.

"Mateo Báez!" he shouted. "Mateo Báez! For the love of God . . ."

"What is it, Don Alejandro?" inquired the hateful voice from the entrance. "I am here."

"Find another bottle," ordered the Spaniard. "Break open the cases. Find another bottle. We'll drink another bottle. Mateo . . ."

"I have two unopened bottles here," replied the other. "Come outside. The moon is rising."

Don Alejandro grunted.

"We'll cut him to pieces tomorrow, Mateo Báez," he declared thickly. "We'll cut him into a thousand little pieces and feed them to the horses. The padre is a majadero. Eh, Mateo? He's lying on my wife's pallet. Perhaps he'd like . . . Where is my wife, Mateo Báez? Eh? Where is . . . ?"

"Where she has been all evening," answered the man with the rotting nose. "In the corral. She's sleeping in the corral."

"Corral," said Don Alejandro stupidly. "Yes, that's right. Corral. Prefers the horses to me. That Otomí fool . . . he's . . ."

"He's watching her," explained the other impatiently. "Come out, now, Don Alejandro. Here are the bottles."

"Bottles," repeated the Spaniard. "That's right. Bottles. Tomorrow we'll slice him into little pieces."

His shuffling steps retreated to the entrance, slowly, stumblingly.

"Keep your eyes open," he said, apparently to the three Indians. "If he stands up, shoot him. If—"

"They will know what to do," broke in Mateo Báez sharply. "They have their orders. Come along. Here . . ."

Don Alejandro's grumbling voice died away.

Juan Diego lay silent in the darkness and watched the tiny flame of the single candle. He had hardly breathed while Don Alejandro was in the cave for he felt that the moment for action had not come. *The wise fox sleeps.* He began to figure out how many men were left now that Jarauta and the recruits had gone. Don Alejandro, Mateo Báez, the three Indians in the entrance, the Otomí watching the corral . . . that meant six. Unless there were guards at each end of the ravine. But Jarauta had said that he would leave only three or four men. He would lay his plans on the assumption that there were no guards. Tomorrow . . . In the daylight . . . Carefully he put his hand up and felt the concealed Colt's revolver. Yes, it was loaded. It couldn't be his own, then, the one he had hurled at Don Alejandro. Where . . . ? Ah. Of course. It was Chepe's gun. The gun that had bewildered Don Isidro's poor Indian. Well. He adjusted the revolver, slipping it farther under his body. He had the feeling that he would not be disturbed again during the night. Don Alejandro would drink himself into insensibility and the Indians, who never seemed to sleep, would guard stolidly, their narrow black eyes watching with the fixity of cats until the sun rose again. It was time to sleep, to rest, to refresh himself, to call the strength and will back into his body. He would make himself sleep. *The wise fox* . . . He shut his eyes and almost immediately fell into a deep slumber.

When he awoke bright sunlight was flowing into the cave and it took him but a moment to realize where he was and that it was late in the morning. There was only one Indian sitting in the entrance but he could hear a murmur of mingled voices outside. He moved cautiously and could feel the comfortable bulk of the revolver close to his side. It gave him a sensation of exhilaration and confidence. Added to this was the welcome discovery that he was no longer in pain. His face was numb but the hot little needles had ceased to exist. The swellings about his eyes had receded so that he could see clearly and the lassitude that had overcome him from loss of blood appeared to have been washed away during his long dreamless sleep. He couldn't tell whether his swift recovery from Don Alejandro's beating was due to Febronio Quijano's cataplasma or his own natural powers but whatever the cause he intended to conceal his renewed strength until the moment to use it came. Therefore, he called to the Indian in a weak voice and asked for water. The Indian spoke to somebody beyond the cave and after a minute or two Mateo Báez appeared bearing a gourd half-full of liquid. He came to the pallet and Juan Diego raised his head with assumed difficulty and a grimace of pseudo pain. The fat fellow tipped the gourd against his face until the brackish stream water ran down his stubbly chin.

"What time is it?" he asked faintly, peering up at Mateo Báez through almost-closed eyes.

A round unblinking stare studied his face but no answer came.

"I'm hungry," whispered Juan Diego.

Mateo Báez emptied what was left of the water in the gourd on the ground and lumbered away, his overgrown buttocks swagging from side to side in the tight velvet breeches. Juan Diego watched him go and made no attempt to call him back. There, he knew, was the most intelligent and dangerous of Don Alejandro's men. He took nothing for granted and he never lost his temper. Don Alejandro might be fooled easily enough but Mateo Báez was always suspicious and on guard. The first bullet in the Colt's revolver would be for Mateo Báez.

Some time after the man with the rotting nose had gone an Indian, a little bowlegged Otomí, appeared with a few cold tortillas and three American army biscuits. Juan Diego chewed them slowly as the Indian fed him bit by bit. Evidently they wanted him to recover a little strength. He tried to speak with the Otomi but the man refused to answer, turning his prematurely wrinkled face aside with a gesture of noncomprehension. After he had passed out of the cave, his splay-toed bare feet scuffling on the rock floor, the young man lay quiet and waited for the next gesture from his captors. An hour passed and nothing happened. Then, another hour. From time to time he could hear voices outside the cave, once in heated discussion, and the scraping of boxes as they were dragged across the ground. The sun seemed to be high in the sky and he judged that it must be about noon. He flexed his limbs and experienced no spasm of pain, nothing but a dry feverish stiffness that gave him the sensation that his legs were jointed sticks of wood. Carefully, watching the Indian in the cave entrance, he worked the Colt's revolver into his camisa until the cold metal pressed against the bare flesh. It was well-concealed there and if he kept his hand and arm over it in a natural attitude of pain in his side he was certain that the bulge would not be noticed and he would be prepared to defend himself, But he must wait for the precise moment.

He had just finished arranging the revolver when the mestizo with the narrow head appeared in the cave entrance and exchanged a few gruff words with the Indian. Then both of them approached the pallet. The mestizo reached down, clutching Juan Diego's shoulder and dragging him roughly to a sitting posture.

"Get up," he said irritably. "We are going to travel."

The young man rose shakily to his feet, pressing his arm and hand closely to his side.

"What is it?" he asked. "What are you trying to do?"

He felt somewhat dizzy but when he took a step he was relieved to discover that he could command all his movements.

"You will find out," grumbled the mestizo, pushing him toward the entrance.

The Indian grasped the young man's arm and he winced dramatically and staggered.

"Don't touch me," he exclaimed. "I can walk without your help. Where are we going now?"

He moved along feebly guided on either side by the mestizo and the Indian. He had the feeling that with every step he took a new strength flowed into his body, a current of energy that he must conceal from the sharp eyes that were studying him. Therefore, he winced and groaned as they led him into the sunlight.

The scene between the rushing stream and the cave was like a set stage. Directly in front of him the swollen waters flashed into white flowers of foam as they split about projecting rocks and on the farther side the dense green-foliaged trees mounted to the invisible lip of the ravine. Doña María Catalina was seated on a rock by the stream and four or five feet from her Mateo Báez stood looking toward the corral. The girl was pale but composed and as her eyes met Juan Diego's concerned gaze she lifted one hand and pushed back the mass of black hair streaming over her shoulder. The gesture was slight and poignant and seemed like a caress to the young man. He felt his heart beating faster and his fingers tightened under his jacket over the hard butt of the revolver. He was convinced that they could speak without words and that she was waiting as tensely as he for the precise moment. That was why she did not look at him.

The round eyes of Mateo Báez swiveled from the corral to Juan Diego's battered features and back again. He was like one of the loathsome watchful zopilotes that perched on the towers of the church in Vera Cruz, staring with lidless eyes at the movement in the plaza and waiting endlessly for carrion. The young man glanced toward the corral, too, and saw the squat figure of Don Alejandro and the little Otomí removing the logs while the half-broken horses tossed their heads and whinnied. Simún's arched neck loomed over the smaller animals and the Spaniard struck savagely at his nose with his whip handle to drive him back. The Arabian reared and kicked at the logs. A tall gaunt Indian with knife-scarred features passed Juan Diego and went into the cave. That would be all. Juan Diego enumerated them quickly in his mind, one man on each side of him holding him upright lightly, two men at the corral, the Indian in the cave, Mateo Báez by the stream, six altogether. Yes, that would be all.

The young man felt his body tightening into a knot of tense expectancy. They were planning to leave the cave and take him somewhere else, a larger guerrilla headquarters, perhaps, or even Jalapa where the thick walls of the old prison would hold him like a beast in a cage. His revolver would be useless there. And if they got him on the back of a horse where they would bind his feet and arms he would be unable even to draw the weapon from its hiding place. He would have to act now. The precise moment was rushing toward him with incredible speed. He glanced again at Doña María Catalina and saw her small profile clear-cut against the farther green. She was like a woman waiting in an agony of suspense, for he could see her clenched hands taut in her lap. Slowly he let his eyes wander about the sun-shot scene. Mateo Báez was continuing to stare from the corral to him and Don Alejandro and the Otomí were drawing aside the last logs and cursing the restless horses. The men on either side of him were waiting stolidly, the hand of the mestizo barely touching his elbow. In the cave there was a scraping of boxes where the Indian with the knife-scarred face was dragging them toward the entrance.

Suddenly Juan Diego knew that it was the precise moment. There would never be a better one.

Drawing a deep breath that set the blood roaring in his head he flung his arms savagely sideways and plunged forward. The mestizo, struck heavily in the chest and caught off balance, went down with a crash and the other guard tripped backward as he tried desperately to retain his footing. He failed and toppled over a large stone. Without pausing to see what had happened to them the young man whipped out the Colt's revolver, ripping a great slit in his camisa, and fired directly into the startled face of Mateo Báez. For a split second the man with the rotting nose appeared to stare with three round eyes instead of two and then his body, as though disjointed suddenly at the knees, the hips and the shoulders, collapsed like an overstuffed puppet. He had not uttered a sound.

Juan Diego felt rather than saw Doña María Catalina beside him and a great clarity that was like an all-seeing eye possessed him. He was aware of everything that was happening on all sides. He was prepared for anything. He saw the mestizo scrambling to his feet and he dropped him with a second shot. The mestizo kicked for a moment as though trying to get rid of his sandals and then lay still. The logs that had barred the entrance to the corral were down and the horses, startled at the loud reports of the revolver, were rushing out. Don Alejandro, mazed by the unexpected gunfire, had turned sluggishly and was trying to drag his heavy pistol from his belt. His mottled alcoholic face and protruding bloodshot eyes were a mask of anger and slow-witted consternation. Juan Diego raised the Colt's revolver with an icy elation but before he could press the trigger the impossible happened. He saw a shining bulk rippling with muscle rear itself by the Spaniard and the downward slash of a sharp hoof. A frightful scream burst from Don Alejandro's viscous red features as he spun and staggered a few steps and then fell spread-eagled upon the ground. The Arabian horse, squealing like a wounded woman, was at him immediately, cutting and kicking with flashing resistless hoofs. Simún had become an elemental fury. The startled Otomí, who had tumbled sideways from the escaping horses, reached blindly for his musket and as his fingers clutched the black barrel Juan Diego automatically shot him through the back of the head. All this seemed to have happened in a lurid instant of miraculous revelation, for the spurt of smoke from the revolver had not disappeared before it was accomplished. Four were dead and two, the man who had guarded Juan Diego with the mestizo and the Indian with the knife-scarred face were running wildly up the ravine toward its narrow end while the panicked horses, now followed by Simún, were bolting out of sight in the thick trees of the opposite direction. The two lovers were alone.

Juan Diego lowered the revolver glanced at it and then thrust it into his belt. He turned to Doña María Catalina.

"I didn't kill him," he said.

It was the first time he had addressed her since that day when she had bade him farewell in the patio at Puebla and he wondered while he spoke why these precise words should come from his mouth. There was something almost triumphal in them as though he had escaped in glory from an inner fear.

She stood gazing at him, a little flushed now and breathing rapidly, her hands clasped tightly across the white chemisette of her Poblano costume. He could find no fear or horror in her eyes. For a moment she did not answer and they remained in an isolated pool of silence while beyond it the thrashing hoofs of the fleeing horses sounded fainter and fainter. Then she nodded briefly.

"It was God who killed him," she replied.

The sound of her voice altered everything and he moved impulsively toward her. She came immediately into his arms and as he crushed her to him in a tight and possessive embrace, the odor of her loose hair filling his nostrils and her firm small breasts pressing against his bared chest where the camisa had been ripped away, he felt a quivering shudder pass through her body and an instant later knew that she was weeping terribly, convulsed with racking sobs that rose in her throat and choked her like the phlegm in a tortured consumptive. He did not say anything. He understood that he could do nothing but hold her close to him. He understood, too, that this was the first time she had wept since Don Alejandro had carried her away from her home and that these tears were the painful cleansing of all that had happened. He thanked God that she *could* weep, that the time for tears had not passed as it had with her mother, with Doña Ágata who had ceased to live and, therefore, to have any need of such cleansing. She still possessed the intense desire to live and her sobs were signs of her deliverance from death. They belonged irremediably to each other and because this was so there was a sort of sad joy in this long-averted weakness. The warm drops that fell from her eyes composed the necklace of love that she was fastening about his throat for all of his life.

Presently her sobs lessened and she lifted her head and kissed him urgently, passionately on the mouth. He could feel her hands tightening upon his back and the tiny sharpness of her nails pressing into his flesh. Her lips, half-open, crushed against his teeth and the honey scent of her breath mingled with his own. Like small arrowheads of fire the nipples of her breasts sought through the thin material of her chemisette the responsive flame of his bosom. He shut his eyes closing out the sunlight and the green fluctuating world, and an ecstasy that was both tender and venereal suffused his taut body. A jangled inconsequence of fragmentary memories rushed through his mind, that first time at Las Golondrinas when she had flung herself against him for protection, the fear that had possessed him at crossing the threshold of the house in Puebla, the day he had seen the drop of blood on her finger, the later day when he had sensed with some embarrassment the reality and desirability of her body beneath the enveloping garments, and then all of them vanished like an exploded liquid bubble and he was back by the rushing stream with the neglected bodies of the dead about them. It was miraculous that they could hold each other so while the blood solidified in the sunlight. It seemed to him, incoherently, that from the passion of death to the passion of love there was but half a step. The spasms of love were a continual dying and a continual search for eternity. One died in the other and was resurrected in the other, and, like death, love was greater than life. It was the final transfiguration. He held her tightly to him in a dream of perfection until her mouth slipped from his own and he felt her arms releasing him and gently thrusting him away. He opened his eyes and saw her face, still stained with tears although she wept no more, half-smiling although her eyes were troubled with a vast concern. The visible world poured into his mind again.

"Your face!" she exclaimed. "Your poor battered face!"

He had forgotten all about his appearance and now he put his hand up and touched warily the lump on his temple, his broken nose and the swollen puffy flesh of his cheeks and split lips. There was pain there, all right, but he thought less of it than how he looked.

"It is nothing," he said, trying to smile. "It will pass in a few days. But I must be confoundedly ugly."

He tried to say it lightly but she did not smile.

"Every time he struck you," she declared, shuddering, "he struck me too. I felt every blow. If I had possessed a pistol I would have killed him."

"It does not matter now," he said stupidly.

"Juanillo," she began and when she used the familiar name for the first time an absurd joy ran flutteringly through his body. "Juanillo, I couldn't do anything. You understood, didn't you? I was afraid that he would kill you."

"I know," he replied. "I was frightened, too. If you had spoken he might have killed both of us."

"I don't believe he ever knew," she remarked quietly, half-turning her head although she did not glance at the hoof-slashed body lying less than thirty yards from them.

"No," he agreed. "He suspected but he never knew. It was Báez who tried to tell him."

"I knew that you would come," she said, following a new line of thought of her own. "I called for you every night. Did you hear me calling for you?"

"I must have," he answered soberly. "There was a voice . . ."

"Juanillo," she repeated again.

He peered at her through his swollen lids.

"I love you," she declared gravely. "You are my life, Juanillo. I love you."

"María . . . María . . ." he ejaculated brokenly but before he could say more she was in his arms again.

Except for the endless rushing of the water it was very still in the ravine before the split entrance of the cave.

"We must make our plans," he said at last as they parted and stood half-smiling at one another.

"Why don't we live in this cave forever?" she asked in a light voice that shook a little.

"We must get away from here as fast as we can," he explained. "This cave belongs to Jarauta. I believe his recruits pass this way on their journey toward the coast. A detachment may arrive at any moment. Besides, two men escaped and are roving somewhere near us in the woods."

He thought it was wonderful to be so practical after what had happened. The feeling of strength that had been with him all morning increased and with it came a sense of mastery. She glanced at him out of her long gray eyes and then, lifting her bright red skirt, sat down on the rocky ground, her fine brown slender legs stretched before her. He knelt down beside her and they clasped hands.

"We have no horses," she announced.

"No," he said. "They've all run away. There were three horses above the ravine . . ."

"Jarauta had two spare horses," she interrupted. "One of his men caught them and brought them in last night."

They were sitting with their backs to the dead mestizo.

"They must have been ours," he declared. "There was David and Chepe and me, you know."

"Yes," she replied in a low voice. "Poor Chepe. Jarauta had him taken down the ravine and buried. He was a good Indian, Juanillo."

"He was a good Indian," repeated Juan Diego.

Then his body tightened.

"There wasn't another man captured . . . or killed?" he asked abruptly. "An American?"

She shook her head.

"I heard of no one," she answered. "Why do you ask? Was there . . . ?"

He drew in a long breath of relief. Then David *had* escaped. If luck was with him and he had recovered his own horse it was possible that he was well on his way to the coast by now. He would be with his own there and would probably return with the Yanqui forces that were moving up along the National Highway. Rapidly, in a few words, he explained about his brother. Doña María Catalina listened attentively but she was not satisfied. She wanted to know everything that had happened since he first heard of her abduction.

He described the long trip from Mexico City to the outskirts of Jalapa avoiding the situation at the house in Puebla as best he could. When he had finished she pressed his hand and looked up bravely into his face.

"Now tell me about my father and my mother," she demanded. "Leave nothing out. What has happened to them?"

He told her. She listened silently and tears brimmed her eyes when he explained Don Isidro's condition.

"He has suffered more than I have," she said when he had finished, "but he will never say so. As for my mother . . . ever since Lorenzo . . ."

Her voice faltered and broke and she glanced down into her lap. Juan Diego sat quiet beside her, an instinctive wisdom keeping his lips closed. The warmth of the sun, moving deliberately to the west, warmed the back of his head and he raised his hand and smoothed down the unruly hair. After she had gained control of her emotions she raised her eyes and met his concerned gaze.

"My father is in no danger," she declared, not as a question but as a reassurance to herself. And then, "What shall we do?"

He was anxious to be practical. He said:

"We can't stay here. It is too dangerous. There are two things that we can do. We can go south until we strike the National Highway, try to get horses somewhere and ride up to Puebla. Or we can travel east through the forests and farmlands until we reach the coast and the protection of the Yanqui troops."

He paused and cleared his throat.

"What would you do?" she asked. "I mean . . . if you were alone?"

"I'm not alone," he replied gravely. "We can travel either way. What do you want to do?"

"Which is the safer way?" she persisted. "We are not so far from the coast here. Isn't it much farther to Puebla? Wouldn't we run the risk of meeting guerrilla bands all the way up the National Highway?"

"It would be more perilous to travel toward Puebla," he explained, "unless the Yanquis have moved up beyond the National Bridge. Yes, there are guerrillas all along the way. But Puebla is your home. Your father and mother are waiting impatiently for you. After all—"

"If you were alone you would go to the coast," she interrupted.

"I didn't say that," he insisted.

She smiled briefly and pressed his hand.

"You will never be a mystery to me, Juanillo," she said. "You are too transparent and I am too wise. We will go toward the coast."

"But, your father . . ." he began.

She interrupted him again.

"My father will be all right," she declared, "and there is nothing now that can help my mother . . . not even I. We are much nearer the coast and your Yanquis cannot be far away. I'd rather meet them than Jarauta's guerrillas."

"After all," he announced with a guilty relief, "it will be a simple matter to send an armed messenger from Vera Cruz to Puebla. And we can go up with the troops . . . or a convoy. I saw a convoy at Perote."

"We will see when we reach the coast," she said calmly.

But he still felt guilty . . . as though he was sentencing Don Isidro to an unwarranted suspense.

"It is quite possible that we *could* get through to Puebla without meeting any danger," he pointed out. "If we find horses . . ."

She shook her head.

"We have ourselves to think about," she declared simply. "We will go to the coast. We will seek the protection of your Yanquis."

It was the second time she had said "your Yanquis." It sounded good. David might have reached the coast. He looked down at her and smiled.

"Would you follow me anywhere?" he asked lightly.

"Your home is my home," she answered.

It sounded like a Roman wedding. He looked at her soberly and nodded.

"And your home is my home," he said.

And suddenly he understood what home was. They sat in silence for a minute or two, still clasping hands and listening to the rapid flow of the swollen stream. The sun moved on toward Puebla and the shadows lengthened. They pointed toward the east, toward the coast, toward Vera Cruz and the blue waters of the Gulf. All they had to do was set their course by the shadows and keep to it and pray for fair weather. And it was not so far to the National Bridge . . . forty miles, perhaps . . . and beyond the bridge were the Yanquis in force. It never occurred to him that she could not walk forty miles through wild terrain. Suddenly he wanted to start. He stood up and drew her to her feet.

"It is time to go," he said. "We must make up a packet of food . . . if there is any . . . and . . . I'll find a pistol and ammunition. I've only two shots left in the revolver."

"There's food in the boxes in the cave," she explained. "Food . . . and aguardiente. I'll see to that. You . . . you . . ."

She turned and ran into the cave. When he was sure that she was out of sight he searched the mestizo's body and found nothing but a knife. He put it in his belt. Then he walked reluctantly to the blood stained mass that had been Don Alejandro and bent over it. The Spaniard had no face at all and far back in the depths of Juan Diego's mind the old memory stirred horribly to brief life. Swiftly, with eyes half-averted, he searched the sprawled body and was surprised to find a Colt's revolver, empty, his own, he imagined, and fifteen or twenty loose cartridges. This was wonderful. He moved away from Don Alejandro and loaded each cylinder of the two Colts that he now possessed. Then he glanced at the little Otomí and decided not to near him. A musket would be too awkward to carry. He walked toward the cave entrance ignoring the body of Mateo Báez the near the stream. There was no time to bury the dead. After a or two Doña María Catalina came out of the cave bearing wrapped in cloth.

She had tied her flowing hair up with a bit of colore kilted her red skirt to her knees. Standing there with soft darkness crowning her small face and her slende below the skirt like the delicate legs of some gracefu more like a child than a woman. There was a pro her that was adorable. He smiled. She accepted t swollen features for what he had intended it t swiftly, wisely, childlike, and then turned in down the bundle of food. She was changed change about her more important than all quite comprehend for a moment. Then flushed; her pale flesh had come to a rosy of the rose-scented patio had changed

She had changed, as it were, in an instant in spite of death and grief and he understood that for the first time he was gazing at the true Doña María Catalina, the awakened child who had never been awakened before. For an instant tears of happiness dimmed his eyes.

"Shall we start?" he asked hurriedly. "It is growing late and we should be some distance from here before nightfall."

She bent and picked up the bundle.

"I'm ready, Juanillo," she replied.

He started to walk up the ravine and she followed, bearing the bundle on her shoulder.

They traveled for an hour through rocky descending woodland judging their direction from the shadows of the trees and when they reached a curious-shaped boulder that was somewhat like a low table he suggested that they rest and have something to eat. The cloth bundle she carried suddenly became a cornucopia of plenty for she drew from it an entire boiled chicken, a dozen tortillas, some chirimoyas and a bottle of aguardiente. They ate like healthy young animals, licking their fingers free of the chicken grease and then finishing the feast with two small draughts of the fiery liquor. As Juan Diego drained his his thoughts reverted to those evenings in Puebla when he had sat late into the evening drinking aguardiente with Don Isidro. Drinking aquardi-nte and talking about patriotism. He had never imagined, even in his 'dest dreams (and he had had some wild dreams about Doña María 'lina) that he would be sitting with her in some unknown thicket th'ast of Jalapa drinking the same burning potion. He had never an 'd anything as desirable as this. The sun had disappeared over to sle'g hills to the west and he estimated that they would have but throug't to travel safely. Then they would have to find some place of time, 'he was reluctant to rise and resume the tiresome trek events that'trees. He felt that moments like these were moments out he could. N'ts that had nothing to do with the slow progression of the rest of his'his life and he desired to stretch them out as long as Catalina. They 'would have pleased him better than to wander for the infinite stars 'half-lost in a strange woodland with Doña María would lull them to s'd travel and laugh and talk by day and at night unknown dangers an'l shine over them and the wind in the tall trees the remaining food an'But life was not like that. Life was filled with think about, too. Thirty-'n and responsibilities. He watched her repack on half a chicken, a handf'it into a smaller bundle. There was that to aguardiente, of course. He 'miles to go (if his judgment was correct) "Are you tired?" he aske'f tortillas and a few chirimoyas. And the ned back against the rock.

She shook her head.

"No," she answered, smiling. "I think that I can walk a hundred kilometers."

"It's not as far as that," he said soberly, "but it is far enough. We'll go on in a little while. We'll walk until it's dark and find some sheltered spot in which to sleep. I wish we had blankets."

"If we lie close to each other we'll be warm," she said in a matter-of-fact voice.

For a moment he was too surprised to speak. Then he recovered himself.

"That is true," he answered in an elaborately casual manner.

All the same, an irrepressible dizziness of expectancy caused the flat rock to fluctuate a little. The idea of her young body stretched beside his own, the warmth of her breath on his neck, perhaps, her hands entangled with his own, grew in him like a wild flower of desire and he found it difficult to think of anything else. Yet he knew that there was nothing strange about it. It was the ordained end of their meeting and it sprang from the dark seed that had been planted in him when he held her in his arms that night in the inner court at Las Golondrinas. He had not known it then but the deep fecund soil of his soul had felt the seed. Awkwardly he endeavored to quiet the expectancy by speaking of other things.

"You have not told me about your abduction," he said, somewhat breathlessly. "How you must have suffered!"

She leaned on the rock with her elbows and cupped her chin in her hands. Shadows from the branches above fell on her face.

"I did suffer," she replied frankly, "but I did not let him see it."

He knew whom she meant by "him."

"I was not asleep when he came," she went on, "although I had gone to bed an hour or two before. It was difficult at the house in Puebla, Juanillo. After the news . . . about Lorenzo . . . came it ceased to be a house of the living and became a house of the dead. My mother passed through every phase of grief until her mind could endure it no longer and she became what you saw. My father did not lose any control of his reason but the blow was terrible, he had placed all his hopes and his eternity in Lorenzo, and I think that he lost his faith in any goodness in the world. As for me, I loved my brother and I wept bitter tears for him . . . but I loved you too, and that gave me á strength of my own. I prayed for you every night, Juanillo, although sometimes I was impatient with God . . . but that was because you were not near me. Why didn't you come to me, Juanillo? I needed you so badly. I . . ."

She paused for an instant and he averted his head because his eyes were filled with tears.

"But, of course, you didn't know," she continued. "We moved about silently in that lonely house, Juanillo, eating little, hardly speaking to one another, listening to the gunfire in the distance and too indifferent to care what it was about. Occasionally the bishop came to visit us but this did not please my father. Finally, the bishop came no more. Life went on like that until the night *he* came. As I told you, I was in bed and I heard nothing until my door was violently opened and he stood there, half-drunk as usual, with that mestizo that you killed beside him."

"Thank God, I killed the dog!" interjected Juan Diego fiercely.

"He stood there," she repeated, "and I knew that he had come for me. I think I had known all along that he would come for me some time. That was why I was so impatient for you to come first. I had considered everything in Apizaco and I had made up my mind to tell you that I loved you and that I wanted you to take me away. You see, Juanillo, I had no shame and no morals. I haven't any now. I think that impossible situations should be cut with a sharp knife. He told me that he had come to claim his wife, and to get up and dress. I asked him where my father was. He replied that he would give me three minutes to get up and dress and that if I was not ready by that time he would go downstairs and blow the top of my father's head off. Then, for some reason, for he has no shame, perhaps it was the mestizo's presence, he closed the door. I dressed as you see me now and went down the stairs with him and the mestizo. I saw my father lying on the floor and three or four men holding Chepe. They took me out into the street and put me on a horse and we rode out of the city. We rode for two days, stopping for food at various huts and finally reached the cave where you found me.

"During that period he never touched me although in the evenings he would talk to me threateningly. He was after money, I discovered, and twice he tried to force me to write a letter to my father demanding a large sum. I refused and once he started forward to beat me but Jarauta intervened and sent him away. I think Jarauta cowed him and I think, too, that Jarauta has his good side although he would never let me speak with him. Apparently, he shunned women. I knew that my only hope of safety was to preserve a cold independent front and this I did. If I had weakened or wept I would have been lost. I saved my tears for you, Juanillo. What he intended to do with me I never found out. There were times when he would talk of Spain and at other times he would speak of Guatemala or Cuba. But he drank constantly, more and more heavily as the days passed, and I knew that this thirst had conquered him. He was hardly able to walk or think in the morning until he had finished half a bottle of aguardiente. By evening he was staggering like a blind man. Sometimes he would be sick in the cave and that was terrible. Once he woke up in a horrible hysteria and swore that the mestizo was a mountain lion that could talk. He tried to shoot him but the pistol was not primed. After that they watched him all the time.

"Then you came, Juanillo. I had been praying for you constantly, calling you silently at night as I lay on the pallet, and when I heard your voice in the cave saying that you had business with Jarauta my heart almost stopped. I had heard the firing before and thought it might be a detachment of Yanquis but before I could rush out from behind the blanket and ask them to help me he and the mestizo bound me to the pallet. It was not until evening, after you had spoken and I recognized your voice, that they released me and brought me out to face you. Oh, my God, Juanillo, how I suffered when he struck you so many times in the face! It took all of my strength to maintain my air of calmness and of never having seen you. Yet I knew that your life depended upon it. If he had entirely believed that man Báez he would have killed you. I was terrified that you might betray yourself and that is why I mentioned the name of San Lorenzo. I thought that it might give you strength. And all the time, Juanillo, I was aching to throw myself into your arms and tell you that I knew you would come and that I loved you. I think that I suffered more than you did, Juanillo."

Having said so much she put her hand over her face and was silent.

"I know you did," he declared gently. "It was my body that received the blows. It was your heart."

They sat in silence for a while.

"Don't think about it any more," he said at last. "It is all over."

She lowered her hand and picked up the bundle of food. The shadows were long now and a blue gloom was creeping upward about the tree trunks. A young breeze blowing from the east brought with it a faint hint of the warmth of the coastal plain. He stood up with her and they went on, side by side, down the ever-descending forested slope. A happy sort of wordless communion enmeshed them both and whenever her arm struck against his a quick spasm of happiness darted through his body. He was intensely aware of her flesh and thought he could smell it, like gardenias, delicate, faint, pervasive, in the gathering twilight. The forest grew more dense as they penetrated into it and the necessity of circling great boulders, sunken hollows and deep fissures made him fearful of losing his course. It would be so easy to travel in a circle. He spoke of this, somewhat tentatively, and she flashed a smile at him.

"It does not matter," she said. "I will set you right by the stars."

"The stars?" he echoed. "Can you read the stars?"

"I know all of them," she asserted confidently. "That was one thing that the padre at Las Golondrinas taught me. He loved God and astronomy and he had a great book, printed in Madrid, full of pictures of the heavens. Don't you know about the stars, Juanillo?"

"Nothing . . . except that they shine," he replied.

Presently they came to a stream and they followed its downward flow for some time. It ran gurgling and sucking over flat stones and around tufts of brush, and he thought, We must be fairly on our course for this water is seeking the lowlands. Perhaps it flows into the Antigua. Partly because of the trees, whose thick foliage intermingled overhead, it was growing very dark and with an inwardly swelling confusion he began to look about him for a possible resting place for the night. They came to a place where the stream had sawn its way through rising ground and so formed two overarching banks partially supported by twisted roots. There would be shelter beneath either bank and some warmth. Water, as well. He stopped and indicated the side that seemed the deeper indented.

"I think we have gone far enough," he said. "There's a place where we can crawl in and sleep."

"Why, it's like a little cave," she cried. "It's perfect."

She splashed through the stream and got down on her hands and knees and worked her way in among the tree roots. He followed more slowly and stood by the lifted jaw of land. Her voice drifted out of the darkness.

"Come in here, Juanillo," she called. "Come and see what a fine shelter this is."

He started to stoop down and then straightened.

"In a minute," he answered in a voice that shook audibly.

He walked down the stream for some distance and after a minute or two came back more slowly. She had emerged from the tree roots and was sitting with her bare feet in the water. Her face was almost indistinguishable in the darkness. He sat down beside her and began to pull off his boots.

"You can't see a thing under the bank," she told him. "It rises into a sort of miniature cave and the roots are like columns going down into the earth. It is hard to get between them but after you do there's a perfect place to sleep."

Her voice was natural and unaffected.

"The ground there was probably washed out during the spring torrents," he said. "The roof is only the mass of earth held by the roots of the trees."

"Thank you, Señor Professor," she replied, laughing. "The roof is only the mass of earth and so forth and so on. Dip your feet in the water and see how cool it is. Do you want me to wash your face?"

"I can wash my own face," he answered, suddenly feeling quite at ease again, "but a multitude of thanks for your generous offer."

His boots off, he thrust his hot feet into the water. It felt wonderful. Bending forward he dipped his hands into the stream and dashed the cool liquid into his face. There was a ripping sound beside him and a small square of thin white cloth was pushed into his fingers.

"Use that," she said in an amused tone. "It is better than your dirty hands."

"Where did you get . . ." he started and then stopped.

"It's just about the last bit of my sayuela," she said. "I've been using it piecemeal for days."

He dipped the torn fragment of her petticoat into the water and mopped his face tenderly with it. All the pain was gone except in the bump on his temple and in his broken nose. These he could not touch without suppressed exclamations of anguish. But the water was deliciously cool and seemed to act like a medicine. Involuntarily he thought of Febronio Quijano who had anointed his face with herbs and brought him the Colt's revolver from Jarauta. Someday he would like to help Febronio Quijano. When he reached the coast he would have a Yanqui army surgeon take care of his nose. When . . . He turned to her in the darkness.

"I hope to find my brother when we pass the Yanqui lines," he said. "You will like my brother."

There was a vague flash of white in the dense obscurity and he guessed that she had raised her leg to wipe her foot or put on her sandal.

"I will like all your family," she said calmly. "Is your brother like you, Juanillo? Does he look like you?"

Family. He had no family. Except David. For an instant his mind dwelt on Santa Anna and it seemed to him that the general was the denizen of another world. Where was he now and what was he doing? It didn't matter. He belonged with things that were ended. With yesterday. And the day before yesterday.

"No," he declared. "David doesn't look like me. He is bigger and better-looking."

"He may be bigger but he can't be better-looking," she announced firmly, putting her hand on his shoulder and rising to her feet. "I'm tired, Juanillo. I'm going to sleep."

"If I went back to the United States would you go with me?" he asked suddenly, the thought popping into his head and out of his mouth before he could stop it.

She stood beside him in silence for a moment and he instantly wished that the question had never been asked.

"Of course," she replied in an altered voice. "I will go anywhere that you go."

She moved away from him.

"I always knew that you would go back," she added, the words half-muffled as she worked her way in among the tree roots.

He sat in the darkness for a long time and then got up slowly, fumbling about him for his boots. He found them and carried them closer to the bank where he set them down. Then he lowered himself to his hands and knees and crawled under the shelving earth, avoiding the stiff tree roots as best he could. There was a rank smell of long-decayed vegetation that made his head swim. He thought of snakes and then dismissed the danger from his mind. After a moment he could hear her regular breathing and he approached her as silently as he could and stretched out on the damp odorous soil. It seemed to him that both of them were enclosed in the womb of the earth and that they were waiting for their day of birth. Perhaps they would be born to-morrow when the sun shone again. He reached out his hands and grasped the sturdy roots and he was sure that he could feel the life in them passing up through their length from the feeding earth beneath and mounting into the green foliage that would curve above him on the morrow. The land. It was always the land. It was before all things and all things, including reptiles, animals, Mexicans and Yanquis, Santa Anna and General Scott, the bishop of Puebla, Don Isidro, David, Doña María Catalina and himself, were but ephemeral shoots of the land. They passed but the land remained and future generations would feed on the land and acknowledge their responsibilities to the land. He inhaled deeply, drawing in the rich rotten odor that was so gloriously sexual in its intoxicating suggestion. Dropping his hand from one of the roots he turned over with a great sigh of contentment, not knowing what he was contented about but sensing that it was something that would last as long as he lived. His hand touched her hair and he heard her move.

"Are you asleep?" she asked in a low tone.

"No," he replied.

"I wasn't sleepy before but I'm very sleepy now," she said in a small voice.

He smiled in the darkness.

"Good night, María," he said softly.

She sighed contentedly and a moment later he heard her deep low breathing, the even sound of one who is sleeping peacefully.

For a while he thought he couldn't sleep and lay staring at the darkness above him. A thousand and one images seemed to be passing through his mind but either his conscious will was too weary to recognize them or they were shapes of the future that he was yet to know.

They were cloudy, indistinct, merging with grayness, but an inner voice appeared to tell him that they were all good, all strong, all important. They belonged to him and he belonged to them. If it was the future he was seeing and yet not seeing then there was but little to fear in it. Finally his mind tired with the eternal procession and a drowsiness, unsought but desired, numbed his senses. A pleasant feeling of expectation like a warm bath flowed along his limbs as he closed his eyes and yawned feebly. He turned on his side with his back to Doña María Catalina and composed himself for sleep. He felt like a man who had done a great day's work. His spirit began to swoon toward that complete nothingness that was deep slumber but before the dark velvet waves closed about him he heard her move again. She turned toward him, moved with a little scratching sound across the earth and an instant later he felt her fit herself against his back, her sleeping breath on his neck, her breasts against his shoulders, her knees matched into the back of his like a completed puzzle. She still slept and it was with her deep regular trusting breathing playing its soft music in his ear that the velvet waves engulfed him.

It was early morning when he awakened for a dim gray light filtered through the tree roots. He discovered that he had changed positions during his sleep for now he was crushed against her back, his knees fitting into the back of hers as hers had fitted into his when he had drifted into unconsciousness. The warmth of her body aroused a small core of fire in his belly. She was still sleeping, the consistent rise and fall of her breast like a tactile rhythm under his hand. Her black hair was all around his face and he thought that it smelt like the cinnamon dulces that were sold in the open market at Jalapa. He lay for a while relishing the new day and then disengaged himself from her carefully so that she would not awaken. She moved a little and muttered a few incoherent words. He rolled sideways, rose to his hands and knees and crept stealthily between the roots toward the daylight. It was not until he emerged from the shelving earth and stood upright by the stream that he dared to breathe freely. Then he felt like shouting with joy.

The fine weather had held. The deep blue of the cloudless sky seemed iridescent with the million golden bees of the early morning sun. The rich green of the leaves arched over the brown pulsating waters of the stream and an infinite choir of birds sang from every branch. He had not noticed the birds yesterday although he realized that they must have been all around him. But now they were musical embodiments of his own exhilaration. Neither had he observed flowers although he saw that they were all around him, growing in clumps between the trees and sometimes rising in vines that clasped the brown trunks and flaring out in blossoms that seemed to be growing from the trees themselves. He saw the pasionaria, the passion flower, the mammoth white bell of the chirimoya, the madreselva which the Yanquis called the honeysuckle, the palma Christi and the wild convólvulo. The crystal-clear air was redolent with their mingled odors. From the luxuriant appearance of these flowers and the flashing colors of the birds as they sped from branch to branch he decided that they were close to the tropical lands. He began to walk down the stream glancing from right to left like a happy hacendado promenading his own estates.

When he thought he was far enough away he sat down on a stone and removed his jacket. The collar was clotted with dried blood and he flung it into the water. Then he unbuckled his belt and put it, together with the mestizo's knife and the two Colt's revolvers, beside him. He pulled the tatters of his shirt off and felt the morning breeze on his bare flesh with a great sigh of pleasure. He stretched his arms and felt strong and happy. It was as though he had been reborn into a new world in a state of virgin innocence and expectation. After a moment he stood up and slipped his breeches and calzoncillos off and walked forward into the stream. The flowing water came halfway up his calves. He stood for a full minute looking down at himself and decided that he was an extremely well-shaped young man. His chest was wide and hairless, his stomach flat, his hips narrow, his thighs sturdy with long muscles and his calves not bulging but well-turned. The ridiculousness of his self-admiration struck him forcibly and he sat down in the water with a splash grinning at the indifferent trees and rocks in a sheepish manner. He had not realized that there was any narcissism in him at all and he wondered briefly what had brought it out. After all, if he had any illusions about his appearance all he had to do was see his own face and they would be destroyed immediately. And he tried to catch his reflection in the stream. But the light was not right or the water was too transparent for all he could see were broken fragments that were not a face at all. He would have to continue to imagine what his face looked like. Putting up his wet hand he touched his features lightly and decided that the swelling had decreased. His broken nose still hurt and so did the huge bruise on his temple and his gums ached but these were superficial injuries in comparison with what he had suffered two days before. Jarauta had been right. He had an excellent constitution.

Settling down into the stream as far as he could he started to splash the cold water over himself and rub his flesh. It felt good. The blood surged through his body with a fresh vehemence and the exhilaration he had felt when he came into the clear day was heightened to a controlled excitement. He began to hum "Adiós" as he cleansed himself. Everything seemed plain and forthright now that he knew what he desired and what he intended to do. It was so simple. He would marry Doña María Catalina and discover the United States and teach the United States to discover Mexico. That was it. He would labor all his life to wed the two Republics, to make them husband and wife as Doña María Catalina and he would be husband and wife. Each had so much to give the other and together they would be an insuperable couple. Mexico was feminine and the United States was masculine. The one was excitable, sensitive, quick to anger and quick to love, sometimes coy and always vivid with human vanities, suspicious, proud, displaying weaknesses, petulant, adorable; the other was harder-willed, egotistic, strong, possessive, sometimes bullheaded, generous, foresighted and smart. Together they would be perfect. Oh, they would have their differences but they would settle them in their own house and never call in any strangers to intervene. They would work side by side, acknowledging their common responsibility to the land and per-fecting the art of existing peaceably and lovingly beneath the same roof. Their single names might be Mexico and the United States but their married name was America.

He recalled now that David had said something to him about going back and telling the Yanquis about Mexico and as he was no longer a Mexican (he knew that quite suddenly and for no specific reason) it seemed the perfect thing to do. It didn't occur to him to consider what he might have done had he lost Doña María Catalina or never seen her again. Neither of those terrible things had happened and he could reason only from what he was and what he possessed on this sunny morning. And he knew that he possessed Doña María Catalina. Everything began in that fact and returned to it again. Love simplified the knottiest problem. And let no one say that he had given up his ideals for love for love had grown out of his ideals and Doña María Catalina in some mystic way was more than Doña María Cata-lina. She was Mexico, too. She was Our Lady of Guadalupe with the eternal odor of gardenias about her name. She was the strength and endurance of the Tarascans of Michoacán who drank the dark wine of San Lorenzo. So wherever he went he would carry his dark foster mother, la morena, with him. With such thoughts, more felt than shaped into actual words, he continued his ablutions. It was like wash-ing the blood and anguish of the past away. The sun climbed in heaven and the day grew warm.

He was about to stand up and wade back to the stone where he had left his garments when he became wildly conscious that he was not alone. He turned his head in a jerky, semiparalyzed manner and saw Doña María Catalina standing by the stone and staring with the frankest curiosity at him. Tiny chills ran up and down his body and he opened and shut his mouth without saying a word. The girl's red lips opened in a delighted smile at his embarrassment.

"Good morning, Juanillo," she said. "Why didn't you awaken me before you crept away? Is the water very cold?"

He mumbled that it was not cold at all.

"Good," she replied. "Then I'll come in, too."

She began to disrobe in the most casual manner, dropping her red skirt and tattered petticoat and pulling the white chemisette over her head. For a moment she stood clad solely in India cotton knee-length drawers, and then, leaning against the stone, she drew them off. When she walked down to the water and dabbled a foot in the shallow stream he knew that she was not naked. She was nude. There was a cool freshness about her young body that dissipated his embarrassment and made her actions seem the most natural in the world. She was small from the finely turned ankles to the thin graceful neck, but she was a woman too. Her breasts swelling delicately into rose-tipped nipples and the curved slope of her hips were potential promises of motherhood. She splashed toward him laughing and kicking the water into his face. When she was within arm's length she sat down and twisted her flood of black hair into a knot on the top of her head. It came to a point and looked comical.

"Have you any soap in your pocket, Juanillo?" she asked. "There's a root that you can wash with but I don't know what it is."

"I don't know what it is, either," he said. "I'm afraid I forgot soap. I left in an awful hurry."

She looked at him sideways and laughed.

"I'll use my hands," she announced. "There's a bit of my petticoat left if you'd like it."

"I've just about finished," he replied.

She began to splash water over herself.

"Then fetch me the petticoat," she ordered, cupping her hands and leaning forward to wet her face.

For an instant he hesitated and then he rose to his feet and went to the stone, picked up the fragment of a garment and brought it back. He thought that it still contained the warmth of her body. She took the petticoat, tore a sizable piece from it and began to scrub her arms and shoulders. He continued to stand and watch her. He was completely at ease again.

"Did you sleep well?" he asked.

"Um," she mumbled.

"María," he said, "will you marry me and go to the United States with me?"

"Of course," she replied. "I thought that was understood."

"I intend to engage in some sort of business," he explained

happily. "Something, perhaps, that will bring us back to Mexico often, maybe every year. You won't be lonesome. You'll see your father and mother constantly. We'll live as though no boundary line existed."

She stood up and continued to scrub herself with the torn bit of petticoat.

"Will you teach me English?" she asked. "I'll be pretty silly in the United States without a word of the language."

"You'll pick it up in a few months," he told her.

It was as simple as that. He watched her for a moment and then waded slowly to the stone and started to dress himself. When she had completed her al fresco bath she left the water, drew on the India cotton drawers and the white chemisette and draped the red skirt about her slim hips. They walked back to the shelving bank hand in hand. Neither one had anything to say to the other in spoken words but their every gesture, their every look, their equal pleasure in the clear day, the sun, the flowers, the birds, the enclosing woodland, became intimate and loving communications. They anticipated each other in a succession of momentary delights and conveyed the most subtle messages by a sort of spontaneous telepathy. This merging of identities, this unity of being, this oneness was love and the rapt mystery of it mesmerized them into a charmed silence that was filled with a million meanings. They drank each other in with adoring eyes. They smiled. They touched hands. Juan Diego knew that he had reached the perfect moment in his life.

After they had eaten a breakfast of the remains of the chicken and a few tortillas they resumed their long walk toward the coast. The direction they took led steadily downward through thick woods and there were moments when the young man was uncertain regarding their progress. They might be going the wrong way. And yet the ground descended, the streams they encountered moved with him and his sketchy knowledge of the sun seemed to indicate that they were traveling eastward, eastward and perhaps a trifle southward. She marched along triumphantly, her black hair piled high on her head and the bundle of food swung over her shoulder. There was a wiry ease about her that delighted him, something Indian although there was no Indian blood in her veins, and he recalled fleetingly and contemptuously the fine ladies he had encountered in Mexico City during the time that Santa Anna was president. They lolled in their carriages and a stroll along the Paseo would have exhausted them. They were artificial and brittle; but Doña María Catalina was real; she was the true Mexico, young and active and filled with the promises of tomorrow.

As they walked they began to converse, asking frank questions and giving long answers. Now that the hush of their ineffable merging had been accomplished they displayed an insatiable curiosity about each other's life and passions and prejudices. Lovers are always like this. It is of supreme importance to find out if the loved one had curls as a child, prefers cinnamon cakes to lemon tarts, writes with the left hand or the right, enjoys Mozart more than Handel, reads Cervantes or Lope de Vega, trusts cats, plays the piano, rides and attends the bull-fights. It is also of supreme importance to confess all these little things, to empty one's self out for the edification of the other like a spilled casket of colored ribbons. Both are delighted for both are exchanging bits of themselves, giving and taking freely and that is the eternal small change of love.

Something that Doña María Catalina said aroused in Juan Diego's mind the reason why Don Isidro had forced his daughter into her unlovely marriage with Don Alejandro and after thinking it over for a moment he decided that she should know it, too. He told her and she listened in silence. When he had finished she did not seem surprised or hurt. She spoke of the past as though it were the past of another woman and explained that she had always known that there was some reason beyond her father's arbitrary desire and that it had never mattered to her what the reason was. "I had no life in those days," she said. "I was an automaton with no desires of my own. I never knew desire until I saw you." Like all lovers he asked the eternal question: "When did you first know that you loved me?" She started to tease him and then suddenly desisted. "It was the day I gave you the rose," she finally replied. "You never gave me a rose," he protested. "I left it in the doorway," she said. Then he remembered. It was the rose he had picked up and Chepe had put in water. "When did you first know?" she asked in her turn. "When you went away from Puebla," he answered. "That was when I really knew. But I think that I fell in love with you that night at Las Golondrinas. I couldn't understand what was happening to me but I knew that something was changing my mind and my life."

By noon they had covered a great distance, Juan Diego estimated it at ten miles at the least, but neither of them was particularly tired. It was like a strengthening tonic to walk through sun-shot trees together and he had the feeling that they could travel a hundred miles without tiring. That, too, is a part of love. The mind becomes regardless of distances when one is looking constantly into the loved one's eyes. The legs move mechanically, the lungs expand, the air is sweet and the heart runs on ahead. Yet they stopped and sat down under a great tree and ate what was left of the food. They pledged each other in aguardiente and when Doña María Catalina tipped the bottle to her lips the liquor ran down her chin and she choked. When she recovered she insisted on another drink and he was surprised to learn that yesterday had been the first time she had ever tasted aguardiente. She had only drunk champagne and wine before and an occasional glass of port or sherry.

After resting for an hour they started on their journey again with nothing but the bottle of aguardiente for supplies. "We'll eat chirimoyas," she said, "and you can shoot little birds and we'll cook them over a wood fire." "Too many chirimoyas are bad for you," he replied, "and I have nothing to start a fire with." "We'll find something," she declared optimistically but he began to worry about the morrow. There was two days' travel, possibly, before them and even that was doubtful. He thought they were moving in the right direction but he was not sure. And at last, for even lovers are human he began to experience a weariness in his legs and could see by her flagging footsteps that she was tiring, too. They traveled more slowly and at mid-afternoon he made her sit down and rest for half an hour. They had gone, perhaps, another five miles. When they started on again he was a trifle grim. She sensed that he was worrying about her but she made no pretense of not being close to exhaustion. The way was more difficult now for they came to a series of ravines where progress was a continual process of scrambling down and then up again.

It was not dark when they came suddenly upon a deserted jacal standing in lonely ruin on a small hill. This was the first time they had happened upon anything even remotely suggesting that there were other human beings besides themselves in the widespread wilderness of trees and rocks. Juan Diego was instantly wary and he drew forth one of the Colt's revolvers as he advanced to inspect the sagging hut. It was quite empty and a part of the low roof had fallen away. Wild vines grew in the one dirt-floored room and there was no door at all. The place had obviously not been occupied for years. It appeared to be the jacal of some Indian who had moved on long before, the ruined skeleton of a habitation that no longer afforded the slightest shelter against the rains and autumn winds.

"We'll remain here for the night," announced Juan Diego after he had satisfied himself that the hut was completely deserted. "You're tired, María."

"My legs are tired," she admitted, sitting down before the gaping door and stretching her brown limbs forward.

He sat down beside her.

"I can hear water running somewhere," he said. "At least, we shall have something to drink besides aguardiente.

"The Indians always build their huts near water," she replied.

With a long sigh of pleasant weariness she lay back and crossed her arms above her head.

"Tell me about the United States, Señor Professor," she commanded. "I'll eat your lecture in the place of food."

Instead of that he started to talk about his feelings concerning the war, of the ideal Republic he had conjured up in his mind, of the vast potentialities of Mexico, of the necessity for a close relationship between the people south of the Rio Grande and those north of it. He tried to explain his feelings about the responsibilities toward the land and why he believed Mexico had forfeited Texas and New Mexico and California. He talked to her as he had talked to his brother in Mexico City and it pleased and fortified him to discover that she understood what he was trying to communicate and agreed with all he said. Twilight crept about the jacal and the twittering birds, calling lonesomely, sought their nests. They continued to converse in low voices, as though the approaching night might be frightened away by too loud a sound, feeling each other out, rushing into immediate agreements, picturing the Mexico that could be and the United States that was. After it was dark Doña María Catalina went to find the invisible but audible water and came back with a smiling face shining with moisture. Quite suddenly, she declared that she was no longer weary. The three hours of rest and conversation had renewed her healthy young body. Juan Diego sought the water and splashed it into his disfigured face. There was no pain there at all now. He could touch the lump on his temple and his broken nose and feel hardly any reaction, nothing but a faint soreness that was as far away as the day before yesterday. When he came back he discovered that she had gone into the jacal. He sat down on the ground and felt the night, cool but not uncomfortable, closing around him like a soft blanket of black fur. If there was a moon or stars in the sky he could not see them for above the jacal bowed the thickly leaved branches of half a dozen trees. He was shut away from the world again as he had been shut away under the shelving bank the night before. But this time it was different. He was out of the womb. He had been born. He felt that he had a raison d'étre. At last he got up and went into the jacal. It was dark and he could not see anything at all.

"María," he called softly, "where are you?"

"Here," she replied in a low voice.

He found her and knelt down beside her and was not surprised to feel her bare arms slide around his neck.

"Juanillo," she whispered, "take off your clothes."

The new day dawned as sunny as the one before.

They dressed, drank stream water, washed their faces and started out again with nothing but the bottle of aguardiente and the deep satisfaction of their consummated love. They had not traveled a mile when

Juan Diego's quick ears caught a sound that was a cross between a wind roaring through tall pine trees and heavy rain falling on wooden roofs. It increased in volume steadily somewhere to the left of them. They stopped in uncertainty and with some fear. It was the first sound they had heard that was not the natural voice of the deserted woodlands through which they journeyed and its very strangeness made it a menace. It was alien, therefore suspect. Suddenly Juan Diego started. He recognized the sound.

"María," he said hurriedly, "remain here while I go forward and see who they are."

"They!" she exclaimed in surprise. "What is it?"

"It is the sound of cavalry," he explained. "At least, it is many horses. Wait here and do not move until I call or come back for you."

He left her standing in bewilderment by a tree and worked his way through the underbrush quickly in the direction of the approaching roar. It did not surprise him to come upon a trail of considerable width that bore evidence of frequent travel. The earth was almost bare of grass and pounded into a hard surface. He understood now why the Indian had built the jacal where it was. He had not been so far removed from civilization, after all, for this was evidently one of the old roads that led down toward the coast. They had probably been moving parallel with it for some time. There were plenty of bushes bordering the cleared ribbon of earth and Juan Diego crouched down among the tallest of them, his Colt's revolver ready in his hand. The noise resolved itself into the mingled clatter of many horses' hoofs and after a minute or so he saw a rising and falling snake of horsemen, riding in couples, bearing down toward him. A rider with a guidon was in the forerank. The moment Juan Diego saw it and darted a quick look at the horsemen he rose to his feet and stepped out into the road and held up his hand. These men were volunteer cavalry of the United States army and judging by their nondescript costumes they probably were Texans. He remembered them all too well from Buena Vista. The leader reined in his horse and held up his hand.

Juan Diego advanced rapidly toward him.

"Can you take me to the coast?" he asked excitedly. "I haven't any horse and I have a young woman with me. I hope . . ."

"Who are you?" asked the leader brusquely.

He was a stout man with red hair and whiskers and he wore a black soft hat pulled over his cold blue eyes.

Juan Diego thought quickly.

"I am Charles Livingston," he said precisely. "I'm the brother of Lieutenant David Livingston of General Scott's staff."

"You look like a Mexican to me," announced the leader. "At

least, what I can make out of your face. What happened to you? Did somebody catch you robbing his house?"

"No, captain," replied Juan Diego. "I've been a prisoner of Jarauta's guerrillas. I want to get to Vera Cruz. Will you—"

"Jarauta!" exclaimed the leader. "That's the murderin' devil that we're after. We've been scourin' these roads for the last three days in search of that fellow. Do you know where he is? Just show us, sonny, and you'll see as fine a hangin' as ever you saw in this God-damned country."

Juan Diego shook his head.

"I don't know where Jarauta is," he replied. "Isn't he at the National Bridge? I understood . . ."

"National Bridge, hell!" snapped the leader. "Joe Lane drove 'em away from there two days ago. They all ran off into the hills. Lane's on his way up the highway now to relieve Puebla. What did you say your name was?"

"Charles Livingston," repeated Juan Diego.

The name sounded funny on his tongue and he had the sensation of traveling under false pretenses. But it *was* his name.

"Puebla?" he said. "Then the war—"

"The war is over," broke in the leader, "but some of these varmints don't know it. They'd shoot their grandmother for a clako."

He turned in the saddle.

"Ryan!" he bawled. "You was at Vera Cruz. Ever hear of a Lieutenant Livingston? First name, David. Supposed to be on the Old Man's staff?"

A young man edged his horse forward.

"Livingston?" he said. "Sure, Captain Hawkins. I heard of him. I seen him, too. Regular officer. I think he's with Lane's commissary in Jalapa now. Don't you remember the feller that rode into our lines a few days ago. Said he wanted—"

"By Jesus, yes!" declared Captain Hawkins. "Sure enough. He wanted half the army to go out searchin' for some fellow."

He leaned over and inspected Juan Diego.

"So you're the fellow, hey?" he asked. "You seem to fit all right. Well, jump up behind Ryan here and we'll get goin'."

"There's a young woman," explained Juan Diego. "I'll want to get her."

"Young woman!" exclaimed the captain. "What in hell are you doing wanderin' around the woods with a young woman? Didn't your maw teach you no better? Well, go get her. We got ten miles to travel before we eat and my men've got awful big stomachs."

There was a snicker and a hoarse voice called, "Not so big as yore big mouth, capt'n."

"I'll hold your pay up for that, Mike Tavis," said the captain equably.

Juan Diego hurried back to Doña María Catalina and explained their good fortune. When they appeared together on the road at least fifty of the sixty men whistled with admiring approval. Captain Hawkins bellowed at them and then dismounted to make an elaborate bow to the girl. Then with Doña María Catalina riding behind the captain and Juan Diego behind Ryan the squadron resumed its rapid trot toward its destination. Once again the young man was riding with cavalry and once again he experienced that exhilaration that only a moving mass of horses could arouse. It seemed to him that he had been snatched in an instant from danger to safety. All questions, food, a place to sleep and protection, were solved now. He glanced over Ryan's shoulder at the girl and saw her turn her head and smile. She felt safe, too. Juan Diego wondered what Doña Ágata would think if she saw her daughter riding with the ferocious Yanquis.

It was near noon when they halted in a large clearing where two white-topped provision wagons and one eight-pounder gun were parked under the guard of some twenty-five men. They dismounted and in a short time were seated together eating hot pork and hard biscuits from a provision box marked "Caffrey and Collis, Army Provisioners, New Orleans." Captain Hawkins came around and explained that he had sent a fast messenger to Jalapa to see if Lieutenant David Livingston was there and then he demanded Juan Diego's story. The young man, careful not to reveal that he was also known as Juan Diego de Béxar, explained the kidnaping of Doña María Catalina and his efforts, with David and Chepe, to rescue her. The captain was full of admiration and amazement.

"It's just like a story in a book, ma'am," he said to the girl. "I suppose you'll marry this fellow now."

"I do not understand," she replied in Spanish, smiling.

"Yes," sighed the captain, "just like a book I read once. I married my old woman because she said she'd take a musket to me if I didn't. And she would, too. She's the orneriest old jennyass in Texas. But she's a good cook and can shoot the eyebrows off a mosquito at fifty yards without injuring the little bastard."

Doña María Catalina did not understand a word of this but she laughed all the same. She liked the captain and thought his red hair and fiery whiskers were wonderful.

It was midafternoon when David arrived and the two brothers flew into each other's arms. David, it appeared, was much nearer than Jalapa; the messenger, in fact, had met him coming up the road to this very camp. Juan Diego brushed away his concern over such minor matters as a bump on the forehead and a broken nose and demanded details of what had happened to his brother since the attack on the cave.

"I saw those horsemen," explained David, "and I knew we didn't stand a chance. I saw Chepe fall and I yelled to you to come back. Then I turned and fairly rushed up the side of that ravine. It wasn't until I reached the top that I discovered you weren't with me. I was tempted to go back but I knew it would be no use and I remembered what you had said about any survivor going for help. I caught my horse and rode south until I reached the National Highway and I galloped smack into a detachment of General Joe Lane's men. They'd already driven the guerrillas away from the National Bridge. I did my damnedest to have the commanding officer, a fellow named Bright, send out strong squads in search of you and he did, at least a dozen of them. They combed the roads and trails and went as far as they could into the wooded country but they couldn't find the cave. I couldn't find it myself. The squads are still out. We were still looking when I met this messenger who brought me here. My God! but I am glad to see you. Now tell me everything that happened."

Juan Diego gave a rapid recital of events. David, he observed, occasionally glanced sideways at Doña María Catalina with a shyness that was unusual in an army officer. He had shaken hands with her and been somewhat stunned by her voluble Spanish. She, for her part, examined him with a friendly intensiveness that increased his shyness. Either David was bashful or he had had extremely limited experience with women. Well, Juan Diego thought, grinning, María would cure him of that. He could see the calculating medicine in her eyes as she studied the lieutenant's somewhat red face.

Two horses had been provided for them and when the cavalcade started for the coast Juan Diego was pleased to observe that Doña María Catalina rode astride, her red skirt caught up and revealing her slender brown legs and sandaled feet thrust into the big stirrups. They rode most of the afternoon, Juan Diego beside David and Doña María Catalina just ahead beside Captain Hawkins, who was regaling her with stories that were completely incomprehensible to her. The two brothers watched the girl as they talked. An hour or so before twilight they came out on high ground, the land fell suddenly away before them and they saw in the near distance the great blue fluctuating waters of the Gulf of Mexico. They had come out above the little seaport of Antigua and in the harbor a large propeller steamer rode lazily at anchor. She flew the Stars and Stripes.

CODA
WASHINGTON

Coda Washington

ABOUT ten o'clock on the morning of March 4, 1857, Tuck, the black servant of the Honorable Alphonsus Ewing, United States senator from Tennessee, was passing the hot biscuits in the dining room of the legislator's house on Lafayette Square in Washington City. A group of gentlemen, several in uniform, was gathered about the large breakfast table and making terrific inroads on enormous platters of ham and eggs. To guard against any inconvenient chill a stack of logs was blazing brightly in the square fireplace. Through the looped curtains of the windows might be seen three victorias, their bored horses, faced toward the Jackson statue, observing Old Hickory with colossal indifference. The click of forks on plates, cups striking saucers and the buzz of conversation frequently punctuated by laughter added a sort of noisy gaiety to the disappearance of the food and a fair proof that all those present were Democrats.

Senator Ewing, long-lipped, ox-eyed and with gray-white hair curling over the collar of his black broadcloth coat, glanced benignantly around the table at his guests. He liked them all and the fact that they would compose an impressive entourage for him when he set forth for the Capitol Building to attend the inauguration of his old friend, James Buchanan, made him like them all the more. He liked company and he liked a string of attendants. The more the merrier. He believed in living his private life in public, that was the least return he could make for the suffrages of his fellow Tennesseans, and he believed in living it up to the hilt. Politics had been his passion and his horn of plenty for twenty years and gregariousness was one of the prime virtues of the successful politician.

He had possessed three other passions but he had outlived them. They were women, whisky and horses. The horses were on his large estate in Tennessee and it was only rarely that he visited them, other interests crowding them out of his busy life. The whisky had gone to his kidneys and his legs, causing the one to grumble and the other to swell. It was with regret that he parted from it. As for the women, he woke up one morning in a strange bedroom and decided that he was too old for them. There was more than regret in this decision; there was acute anguish. Politics remained. Thank God for that, he thought.

No matter how old and senile he became he could always be a politician in the United States.

Yet he was a generous warmhearted old fellow with the best intentions in the world. Being smart had never curdled his milk of human kindness. He had been careful never to marry a wife and, therefore, never to betray one. And if for a decade or two he changed his housekeeper at least once a year that was his own business. They were all single women, anyway, and old enough to know a hawk from a hand saw. Besides, he always treated the wives of his friends and acquaintances with an elaborate courtesy and instinctive delicacy that won the enthusiastic approval of the husbands as well as the wives. In Nashville this had got him a lot of votes. And once, Andy Jackson, whose metal figure was out there in the square, had clapped him on the back and told him, with an admiring oath, that he was one of nature's noblemen and that he had better get rid of Miss Lucy Lantrum, who was his housekeeper at the time, because she made damned bad rabbit stew. The senator got rid of Lucy although when he thought of her he never thought of stew. When he ran the second time for office his backers proclaimed him as "Alphonsus Ewing, Nature's Nobleman and Tennessee's Gift to Washington." He won hands down.

One had to go no further for a proof of his essential goodness of heart than to point out his adopted son, David Livingston, whom he had brought to Tennessee from Texas in the wild days of the Alamo and Goliad and reared from a ragged orphan boy to a distinguished young officer in the United States army, educating him through private schoolmasters, wangling an appointment to West Point for him and getting him on Zachary Taylor's staff during the Mexican War. Here was goodness with a vengeance and if the young man reflected credit on the senator so did the senator exert influence for the young man. And if one *did* want to go further, then that pertinacious one might point to David Livingston's younger brother, Charley, who had come up from Mexico with his gray-eyed young bride in 1847 and been taken promptly to the ample bosom of Alphonsus Ewing and installed as a permanent part of his household. In other words, the senator, not having a family by natural means, secured one, so to speak, by negotiation. One had to admit that Nature's Nobleman had a heart of gold that was as big as all creation. True enough, the younger Livingston, "the Mexican one," as Washington and Tennessee neighbors called him for a long time, turned into a successful businessman. He organized an export and import house with his Mexican father-in-law (the firm of Núñez and Livingston, with offices in Mexico City, Puebla, New Orleans and Baltimore, was extremely well-known during the fifties) and let the senator in as a silent partner and he cleared up a tidy sum in profits for which he did nothing at all. But that cast no aspersion on his goodness. It merely testified to his luck and foresight.

There was reason and justice, then, in his pleasure as he glanced benignantly from face to face on this March morning that would witness James Buchanan's inauguration as president of the United States in succession to Franklin Pierce. Both his adopted sons (for he had lost no time in adopting the Mexican Livingston too) were present and so was the Mexican father-in-law, Don Isidro Núñez de Haro, who had some more to his name which the senator always forgot. The aging legislator observed them with large approving eyes. They were nature's noblemen, also, and he had told them as much for he believed in rolling periods and orotund phrases. They were all good to look at. David Livingston, wearing the insignia of a captain (the senator hoped to change it to the insignia of a major as soon as he talked with the new secretary of war, John B. Floyd), looked very stalwart in his well-tailored uniform, decorations and small silky side whiskers. He was a born officer and that meant that he was well-disciplined and obedient to his superiors and not blessed with too much imagination. Charley Livingston, whom his pretty birdlike wife always called Juanillo or Juan Diego, was spotlessly garbed in a dark clawhammer coat, a white watered-silk waistcoat and a rich black stock decorated with a pearl tie pin. He was the handsomer of the two brothers, the senator thought, and if it weren't for that dip in his nose where it had been broken some years ago he would look like a dynamic young actor. Charley was fond of bright colors and highly seasoned foods. He was not often at home now and it was a pleasure to see him devour the ham and eggs with the same gusto that he brought to Mexican concoctions. As for Don Isidro Núñez de Haro (this, by the way, was the third time the senator had seen him during the past ten years), he was a veritable giant of an old fellow, as big as Sam Houston, and it was a damned shame that he was forced to swing himself along between two great apple-wood crutches. One leg and hip were completely paralyzed. But there was tremendous vitality in Don Isidro and he worked mightily to enlarge the now friendly intercourse between the United States and Mexico.

The senator, himself, had never visited Mexico. However, he remembered the Mexicans from his residence in Texas back in 'thirty-five and 'thirty-six and he was inclined to be prejudiced against them. That fellow, Santa Anna, for instance . . . It was Charley who fought stoutly for the Republic south of the Rio Grande, admitting its flaws, to be sure, but talking up its virtues, pointing out its potentialities and insisting on the necessity for a close brotherly relationship. Indeed, Charley would talk your ear off the minute Mexico was mentioned. He plagued the senator to introduce into the Halls of Congress all sorts of impossible legislation calculated to bring the two Republics together, the abolition of duties, an offensive and defensive alliance, the exchange of students, a publishing house that would print all sorts of books, histories, romances, biographies and economic treatises in two languages, Spanish and English, and distribute them in both countries, the obligatory teaching of Spanish in the public schools and colleges of the United States and heaven knows what else. Of course, the senator couldn't do that. His Tennessee constituents would never stand for it and it would never do to be labeled a Mexico-lover. Yet there were moments when Charley sounded extremely convincing. He had a way of describing a sort of ideal Mexico that drew its virtues and strength from the land and had as much to give to civilization as the United States. He mesmerized you with this dream country until you remembered that your own country was God's gift to the world and possessed in itself all the virtues and all the strength and all the civilization that were really worth-while on the face of the globe. Why worry about other countries? Let them mind their own business and we would mind ours. And if anybody tried to pluck a feather out of the eagle's tail he'd better look out for his skin. Besides, the senator had tried chile con carne and didn't like it. It burned his tongue. Those infernal foreign dishes . . . not a bit like plain roast pork and mashed potatoes. All the same . . . Charley was a good talker. It was fun to listen to him even if you didn't believe a word he said. Americans were open-minded.

The senator, as he turned his head from side to side to listen to and acknowledge the conversation of his table neighbors, never lost sight of his three favorites. It wasn't often that they were all together at the same time and when they were it was usually for some unique occasion such as this inauguration. David, who was on a short leave from San Francisco, was assigned generally to some post in the back of beyond. When he talked to Floyd, the senator thought, he'd put in a word to have the boy transferred to Washington City. It was time that David married, anyway. He was in his middle thirties now. Charley and his wife (and their little boy, too) were in Mexico as much as they were in Nashville or Washington. And this was only the third visit that Don Isidro had paid to the United States. The senator recalled the first two without an effort. There was the marriage of Charley and María; that had been in January, 1848, and the big Mexican, pale and wasted, had been practically carried by two body servants. Then there was the birth of Charley's boy, Lorenzo. That was in November, 1848, and María's father had come again, come with speed, too, for he arrived little more than two weeks after the infant had emitted his first howl. Don Isidro had been much stronger then. It was during this visit that the plans for the export and import house were laid and within a year the firm was established and growing by leaps and bounds. After that Charley and María passed six to seven months in Mexico each year. It appeared to be a life that pleased them both, this having a foot in each country, as it were. And now little Lorenzo would be nine years old in November. Time certainly passed with unbelievable speed. The senator felt like Doctor Pangloss as he leaned back in his chair and listened to the laughter and chatter about him. There was that captain, that friend of David's who had come on with him from San Francisco, what was his name? . . . Cousins, that was it, Cousins. There was a lot of bounce in Captain Cousins.

Charley and Don Isidro, regardless of the hubbub about them, had their heads together in a close conversation. They were speaking Spanish.

"I'll look into it," the Mexican was saying. "There's no reason why we shouldn't ship from the west coast, Mazatlán, say, to San Francisco, as conveniently as we do from Vera Cruz to New Orleans and Baltimore. Of course, we'll have to build warehouses."

"Will that cost much?" asked the younger man.

"It depends," replied Don Isidro. "It depends on whether we build with stone or lumber."

He leaned back and sighed, his heavy underlip thrusting out as the exhaled air whistled through his mouth.

"Juanillo," he said abruptly, "do you know what date it is?"

"Why, yes," answered the other with some surprise. "It's March fifth. Why?"

"It is eight years ago today that Doña Ágata died," explained the Mexican shortly.

"March, 'forty-nine," acknowledged his son-in-law soberly. "You are right."

Don Isidro rubbed the white scar on his forehead.

"A lot of water has flowed into the Gulf of Mexico since then," he said gravely.

Charley nodded.

"Yes," went on Don Isidro in a brooding tone, "a lot of water. Well, it was all for the best, I suppose. She is happier where she is . . . with Lorenzo. It won't be long before I join them."

"Anda!" exclaimed the younger man. "Why do you talk like that? You know as well as I do that you'll live practically forever. You're like the Pyramid of the Sun at San Juan Teotihuacán. Except for the paralysis you're as strong as a bull."

"It's not my body," declared Don Isidro. "It's my mind. It's getting tired. But let it go. I'll live a few more years, I imagine. I'm like that . . . slow-witted . . . never knowing when I'm through. Or perhaps it's the ham and eggs that has put me out of sorts. I detest ham and eggs."

"And there isn't a bottle of aguardiente in the house," remarked Charley, smiling.

The corners of Don Isidro's lips twitched upward.

"Oh, yes, there is," he said. "I brought one in my traveling bag. I don't like your whisky. It tastes like furniture varnish. Is María Catalina going to see your new president sworn into office?"

"She wouldn't miss that," answered Charley. "The ladies will come down in a few minutes and then we'll all leave together. It's not like an inauguration in Mexico City, is it?"

"I haven't heard of anybody being shot yet," declared Don Isidro dryly. "But if your abolitionists continue as they have been going on lately I expect to hear of a lot of Yanquis being shot. What does Old Blunderbuss think?"

It was his name for Senator Ewing.

Charley's face clouded.

"He thinks that everything can be controlled in committee rooms," he explained reluctantly. "He believes that the country can find a way out, a compromise or something. Anyway, Buchanan is a nice old man."

Don Isidro grunted.

"You can't control the passions of men in committee rooms," he announced, "and there comes a time when compromise is the ultimate affront. I'm only a poor benighted Mexican but it seems to me that you have been trying to live here for some time under two standards. It's like trying to drive a carriage whose pair of horses is pulling in different directions. It won't work. This matter of slavery is going to split you in two as cleanly as a butcher divides the carcass of a steer."

"It's more than slavery," said Charley, "although, I suppose, that is the prime reason for our difficulties. There are States' Rights as well."

"States' Rights," grumbled Don Isidro. "Where does Old Blunderbuss stand?"

"Oh, he believes in States' Rights," declared his son-in-law.

"To the point of secession?" demanded the Mexican.

"Yes," replied Charley.

"You're as badly off as we are," announced Don Isidro with emphasis. "In the south you justify secession; in the north you insist that it is treason. You make a compromise and then you break it. Every section thinks of itself first of all and the entire United States last of all. What are you going to do? What do *you* think, Juanillo? Do you believe in secession?"

"I don't think I do," said the younger man slowly. "This is one country. It was one army that fought for its independence and . . ."

"That, if you remember, was what we believed in Mexico," broke in the Mexican. "We didn't recognize the secession of Texas and we fought for it. You Yanquis argued us into the position of tyrants. We had no right to try and prevent our own breaking away from us. But let your own try to break away and all hell will be let loose. It depends whose leg is wearing the boot, doesn't it?"

His voice was raised and several of the breakfast guests were eying him with some curiosity.

"Shhh, taita," exclaimed Charley quickly. "The war is over."

"Our war is over," said Don Isidro, "but yours has just begun."

He pushed his plate away with some disgust.

The senator's mellow voice boomed across the length of the table.

"Don Isidro," he called, "tell me, what do you think of Washington? How does it compare with your Mexico City? I know you haven't been here for a long time so . . ."

"I've never seen so much mud and so many unfinished buildings in my life," answered Don Isidro in testy curiously accented English. "Wherever one looks there are piles of lumber, blocks of granite, donkey engines and workmen's sheds. And that awful scaffolding around the dome of the Capitol. Why, it looks—"

"Yes, yes, yes," interrupted the senator with some haste. "Of course, we are in process of building. We are growing every day, you know. This great Republic cannot stand still. The winds of the Future . . ."

His voice rumbled on and Captain Cousins, who was seated opposite Charley, leaned across his empty plate.

"Do you two talk business all the time?" he asked. "What is it now? Ingots of silver or bananas?"

"We were discussing jalap," responded Don Isidro unsmilingly.

"Hmm, jalap," repeated Cousins. "Very efficacious, jalap. I wonder that our War Department doesn't employ it as an offensive weapon."

At that moment there was a great rustling of skirts and half a dozen women swept into the dining room. There was a jabber of voices as the men rose hastily to their feet. The senator, with agility surprising for his age, was already bowing over the extended hand of a buxom lady in enormous hoops and a cashmere shawl. Charley watched María come toward him smiling in her gray merino pelisse and black beaver hat with plumes. She was buttoning her silk gloves. He noted as he had noted a thousand times before how eternally young she seemed every time he saw her and the old inward excitement throbbed again in his breast. He pushed his way toward her and then stopped as three or four men, including his brother and Captain Cousins, closed about her like a protective guard. He knew that she was gazing past them at him with a glint of mischief in her long gray eyes. Oh, all right, my young lady, he thought, and turned with elaborate nonchalance to help Don Isidro get to his feet.

"María is looking very well," remarked her father with a half-smile.

"She is enjoying the best of health," replied Charley.

At that instant he heard her calling him and nearly tripped over a chair to get around the table.

Don Isidro stood alone, sagging on his crutches, and waiting to be piloted to one of the victorias.